THE SNOW MOUNTAIN

The
Snow Mountain

Catherine Gavin

CORONET BOOKS
Hodder Paperbacks Ltd., London

To Helen Peers

Copyright © 1973 by Catherine Gavin
First published 1973 by Hodder and Stoughton Limited

Coronet edition 1975

Printed and bound in Great Britain for
Coronet Books, Hodder Paperbacks Limited,
St. Paul's House, Warwick Lane,
London, EC4P 4AH
By Cox and Wyman Ltd, London, Reading and Fakenham

ISBN 0 340 19681 5

PETROGRAD 1914-1918

CATHEDRAL

FORTRESS OF
ST PETER & ST PAUL

NEVA

TRINITY
BRIDGE

BRIDGE

EXCHANGE

RIVER

VASSILI
ISLAND

PALACE BRIDGE

SUMMER
GARDEN

MARS'
FIELD

MILLIONNAIA

MOIKA

WINTER
PALACE

PALACE
SQUARE

MICHAEL
GARDEN

ADMIRALTY

ALEXANDER GARDEN

NEVSKI

INZHENERNAIA

MICHAEL
SQUARE

ITALIANSKAIA

EUROPA
HOTEL

PROSPEKT

MORSKAIA

MOIKA CANAL

K A Z A N S K A I A

CATHERINE CANAL

NEVA

BAZAAR

SADOVAIA

ANI
PAL

S P A S S K A I A

SADOVAIA

FONTA

| 0 | ¼ | ½ | 1 |

Mile

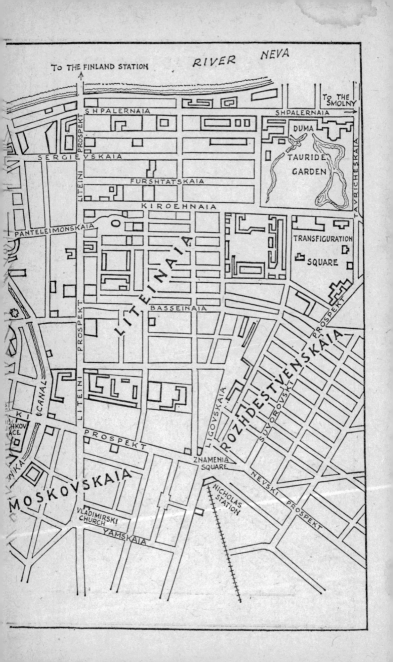

CHAPTER ONE

THERE was one day, and perhaps only for an hour of that one day, when they were all within sight of each other on the broad expanse of water where the Neva flows into the Gulf of Finland. Some of them had not yet met. They were strangers among the thousands of Sunday holiday-makers who had come out from St. Petersburg in the ferry steamers which normally plied between the islands, and in light craft of all sorts, to see as much as they could of what the Russian newspapers had been calling for nearly a week an historic occasion. But the Grand Duchess Olga was there, happy and excited, aboard the little *Alexandria,* and so was Simon Hendrikov, in the bodyguard of her father, the Russian Czar. Simon's parents and the two schoolgirls in their charge were on the deck of a steamer close behind the barrier of river police boats guarding the waterway along which the imperial yacht would pass. And Richard Allen was there, waiting inconspicuously aboard the British flagship, HMS *Lion,* long before Joe Calvert, who knew none of them as yet, moved away from the parapet of the Nicholas Bridge.

The Czar of All the Russias and his family were going to lunch aboard the *Lion* with the British Admiral and his officers. This was the historic occasion, the apex of a week of tremendous celebrations in St. Petersburg marking the visit of the First Battle Cruiser Squadron to Kronstadt, after a long goodwill voyage begun nearly five months earlier at the French port of Brest. The Royal Navy was showing the flag in the North Sea and the Baltic, and on this same Sunday when Sir David Beatty was to play host to Czar Nicholas II, Admiral Sir George Warrender was receiving the German Kaiser aboard his own flagship at Kiel. In Russia the Duma, which had suffered many things at the hands of the Czar since its mild attempts at parliamentary government began, had stolen a march on him by sending a delegation to greet Admiral Beatty at the Gulf port of Reval; but this was only a prelude to the festivities at St. Petersburg. All the British ratings had been entertained by the Russian Admiralty in the People's Palace. The Municipality gave the officers a banquet at the Tauride Palace, in a setting even more splendid than that of the luncheon party previously given by the Czar in his own home at Czarskoe Selo. Now, after a week of rising excitement, of feasting carried out in perfect June weather, came the imperial visit to the squadron at Kronstadt, to be followed later in the day by a Royal Navy ball.

Of all the group of young people whom fate and history were to link together, Joe Calvert was the one who saw and heard the least that day. This was because he started for Kronstadt late and unprepared, without binoculars, a young man who had spent exactly five days in the Russian capital as a vice-consul of the United States of America. He had gone with one of his new colleagues to the Nicholas Bridge, joining the crowds looking on and even cheering as the two British light cruisers berthed in that stretch of the Neva got under way, dressed overall, and departed to join the rest of the squadron at Kronstadt.

'Just listen to the girls!' he said, as squeals and shrill good-byes broke out. 'They won't forget the Limey sailors in a hurry.'

'Jack ashore!' said Edward Murchison. 'Jack's going to remember Petersburg as a wide open town, a damn sight better fun than Devonport on a wet Saturday night. Or even Newport News, for that matter.'

'Petersburg put on a great show for them, you've got to allow.'

'Sure did,' said Murchison amiably. He was pleased with himself and with the world. He had served two years in the American consulate at St. Petersburg, and had earned so many reprimands from the consul that he had more than once feared his next posting would be to Siberia, and behold! his orders had come through for Berlin and a return to the western world. He had never even attempted to understand the Slav mentality, and yet, with this kid already on the spot to take his place and his bags packed to go, he was inclined to envy Joe Calvert, who had the whole Russian experience before him. He wondered what Calvert would make of the alternate brilliance and fecklessness of a society in which he might or might not find a place, the snowy winter streets and the white nights of midsummer, the ballet and the gipsy singers, all backed by the daily drudgery of the consulate.

'What do you say we follow them downstream for a bit?' Joe Calvert said. He was fascinated by the sight of the two cruisers, running west between the rose-purple of the granite embankments on the city side and the rose and white façades of the university on Vassili Island. 'Come on, Murchison! The fun's all over here, and there's still time to catch that steamer by the steps.'

'What, that leaky old ferry?' But Ned Murchison, after consulting his watch and reckoning that they could 'just make it' before the Czar's arrival, allowed himself to be persuaded. He was sentimental, although he would never have admitted it, about going on one last trip down river, looking back beyond the Nicholas to the Trinity Bridge, to the Alexander, to all the bridges of the Neva which opened to let the freighters go upstream; looking back at the statue of the Bronze Horseman and the slim golden spires against the blue. Unsentimentally, he warned Joe Calvert to look out for his watch and wallet and keep his jacket buttoned up, as they ran down the granite steps and aboard the crowded ferry, where a shaggy man in an embroidered peasant blouse was playing the fiddle on the after deck, and some girls were already dancing. In fact the jackets of both young men were buttoned almost to their choker collars. They were tall and lanky, American dandies of 1914, immaculately turned out in light grey suits and straw boaters.

Joe Calvert's name, which was to become familiar and sometimes execrated in St. Petersburg, was only known to two persons in the crowd that day. Madame Hendrikova, the language teacher, had heard it from the American consul, who wanted her to give the new arrival Russian lessons, and she had mentioned it to her husband, the professor. As it happened, the Hendrikov party was not far away from Joe when the ferryboat shut off her engines at the order of a police patrol. Professor Hendrikov had reserved places for his wife and the girls in one of the pleasure-boats chartered by the university for the occasion, and from the deck of this craft, lying low in the water, the two schoolgirls looked up curiously at the noisy crowd aboard the ferry, and the bottles of vodka being handed round. Madame Hendrikova signed to them to move away from the rail and under the shelter of an awning.

'But mother, we can't see anything, back there!' protested her daughter.

'I promised your headmistress you wouldn't make yourselves conspicuous, when I asked her for a holiday.'

'It's not as if we were wearing our Xenia fancy dress,' said the other girl defiantly. They had been close friends for several years, Darya Hendrikova and Marya Trenova, Dolly and Molly to their classmates at the Xenia School, and although the friendship had begun to wane they were united that day in the silent determination to see Lieutenant Simon Hendrikov in the uniform of the Garde Equipage.

On the other side of the police barrier, on the deck of HMS *Lion*, Richard Allen was waiting for the show to begin in far greater comfort than Joe Calvert or the Hendrikov party. It was like him to be at the centre of events, ostensibly in attendance on the British Ambassador, while back in the embassy on Suvarov Square some junior members of the staff who had not been invited to the revels wondered resentfully how Captain Allen had got away with it again. With the modest posting of temporary military attaché, Captain Allen kept his distance from the Ambassador, while giving his full professional admiration to Sir George Buchanan's fine appearance in his gold-laced diplomatic uniform, and the poise of Lady Georgina, his stately wife.

'Who did we pull out of the imperial lucky dip today?' he inquired *sotto voce* of a young man in naval uniform, who answered with a smothered laugh:

'His sister and the Kirills: it might have been worse.'

'Not much worse.' Captain Allen surveyed those members of the Romanov family who had been invited to meet their august relatives under the protection of the British flag. The Czar's younger sister, Olga Alexandrovna, was likely to be a popular guest, especially as she had turned up alone, without either her husband, the much disliked Prince Peter of Oldenburg, or the handsome colonel who was the third member of their unconventional ménage. A rawboned rangy woman in her middle thirties, with a plain face and an underslung jaw, she was talking pleasantly to one of Beatty's flag officers: her laugh rang out from time to time. No problems there, thought Richard Allen, and looked thoughtfully at the Grand Duke and Grand Duchess Kirill. They were talking to nobody, but

standing a little apart, she with the look of offended di
only too familiar on the faces of the imperial ladies. Th
marriage had been a resounding scandal of some years back,
when she, as a divorced woman, had married the Czar's cousin
Kirill, the scandal being compounded by the fact that her div-
orced husband was none other than the Czarina's brother.
They had been banished from the Empire by the Czar, and
although he relented after a time and permitted them to return,
the wrong still rankled in his wife's unforgiving heart. All the
British diplomats aboard the *Lion* knew the problem, the more
acute to them because the Grand Duchess Kirill had been born
a British princess: either the Czarina would ignore her former
sister-in-law or she would favour her with the frigid smile that
blighted conversation. The very best that could be hoped for,
thought Richard Allen, was that the former sisters-in-law
would kiss the air four inches from each other's cheeks and call
each other by their nursery names. He was never sure of his
ability to keep his own face straight when he heard the Czarina
addressed as 'Sunny' — she who looked so miserable, or the
Grand Duchess called 'Ducky', when her long neck and dra-
matically poised small head occasionally made her look like an
indignant swan.

'Did we have to have the Kirills?' he said, still in a lowered
voice, and the naval attaché reminded him:

'Of course we did. He's the commander of the Garde Equi-
page, and he'll probably be the next chief of the naval staff.
And anyway, who else is there?'

Richard Allen shrugged. He knew as well as the other man
that the Czarina, Alexandra Feodorovna, had quarrelled with
nearly every member of her husband's family since she entered
it twenty years ago. With some, the quarrels had been on re-
ligious grounds, with others because of what she called loose
living — and no doubt about it, outside the charmed circle of
the ruler and his family, the Romanovs had a talent for living
loosely. His uncles, his cousins, even his only surviving
brother, had bedevilled the Czar's peace of mind with their
morganatic marriages, their bastard children who had to be
legitimised and ennobled, their years of foreign exile until the
inevitable pardon was forthcoming. Who, in such a crew, could
be invited to meet, or particularly wanted to meet, the religious
and strait-laced Czarina?

13

s all gone well so far,' said Allen. 'I'd like to see this
rticular show go with a swing.'

'I think we can safely leave that up to Beatty.'

'To Beatty and the girls.'

'The little Grand Duchesses? The older two?'

'All four of 'em, from what I hear. People say they were
wonderful hostesses at the Czarskoe Selo lunch last Wednesday.'

'I expect it was a change for them. Poor little devils, they
don't have much of a life!'

By way of reply, Richard Allen silently indicated a small
yacht which had appeared on the bright waters of Peterhof
bay. It was nearly eleven o'clock, and all through the British
squadron crisp orders rang out. Aboard the flagship the marine
band lifted their bugles to their lips. The guests drew back in a
semi-circle behind Admiral Beatty and his flag officers. It was a
great moment for Sir David Beatty, who had scored a huge
personal success in Russia, where since the disasters of the war
with Japan the image of an admiral was that of an obese elderly
man with a white beard and a marked incompetence in sea-
faring and the art of war. Admiral Beatty was only forty-three,
and looked much younger, clean-shaven and debonair, with his
headgear set at the famous 'Beatty tilt'. There were cheers
from the Russian pleasure-boats as he stepped forward, and
the twenty-one gun salute began.

'Here they come, bang on time,' said Ned Murchison.

'Say, I read where the Czar had a terrific yacht,' said Joe
Calvert. 'I never knew he travelled in a paddle-wheeler!'

'That's the *Alexandria*, she's only a tender. The *Standart*
can't put in to Peterhof, and neither can the *Polar Star*.'

'Peterhof's the summer palace?'

'One of them. Watch him now!'

Nicholas II swung himself nimbly up to the frenetically
holy-stoned deck of HMS *Lion* as the bosuns' pipes shrilled
and the imperial standard was broken out. He was wearing the
British uniform of an admiral of the fleet and all his British
decorations. As always when the Czar appeared before a
British regiment or ship's company, however disciplined, there
was a perceptible wave of recognition that the Russian ruler
was so like George V as to pass for his twin brother. They had
the same neat features, inherited from the Danish sister prin-

cesses who had given them birth, the same short, slight bodies and the same trim brown beards. Only the Czar's dark eyes, unfathomable and sad, were in striking contrast to King George's straight blue gaze.

The Emperor and the Admiral saluted and clasped hands. It was the high point of the occasion, urgent in its symbolism, and yet the eyes of all the spectators were already turned on Alexandra Feodorovna, waiting to follow her husband. Then there were murmurs from the critics on ship and shore, and no applause: the Czarina, with her talent for doing the wrong thing, had hidden her face from her husband's subjects behind a white lace parasol.

There were other critics, like Professor Hendrikov, who were talking instructively about bread and circuses. St. Petersburg had been convulsed for a month past by strikes and lockouts, when the shrieking streets had been cleared again and again by Cossack charges, and only the arrival of the British sailors had changed the ugly mood to one of holiday. 'Beatty's visit is worth its weight in gold to Nicholas,' said Professor Hendrikov, but neither his daughter nor her friend was listening. The girls had taken off their hats, much to Madame Hendrikova's displeasure, and Dolly's fair curls were pressed close to Mara's sleek dark head as they craned their necks to look at the *Alexandria*.

'Oh mother, I can see Simon, close beside Her Majesty!' gasped Dolly, who had the binoculars. 'Don't you want to look?'

'Let Mara have the glasses first, dear.'

'I don't need them, thank you, Vera Andreievna, I can see quite well.'

'Then you must have exceptionally long sight,' said Dolly's mother with a smile, and Mara blushed. It was true that she could see Lieutenant Simon Hendrikov, although the other officers standing to attention on the *Alexandria*'s deck were almost a blur: the long vision which made his blunt features clear to Mara Trenova was the vision of first love.

The transfer of a tall woman of forty-two, for long a martyr to sciatica, from a paddle-wheeler in mid-channel to the deck of a battle cruiser was not easy to accomplish gracefully, and the Czarina appeared to hesitate, but a gloved hand appeared from nowhere — as a white-gloved hand always did — to take the furled parasol, and Alexandra's huge picture hat was not even disarranged when she appeared on the deck of the *Lion* and graciously extended her own hand for Admiral Beatty's kiss. The spectators watched eagerly to see who would follow her up the awning-protected companionway. There had been very little cheering for the imperial couple: now there was a groan of disappointment, like a long sigh or growl coming over the water, when no small boy in a sailor suit appeared behind his mother.

'The Heir? Where's the Heir?'

'Where's Alexis Nicolaievich?'

'What are they saying?' Joe Calvert asked.

'They want to see the boy — the Czarevich,' said Murchison. 'I guess he's sick again. He doesn't often get to appear in public.'

'Is that right?' said Joe. 'I knew he had one bad illness, was it a year ago, and that monk fellow, Rasputin, cured him; I thought it was for keeps. Will Rasputin be along with them today?'

'Keep your voice down, for God's sake,' said Murchison between his teeth. 'Don't ever mention that name in a crowd like this!' And lowering his own voice, he said in a whisper, 'He's in Siberia.'

'Where's the Heir, the pretty dear?' said a fat woman wedged close to Joe, whose shawl smelt abominably of fish. 'Where's little Alexis?'

Obviously not to be seen that day. Not even carried in the arms of his *diadka*, the sailor nurse who had carried him, before the eyes of a horrified people, through all the previous year's celebrations of the Romanov tercentenary. The thousands who stared at the nine-year-old Alexis had seen only a pale face beneath bright hair, a thin hand clutching the *diadka*'s shoulder, and then the pathetically dangling legs. Last year's rumours sprang to life again in the boats behind the police barrier, well out of bomb and hand grenade range: helpless cripple, semi-paralysed, idiot child, unfit to reign.

But there came the four Grand Duchesses to take their places behind their father and mother. Across the heat haze rising from the water, they could be seen only as a dazzle of white dresses and white picture hats as big as the Czarina's. Olga and Tatiana wore hats adorned with white ospreys, while the two younger girls, Marie and Anastasia, had wreaths of white and pink roses instead of feathers. The four sisters, so near in age (the eldest eighteen, the youngest just thirteen), were not quenched by the over-elaborate fashions of the times. They were overflowing with health and good spirits and the absolute assurance of enjoyment ahead. The Family enemies relaxed into smiles, the British naval officers and diplomats were beaming, and it was with difficulty that the ship's company looked solemn for the playing of the two national anthems. The Czar, like the Admiral, stood stiffly at the salute. But his sombre eyes looked away from the flags and the bunting, past the Russian double eagle and the white ensign, down the hidden years into the future.

Far away from St. Petersburg, another luncheon party had been arranged for a royal personage. He and his wife, who did not share his titles or his honours, were to be the principal guests at a banquet in the Governor's Residence of a small provincial capital which had been for four hundred years under Turkish rule.

Forty years of western influence had enlarged the population and added some new buildings to the dusty little town, but had hardly altered its appearance. Mosques and minarets still lifted their heads beneath the mountain peaks, and the Turkish bazaar was still a centre of the local life. But there were new influences at work in the town, influences which had seeped across the border from free Serbia, and these went by the name, at least, of liberty and independence. The prince in whose honour the banquet was to be given appeared to some to be an obstacle to these influences and a monster of reaction.

He had known, for he was not a fool, what he might be risking by going to the mountain town, and one threat to his life was made when his procession started on that Sunday morning. But he survived to take the route to the Residence, a route about which there had been some difference of opinion, and it took him past a modest provision store, outside of which stood a nineteen-year-old boy armed with a pistol. There the prince and his wife were shot dead, and by the time the first toast was drunk aboard HMS *Lion* their bodies were lying on two iron bedsteads in the Residence, strewn with flowers hastily taken from the vases arranged along the luncheon tables in the hall below.

17

The news travelled slowly beyond the mountain range. In the town of fifty thousand persons the mayor, the chief of police and the military governor were all disputing responsibility for the security arrangements which had so sensationally broken down, and there was an outbreak of street rioting and looting which did nothing to help the authorities in their attempt to round up the criminals. The youth who fired the two fatal shots had been seized and beaten up by the police, but refused to implicate others in the plot, although at least one had been caught when he jumped into the dry bed of the Miljacka river, after swallowing a cyanide capsule which failed to work. It was some time before the news of the double murder was telegraphed to Austria, whence the dead man had come. It had not even reached Vienna when Lieutenant Hendrikov and his brother officers of the Garde Equipage ate lunch ashore, listening to the sound of music floating across the water from the British ships.

The *Alexandria* had been ordered to return to HMS *Lion* at half past three, but it was almost half past four when the imperial family was ready to embark. The Czarina came aboard exhausted, and was helped by a maid of honour to a comfortable wicker chair, but the Czar appeared to be in excellent humour, and his four daughters were in wild spirits. They all crowded to the rail, laughing and waving their bouquets as their new English friends cheered them on their way. Then there was a concerted rush to put the flowers in water, for the pretty girls, always kept in the background, were touchingly grateful for any little presents they received. The bouquets, very wilted as to petals, were reverently arranged in vases on the Czarina's table. She complained of the strong perfume.

'You're so tired, mother,' said the Grand Duchess Tatiana, carefully arranging cushions at the Czarina's back. 'Wouldn't you like to have some tea?'

'I'd rather wait till we get home.' Alexandra paused, frowning, to listen to her husband teasing his daughters.

'Oil on Mashka's dress,' he said with mock severity. 'The Imp has a run in her stocking, and even Tania has coal dust on her shoes. You three look as if you'd been in the stokehold.'

'So we were, all except Olga,' said Maria.

'Olga stayed on deck, flirting with Georgie Battenberg,' said Anastasia, and Mademoiselle Schneider, in attendance on the

Czarina, said 'Girls, girls! Young ladies, if you please!' But this was automatic, and made no impression; teasing about flirtations, like the flirtations themselves, was encouraged by the parents of the four Grand Duchesses, as a normal and innocent outlet for the romantic ideas of growing girls.

'I don't care,' said Olga, 'Georgie was so nice today, they all were.' She took off her matronly hat with a sigh of relief, and stabbed the two pearl-headed hatpins through the crown. 'Thank goodness we don't have to be dressed up any longer! But I hate to have the party over, it was such fun.'

'Why should it be over?' cried Anastasia. 'The Imp' was the most daring of the sisters, and often showed the most initiative; now she began to clamour for just one hour's extension of their outing, just a short sail across the Gulf and back before they need go home!

'What does mamma say?' asked the Czar, and his wife, supine in the wicker chair, turned her careworn face to his.

'Baby will be missing us,' she said.

'He's got half a dozen people to amuse him,' said the Czar. His manner was unusually breezy, as if the British admiral's uniform he wore, and the company of King George's officers, had been a stimulus to his reserved personality. He bent over Alexandra's chair, and with his fingers made a bracelet round her wrist. 'I do think we might run over to Terijoki and back again, just to get the fresh air. And the girlies would enjoy it.'

In the scales Alexandra perpetually balanced in her mind, the claims of the girlies were as nothing compared to the claims of Baby, as she still called her growing son. But the touch of her husband's fingers, the rarity of his caress in public, at once stirred the deep sexual response Nicholas could always arouse in her. With a blush, and a submissive smile, the Czarina said, 'Well, just for an hour then. Tatiana, tell them to bring us tea.'

There was no room for tea-tables and the elaborate service of the *Standart* aboard the little *Alexandria*, but tea was served in glasses, quickly and informally, and within twenty minutes after the imperial guests had left HMS *Lion* the paddle-wheeler was passing Tolbukin Light, where the British squadron was half hidden by the fortifications of Kronstadt. It had been a very hot day, and the Czarina owned the sea breeze was refreshing, the breeze which lifted the flattened gold hair of the Grand Duchess Olga and stirred the white laces at her throat as she stood by the rail with Lieutenant Simon Hendrikov.

It was an article of faith among all the young officers of the Guard that the Czar's second daughter, Tatiana, was the most beautiful of the four sisters. Marie, called Mashka, or sometimes Bow-Wow, was at fifteen much afflicted by puppy fat, and Anastasia, the Imp, offered no certain promise of beauty. But Tatiana Nicolaievna, at seventeen, was said by the older courtiers to be even more beautiful than her mother, in the legendary days when the Czarina, as Princess Alix of Hesse-Darmstadt, was the admired 'Sunny' of a little German court. Tatiana's red-gold hair was richer in colour than her mother's, her eyes a warm amber instead of Alexandra's cold grey-blue, and her smile was warm and loving. Simon Hendrikov, like his brother officers, admired her from afar. But the one he adored was her older sister, less classically beautiful with her tip-tilted nose and Slavic cheekbones, but also less acquiescent and far more exciting in the vivid shift and domination of her moods.

'Why didn't you come aboard the *Lion*, Simon Karlovich?' she was saying, in the impulsive way some of the courtiers called abrupt. 'You met the English officers last Wednesday, didn't you?'

'My orders were to return to shore, Your — Olga Nicolaievna.' Lieutenant Hendrikov had served in the *Standart* for only three months, not long enough to be accustomed to the order never to say 'Your Imperial Highness' when talking to the girls.

'But you're going to the ball tonight, I hope?'

'I was lucky enough to get one of the invitations, yes.' Simon took his courage in both hands. 'Madame — Olga Nicolaievna — may I have the very great honour and pleasure of a dance with you?'

The girl stared at him in honest surprise. 'Why so formal? Of course I'd love to dance with you again, Simon Karlovich, but you see ... my sister and I aren't going to the ball aboard the *Lion* after all.'

'But I understood you — '

A smiling mask seemed to have dropped over the pretty face

of the Czar's eldest daughter. 'There will be two thousand guests in the British ships tonight,' she said. 'It was thought — not really advisable for us to go.'

The young man understood at once. Although the 'white nights' were not yet over, there would be two hours of darkness in the Gulf of Finland. There would be shadows, patches of light and shade beneath the fairy lamps, along the decks of the two battle cruisers which were to be lashed together for the final entertainment Admiral Beatty intended to offer to all those who had shown such lavish hospitality to the men under his command. There were, aboard the cruisers, too many places where an assassin, come aboard in the great crowd of guests, could lurk until he found the right opportunity to fire at, to draw his knife on, just one girl, or one of two girls, whose only crime was to bear the name of Romanov.

He felt rage rising in his heart. But Simon Hendrikov had been well schooled since he joined the *Standart*; he too could smile, and affect nonchalance in the presence of the constant menace which hung over the heads of those he had sworn to serve. He said, 'The Admiral and his officers will be very disappointed.'

'Oh, so are we all! My little sisters pestered the life out of our cousin, Prince George of Battenberg, wanting to know how *Lion* was to be "tied up" to *New Zealand*, as they called it, and how the guests were going to get from one ship to the other, and what they were going to have for supper — that was Mashka, of course!'

Olga looked smilingly over her shoulder at the plump girl, who was sitting between her father and mother at the flower-laden table, and enjoying a plate of cream cakes.

'I don't know about the supper,' Simon said, 'but I did hear the Englishmen were having trouble in getting enough champagne for the ball tonight. After all the Petersburg hospitality, supplies are beginning to run short in the city.'

'Perhaps it's a good thing they're leaving soon. Are you going in the *Polar Star* to Björkö, to see their tactical manoeuvres?' She stumbled over the technical words, and laughed at herself.

'On Wednesday, yes.' The young man spoke so glumly that Olga laughed again, at him.

'Cheer up, Simon Karlovich, don't look so sad! I'll keep that dance for you, next time we're at a ball together. Maybe next winter, when the court balls begin again, or maybe sooner, who can tell?'

'Are there going to be court balls next winter? Really?'

'Yes, really, didn't you know? The Czar and the Czarina' (the girls always spoke of their parents by their titles) 'decided long ago that as soon as my sister Tatiana was seventeen, we could start going to balls together. We did go to two last winter, but they weren't our *own* balls of course. Next year they will be.'

'And given in the Winter Palace?'

'Just as they were in the Czar Alexander's time.'

'May I take your tea glass, Olga Nicolaievna?' Simon asked.

'Thank you.'

The glass in its wrought silver holder, was put on a tray carried by one of the sailor servants, and Simon again looked into Olga's eyes. She was a tall girl, and he was not much over medium height, strongly built rather than slender: on a ballroom floor, he remembered all too well, her face was very close to his.

'Thank you for your promise, Olga Nicolaievna,' he said. 'But at the Winter Palace, I'm afraid, you'll be too far away from me. You'll be near the thrones, with princes begging you to dance with them — it won't be like our last waltz at Livadia, fifteen days ago.'

'Exactly fifteen days ago? Are you sure?'

'It was the night before the *Standart* sailed for Constanza, I know that.'

'Oh, Constanza!' Olga, to her annoyance, felt her cheeks grow warm. 'Is it really only two weeks since we all went to Rumania? It seems much longer, doesn't it? Such a lot of things have happened since.'

'Things have happened to *you*, Olga Nicolaievna?'

She heard the new, rough note in his voice, and thrilled at the thought of telling Tatiana all about it, in the bedroom which they shared at Peterhof. The sisters loved to gossip about their carefully permitted flirtations, and this was flirtation with a vengeance, something more in earnest than Olga had ever known before. She said,

'I mean, there's been so much to do, since we came back!

First there was the King of Saxony's visit, well, I know that wasn't very exciting; and then this wonderful time with the English squadron, and next month the French President is coming on a state visit, and Tatiana and I are going to ride with the Czar at the grand review!' She clapped her hands. 'It's almost too much for just one summer!'

'So you're happy, Olga Nicolaievna?'

'Why shouldn't I be?' she said, with a quick return of her imperious manner. 'I have everything in the world to make me happy; everybody tells me so! Look, Simon Karlovich, we're nearly at Terijoki, see the club-house and the church! Come and look, you two; you wanted to see Terijoki, didn't you?'

Not only the two younger girls, but the Czar himself, who had been walking up and down the deck with one of his officers, came up to stand beside Olga at the rail, and Simon respectfully drew back. The Grand Duchess Tatiana remained beside the Czarina's chair, and fanned her mother with a small silk fan.

'Nice place, Terijoki,' said the Czar. 'I had some first-rate tennis there last year.'

From the water the little Finnish town looked charming, with the tall steeple of the Orthodox church rising three hundred feet above the harbour. Terijoki was in the Czar's Grand Duchy of Finland, only three miles by land from the Russian frontier posts, and a favoured spot for the rich inhabitants of Petersburg to build their summer dachas. The members of the Terijoki Yacht Club had set their club-house behind green lawns running down to the water's edge, covered, on this hot June Sunday, with tea-tables shaded by gay parasols. The little *Alexandria* could go so close inshore that the imperial ensign was clearly seen from the club-house, and the members left their tables and hurried down to the edge of the lawn to cheer their monarch and his family. The Czar saluted automatically. The three Grand Duchesses waved their handkerchiefs; they loved to be recognised and feel part of the people, but the Czarina called her younger daughters to her side. She detested any appearance of what she called 'currying favour', or even worse, 'courting publicity'.

The *Alexandria* turned away to port, and Anastasia, on her way to rejoin her mother, said sorrowfully, 'Must we really go back to Peterhof now, papa?'

23

'What an Imp you are! Of course we must. Here ends your cruise in Finnish waters, girls, but don't be down-hearted! We'll be off to sea in the *Standart* in another couple of weeks.'

The Czar, with a smile for Simon Hendrikov, resumed his walk. He was fanatical about his need for exercise, and five hours of near-immobility aboard HMS *Lion* had tried him severely. Olga laughed at the expression on Lieutenant Hendrikov's face.

'Are you glad to hear about the *Standart*, Simon Karlovich?'

He made her a little bow. 'Very glad.'

'But you knew it was on the programme, didn't you — the summer cruise?'

'On the programme, yes, but you missed it out of your wonderful summer, Olga Nicolaievna. You jumped straight from Admiral Beatty to President Poincaré, and for all I knew the cruise had been cancelled —'

'Why should it be?'

'In case somebody might be coming from Rumania.'

Simon Hendrikov knew that he had been presumptuous when he saw the Grand Duchess Olga's dark brows, so much darker then her fair hair, meet in a straight line across her eyes. But she ignored his stammered words of apology, and smiled again, saying, 'I can't imagine anything at all that would make the Czar cancel the summer cruise. It's the best thing that happens in the year, for him and the rest of us. We're going to Björkö first, where you'll see the British squadron at their manoeuvres on Wednesday, and then right down the Gulf to Hangö Head. Have you ever been there, on your own, I mean? It's your first tour of duty on a *Standart* cruise, I know.'

'I've never been to Hangö, Olga Nicolaievna. But I do know Björkö, as it happens. My father and mother have a little dacha in that direction, not far from Koivisto village.'

'They have? Could we go and see it? Would your parents mind? We've none of us ever been inside a real country dacha, just those awful villas that pretend to be dachas, between Czarskoe Selo and Pavlovsk. Where is yours? Is it far from the harbour? Could we get there on foot?'

The torrent of eager questions fascinated Simon. He had

been for too short a time in the imperial entourage to know what boundless curiosity the four Grand Duchesses, and even their little brother, felt in the homes of everybody who lived outside the court circle. During the two months spent at Livadia, their palace in the Crimea, while the *Standart* was in harbour at Yalta, there had been little opportunity for the girls to go about among the people: they went, guarded always by the security police and in automobiles, from one princely Crimean estate to the other. But a dacha, his father's little dacha by the river-side — that his princess should want even to look at it was outside his scope of belief. He managed to say that his parents would be honoured beyond words —

'But they're not there now, are they? I thought your father was a professor in St. Petersburg.'

'So he is. They went there with my sister Dolly at Easter, when I was at sea ... and to tell you the honest truth, Olga Nicolaievna, I don't know what sort of state the place is in, shut up since the spring ... I'd have to arrange to get it cleaned, and everything.'

'Oh no, that would spoil it all! People are always cleaning up for us, and putting out flags, and offering us the holy ikons, and turning out the guard. Couldn't we just walk to your dacha at Koivisto, and take a picnic basket from the *Standart*, and have tea there? My sisters would be absolutely *thrilled*, and so would Alexis be, I know.'

After all, he thought, she was still a schoolgirl, with a schoolgirl's sudden enthusiasms, in spite of the voyage to Constanza and the rumours of her engagement to the Rumanian prince which had aroused his jealousy. He said,

'As far as walking goes, that's easy; you wouldn't even have to go through Koivisto village. There's a path from the shore along the riverside, and it isn't far. But remember, won't you, that it's just a little place, a little wooden cottage, not a grand dacha like the ones round Terijoki—'

'That doesn't matter! It'll be such fun to look forward to! I'll tell the others as soon as we get home. We'll keep it a secret, won't we, Simon Karlovich — my sisters and I, and you and Alexis, nobody else?'

'As Your Imperial Highness wishes.' He couldn't help but call her that, she was his princess, who talked to him, and would let him walk with her by the river of his boyhood holidays, and he stood at the salute as she smiled and turned away. The *Alexandria* was coming up to Peterhof quay, and the Czarina was being helped out of her wicker chair. The last thing he heard Olga Nicolaievna say as she joined her sisters was, 'What have you all done with my horrible hat?'

The sightseers who went out from St. Petersburg to look at the British officers and their imperial guests made their way back to the city long before the first course was over at the luncheon tables aboard the *Lion*. Slowly, on that hot afternoon, the capital filled up again: family parties strolled in the Summer Gardens or in Mar's Field, and young people studied the shop windows in the Nevski Prospekt. The factory workers and mechanics went back to their crowded homes on Viborg Side or the Lines near the Maly Neva. By contrast the Austrian capital was empty when the news of the double murder in the mountain province reached the city. The news of the tragedy had to be broken first to the Emperor, Franz Josef, for the dead man had been his heir-apparent, and the eighty-four years old Emperor was on holiday at his favourite place, Bad Ischl. His subjects had a carefree afternoon in the Weinerwald or the Semmering, drinking wine in the flowery gardens of rustic inns and listening to music. They trailed back to the city in the early evening, young girls arm in arm with their sweethearts, and young fathers carrying sleeping children on their shoulders. By that time the telegraph had begun to send its message of murder across the world. It reached the Czar and his ministers, the British Admiral and his officers, when the great ball aboard the two cruisers had just begun. It reached the young Grand Duchesses in their protected home at Peterhof, and it reached some to whom the name of murder was not horrible, in the slums of Petersburg. Soon the whole world knew that a student terrorist, of the same breed if not of the same nation as those who had hunted the Romanov Czars for so long, had shot and killed the Archduke Franz Ferdinand, and his wife the Duchess of Hohenberg, in a place few people had ever heard of called Sarajevo.

CHAPTER TWO

The Hotel Europa, seventy-five years old in 1914, continued to be the most fashionable hotel in St. Petersburg. Connoisseurs in living might extol the cuisine and the general unpredictability of the Hotel de France on the Morskaia, and the new rich of the rising business community might prefer to spend their money and show off their women in the Astoria, but neither could seriously challenge the Europa. It had been built as part of Rossi's great complex in the heart of the capital, with the park, the squares, the theatres all harmonising in their architecture and their façades of yellow ochre, and on the hot July night when Joe Calvert came in from the Nevski Prospekt some of the dust from the street seemed to be dyed the same gold in the westering sunlight. He stood blinking on the threshold of the bar. It was entered from the lobby of the Europa, through the main door on a street leading to the former Michael Palace, but the tall windows opened on the Nevski Prospekt, and they were open now, in spite of the noise of trams and droshkies, to let the warm summer air come in.

Joe surveyed the place with well-concealed amusement. The words 'American Bar' had recently been added, in gilt letters, to the glass doors, but the interior was like no saloon he had ever seen in America. The long mahogany bar, the brass rail, the white-coated barmen and the array of bottles behind them were not to be found in the Europa, where the atmosphere was more like that of an English club. Waiters in tail coats moved quietly between the tables and the heavy saddlebag chairs, set not too close together in a room heavy with the scent of Russian cigarettes and bright with the uniforms of a colourful army. There were no women to be seen. Ladies, sometimes perfectly respectable ladies, took tea in the Palm Court of the new Astoria; the Europa's bar, whether American or not, remained a strictly masculine preserve.

'Are you making up your mind to have a drink, Mr. Calvert?'

27

said a voice from behind the pages of *Vechernaya Vremia*, and Joe turned round with a smile.

'Oh, good evening, Captain Allen. Sorry I didn't see you at first. How are you?'

'Very well, thanks. Won't you join me, unless you're meeting somebody?'

'Nobody at all.' Joe Calvert settled his long body behind the corner table where the man from the British Embassy was watching him with quizzical eyes. Captain Allen was as unobtrusive as ever in a dark civilian suit, with his blond hair carefully brushed and his blond moustache close-clipped. His nondescript face reminded Joe of the rubber toys of his childhood, which could be squeezed into any shape by skilful fingers.

'How about some vodka?' Richard Allen said, beckoning to a waiter. There was a small carafe of vodka in a bowl of ice, with one glass, on the table, flanked by another ice bowl containing a little pot of caviar, and a plate of sliced black bread.

'Vodka seems to be an acquired taste, and I haven't acquired it yet,' said Joe. 'I'd like a sherry cobbler.'

'Do you think they'll know how to mix it, here?'

'Oh, they should,' said Joe softly. 'I gave them a lesson myself, a few days ago. No point in calling it an American Bar if they can't mix American drinks, is there?'

Captain Allen laughed. Young Calvert wasn't quite the 'new boy' he had thought him at the American Embassy reception last night, when the consular staff, pressed into service for the Fourth of July, had been over-eager in trying to make things go. Young Calvert looked fine-drawn and pale this evening, as if the rising tension in St. Petersburg had communicated itself at last to the one foreign colony which had remained in splendid isolation since the murder at Sarajevo.

'That was a very good party your chargé d'affaires gave us yesterday,' he said. 'I enjoyed myself.'

'Why, thanks. We did our best, Independence Day and all that, but we couldn't measure up to the great shows you people put on when the Navy was here. Congratulations, by the way; I hear your Admiral was a roaring success in Moscow.'

'Roaring being the appropriate word,' said Allen. 'He's got a fine, powerful voice, has Admiral Beatty, and the story goes that when he spoke out of doors in the Sokolniki Park he could be heard inside the Kremlin. Anyway he made a great impression, and we've all survived — even His Majesty. 'I suppose you heard about the Björkö foul-up, at the tac. exercises in close order?'

'I did hear there was some trouble aboard the *Polar Star*,' said Joe discreetly.

'That's putting it mildly. The damned yacht sailed too close to the cruisers, and was nearly swamped in the wash when they turned. The Czar and his entourage were clinging to the rail, knee deep in water, God knows how they weren't drowned.'

'Sounds like a court of enquiry for somebody.'

'Not necessarily. It's only a few years since Admiral Nilov ran the *Standart* aground, and all the imperial family had to be taken off in boats. Aground in the Gulf of Finland, on a summer cruise! The Czar himself stopped the Admiral from committing suicide over that one, and there was never any question of a reprimand.'

'The Czar seems like a pretty cool customer.'

'Cool, or apathetic.' Captain Allen paused while the waiter put Joe's sherry cobbler on the table. 'There's an element of farce in the Russian character, as you'll soon find out. They put on great shows and ceremonies, and then something goes wrong out of sheer inefficiency, as it did aboard the *Polar Star* last week, and everybody behaves like knockabout comedians in the music halls.'

'It might be rather an endearing trait.'

'I certainly hope they'll stick to the comedy line for the next few weeks.'

'Even during the French state visit?'

'There'll be some unrehearsed funny turns during that visit too. By the way, what are they saying in France about President Poincaré's trip to Russia? Your last posting was to Lyon, didn't I hear you say last night?'

'My last posting and my first, I only left Washington in January '13. Well, I can't say there was much interest expressed in Lyon, one way or another, but I had Paris leave before coming here, and the Parisians were full of it; some approved, but the Socialist newspapers were dead against it. Said the French President ought not to consort with — you know the sort of stuff they write,' said Joe, looking cautiously around. The bar was full of Russian officers, none of whom showed any interest in the two foreigners in their quiet corner.

'I know the stuff all right. But talking about consorting, quite a lot of people here see it the other way round. The monarchists are saying the Romanov ancestors will turn in their graves when Nicholas welcomes the president of a republic to his palace. However, there's nothing they can do about it, France is the ally of Russia, bound by solemn treaties going back to the last reign. Then the Socialists — Social Democrats *and* Social Revolutionaries, argue like their comrades in France. They think the alliance with France is bound to lead to war.'

'But isn't your own country part of that alliance?' asked Joe Calvert.

'Of the Triple Entente, yes,' Richard Allen said.

'Meaning just good friends, eh?'

'Something like that.'

'And what are we?'

'The Americans? Nothing, so far. But you just might be called upon to keep the ring in Europe, one of these days.'

'That's not very likely.'

'We shall see. I'm glad President Wilson has appointed an ambassador to Russia at last. Not that your chargé d'affaires hasn't done extremely well, but still — two years without any ambassador at all, and only because your Congress revoked some eighty-year-old trade agreement with the Russians, that everyone here had forgotten for generations!'

'It was a pretty convincing vote by Congress — three hundred to one, as I recall.'

'When do you expect the new man in St. Petersburg?'

'Mr. Marye? Not for a while yet. The Senate has to advise and consent to his appointment first. He'll probably arrive at the end of September or the beginning of October.'

Richard Allen considered that, with his pale eyes as round as glass marbles beneath lifted brows.

'So there'll be no American Ambassador in Russia for the next eight weeks. Too bad!'

'There won't be much doing in the holiday season.'

'I'm not so sure. What are they saying at your shop about the murders at Sarajevo?'

'Oh that.' At Joe's shop, if by 'shop' Allen meant the US consulate, the current problem had nothing to do with international politics, but with the labour troubles of an American concern called the Stepeezi Shoe Company, recently established in St. Petersburg. Joe had spent the afternoon drafting a memorandum to the parent company in Philadelphia. It was written on approved consular lines and he was rather proud of it, but it was hardly on the level of a Note exchanged between the Great Powers. 'Sarajevo?' he said, 'you should have asked our chargé d'affaires about that, last night.'

'I did,' said Captain Allen, 'but every day counts in a Balkan crisis, and it's a week since the Archduke and his wife were killed. I don't like the way the Austrians are hanging in the wind. If they want to pin the final responsibility for the murder plot on the Serbian government, I should have thought both the Ballhausplatz and the Hofburg would have shown their hands by now. After all, Franz Ferdinand was the heir-apparent to the throne of Austria-Hungary.'

'You wouldn't think so by the way they buried him,' said Joe. 'A scrambled lying-in-state and a midnight drive through a thunderstorm to a private vault at Artstetten. I read in our press digest that the coffins were nearly toppled into the Danube before they got there.'

'Yes, well, that's the Austrian idea of drama, they've never recovered from Mayerling. And the Archduke wasn't really popular in Vienna. That morganatic marriage stuck in more throats than the Emperor's.'

'Well, if he wasn't all that important, why should they want to involve the Serbs in it? They've got three of the Bosnian gang in custody now, and this fellow Princip is known to have done the actual shooting—why not just string him up, and call it quits?'

'Because unfortunately,' said the Englishman with a wry smile, 'we're dealing with the Near East, not the Wild West. Will you excuse me, please?' He got up and shook hands with a tall Russian officer, who had greeted him on his way out of the bar. They chatted for a few minutes, which Joe employed to order the little carafe of vodka to be refilled.

'That's very kind of you,' said Allen, sitting down again just as the waiter's careful pouring ended. 'I hope you'll forgive me for not introducing you to Count Bronski. He doesn't speak a word of English, and unlike most of them he doesn't speak French either.'

'I was admiring your Russian,' said Joe. 'I saw you were reading the evening paper when I came in, but the way you

31

speak it — gosh! How long have you been attached to the British Embassy?'

'Oh, not so very long on this tour of duty,' said the Englishman easily, 'but as a matter of fact I was born here. My father came from Lancashire: he set up some of the modern textile mills in Russia, in the Czar Alexander's time.'

'That sure gave you a head start with the language. And maybe you could advise me — ' Joe looked at his pocket watch. 'Or am I detaining you? Maybe you're expecting friends, or going out?'

'I *am* expecting guests, and we're dining at Cubat's. But being Russian, they'll be at least an hour late, so there's no hurry. You're taking a long time to finish your sherry cobbler.'

'Well, I — the thing is, I've been invited to my language teacher's house tonight.'

'Ah, you've acquired a language teacher. Good.'

'And as people here seem to eat at all hours, I don't know if I'll be crashing into the middle of *their* dinner, or have to hang around until they finish it, or just go hungry.'

'That depends on the man who's going to teach you Russian,' said Allen, looking amused.

'It's a lady. Madame Hendrikova, she lives on Vassili Island.'

Allen whistled. 'You must be quite a linguist, Mr. Calvert. Vera Andreievna can pick and choose her pupils, and one thing she insists on, they must all have what she calls a language brain.'

'You make me feel as if I were going to sit an exam tonight. So you know Madame Hendrikova?'

'Only very slightly. I've been to their apartment twice, but that was as her husband's guest, not hers. And I haven't met any of the family. I believe there are two very pretty daughters, and a son in the Marine Guards, but I imagine they fight shy of papa's political evenings.'

'I thought the husband was a history professor.'

'*And* by way of being a politician. Rather a swell in his day, an elected member of the First Duma, but after that little flutter in the parliamentary line was closed down by imperial ukase, Karl Hendrikov was warned that he would lose his professorship if he went on with it. I suppose he's what we'd call a Liberal, and you a Democrat; at any rate, he still writes for the

32

Liberal paper, *Rech*, and Vladimir Nabokov was one of the guests the first time I went there. Nowadays he seems to have taken up with Kerensky, the Labour leader — the barrister who made such an impression in the Lena Goldfields case. You won't meet Monsieur Kerensky tonight, though. He's politicking somewhere in Siberia. According to the papers, he was attending a schoolteachers' congress on the day Franz Ferdinand was shot. At a town in the Urals called Ekaterinburg.'

'That's all right with me,' said Joe. 'I don't feel equal to meeting any Russian politicians yet, Liberal *or* Labour.'

'You'll have a very pleasant evening. They'll probably ask a crowd of relatives and friends to meet you, and the samovar will be filled and refilled until midnight. You're wise not to have any dinner! But let me get you another of those cobbler concoctions. By the way, I thought you Americans went in for cocktails, made with gin?'

'Oh, we do,' Joe Calvert assured him. 'I was just keeping my head clear for Madame Hendrikova. No, not another, thanks. And thanks for the briefing, too. I think I'll go up to my room and have a wash.'

'That's right, you're staying in the hotel, aren't you?'

'Only until I find a flat. And I suppose that means until I can speak enough Russian to hire a maid.'

'It won't take you long. I've got a small flat of my own in the Italianskaia, about five minutes' walk from here. Number 365, an easy one to remember, just think of the days of the year. After President Poincaré gets safely back to Paris, maybe we could fix up a bridge four there some evening?'

'I'd like that,' said Joe, shaking hands. 'But poker's my own game.'

'I rather thought it might be.'

The Hendrikovs lived in the Fourth Line of Vassili Island, a wide street set at right angles to the University Quay, where two rows of tall apartment buildings faced each other across stone pavements with grass verges planted with linden trees. The limes were just coming into flower, and the sweet scent of the blossom was mixed with a faint but distinct smell of salt sea and tarry ropes. Joe sniffed it appreciatively as he paid off his driver. The Hendrikov flat, he was told by an obsequious

33

porter, bowing very low, was two stairs up, if the *barin* would give himself the trouble to ascend the staircase, since alas! there was no elevator. The stairs were well carpeted, and solid mahogany doors indicated that there were two apartments on each floor. He rang the Hendrikovs' bell. A tidy girl with a broad face and her hair in two plaits, wearing a white apron, curtseyed as she opened the door. He hung his straw boater on a stand in the hall and was shown into a pleasant family room where two girls rose to greet him with curtseys far more graceful than the maid's.

'Good evening,' Joe said as he made his bow. 'My name's Calvert, from the US consulate. I've an appointment with Madame Hendrikova . . .'

'Good evening, sir,' said the fair girl politely. 'Please sit down.'

'Thank you.' The two girls had been sitting at a round table, covered with a red plush cloth, with open books before them. Joe took a chair opposite, and said, rather at a loss:

'Uh — it's been a beautiful day, hasn't it?'

'Beautiful,' the dark girl repeated. He could have sworn they were laughing at him. As a rule Joe was immediately at his ease with girls, but there was something disconcerting in the way those two were staring, as if some strange creature had been released in their familiar room. And yet they were very attractive, the fair one, with her curls tied back by a black ribbon bow, extremely pretty; the dark one, with her black braids wound round her head, also pretty in a more severe style. They had the same hazel eyes, neither brown nor green, and on the strength of that resemblance Joe decided to say:

'Are you Madame Hendrikova's daughters?'

'Oh no, sir,' the fair girl managed to say, 'my older sister Betsy is married, and lives in Denmark. I'm Darya Hendrikova, and this is my friend Marya.'

'Mara Trenova,' the dark girl said. 'We are pupils of the Xenia School.'

'Is that a boarding school?' said Joe.

'Yes, but now we have holidays.'

'I see,' Joe glanced round the room, seeking inspiration for what he could say next. It was well furnished in mahogany, with glass-fronted bookcases, a mirrored sideboard and a china cabinet, but there were also some execrable examples of still-

34

life painting which included one enormous canvas, a 'problem picture' of the Nineties, representing a young woman with a baby at her breast and no wedding ring, staring morosely into a dying fire. No inspiration there! Joe was about to venture, 'Are you going on to college?' when Darya helped by saying, 'Please to excuse my mother. She had another pupil, but I think now she is coming.' The sounds of farewell, and of doors shutting, could be heard from the hall. In another moment a little stout lady, with fair greying hair screwed up on the top of her head, and her face pink from exertion, burst into the living-room.

'My dear Mr. Calvert,' she said effusively, 'I'm so sorry to have kept you waiting. My last pupil was over half an hour late for his lesson. I hope Dolly and Molly have been entertaining you?'

'They've been very nice,' said Joe, and Dolly said something in Russian which made her mother turn on her with a snap.

'Dolly, it's very rude to speak your own language in front of somebody who doesn't understand it!'

'What did she say, madame?'

'Please excuse a silly girl, Mr. Calvert. You are the first American my daughter ever saw, and what she said was that you don't look at all as she expected.'

'I should have worn a war-bonnet and wampum, maybe,' said Joe good-naturedly.

'Aha! You can be silly too! This is well,' said Madame Hendrikova. 'Come now, we must talk about your work. I have a little room far, far away,' she waved her hand to indicate the other corner of a not very large flat, 'where I receive my pupils, but tonight we shall sit in my husband's study. He too has been looking forward to meeting you.'

With another snap of 'Dolly! tell them to make the tea!' the little lady ushered Joe through a connecting door into a room lined with books on open shelves where Professor Hendrikov rose courteously from behind a laden desk. He was not a tall man, though decidedly taller than his wife, with a high scholar's forehead, growing bald, and clumps of hair arranged behind his ears. With his greying moustache and imperial, and something flowing about his collar and tie, he reminded Joe of a bust of Shakespeare which had stood in his school library at home.

It was about Joe's home that Professor Hendrikov began to

35

talk gently, discovering that he was an only son, that his father had 'sort of retired', while his mother was active in women's club affairs, and getting some idea of the home in Baltimore, Maryland, where Joe had been born and his parents still lived. He nodded approvingly at Joe's description of the brick-paved streets, where the old trees thrust their roots up strongly and made the bricks uneven, and the suburban houses with wide stoops and porch swings where pretty girls and their beaux sat on summer evenings, playing mandolines and sometimes singing in harmony, while younger kids played in the middle of streets where only an occasional horse and buggy ever came.

'And you're a university graduate, I'm told?' he said.

'Yes sir, AB Princeton. Princeton 1911, I majored in French Civilisation.'

'Dear me,' said Professor Hendrikov. 'Already we have something in common. My own subject is French history, from the Revolution to the present day.'

'*Donc, attention, monsieur!*' interrupted Madame Hendrikova, '*parlons français!*'

'*Bien madame.*'

She led the American briskly through an account of his daily life in Lyon and his short holiday in Paris, and then exclaimed '*Assez!* The grammar is very good, the accent not; I think we shall work in Russian-English, not Russian-French.'

'That's fine with me,' said Joe. 'I wasn't planning on working any other way.'

'Then the sooner we start the better. Normally I see my students twice a week, Mr. Calvert, but you I should like to see three times a week for what remains of this month, until we go on holiday to Finland.'

It was agreed that Joe should come to the flat on Mondays, Wednesdays and Fridays, beginning next day at six o'clock.

'It's really very unfortunate,' fretted Madame Hendrikova, 'that you're starting on the eve of the holiday season. We go to the dacha in one month from today, Sunday the second of August; would it be possible for you to come and spend a week with us at Koivisto, talking nothing but Russian, as far as you are able?'

'My dear Vera,' said her husband, 'you're forgetting that Betsy and Hans are coming all the way from Copenhagen to spend August with us, and you've already invited so many

36

relatives we'll have to board them in the village. I don't think that would appeal very much to Mr. Calvert.'

'It's very kind of you, madame,' said Joe, 'but in any case it wouldn't be possible for me to get away from Petersburg. I'm the new man here, and the junior vice-consul; my Paris leave is all I rate this year.'

'Then I shall set you a great many exercises to do in August,' said his teacher. 'And now come and have some tea.'

When they returned to the living-room the table had been spread with a white cloth, and Dolly was presiding over a samovar set at one end. To Joe, the room seemed to have filled with people all talking at once, who presently resolved themselves into Cousin Timofey, a violinist under Glazunov at the Conservatoire; Cousin Arkadeiv, a laboratory assistant to the great Mendeliev; Cousin Boris, who was a junior curator at the Museum of Russian Art, and at least four plump female cousins dressed up for the occasion in evening blouses bedecked with lace inserts and tucks. They spoke in French to Joe, and were all very friendly and welcoming, a great deal more so than the stuffy businessmen of Lyon, not one of whom would have dreamed of inviting a young American into their bourgeois homes.

The maid and another girl of the same sturdy peasant type came and went with platters of food, until presently the whole table was covered. There was a dish of sliced white fish of some unfamiliar sort, and another of Baltic herring; various salads, including cucumber with an oil dressing, and cubed beetroot; black bread, and bread sprinkled with poppy seeds, and saucers of raspberry jam, which some of the company mixed with their tea instead of lemon. Dolly Hendrikova left her place behind the samovar to offer Joe a plate of ginger snaps, bought especially for him, she said with her little curtsey, at the English Shop on the Nevski Prospekt.

He looked up at her, smiling. She was really very pretty, with those clear eyes, and the soft features on which life had left as yet no mark, and the fair shining ringlets which had escaped from her severe black bow.

'You have such ginger cakes in Baltimore?' asked Cousin Timofey, and to please Dolly Joe said yes, monsieur, he was crazy about them, and took a second from the plate she had left near him.

37

'Russia must be very strange to you, monsieur.'

'It is, a bit, but I hope to be here for a good long while, and see something of the country.'

'What do you find most difficult to get accustomed to?' persisted Timofey. 'The food? The wine? The hours we keep?'

'The calendar,' said Joe unexpectedly.

'The *calendar*?'

'You know why. It's the fifth of July in America, yesterday was our Independence Day, but here it's only the twenty-third of June. I've been in trouble at the consulate already, for getting the dates mixed up.'

There was a general laugh, under cover of which Joe thought he heard Professor Hendrikov mutter, 'I wish we could put the calendar back to the first of June, for all of us.' But he was not sure that he had heard aright, for Madame Hendrikova, reverting to English, broke in emphatically:

'There now, Mr. Calvert, we've found a good topic for your first Russian lesson: after the alphabet, the days of the week and the months of the year. But tonight already, you shall learn how to address Russians, and be addressed: you shall no longer say to me, Madame Hendrikova, but Vera Andreievna, using the patronymic; and to my daughter, Darya Karlovna, and so on. You shall use each time the person's Christian name and his father's name; it is more correct Russian usage than the other.'

'But what if you don't know a person's father's Christian name?' parried Joe.

'Then you shall listen until he is called by it, and then you shall remember it. Now we take your own case. Your Christian name is Joseph, so?'

'Right.'

'And your father's?'

'It's George, as a matter of fact. George Alexander Calvert.'

'Thus we see,' said his new teacher, 'that your name in Russian is Yusuv Yurievich, and so, from now on, you shall be known here.'

'To Yusuv Yurievich!' cried the musician, raising a glass of what looked more like yellow wine than tea. But the rechristened Yusuv said very decidedly:

'I'm sorry, madame, but I don't think I'd know myself as

38

Yusuv What-d'you-call it. I'll go on being plain Joe Calvert, if you don't mine.'

There was a shout of laughter, even louder than before, and though Madame Hendrikova shook her head, the American was pleased. He had asserted himself, and they liked him for it; Joe felt himself accepted into the friendliest group he had yet met in St. Petersburg. The talk broke out again like Niagara Falls: it was almost a shock when a new, deep voice cut through the gabble and a young man said from the door:

'What a row you're all making! I could hear you from the end of the Fourth Line!'

Simon Hendrikov told the droshki driver to wait for ten minutes, say a quarter of an hour, and when the man demurred he offered him double fare for the return trip to the Morskaia, which was accepted. A young officer going to one of the smart clubs or hotels on that fashionable street would be good for a big tip as well as double fare when the drive was over, and the *isvoschik* got contentedly down from his seat and gave his scraggy horse a nose-bag. On his way to the front door Simon looked up at the unlighted, open window on the second floor, and listened for a moment to the babble of talk. They were sitting in the dark as usual, smoking and talking about art and the artist's duty to his public, or so he was prepared to bet. Indoors, the staircase was well lighted, and as he reached his own landing a man in naval uniform came running downstairs from the floor above. He wore the badges of a commander's rank. Simon saluted, received a pleasant 'good evening' and, while feeling for his latchkey, watched the stranger go downstairs and out of the building. There had been something oddly familiar about his face.

He opened the living-room door without a sound. There they all were, his family and the cousins, the eternal hangers-on, their faces only visible by the tiny points of light from their cigarettes. He told them he could hear the row they were making from the end of the Fourth Line, and flicked the electric light switch by the door.

'I wish you wouldn't do that, boy!' The professor was blinking in the crude white light. Suddenly they were all shown at their worst, sitting round a littered table with dregs in their glasses, the women with tousled hair, the men irritable. Simon himself was immaculate in his summer uniform. He had square features, crisp hair more chestnut than brown, and clear hazel eyes like his sister's. His mother said, 'You're late.'

'I know, mother, but something came up at the last moment, I'm very sorry.' Simon pulled his sister's hair, said something in Russian to Mara which made her smile, and then went round the table greeting all the company in French and kissing the hands of the ladies. He shook hands with Joe Calvert and bade him welcome to St. Petersburg. It was a finished performance of ease and good manners, but Simon Hendrikov's restless impatience was clearly held in check beneath the surface.

'Father, could I speak to you alone?' he said when the circle of the table was complete. 'I've got a droshki waiting, I mustn't stay too long.'

'But Simon —' Madame Hendrikova was silenced by her husband's gesture. 'Come into my study, boy,' he said very gravely indeed.

'I've told them to make fresh tea for Simon, mother,' said Dolly, pulling a heavy brass ceiling lamp down to the table. Joe jumped up to help her, and some of the women began lifting the scattered plates from the centre of the cloth.

'Don't trouble, Mr. Calvert, I know the way of it,' said Dolly. She held a match to the lamp wick and replaced the large white shade. A smell of paraffin, accompanied by a soft golden light, diffused itself through the friendly room. Dolly switched off the lights in the chandelier. 'Papa is so old-fashioned,' she confided to Joe, 'he likes the oil lamp better than anything more modern.'

'I don't blame him.' But the spell was broken. One or two of the women murmured that they ought to be going home.

'Nonsense, it's not eleven o'clock yet,' said the hostess automatically. 'Simon and his father won't be long, I'm sure.'

'Are you?' said Cousin Timofey. 'Simon looks wrought up enough to be breaking the news of a general mobilisation.'

'Good God!' said the museum curator. Two of the older women crossed themselves, and Simon's mother, very pale, told Timofey that was a horrible thing to say. It was over in a moment, for Simon and his father came back smiling, the young man putting something in his pocket as he closed the study door.

'You must sit down and drink a glass of tea with us, Simon,' said Madame Hendrikova, imperative in her relief.

'All right then, but I really mustn't stay more than a few minutes. I'm invited to supper at the Yacht Club, and I don't want to be late.'

'The club on Krestovski Island?' asked the professor.

'No, father, the Yacht Club on the Morskaia.'

'And then on to the gipsies, no doubt,' said Mara Trenova.

Simon gave her an indifferent look. 'Possibly,' he said.

Joe Calvert missed none of it: the delight of the liberal professor at his son's entrée to the most exclusive club in Petersburg, and the disappointment in the girl Mara's face. She came here to see him, and now he's walking out on her, Joe thought. Too bad!

Dolly intervened hastily. 'Well, as long as you *are* here, give us some court gossip,' she said. 'When is the Grand Duchess Olga's engagement to be announced?'

Simon was fitting a black Russian cigarette into an amber mouthpiece.

'What engagement is that?' he said.

'Oh, come on, now!' 'Simon, don't be silly!' The voices broke out in a gush of relief, as if a court romance put the hint of war a long way off. 'We all know you went to Constanza for the great meeting with Prince Carol, and that she liked him very much —'

'She *met* Prince Carol at Constanza, that's all anybody knows.' The young officer scowled. A handsome kid with one hell of a temper, thought Joe Calvert; with that build he should be useful in a scrap.

'I heard Olga Nicolaievna was going to marry the Prince of Wales,' said one of the ladies.

'But Monsieur Sazonov prefers the Rumanian match,' said Professor Hendrikov. 'Our foreign minister thinks it would advance Russia's plans in the Black Sea. On to Constantinople! The old Byzantine dream will never die.'

'Are princesses still made to marry for political reasons? Sounds like the Middle Ages,' said Joe.

'The Romanovs are *living* in the Middle Ages,' said Mara.

'The Empress Dowager has a great deal more influence in the family than Sazonov,' said Madame Hendrikova, 'and *she* would like to see her eldest granddaughter married to the future King of England.'

'I've been told,' said Cousin Timofey, 'that the young lady herself favours the Grand Duke Dmitri.'

Simon pushed his chair back and got up. 'What a pack of gossips you all are!' he said. 'Next time I'm here, I'll expect to find you holding a spiritualist seance, or telling fortunes with the tarot cards.'

'And you get plenty of occult influences at court, don't you?' Mara said.

'You know nothing whatever about the court, Mara Ivanovna,' Simon retorted. 'Mother, I must go. I'll leave the rest of you to your old wives' tales. Good night!'

'Simon darling, when shall we see you again?'

He was too warm-hearted to resist the appeal in his mother's voice. He stooped and kissed her.

'I hope to get a few hours' city leave before the cruise to Finland starts, but I'm not sure. They're keeping us pretty close to barracks this week. Oh, that reminds me! I meant to ask you something, mother.'

'Yes, what is it, dear?'

'Those new people who moved into the flat just overhead, have they a son in the Navy?'

Madame Hendrikova laughed. 'What an idea! The Martovs have a son in the cradle, barely three months old. They're quite a young couple; but of course you haven't seen them yet. What made you think they had a son in the Navy?'

'Oh, nothing. Just a man I met on the stairs, he must have been a visitor. He reminded me of somebody, that's all.' Simon twisted the door handle irresolutely. 'Well, good night again.'

'Good night, Simon Karlovich.' It was almost a chorus, and after that nobody spoke until the door of the apartment closed. Then Cousin Timofey said with a sarcastic laugh:

'Who would have thought your son would turn out to be such a supporter of the court, Karl Leontovich? Simon has become a monarchist since he was promoted into the *Standart*.'

'Imperial favour means a lot to a young man with his own way to make in the service,' said the professor.

'How does Simon stand in Rasputin's favour?'

What might have been an argument was stopped by the girl Mara. She got up, and looking only at Madame Hendrikova, said, 'Many thanks for your hospitality, Vera Andreievna. I really must go home now, I live so far away, and my mother will be anxious about me.'

'May I have the pleasure of seeing you to your home, Mara Ivanovna?' said Joe. He didn't know what prompted his offer, the girl might live ten miles out in the country for all he knew, but he didn't like to see a woman humiliated, even if it was her own fault for showing her feelings all too plainly, and then needling the guy until he turned on her in front of everybody. Anyway it was a good move, because Mara smiled, and the other Russians burst into a shout of laughter. 'Aha! he has begun to use the patronymic!' 'Your pupil will do you credit, Vera Andreievna!' It was a small joke, but they made the most of it to relieve the tension which Simon had brought into the room.

'Please don't worry about me, monsieur, I'll get a tramcar at the bridge,' said Mara.

'Let us all three walk along to the new bridge together,' said the professor. 'We can hardly expect our foreign guest to know one bridge from another yet.'

His getting up was the signal for a general departure. Mara went away with Dolly, and came back wearing a tightly fitting blue serge jacket over her dress of the same material, and a cream straw hat not unlike Joe's own. The professor took up a shapeless homburg, and while the other guests lingered chattering on the landing, they went out together to the Fourth Line. Here, after the dimness in the linden-shadowed living-room until Simon's entry, it was surprisingly light.

'Not as light as it was two weeks ago,' said Professor Hendrikov in answer to Joe's comment. 'If you had been here at the time of the summer solstice, you could have stood on the Neva bank and seen the sun sinking into the Gulf of Finland while the light of a new day was dawning in the east. But I think that at the beginning and the ending of what we call "the white nights" the colours are even more subtle than at the melo-dramatic moment of the solstice.'

He was right about the subtle colour of the white night. From Strelka Point the river and the city seemed to have taken on the colours of a clouded pearl, shading through rose to lilac

43

above the deep violet of the granite embankments. The sky above was palest grey, pierced on each side of the Neva by the golden spires of the Admiralty and the Cathedral of St. Peter and St. Paul.

'Listen!' said Mara Trenova.

A carillon, delicate but insistent, rang across the river from the cathedral belfry.

'It's a tune, isn't it?' said Joe.

'It's the chime of *Gospodi pomiloui*, "Lord have mercy upon us",' said the professor. 'It rings every quarter hour. If we waited here for another quarter, we should hear the hymn the bells play at midnight. *Kol slaven nach Gospod v Sion*, "How glorious is our Lord in Sion". My wife shall teach you the Russian words.'

Joe glanced down at Mara. She was looking up the broad reaches of the Neva, and he could see tears on her black lashes. Instinctively he slipped his hand through her arm. She looked up at him, surprised, and her face softened in a smile.

'Shall we walk on a little ways?' said Joe. 'There's another tram stop at the far side of the bridge.'

'I'd like to.' Mara said nothing more about her mother's anxiety. Walking slowly, the girl between the two men, watching the deepening of the grey light on the stone harmonies which the Romanov empresses and their architects had built to realise the great Peter's dream in granite, stucco and water, they passed through the squares beyond the bridge into the Nevski Prospekt.

'Now I know where I am,' said Joe. 'Here's the Morskaia, with the Astoria Hotel at the end of it, and once we're across the Moika canal, the Europa's just a few blocks further on. Say, the Petersburgers certainly enjoy taking a walk at night!' The Nevski was almost as crowded at midnight as in the early evening. The shop windows were lighted and electric lamps shone down on the steady movement of trams and traffic.

'Walking by night is one of our pastimes, winter or summer,' said the professor. 'You'll soon know your way around St. Petersburg, Mr. Calvert!'

'Do you know the names of all the canals?' asked Mara. She had slipped her hand from Joe's arm when they entered the Nevski Prospekt.

'I know three. We've crossed the Moika, we're coming up to

44

the Catherine, and the Fontanka's quite a distance down the avenue. Professor, I wish you'd tell me the name of that church on the canal bank. It's different from all the other buildings in the city, and yet it looks familiar, somehow.'

The professor smiled. 'That's because you've seen pictures of the church of St. Basil in the Kremlin. They're very much alike — this one is called the Church of the Resurrection — and I agree with you, it is not in keeping with all our eighteenth-century and neo-classical façades.'

'The Byzantine dream again, eh?' said Joe, studying the domes and Greek crosses, the polychrome rhomboids of blue, green, yellow and amber, all shifting in their colour values as the electric lighting from the Prospekt challenged the darkening night. 'Is it a very old church?'

'One of the newest in the city,' said Mara. 'The Romanovs put it up in memory of Alexander II, on the spot where he was killed. Its other name is the Church of the Spilled Blood.'

'Killed?' said Joe. 'You mean murdered.'

The professor interposed. 'It's an old story, Mr. Calvert, and not one we should be proud to tell our foreign friends. A story of student terrorists, led by a fanatic from Odessa — '

'And by a girl from the aristocracy, Sophia Perovskaia,' said Mara. 'After they killed the Czar, she was hanged for her share in the plot. Imagine the cruelty of hanging a woman!'

'If you plan to blow up an emperor, you'd better be prepared to pay the price,' said Joe. 'Murder solves nothing, Miss Trenova! Do you think the shots Princip fired at Sarajevo last week will give the Bosnians their independence?'

'I admire Sophia Perovskaia,' said Mara violently, 'and I honour Gavrilo Princip for what he did. The Bosnians have lived under an imperial tyranny for too long — just as we live in Russia. Oh, what's the use of talking, I'll only make the professor angry! Thank you both for escorting me — and good night.'

Before either man could stop her Mara ran across the street, dodging the traffic, and they saw her boarding a tram on the far side of the Nevski Prospekt.

'That was an abrupt departure,' said Joe drily. 'Has she really got a long way to go? Will she be all right?'

'Of course she will. She doesn't like any of us to escort her to her own front door. Poor Mara! She lives in a miserable

45

neighbourhood, and she's alternately proud and ashamed of it.'

'She wasn't ashamed to say she honoured the Sarajevo murderer.'

'Poor girl,' the professor said again, 'I don't think she quite knew what she was saying. She's very unhappy about her own future, now that she's come to the end of her schooldays and has no prospect of going on to the university — but Mara Ivanovna's personal problems can't possibly interest you!'

'I want to understand, if I can, sir. But you mustn't stand here by the canal, being jostled by all these night walkers! Come back with me to my hotel and let me offer you a drink before you start back home.'

He wanted the drink, he didn't want to go on talking; even for a young man of twenty-five it had been a long day, with the routine office work overlaid by a host of new impressions, but the Russian jumped at the chance of continuing the conversation. When they were settled in the Europa bar, as crowded still as when Joe sat there with Richard Allen, and now enlivened by the sound of orchestral music coming from the supper room, he observed with a sinking heart that Professor Hendrikov looked fit for another hour of talk.

'You are right,' the older man was saying earnestly, as he sipped appreciatively at the brandy Joe had ordered. 'You want to understand, you ought to understand this country where you have been appointed to serve your own. And I believe Mara Trenova's story may contribute just a little to your better knowledge of our difficulties. To begin with, her father, Ivan Trenov, was a schoolmaster here in Petersburg. I knew him very slightly: he was a clever man. Very active in the Teachers' Union, but apart from that not politically inclined. Now, after the troubles in 1905, when between the Duma and the *zemstva* — rural councils you might call them — it seemed as if Russia was set on a more liberal course, an imperial edict invited the Teachers' Union to propose any reforms they wished to see in our school system. Trenov was one of the authors of the proposals finally submitted. They were studied by the Czar's ministers, if not by the Czar himself, and they were used, Mr. Calvert, each separate reform in the petition — remember one may only address the Czar as a petitioner — was used as a weapon to attack the very men who had drawn it up. Many teachers were arrested, many more lost their jobs. As my talented young friend Alexander Kerensky says, it was a trap for those who had taken the word of the Czar at its face value.'

'Was Mr. Trenov among those arrested?'

'He was. His case was heard, with others, by the Court of Appeals, and he was among the majority who were acquitted. But not one was reinstated in his old position; there was no job anywhere for those men in our Russian schools. Trenov kept his head fairly well until he realised the truth. Then he went back to the law courts, demanding justice; was arrested again, resisted arrest, and wounded a police officer — the wretched man was armed — and after another trial he was exiled to Siberia.'

'Is he still in Siberia?'

'His conduct on the march was such that he was sent to the prison reserved for our most dangerous convicts, on Sakhalin Island, and he died there three years later.'

Joe drew a long breath. 'When did all this happen, sir? How old was Miss Trenova at the time?'

'Let me see. The Court of Appeals heard the teachers' case in 1907, as far as I remember. Mara Ivanovna is nineteen now, so she would have been twelve then. Left virtually fatherless at twelve years old! I don't know how she and her mother would have survived if it hadn't been for some old cousin, a wealthy woman, who paid for Mara's education at the Xenia School. I believe the mother has a tiny annuity; enough to live on by herself in their pathetic flat near the Vladimir church. Indeed I think the mother spends most of her time at church, or attending funeral services, to hear the priest singing the *panikhidia,* and reciting the *kontakion* with the rest of the faithful.'

'Poor woman. It's a tough story, professor, and I can see how it would make Trenov's daughter very bitter, but even so, it's not an excuse for condoning murder.'

'That affected you unpleasantly, I see. Wild talk, Mr. Calvert! I'm accustomed to it from my students. Nine times out of ten it means nothing.'

'But what if the tenth man is Gavrilo Princip?'

'Ah.' Professor Hendrikov looked cautiously around the American Bar. There were fewer officers than there had been earlier, and three tables had been pushed together to accommodate a large party of men in white tie and tails, some wearing decorations and all absorbed in their own conversation. 'Princip, yes. He set a match to a bonfire last week in Sarajevo: let us pray that the fire brigade comes along and puts it out before the flames are out of control.'

'You don't really think the assassination will lead to war, do you?'

'We shall know better in a day or two.'

It was exactly what Captain Allen had implied, when he wished that 'the Ballhausplatz and the Hofburg would show their hand'. Joe shook his head doubtfully. 'Even so,' he said, 'it would only be another little Balkan war like last year and the year before. I have an uncle in the State Department. He's got one of the desks in the East European section, and his view is that the Balkan wars can always be localised: the real danger in that area is Turkey.'

'I must respect the views of the State Department,' said Hendrikov politely, 'but speaking as a mere citizen of Petersburg, I saw and heard some alarming things in this city during the last "little Balkan war" as you call it. The Bulgarians were the heroes of the hour then; now, of course, if the Austrian government can pin responsibility for Gavrilo Princip's act on Serbia, it'll be the Serbs. But last year we had a hothead from Bulgaria as the guest of the city, a general no less, called Radko Dmitriev, and he made speeches about the great Slav brotherhood, and how Russia alone had the right to interfere in the domestic quarrels of the Slavs. Of course he was only drumming up help from Russia for the Bulgarians, but he did go so far as to promise to lay Constantinople at the feet of the Czar ... and His Majesty has always been a dreamer of the Byzantine dream.'

'That's very interesting, and I wish we had more complete reports of all that in Washington, but in any event the Russians didn't march, and the war was localised and ended quite soon. Why shouldn't it happen that way again?'

'It should,' said the professor heavily. 'If only we had stronger men at the head of affairs. Sazonov is very clear, but the cabinet is responsible to the Czar and not the Duma: they will be overruled if the generals can overpersuade the Czar. I wish Stolypin were alive today. He was a man of great authority.'

'Stolypin was the prime minister. But my God! he was assassinated too!'

Joe Calvert's head was aching, and in spite of the long brandy and soda his throat was parched. He thought sheer fatigue must be responsible for his sudden qualm of fear.

'Stolypin died in hospital, after a murderous attack upon him in Kiev,' said Professor Hendrikov. 'In Russia, all too often, the good men die young.'

CHAPTER THREE

THE fine summer days went quietly by, and the diplomats breathed more easily. It began to be hoped that the Sarajevo murders would be indemnified by the payment of some sort of reparations by Serbia, and of course by the execution of the young men now held in custody. What was not immediately known was that there had been a quiet exchange of letters between the aged Austrian emperor, Franz Josef, and his good friend and ally, Wilhelm II, the German Kaiser. The old man wrote to his ally a few days after the double murder, personally and almost ruminatively, to say that his primary policy objective in the affair must now be the isolation of Serbia. To which the Kaiser, with the full approval of his Chancellor, Bethmann-Hollweg, replied that Austria could count on Germany's full support if punitive action against Serbia should bring her into conflict with Russia. He added a few days later that his support would be forthcoming even in the event of 'a European complication', for the price of German support of Austria-Hungary in the Balkans was to be Austrian support of Germany against France.

Thus the famous 'blank cheque' was issued, a document which was literally a matter of life or death to millions of men and women who were young in 1914, and who were then, in their various ways, enjoying the pleasures of a remarkably warm summer. In Britain the perennial trouble in the Balkans seemed remote. Britain's troubles lay nearer home: there was a threat of civil war in Ireland, where Ulster was preparing to resist Home Rule. Sir Edward Carson's speeches encouraged the formation of an Ulster Provisional Government, and sums of money collected in America encouraged the arming of the Irish National Volunteers. This did not spoil the average Englishman's enjoyment of a sporting summer, in which the fight between two famous boxers, Georges Carpentier and 'Gunboat' Smith, aroused at least as much interest as the strife beyond the Irish Sea. A torrid Henley was followed by the tennis championships at Wimbledon and the Eton and Harrow match at Lords. Society went to the Rose Show in Regent's Park and looked forward to the state ball at Buckingham Palace and the naval review at Spithead towards the end of July; meanwhile, the fruit ripened in the Kentish orchards, and trainloads of happy Cockneys went off on their annual cherry-picking holiday. Across the Channel a sex drama, revealed when Madame Caillaux, the wife of the Finance Minister, shot and killed the editor of the *Figaro*, was absorbing the attention of the Paris press.

Even in Russia, where the Czar and his ministers conferred daily on the Balkan situation, a new sensation had eclipsed the assassination of Franz Ferdinand. This was an attempt on the life of Rasputin, the *staretz*, or 'man of God', whose influence at court was believed by most literate Russians to be the influence of the devil. Joe Calvert had been warned, aboard the ferry bound for Kronstadt, not to say his name aloud in a Russian crowd, and this no doubt was wise advice to a foreigner, but the name, in all its variants, rang in the streets of every city in Russia when it was known that he, Grigori Efimovich Novik, Grisha, called Rasputin, had been stabbed in his home village of Povrovskoe by a young woman who drove a knife into his stomach, with a cry of 'I have killed the antiChrist!' Rasputin was in hospital in Tiumen, and lay there at the point of death; about his assailant the reports were far less clear. Her name was given as Khinia Gusseva, her age as twenty-six. She had been taken to prison, she had been taken to a lunatic asylum, she had been torn to pieces by the devoted villagers of Povrovskoe. She had been paid to kill Rasputin by his enemies, said one report. Another said she was a Petersburg prostitute who had been rejected by Rasputin after sharing in many of the orgies which went on at his apartment, or in the bath houses of the capital. All of these reports were censored by the Czar's police, and the news telegraphed round the world was that the stabbing of Rasputin was the act of a madwoman.

The ship's officers and members of the Garde Equipage assembled on board the imperial yacht *Standart* on the day the news was released were a silent company. Sidelong glances and one or two bawdy references to Gusseva were as far as anyone cared to go in comment. Simon Hendrikov, after only three months' service aboard, had not yet decided which of the naval officers owed their appointments to the Czarina's interest — this meant they venerated, or said they venerated, Rasputin as a holy man — and which of them, being there by merit or seniority, were prepared to jeer at the priest's convenient doctrine of committing the sins of the flesh deliberately, in order to obtain salvation. It was part of the wretched web of intrigue which the Czarina's faith in Rasputin had woven about the court that even in her floating home, the *Standart*, which her children preferred to all their father's palaces, there could be no honesty between one man and another.

It was the day appointed for the start of the cruise down the Gulf of Finland, and as the morning passed without orders from Peterhof it began to be rumoured that the cruise would probably be cancelled. Rasputin must have died in Tiumen, the grief-stricken Alexandra Feodorovna must have refused to consider a holiday: the only matter for conjecture now was, one humorist dared to say, how long would the court mourning last? Simon could tell, by the look on several faces, that there were still officers in the *Standart*'s company who would exult in the death of the Czarina's evil angel.

Shortly after midday it was announced that the summer cruise would start as planned, but with a few hours' delay to enable the Czar to visit the new dry dock at Kronstadt. Simon's spirits rose immediately. Since going to his home in the Fourth Line to ask his father for the key of the dacha at Koivisto, he had thought of nothing but the picnic so impulsively proposed by his princess, and how it could possibly be brought about. He was no more interested in the knifing of an unsavoury religious maniac in Siberia than in the assassination of the Austrain Archduke; at twenty-three, his heart was set on just one thing: the chance to spend an afternoon in the company of Olga Nicolaievna.

It seemed hours before the *Alexandria* came alongside, and he saw her on deck, standing rather in the rear, with her head bent over the stiff bouquet of carnations which told him that the eldest Grand Duchess, instead of her mother, had accompanied the Czar on his tour of the dry dock built to accommodate two newly purchased Dreadnoughts. The Czarina was sitting in a deck-chair, listening to a fat, pasty-faced young person called Anna Virubova, her closest woman friend. The Heir to the Throne was standing at the rail between his father and one of his two sailor nurses, waving and laughing to his friends, the whole ship's company of the *Standart*, and at the sight of his happy face the long tension of the day was suddenly relaxed.

Alexis Nicolaievich was nearly ten years old, and tall for his age. He had inherited his mother's grey-blue eyes and red-gold hair, which in the boy might darken to copper as he grew to manhood. Whatever ailment had kept him from the luncheon in HMS *Lion*, he now appeared to be the picture of health, and although he was rather pale, his clear complexion gave the lie to the persistent rumour that he had been born with one skin too few.

From the deck of the little *Alexandria* he looked up delightedly at the splendid Danish-built *Standart*, sleek in her black paint with the gilded bowsprit and stern, and started up the ship's ladder behind his father, at the very moment the Czar was piped aboard. Nobody really saw how the accident happened. The sailor attendant, Derevenko, was close behind the child, and a petty officer called Gordienko had stretched out both hands to help Alexis aboard, when suddenly he seemed to slip between the two men, and stumbled heavily on one rung of the ladder. He was saved from sprawling by the petty officer, but his involuntary 'Oh!' reached the ears of his father, who was shaking hands with Commander Sablin.

'What happened, Alexis?'

'Nothing, papa. I hit my foot against the ladder, that was all.'

'What a silly thing to do.'

'I'm *all right*, papa.'

'Of course you are.' But the Czar took the child's hand and held it tightly until the ladies and his personal staff had come aboard. Then, when the formal greetings were over, he marshalled them all below, and to the disappointment of the officers the imperial family was seen no more that evening.

It was perhaps understandable, for a stiff breeze was blowing up the Gulf of Finland, and even the splendid steam yacht was rolling a little as she headed west by south. The escort of torpedo boats, the only security measure the Czar permitted on those cruises, was bucketing up and down along the line of the

53

horizon. So the white awnings above the decks were furled, the folding chairs and tables put away, and no pretty girls appeared to ask eager questions about navigation or renew acquaintance with old friends. The balalaika orchestra was summoned to one of the ornately furnished saloons, but only played for half an hour, the Czarina complaining of headache, and the stewards, sent to offer evening tea, reported that everyone had turned in early. Simon Hendrikov did the same. He slept soundly, happy in the knowledge that his princess was not far away, and awoke once only during the night, when he thought he heard a child screaming in pain. But all was silent, except for the normal sounds of a ship at sea, and Simon dismissed the dream, to sleep again.

The wind fell during the early hours of the morning, and when the Czar came on deck for his usual brisk constitutional the *Standart* was lying in a beautiful little Finnish bay, where the birch woods came down close to the water's edge. He chatted amiably with the officers of the Garde Equipage, and groaned audibly when the courier boat from St. Petersburg came alongside with the morning's load of letters, reports, and documents requiring the signature of the man who, in spite of the Duma and the Council of the Empire, was still the final arbiter of all affairs in Russia. When the Czar went to his private quarters, Marie and Anastasia came on deck. They had friends among the sub-lieutenants, and presently a noisy game developed, involving the squealing and shouting and racing round the housing which their parents not only tolerated but encouraged aboard the yacht. It was in the middle of the fun, when Simon for some reason was required to time their activities with a stop-watch, that he received an unexpected summons from the Grand Duchess Tatiana.

He turned over the stop-watch to another man, and went below with his uniform cap under his arm, following the steward who had been sent to fetch him through the magnificent suite of saloons until they came to a cabin fitted up as a writing room, where Tatiana Nicolaievna was sitting behind an ormolu desk. One of the young officers from the wireless cabin was standing at attention by her side.

'Good morning, Simon Karlovich,' she said with the smile and the studied charm so oddly mature in a girl of seventeen, so often contrasting with her sister Olga's more slapdash ways.

'Will you excuse me one moment? I've been writing telegrams for the Czarina, and they must go at once.' She counted the sheets of paper, while Simon thought what a picture she made, with that glorious hair against the emerald green silk hung instead of paper on the walls of the writing room. He had time to wonder how many of the telegrams were directed to the hospital at Tiumen, where Rasputin (so the men in the courier boat had said) was beginning to rally from his stomach wound.

'Ten, that's right. These may go off now, and thank you, Ivan Ivanovich.'

When the wireless officer had left, the girl relaxed in her velvet armchair, and smiled again at Lieutenant Hendrikov. 'I want to give you a message from my sister Olga,' she said. 'She's sitting with our little brother. I don't know if you heard that Alexis wrenched his foot rather badly as he came aboard yesterday, and Dr. Botkin wants him to stay in bed all day.'

'Wrenched his foot? Just coming up the ladder?' He couldn't help saying it, or seeing how the smiling mask came down over Tatiana's lovely face, just as it dropped over Olga's when she talked by implication of security at the British squadron's ball.

'Yes, it was most unfortunate,' the young Grand Duchess said. 'Especially since we're now so near your home, I mean your father's dacha in Finland, which my sister says you kindly invited us all to visit!'

'Your visit would be a great honour for my family and me, Tatiana Nicolaievna.'

'Then shall we arrange for this little excursion to take place today, Simon Karlovich? The Czar has given his permission, and perhaps you could arrange with Commander Sablin about the launch, and where you would like to be put ashore?'

Simon bowed. He had an intuition that the prompt arrangements for what was to be a surprise picnic had been devised as a means of getting the noisy youngsters ashore and procuring silence for the boy who didn't seem able to stay well for a couple of weeks on end. He said, 'I will make all the arrangements, Your Imperial Highness. At what time would it be convenient for us to start?'

He had to use her title, all orders to the contrary: there was something regal about this girl with the red-gold hair, who was

55

planning his day for him, and for her sisters, with such aplomb. He remembered having heard that Tatiana was sometimes called 'The Governess' by her sisters, because of her ability to plan for them, her fondness for timetables and exactitude — the exactitude which made her say immediately:

'That depends on the distance between your dacha and the anchorage, Simon Karlovich. As far as my sisters' leisure is concerned, I should say about half past two.'

It was barely half past two when three glowing girls came on deck to join him, the 'Little Pair', as Marie and Anastasia were called in the Family, childishly dressed in pinafore frocks with wide sailor hats, and carrying osier baskets. Olga Nicolaievna wore a white middy blouse with a navy blue tie and a white duck skirt. All three were wearing white buckskin shoes with heavy leather soles.

'Simon Karlovich! Are those the right kind of shoes?'

'We could wear our tennis shoes, you know!'

'Is it far to the dacha? Are we going into the village? Are there other people living close to you?'

'Be quiet, you two,' said Olga. 'Simon Karlovich, my sister Tatiana is so sorry she can't join the party. She really feels she ought to stay aboard with the Czarina and my brother.'

'How is Alexis Nicolaievich feeling now?'

'Very sorry for himself,' said Olga frankly, 'but Dr. Botkin thinks he'll be much better in the morning.' She turned to the man who was waiting to help her down into the launch. 'You're Petty Officer Gordienko, aren't you? I do hope you aren't blaming yourself for my brother's stupid accident?'

The man saluted and said nothing.

'Because it was all his own fault really,' Olga went on. 'He was so excited about the cruise he simply didn't look where he was going; I think he must have picked that up from me!'

Gordienko bowed. He said to Lieutenant Hendrikov: 'At what time shall the launch return, sir?'

Simon looked enquiringly at the Grand Duchess. 'Shall we say five o'clock? It's not quite half an hour's walk to the dacha, twenty minutes if we walk fast.'

'But we don't want to walk fast, this is our holiday! Five o'clock will be quite soon enough.'

'Five o'clock, Gordienko.'

'Very good, sir. And which of the men shall go with you, to carry the basket?'

'I'll take that myself.' Simon already carried beneath his arm a large box wrapped and tied by a famous Petersburg confectioner, at which the Grand Duchess Marie's huge blue eyes — 'Marie's saucers' as they were called in the Family — grew wider than ever in anticipation.

They were set ashore in a sandy cove, one of the many which broke the rugged Finnish coastline, with no sign of life about it, not even the wooden sauna which would have revealed the presence of a summer dwelling hidden by the evergreens. A narrow path led from the cove up through the trees.

'Where exactly are we?' Olga said. 'I know we haven't passed Björkö yet.'

'No, we cruised across the Gulf to the southern shore last night, and then turned north. We're about one mile west of Koivisto village, call it thirty miles east of Terijoki.'

'It feels like three hundred miles from Terijoki. Remember the Yacht Club, and all those smart little tables on the lawn? This is the real country, isn't it?'

'I'm glad it pleases you, Olga Nicolaievna.'

'I love the Finnish countryside.'

It was impossible to hurry along that path, which wound between thickets of pine and birch until it emerged upon the bank of a river, little more than a trout stream, which flowed to the sea through stony shallows and deep pools of clear amber water. There were wild flowers growing in profusion, which made Marie and Anastasia begin excitedly to plan how they would fill their baskets, and there was above all, hardly broken by their chattering, the deep and healing silence of the Finnish woods. Olga walked very quietly on the carpet of pine needles. Simon brought up the rear, carrying the picnic basket, which was heavy: he was glad when they reached the clearing where his parents' summer cottage stood.

He had been right in telling Olga that it was not in the least like the smart villas at Terijoki. The Hendrikov cottage was built of pine logs, hand hewn, with a stone chimney at one gable end and a pile of firewood at the other. A flight of four wooden steps led up to a verandah with a shingle roof, protecting the door, on each side of which a small window of four square panes gave the front of the cottage something of the simplicity of a child's drawing. There was no attempt at a garden, but the grassy ground which sloped very gently to the river had been roughly scythed, and smelt of new mown hay.

'Is this it?' 'What a marvellous place!' 'Oh, Simon Karlovich, aren't you lucky!' The enthusiastic exclamations broke out behind Simon as he laid down his burdens and produced the key he had requested from his father. 'Just a moment,' he said hurriedly, and this was the anxious moment, when he let himself into the cottage without knowing what state it might be in. Madame Hendrikova had long ago decided that as a member of the intelligentsia she had a soul above house-keeping, and the occasional country girl who was all the help available in Finland appeared to share her views. But Dolly's neat hands must have been at work before they left at Easter, for the living-room was very tidy, and across the tiny hall he could see through an open door that his parents' bedroom was in good order too. The place was hot and stuffy, but that was remedied at once by throwing up the sash windows, and then his eager guests were jumping up the steps to join him.

'It really is delightful, Simon Karlovich,' was Olga's quieter comment while her sisters squealed their admiration, and Simon looked round the log-walled living-room, hung with *rya* rugs in vivid colours, trying to see it with the eyes of a girl accustomed to the formal grandeur of Peterhof and Czarskoe Selo. There was a long table in the middle of the room with a runner of Finnish linen down the middle and set about with stools, and a copper lamp swung on chains directly overhead. There was a magnificent stone fireplace, with iron firedogs set wide enough apart to hold six-foot logs, with a bearskin stretched in front, pale brown on the back and shading to cream on the extended paws. A small brick cooking stove, also wood-burning, was built on one side of the great stone hearth.

'And where does everybody sleep?' said inquisitive Marie.

'Mashka, I really am ashamed of you — '

'But Olga, it's the very first time we've ever been in a real house!'

'My parents sleep across the hall, Marie Nicolaievna. There's nothing much to see but beds and books.'

'What a lot of books!'

'My father uses this for the overflow from our flat in Petersburg.'

'He must be *very* clever to have read all those.'

'And just look at the beds, so cosy, with those lovely puffy quilts,' said Anastasia. 'You should see the beds we have to sleep on, Simon Karlovich!'

'*Anastasia!*'

'Well, what's wrong with that, everyone must sleep somewhere,' said the *enfant terrible*. 'We sleep on beastly little camp beds at home. Because the daughters of Alexander the First did it, we have to do it too!'

'Well, never mind about all that, let's think about having tea,' said Marie, to cover Olga's vexation.

'Tea already!' the latter said. 'Why, it isn't half past three!'

'We ought to get started on it,' said Marie. 'You never know, somebody might be sent to fetch us back —'

'That's true. Let's see what's inside our basket, then.'

The picnic basket, opened on the greensward, was found to contain two kinds of sandwiches and a large plum cake. There were also glasses, carefully packed, china plates and linen napkins, and to Anastasia's despair, a vacuum container full of milk.

'But we ought to have *tea* at a picnic!' she protested.

'We can make tea indoors,' said Simon recklessly. 'My mother has a spirit stove somewhere. I'm sure I can find it, the fire would take too long.'

He found it easily inside the wooden dresser, and his delighted visitors, rummaging, discovered a teapot and teacaddy, which Olga appropriated, and Finnish pottery mugs, pronounced to be 'much nicer than those rotten glasses from the yacht'. The tea was infused, the long table set, and next to the cut cake in the centre of the linen runner Simon set the box of chocolates which he had brought from St. Petersburg.

'Two chocolates each after tea, girls, and we'll take the rest home to Tania and Baby,' Olga said.

'Huh!' said Anastasia. 'Baby won't be allowed to eat sweets today.'

'Why not?' asked Simon. 'I should have thought chocolate was just the right prescription for a wrenched ankle.'

'He'll enjoy them tomorrow,' said Olga, with an imperceptible glance of warning at her sister. 'Have some more cake, Simon Karlovich.'

'It *is* good,' said Marie, helping herself. 'We get much nicer teas on the *Standart* then we do ashore.'

'That's because we always have some horrible cakes that Catherine the Great enjoyed,' said Anastasia.

'This is my sister's day for giving us a lecture on Russian history,' said Olga lightly. 'Now who's going to do the washing up?'

'Washing up?'

'Yes, of course; we can't leave this lovely place untidy.'

'But we've got to go now, and make the posies for mamma and Anna.'

'Dishes first.'

Eventually they all did the washing up, by the simple process of rinsing the mugs and plates in the river and drying them with one of the table napkins. Then the two younger girls caught up their osier baskets; they were impatient to be off.

'Where does that road lead to, Simon Karlovich?' asked Olga, pointing to a road of sorts, many times broader than the track from the shore, which began at the cottage clearing.

'First to a farm, and then across the river by a bridge, and then back on the other side of the water to Koivisto,' Simon said. 'That's the way my parents drive up, when they come here on holiday.'

'I see. All right, you two, keep to the road or the river bank, and don't go out of sight, please.'

'Oh, but Olga, we want to go into the woods to gather berries.'

'The bilberries aren't ripe yet, I saw them all green beside the path.' She turned to Simon as the girls ran off. 'What a blessing it isn't the mushroom season. We wouldn't have been able to keep track of them then.'

He was enchanted by the way she said 'we', for the first time linking them together, two adults, jointly responsible for two harum-scarum children.

'Where would you like to sit, Olga Nicolaievna? You haven't got a hat, and the sun's so strong.'

'I love sitting in the sun.' But she got up, and moved to the verandah, folding her white skirts carelessly to sit down on the top step, motioning to the young man to sit on one of the steps below.

'There's just one drawback to your paradise,' she said. 'The midges. Wouldn't you like to smoke?'

'If I may.'

'Of course. And since there's nobody here to be shocked, I think I'll smoke myself.'

Simon got up at once to offer her his cigarettes and strike a match. She looked up at him with a smile. He was very good-looking, with his chestnut hair growing so crisply above his broad forehead, and his clear hazel eyes, but the Grand Duchess Olga saw handsomer men every day of her life among the officers of her father's Guards. What appealed to her in this man was his solidity, not only the strength of his square shoulders and vigorous body, but in the feeling he gave her that here was a man to be relied on. She leaned backwards in a luxurious stretch, and said,

'How marvellous to get away from the botanists!'

'What botanists, Princess?'

'Don't you know that expression? That's what the Czar calls the plain clothes police, who're always slinking about when he goes on his long walks. He says he can spot them a mile away, peering at flowers and pretending to be interested in shrubs. You must have seen them in the Crimea, Livadia was swarming with them!'

'I suppose I did.'

Simon sat down again and looked away from her, across the shining river. He was remembering, almost with guilt, the hour he had spent in the Commander's cabin after his talk with Tatiana, drawing a map of the route they would take from the launch to the dacha and back, showing the farm and Koivisto village, and answering detailed questions about the Finnish farmer and his family, their names and ages, but quite unable to give answers about their political opinions, about which he knew nothing. Olga might think, poor darling, that the summer woods were free of 'botanists', but the invisible guards were bound to be there, the bars were still up round the golden cage. He muttered something like, 'It's better to be careful.' He was remembering that this young girl, when she was younger still, not yet sixteen, had been a witness of Stolypin's murder in the theatre at Kiev. Everybody knew the story, how the murderer and his victim, dabbled with blood, had been removed, and the horrified audience, streaming back from the stairs and foyers (for it was an interval) had poured into the auditorium, believing that the Czar himself was shot. Then, while they sang the national anthem, spontaneously, full-throated, while the

61

fourteen-year-old Tatiana cried hysterically in the anteroom, the Grand Duchess Olga stood steadfastly beside her father in the imperial box, as proud a Romanov as any woman who ever graced the throne. He said, trying to speak naturally, to pick up the cue she had given him about Livadia:

'Do you think you'll be going back to the Crimea, later in the year?'

'It isn't very likely.'

'But — it was announced that Prince Carol of Rumania, and his mother, the Crown Princess, would be returning your visit to Constanza.'

'How you harp on that visit to Constanza! It only lasted for one day.'

'I was in hell that day ... because everybody said your engagement would be announced at the end of it.'

'That was the idea, I believe.'

'So what happened? For God's sake tell me what happened, Princess!'

'Why do you call me Princess, Simon Karlovich? You know my name, why don't you use it?'

'Because you *are* a princess, just a girl: Grand Duchess seems so old and settled, it makes me think of a tall, stout lady, very proud and hung about with jewels, giving orders to everybody — not like you.'

In spite of herself, Olga giggled. 'You're drawing a wonderful picture of somebody I know.'

'Please don't tease me, Olga Nicolaievna, it means so much to me.'

She relented. 'Very well, I will tell you, and why shouldn't I? Some of my real friends know, and you are my friend, aren't you? We sisters think of everybody in the *Standart* as our good, true friends — and you'll never know how glad I was to get back aboard the *Standart* after that horrible day at Constanza. Poor people — they put on such a show for us, building that wretched pavilion specially, down by the sea; and the old Queen, Carmen Sylva, had forgotten her Orders, and the King was furious with her ... and then Prince Carol, and the awful proposal. I asked for time to think. So Monsieur Sazonov said his say, about how much I could do for Russia as Queen of Rumania — and of course Carol's wife will be Queen some day — and the Czarina had a heart attack, at least she said it

62

was a heart attack, and it was only papa, I mean the Czar, who stood by me. He said he would never force me into a marriage against my will, and he knows I never want to marry any foreign prince, and have to make my home away from Russia. Why should I, Simon Karlovich? After all, I *am* a Russian, and I mean to live and die in Russia!'

She was a Russian of the Russians then, in spite of all the German blood, going back through generations, which the spiteful said had drowned the tiny proportion of Slav blood left in the reigning house. She was a Russian, and also a thorough Romanov: through the girl's young face came the look, the features pictured on a hundred canvases in the galleries of the Winter Palace; and in a gust of admiration and relief Simon Hendrikov seized her hands and began to kiss them.

'So they sent my answer to Bucharest, and Prince Carol and his mother won't come to Livadia this year ... Oh, Simon Karlovich, why does it mean so much to you?'

He lifted his head from her hands and said hoarsely:

'Because I want you to stay my princess — stay a happy girl — because I can't bear to think of you as the wife of any man.'

It took a moment for the full sexual implication of his words to reach her. It was the physical relationship, from which she had shrunk with Prince Carol, which had roused this storm of feeling in the young man almost kneeling at her feet. Olga's first impulse was to pull her hands away, to run to the river, calling to her sisters that it must certainly be time to start back to the launch. But then it was too late, for Simon Hendrikov was kneeling no longer. He rose and pulled her up into his arms.

It was not until after she had gone to bed, and was listening to Tatiana's quiet breathing in the next berth — 'the Big Pair' were sharing a cabin as they shared a bedroom ashore — that Olga was able to live in memory the thrilling moments of Simon Hendrikov's embrace. It had literally lasted for moments only, for he released her as soon as they heard the sound of the young voices coming round the bend of the river. Then Olga went to meet the girls with exaggerated praises of the wildflowers they had found, and Simon, at Anastasia's

63

suggestion, went back into the dacha to see if he could find some sewing silk to tie up the posies. He found it in Dolly's neat workbox, in the back bedroom she had been accustomed to share with her sister; looked into his own small bedroom, and wondered what his father would say if he knew who his guests were on this summer afternoon. He had told the professor that he wanted to give Captain Prince Somebody a few hours' fishing — he knew that for a title his father would give up half a dozen keys.

They were all sitting on the grass when he went out with the green silk reel, and Marie had begun to arrange the harebells, the trefoil and campion into the little nests of coloured mosses which her strong hands wove with such delicacy. The four little Finns from the farm were sitting cross-legged, and devouring plum cake.

'They can't speak Russian,' said Anastasia.

'Their parents can, I know.' To Olga, lining the osier baskets with bright moss, Simon's voice sounded forced and far away.

'May we give them some of your lovely chocolates, Simon Karlovich?'

'They're your chocolates now, Marie Nicolaievna.'

'Two each, then,' said Olga. 'Just what we had ourselves, share and share alike.'

The silent little, tow-headed Finns looked blissful as the young ladies gave them the chocolates. They hung about, waiting for whatever might happen next while the Grand Duchesses had one more look inside the dacha ('just to remember everything') and then stood waving while Simon's party went off back down the path. The Finnish children were a help, thought Olga, as the *Standart*, that floating palace, steamed west and by south again towards the roadstead of Reval. They made everything seem so ordinary.

Everything was normal, too, though in a tragic way, when they were back aboard the yacht. It only required the deep, anxious silence which hung over the imperial suite, and the lady-in-waiting on duty rising with her finger to her lips as the girls entered, to tell them that their brother was no better, and Tatiana coming in pale and despairing, whispered that he was worse.

'Is it as bad as the Spala time?' asked Olga, when the older sisters were alone in the stateroom. They both dreaded a recurrence of the fearful attack of 'internal bleeding', as they had been taught to call it, which at Spala in Poland, in 1912, had left Alexis crippled for a year.

'Oh, we must pray it won't be nearly as bad as that!'

'But we do pray, Tania: if our prayers were heard, he'd be the healthiest boy in all the world.'

She was unknotting the sailor tie, unfastening the middy blouse and the white skirt stained with grass. 'The Little Pair want to give him their flowers and sweets, can they?'

'Mamma won't let anyone but herself see him tonight.'

'Oh Lord,' said Olga with resignation. 'So we're in for it all over again. Why doesn't papa order them to put about and take us back to Peterhof?'

'The doctors are here on board with Baby. There's nothing they can do for him at Peterhof that they can't do here. And think of the publicity, just before the French state visit!'

'Of course, we can't risk the publicity, can we?'

The four sisters had been trained from their brother's babyhood to keep him from bumps and bruises. That bump against the ship's ladder, which would have meant nothing to any one of them, had resulted within two or three hours in a dark blue swelling over the place where his ankle struck the wood, then in further swelling and intense pain as the bruised blood seeped into his ankle joint and then through the tissues of his leg, which was already hideously cramped against his abdomen. The girls had petted him and prayed for him through all his attacks, had sung lullabies and told him fairy stories, even wept for his pain, but thanks to their mother's excessive prudery in physical matters, they had never been told, in so many words, the nature of his malady.

'How's mamma bearing up?' Olga picked up her white cambric dressing gown, and heard someone turn on the bath water in the next cabin. Her hands still smelled of moss and flowers.

'Mother? Wonderful with Baby, of course, she always is, but feeling so wretched and depressed. As she says, if only Father Grigori were well and close beside us, or even able to remember us in his prayers!'

'*Can't* he remember us in his prayers?'

'He's only been conscious for short intervals since they took

65

him to hospital. But Ania had a much more hopeful telegram from the chief surgeon, just over an hour ago.'

'So they think he's going to live?'

'Oh yes, he'll live, thank heaven.'

'Well, good, in a day or two he'll be able to telegraph himself. After all, Grigori Efimovich was in Siberia when Alexis was so ill at Spala. He cured him by telegram that time; why shouldn't he do it this time too?'

'What an unfeeling thing to say!'

Olga considered that judgment, hours later, after the wretched evening had worn away. The Czarina remained by her sick child's bed, the Czar escaped to dine in the mess, while the girls sat on deck and chatted quietly as the *Standart* sailed into the twilight. No, she was not unfeeling — unsympathetic, perhaps, to her mother's cult of Rasputin, whose magnetic eyes and shaggy, greasy locks had become increasingly repulsive to the adolescent girl. But her deepest feelings had been aroused that day, and as never before, in the arms of Simon Hendrikov.

His kisses were not the first to kindle her Romanov blood. At her very first dance, on her sixteenth birthday, Olga had given her lips trustingly and happily to the young prince, little more than a boy himself, whom she believed her parents had chosen to be her husband. It had been the perfect setting for romance, like a scene in one of the English novels the Czar liked to read aloud to his family, among the roses and heliotropes of Livadia, high on a marble balcony above the sea. There had been other episodes since then, the natural outcome of the carefully encouraged flirtations, but none of them had so much moved her, had so kindled her sexuality, as that brief embrace in the wild Finnish countryside, under the pale skies of the north. Olga fell asleep wondering how Simon would look, what she would say, when they met on deck next day.

But the next morning was given up to pomp and ceremony, in which the Grand Duchess and the Marine Guards officer each had different parts to play, when the Czar received the mayor and military governor of Reval aboard the *Standart*. The Czarina came on deck and walked through her own part in the ceremonial, and when it was over Olga and Tatiana were allowed to sit with their little brother while the pale empress sat in the fresh air on deck. Alexis was out of pain, for the doctors had unwillingly given him morphine at midnight, but sleepy and very languid. Tatiana brought her balalaika and played to him softly. Both girls thought it a great advance, a hopeful sign, when the boy's heavy lids were raised and he said, in almost his normal voice, 'I think I'd like to learn to play that thing!'

He was able to be dressed in his sailor suit, although the cap with its brave *Standart* riband lay pathetically askew on his bright hair when Derevenko carried him on deck as the yacht entered Peterhof bay. The unsuccessful cruise had lasted only six days instead of fourteen, because of the French state visit, although it was understood that this was only an interruption. The Czar said as much, talking cheerfully to Commander Sablin at the approach of the tender, and as the imperial ladies went down the line of officers, saying goodbye, Simon seized his chance to say to Olga when he bent over her hand:

'I look forward to the next part of the cruise, Princess.'

'I hope we can begin again where we left off,' she answered, and hid her smile at the quick look of delight in his eyes. The Czarina, immediately ahead, heard nothing: she was saying lugubriously to Anna Virubova that she didn't think they would ever be all together in the *Standart* again.

'Speak for yourself, my dear,' said the Czar. 'I'll be at sea tomorrow, for the welcome to President Poincaré.' He was quite nonchalant about the French state visit, although the courier boats had brought him reports twice daily about the increasing tension in the capital. While the investigation of the Sarajevo murders was still being studied in Vienna, the President of the French Republic was not a welcome guest in Petersburg. Raymond Poincaré, a Lorrainer, had seen the province of his birth invaded by the Prussians in 1870 and torn from France by conquest: for him, even more than for most of his French contemporaries, 'the gap in the Vosges' was a phrase full of poignant meaning. To fill that gap, to bring Alsace and Lorraine back to France, was known to be the aspiration of Poincaré and other Frenchmen sworn to *la revanche*: might this honoured guest not use his visit to France's ally to persuade Russia into a war with Germany? The Cossacks were clearing the streets of the capital of anti-Poincaré demonstrators while the Czar and his family entered the immense grounds of Peterhof and were driven to their summer home at Alexandria Cottage.

It was a cottage only by courtesy, being more like a large country house, but compared with the other imperial residences it was a gay and frivolous little dwelling in a mixture of styles. There were mullioned windows wreathed in creepers, there were white-painted balconies with blue curtains and pink and white sun screens in a bright contrast to the yellow stucco of the house. It looked both welcoming and peaceful to the travellers from the *Standart*, for the gardeners usually working beneath the rose pergolas and linden alleys had been drafted to swell the army of men who were bringing the lawns, the avenues and the fountains of Peterhof to the last pitch of perfection in honour of President Poincaré.

The elected head of the French Republic was to stay in Peterhof palace itself, the supreme achievement of the great Peter and his challenge to Versailles; and there on the next evening, following his safe arrival on board the battleship *France*, Monsieur Poincaré was entertained by the Czar at a banquet in the Empress Elizabeth salon. For the young Grand Duchesses the chief pleasure of this occasion was the sight of their mother restored for a few hours to her legendary beauty, with her splendid cold profile and glorious hair enhanced by the traditional dress of a Russian empress. Alexandra Feodorovna wore a diamond tiara over the long lace veil which fell over bare shoulders, revealed by her low-cut brocade gown, and above a many-stranded diamond collar and necklace, ropes of pearls, her favourite jewels, reached almost to her waist. It was a hot evening, and when she held out her hands to her younger daughters, who had begged to clasp the pearl and gold bracelets on her wrists, they were shocked by the chill of their mother's touch.

The next day the French President visited St. Petersburg, and as a protest demonstration the tramcar and train drivers went on strike. This was no inconvenience to Monsieur Poincaré, driving up the Nevski Prospekt in a carriage and four: he smiled affably and raised his silk hat repeatedly to the cheering groups paid and stationed at every corner by the police. It was an inconvenience to Richard Allen, who, unable to find a droshki, had to walk some distance between his flat on the Italianskaia and the British Embassy, and also to Mara Trenova, who had to walk still further from her depressing home near the Vladimir church to the equally depressing classroom where she was taking lessons in shorthand and typewriting. Her fellow-students were as discontented as herself, young men and women who had been unable, for a variety of reasons, to enter the university, and were starting adult life with a grudge against society. In the shabby tea-room to which they repaired at the end of the day, they eagerly discussed the strikes which were said to be breaking out in the major factories of the capital and the rumours of a general mobilisation which had been rife for some days past. They carried their rumours and complaints home with them, to be repeated in the cheap food stores and round the supper tables of the poor and the dispossessed. But President Poincaré held a grand diplomatic levée at the Winter Palace, at which the only guest who appeared to be under some constraint was the envoy of Austria-Hungary, and drove back in state to Peterhof when the day was over.

Those responsible for his safety began to breathe more easily. The worst was over. There had been no 'incident' in Petersburg, not even the shadow of another Sarajevo, and nothing lay ahead until the hour of his departure but the long series of ceremonial occasions, toasts, and protestations of undying friendship between France and Russia. There was a luncheon given by the Czar at which no ladies were present, there was the singing of the Evening Hymn by the Guards in the summer camp at Krasnoe Selo, and finally, on the morning of the last day of the state visit, there was to be a great review of those same Guards, the flower of the Russian Army.

The Grand Duchesses Olga and Tatiana waited in one of the wooden dachas, which were part of the cantonments at Krasnoe Selo, to play their part in the review. From earliest childhood they had been present at the summer manoeuvres which their father enjoyed so much, feeling himself to be a soldier among soldiers and at his ease, but this was the first time that, as the Colonels-in-Chief of two crack regiments, they would ride alongside the Czar as he reviewed his troops. The little room where they stood waiting, with its one window looking into a clump of birches, seemed to be remote from the great camp, but in fact the girls could hear all the noise of the preparations, from the moving into place of the cavalry regiments to the sound of carriage wheels as the privileged spectators were driven up to the grandstand.

'How much longer, Tania?' said Olga, going closer to the open window. 'It's terribly hot in here.'

Tatiana consulted her wrist watch. 'Fifteen minutes, if they're punctual . . . Olga, *don't* lean on the window sill! You're sure to get a smear or dust on your sleeves, or something!'

She herself was immaculate, standing just as her mother's dresser, lent for the occasion, had made her stand while the heavy uniform was smoothed and folded to her slenderness. Olga scrubbed at her elbows with her handkerchief and pulled her tunic down. 'No harm done,' she said nonchalantly. 'Do you think we dare undo our collars?'

'No, the hooks are far too stiff to fasten again. It *is* hot, though!' The tunics of their regiments, worn above dark riding skirts, were far heavier than their usual summer dresses, Olga's with frogs across the breast and embroidered cuffs, Tatiana's with heavy epaulettes. On a table in the centre of the room lay their white gloves and riding crops, beside Tatiana's Uhlan helmet with its drooping plume and Olga's Hussar hat with its thick chinstrap.

'I wish mamma was here,' said Tatiana. 'She told me this morning she hadn't been inside this place for years.'

'She's got to drive with Monsieur Poincaré. But isn't it odd to think that she and father actually lived here, nineteen years ago, the whole summer before I was born? I bet they were happy then, don't you?'

'They're very happy in each other now.'

'Yes, but —' There was no need to elaborate upon that 'but'. Olga looked round the little sitting-room, so unsuitably furnished for its country setting. The young Empress of Russia had exercised the fatal taste of all minor German royalty for the London furniture of the Nineties, and had shopped extensively on the Tottenham Court Road.

'The place looks all wrong somehow. Not a patch on the Hendrikovs' dacha at Koivisto.'

'That really impressed you, didn't it? Listen — are they bringing up the horses?'

'No, but somebody's creaking about outside.' Olga opened the door leading to the little anteroom, where an ADC remained on duty. He had his back to the Grand Duchesses, and seemed to be barring the way to a plump woman with an ingratiating smile.

'Anna Alexandrovna, what are you doing here?' demanded Olga.

'Oh, my darlings, I only came to wish you luck — '

'It's all right,' said Tatiana quietly. 'Madame Virubova may come in.' And, as the ADC stood aside, she added,

'I should have thought you'd be in the grandstand by now, Ania.'

'But my place is reserved, Tania dearest; I can climb up there at the last moment. I can wait here for ever, if there's the least little thing I can do for you.'

'What should there be?' said Olga indifferently. She turned back to the window and took a deep breath of the fresh air.

'But aren't you, confess now, just the least little, teensy weensy bit nervous?' said Madame Virubova.

She had a curious way of talking, as if her tongue were too thick for the small mouth in what was still a babyish face, overlaid by fat. There was the same disproportion in Madame Virubova's figure. At thirty-two she had sloping, girlish shoulders above a short torso and huge thighs, painfully outlined, on this blazing July day, by her clammy, clinging chiffon skirts. She had taken off her gloves, and Olga shied away from the moist pink fingers stretched out to her own breast.

'Don't touch me, Ania. You know I hate being pawed about.'

'Angel, I think you must be a wee bit uncomfy, because your ribbon is askew — '

'Leave it alone!' The mirror showed Olga that the scarlet ribbon of the Order of St. Catherine, which with its diamond star was the prerogative of the empress-consort and her daughters, lay in a perfect line across her tunic.

'You're terribly excited, pet, and I don't wonder. I told your dear mamma only this morning that you ought to have had a chance to practise for such a grand review.'

'We don't have to practise,' Olga said. 'It comes to us quite naturally.'

'Very well, girlies. I see you haven't any use for your poor old faithful Ania. But do do your best, won't you, out there in front of all those men? Don't do anything to spoil your father's memories of Krasnoe Selo!'

'What do you mean by that?' said Tatiana. 'You mean when he lived here with the Czarina, long ago?'

71

'I mean his happy days with Mala Kchessinskaia.' Anna Virubova kissed her hand to the two girls, and manoeuvred her spreading hips through the doorway. Olga shut the door behind her with a bang.

'You were awfully rude to her, Olga.'

'I don't care, she makes me sick. How mother can bear to have her about, I simply do not know.'

'Oh, come on now, you used to enjoy going to parties at her house when we were little.'

'My sense of smell can't have been developed in those days. When do you suppose she washed her armpits last?'

A heavy knock on the door changed Tatiana's shocked '*Olga!*' into 'Five minutes! Let's put on our helmets! We can't keep papa waiting!'

'We won't.' The chinstraps were adjusted, the white kid gloves pulled on. A long look in the wall mirror was entirely reassuring. But before they left the close little room, which now indeed smelled far from fresh, Olga said uncertainly:

'What do you suppose she meant about Kchessinskaia?'

'The ballerina?'

'Who else?'

'Oh, don't fuss about it, Olga, you know how Ania likes to drop little hints which never mean anything! And everybody knows that Kchessinskaia — '

'Is Cousin Andrei's mistress,' Olga finished for her. 'And has been, almost since the time that I was born.'

The vast parade ground at Krasnoe Selo was hardly an amphitheatre, but the ground sloped at either end into a rise where, at the end where the cantonments were established — the headquarters, barracks, dacha, church and theatre — a grandstand had been put up for the guests at the review. It was already filled with women in picture hats and their escorts, many in brilliant uniforms, when a barouche drawn by four grey horses and escorted by Cossacks came up the long avenue and halted beneath a silken canopy. In it were the Czarina and the President of the French Republic, and facing them, the young Grand Duchesses Marie and Anastasia.

In the silence of almost reverent attention sixty thousand troops, horse and foot, stood fast while the Czar and his elder daughters rode on to the parade ground. The regiments stretched out as far as the eye could reach, to the belt of trees which marked the summit of the rising ground at the far side, and only the faint but constant jingle of harness was heard as the Czar halted and raised his hand in salute. Two little white-gloved hands flashed up behind him as a massed military band broke into the 'Marseillaise', and the French President stood up in the barouche with his silk hat in his hand. While the Czar's mount fidgeted and tossed her head, the black and the bay which carried the Grand Duchesses stood motionless during the playing of the French and Russian national anthems. Then the imperial riders, saluted and escorted by the generals of the Guards, turned to pace along the front rank of the foremost regiment, while the band played the traditional '*Kol slaven*', the hymn which the fortress bells of St. Peter and St. Paul played at midnight and noon.

The Czar, surrounded by his generals, wore the uniform and insignia of a colonel of the Regiment of the Transfiguration. It was the highest rank he had reached during his father's reign, when after training in the Hussars he had been gazetted colonel in the Preobrazhenski, and out of sentiment he had promoted himself no higher when he became Czar. The Transfiguration Regiment was in front, with the girls' regiments immediately behind: Olga's Hussars of Elizabeth-grad, Tatiana's Uhlans of Vossnossensk. All the three regiments were inspected by the Czar. The spectators, through the binoculars which became necessary, saw Tatiana's face grow pale with nervousness and assume some of her mother's hauteur: Olga was flushed and smiling. Before the review began she had been innocently excited at the thought that Simon Hendrikov would see her mounted, dressed as a soldier, wearing the Order of St. Catherine, but as she rode down the lines behind her father she was too much carried away by the vastness of the assembly to think of any one man in it. Under the wide pale Russian sky, in the huge plain that smelt of dust and harness oil and horse manure, secure in her side saddle on the familiar black mare, Olga Nicolaievna knew a physical felicity only matched by the exaltation of her mood. As they turned and rode back to the saluting base, to the silk-canopied barouche where her mother's parasol dipped in approval, to the smiling faces, becoming more distinct, in the red and gold draped imperial stand, Olga's heart was beating faster in the first public triumph of her life.

The march-past began, and now, in honour of the French President, the Russian troops came up in quick time, to the tune of the 'Marche Lorraine' followed by 'Sambre et Meuse'. Some of the better-informed Russians in the grandstand shrugged their shoulders: they knew that these were melodies to which the soldiers of France had traditionally gone into battle, but not all the company grasped that significance — the tunes were catchy, that was enough. The infantry marched past in faultless alignment, by columns of four, of eight, sixteen, thirty-two; the regimental colours were dipped to the Czar and his daughters, a group as motionless as Peter the Great and his bronze horse miles away on the Neva embankment. And the French President, who had been visibly moved at the playing of the 'Marche Lorraine', said to the Czarina:

'Your daughters are magnificent, Madame — all your daughters!'

The younger girls giggled, and the Czarina, with the pinched and patronising smile of which Poincaré had had more than enough, replied, 'My older girls are very fond of riding, and His Majesty is the best of teachers.'

'And you, *Altesse*,' persevered the President, smiling at Marie, 'do you enjoy riding too?'

'Very much, Monsieur le Président.'

'Oh, but my sister's a terrific gymnast!' burst out Anastasia. 'She's very strong. She can lift a man right up off the ground — an ordinary-sized man, that is,' she concluded, with a doubtful glance at the President's bulk.

Poincaré's lips twitched. 'Your Imperial Highness has inherited the prodigious strength of the Czar Alexander II,' he said to Marie. 'I shall have to be very careful not to offend you!'

Alexandra Feodorovna closed her eyes. Tormented by headache to the point where the flags and the uniforms turned in her brain like a vast wheel of colour, she found it no longer endurable to look at the tableau of her husband and the girls on horseback. They were more relaxed now, and Nicholas had turned from one to the other with a smiling remark as the long lines of marching men advanced and wheeled. She saw Tatiana smile in return, and that was bearable, for Tatiana was her favourite daughter, and there was something deeply satisfying in seeing her own young beauty revived in the slender girl on the bay mare. But Olga's gay glance at her father gave his wife a pang of jealousy which, as she looked at them once more from beneath her tilted parasol, she told herself was jealousy for Alexis. Olga's strong, slim shoulders in the military tunic, Olga's strong legs just moulded by the riding skirt, were to the mother's obsessed mind an insult to Alexis. He had never sat a horse and never would. He walked in the gardens, when he was well enough, holding the bridle of Vanka, the donkey bought for him at Cinizelli's circus. Sometimes, with his sailor nurse in close attendance, he drove little Vanka in a donkey cart. But the doctors were absolute in forbidding him to ride. It was Olga, not Alexis, who rode beside their father to review the troops.

The Grand Duchess Marie unobtrusively passed a bottle of smelling salts to the Czarina.

'It's nearly over now, mamma,' she said gently. 'Do watch the cavalry!'

The bugles were shrilling for the sensational finale of the Guards' review, when the cavalry regiments charged en masse towards the saluting base. They came shouting, and with such élan that spectators who were at Krasnoe Selo for the first time shuddered at the thought that the Czar and his entourage would be swept aside or ridden down by an irresistible tide of horses and men. Then at the last moment the riders checked, the horses in the front rank curvetted in a salute, and silence fell over the sun-soaked plain. The voice of the Czar was clearly heard in the traditional shout of approval:

'Well done, children! Well done!'

And sixty thousand men gave the deep-throated reply:

'Happy to serve Your Imperial Majesty!'

CHAPTER FOUR

JOE CALVERT was glad the tramcar strike had ended. On the morning after the battleship *France* sailed from Kronstadt, carrying President Raymond Poincaré on his next state visits to the northern capitals, Vice-Consul Calvert, that tiny cog in the diplomatic machine, caught a tram outside the Europa at eight in the morning and went off to his Russian lesson.

With the permission of his consul, he had arranged to visit Madame Hendrikova at half past eight on three mornings a week. It meant arriving late at the consulate, but Joe had already seen enough of Russian unpunctuality to realise that a lesson set for six in the afternoon might not begin until seven, as her tardy students prolonged Madame Hendrikova's working day. And both she and Joe were fresh, first thing in the morning, ready to do a good hour's work in her little room at the far end of a corridor, where the only sounds were the footsteps of the Lettish servants going between the kitchen and the living-room. There, Joe supposed, Dolly and her father were having breakfast, but he neither saw nor heard them; after having been catapulted into the family life of the Hendrikovs his own plan for work now kept them at a distance. By and by, but certainly before they left for Finland, he wanted to invite Dolly and her parents to dinner and the French play at the Alexandrovski theatre. He was hardly up to a Russian performance after barely three weeks' instruction in that language, but he knew he was making progress, although his teacher was sparing of her praise.

He had mastered the Cyrillic alphabet and its pronunciation, and was acquiring the rudiments of the complicated grammar, with a small vocabulary. Joe Calvert had no difficulty in reading one word on the billboards outside the newspaper kiosks as the tram went along the Nevski: *Voina! Voina!* That meant 'war', he knew; but the papers could hardly be announcing an outbreak of war, for there was no undue concern on the faces of his fellow passengers. They wore the blank look of indifference Joe had become used to in a certain element of Petersburg society, and he supposed, at that hour of the morning, they were minor members of the empire's vast bureaucracy going unconcerned to their routine work.

When he reached Vassili Island he was sufficiently disturbed to buy a copy of *Novoie Vremia*, and was feeling in his pocket for change when he heard his own name spoken breathlessly and found Dolly Hendrikova at his elbow.

'Oh, Mr. Calvert, are *you* buying the newspaper?'

'Yes, though I can't read much of it yet, Darya Karlovna —'

'Father sent me out to get the special edition —'

'This is an extra? Because of this word here, *voina*, war?'

'One of his friends at the paper telephoned —'

'You mean war's been declared?'

'No, thank God, no! This says "Danger of war", not "Declaration of war" —'

She was out of breath and flushed with hurry; pretty Dolly, in a blue cotton dress without hat or gloves, and little wisps of fair hair escaping from the tortoiseshell clasps meant to hold her curls in place. Joe saw with amusement that she was wearing a scuffed pair of dancing slippers, as if she had been sent off half-dressed along the quays.

'Come on,' he said, 'we'd better get along to the flat and out of this crowd; see, everybody's going to work as usual.'

Dolly looked at the office workers making for the Exchange and the Academy of Science, and nodded in agreement.

'So they are,' she said, 'and you're coming to your lesson with my mother?'

'That was the idea. And maybe, as we go, you'd tell me what the trouble is? People have been talking about the danger of war for nearly a month now —'

'Yes, but *last* night,' said Dolly earnestly, 'in the *middle* of the night, they waited until the French President had sailed from Kronstadt, the Austrians sent an ultimatum to the Serbian government. My father says if the Serbs don't accept it, it means war.'

'But what was the ultimatum?'

'It's in the newspaper. Oh, let's hurry, please!'

In her flat-heeled slippers Dolly was almost running over the uneven paving, and Joe remembered to ask:

'How is your friend, Darya Karlovna? I mean your school friend, Miss Trenova?'

'I haven't seen her for a week. She's doing a secretarial course, you know.'

'So your mother told me.'

'One of the visiting lecturers at school promised to find a position for her, as soon as she's qualified.'

'That's good.' They were in the Fourth Line by this time, and Professor Hendrikov's grey head was to be seen at his study window. Dolly waved the copy of *Novoie Vremia*, which Joe had passed on to her. The porter, with his most obsequious bow, opened the front door for them.

Madame Hendrikova, without waiting for the slow Lett maid, pulled open the door of the apartment. 'You had Mr. Calvert to look after you,' she said to Dolly. 'That was good.'

'I'm glad I was early this morning,' said Joe.

It was still not half past eight, but Madame Hendrikova was ready for her day's teaching, every hair in place, a plain silver watch pinned to her white blouse, and her satin belt drawn taut above her sweeping skirt. 'You must have a cup of tea with us, Mr. Calvert,' she said calmly, 'and my husband will tell us the news from Vienna.'

She took a fresh teacup and filled it from the samovar, indicating to Joe and Dolly that they should sit down at the breakfast table. The chair the young man took was the one occupied by Simon Hendrikov during his brief visit to the supper party late in June. Joe remembered Madame Hendrikova's distress at the mere hint of a general mobilisation, and marvelled at her calm when the hint seemed so likely to become reality.

'May I have some more tea too, mother?' said Dolly. 'I'm so thirsty.'

'No wonder; you ran out before you'd finished your breakfast.'

They smiled at each other, and Dolly, after a furtive glace at the sideboard mirror, pushed back her dishevelled hair with her fingers. Professor Hendrikov, almost as untidy as his daughter in a shabby alpaca jacket, had been scanning the newspaper closely since he took it from Dolly's hand. Now he looked over his spectacles at his wife and said:

'It's all pretty much as Kolia told me on the telephone. Except that the ultimatum wasn't sent to Belgrade in the middle of the night, as I understood him to say, it was sent yesterday evening. But here comes the bombshell. Austria requires a judicial investigation in Serbia itself, conducted by Austrian officials as well as Serbs — ' He threw up one hand in a gesture of despair.

'A new investigation into the plot?' said Joe.

'Yes.'

'And you think the Serbians won't accept the Austrian officials?'

'I'm certain they will not. It would be too great a blow to their national pride and sovereignty.'

'Maybe they'll swallow their pride rather than risk a war.'

'They swallowed their pride in 1908, when the Austrians annexed Bosnia and Herzegovina. They won't do it a second time.' Professor Hendrikov struck the table suddenly, so that the china rattled, and raised his voice. 'What a farce! What an imposture! The Emperor Franz Josef has one foot in the grave, and the King of Serbia is deranged to the point where his son has just been named as Regent. Why should two old dotards gamble with the lives of a whole generation of young men?'

Joe Calvert looked at Dolly and her mother. Both were pale, and the girl's eyes were full of tears. It's the son, of course, he thought, that kid in the Marine Guards, they're thinking what he's in for, if the Serbs reject this damned silly ultimatum. He felt out of place, the neutral, the citizen of a great republic above and beyond a squabble in the Balkans. He said to Madame Hendrikova:

'It's very upsetting news, madame, and I'm sure you don't feel like giving me a Russian lesson this morning. Let's just cancel this one, and try again on Monday.'

'Certainly not!' The little lady got up briskly, and Joe jumped to his feet. 'There is nothing like hard work in a crisis, monsieur, and I hope you intend to work hard this morning. I set you a lesson on the use of adjectives — hard, soft and mixed.'

'I've studied it, madame.'

'Then come along; we're ten minutes late already.'

But before Joe followed his teacher to her workroom he said to her husband:

'Look here, sir, I know I'm only a greenhorn, and maybe I'm

79

too optimistic, but I don't see why this ultimatum *has* to lead to war. Maybe the Serbs will be sensible, and accept all the terms, or maybe the Great Powers will take the whole thing to the Court of Arbitration at the Hague and settle it round a conference table like the Agadir crisis. Say! Is there a time limit to that ultimatum?'

'Forty-eight hours.'

'Well, the great thing is to keep them talking and not shooting off any guns.'

'Yes, but the very timing of the ultimatum shows the Emperor and his friend the Kaiser want to prevent talks between the allied Powers. Sent at the very end of Poincaré's visit, making it impossible for him to consult the Czar! Sent when the French chief of state and the French prime minister are both out of the country together and on the high seas —'

'But good Lord, sir, don't they have wireless telegraphy aboard the *France*?'

'You mean nations should take great and vital decisions by wireless telegraphy?'

'Why not, if it's to stop a war?'

Dolly looked up, and she was actually smiling. 'It's no use,' she said. 'Papa thinks of statecraft in terms of pens, ink and paper. And speeches in the Duma, very correct and proper.'

'Oh! Well! I'm keeping Madame Hendrikova waiting. Maybe we could have another talk on Monday?'

Joe saw as he left the room that Dolly had gone to her father's side and put her fresh cheek against the lined cheek of the history professor whom History had overtaken.

Street fighting broke out again in Petersburg that day. The bridges of the Neva were raised to keep the workers on the Viborg Side from demonstrating in the main arteries of the city, and heavy police casualties were reported at the council of ministers presided over by the Czar. No time was wasted on such domestic details by Nicholas II and his councillors, who like every other cabinet in Europe were concerned only with the Austrian ultimatum to Serbia. It was impossible to hold their meeetings at Alexandria Cottage, and the Czar walked to and from the great palace, reluctantly leaving the summer warmth of the long avenues for the council chamber.

His daughters, confined to the environs of the Cottage, lamented their father's absence as much as his decision to postpone the second part of the summer cruise. He was the best of playfellows in his leisure hours, and without him Marie and Anastasia took to the tennis court and played endless singles, complaining of the heat. Even when they stopped to mop their faces and drink lemonade they had nothing to say about the business which kept their father at Peterhof. The Czarina stayed with Alexis, who was still confined to bed, and Tatiana was in devoted attendance on her mother. No one seemed to realise the gravity of the situation but Olga. The young Grand Duchesses were not encouraged to read the newspapers, but the papers were there, on a table in the little library, and she read them in the peaceful, silent afternoons, to the thump of tennis balls and the pleasant sound of a pony, wearing leather boots, drawing a mower over the lawns round Alexandria Cottage.

Olga was thankful for two mercies, not small: that Father Grigori, called Rasputin, was far away in Siberia, and that Anna Virubova, although much closer to hand, had gone home to her own little house at Czarskoe Selo, for those were the two who most regularly encouraged the Czarina to meddle in politics. So far she was keeping quiet, even at the family tea which her husband never missed, although many more dispatches than usual were brought in while they sat over the teacups. It was a sight to which all the girls were accustomed: the ADC on duty bringing in the news agency digests for the next day's press in their long white envelopes, and their father pulling at the thread of orange-coloured silk passed under each seal for easy opening. He read each report as calmly as he had always done, and folded it with care, but without making any comment on the contents. Alexandra Feodorovna watched him intently, but she asked no questions: Nicholas II had been brought up to believe that it was discourteous to mention politics in the presence of ladies.

It was Olga, impulsive as ever, who made the first oblique comment on the painful situation. On Saturday, when the forty-eight hours of the Austrian ultimatum were beginning to run out, the Czarina lunched with her girls on one of the pleasant balconies of the cottage. A vegetarian herself, and proud of the fact that she took no interest in food, she ate only a few mouthfuls and drank a sip of mineral water, and even the healthy appetites of the girls were quickly satisfied. At last Alexandra Feodorovna, abandoning her pretence of tranquillity, said to Olga:

'I feel so much for poor dear Helen today! Write her a little note of sympathy, Olga, and a courier can take it over to Pavlovsk.'

'Which Helen?' Olga said perversely. 'Cousin John's wife?'

'Don't be silly, dear; yes, Helen of Serbia, of course. Poor thing, my heart bleeds for her, a stranger in a strange land —'

'She's been married to John Romanov for at least three years, mamma.'

'But I'm sure her heart is in Belgrade today, where her poor father is so much afflicted, and her brother the Regent faced with such a terrible responsibility! Tell her we are all thinking of her and her gallant little country —'

'I don't think I can quite say that, mamma.'

'What *do* you mean?'

'I think Serbia has been a very quarrelsome little country, since old King Peter came to the throne. And we all know *how* he came to the throne — after King Milan and his queen were stabbed and hacked to death in their own palace, only ten or eleven years ago.'

'Olga! Where did you hear such a horrible thing?'

'It's a matter of history, mother.'

'But I thought you were so fond of your cousin Helen!'

'I am, I like her very much. But I don't see why Serbia should be called a gallant little country just because one of the princesses married our cousin John!'

The Czarina closed her eyes. 'Please don't argue, Olga,' she said. 'Write as I tell you, and sign all your initials, in that pretty way I like so much. Go indoors and do it now.'

The Grand Duchess Olga obeyed. She wrote a few affectionate lines to the anxious young princess at Pavlovsk, in the firm, almost masculine hand with the wide spaces between the words which was her characteristic. But she omitted the girlish signature of OTMA, which the four sisters had adopted from the initials of their names, and almost for the first time in family correspondence signed herself 'Olga' with the broad sweep of a ruler signing a document of state.

It was a firmer signature than the 'Nicholas' which her father appended, some hours later, to his order for the preliminaries to mobilisation in four military areas of Russia. For the Serbian government, after long deliberation, refused the one clause in the ultimatum which demanded an Austrian share in a new judicial investigation. When this refusal was sent to the Austrian envoy in Belgrade he immediately asked for his passports, and diplomatic relations with Serbia were broken off.

It had been the tradition through more than one reign that the Krasnoe summer ceremonies should end with a performance in the little theatre, presented by the new graduates of the Imperial Ballet School. This year, on the hot July evening when peace hung in the balance, there were to be two additions to the programme: the great aria from Glinka's 'A Life for the Czar', and the mazurka from Act II of the same opera, to be danced by Mathilde Kchessinskaia.

When the Grand Duchess Olga was told that, as had happened at several of the summer ceremonies, she must take her mother's place at the theatre, she felt a double surge of pleasure. Anna Virubova's poisoned words had left enough impression for the girl to wish to watch her father as he watched the dancer, but above all, the pent-up anxiety of the previous days made her long for a private word with the Czar. As it turned out, she was dressed and sitting in the motor for ten minutes before Nicholas came to join her, and then he was followed by the ADC on duty. With the brief remark, 'More rotten telegrams!' the Czar switched on the roof light of the car, dispelling the gentle summer dusk, and all through the short drive to Krasnoe Selo he read the telegrams one by one, making very brief notes on each with his gold pencil, and handing it over to be filed in a leather wallet by the ADC. It was impossible to interrupt him, and Olga sat silent while they drove through Krasnoe Selo, the Red Village, until they reached the theatre. There the court official who was also the theatre director was waiting, with a bouquet of roses for the young Grand Duchess in his hand.

It was a quaint little place, like an overgrown dacha, with fretwork carving and a curtained piazza set about with pots of flowers. Protocol required that certain courtiers should greet the monarch in this piazza, and then the Czar and his daughter entered the theatre by a covered private way which led past the stars' dressing-rooms, where lights were shining behind drawn blinds. The anteroom to the imperial box was so bright that Olga's eyes were dazzled: she was aware of ladies curtseying, and then all other impressions were obliterated as Simon Hendrikov stepped forward to take her light cloak from her shoulders.

She gave him her hand to kiss, and said:

'I hardly expected to see *you* here.'

'I moved heaven and earth to be posted to the theatre guard tonight.'

'I mean, I didn't expect you to be still at Krasnoe Selo.'

'We're moving off to Petersburg tomorrow.'

'Oh, then you'll see your family. Unless they've gone to the dacha already?'

They smiled at one another, as much alone in that crowded anteroom as if they stood again among the wild grasses by the Finnish river.

'My family? I don't think they plan to go to Koivisto yet ... I saw you at the review, Olga Nicolaievna. You looked marvellous.' His eyes said, And you look marvellous tonight.

'I'm afraid the *Standart* cruise is off for the time being,' said the girl.

'It was in the orders of the day. I suppose it can't be helped. But if all this blows over —'

'Oh, Simon Karlovich!' said Olga, very low, 'pray, pray that it will!'

'Come along, my dear,' said the Czar at her elbow. 'Ten minutes late already, and I asked for a short programme tonight!'

In his terrible preoccupation, Nicholas had hardly noticed how the girl was dressed. Now, as he handed her to the front of the imperial box, he was at once aware of a hum of pleasure and approval, as the very critical audience assessed the charm of that young figure in a simple, pink chiffon dress, bowing and smiling to them all. Olga's only ornaments were a single strand of pearls, banding her upswept golden hair, and the bouquet of roses which she carried in her left hand. The unexpected meeting with Simon had left her flushed and pleased.

'How very nice you look,' murmured the Czar. 'Young Hendrikov seems to be badly smitten. Are you going to turn out to be a heartbreaker, my dear?'

It was the familiar tone of family banter, but Olga was glad that the house lights were dimmed at that moment, and the orchestra began an overture. The performance started, no better and no worse than others she had seen before, with the new graduates of the ballet school dancing in the perennial hope of imperial patronage as eagerly as if no Serbian batteries were being mounted along the high frontier on the way to Sarajevo. When the interval came she and her father remained in the imperial box; cousins came and courtiers came, and made their bow, leaving the girl just time to say,

'I'm looking forward to Madame Kchessinskaia's dance.'

'But you saw her dance the mazurka last year, at the Maryinski.'

'I missed most of it. Don't you remember? Mamma felt faint, and Tania and I went back to the anteroom with her.'

'So she did, poor mamma.' The Czar spoke abstractedly, and Olga wondered if he realised, as she had come to realise, that her mother's faintness and palpitations always came on when she herself was not the centre of attention. But, on that night of the tercentenary celebrations at the Maryinski theatre, had Alexandra Feodorovna had a special reason for resenting the dancer's presence on the stage? She said breathlessly:

'Do *you* admire Kchessinskaia's dancing?'

'She's Russia's only *prima ballerina assoluta*, dear.'

'Yes, but, some people say her style is terribly old-fashioned, and too formal and cold for modern audiences. Do you agree with that?'

'I must say I prefer the old choreography to the new.' It was one of the Czar's characteristically noncommittal answers, and Olga was surprised when he went on to say, 'It was in this very theatre that I saw her dance before the public for the first time.'

'Madame Kchessinskaia? When was that — before you and mamma, were married?'

'Oh, long before. About a thousand years ago.'

'You're not very flattering to the lady. Why, how old is *she*?'

'She must be over forty now.'

But the dancer, revealed in a shaft of golden light when the curtains swept aside, looked little older than a girl. She was small and slim, with a piquant face and brilliant eyes, and the mazurka which she had danced so often was out of all her repertoire the theme best suited to her genius. Mala Kchessinskaia was of Polish blood, and the celebration of a Polish triumph in the scene of the mazurka struck an emotional fervour from her performance which overshadowed its technical skill. She curtseyed her thanks for what was very nearly an ovation without glancing in the direction of the imperial box, where the Czar, after applauding politely, sat with his hand covering his bearded mouth.

The real ovation came ten minutes later, when the greatest baritone in Russia finished Glinka's magnificent aria in which Ivan Susanin, surrounded by the enemies of his young emperor, proclaims his duty to give his life for Russia. It was the final expression, the emotional catharsis, of what every man and woman in the threatre had felt under the mounting pressure of the passing days. They stood up to cheer the singer, they turned spontaneously to cheer the Czar. In a moment the evening became his triumph, as the theatre echoed to the national anthem.

And when his daughter followed him down the covered way which led past the stars' dressing-rooms, she saw him look across the courtyard at one window, and lift his hand to his cap in a salute to Mala Kchessinskaia, who stood there silhouetted against the lighted room with her own hand at her lips.

It was a fleeting impression, only visible to Olga's watchful eyes, and swiftly obliterated by the scene in the piazza. The ADC who had accompanied them to the theatre was there, with a new sheaf of telegrams in his hand, and the Grand Duke Kirill and his wife were there with one or two other members of the Family. It was Kirill who took the Czar aside and spoke to him urgently: Olga could hear nothing but names — 'the Kaiser — the German Ambassador — Sazonov' — and then her father glanced in her direction.

'Kirill and Ducky will take you home, Olga. Tell mamma I'm going straight to the palace to hold an emergency council; I hope it won't last long.'

With that he got into the car waiting with its motor running in front of the rose-hung door, and the Grand Duke Kirill, with cold ceremony, bowed Olga into his own limousine. His stately wife took her place beside the girl. She felt tongue-tied, a schoolgirl again on the short journey home, during which only the performance was discussed by them, in words suited to the understanding of a child of ten. Olga almost ran into the hall of Alexandria Cottage as their motor drove away.

The Czarina appeared at once from one of the reception rooms. She was wearing a robe of heliotrope silk, cut in the flowing style she preferred, neither a teagown nor a negligée, which gave her a look of perpetual invalidism.

'Where's your father?'

'He went straight to the palace to hold an emergency council.'

'At this hour of the night?'

Olga glanced at the clock. It was after midnight.

'Has there been more news from Vienna?' demanded the Czarina.

'I don't know, mamma. I only heard them say something about a message from the Kaiser.'

'That madman!' exclaimed the Czarina. 'He's at the bottom of all this, of course! Nastia' (to the lady-in-waiting who had followed her into the hall) 'I want to telephone to the palace at once!'

'Mamma, do you think that's wise, if they're in conference?'

The Czarina wrung her hands. 'Heaven knows what may be decided, if I'm not consulted! Oh, if Father Grigori were only here!'

Olga looked round the hall. They were not alone — but then they never were alone; besides the alarmed lady-in-waiting there were two footmen on duty, immaculate in livery, their hands encased in white cotton gloves, and an ADC was standing at attention on the landing upstairs. 'Where's Tatiana? Gone to bed?' she asked.

'Yes, she went to bed an hour ago, she wasn't feeling well. You run along now, lovey, and don't wake her up to start gossiping.'

'I never felt less like gossiping in my life.' But the Czarina had no more attention to give to the daughter she had dismissed like a tiresome child. As Olga went upstairs, trailing her cloak, with the roses of her bouquet dropping petals on every step, she heard her mother saying eagerly:

'Nastïa! Get Anna Alexandrovna on the telephone! Arrange for a car to bring her here as soon as possible!'

But it was not until many hours and several telephone calls later that Anna Virubova arrived at Alexandria Cottage. The Czar himself had come and gone by that time, arriving in the dawn and breakfasting alone with his wife before returning for a long morning's work at Peterhof. The cars came and went along the avenues, bringing new counsellors in and out of uniform to discuss the news already being flashed around the world: the declaration of war on Serbia by Austria-Hungary.

By the time that Madame Virubova came the Czarina was distraught, and her daughters shocked into silence. They submitted to be kissed and cried over by the plump, untidy woman, and then sat down near the drawing-room window, making a pretence at embroidery, while their mother whispered with her Ania at the far end of the room. They were sewing in silence when the car came up the drive and Nicholas II got out alone.

'There's papa!' called Anastasia, jumping up and scattering the basketful of sewing silks.

'Wait!' said Olga. 'Wait until he comes to tea.' It was nearly five o'clock, and two footmen had already come in to arrange the tea-table.

From the window, the girls saw their father stoop to pat two of his favourite collies, decoratively grouped beside the open door, and then they heard his footsteps, heavy and slow, crossing the hall and diminishing on the stairs.

'Let's put our work away,' suggested Marie. 'Papa won't be long.'

The clock struck five, and Alexandra Feodorovna came forward, with Ania at her heels, to light the spirit-lamp beneath the silver kettle. The women waited in silence until the lid began to dance.

'Shall I make the tea, mamma?' asked Olga.

'We'll wait a few minutes longer for papa.'

They waited. The gold clock, adorned with tiny statuettes of Cupid and Psyche, struck the quarter after five. The Czarina, with a sigh, turned down the flame beneath the kettle.

'Papa was alone, wasn't he?' she said.

'He came in alone, mamma.'

'Tatiana, run, darling, and remind him that it's tea-time.

Tell him Ania is here, and wants very much to see him.'

'I'll go!' said Olga, before her sister could get up. It was the chance to speak to her father alone for which she had been waiting since they drove together to the theatre at Krasnoe Selo. She ran upstairs, along a corridor, and stopped at the study door before which, even in the informality of Alexandria Cottage, two gigantic Ethiopians in their picturesque dress stood guard. Olga looked round for an ADC on duty: there was none.

The Ethiopians bowed to the Czar's eldest daughter, but stood squarely in front of her father's door. Men of their race had guarded the privacy of the Russian monarch since the days of Catherine the Great, and they were jealous of their privilege. But when Olga said urgently: 'I have a message from Her Imperial Majesty!' the men bowed low, and simultaneously opened the two leaves of the gilded door.

The Czar's study was a pleasant, airy room, with large windows giving a fine view of the Gulf of Finland. Besides the neatly arranged desk it contained one table covered with papers, and another nearly concealed by an ordnance map of Turkey and the Balkans. Engravings of military subjects hung on the walls, and the furniture was very simple. There were half a dozen leather chairs and a deep sofa, in one corner of which the Czar was half sitting and half lying. His uniform tunic was open at the throat, and his face was more haggard and worn than Olga had ever seen it. On the table near his hand was a tray with cognac and seltzer water, and a half-empty glass showed that the Czar, the most abstemious of men, had felt the need of a stimulant.

'Papa, I'm very sorry to disturb you, but mamma said —'

'You don't disturb me, dear; come in and sit down.'

Looking at those burning eyes she felt helplessly certain that the worst had happened, and Russia was at war. But she plunged on with the message:

'Mamma said to tell you that Ania's here, and wants very much to see you. We hoped you'd come to tea —'

Nicholas managed to smile. 'Ania can wait,' he said. 'How nice and cool you look! Sit down and tell me what my girlies have been doing all this long hot day.'

'Papa, please don't make babies of us all. Please tell me what is happening. I must know, I have a *right* to know,' said Olga, more vehemently than she meant. 'Has Austria declared war on Russia? Have you ordered a general mobilisation?'

The Czar sat up and drained his glass. 'We're not at war,' he said, 'don't worry your pretty little head about that.'

'I asked you not to treat me like a child, papa. After all, I'll be nineteen in November.'

'You still seem like a little girl to me.'

'But only a few weeks ago you thought I was old enough to be married, didn't you?'

'I told you I would never force you into marriage, Olga, and I kept my word.'

'I know you did, but at the beginning you thought it would be all right to give me in marriage to a boy I hardly knew, and send me off with him to a strange country, away from all of you! If I was old enough to be the Princess of Rumania, surely I'm old enough to know what's happening to my own country?' She used the word *rodina*, motherland, and saw the exhausted man before her bite his lip.

'Very well,' he said, 'you know, of course, that the Austrians have declared war on Serbia. They ordered a general mobil- isation this morning. And very much against the will of my military staff, who wanted us to reply in kind, I ordered a partial mobilisation of our army.'

'What does that mean, exactly?'

'It means that thirteen divisions will start moving west to the Galician frontier.'

'Including the Guards we reviewed at Krasnoe Selo?'

'Including certain Guards divisions, naturally.'

'But the Austrians aren't threatening *us*!'

'Not directly. Not today.'

'And if they don't attack us, ever, could you order those thirteen divisions back to barracks — back to all the towns and provinces they came from?'

'In theory I could, but technically it would be very difficult. It's a problem of train transport, which I doubt if you would understand.'

'Father, it would be better to send these men home if they had to walk every mile of the way, rather than send them to the front to die for Serbia.'

'Now you're talking foolishly, my dear. Hadn't we better go to tea?'

'Please wait.' Olga had not accepted the invitation to sit down. Now she moved across the room to where a huge globe, mounted in a brass stand, stood between the two long windows.

'You know,' she said, and spun the globe as she spoke, 'I'm old enough to remember 1905.'

'Are you really?' said the Czar, with an attempt at a light tone.

'Yes, really. I was just the same age then as Alexis is now, and he's supposed to be very bright. I'm sure he'll be able to remember 1914 all his life.'

'And what does my equally bright Olga remember about 1905?'

'I remember the troops leaving for the war against Japan, dead drunk. I remember the troops coming back — those who came back — maimed and blinded. I know Japan defeated us terribly at Mukden, and destroyed our navy at Tsushima Bay. What will happen if the Japanese declare war on us again, and attack us in the east while our army marches west?'

'God's will be done,' said the Czar, and stood up stiffly. 'I learned long ago to bow myself to His punishments.'

'But that's just fatalism, father! Don't you believe God expects us to work to help ourselves?'

'Somebody has been teaching you Protestant doctrines,' said Nicholas dryly. 'Speaking of which, I'm a great deal more concerned about the British than I am about the Japanese. I'm waiting for my beloved cousin Georgie to announce his intention of standing by France and me — '

'But the King of England has to wait for his parliament to decide, doesn't he? We learned that in our history class — '

'That's their beastly idea of liberty,' agreed the Czar. ' — Sunny, my love, I'm so sorry to have kept you waiting!'

The Czarina, with a swirl of draperies, was in the room, red patches on her cheeks and neck marking the nervous rash which afflicted her in moments of extreme stress. Her confidential friend, perspiring and humble, curtseyed deeply to the Czar.

'We couldn't wait any longer, Nicky,' said Alexandra Feodorovna. 'Ania had a telegram from Our Friend, from Father Grigori, with a message for you which you ought to read at once . . . Olga, go downstairs, and supervise the children's tea.'

'Olga has taken to grand strategy like a duck to water,' said the Czar. 'I don't think Father Grigori can have anything to say to me that she can't hear too. Where is this telegram?'

The Czarina had it ready in her hand. Nicholas took the message — it was very short — and the colour rose in his pale face.

'Is this impudent telegram in answer to one from you?' he asked his wife. She, in her turn, coloured at his tone.

'Ania telegraphed to Tiumen on my behalf,' she said. 'After the Austrian declaration, I thought Our Friend ought to know that we are truly horrified at the very thought of war. I begged him to help us with his counsel — and you have it there.'

Nicholas turned to Madame Virubova, who had burst into tears.

'Anna Alexandrovna,' he said icily, 'will you in future remember that I am capable of ruling my country without your interference, or that of Father Grigori? I shall destroy this piece of impertinence, and as a kindness to you both I'll try to forget that it was ever sent.'

'What does it say, father?' Olga asked, and ignoring his wife's gesture of protest the Czar read Rasputin's telegram aloud:

'Let Papa not plan war, for with the war will come the end of Russia and yourselves, and you will lose to the last man.'

CHAPTER FIVE

AUSTRIA-HUNGARY declared war on Serbia on July 28 by the western calendar, exactly one month after Princip fired the fatal shots at Sarajevo. But whereas the opening crisis had been counted in days and weeks it was now counted by hours, and the Czar's insistence that the mobilisation of his army should be only partial proved as ineffectual as Olga's pathetic suggestion that if there was no attack from the west the Russian troops might walk home if train transport failed.

When the Austrians presented Europe with a *fait accompli* by bombarding Belgrade on the next day, Nicholas II could not stand out against his eager generals. At dawn on Friday, July 31, the general mobilisation began in Russia, along the East Prussian as well as the Galician border. The immediate result was general mobilisation in Germany, and an ultimatum from Germany to Russia to stop the preparations for war. When the ultimatum expired at seven o'clock on Saturday evening, Germany declared war on Russia.

At almost the same hour, hundreds of miles to the west, there was a sudden alarm in Luxemburg, the tiny Grand Duchy which lay between Belgium and Germany. There was a point in the Luxemburg territory — barely one thousand square miles in extent — where the railway lines from Germany and Belgium crossed, and this railway station with its adjacent telegraph office was invaded and occupied by a German lieutenant and one infantry company of the 69th Regiment. The station was called Les Trois Vierges, the virgins being Faith, Hope and Charity.

It was a miniature act of aggression, with very little damage done, for the Luxemburg army was barely three hundred strong and composed largely of postmen and railway workers. But it was none the less conclusive, because the neutrality of Luxemburg had been guaranteed by all the Powers, including Germany, and the young girl who was the ruler of the little country was justified in asking the German soldiers to withdraw. But the Germans stayed.

The Czar told his family the sad little story late in the evening, while he waited to give an audience to Sir George Buchanan, the British Ambassador. He still had no great hopes of help from Britain, where the cabinet was in almost continuous session, although the French were standing firm to the Russian alliance and had mobilised during the afternoon. 'Probably only another beastly telegram,' he said of the message which the ambassador was bringing from King George V. Tonight, at least, the Czar did not take refuge in his study. He had spent half an hour with his boy, and then seemed glad to sit in the last amber of the sunset with his wife and daughters, forbidding the lamps to be lit. In the dusky drawing-room, where her husband's cigarette made a little point of red, Alexandra Feodorovna was all loving attention and all patriotism. She had had a bad fright when Nicholas tore up Rasputin's telegram in a weak man's sudden gust of rage: tonight, with the die irrevocably cast, she stormed at her cousin the Kaiser, the arch-plotter behind the senile Austrian emperor, and lamented the bad luck which had sent the Czar's mother, the Empress Dowager Marie, travelling home across Germany at such a time.

'She's not alone, Sunny,' the Czar reminded her. 'Xenia is with her, and all their people; they'll be well taken care of, I'm sure. Their special train may even be at Wirballen by this time.'

'But what if they stopped in Berlin to see Felix and Irina? Really I think *they* might have left for home as soon as the Austrians issued that wicked ultimatum! So inconsiderate of Felix not to be more careful of Irina, in her state of health!'

In the half dark, side by side on the sofa, Marie and Anastasia unobtrusively nudged each other. Their cousin Irina, daughter of their father's sister Xenia, had recently married Prince Felix Yusupov, and in their experience whenever a young married woman was 'in a state of health' it meant a baby was on the way. For both girls, but particularly for Marie, weddings and the subsequent arrival of babies were the two most important topics in the world.

'Don't worry too much about Motherdear,' said the Czar. He knew only too well his wife's steady jealousy of Motherdear, as the Empress Dowager liked her children to call her: it had been one of the penalties of his early married life. To cover her insincerity he began to tell his daughters about that other family of royal girls in Luxemburg, and the ordeal which the eldest, still only twenty, was facing on that July night.

'Are they related to us, papa?' asked Marie.

'Are they, Sunny? Haven't they relatives in Baden?'

'I only know that this girl's mother was a Braganza.'

'But why should the Germans invade Luxemburg?' asked Tatiana.

'They want to cross Luxemburg and Belgium to invade northern France,' said her father.

'Why don't they just cross the Rhine?' asked Olga pertly.

'Because it would take them too long to reduce the forts the French built along their eastern frontier after they lost Alsace and Lorraine. Now, chicks, I've got to see that tiresome ambassador —'

'Come on, girls,' said Tatiana, rising, 'let's go to bed.'

They wished their father good-night affectionately. There had been tears earlier in the evening, when the Czar told them war was declared, but now all four were too tired to show emotion. They kissed their mother's hand and left the room.

Olga halted in the hall.

'I wonder if there are any pictures of that Luxemburg girl in the library. Let's have a look and see.'

'But all our photograph albums are at Czarskoe Selo,' objected Marie, a devoted collector of the family snapshots.

'There wouldn't be any in *our* albums, silly, but I think I know where to find one in papa's collection,' said methodical Tatiana.

'Oh, don't let's start hunting for photographs tonight,' whined Anastasia. 'I'm so sleepy. I want to go to bed.'

'You want to look your best at the Winter Palace, do you?' said Olga.

'That's not *fair*!' said the child, flinching at the tone. 'I think it'll be *awful* at the Winter Palace tomorrow with all those people staring!'

'Staring at papa, perhaps, but not at you.'

'Here you are,' said Tatiana, lifting a green leather album from one of the bookshelves. 'I knew I saw it here ... Oh, thank you!' The inevitable pair of white-gloved hands took the heavy album from her own; a footman, accepted rather than recognised, had been switching on the lights in the library.

'Put it on the round table, please . . . What a neat index papa keeps! "Marie Adelaide, Grand Duchess of Luxemburg, born 1894" — just a year older than you, Olga! "Succeeded 1912", yes, he did say she was twenty now. Page sixty-three.' She turned the pages of the Czar's neat collection of pictures presented to him by minor foreign royalties. The Grand Duchess Marie Adelaide had signed the stiff cabinet photograph taken on her accession day, showing a girl with a sweet, serious face, her hair puffed out over a wire frame under a top-heavy hat.

'That hat's even worse than ours.'

'But she looks rather nice, doesn't she?'

'I wonder why she isn't married.' That was Marie, of course; but Olga, pointing to the opposite page, said, 'Here she is with her sisters.'

The sepia print, obviously reproduced from a painting, was captioned 'Christmas at Castle Berg'. It showed six girls, scarcely a year apart in age, wearing tailormade costumes and flat, round caps, standing round a little donkey cart laden with Christmas trees and gifts for the poor.

'Six of them!'

'*Les six vierges,*' said Anastasia with a giggle.

'And they haven't got an Alexis, bringing up the rear.'

'That's why Marie Adelaide's the ruler, isn't it?'

'So papa explained.'

'I didn't know girls *could* be rulers.'

'What about our great-grandmamma, Queen Victoria?' asked Tatiana.

'Oh well, that's history,' said Anastasia, and yawned. The younger girls' interest in the Grand Duchess of Luxemburg was yielding to fatigue, and they were ready to follow Tatiana through the far door of the library and up the private staircase to their rooms. But Olga sat on at the round table with the pictured face of that other girl before her, the girl who, with her little army of market-gardeners and postal clerks, had suddenly become the symbol of resistance to German aggression. And for the first time in her eighteen years Olga Nicolaievna wondered what it would be like to be a ruler — and a girl.

The thought of Marie Adelaide was still uppermost in her mind when they all met for a hasty breakfast before the age-old ceremonial of a Romanov Czar at war laid its iron hold upon them, and she gasped with pity when her father told her that the whole of Luxemburg, capital, villages and countryside, was now in the hands of the Germans.

'Oh, the poor girl! She couldn't hold out against them?'

'It would have meant a wholesale massacre.' The Czar rose from the table with a word to his wife, and left the room abruptly. Alexandra complained,

'How can you talk about Luxemburg, Olga, without even asking about poor granny?'

'Is there news of granny? Has she reached the border safely?'

'Your grandmother is still in Germany,' said the Czarina, with an awful calm. 'We've just heard through the Danish Embassy that she was arrested in Berlin by order of the Kaiser.'

'Granny's in prison? I don't believe it!'

'She's under arrest at the station,' said Tatiana. 'She's with Aunt Xenia, in their special train.'

'I don't blame Olga for refusing to believe it,' said her mother. 'To me it's absolutely incredible. Imagine a monarch arresting an empress! Willy must have gone out of his mind.'

'Granny under arrest!' repeated Olga. 'But what does father mean to do? How can we get her home again?'

'Naturally the Danish relatives are doing all they can.'

'I'm sure they are.' It was no time to speak of the British relatives, although the Empress Dowager had been visiting her sister, the widowed Queen Alexandra, in Britain before she started back to Russia via Berlin. It was quite evident, from the silence of the Czar himself, that the British Ambassador had brought him no satisfactory message in the night hours. Olga took a sip of tea and pushed away her plate.

'Don't let it destroy your appetite,' said Marie. 'I'll back granny against the Kaiser any day.'

'I'll back granny against the whole German army,' said Anastasia, and even the Czarina smiled. She reminded the girls that they must leave for St. Petersburg in just over an hour, to attend the ceremony of the Czar's oath to the Guards, and must try to cheer up Alexis, once again to remain behind in bed, before they left.

The girls were already in their little brother's room when

their father joined them. Nicholas had been working with his secretaries, going over what must be done that morning in the Winter Palace, and studying the first plans for the more complicated rituals and ceremonials which awaited him in Moscow. He had been persuaded, much against his wife's will, to receive the members of the Duma, that debating society — for it was very little else — with which he was so frequently in conflict; and this was an innovation which had to be planned with no guidance from protocol. From his study he had been called to his wife's dressing-room, to discuss what jewels Alexandra should wear for her first appearance before the mass public for over a year. Against the opinion of the Mistress of the Robes, who argued for a rope of pearls at least, he upheld the Czarina's wish to wear no ornaments of any kind on a progress which would take them by water to St. Petersburg, and then on foot through what might well be hostile crowds.

'Her Majesty will wear jewels in Moscow, but not today,' he told her attendants, as he dismissed them from the room. Then he took the trembling woman in his arms and kissed her passionately, whispering that she must be calm, and help him through his ordeal at the palace, that he relied upon her absolutely, in all things ... and knew, as he felt her immediate physical response, that he had one hold over her which never could be broken while they lived. He had withheld his caresses since the affair of the telegram from Rasputin, not by calculation but from sheer fatigue; Nicholas realised now, as he heard her broken murmurs of forgiveness, that she had gone in fear of his displeasure for days past. He forced her mouth open with his lips, and moulded his body close to hers, so that when he released her she looked at him with the adoration of a bride and whispered, 'Such kisses — and in the daylight too! Sweet Childie, how happy you make me!'

So she was happy, for an hour at least, and as the Czar paused outside his son's bedroom door he knew that Alexandra was not the only one; the sound of happy laughter was coming from inside. His sweet silly girls were certainly amusing their brother, for Alexis's laugh rang louder than the rest.

They must have been acting some sort of charade for him, as the Little Pair, especially, loved to do, for they were all standing against one wall, while Alexis, giggling, was propped up on his pillows. Monsieur Gilliard, his Swiss tutor, was smiling by the bedside, with what looked like a picture book in his hand. He rose and bowed when the Czar came in.

'Well, young man,' said the Czar fondly, 'what are you up to, this fine morning — teasing your sisters?'

'They look so funny, all dressed up with their hats and gloves on,' said the little Czarevich. 'But they do look very nice and tidy, and I'm proud of them!'

'Thank you, Sir,' said Anastasia, dropping a curtsey.

'Only why can't I go to the Winter Palace too?'

'Because you want to go to Moscow, don't you? The doctors say if you have a few more days' rest in bed, you'll be quite able for the journey.'

'It's always a few more days,' said the child.

The Czar glanced at the young tutor. 'How was the walking exercise this morning?'

'Very promising, Sir. Alexis was able to walk right round the room between Nagorny and myself.'

'So you see, Alexis! You'll be running about and playing again in no time,' said his father. 'And while we all go off to work, you're having a marvellous holiday from lessons —'

'I was doing my lessons when all these girls came bursting in.'

Monsieur Gilliard held up the book with the bright cover. 'We were reading *Heidi*, in the French translation,' he explained. 'Alexis is making good progress in his French.'

'*Heidi*'s a girl's book,' said Marie.

'I don't care, I like to read about Peter scrambling on the mountain with the goats,' said the boy who was never allowed to scramble unless someone held his hand. 'Papa, can I have a pet goat when I'm quite well again?'

'It seems to me you've got a sizeable menagerie already.' The Czar surveyed the big grey cat, sleeping through all interruptions at the foot of his boy's bed. There were three dogs in the room, one asleep — Ortipo, Tatiana's bulldog, which snored — Eira, the Czarina's snappish little Scotch terrier, and Joy, the King Charles spaniel which Alexis loved best of all. 'What would you do with a goat, boy?'

'Milk it, like Heidi and Peter did,' said Alexis, and the laughter began again, so that the Czar told his daughters rather sharply that enough was enough, and they were supposed to leave for Petersburg in five minutes.

'Why do they get to go in the motor today, and not in the yacht with mamma and you?' the boy said, as his sisters came up to kiss him goodbye.

'Because we want them to be at the palace when we arrive,' said the Czar. But when the girls had gone, and Monsieur Gilliard had tactfully left the room, he took his son's hand, with the long fingers so like Alexandra's, tenderly in his own, and said,

'I wish you were a bigger boy, Alexis.'

'And a stronger boy — don't you?'

'You're getting stronger every day. I mean, if you were older, if you were sixteen and had taken the oath of allegiance to me, you could have joined me in the oath I must take to the Guards today.'

'Monsieur Gilliard told me what you were going to say.'

'Will you think about it, Baby, while I'm gone? And pray for me?'

'I'll pray for you and Russia,' said the child.

'Alexis has a lot more nerve than we have,' said Marie, as the motor rolled down the avenues of Peterhof. 'He asked point-blank what we've been wondering about — why we're going to town ahead of papa and mamma.'

'You heard what father said,' Olga reminded her. 'It's because they want us at the palace before they get there.'

'Yes, I know, but why? We always follow them, walking two by two, just like the pictures of those English girls in the school stories Aunt Victoria sends us.'

'Pooh!' said Anastasia with her sharp look, 'I've worked it out already. If they appear alone, without any of us tagging along behind, it won't be so noticeable that Alexis isn't there at all. You know that's what worries them really; we don't count.'

'We're on our way to a religious service, Imp,' said Tatiana. 'It's hardly the time to be sarcastic, is it? Especially when we think about poor granny.'

The Little Pair subsided, as they always did when 'The Governess' took that tone, and the two older girls exchanged glances. They knew, if the younger ones did not, that there was another possible reason for the change in their routine. Four girls in white dresses, walking for however short a distance through a city seething with discontent, were simply four more targets for a bomb or a bullet, and while Olga and Tatiana had learned to master fear for themselves since Stolypin was murdered before their eyes in the theatre at Kiev, they were both sick with anxiety for their father and mother. This visit to the Winter Palace for the ceremony announcing the beginning of a war would be almost the first the sovereigns had dared to pay to their former home for nearly ten years.

The little procession of three motor cars took longer than was necessary to reach its destination, for the drivers kept away from the main arteries of the capital and chose side streets along a route decided on at the last possible moment. The girls tried to recognise the few familiar landmarks through the smoked glass windows: there were none until they came to Suvarov Square, with the British Embassy on one corner and the Marble Palace on the other, and the spire of Peter and Paul rising into the summer blue on the far side of the Neva. From there it was a short drive along the quays, past the magnificent homes of their kindred, with nearly every one of whom the Czarina had systematically quarrelled, to the river entrance of that great palace, with its thousand rooms, its hundred staircases, which Rastrelli had built for a Russian empress and autocrat.

The aged Mistress of the Robes and the Governor of all the Imperial Palaces, General Voieikov, got out of the first car and stood ready to greet the Grand Duchesses: the armed police guard got out of the third car and closed in behind the girls, who were scarcely given time to notice, as they ascended the short flight of steps, that a dense crowd had already gathered on the Palace Quay.

'How many people have been invited to the ceremony?' Olga asked the Governor as he escorted her through the hall leading to the Ambassadors' Staircase. It was empty except for a guard of the Cossacks of the Escort, standing between the pillars and at regular intervals up the grand staircase itself, their red caftans vivid beneath the white stucco angels which started from the walls.

'Five thousand, Your Imperial Highness, and most of them — using another entrance of course — have already taken their places in St. George's Hall. Outside, I'm told there are a hundred times that number in the Palace Square.'

'How strange that everything should be so silent here.'

'The walls are very thick, *Altesse*.'

Down corridors between those thick walls, which for two hundred years had held so many secrets of blood and lust, the four sisters were conducted to a suite of rooms which had been the private apartments of their great-grandfather, the Czar-Liberator Alexander II. Their maids were waiting in the dismal Blue Bedroom where his neglected wife, the Empress Marie, had dragged out her last days, to offer basins of scented warm water, damask towels, eau de cologne, hairpins and curling tongs, as toilet necessaries after the short motor drive from Peterhof.

'She didn't have much of a view, did she, great-grand-mamma Marie?' said Anastasia, going to the window. It over-looked a cheerless stone courtyard and another wing of the vast palace, in which the anonymous windows were shrouded with thick net. There was nothing to be seen but a patch of blue sky overhead, such as a prisoner might have pined to see.

'The Empress Marie Feodorovna was a sad invalid,' said Madame Narishkina, the Mistress of the Robes. 'But also a model of deportment. An example to *you*, Anastasia. Come into the Gold Parlour, young ladies, if you please.'

In the immense parlour a table had been spread with more unnecessary luxuries in the shape of candied fruits and violets, and rich little cakes such as the girls were never allowed to have at home. Marie stripped off her gloves with enthusiasm.

'Mamma and papa were married here, weren't they?' she said when she had enjoyed two glacé apricots and a macaroon. 'No, not here in the Gold Parlour, silly! In the chapel, of course.'

'Yes, and they *saw* each other for the first time in the chapel, when Aunt Ella was married to poor Uncle Sergei.'

'I remember Aunt Ella telling us that.'

'Mamma was only twelve.'

'But where *is* the chapel, Olga? Do you know?'

'I was taken there once or twice when I was a little girl, but I couldn't possibly find my way back there alone.'

'Mamma was dressed for her wedding in the Malachite Hall,' said Marie, reverting to her favourite subject. 'Shall we see that today?'

'Yes, we shall,' said Tatiana. 'You'll see the Empress Anna's mirror where mamma watched her reflection when they put the bridal diadem on her head. As you will too, Bow-Wow, when your turn comes.'

'Oh-h!' said Marie blissfully. 'But don't you have to wear false hair?'

Olga bit back a laugh. Somehow it was impossible to picture Fat Little Bow-Wow decked out in the traditional cloth of silver and red velvet mantle of a Romanov bride, with the artificial ringlets framing her round, honest face.

'Well, I must say, our ancestors had more room in their palace than we have in ours,' said Anastasia. 'No wonder great-grandpapa Alexander was able to keep his mistress and three brats in a set of rooms right over his poor wife's head!'

'Anastasia!' 'Anastasia Nicolaievna!' Both Tatiana and Madame Narishkina fell upon the culprit, and How dare you use such language, and Who told you such an abominable story, mingled with Marie's giggles, and Anastasia's spirited defence.

'Well, he married her, didn't he, just as soon as his wife died? She was his morgantic, no morganatic, wife, just the same as the Archduke's, that we were all so sorry for when he was killed at Sarajevo, wasn't she? And she was lovely, Princess Catherine Dolgoruki — '

Olga moved away, out of earshot of the inevitable lecture on behaviour befitting an Imperial Highness which Madame Narishkina was preparing to deliver, and went into the next room, which, although small, was known as the White Ballroom. It was almost bare of furniture, except for the gilt chairs set round the walls, and the iridescent sparkle which the sunshine struck from the prisms of the chandeliers was reflected in the inlaid parquet of the floor. Olga would have said the room was empty, although in fact there were footmen as well as Cossacks on duty, motionless and unobtrusive. She was quite unaware that their eyes followed her as she walked gracefully down the room and looked across the Neva to the bridge.

Candied apricots and court gossip — they seemed to sum up the future that had been waiting for herself, when she emerged from the schoolroom less than six months before. And now Russia was at war, bound no man knew where, and least of all the man, who, his daughter's newly critical heart told her, had drifted or been urged downstream into the worst danger of all. The Grand Duchess Olga wished passionately that the Czar's first act, after Germany declared war, had not been to seal himself to the fight in this ancient palace where he and his were surrounded by so many emblems of death. She was not a fanciful or a superstitious girl, having inherited the strong nerves and commonsense of the indomitable little lady who even at that moment was sitting in her train at a Berlin railway station, ignoring the insults and obscenities hurled by a mob of German louts from behind a police barrier only two yards away. But the Winter Palace had never been a fortunate home for the Romanovs. Here the terrorist Khalturin had tried to blow up the state dining-rooms, with Alexander II inside, and had succeeded only in killing innocent soldiers and servants instead. Here Alexander II, after escaping so many attempts on his life, had been brought back to die after the bombs were thrown on the spot where the Church of the Spilled Blood now stood, and had died in the arms of his morganatic wife, the Princess Catherine Dolgoruki. And there were other, and worse, associations than the tale of royal assassinations. When Olga told her father that she could 'remember 1905', she had spoken only of the war with Japan. But she could also remember, as a terrified child, hearing what happened outside the Winter Palace on the Bloody Sunday of that unhappy year, when a procession of workers, crossing the Palace Square to present a petition to the Czar, had been fired on by the troops and ridden down by the Cossacks, so that a peaceful demonstration had turned into a near-massacre. Olga could remember the courtiers saying that the Czar was not to blame, he was at his palace in the country: it was his uncle, the Grand Duke Vladimir, who had given the fatal order to fire on the crowd. But the Czar, as Autocrat, was ultimately responsible, and although Bloody Sunday had led to the October Manifesto which ended the autocracy and led to the establishment of the Duma, more than a year elapsed before Nicholas II dared to set foot in his loyal capital of Petersburg. Now here, nine years later, was another Sunday, bloodier in its implications than any which had gone before, and what sort of reception would the Czar and his consort have today?

Tatiana came up behind Olga and slipped her arm round her sister's waist.

'The general wants us to take our places in St. George's Hall,' she said.

'I want to see papa and mamma disembark.'

'I do too.'

'They can't be much longer, can they? ... What's that noise?'

It might well have been the roar of an angry crowd. Tatiana turned imperatively to one of the waiting footmen.

'Open the window, please!'

The man wrestled with the single pane set in the double window, which could admit fresh air to the White Ballroom on a winter day. Now the warm breeze of summer rose off the Neva, lined on its further shore by spectators, and there was no mistaking the sound which greeted the *Alexandria*, just visible below the Palace Quay.

'They're cheering! Oh, thank God!'

Olga clutched her sister's hand. In the eager clasp they both betrayed the depth and secrecy of their anxiety.

Between the escorting police boats, up the river teeming with craft, the *Alexandria* reached the landing stage, and the Czar and Czarina stepped ashore. Alexandra had made a supreme effort to be gracious and to conceal her own tortured anxiety. She was smiling as she laid her hand lightly on her husband's arm, as it had lain at their wedding and their coronation, and allowed him to lead her towards the palace he had once intended to be their married home. She was dressed in white, with a long white ostrich boa on her shoulders, and wore a tulle hat which showed her red-gold hair.

'Doesn't she look wonderful today?' said Tatiana.

'Yes, she does.'

'Come on, you two!' called Marie from the ballroom door. 'Or else the general will have a fit!'

General Voieikov, trying to conceal his impatience, led the girls quickly through the maze of corridors and reception rooms to St. George's Hall. From the great room of state, where five thousand men in uniform and women in gala dress had assembled, there came a murmur of anticipation which echoed the sound of cheering from the Palace Square. Although the ceremony was to be religious, with an altar set up in the hall to hold the ikon of the Virgin of Kazan, brought from the national sanctuary on the Nevski Prospekt, it was not possible for five thousand members of the Russian nobility to maintain a devotional silence for long. They moved and murmured, chattered, criticised, acknowledged the presence of their friends with waves or bows, while those nearest the closed french windows jockeyed for position to see the vast crowd in the enormous square.

The young Grand Duchesses (walking, to Olga's irritation, two by two like the English schoolgirls of Marie's joke) were led to their places at the left of the altar. There they were hemmed in by the Family, led by the stately Grand Duchess Marie Pavlovna, known to the girls as Aunt Miechen, who considered herself to be, after the two empresses, the third lady in the land. She gave them an all-embracing, condescending smile; and Olga, smiling back, remembered with secret amusement Simon Hendrikov's definition of a Grand Duchess as 'a tall stout lady, very proud, and hung about with jewels'. Aunt Miechen to the life! She remembered that Aunt Miechen's husband, now dead, was that Grand Duke Vladimir who had given orders to open fire on Bloody Sunday.

There was someone else in the serried ranks of the Family whose smile was instant and affectionate. The Grand Duke Dmitri, tall and fair and engaging, wearing the uniform of the Chevalier Guards, gave Olga the encouraging nod of an elder brother, which was how when they were children — he being only four years her senior — she had been taught to regard him. There had been a later time, at that first dance at Livadia and for a while thereafter, when Dmitri's kisses, his gaiety, and his attentive companionship had led the adolescent girl into a happy fantasy of becoming, some day, Dmitri's wife. The realisation that the dashing young cavalry officer, the toast of the Petersburg nightclubs and the theatre dressing-rooms, would never feel more than a cousinly affection for a girl whose upbringing was more like that of an English parsonage than a Russian court, had brought Olga some pain and even some secret tears. She had conquered her feeling for him in silence: it was still strong enough, as the Orthodox clergy's processional began, with chants and swinging censers, for Olga's first prayer to be for Dmitri's safety.

The Czar and his consort entered St. George's Hall, where now at last five thousand Russians bowed and crossed themselves in devout unity. Alexandra's public smile had disappeared, but she was more composed than many of the witnesses had expected, and during the long Te Deum she was ready with a grave but encouraging look whenever her husband seemed to ask for her support. The chants, the ritual took their prolonged way, and St. George's Hall grew thick with incense. Then the court chaplain read the manifesto by which the Russian Czar informed his people that the country was at war. Nicholas stepped towards the ikon of the Virgin of Kazan. A copy of the Gospel was held out to him, and he solemnly laid his right hand upon it.

'Officers of my Guard, here present, I greet in you my whole army and give it my blessing. I solemnly swear that I will never make peace so long as one of the enemy is on the soil of the motherland.'

It was the oath which his ancestor, Alexander I, had sworn when the enemy was Napoleon Bonaparte — an oath redeemed by Russia's victory. To all his hearers, superstitious and dependent on signs and tokens and influences both mystical and occult, the words seemed like a happy omen. Nicholas himself seemed to have gained in stature by repeating them. With his curiously impassive dignity he walked down the hall, the french windows being opened at his approach, and passed alone out to the balcony.

He stood there, dwarfed by the gigantic pillar in the square raised to the memory of that same victorious ancestor, between the People outside and the Court within, while the Court applauded, and the People yelled themselves hoarse. They cheered their beloved Little Father as he had never been cheered in his life before. They roared their execration of Germany and their confidence in the might of the Russian army. And then, in the square where the workers had fallen under the bullets of 1905, and while the bells of Peter and Paul chimed, 'Lord, have mercy on us', they sang the national anthem.

God save the Czar! For that day, at least, Bloody Sunday was forgotten.

CHAPTER SIX

Among the assembly of Russians invited to listen to the oath taken by Nicholas II, there was only one foreigner. He was the French Ambassador, Monsieur Maurice Paléologue, representing Russia's great ally. Within two days Russia had other allies, one a little nation fighting for its life, which was Belgium; the other, the guarantor of that little nation's independence, which was Great Britain.

The game of ultimatums was nearly over. During all that Sunday when St. Petersburg clamoured its enthusiasm for the war, the King of the Belgians and his ministers discussed the reply they should send to the German government, which demanded free passage for its troops across the little country. Next day, the day that Germany declared war on France, King Albert, his cabinet and his parliament resolved to resist the German invasion. Belgium had six army divisions and Belgium would fight.

That Monday was a Bank Holiday in England, traditionally a day for going to the seaside. Some Englishmen went in other directions, as Reservists and Territorials were called up, and all the members, without exception, of the House of Commons assembled in the historic chamber to hear the Foreign Secretary declare that it would be a sacrifice of Britain's good name and reputation before the world to run away from the obligations of the Belgian Treaty. The tumultuous applause of the vast majority of the House indicated its complete approval.

At eight next morning, August 4, the Germans invaded Belgium, and later in the day the British ultimatum was received in Berlin. It charged Germany to uphold the treaty of Belgian neutrality, signed in the previous century by Prussia among other powers. The German Chancellor dismissed the treaty as 'a scrap of paper', and no answer was sent to the British ultimatum. With a much briefer time-limit than the ultimatum sent by Austria-Hungary to Serbia, the British challenge expired at midnight. Britain declared war on Germany, the last knot in the rope of alliances and ententes had been tied, and the midnight bells rang out across a continent under arms.

At the American Embassy and consulate in St. Petersburg, by comparison with these excitements, all was stagnation. President Wilson had given a press conference on the day Germany declared war on France, but on August 6 his wife died, and for the period of her funeral there was no further statement from the White House. Joe Calvert, professionally concerned only with the fortunes of an American sewing-machine company's Russian outlets, was delighted to hear Richard Allen's voice on the telephone one mid-August morning.

'Joe? You free for lunch today, by any chance?'

'You bet I am!'

'Care to come along to my place, about one o'clock?'

'It's a date.'

Their few brief conversations had always been in this laconic style, due as much to the erratic Petersburg telephone system as to their respect for official business, as the friendship developed between the two young men. Thus they had arranged meetings at the Mourina golf course, laid out by the British colony about twenty miles from the capital, and evening poker sessions at Richard Allen's flat. This was the first time Joe had visited the flat by day, and as he walked along the Italianskaia he thought how splendid the street was, with its harmonising façades of yellow ochre, compared with the shabbiness of his new friend's home.

Captain Allen's flat was decidedly a bachelor establishment, kept barely tidy by an elderly daily maid. The living-room, which had two windows on the Italianskaia, gave absolutely no indication of its owner's tastes and personality, except for a few books by William Le Queux and E. Phillips Oppenheim, and a china tobacco jar with a regimental crest which stood next to a rack of well-seasoned pipes on the writing desk between the two windows. The table used for the card games was now covered with a coarse linen cloth and set for luncheon with a modest selection of *zakuski*, the Russian hors d'oeuvres, the inevitable vodka decanter, and a large glass jug into which, when Joe arrived, his host was pouring bottles of chilled Danish beer.

'That looks good, on a hot day like this,' said Joe as they shook hands.

'I remembered you weren't very keen on vodka. Pull up a chair, Joe, and fill your plate. There's nothing coming but boiled sturgeon and potatoes, the only dish Varvara knows how to cook.'

'This is very good.' Joe helped himself to caviar, and took a gulp of the cold beer. 'Say, Dick, I wanted to call you days ago, but I figured you'd have too much to do to spare any time for poker. Fact is, I wanted to tell you how right you were, that night we met back at my hotel, when you talked about America having to keep the ring in Europe, one of these days —'

'Was that what I said?'

'You sure did. And right off, President Wilson told the press that the United States stands ready to help the rest of the world as a mediator in this great international crisis — wasn't that what you meant?'

'Something like that.'

'Well, anyway, you were pretty smart. You saw the war coming, when I just couldn't believe it, and now you people are in it yourselves, right up to the neck.'

'In your own words, Joe, we sure are.'

'Anyway, you're the heroes of the hour in Petersburg.'

'We've Admiral Beatty and his jolly tars to thank for that. More beer?'

'Please.' The cool gold Tuborg foamed in the fluted glass. 'Say, are you going to Moscow for the imperial visit?'

'Me? Good Lord, no! That particular junket's only for top-drawer diplomats, not for the likes of me. And what a waste of time the whole dead ceremonial is — the Czar going off to Moscow to ask God's blessing on the war, and drag his family round every shrine and chapel in the Kremlin, when he should be here in Petersburg, taking advantage of the goodwill of the Duma.'

'The Duma certainly seems to be solid for him right now. But so does everybody.'

'Yes, Nicholas is riding high, but how long will it last? I wouldn't bet on his popularity after the first defeat. Just one defeat like Liège —'

The slipshod maid brought in the fish platter and a pot of coffee, which she deposited with a grunt by her employer's hand, and the conversation turned to the German capture of the great fortress of Liège, which the Belgians had believed to be impregnable. And as they talked, Dick Allen studied his guest's face, so open, even ingenuous; the brown eyes so candid: was it really possible, when it got down to brass tacks, to convey to this boy a disingenuous suggestion, on which much might yet depend? He stirred his coffee thoughtfully.

'Joe, have you found a flat yet?'

'I only wish I had! I've looked at more dumps from the office list, and they're either miles out, or filthy dirty, or I'm expected to muck in with the family ... I don't know what to do. I can't go on living at the Europa much longer, it's in a higher bracket than my allowance scale. The other guys are beginning to think I'm a millionaire —'

'How would you like to take over this dump of mine?'

'*This* flat? But what about you?'

'I'm going away from Petersburg for a bit.'

'Back to England?'

'Why to England?'

'I thought you might be going back to rejoin your regiment.'

'I haven't been any use to the regiment since I stopped a Boer bullet at Spion Kop. You haven't noticed? I still limp a bit when I'm tired.'

'I did notice, on the golf course; I thought you'd a stone in your shoe. The Boer War, eh? You must have been just a kid.'

'Twenty-one. But that's water under the bridge, old boy; I'm leaving Petersburg because I've been posted. I'm going to the Legation at Stockholm.'

Joe nodded. It seemed to him like a demotion, this transfer from one of the nerve centres of the spreading war to a remote and neutral country like Sweden. He thought it tactful to say nothing.

'I don't want to give up the flat,' Dick Allen was saying in his placid way. 'It isn't up to much, I know, but I've got all my stuff here — I hope you don't mind that — and I'd like to be able to come back some day. And it *is* very central and convenient.'

'What would you want for rent?'

'Well, first you ought to look at it, we'll do that in a minute.

You've seen the bathroom, the kitchen's not much better, but Varvara knows her way about in it, and I think she'd like to keep the job. There's a fair-sized bedroom and a little one, both looking out on the courtyard, and that's all. I certainly wouldn't want a big rent from a careful tenant.'

He named a weekly sum which made Joe raise his eyebrows. 'That's less than I'm paying for my cubbyhole at the Europa.'

'Wait until you see the bedrooms. The little one's just a cubbyhole too.'

The old-fashioned flat was speedily inspected. There was a single wardrobe in each of the bedrooms and built-in cupboards for linen and china in the hall.

'And what's that door?'

'That? It's the door on to the service stairs. They're supposed to be used for deliveries, but the tenants are always complaining that the delivery men use the front entrance.'

'And the stairs lead up from the courtyard?'

'That's right.' They went back to the living-room, and Dick Allen started to fill a briar from the tobacco jar. Joe waited until the match was struck.

'Look here, Dick,' he said, 'I'd like to rent your flat, it's very much the sort of place I'd hoped to find. But the rental you're asking just isn't realistic. Where's the catch in the deal?'

'There isn't any catch,' said Dick. 'There is just one slight string attached.'

'Let's hear about it.'

'I might have to come back from Stockholm, from time to time. And then, if it wouldn't cramp your style in any way, I'd like to be able to use the smaller bedroom. I'd like to keep one key, and come and go without bothering you or Varvara —'

'Or any of the neighbours?'

'Well, yes.'

'Because you'd be using the service stairway.'

'Exactly.'

Joe squared his shoulders. 'Now get this,' he said, 'I wasn't born yesterday. I may be just a freshman around here, but I do know that a foreigner renting a Petersburg apartment has his name on the police files, and may be liable to police surveillance. What you're asking me to do is to front for you, whatever it is you're up to; and when all is said and done I'm an officer of the American Foreign Service, a low man on the totem pole of a neutral power. I can't, and I won't, cover for anything I don't understand. I think you'll have to tell me more about your job in Stockholm.'

'Assistant military attaché, the same as here.'

'I don't think,' said Joe Calvert, and his Maryland drawl was suddenly very pronounced, 'that you British really need such a heavy military representation in a neutral country like Sweden. One military attaché would seem to be enough.'

Dick shrugged. 'Then let me put it this way. Very few men among our allies — very few, that is, in Russia, and certainly none in gallant little Serbia and gallant little Belgium, have twigged that this is going to be a war of propaganda as well as a war of manpower, transport and weapons. But we know how good German Intelligence is, and how long their brightest boys have been working on the idea of starting revolution — yes, actual revolution, the overthrowing of the state — behind the frontiers of their enemies. We're vulnerable in Ireland, where the Germans counted on civil war, in British India and in Egypt. But Russia is the most vulnerable of the lot, especially in Poland, Finland, and perhaps the Caucasus and the Ukraine. Joe!' he said emphatically, 'what I'm going to tell you now might be considered classified, but I have to take the risk: after all, it's something the American Foreign Service has probably worked out for itself: five of the German Embassies in Europe are key points in the propaganda network. Stockholm is one of them. As you know, Baron von Lucius is the ambassador to Sweden, and he has a staff of the Kaiser's best men around him. We've decided to increase our representation in Stockholm, just to keep pace with them, and that's the reason for my transfer. I may have to act as a courier between there and here from time to time, or the King's Messengers may act as liaison officers instead: it's as simple as all that.'

'Very simple indeed,' said Joe, 'unless you use the word "espionage" instead of "propaganda".' He laughed. 'All right, Dick, you don't need to tell me any more. When do you expect to leave St. Petersburg?'

'Next week — the twenty-second.'

'Then it's a deal. I'll take over the flat on the twenty-third, for one quarter only, and we'll see how things work out.'

'Good enough!'

'The way people are talking, the war mayn't even last three months. The Russians say they'll be in Berlin in six weeks' time.'

'And the Germans are planning to celebrate Christmas in Paris. God! Lord Kitchener's the only realist among the lot. As soon as he took over at the War Office, he said he would begin his plans on the assumption that the war would last three years.'

'Three *years*!'

'Or maybe four.'

Simon Hendrikov was one of the few young Russian officers who was not convinced of a lightning victory. He was indeed profoundly depressed when he returned to his parents' home in the Fourth Line on the night before his entrainment for the front, although with true Russian fatalism he accepted the destiny which had placed him in the one battalion of the Marine Guards called up for active service. The *Standart* had been laid up for the duration of the war, and the Grand Duchess Olga was with her family in Moscow.

As he turned in at the gate he saw another officer emerging from the building, and recognised the man who had passed him on the stairs a few weeks earlier. As Simon saluted briskly the other man stopped, and after saying 'Good evening!' in the same pleasant way he added, 'Haven't we met before?'

'We've seen each other, sir, right outside my own front door.'

'Oh, you live here, do you? Then you're Professor Hendrikov's son; my cousin Madame Martova told me about you. My name's Yakovlev, Commander in the *Askelod*.'

'A cruiser, isn't she? Wasn't *Askelod* one of the guard ships when His Majesty opened the new dry dock last month?'

'Yes, and I remember now, you were one of the Garde Equipage on duty.'

Commander Yakovlev was very frank and agreeable, much more so than Dr. Martov or his wife, as far as Simon knew the Martov neighbours. It was unusual for a naval officer of higher rank to be so pleasant to an unknown junior, and Simon wished the commander, 'Good luck, sir!' with sincerity. But as he went upstairs he was still haunted by the man's resemblance to somebody, and somebody in the Service at that. Out of uniform the resemblance would have been less striking. Then he dismissed the matter as he entered the flat, and Dolly came running to meet him, jumping up to kiss him and clasping her hands behind his neck.

'Here, you're choking me!' Simon protested. 'Look at you, all dressed up! Are you going to a party?'

'Mother and I are going to dinner with Plain Joe Calvert!'

'With *who*?'

'You know, the nice American who's studying with mother. You met him the first night he came here, before the cruise.'

'Tall, dark, speaks good French? I remember him.'

'He's asked us to dinner at the Europa, along with a friend of his from the British Embassy, who's going off to Stockholm.'

'Simon! my dear boy, what a nice surprise!' said his mother, who had hurried from her bedroom at the sound of his voice. 'What a shame we'd planned to go out! Of course we could cancel it, couldn't we, Dolly?'

'Cancel it?'

'We could telephone to Mr. Calvert and explain about Simon's visit — '

'But mother, he's got seats for the theatre! And we can't telephone to Mara, to tell her not to meet us outside the Gostinnoi Dvor!'

In the face of Dolly's open disappointment, Simon took a quick decision. There was no need to tell his family that he was on entrainment leave; that could wait until the early breakfast time, and then, as soon as the fuss started, he would be gone. 'You mustn't give up a theatre evening on account of me,' he said. 'I've got an all-night pass. Go ahead and enjoy yourselves, and I'll have something to eat with father. Where is he, by the way?'

'At the Public Library. Oh, Simon, this does seem so unfair to you! Should we call Cousin Timofey or Cousin Boris, and ask them to come round and entertain you? Papa is so depressed these days. Mr. Calvert invited him too, of course, but he says it's the wrong time to be going to parties — what do you think?'

'I think Petersburg's gone party mad, and father doesn't know there's a war on,' said Simon lightly. 'It'll be nice to spend an evening with him, just the two of us, and we'll have the samovar boiling when you come back. And mother, shouldn't you finish dressing if you're going out to dinner?

Dolly looks all ready for the road, so don't you want me to get you a droshki?'

'Lena went out to fetch one.' When the flurry of departure was over Simon went into his own narrow bedroom to change out of uniform. As he put on an old pair of trousers and a soft peasant blouse of the sort he wore at the dacha he wondered how many of his brother officers, on their last all-night leave in St. Petersburg, would be spending it exclusively with their families. He had been invited to join more than one group, bound either for the Islands and the gipsy singers, or for Cubat's restaurant and the ladies of the town, and when he thought of an evening alone with his father, who always talked above his head, Simon half regretted his refusal. But then no girl would do but the one girl, in rank so far above him, unattainable, who was now taking part in that foolish charade in Moscow; and he sat down on the edge of his bed with the embroidered shirt in his hands, to think of their last meeting. All the officers and ratings who had served in the *Standart*, from the Black Sea duty earlier in the summer until the cruise to Finland, had paraded at Peterhof quay to receive the farewells and good wishes of the imperial family before dispersing to their different barracks. Olga Nicolaievna had come down the lines of men in blue immediately behind her father and mother. He heard her greeting the senior officers much as her parents did: 'We'll be thinking of you' — 'Good luck!' — 'May we meet again soon.' But when she came to him, Simon saw the golden head droop and the blue eyes mist over, and when she held out her little hand for his kiss he heard Olga murmur, 'God bless you, Simon Karlovich!' It was all he needed, of pleasure, feasting and love, before leaving for the front.

He had been so casual, and so prompt in sending his mother and Dolly off to Joe's dinner party that neither one suspected that this leave was the last, and Dolly chatted happily as they drove down the Nevski Prospekt to the big bazaar opposite the Europa Hotel. Mara Trenova was waiting there, for Madame Hendrikova had insisted that the two girls must enter the hotel together, and under her chaperonage. Joe and Dick Allan were waiting for them in the lobby. Joe was unusually nervous; he had invited Mara Trenova at Dick's own request, and was uncertain how that unpredictable young lady would choose to behave in company.

'Don't you know some nice English girl you'd like to have meet the Hendrikovs?' he pleaded when the farewell party was being planned.

'I'd like to meet Ivan Trenov's daughter, and see if she runs true to form. Her father was a bit of a firebrand, I've been told. Is she?'

'I think she's a bit of a pill,' said Joe, and then, repenting, 'No, she isn't really. She's an attractive girl, and clever too, I think. But if one of us says something that doesn't please her, she's quite capable of getting up and walking out of the restaurant and going home.'

'That wouldn't worry the other diners, Russians love scenes. Go ahead and invite her, Joe!'

So now he was ushering Madame Hendrikova into the Europa's vast restaurant, one stair up and with its ceiling two storeys high, and the girls were walking behind their chaperone as demurely as if they were once again the Dolly and Molly of the Xenia School. All the ladies wore high-necked dresses, but no hats, and for the first time since he had met Dolly, Joe saw that her curls were brushed up and pinned on the top of her head. Mara's dress was plain, but her manner was relaxed, and she obviously intended to be a charming guest. As the food and wine were brought Joe realised that another person determined to be charming was that usually lackadaisical individual, Captain Richard Allen. It was strange how a well-cut dark suit, starched linen, and a touch of pomade on his hair and moustache seemed to have transformed him into a man about town. Dick's French was not as good as his Russian, but fluent enough to allow him to embark on a series of jokes and anecdotes which started off the evening well.

Mara and Madame Hendrikova listened with amusement, but Dolly looked round the room very often, and twice whispered to Joe that it was wonderful. The place indeed was crowded with handsome men and women who were apparently determined to forget the war, and the orchestra was playing selections from *The Merry Widow*. There was champagne on every table, and Joe had ordered it as a matter of course. Dolly's hazel eyes sparkled as she took her first sip, and wished Captain Allen a safe journey to Sweden.

The conversation turned to the stage, and the French play they were to see at the Alexandrovski theatre. On this Mara was opinionated, and spoke rather too long about Meyerhold's theory of audience participation, but the only slight ruffle on the surface harmony came later, and was innocently caused by Joe himself. In one of the pauses between the courses he asked Mara how her secretarial training was progressing.

'Pretty well, I think. The instructors say I have fair speeds already, in both shorthand and typewriting.'

'Great, and you must be pleased to know you've got a job waiting for you.' He meant to add, 'When exactly do you graduate?' but she interrupted him with:

'Who told you I had a job waiting for me?'

'Darya Karlovna said something about it.'

'What a chatterbox you are, Dolly!' It was said with a touch of the cold venom which had repelled Joe when Mara condoned the Sarajevo murders, and Dolly said defensively:

'I only told Mr. Calvert that one of our lecturers had promised to find a position for you. I didn't know it was a secret. I didn't even mention the person's name.'

'Of course it's not a secret,' said Mara, and was able to smile. 'It was Professor Rostov who kindly offered me his help. He was a friend of my father's, in their student days.'

'Which Rostov is that — the historian?' said Richard Allen.

'No; Lev Andreivich Rostov, the distinguished chemist.'

'Is *he* teaching at Xenia now?'

'Oh, certainly not. He came just once, as a guest lecturer, when he was on a short visit to Petersburg. He works in Stockholm now. Perhaps you'll meet him there, Captain Allen.'

'I wouldn't know how to talk to a distinguished chemist.'

Then the cutlets were served, and Joe turned to Madame Hendrikova with a question about the dacha at Koivisto. 'My daughter Betsy and her husband are staying there,' she said. 'We want to wait here until we know what Simon's orders are. Of course we hope he'll remain in Petersburg for as long as possible.' It was the only reference to the war which had been made so far, except for Madame Hendrikova's warm greeting of Dick Allen, when Joe introduced him. 'I'm proud to meet one of our allies, monsieur,' she had said. 'I've always admired Britain; now, more than ever.' But Dick had only bowed and smiled; he had not made any comment on Britain's entry to the war, although every day now the trains which had carried

the cherry-pickers to Kent in July were carrying the Briti[sh]
Expeditionary Force to the ports of embarkation for the Co[n]-
tinent. In the company of three Russian women, two of the[m]
very young, the Englishman and the American had steered th[e]
conversation clear of politics, so that Joe was taken by surprise
when Dick said, over the coffee:

'You must have brought your new student on very quickly,
madame, since he's already taken to attending the sessions of
the Duma.'

'The Duma!' said Madame Hendrikova. 'You never told me
that!'

'Captain Allen exaggerates,' said Joe. 'I attended *one* session
of the Duma last week, and as I understood about two words
out of every hundred, I didn't tell you because I thought you'd
laugh at me.'

'Have all foreign consuls the entrée to the Duma?' asked
Mara.

'I doubt it, Mara Ivanovna. I'm afraid I was a little above
my station, but I did manage to get a pass for the diplomatic
box at the Tauride Palace, when they were debating the war
credits. I couldn't understand much of it, but I could watch
their faces, and find out what the Deputies look like, what they
sound like — the men I read about in our press translations
every day.'

'I think that was very clever of you,' said Dolly. 'But how did
you find out what was happening?'

'From a Frenchman sitting right next to me. He explained
that the Socialists were refusing to vote the military credits,
and that worried me some, because in Germany the Socialists
did vote the war budget, same as all the other parties. But it
seems to be true enough, because it was repeated in our press
digest next day.'

'Did your press digest give our Social Revolutionary party's
reasons?' Mara asked.

'Not in so many words, no. Those digests have got to be kept
short.'

'I can tell you in so many words,' said the girl, and again the
flash of her dark eyes was cold. 'The SRs refrained from voting
the war credits because they refuse to accept responsibility for
any Czarist policies. And the spokesman said, "We invite
democracy to defend its native soil against invasion. *Workers*

119

While the Czar and his retinue paced through the Moscow
ceremonies, which had more than a touch of the old Byzantine
splendour about them, the Grand Duke Nicholas Nicolaievich,
an experienced soldier, assumed the supreme command of the
army and established his GHQ, called the Stavka, on the
Moscow-Warsaw railway at Baronovichi. There was nothing
to fear on the eastern front, for in spite of Olga's forebodings
Japan had declared war on Germany. In the west Italy, allied
by previous treaties with Germany and Austria-Hungary, decided on neutrality and the strategic advantage of sitting on the
fence.

Along with this good news, the imperial family were thankful to know that the Empress Dowager, after her ordeal at the
station in Berlin, had been allowed to journey on to St. Petersburg via the Scandinavian countries with her daughter
Xenia, her grand-daughter Irina, and Irina's husband Prince
Felix Yusupov. They were all safe at the Anichkov Palace,
tired and angry after their adventure, and the Empress Dowager, furious with the Kaiser, could hardly wait for the Russian
victory parade through Berlin. It *must* happen before Christmas, everybody said so; the Allies in the West had great faith
in 'the Russian steamroller', which was the new propaganda
phrase. And with the slow, cumbrous advance of a real steamroller the Russian armies moved forward to East Prussia and
Galicia, groping for the enemy.

As soon as the fighting began, the Czarina threw herself
heart and soul into humanitarian plans. In her early married
life she had tried to improve the hospital services of her new
country, and her working guilds, summer crèches, and ortho-
paedic institutes for children had been heartily ridiculed by
Petersburg society. Now, while her daughters pestered her to
let them learn to drive ambulances, to go to the front as nurses,
or even to practise pistol shooting, she conferred alone with her
sister Elizabeth, the head of a successful nursing sisterhood in
Moscow.

Elizabeth, or Ella, of Hesse was the childless widow of the
Grand Duke Sergei, the Governor of Moscow, who during the
revolutionary troubles of 1905 had been blown to shreds by a

terrorist's bomb. Ever since, the Grand Duchess Elizabeth had worn a most becoming habit and a sweet martyred smile, but she had her full share of Teutonic efficiency, and was of real help in organising her sister's always emotional plans. The Grand Duchesses were only told that their share in the plans would be explained as soon as they got home.

They knew already that the Winter Palace, which was to have been the scene of Olga and Tatiana's brilliant début, was being transformed into a vast depot for medical supplies and surgical apparatus, and that the splendid Catherine Palace at Czarskoe Selo, the Czar's Village, fifteen miles from St. Petersburg, was to become a military hospital. But there were no changes as yet at the Alexander Palace, joined to the Catherine by vast and linking parks, and this was the home they were bound for, the palace they knew and preferred to any other. The first hour after they got back from Moscow was spent romping through the familiar rooms, greeting the entourage, the servants, the officers of the Guard, and petting the beloved cats and dogs which had been brought back from Peterhof. They were all children again for that one hour, perhaps for the last time in their lives.

One of the uncomfortable aspects of the imperial family's housekeeping was the parents' decided preference for eating in almost any room other than the formal dining-room in their private apartments. That night the Czar's choice fell on the library. Alexis, exhausted after the trip from Moscow, was having supper in bed and feeding titbits to his adored spaniel Joy, and without his chatter the library's sobriety had a calming effect upon the girls. They were ready to be attentive when, the folding table having been taken away by the footmen, the Czar said gravely:

'My dears, you realise that I'll have to be away from home a great deal in the future.'

'Oh papa, must you?'

'Of course. I'll have to be at GHQ very often, and visiting our brave soldiers at the front. So I think there are some things we ought to settle as soon as possible.' He cleared his throat. 'Mamma and I have been so touched, so comforted, by your willingness to help us now in any way that young girls can. And this is one way we talked over with your aunt Elizabeth: the provision of hospital trains for the wounded.'

'A hospital in a train!' marvelled Anastasia.

'You know there has been heavy fighting in East Prussia—'

'But we're winning, papa?' said Tatiana.

'It's certainly a very hard-fought fight,' said the Czar in his oblique way. 'And that means a heavy casualty list. The Commander-in-Chief tells me trains converted to hospital use are needed urgently. Mamma and I are each donating one such train: may we give four more, at your expense and in your names?'

'Oh papa, *yes*!' 'What a marvellous idea!' 'And one for Baby, too!' The happy clamour brought a smile to the Czar's drawn face. But Olga said,

'How much would it cost?'

'You don't mean you would *grudge* the cost?' said the Czarina.

'Oh no! Please!' Olga flushed with dismay. 'I only meant, can we really afford it?'

'Most certainly you can.'

'Well but, papa, how are we to know? We only get twenty roubles a month each, for pocket money. I asked Mr. Gibbs, and he said that was two pounds in English money, or ten dollars in American, which really isn't very much.'

'Is there a single want of yours which isn't satisfied?' flashed the Czarina. 'You have dresses, furs, jewels —'

'Yes, I know, mother, but sometimes I think it would be fun to go into the Gostinnoi Dvor and buy a pair of gloves I chose myself.'

The Czar held up his hand. 'That's beside the point,' he said. 'Each one of you girls has an annual income from the Apanages established by the Empress Catherine II. It's administered for you by a special office of the Household, and the accounts will be rendered to you as you attain your majority. Does that satisfy you, Olga?'

'Well, I *must* say,' the Czarina interrupted, 'when I was a girl in Darmstadt, my sisters and I were never present at any discussion of money matters —'

'No, mamma,' said Tatiana hastily, and gave a slight shake of her head at Olga. She knew, as if she had shaped the words herself, that her quick-tempered sister was about to say, 'I don't suppose there was much money to discuss at the court of Hesse-Darmstadt!' The tactful girl went on:

'Thank you so much, papa, for explaining it all to us, and of course we'll be delighted to donate the trains. But we do want to work ourselves as well. I know you laughed at us for wanting to go to the front, but surely we can do war nursing here at home?'

'I think you can, lovey, and that's what mamma has in mind for you.'

'The Big Pair and I are going to be nurses,' said the Czarina impressively. 'Tomorrow morning we'll go over to the other palace and meet the lady who's going to instruct us — not a nurse, but a qualified surgeon, one of the best in St. Petersburg. And when we've passed our examinations, then we'll be able to work as nurses in the wards.'

'But mamma, you're a wonderful nurse already,' said Anastasia.

'I've certainly had enough practice with you children,' said her mother sadly. 'But for military nursing we must study anatomy and physiology, and operating theatre techniques, and much else, before we can really help our brave wounded. And isn't that just what you wanted, girls?'

'Oh yes,' said Olga from her heart, and Tatiana kissed her mother's hand. But the Little Pair set up a clamour: 'What about us?'

'You can make bandages, and sew for the troops. But you're too young to be nurses; yes, Mashka, fifteen really is too young.'

'Well, it's too bad,' said the honest girl, 'because I was planning to be a heroine.'

'What sort of a heroine, Bow-Wow? A lady soldier?' teased the Czar.

'No, a historical heroine like in our English story-books. They're all about girls who refused to betray state secrets, even under the threat of torture — real heroines.'

'You'd better stick to your sewing basket,' Olga told her. 'Because we don't know any state secrets, and no one in the world is going to torture us.'

'It was only a joke,' said Marie humbly. But the Little Pair felt no temptation to be funny next morning, when they were left behind in their schoolroom for a French class with Monsieur Gilliard, while their sisters started on a new career. Nor did the Big Pair feel anything but solemn when they were conducted through the magnificent rooms of the great palace which Rastrelli had built for Elizabeth I, and which had been added to and made even more magnificent by the imperial Catherine whose name it bore. The girls knew the state rooms well, although in recent years these had only been used for family baptisms or weddings, and it was strange to see the rooms, with their gilded walls and painted ceilings, set out with high, hard hospital beds. In the operating theatre, which made Tatiana shiver, they met the lady of title who was not only a surgeon but a surgery professor, and liked the way she spoke to them as students and not as Imperial Highnesses. They were given textbooks, and told to go home and study them in preparation for some practical instruction that afternoon.

After that it was only a matter of hours before even the hands of two inexperienced girls were useful when the first ambulances drew up before the Catherine Palace hospital. The fighting in East Prussia flared into a six-day battle in a wilderness which the Germans decided should be called Tannenberg. In Galicia the Russians won a victory at Lemberg for which bells were rung in a capital which had changed its name from St. Petersburg to Slavic Petrograd, and in the rejoicings it was easy to make light of the defeat at Tannenberg — a battle which had made the Germans order six corps eastward from the fighting on the Marne meant to end in the fall of Paris. Certainly the Allied High Command in France was not at once aware of the significance of Tannenberg, in which the proud façade of Russian patriotism was wrecked.

The occupants of the Alexander Palace were almost as well protected as the Allied High Command from a knowledge of the meaning of the Tannenberg disaster. There were only so many casualties which the Catherine hospital could hold at any one time, only so many hospitals in Petrograd which the Czarina and her daughters could visit. They had not yet seen the hideous confusion of the front, where men died for lack of medical care and horses in the antique ambulances fell dead between the shafts as they dragged their loads of wounded to the railhead. They saw enough, within the rococo rooms of their ancestral palace, to turn Olga and Tatiana Nicolaievna from girls into women.

In the days after Tannenberg they worked all round the clock at the task they had assumed. In their off-duty hours, they went to their sitting-room (or sometimes to their bedroom, for their mother often invaded their sitting-room, to scribble her endless letters on their own chaise-longue) and asked each other questions from their lecture notes and textbooks. It was Tatiana, with her practical mind, who assimilated scientific knowledge faster, but Olga was the steadier in the wards, the calmer and more warmly compassionate in the face of sights and sounds which could not be kept from the knowledge of Imperial Highnesses. And when the long day came to an end they were ready, although the Czarina often protested, to return after dinner to the Catherine Palace and take their turn at washing the instruments used in the operating theatre, which was always in service.

They were very simple girls, and hardly understood, as yet, that the war had brought them a new freedom, being discovered by thousands of other girls in the sheltered homes of Europe. The Czar's daughters had never been allowed to make any friends of their own age — 'For surely,' the Czarina often said, 'four sisters are quite enough company for one another!' — and now they had other young nurses to talk to, and drink tea with when they had ten minutes of leisure; and young army doctors, to whom they gave the same eager friendliness as the officers of the *Standart*. They were free to come and go between the palaces, unescorted for the first time in their lives, with only the sentries presenting arms at the gates, and the Cossacks of the Escort, patrolling the avenues day and night at a distance of fifty yards apart, to remind them of their rank. And their mother, whose possessive jealousy had kept them tied so close to her, was now unable to account for every moment of their days.

The Czarina was in better health than for some time past. She still complained of sciatic pains, but said no more about her palpitations, nor of her heart, which apparently could not only enlarge or contract at will, but even move from one side of her body to the other. She had reacted emotionally to the defeat of Tannenberg, and while her husband reminded his family that he was born on the birthday of the long-suffering Job, and repeated with the prophet, 'All the evils I foresee descend upon my head', the Czarina valiantly told her children:

'We did everything we could to avert this war, and so we may be certain God will give us victory!'

There came a night in September, with the first breath of autumn chilling the long hot summer of 1914, when the Grand Duchess Olga, returning alone from the hospital to the Alexander Palace, was ushered in by the side door and climbed the long flight of stairs leading to a gallery where sentries stood between the marble statues on the upper floor of the private apartments. There a footman, sweeping off the hat with coloured feathers worn by tradition since the Empress Elizabeth's reign, informed her that the Grand Duchess Marie wished to see her 'on an important matter' as soon as she returned.

'Ask Her Imperial Highness to come to me.'

Olga went into her sitting-room, hiding a smile. Fat Little Bow-Wow's important matters — she probably had an essay to write for Professor Petrov and had stuck in the middle of it! She took off the cape she wore above a plain white overall, and flung herself down in one of the chintz-covered armchairs. She noticed that the cretonne screens round the tall porcelain stove had been removed and that there was a faint warmth in the room.

'Can I really come in, Olga?' Marie, at the door, was certainly wearing an important face.

'Of course you can! Is anything the matter?'

'Where's Tatiana?'

'She hasn't finished yet, the car went back to fetch her. I came right home to have a bath, as soon as I was through.'

'You're tired.' Marie came to sit on the arm of her sister's chair. 'Was it awful today?'

'Pretty awful. Be a pet, Mashka, and take my hairpins out.'

'I will in a minute. But I've got a message to deliver, to you and Tatiana.'

'Who from?'

'Father Grigori.'

Olga sat upright. "Has *he* been here?'

'About an hour ago. About half past nine. He was very sorry to miss seeing you.'

'Who *did* he see?'

'Why, papa and mamma, and Baby of course, and us. And Olga, he kissed Anastasia and me!'

'Kissed your lips?'

'No, he kissed us on the forehead, like he does Baby, and gave us his blessing.'

'He should have been down on one knee, kissing your hands.'

'He doesn't even do that to mother.'

Olga sighed. 'You'd better tell me all about it,' she said. 'How was he looking?'

'Just the same as ever, with his high boots and peasant blouse — you know. Mamma seemed so happy to see him again, and kept telling us it was a miracle. She sent for us, after he'd been with Alexis — I mean we went down to the drawing-room, and they were all three there, papa, mamma and Father Grigori.'

'And did papa seem happy too?'

'Oh yes, very. Why?'

'Because I know he wasn't pleased with a message Rasput — Father Grigori sent him, just before war was declared.'

'Papa told us Alexis was asleep when they went into his room. So Father Grigori said not to wake him. He made the sign of the cross over his head, and whispered, "Now the Little One will soon be well." Then mamma kissed Father Grigori's hand, and cried.'

'But Alexis *is* quite well again.'

'I know. He was playing outdoors with Joy all afternoon.'

The dark blue eyes met Olga's in a searching look. It struck the elder sister that Fat Little Bow-Wow was not quite the harum-scarum schoolgirl she had been. She's beginning to watch and wonder too, she thought, and saw that the round childish face was thinner, the Slavic cheekbones more clearly defined, since Marie had started out to be a heroine by curbing her appetite for chocolate and cakes.

'Father Grigori has a talent for turning up every time that Alexis is really on the mend,' she said. 'But what was his message to us?'

'He said he was very pleased you'd started to train as nurses.'

'That was kind of him.'

'But he wants you to visit the hospitals in other cities, not just in Saint — Petrograd; with mamma, of course, and he wants you always to wear your uniform as Sisters, with the red pectoral cross.'

'What nonsense,' said Olga. 'Dressing up to visit other

people's hospitals, indeed! Anyway we're only allowed white overalls until we've passed our certificate exams.'

She stood up, shaking down the rumpled overall, as if she meant to argue this point with Rasputin then and there. 'Is he still in the palace?' she asked.

'He went away with papa and mamma to pay a late call on Ania.'

'Oh —' Olga nearly said, 'Oh no! So that's going to start all over again!' It had been one of the blessings of the Czarina's preoccupation with war work that she had practically suspended those evening visits to Madame Virubova's discreet little house at the corner of Srednaia Avenue, just outside the palace grounds, which were the subject of gossip, as Olga well knew, to the imperial entourage. If she meant to drag the Czar to the Srednaia again, with Rasputin leading the way — ! 'Sorry, Mashka,' she said, 'I didn't quite hear what you were saying.'

'You were whispering too.' But Marie did not raise her voice: whispering seemed to have come into fashion in the Alexander Palace since Rasputin's return. 'I only asked you why mother makes such a fuss of Ania, when she's usually so strict about divorce.'

'Oh, but the Virubov marriage was dissolved, they weren't divorced. And anyway, the poor man's gone. He had a terrible experience at the battle of Tshusima Bay, and went off his head soon after they were married. I was about twelve then; I remember him being sent away to a sanatorium in Switzerland.'

'Yes, but why should mamma call Ania "Our eldest daughter"? She has a very nice father and mother of her own.'

'But *our* mother feels responsible for the whole thing. Ania had fallen in love with General Orlov, and mother thought he was too old for her. So she urged her to marry Lieutenant Virubov, and ever since, she's felt guilty about the consequences.'

'Ania's always falling in love with somebody,' said the Grand Duchess Marie. She looked at the double doors of the sitting-room, and lowered her voice further still. 'Olga, don't be angry — but honestly I sometimes used to think she'd fallen in love with father.'

The Czar went off to Baranovichi, and in his absence Rasputin did not appear at the Alexander Palace. Nor did the Czarina pay any evening visits to 'Our Lady of the Avenue', as some of the courtiers called Ania Virubova. She sat at home with her girls, sewing, and writing her name on the holy pictures they all signed in turn, which were intended for the troops. But Ania was with her for part of every day, and most often when the Czarina visited the restored crypt chapel beneath the palace hospital, where rapt with religious exaltation she would lie on the cold stones to pray.

Insidiously, through Ania's messages, Rasputin's influence was re-established. As he suggested, Olga and Tatiana went with their mother to visit hospitals behind the lines as soon as they passed their nursing examinations at the end of October, earning the right to wear white veils, and the nursing sisters' white aprons with scarlet pectoral crosses. They went to Vilna, where the Czarina's sciatica was so acute that she had to be carried up the hospital stairs, an unregal progress which mystified the soldier patients. They went to Pskov, where the Grand Duke Dmitri's sister Marie, known in the Family as Marisha, was on the staff of a huge hospital of twenty thousand beds. These were all filled. The sight of the wounded lying on pallets along the corridors, and the misery of the refugees wandering homeless, drove Olga frantic for fresh opportunities for service.

'Tania and I want to help the old people, mother. And the babies! Nobody's doing anything about them.'

But this had not been foreseen by Rasputin, and Alexandra Feodorovna snubbed her impetuous daughter.

'You always want to run before you can walk, Olga. Try to become a really good nurse; that's quite enough for a girl barely nineteen.'

'Marisha isn't only nursing, she's helping to *organise* that enormous hospital. You said yourself she was fighting a good fight against incompetence. And she's only five years older than I am.'

'Five very important years in a young woman's life. You're an inexperienced girl compared with Marisha.'

'Yes, well, Marisha's been married and divorced and had a baby. Is that the right experience for running a hospital? Do I have to be married and divorced before I can run a charity?'

'I shall talk to your father about the wilful, disagreeable spirit you're showing these days — '

'All right, I want to talk to him myself.'

As usual, it was the diplomatic Tatiana who did the talking, at the first family dinner after Nicholas II returned from his latest trip to GHQ. Her gentle 'We only want to do more to help you, papa,' was far more persuasive than Olga's excitement, and the Czar looked hopefully at his wife.

'What do you says, Alix? Really I think we might let them be seen and heard a little more.'

'But what in the world could they do? Olga is far too young to preside over a sewing circle, as Motherdear did in the war with Japan.' The girls burst out laughing, and even the harassed Czar smiled.

'Frankly I don't see Olga presiding over a sewing circle at any age,' he said. 'But I don't see why they shouldn't be the nominal heads of two of the relief committees.'

'Your sisters are the proper persons to take charge of the relief committees,' said the Czarina. 'If Olga Alexandrovna had remained in her married home instead of going off to nurse at Kiev — '

'My sister Olga is doing very well in her hospital at Kiev, I saw that for myself three weeks ago. And Xenia is too busy to do war work, with that great household of boys — '

There was nothing, and her husband knew there was nothing, which silenced Alexandra Feodorovna more completely than an allusion to the Grand Duchess Xenia's large family of sons. Her first child had been a girl, Irina, born in the same year as Olga Nicolaievna. Then, while daughter after daughter was born to the Czarina, waiting in hope and despair for a son and heir, Xenia had given birth to no fewer than six sons, big, noisy, healthy boys whom the Czarina, in her terrible jealousy, had declared too rough to be fit playmates for her own ailing Alexis. She sat sulking now, while the girls overwhelmed their father with thanks, and finally said crushingly:

'Well, I hope you're satisfied, Olga. I think you must want to curry favour and court popularity, like your Aunt Miechen. Isn't it enough that your new photographs are on sale at every street corner in the Nevski Prospekt?'

'Like the Biograph Girl's!' said Anastasia, and the Czarina's sarcasm was drowned in happy giggles as the family got up from table. It was very soon settled that Olga should be the president — the 'nominal president', her mother insisted, of a relief committee for soldiers' families, while Tatiana took on a committee for refugees. It was a new escape for the girls to go at least once, and more often twice a week to the Winter Palace, where the committees met and donations were received. They drove to town accompanied only by one of their mother's younger ladies-in-waiting, and at the Winter Palace they quickly dispensed with protocol and fuss. The members of Petrograd society who had joined the relief committees because it was the fashion to be charitable without getting one's hands dirty, were soon amazed at the programme of work laid out for them by two very young and very determined girls who, so far from being 'nominal' presidents, sheltering under the wing of some white-haired general, stood up and addressed their committees with clarity and force. 'True Romanovs both,' was the general opinion. 'How very different from their wretched mother!'

Eight hours a day in hospital, four hours a day on the committee work — it was enough to give Olga Nicolaievna dreamless sleep at night, unplagued by thoughts of the Galician front into which Simon Hendrikov and his brother officers of the Garde Equipage had disappeared weeks ago. Perhaps only the girls and Alexis slept soundly during those November nights at Czarskoe Selo, after the new offensive on the western front had fallen into bloody collapse, and the Russian High Command turned to face a new threat to the south and east. In the Ottoman Empire, Enver Pasha and his Young Turks had dragged the Sultan into the war on the side of Germany, and while the winter snows began to fall on the great plain of Petrograd, Russian troops were struggling through blizzards in the mountain passes of Eastern Armenia. By Christmas, the date each belligerent had sworn to celebrate in the enemy's capital, it was clear that Lord Kitchener had been right in predicting a long war. In western Europe the trenches, waterlogged and rat-ridden, stretched from the Channel to the Swiss frontier, and the terrible toll of First Ypres had been added to the casualty lists. The Russians had lost over a million men. And steadily new volunteers joined the ranks, above all from the British Empire, where young men were still loyal to the motherland. They called the war 'the Great War' now, for it had become a continental war in which two men had already been forgotten: Franz Ferdinand in his tomb at Artstetten, and Gavrilo Princip, rotting in his Austrian prison.

CHAPTER SEVEN

IN Petrograd, in early January, the wan daylight did not filter through the falling snow until nine o'clock in the morning, and many shops and places of business did not open their doors until ten. There was plenty of time, said Madame Trenova, for Mara to accompany her to a brief memorial service in the Vladimirski church, a *panikhidia* for three young men of their neighbourhood who had fallen on the Turkish front.

'I wouldn't call any of your services exactly brief, mother. And I don't want to be late at the office,' said Mara. She was standing in front of a little cracked wall mirror in the kitchen which was also their living-room and her own bedroom, pulling a woollen cap down over her ears and adjusting its strings inside the narrow fur collar of her black cloth coat.

'You needn't stay for the mass, dear. But it would please the boys' mothers so much to see some young people present. So dreadful not to have a proper funeral!' whimpered Madame Trenova. She was a tiny, mouse-like woman, darting round the small apartment with something of a mouse's agility, piling the teacups into a basin to wait for water from the tap on the landing, and slipping into her own slit of a bedroom for a thick scarf to twist round her head. Without a hat she looked like any of the shawled, shabby women who thronged the stone stair-case of the apartment building on Yamskaia Street which had been her refuge since Ivan Trenov was marched off with the convict gangs to die at Sakhalin.

'Come along then, at least it isn't far,' said Mara, for the Church of Our Lady of Vladimir occupied most of the huge square near their home. Crossing the street, she took her mother's arm, for the square as usual was crowded and the going difficult on the lumpy, frozen snow. There were crowds outside the small shops and round the fish and vegetable barrows by the church; crowds not yet formed into orderly patient queues, although food shortages were now beginning to be felt. There were hawkers' carts, and vendors of old clothes with ten capes on their backs, four fur hats on their heads; and in the grey-faced, dark-clothed crowd there were also women pickpockets and men who, in spite of the wartime ban on vodka, had somehow contrived to become uproariously drunk. The scene through which Mara piloted her mother might have been sketched by Dostoievski, it was the St. Petersburg of Raskolnikov and Prince Myishkin, and Dostoievski himself had died in the Yamskaia, in a flat very little more luxurious than Madame Trenova's mousehole. The two women loosened their coat collars thankfully in the warm air of the church.

'Are you coming home to lunch today, Mara?' her mother whispered, before they went inside the nave.

'I shouldn't think so. This is press day, don't you remember? We'll probably all go out and have a bite at "The Red Sarafan".'

'Well, be sure to have a proper meal, you're getting much too thin. Don't let them work you too hard . . .'

Any bite at 'The Red Sarafan' would be more filling than a midday meal at the flat, which usually consisted of a bowl of soup or kasha and a small piece of smoked fish, a scanty diet for a girl who for years had been fed on the good plain fare of the Xenia School. Mara said nothing, but let the familiar whimper about overwork die away as she piloted her mother to the ikon of St. Dmitri. One of the dead soldiers had been called Dmitri, and there the mourners had gathered, most of them in tears. Madame Trenova's easy tears began to flow too, and Mara lit a candle and put it in her mother's hand.

There were sorrowing groups in other corners of the church, and a constantly shifting line of shawled women standing with clasped hands and moving lips before the great golden ikonostasis, representing the temple veil, which stood between the altar and the nave. All three gates were shut: the two through which the deacons might pass during the rites of worship, the third which opened only to the priest or to a Czar on the day of his coronation. Above the flickering candles Mara Trenova studied the glory of gold and imagery which was almost the only colour in the lives of the drab women standing or kneeling below it. She had seen the doors of the ikonostasis open many times, and had once truly believed that when the priest's gate was opened after the consecration, the sight of the altar beyond was the revelation of heaven to the faithful. She believed in nothing now, except that religion was the opium of the people, and the words of the priest, singing the *kontakion*, meant less than nothing to Ivan Trenov's daughter.

Give rest, O Christ, to Thy servant with the saints:
Where sorrow and pain are no more;
Neither sighing, but life everlasting.

It was the right time to go; the mourners were all absorbed in the chant and would never miss her. Mara touched her mother's arm, made a little movement of her head towards the door, and went away down the stone flags on tiptoe. The priest was still singing, inaudible by the time she reached the door, but whether she believed in them or not she knew the words by heart:

All we go down to the dust.
And weeping o'er the grave we make our song:
Alleluia! alleluia! alleluia!

As she hurried back across the square, a clock above the market stalls reminded Mara that the girls of the Xenia School must then be filing into their chapel, a copy of the Church of the Nativity at Bethlehem, to sing their morning hymns. She could picture Dolly Hendrikova, condemned to another year of school, trailing the absurd skirts of the school costume along the steps of the great grey marble staircase and shivering, as they all did in January, in the low-cut boned bodice and the white lawn sleeves and apron. She was delighted to be done with all that mummery, and she didn't care if she never saw the Hendrikovs again, or Plain Joe Calvert either, with his champagne and his Hotel Europa dinners. Now she was a worker, and though her hands were stained with nothing worse than carbon paper Mara felt, every time she went down on an errand to the printers in their cellar below her office, that she was one of a community of real workers, proletarians, just as every time she joined in the arguments over the tea glasses and *pirozhki* in 'The Red Sarafan' she felt herself accepted by creative artists. Alleluia! Alleluia! Mara Trenova was free at last.

The publishing house where Professor Rostov had found her a job was within walking distance of her home, occupying nearly the whole of one of the short, dingy alleys near the Nicholas station, off the Znamenia Square, one of the beating pulses of Petrograd. Known as The Children's Castle, it published school textbooks and juveniles, but was best known for its pocket editions of the Russian classics which, on thin grey paper and in type small enough to strain any child's eyesight, were sold tied up in orange ribbon with slabs of chocolate by the leading confectioners of the capital.

Almost as bland as the 'candy classics', as they were known to the trade, was the children's magazine put out monthly by the house, and a weekly review for adults which went out to a fairly large mailing list, and which was known as *Castle Comments*. When Mara was getting her bearings in her new job, she was surprised to find that so much business was done through the mails, for large consignments of the pocket classics, orange ribbons, chocolate slabs and all, were sent off regularly to addresses in the country, and the readers of *Castle Comments* were assiduous in writing to the editor, Jacob Levin. The review was the reverse of *avant-garde*. The criticisms of music and the ballet were fresh and interesting, but no historian more recent than Karamsin, no poet more revolutionary than Zhucovski, was ever made the subject of a leading article. It appeared that admirers of Karamsin and Zhucovski were numerous in the provinces, and the letters to the editor were full of page references and paragraph numbers which Mara was expected to check and compile for Jacob Levin. She had been his secretary for nearly three months.

He was not in the office when she arrived breathless from the Vladimir church, but this was normal on press day, when he and his elderly assistant came in at the same time as the printers. Their coats and fur hats were hanging on the wall of the big, dingy office on the second floor, and the clatter and stamp of the antiquated Wharfedale presses could be heard and felt all through the building. She stole a quick glance at the newspaper on Levin's desk. The headlines scarcely ever varied. Retreat — Strategic Withdrawal — Commission Demanded by the Duma — Lack of Air Support in the North — she could have written them blindfold. Mara tackled a basketful of morning mail.

It was not until Sergiev brought her a glass of tea from the samovar which bubbled continually at the end of the corridor that Mara Trenova realised she was famished, and that the morning hours had sped away.

'Thank you, Sergiev,' she said gratefully. 'Mr. Levin's staying down there a long time, isn't he?'

'He had a row with the foreman printer,' said Sergiev. 'One of the presses broke down in the middle of the run.'

'It happens every week, doesn't it?'

Sergiev laughed hoarsely. He was an uncanny creature, barely four feet tall. Sergiev was a hunchback, with a lined and twisted face: he might have been any age from fifteen to forty, and was employed at The Children's Castle as a copyboy and general drudge.

'Every week, and Mr. Levin fixes it.' he said. 'Have you heard what the carters are saying in the alley?'

'No, what?'

'They say the German woman has been shot.'

'What German woman? Sergiev! Not the Czarina?'

The hunchback nodded. 'It happened out at Czarskoe Selo. Six thousand men she had to guard her, I've heard tell. Police and soldiers. Cossacks, Garde Équipage and all. But they got to her, oh yes, they got to her . . . just as they'll get to *him* some day.'

'Is she — dead?'

'Dead or dying, does it matter?' Sergiev looked gloatingly at the pale face close to his own. 'This is good news, not?'

'I suppose so. But who did it, Sergiev? Have they caught the assassin? Was it at the hospital, or in the grounds, or where?'

'Does it matter?' he said again. 'Think of it, Mara Ivanovna! Rasputin's crowned mistress — gone!'

'I wish *you'd* go, and find out the details. It's probably only a silly rumour,' she called after him, as Sergiev tossed his huge head and left the room. Why she added that, she didn't know; she was shocked, and there was no reason to be shocked, for death always stalked the Romanovs, and Alexandra Feodorovna deserved it more than most. Still, Mara's head was throbbing as she rolled fresh paper and carbons into her high typewriter, and when she had written the date under the letterhead she took her hands from the keyboard and pressed them to her brow, and thought of a beautiful and tragic woman, lying dead.

She heard Levin's heavy step in the corridor, and the creak

of the opening door, but although she raised her head Mara neither rose nor turned round. In a moment she felt the touch that made her shiver, the caress of a maimed hand on the nape of her neck, and she said, 'You startled me.'

'Don't be silly, you were expecting me, weren't you?'

'Yes.'

She felt Levin's indrawn breath above her hair. 'You reek of incense, girl, where have you been?' he said easily, as he moved round the desk to his own big chair.

'Mother dragged me to a service at the Vladimir this morning.'

'Aha! That accounts for it. Now let's get to work.'

Mara passed a file of letters and notes on copy paper across the desk, and he read them quickly. Jacob Levin was a short, powerfully built man, with greying hair cut as short as possible, and a square, self-contained face. The top joints of the middle finger of his right hand were missing, the result of an accident when he was a journeyman printer in Odessa. Mara had at first found the stump repellent; she came to have a perverse pleasure in watching how dexterously he held his pen.

'Right; now take dictation, please.' He began to talk, not too quickly, expanding the annotations he had made upon the file; and as he dictated he watched Mara Trenova, with her dark head and sharp profile bent over the shorthand notebook. He thought she was shaping up very well indeed.

Rostov had ended a short written report on her background with the words, 'Clever, conceited, resentful and deprived — could become a useful recruit, with the proper training.' Levin was an experienced trainer. Offhand and impersonal, he had let the girl settle to the office routine for a few weeks. Then he took her along to 'The Red Sarafan' and waited while Mara Trenova adapted to the group of failed authors, unpublished poets and hack reviewers who made the restaurant their rendezvous. One night, when after two glasses of yellow wine she had become voluble and excited about the latest rumours of corruption in high places, he had escorted her home with her cold hand comfortably tucked inside the pocket of his greatcoat, and asked her pointblank:

'Are you going to fritter away your time jabbering about politics, like that crowd in the "Sarafan", or do you mean to do something about it?'

Mara told him proudly that she intended to apply for membership of the Social Revolutionary party. He barked with laughter.

'The SRs! Why the SRs?'

'It was my father's party, when he was alive. And I think the SRs mean to do most for the people.'

'For the peasants, or so they say. They don't reach the proletariat of the factories.'

'Well, at least their leaders are in Petrograd, and not in Zürich or Geneva, like the Bolsheviki.'

He had stopped at a street corner then, and taken her by the shoulders. 'I bet you heard that argument at one of Professor Hendrikov's social evenings,' he said. 'I can just see you, lapping up his milk-and-water liberalism.'

'But Professor Hendrikov isn't an SR. He was elected to the First Duma as a Constitutional Democrat — a Kadet.'

'He has plenty of SR friends, though: he practically thinks he invented Alexander Kerensky. Was *he* your inspiration, Mara? Kerensky? He's young, and not bad-looking in his way; a lot of girls have fallen for him.'

She was quite oblivious to the cold and the snow, he saw with professional approval. Exalted by her own fervour, she told him that her inspiration for years had been the great women of the SRs, who had conspired, killed, borne torture and exile, even gone to execution, so that some day Russia should be a better place to live in. The names came tumbling out, Vera Figner, Vera Zazulich, Perovskaia who had died for her share in the assassination of Alexander II, Dora Brilliant who had helped Kaliaev, the killer of the Grand Duke Sergei, Maria Spiridonova, for the past eight years an exile in Siberia ... Levin had kissed her then for the first time, roughly, their cold faces colliding rather than caressing, to put an end to the scene.

He remembered it, as he watched her across the desk, and when he finished dictating and took out his cigarettes he said casually:

'There's a rumour floating around the building, about an incident at Czarskoe Selo —'

'An *incident*! Sergiev told me the Czarina had been murdered.'

'The Czarina, did he? We'll have to get Sergiev to churn out some fiction for our readers, one of these days. The way I heard the story, it was the Czarina's dear friend, Madame Virubova, who was the victim of — circumstances.'

'I told Sergiev to go out and get the facts. He must have gone to buy an evening paper.'

'He won't get any facts from the newspaper, if the censorship has been clamped down. Cigarette?'

'No thank you.'

'Mara. Was that why you were looking like a sick cat when I came in — because you thought the German woman was dead?'

'Why should I care about her death?'

'What was the matter with you, then?'

'I was just trying to picture — trying to imagine what it would be like to be the — the person who put a weapon in her pocket and went out deliberately to take a life — '

' "In *her* pocket." Still thinking of the great SR heroines?'

'Perhaps I was.'

'Have *you* ever handled firearms?'

'Never in my life.'

Levin drew a Nagan revolver from his jacket pocket and laid it on the desk between them. Mara looked at it fearfully.

'Is it loaded?'

'Yes, of course it's loaded, not much use if it weren't. Pick it up. Like this, see? You've got five fingers, not like me.'

The mutilated finger seemed to be no handicap as Levin's hand closed on the revolver. He pushed it closer to the girl. Mara Trenova took it up cautiously and without touching the trigger. It was warm with the heat of Levin's body.

'It's very heavy.'

'Too heavy for you, maybe. All right, now you've got something like the feel of it, and if it stops snowing I'll take you out to the marshes on Sunday and teach you to fire it. Where the hell has Sergiev got to?' Levin put the weapon back in his pocket and opened the office door. 'Hey! You out there! Anybody seen Sergiev? Eh? Oh, he's coming.'

The hunchback came stumbling in, carrying a newspaper. 'I went over to the station, and then I had to wait for the delivery truck,' he grumbled. 'And it's not the Czarina they got, it's the Virubova woman.'

'As I could have told you, you damned fool, if you'd come to me with your silly story. Clear out now, and get your dinner, I'm too busy to be bothered with you.'

Mara was rubbing her right hand, still tingling from its contact with the gun. 'So it's actually in the paper?' she asked.

'Yes, here it is, page four, they've been told not to give it much of a play. Mara! They claim it was a rail accident, not far from the station at Czarskoe Selo.'

'A *rail* accident! Not an attempted murder?'

'Listen to this. Yesterday afternoon, a number of passengers were injured, etc., including Anna Alexandrovna Virubova, daughter of, etc., a former maid of honour to Her Imperial Majesty (now a matron of dishonour, they might have said), trapped under wreckage, etc., received nearly fatal injuries but has survived the night. Well! That should put a stop to Her Imperial Majesty's cosy evenings with Rasputin, for some time to come!'

'What about the other people who were hurt?'

'Just a list of names, mis-spelled; what more did you expect for the common herd?'

'But what caused the accident?'

'Doesn't say. An accident, eh? on the best policed line in all Russia. Couldn't have been a bomb on the line, or a length of track torn up, or a grenade thrown from the embankment. Perhaps it *was* an accident — maybe the driver was drunk.'

Mara shook her dark head. 'It's never an accident,' she said positively, 'when it's anything do to with one of *them*.'

But it can't have been an accident. The Grand Duchesses Olga and Tatiana, looking at each other aghast in one of the hospital offices in the Catherine Palace, shared the thought of Mara Trenova, although they were careful not to put it into words. If one of them had spoken out, it might have been to say, 'Do you suppose it was something meant for *us?*'

They knew much of the long record of terrorist activities against the Romanovs when the imperial family travelled by train. Bombs on the permanent way, bridges blown and dynamite charges left in tunnels had been part of their forebears' occupational hazards, culminating in the tragedy near Borki in 1888. They knew every detail of that attempt, which caused nearly three hundred casualties, because their father had been in the train, a young man of twenty, and he had often told them how his own father, the Czar Alexander III, a man of colossal strength, had saved his wife and children from maiming and suffocation. They were in the dining car when the terrorists blew up the train. The Czar had taken the whole weight of the iron roof on his powerful back and shoulders, allowing his family and their attendants to crawl to safety, but sustaining the damage to his kidneys which brought about his early death.

There had been no man of similar strength in the train wreck outside Czarskoe Selo, and now Anna Virubova lay unconscious, her left leg broken, her right thigh crushed, and with multiple injuries to her head and shoulders.

'The Czarina wishes absolutely to send for Father Grigori,' said Tatiana, in the soft voice which could be as implacable as her mother's when she chose.

The army doctor who had brought them to the little office where one of the few telephones in the palace hospital had been installed, sighed and shook his head.

'Her Majesty was in a state of acute hysteria,' he said. 'She became much calmer as soon as His Majesty the Czar arrived. The interference of another person — *any* other person — might easily revive her distress.'

'The Czar also wishes Father Grigori to be sent for. Not on my mother's behalf, but on the patient's.'

'The patient should be left in peace for her last hours. You heard the opinion of three doctors, nurse: Madame Virubova is dying.'

'My brother has been at death's door more than once, and Father Grigori's prayers have saved him.'

'Then the telephone is at the disposal of Your Imperial Highness.'

'Thank you.' Tatiana ignored the sarcastic tone. She called the switchboard operator and gave the number of Rasputin's flat in Petrograd. The doctor listened. She knew the number by heart, of course, no hesitation there! He remembered the rumours circulating about those two pretty girls and Rasputin. The fellow had slept with them both, and their mother too: soon it would be the turn of the younger ones. Disgusting if true, revolting if lies! Tatiana was saying:

'When? About an hour ago? No thank you, I'll see to it myself.' She turned to Olga. 'His housekeeper says he's at a dinner party at the Hotel Europa. One of the cars must go in and bring him here at once.'

'Doctor — ' said Olga appealingly, and the doctor, with an unwilling bow, said he would attend to the matter. 'But may I remind you, nurses, that this is a military hospital, where discipline can not be disrupted for the sake of one civilian patient? Or two, however exalted the second one may be? You both left your duties to comfort Her Imperial Majesty. Now you will please return to your wards immediately.'

'How rude he was to us!' said Tatiana, in the corridor, and Olga wondered if they could blame the man, when her sister lingered until she saw an orderly on his way to the stable garages, where the imperial cars were parked. She fully expected a few angry looks when she returned to her own ward, for the patients' supper had been served while the girls tried to calm their frantic mother, and one young nurse muttered 'Don't *hurry*, will you?' when Olga arrived only in time to help with the removal of the dishes. But then quiet fell on the ward as the patients, all surgical cases, were settled for the night, and the lights were dimmed, and the nurses left on duty sat down by their tables to sew before each in turn went to her own supper.

Olga, because of her long absence in the late afternoon, was the last to go, and there was no one in the little refectory but two servants who brought her food and tea. No sign of Tatiana, no one to tell her if Ania Virubova was alive or dead; the Catherine Palace was as silent as it had been for many years before the war. She looked at the watch pinned to the bib of her apron. If Rasputin really was at the Hotel Europa, and not carousing in the city, there was almost time to have brought him to his devotees by now. Olga crossed the great landing and gently opened the small shutter which allowed her to look out of the heavily covered window. It was a clear, sparkling night with no snow falling, and she could see all down the gardens, where the trees were heavy with snow, and all the follies, statues and bathhouses of the Romanovs were encased in wood against the bitter frost. One of the imperial cars came up the driveway, where even the wheels of the ambulance had not broken the snow crust, and stopped, just below Olga's window, at the steps leading up to the main entrance to the palace. She watched, sick with foreboding, while Rasputin got out.

Dressed for his dinner party, he was not wearing the rough peasant clothes which appealed so much to his imperial patrons. His tall figure was clad in a long tunic of purple silk, with a jewelled belt, breeches of fine cloth, and high boots of the finest polished leather. In the starlight his long black hair shone with brilliantine. He stood on the bottom step, looking up at the splendid palace as if he owned it, and spread his arms out, Olga thought in rehearsal of a blessing, like the wings of some gigantic coloured bird. Or it might have been in an attempt to keep his balance, for as a footman left the seat beside the driver and came running round the limousine to put a fur *shuba* round Rasputin's shoulders, the monk staggered and caught at the fellow's arm to steady himself. To the watchful blue eyes at the window, it was clear that the holy man was drunk.

It was not until much later, when he called them into his own study, that Nicholas II described to his elder daughters the miracle that 'the man of God' had wrought in what was all but a chamber of death. The Czarina was already in a drugged sleep, and the girls more exhausted by her emotion than by their long day's work, but the usually impassive Czar was strangely excited as he told how Rasputin entered Anna Virubova's room, ignoring everyone but the woman in a coma on the hospital bed.

'Poor mamma knelt to him and tried to kiss his ring,' said Nicholas II. 'But he withheld his blessing. He didn't call her "Matushka Czarina", Mother Empress, as he usually does, nor bow to me and call me "Little Father", he simply fixed his glowing eyes on Ania, and held out those wonderful long hands towards her. Then he said her name, "Annushka!" three times over, and her eyes opened and she recognised him. She whispered "Father Grigori!" and he said "Rise!" '

'He didn't say "Arise, take up thy bed and walk," by any chance?' said Olga, and Tatiana quickly covered the levity.

'But poor Ania couldn't rise, could she, papa?' she said.

'Those idiots of doctors told us she would never move again. But at the sound of *his* voice she lifted her head and shoulders from the pillow, she even smiled. One of the doctors came forward to take her pulse, and poor mamma got up and tried to speak. Then Father Grigori said, "You will keep her. Russia needs her still!" and fell back against the wall with the sweat pouring down his face. I thought he would be the next to faint — '

'I hope they gave him something to drink,' said Olga.

' — They brought him wine in the ante-room, and mamma and I said a prayer of thanksgiving with him. Oh, how grateful we should be, my darlings, for the divine intervention that saved his life last summer! I may have been born on the birthday of the long-suffering Job, but tonight I have been privileged to be the witness of a miracle.'

The daughters kissed their father's hand and went to bed almost in silence. Tatiana went to sleep at once, but Olga lay awake for an hour, trying to think what this new victory for Rasputin might mean for all of them, and wondering if there would be an investigation of the railway accident and what it would reveal. She might have been comforted if she could have heard the doctor who had spoken so bluntly about hospital discipline telling a colleague about Rasputin's 'miracle', ending with the words:

'It was the clearest — the very damnedest — case of hypnotism I ever saw.'

Hypnotised or not, Anna Virubova recovered. The news was broken to her that even when discharged from hospital she must spend weeks in a wheel-chair, or on a couch; when she began to walk it would be on crutches, and she might never walk without a support again. Ania accepted the verdict with pious resignation. She had regained the full attention, even the doting care, of Alexandra Feodorovna, and in spite of the pain of her terrible injuries her fat face lit up with pleasure when the Czarina sat down beside her with a bowl and spoon, and fed her as tenderly as she had fed her own babies.

Every bed in the palace hospital was needed for the wounded, and as soon as possible Ania was taken by ambulance to her own little house, where a nurse called Sister Akulina was detached from the hospital to care for her. Soon 'Our Lady of the Avenue' had a new entourage, all followers of Rasputin. Sister Akulina, a Siberian, had been cured of convulsions by Rasputin when he visited her convent near Ekaterinburg, and Peter Badmaiev, sometimes called a Siberian and sometimes 'a Mongolian herbalist', or even a Tibetan, came at Rasputin's instance to dose Ania with some of his brews made from wild plants and herbs. Anastasia, the first of the Grand Duchesses to meet Badmaiev, reported to Olga that he was 'a funny little man, with a tall peaked hat', who had made her taste a drop of some dark green stuff called Essence of Black Lotus, which made her feel quite funny.

'I don't think mamma and papa would like you to drink some queer stuff out of bottles, unless Dr. Botkin knew and approved.'

'Oh, but papa had some too! He drank a wine glassful of Tibetan Elixir and enjoyed it. Peter Alexandrovich says it'll make him sleep better when he's at the front.'

Olga said no more. She thought there must be a queer new group at the little house on the avenue, where the Czar and Czarina visited every night — they who visited nobody — and where she never went herself if she could help it. Olga was too kind-hearted not to be sorry for Ania, a grotesque figure with her heavy and now twisted limbs sprawled on the sofa, but she always felt stifled if she spent longer than twenty minutes in the little sitting-room which was at once cold and heavy with the stale smoke of innumerable cigarettes, and where three of the four walls were covered with enlargements of Ania's own snapshots of the Czar. As for Alexis, he was not allowed to visit Ania at all, much as she begged to see him. He had been ill so often himself that he was very sensitive to the suffering of others, and would certainly have cried himself sick if he had seen her in the first weeks after the accident.

The boy was now quite well and strong, and growing fast. He had begun to learn English and the balalaika, and enjoyed playing in the snow, especially with a captured German machine-gun which the Commander-in-Chief had sent him in the early days of the war. The great improvement in Alexis was the chief gain of late January and February, while the military situation deteriorated on all fronts, and the Duma, outraged by the incompetence which was sending Russian troops unarmed to their deaths, was clamouring for the creation of a War Council on a broad basis, to include Deputies, bankers, industrialists and representatives of the war ministry.

The Duma and the Czar had long been irreconcilable, all the more so because in the Czar's own home his wife kept insisting that the manifesto which created the Duma had been 'wrested from him' in the aftermath of Bloody Sunday, and that in the eyes of God he was still the autocrat of his anointed coronation. She told him a good deal more than that in the weeks following Rasputin's 'miracle', and now her criticisms were not kept to their private hours, but voiced in front of the embarrassed girls.

She began, characteristically, by criticising various members of the Family. It was a sore point with the Czarina that Nicholas II had recalled his brother Michael to Russia at the beginning of the war. The Grand Duke Michael, known to his relatives as Floppy, was an exile for the usual Romanov reason of a morganatic marriage, in his case with the extra distinction that his wife, Countess Brassova, had been twice divorced before the birth of their illegitimate child. But the Czar was determined to forgive 'Misha' and have him back, and now Misha, or Floppy, was commanding a division in the Caucasus, a long way from the salons of Petrograd or the Puritan lady of Czarskoe Selo. There were other targets, nearer home, for her growing malice. The Grand Dukes came under steady fire: Dmitri, once a great favourite, 'now so *fast*, and coming on leave so often, he ought not to have the honour of being your aide-de-camp, Nicky,' Sergei, 'mixed up in that dreadful artillery scandal,' Kirill. 'using his position at the Stavka to connive with Nikolasha.' And Nikolasha himself, the C-in-C, 'incapable of winning a victory.' and 'trying to undermine your popularity with the troops.' The young Grand Duchesses saw a case of pathological jealousy developing at their family table, day after winter day.

The Czar bore it all calmly enough until the day came when the hysterical woman attacked Mala Kchessinskaia, and then the worm turned. In the Duma and the popular press there was a mounting outcry against the War Minister, who was held responsible for the terrible shortages of munitions, artillery, and even food and clothing for the troops. But the War Minister was a strong adherent of Rasputin, and so in the Czarina's eyes could do no wrong. She asked point blank that the Minister of Justice should take proceedings against certain persons who had accepted bribes for placing orders for artillery with different firms in Russia and abroad. And among them she named Madame Mathilde Kchessinskaia.

The Czar laid down his table napkin (they were about to finish luncheon) and said, 'I really don't believe that's true, Alix. Kchessinskaia has no need to take bribes from anybody,

147

she must be one of the highest-paid dancers in the world.'

'So brave to go *on* dancing, at her age,' said the Czarina. 'But perhaps she doesn't get all the money she needs from her protector, your cousin Andrei.'

'She was dancing like an angel, only last July at Krasnoe Selo,' said Olga, and her father gave her a grateful glance.

'I don't think these details can really interest the younger ones,' he said, though 'Marie's saucers' were round with the determination not to miss a word. 'Have you any documentary evidence of this bribe-taking — names, dates, places, that sort of thing?'

'One doesn't need documentary evidence when a matter like this becomes common knowledge!'

'I think you'll find the Minister of Justice will,' said the Czar, 'before you can persuade him to take legal action against your "certain persons". As for Mala Kchessinskaia, she isn't even a business woman, let alone a cheat. I remember the night I met her first — long before you and I were married, Alix — and my father said to her, a lovely girl of eighteen, "Be the glory of our Russian ballet!" And that's exactly what she has been, and *all* she has been, from that day to this.'

He left the table with a bow to his wife and went to his study; the girls scattered hastily to their different occupations. But before the Czar left for the front that night he kissed his eldest daughter with especial tenderness, so that she knew her few awkward words of championship had touched his heart. She must have been uppermost in his mind on his journey into Poland, for his first letter from the front, addressed to the Czarina, was so completely lacking in the usual endearments and implicit sexual allusions that she showed it at once to Olga and Tatiana.

My beloved Sunny [the Czar wrote from Warsaw]

I wish you would direct the Zemstvo Red Cross to look at once into the situation of our wounded in this area. I was horrified to find upon arrival at Warsaw that nearly twenty thousand wounded from the recent battles have been lying untended in and around the Vienna railway station for several days. I personally ordered up all the available ambulance trains, and into Olga's train, which happened to be the first to arrive, I put several wounded officers known to me, among them Olga's old flame from the *Standart*, Lieutenant Simon Hendrikov He has a severe chest wound, and the doctors don't hold out much hope for him, but the train will go straight through to Czarskoe Selo, and you may be able to patch him up. The courier is leaving now. I will write tomorrow.

Your loving old hubby,
Nicky.

CHAPTER EIGHT

OLGA was thankful that this letter arrived so late in the evening that she soon had a chance to be alone. When the Czar was at GHQ the two elder girls had to sleep with their mother in turn, in the big double bed in her bedroom on the ground floor. It was too cold for their Russian blood in the winter, for the Czarina shared the liking of her grandmother Queen Victoria for cold and draughty rooms, and they were often awakened during the night as the restless woman turned on her pillows, or tiptoed in and out of the private chapel by a door on the right side of the bed. On this particular night it was Tatiana's turn to sleep downstairs, so Olga had the comfort of solitude in a warm room, with the door of the porcelain stove open to show the burning birch logs, and the snoring of the bulldog, Ortipo, the only sound in the February night.

She sat, propped up on a hard pillow, in the narrow bed prescribed for her by tradition, with the bright hair Simon had loved spilling over her white nightgown, and thought about the hospital train which her money had bought and which bore her name, crawling across the frozen countryside from Poland into Russia. She thought of the young officer who had kissed her hand in farewell six months before, and of whom she had heard nothing, enquired nothing, until now when by the most fortunate of all chances he was coming back to her. *If* he came back to her — if the doctors were wrong, as they had been wrong in Ania's case, about his chances of survival. If he were to come back only to die.

Olga Nicolaievna had seen death in many forms since the summer evening when sixty thousand men, vigorous and well, had shouted, 'Happy to serve Your Imperial Majesty!' The first time, death had come horribly to a soldier on the operating table, in the middle of surgery intended to save his life, and Olga, threading the needles in the operating theatre, had watched appalled as the red tide of a violent haemorrhage flowed across the table and dyed the sterile sheets. Since that day, at the end of November, she had watched others die more slowly and more tranquilly, often feeling a sense of total unreality as death came into the clean, well-tended wards so far from the battlefield. And Simon had been one of those who had lain for days without attention, not even on a pallet in a hospital corridor, but among other wounded men laid out like half-slaughtered animals in a railway yard. 'If only I were older,' she thought desperately. 'If only there was more that I could *make* them do!'

She knew already — she could not fail to know — the real power she exercised over the very limited public she was allowed to meet. At a big war charities concert given in Cinizelli's circus a little surprise had been sprung upon her — probably by Aunt Miechen, who enjoyed showing up the inefficiency of what she called 'The Grand Court' — in the presence, which she had not expected, of all the ambassadors and Ministers in Petrograd. Before the performance, the Grand Duchess Olga had 'made the circle' for the first time in her life. Young, blushing but very dignified, she had remembered all the names and faces, had said something appropriate to each one, and at the end even Aunt Miechen had swept her a little curtsey of approbation. The experience had lent her courage to ask the huge audience to give generously, and the giving had exceeded all expectations.

It was the same, on a smaller scale, at her weekly meetings in the Winter Palace. People gave large purses to the young Grand Duchess, and like Tatiana with her Refugee Committee, she checked the accounts most carefully, and kept lists of the various relief centres to which the money was destined. But how could she be sure that the money ever got there — that it didn't stick to a score of paws along the line, just as surely as the credits voted for armaments had gone in bribes and faked manifests? How could she, at nineteen and unmarried, embark on such a career of active good works as had already earned for her mother and Aunt Ella the ridicule of Russian society? How could she get away from society, and reach the people?

On her bedside table Olga had several volumes borrowed from her father's library, dealing with recent Russian history and Russian thought. She found them heavy going, for as the best of her tutors had noted, the Grand Duchess Olga's intellectual powers — much greater than those of her sisters — had

151

never received the right nourishment and training. But the librarian was delighted to lend them. Every month he sent what he considered the twenty best books published in several languages to the Czar's study; every month the books came back with the pages uncut. The Czar said he had no time for reading now; and in any case his tastes ran to English lady novelists with such melodious names as Mrs. Henry Wood, Mrs. Humphrey Ward, and Florence L. Barclay. So the librarian, bored with inactivity, was delighted to advise the Grand Duchess Olga, and even to let her take away — surreptitiously — a copy of *Anna Karenina,* prohibited by her mother as likely to cause 'unhealthy curiosity'. *Anna* had gone back as furtively as she had come, Olga's healthy sexual curiosity not having been much enlightened thereby; but the romantic poets remained; respectable as Russian classics, they were always on Olga's bedside table.

It was to Lermontov that she turned when the logs burned low, and the sleeping dog stretched himself full length on the rug. There was something in her father's letter that had made her think of a Lermontov poem about a soldier, which she had learned for recitation to Professor Petrov when she was twelve. The soldier had been shot in the chest like Simon Hendrikov. Olga had forgotten the title, but the verses began:

> I want to be alone with you
> A 'moment quite alone

and she found them easily in the book on her table:

> And yet if someone questions you
> Whoever it may be —
> Tell them a bullet hit me through
> The chest — and did for me.
> And say I died, and for the Czar,
> And say what fools the doctors are,
> And that I shook you by the hand,
> And spoke about my native land.

' "And say I died, *and for the Czar,*" ' she repeated aloud, and oh God! what a long way they had all come from that night in the rose-decked theatre at Krasnoe Selo, when the audience rose cheering at 'A Life for the Czar'! How many lives given already? How many more to lose?

Simon Hendrikov's battalion had been moved up to the line of the Vistula during the abortive advance of November, and there it survived until the engagement which reduced it to the strength of a single company. He vividly remembered being brought in to Warsaw, and laid on the floor of what had once been a station waiting-room, so it seemed logical to suppose he had been taken away from there by train. But of the train itself he could remember nothing, except a great deal of pain and jolting, and the occasional comfort of some cool liquid held to his mouth, until he became aware that he was in a clean, high hospital bed with white muslin screens around it, under a lofty ceiling where naked Loves and Graces played in a transparency of milky cloud. His right shoulder and arm were splinted, his wounded breast very tightly bandaged, but his head was almost clear. He said to the man in a white coat, with the stethoscope dangling round his neck, 'Where am I?'

'In the Catherine Palace hospital at Czarskoe Selo.'

'They brought me here from Warsaw? So near Petrograd? My family — ?'

'Your family knows your whereabouts, lieutenant. They'll be allowed to see you in a day or two, if all goes well.'

'Why not — today?'

'We've got to get you in better shape first. Don't worry, you'll be taken good care of. I've got you down on my list as a PP, so you get top treatment, Lieutenant Hendrikov.'

'What's a PP?'

'Palace Pet. Sent on to us by order of the Czar, travelling in the Grand Duchess Olga's hospital train, enquired for every few hours by the most exalted ladies in the land — we know the form! Now just let me listen for a moment, and then you can go back to sleep.'

He moved the stethoscope over Simon's bandaged chest, and nodded. 'You've been very lucky. The bullet smashed your shoulder-blade but missed your lung. Expect you'll have some trouble with the arm for a bit, but it'll come all right in time. Now here's Nurse Vera with some liquid nourishment. Good-bye.'

A little dark-haired nurse held a feeding cup to his lips with something bland and warm in it, and while he was trying to tell her that she had the same name as his mother Simon drifted off into a haze from which he was only roused by a cool wet cloth on his forehead and the sensation that his bandages were being undone. He opened his eyes to see a tall ward sister, with grizzled hair, lifting away the sterile dressings.

'I'm afraid this will be uncomfortable, lieutenant; I'm sorry,' she said, not unkindly. '. . . Now hold the bottle steady, nurse, and pay the tape out evenly.'

The treatment prescribed for a chest wound, still in danger of septicaemia, was to plug it with medicated tape taken from a bottle of disinfectant. Simon bit his lips on a groan. His eyes filled with water, and through the blur he saw a face he knew, intent on nothing but the task in hand. The sight connected with the doctor's words 'The Grand Duchess Olga's hospital train', and Simon said tentatively:

'Princess?'

'No talking please,' said the ward sister. 'The dressings, nurse.'

But when the bandaging was done to her satisfaction she went away at once, and the young nurse, clearing the dressings tray, had a moment to bend over Simon and whisper, 'I'm Tatiana Nicolaievna. My sister and I are very glad you're safe!'

'Is she here? The princess?'

'She'll come to see you in the morning. Now try to rest.'

He rested, ate a little solid food, drowsed, asked to be shaved and was refused; slept. And in the morning there she was, and he wasn't dreaming. His princess, dressed in white, just as he remembered her, was standing beside his bed.

'How are you, Simon Karlovich?' It was the most conventional of greetings, but her lips were trembling, and Simon could only gesture with his left hand. Olga guessed what he wanted, and put her own hand in his, so that he could carry it to his lips and kiss the palm and fingers, rougher than they had been. Then she put one hand on his hot brow, and stroked his unshaven cheek, and Simon whispered, 'My darling — *dushenka moya* — ' Then he saw her tears, and could say no more.

But that was the only moment of weakness. Next morning when she came Simon was better, all the better for being shaved, and very thankful to be shaved, since Olga was accompanied by the Czarina, herself looking worse than some of the patients, and leaning heavily on a stick.

'My poor boy,' said the Czarina, in the motherly tones her children loved when they were ill, 'we are all so sorry for you! So very glad you're off the danger list today!'

'Thanks to Your Imperial Majesties,' said Simon, with the slight movement of his head which had to do duty for a bow.

'Do you feel much pain in your shoulder this morning?'

'I don't feel much of anything, Madame.'

'And your arm?'

'I don't seem to be able to move it yet, but the doctor says that'll come.'

'Of course it will. And now a happy surprise! Your own mamma will soon be here to see you. I sent a car into Petrograd to fetch her, half an hour ago.'

'I don't know how to thank Your Majesty for so many kindnesses.'

'We have to take specially good care of our old friends from the *Standart*.'

He was a Palace Pet, no doubt about it. Simon could see in his mother's eyes that she thought so too, when she told him about the telephone call from the Czarina's lady-in-waiting, and the limousine with the footman which had so impressed the porter of their apartment building in the Fourth Line, and of the kind promise that his father and Dolly should be brought to see him next day. Not a word — and for this Simon adored her — did Madame Hendrikova say of the long winter of anxiety, and of the terror they had all felt for him after the last fighting on the Vistula; no, Simon was on the mend, thank God, and they could now look forward to the future.

But after this promising beginning Simon suffered a relapse, and some days of fever and great pain went by before his father was allowed to see him along with Dolly, on a special day's leave from school and revelling in the comforts of the palace hospital as she had once revelled in the luxury of the Europa restaurant. She was wild to leave school and start war nursing.

'It's a nasty messy job, Dolly, you wouldn't stand it very long.'

'Other girls can stand it, so why not me?'

'I suppose that means Mara Trenova has started nursing, and so you do too.'

'Mara? No, she really did get a job. I saw her at Christmas

and she said how busy she was. And once I saw her on the Nevski with a rough-looking man, an older man — she was so busy talking to him that she didn't see me.'

'I feel sorry for that poor little mother of hers,' said the professor. He kept still while Dolly chattered, with eyes only for his boy. He hardly realised who the young nurse was who came in so quietly, until he saw his daughter rise and sweep the newcomer her graceful Xenia curtsey. Then he got up hastily and bowed, while Simon said:

'Your Imperial Highness, may I present my sister Darya, and my father, Professor Hendrikov?'

'I'm so glad to know them both,' said Olga with a smile. 'Do forgive me for interrupting you! Our chief surgeon sent me with a message to you, professor. She would like to see you before you leave the hospital.'

'Your chief surgeon is a lady, Madame?'

'A very clever and capable lady, sir.'

'I hope this doesn't mean she has bad news for us?'

'I'm sure it doesn't,' Olga smiled. 'The lieutenant is making very good progress now. But Darya Karlovna!' looking at the blushing girl, 'you and I have met before. Didn't you present a purse of money to me, from the girls of the Xenia School, after the concert in the circus?'

'Yes if you please Your Imperial Highness,' said Dolly in one breath, and her brother came to her rescue.

'Dolly is envious of the young nurses here, Madame. She seems to have ambitions in that line herself.'

'Have you really?' said Olga. 'But aren't you still at school?'

'I'll be eighteen in March, please Your Imperial Highness, and my father says I can leave school at Easter, if I pass all my exams.'

'Then let's see what can be done at Easter,' Olga said. 'I'm sure you'd like Darya Karlovna to work near her home, professor? My cousin Dmitri Pavlovich has put his home on the Palace Quay at the disposal of the British Red Cross, and I know the charming English ladies taking charge of it are looking for Russian probationers. Will you allow her name to go foward — if she passes her exams?'

It was said with the smile Simon adored, so saucy and so lively, with the flash of perfect teeth in the pretty Russian face, and Olga quickly cut short their thanks. 'The orderly in the corridor will take you to the chief surgeon when the visiting hour is up,' she said. 'Good evening to you all!'

'Isn't she *wonderful?*' whispered Dolly, when the light footsteps died away across the ward.

'No Romanov ever came in a more charming guise,' her father said.

'You should have *seen* her at the circus, Simon! She was wearing the most beautiful blue dress — '

'I've seen her a hundred times wearing beautiful dresses,' Simon interrupted. 'Last summer, before this rotten mess began.'

'Does she nurse you herself?' said Dolly.

'God forbid!' Simon closed his eyes. It was bad enough to have Tatiana Nicolaievna at his bedside twice a day, assisting in the painful stuffing of his wound with tape. But to have Olga involved in the intimacies of the bedpan and blanket bath was worse than unthinkable.

Professor Hendrikov thought they were tiring the boy. He told Dolly to kiss her brother, and took her to wait in an anteroom while he went to see the surgeon-in-chief. Installed in one of the smaller reception rooms of Catherine the Great, where the modern desk and filing cabinets were in odd contrast to the baroque splendours of the walls and ceilings, the princess told him that his son's right arm was at present entirely paralysed, but that when the wound was sufficiently healed the paralysis might be overcome by 'electric therapy'.

'It is a new technique in Russia, at least in military hospitals,' she said. 'As a matter of form I should like your consent to its use on Lieutenant Hendrikov.'

'I'll consent to anything that'll do him good. Electrical techniques, eh? Isn't the apparatus very difficult to install, in an eighteenth-century palace?'

'I believe there have been certain problems,' admitted the princess, 'but our engineering section solved most of them within the first three months.'

'I'm inclined to wish I had been allowed to visit the Catherine Palace before the engineers took over.' The professor hesitated. 'Equipping it as a hospital must have cost a fortune.'

'It most certainly did.'

'At the public expense, princess?'
'Entirely at the expense of Their Imperial Majesties.'

New morning Simon's bed was rolled out of the screened alcove and into a long ward where it became one of twelve beds, arranged in two rows of six. Here he had the company of other men, just when he felt ready for it, but with no special privileges of receiving visitors, imperial or family. The only suggestion that he was still a Palace Pet came from the doctor who had given him the nickname, and who, on his first visit to Simon in the ward, remarked as he moved away:

'Remember, if you want some hypnotic treatment, lieutenant, we've a direct line to Rasputin.'

The man in the left hand bed snickered, the one in the right said 'Hush!' and the doctor was out of earshot before Simon found the right retort. He had heard the rumours about Rasputin and the Czarina — who had not? but he had never expected to hear, in an imperial palace, the kind of gibe that would have brought dirks out of their scabbards in the Marine Guards barracks. He himself was a model of frozen respect when the Czarina, tired and limping, made her next round of the wards. He saw that, however tender and maternal she could be when alone with a man on the danger list, her invincible stiffness and reserve prevented her full communication with badly wounded men. He remembered those, flung with himself into the charnel house of the railway station at Warsaw, who had raised themselves to kiss the Czar's shadow as he passed.

Alexandra Feodorovna, as a nursing sister, was still the empress he had known from afar at Livadia and aboard the *Standart*. She had the same pinched smile for every man she spoke to, and the same mechanical form of words. That morning it was, 'Are you feeling a wee bit more comfy today?' and Simon could see some of the men winking behind her back as she walked down the line of beds. That day each man received a holy picture, signed on the back by the Czarina and her children, and obviously much care had been taken to fit the pictures to the names of the patients. Simon was touched to receive the image of the Apostle Simon Zelotes, and propped it respectfully against a little flower vase on his bedside table.

The Grand Duchesses must have been kept busy in their

own wards, for Olga no longer accompanied her mother, and the taping of Simon's wound was taken over by Nurse Vera. As he grew stronger every day, the fact of not seeing her became a mild obsession: he could hardly believe that she had stroked his gaunt cheek and let him call her 'darling'. All winter long, in the snow and slime of the front, Olga had been the vision of his romantic idealism. He had believed in her as a spirit, just as many young men in other lands believed in the Angels of Mons. But now he had seen her again, neither an angel nor a princess, but simply a tired young nurse with a bedraggled apron, and a veil not as crisp as it might have been, and desire moved again in Simon Hendrikov's body, and the days without her took a long time to pass.

Presently he was promoted to a wheel-chair, and passed the mornings in an oval room, ornately decorated, which looked out through tall windows down the avenue leading from the main entrance to the palace. Here as many as fifty men, walking wounded or in wheel-chairs, could gather round tables laid out with table games like chess and dominoes, magazines and playing cards. These were largely neglected for the favourite Russian pastime of talking, and talking, of course, about the war. There was resignation rather than defeatism in the talk, for although the thinking of all of them had been conditioned by the débâcle of Tannenberg, although the first great flame of patriotism had been extinguished in 1914, never to be revived, there was a degree of optimism in the air. Two million more Russian recruits had been called to the colours, and the Grand Duke Nicholas was preparing for a new advance. The British and French, with troops from the British Empire, were about to come to Russia's aid in the Turkish campaign by moving in to the Black Sea, so that the capture of Constantinople, the realisation of the Byzantine dream, seemed to be a matter of weeks. By the time Simon's electrotherapy treatments started the Russians had captured the great Austro-Hungarian fortress of Przemysl, and the victory bells were ringing in Petrograd for the first time in many months.

There was always the ominous undertone that even though Galicia was entirely conquered, it had been by the bayonet and not by fire-power, while only force of numbers and great courage had taken the Russians across the Carpathians and into the vast plain of the Danube which lay below. But the overtone was all exultation, and Simon Hendrikov's exultation was that he now saw the Grand Duchess Olga every day.

The new electrotherapy wing had been installed in the Cameron gallery, which her Scottish architect had added to the great Catherine's palace, and the door of Olga's ward was set at right angles to the circular ante-room, hung with portraits of the nineteenth century, in which the patients waited to be summoned to their treatments. It was easy for Nurse Olga to slip out for a few minutes, once the timetable was established, and chat with Lieutenant Hendrikov, so far improved by now that he was wearing uniform, with his arm in a sling, and able to walk to the electrotherapy department on his own two feet.

In those brief meetings they took up their friendship again, as it had been in the previous summer at Livadia, but now as two human beings, not as the pretty princess and the dashing lieutenant of an operetta. The old etiquette was forgotten, for Olga insisted that Simon, as a patient, should remain seated, while she stood by the door left ajar 'in case ward sister pounces!' she said. And every time he went back to his own ward Simon Hendrikov wished that she was just Olga Romanova, an ordinary girl, a young nurse of the kind Dolly was cut out to be, warm-hearted and true; and that theirs could be the very ordinary romance of a wounded soldier and the girl he met in hospital.

But she was Olga Nicolaievna, the eldest daughter of the Czar.

The reminders of it were everywhere, in this resplendent palace of her ancestors.

Even the nineteenth-century portraits in the ante-room reminded him that the Romanov line went back for three hundred years, through Russia's greatest era of expansion and power. They were not good paintings, and some of them were highly imaginative, but the more recent ones had the merit of showing members of the Family in their younger days, before they assumed the sceptres and sashes of authority. One or two of them reminded Simon of Yakovlev, the naval commander he had met in the Fourth Line, and who now presumably was aboard the *Askelod* off the Island of Lemnos, the cruiser having been sent to represent Russia in the Allied attempt to force the Dardanelles. Yes — he had caught the resemblance at last: Commander Yakovlev had a certain look of Alexander II, the Czar-Liberator, and perhaps even more of Alexander III, who had been Olga's grandfather.

The Romanov look, written clearly on her own face.

Well, the Grand Dukes had scattered their seed lavishly across Russia; there was no reason why Yakovlev should not be a Romanov by-blow. But Olga's was the blood imperial: her place was in the circle round the throne.

She looked very little concerned with her imperial heritage on the bright day at the end of March when she met him, not — as so often — before his treatment, but afterwards, just as he left the electrotherapy department.

'How would you like to go for a drive with me, Simon Karlovich?'

'A drive? This morning?'

'Yes, quite a lot of the other men have been out since the weather turned so fine.'

'I know — but you did say a drive *with you*, didn't you?'

'Sister has given me the rest of the morning off, and the doctor says you can go. I wish we could take a sleigh and a troika, but the cold and the jolting might be too much for you. We'll take a limousine, and go gently round the parks. If you would like, that is.'

'If I *like*!'

'Then we'll meet on the ramp in twenty minutes, and Ivan will take care of you.'

There was always an Ivan, not very far away, and although the hospital orderlies didn't wear white cotton gloves like the palace footmen, there was always a pair of hands ready to serve an Imperial Highness. The orderly made Simon sit down, brought him his own uniform cap and gloves, a heavy hospital cape, a scarf and a pair of felt *valenki* big enough to fit over his hospital shoes, and finally, against Simon's rising protests, a wheel-chair, in which Lieutenant Hendrikov was taken into the fresh air for the first time in many weeks.

The big car with the imperial arms on the door was waiting on the ramp built for the convenience of Catherine II in her unwieldy old age, and Olga got out to help Simon, hampered by his splinted arm, to climb inside.

'Roll up the window, Ivan,' she said imperatively. 'The lieutenant must *not* catch cold.' She told the driver, 'Go very gently round the parks, and then bring us back to the hospital.'

The orderly, before closing the door, put two cushions deftly behind Simon's shoulder and splinted arm, and laid a fur-lined lap robe over his and Olga's knees. The big car glided down the ramp and started along the roads through the park, which were kept sanded for such outings. The snow sparkled in the sunshine with iridescent lights of pale gold and blue: the surface was still hard, but the sheathes of ice were dropping off the birch twigs, and the twitter of birds was beginning to be heard.

'This is wonderful,' said Simon Hendrikov.

'I thought you'd like it. But are you quite comfortable?'

'Very, thank you, except that I'm wrapped up like an Eskimo.'

Olga laughed. 'We mustn't risk a chill for you. Have you ever been in the park before? It used to be open to the public at certain times before the war.'

'I came here just once with my father, when I was a little kid. He used it for a history lesson, of course.'

'I'm not too sure of all the history myself. But look, there's the Chinese Pavilion, doesn't all that red and gold look pretty in the snow? And the Turkish Bath with the pink minaret on the other side of the lake? They didn't care how they mixed up styles and places, did they?'

'I remember the "Girl with a Pitcher" best, from the Pushkin poem.'

'Do you love Pushkin too?'

'I do, in spite of having to learn reams of him by heart at school.'

A plate glass partition divided them from the chauffeur in the imperial livery. Olga picked up a speaking tube and told the man to take the road leading past the 'Milkmaid' statue.

'There she is, your Pushkin heroine!'

But Simon had no eyes for the 'Girl with a Pitcher'. He had Olga beside him, living and warm, with a sable coat concealing her white uniform, and a peaked sable hat instead of her nurse's veil. He said impulsively: 'How lovely you look in furs! I never saw you wearing furs before.'

'It was summer when we met first, Simon Karlovich.'

'At Livadia. But that hat — it does look a bit like uniform. It makes me think of the morning you rode on to the parade ground at Krasnoe Selo, and your regiment cheered you —'

Olga said quietly, 'Do you know that the Hussars of Elizabethgrad were completely wiped out at Tannenberg?'

Simon held out his hand to her, on top of the lap robe, and she put her gloved hand into it. She sighed, and then he realised how tired she looked: pale, with shadowed eyes, and he blurted out:

'You look absolutely exhausted.'

'What a nice compliment.'

'It is; I know you're tired because you're doing far too much. How many hours did you spend in hospital yesterday?'

'I *am* a little tired, that's why Sister gave me half the morning off, but it's nothing to do with the hospital. I had to go into Petrograd last night to help my sister Tatiana, and we didn't get back until nearly two o'clock.'

'Help her, what with?'

'She's chairman of the Refugee Committee, it's a terrific job. And so many refugee trains came in yesterday afternoon that the committee simply couldn't cope: the shelter at the Narva Gate was overflowing. We ordered the emergency barracks on Golodai Island to be opened, and somehow they got food and bedding for them all.'

'Who's "they"?'

'Some of Tatiana's committee, and some Americans who've started working for it too. The American Ambassadress brought a motor car full of tinned food, and a Mr. Calvert from the consulate helped to distribute it. He's a man about your own age, very tall.'

'I think I know him, Joseph Calvert, dark-haired, with a sallow face? He's been taking Russian lessons from my mother.'

'Really? He speaks Russian very well. And he was a great help at the barracks — I liked him.'

'But it took you and Tatiana Nicolaievna to get the barracks opened. You were the only two who could really cope?'

'Oh no, but when we're there the others work harder, instead of just — philosophising. Sometimes I think we Russians are rather too fond of talking, instead of doing.'

'You ought to be at one of my parents' evening parties. Talk about talk!'

'I'd love to come! I'd love to see your home in Petrograd. Is it as nice as the dacha?' Simon smiled and shook his head.

The car had left the Catherine park, and crossing the avenue went into the other vast park which surrounded Olga's home, Quarenghi's masterpiece in honey-coloured stone, with its two wings balancing the central building, reached through the state entrance by a flight of steps and colonnades.

'It really looks prettier in summer,' said Olga apologetically, 'when the deer are wandering about the park, and the swans are on the lake. Still, the children enjoy skating in the winter — '

'Don't you?'

'I've no time for skating any more.'

They had been driven round the front of the palace to the garden side, where the flower-beds were covered with fir branches against the frost and the captured German machine-gun, prominently displayed, was protected by a tarpaulin. Beside the lake a miniature toboggan run, perhaps twenty feet high, had been constructed on a wooden framework, the top of which could be reached by a fireman's ladder.

'Why, there's Alexis Nicolaievich!' said Simon. 'Playing on the snow mountain.'

'He's crazy about snow mountains, we all are,' said Olga. 'But as he told me this morning, "it's no fun without papa".'

'Let's stop and watch them, may we?'

'If you're sure you won't be chilly?'

'With all these wraps, *and* a footwarmer?'

The car came to a standstill. Across the snow they saw Alexis appear at the summit of the snow mountain, and set his toboggan at the top of the ice chute, which was about three feet wide. A tall man in sailor's uniform sat firmly down on the long toboggan and took Alexis in his lap. With a squeal of delight from the boy they shot down to the bottom, where another man in a fur cap and fur-collared overcoat helped Alexis to his feet. Clapping his hands, the boy ran off round the base of the mountain to start all over again. He was quickly pursued by the sailor.

'That's not Derevenko, is it?' asked Simon.

'No, that's Nagorny, it's his week on duty. He takes such good care of Alexis!'

Simon remembered the last cruise on the *Standart*, and the

little boy's accident on the ladder. 'Is it quite safe for Alexis Nicolaievich?' he said uneasily.

'Oh quite; he's not allowed to go down alone. You should see him with Marie, she never brakes with her heels, and Nagorny does.'

'He's looking splendid, and he's having great fun,' said Simon. 'I was crazy about snow mountains myself, when I was a kid.'

'Really? Where was yours?'

'Well, we didn't have a private one, we went to the public parks. The best snow mountain in Peters — Petrograd, is always the one in the grounds of the Tauride Palace. It's about three times as high as yours.'

'Yes, well, there aren't so many grooms this year, to keep the buckets of water going. This one looks a bit patchy to me already.'

But now the attention of the Czarevich had been attracted to the stationary car, and he came running up, waving to his sister. Nagorny was running alongside, and the other man was not far behind Nagorny. It struck Simon Hendrikov that they were a lonely little group, hurrying across the expanse of snow with the great bulk of the palace behind them, and a spaniel, barking, bringing up the rear.

'Olga, come and play on the snow mountain!' The child stopped, embarrassed at the sight of his sister's companion, and Olga opened the door on her side of the car.

'Alexis, this is Lieutenant Hendrikov. You remember him last summer at Livadia?'

Alexis bowed.

'I remember you, lieutenant, and my sister Tania told me all about you. She said you'd been wounded, but you were very brave and didn't cry.'

'Well, no,' said Simon awkwardly.

'Where are you going to? Can I come for a drive with you?'

'We're on our way back to the hospital,' said Olga.

'Well, just *to* the hospital, then, and home again,' said the child, sure of his welcome, and climbing into the car.

'Be careful! Don't jostle Simon Karlovich's arm, whatever you do!'

'And Zilchik and Nagorny must come too.'

'The more the merrier,' said Olga resignedly. 'Lieutenant Hendrikov, this is my brother's tutor, Monsieur Gilliard. (Alexis, you are *not* to call him "Zilchik"). Nagorny, get in front beside the driver. Oh, not the dog too!' — for Alexis, with a shout of 'Joy! Joy!' was dragging his pet into the car. The dog, which had been rolling in the snow, immediately jumped on to the lap robe.

'We're imposing on you, Olga Nicolaievna,' said the Swiss tutor, as the car started, 'but you know how Alexis enjoys even a short spin —'

'Of course I do. But I thought you were going for a drive every afternoon in this fine weather?'

'We drive thirty versts some afternoons,' said Alexis to Simon. 'Where were you wounded, Simon Karlovich? Does your arm hurt you much?'

'On the Vistula, Alexis Nicolaievich, and it's getting better all the time. What do you do on such long drives?'

'I'm studying the railway system of the Petrograd suburbs,' said the boy importantly. 'Zilchik won't allow me to go into the city.'

'There are plenty of railway lines to study outside Petrograd,' suggested Simon.

'Oh yes, and I make notes of the bridges and tunnels, and the stations, and the repairs to the tracks, and everything.'

'I'm afraid it's only lessons in a pleasant form,' said Monsieur Gilliard, 'but it's excellent practice in mapping and memorising details, and we enjoy talking to the people we meet, don't we, Alexis?'

'Have you a model railway, Alexis Nicolaievich?' said Simon.

'Yes, a huge one, all over the schoolroom floor. I move my troop trains on it, and my hospital train too.'

'You'll be a great soldier, when you're a man.'

The boy hung his head in the sudden shyness of ten years old. Then he recovered, and gave Simon his sister's saucy smile, which in his rosy face was a boy's grin, and said:

'Anyway we take a different route each day, and the policemen can't keep up with us, it's lovely!'

They had made a short circle of the park, and the car stopped again near the garden entrance of the palace. The Czarevich and his party got out with many goodbyes and thanks, the boy turning to wave several times before he trudged off across the snow, with his hands deep in his overcoat pockets.

'He's grown a lot this winter,' Simon said. Olga was picking wet brown and white hairs off the lap robe.

'That miserable dog!' she said. 'I wonder Alexis doesn't take *him* down the snow mountain.'

'I don't think anybody'll go down this snow mountain again, unless the frost comes back,' said Simon. 'Look, it's beginning to melt.'

The sun of an early spring, even of the chilly Russian spring, was at high noon. The fir trees round the lake were shedding their loads of embossed snow, and where the ice chute had been patchy there was now a tiny rivulet of water.

'It doesn't matter,' said Olga, and slipped her hand once again into Simon's. 'It only means the winter's over now.'

CHAPTER NINE

On the night Richard Allen returned to his flat in Petrograd the spring thaw was well established, and a steady rain was washing the last grimy slush from the pavements of the Italianskaia. There were few pedestrians about at ten o'clock, and Joe Calvert, waiting in the living-room with a good fire in the stove, imagined that every footstep, heard so faintly through the double windows, marked the arrival of his friend.

The flat was still very much a bachelor apartment, and Joe had added very little to it except a score of books and a few prints of old St. Petersburg. The belongings left behind by Captain Allen — referred to as his 'stuff' — had not amounted to much beyond his golf clubs and his fishing tackle, for Dick had been a dedicated fisherman in the rivers of Finland on his occasional summer leaves. Joe had bundled this sporting equipment, along with a butterfly collection which surely dated from Dick's schooldays, into the wardrobe in the smaller bedroom. Nobody had occupied it during his tenancy, which had been extended for a further six months after the original three. Nor had he heard anything of his landlord, barring an exchange of letters about the extension of the lease, until Dick's telephone call had reached him at the consulate in the afternoon.

The ring at the front door bell took him by surprise. The bulky figure on the landing surprised him too, and he said, 'Good evening, sir,' in Russian, uncertainly, and then the man took off his fur hat, laughing, and was Dick.

'You son of a gun,' said Joe, punching the visitor on the arm as he took him into the lighted living-room, 'what's happened to the cloak and dagger stuff? I was expecting you to tippy-toe up the back stairs and slide through a secret panel in the service door.'

'I took a chance,' said Dick. 'D'you think any of the neighbours would have recognised me?'

'No,' said Joe more seriously, 'there's not much fear of that.

Put on a bit of weight, haven't you? And how about that beard?'

In the light of the crude electric chandelier he saw a Russian *bourgeois*, a stout, prosperous merchant in a fur-collared coat, with a well-trimmed moustache and beard — surely darker than the moustache Joe remembered — and gold pince-nez. Dick laughed.

'The beard I can't remove without a razor. The overweight is easily disposed of.' He took off the heavy overcoat, and the padded jacket and waistcoat underneath, and stretched luxuriously.

'That's quite a load to carry around,' he said, flinging the garments on a chair. 'Well, Joe, and how are you? Got a drink for me?'

'Sure, the vodka's all ready, and I've even got some ice.' Joe indicated a drinks tray, waiting on the writing desk.

'Vodka, eh? Breaking the wartime prohibition order?'

'Doesn't affect me, this is one of your own bottles,' Joe retorted. 'Thanks for leaving me the bar.'

'What's that you're having yourself?'

'Imported bourbon and branch water. Even the consular staff lives in luxury since the new ambassador took over.'

'Mr. Marye. I hear he's doing very well, and I hear great things of *you*, Joe.'

'You must be well informed in Stockholm. You came on from Stockholm, I suppose?'

'Actually I've been in Moscow. Came up on the night train, in time for breakfast at the Astoria.'

'It was nice of you to call me, especially when you didn't have to. It was part of the deal, wasn't it, that you were to keep your key, and come and go whenever you wanted?'

'Yes, but I wanted to be sure of seeing you, and I didn't want to upset any of your private plans.'

'Such as?'

'Such as having a pretty lady to dine and sleep.'

'That wouldn't have happened. I might have had some guys in for a poker session, but that's about all.'

'Leading a celibate life, are you?'

Joe shrugged. 'I wouldn't say that, exactly. But there's been nothing — nobody — that mattered at all.' He grinned. 'Maybe I'm waiting for Dolly Hendrikova to grow up.'

'Ah! How is that sweet child?'

'She's just started nursing at the Grand Duke Dmitri's hospital.'

'*His* hospital?'

'Well — his palace. The British Red Cross project. Dolly's brother's in hospital right now, out at Czarskoe Selo. He was wounded on the Vistula, end of January or beginning of February, I forget.'

'It seems a long time since your party at the Europa.'

'Doesn't it, though?'

'Have you seen much of the other girl, Mara Trenova?'

'Just once since then, at the Hendrikovs' Christmas party. She's going great guns in some publishing house, The Children's Castle I think it's called.'

'H'm, the "candy classics". That sounds rather a sugary diet for the fiery Trenova.'

'Top up your glass, Dick?'

'Thanks.'

Joe had been in the Foreign Service long enough to know that the preliminaries were now over. When he thought the friendly silence had lasted long enough, and Captain Allen, predictably, had filled and lit his pipe, he said easily:

'So what brings you to Petrograd, Dick? You're not going to throw me out of the flat, I hope?'

'Can't, until the end of May, and don't want to anyway. You like it here, eh? Old Varvara looking after you all right?'

'She gets by.'

'Good. As to what brought me back to Petrograd, well, that's quite a long story. And I can't even begin to tell it you until I know if you still feel the way you did last August.'

'In relation to the war?'

'In relation to American neutrality. You remember the day I offered you a sub-lease of the flat, you reminded me that as an officer of the American Foreign Service you couldn't "front" for anybody — I think that was your word — unless you knew what you were getting into. Do you still feel that way?'

'Look,' said Joe, 'we had no ambassador in Petersburg at that time. Petrograd I mean, damn it! Things have been a lot different since Ambassador Marye came. He really got the American colony together and started to organise charities. There's an American hospital for Russian wounded now, and an American crèche for babies, sort of tied in with the Grand Duchess Tatiana's Refugee Committee; it seems to me we've come out pretty strong on the Russian side.'

'Yes, but only for Russian charities, Joe! What about Russia in the war against Germany?'

'Now see here,' said Joe, 'President Wilson spelled out where he expects us to stand on that, just about the time you left for Stockholm. I think it was the first public statement he made after his wife died. He said, "Americans should be neutral in fact as well as name, impartial in thought as well as action." I know those were the words, I memorised them.'

'Yes, I remember,' said Richard Allen. 'Well?'

'But Mr. Page, our ambassador to the Court of St. James, he came right out and begged to disagree. He said, "A government can be neutral, but *no man* can be." And he'd been a very close friend of President Wilson.'

'It sounds like the end of a beautiful friendship to me,' said Dick flippantly. 'Joe, I think I see what you're driving at. You've come down on the Page side, and not on the President's?'

'As a man, I have. Way I see it, the Germans have been the aggressors all along the line. They want to take over the world, and sooner or later we'll have to line up with the guys who're out to stop them. That's my own opinion, Dick, in confidence, strictly unofficial; but just remember, I want to help every which way there is.'

'Thanks, Joe,' said the Englishman. 'That makes things easier.'

He leaned forward in the creaking wicker chair.

'There's one thing I want to ask you first, and then I'll tell you my story. Did you ever hear of an organisation called the Green Men?'

'Here in Petrograd?'

'Or in Moscow, or anywhere in Russia.'

'Would they be Moslems?'

'I hardly think it's likely. Why?'

'Green's the Prophet Mohammed's colour, and there's been a lot in the press about the new mosque near the Finland Station.'

'Apart from that, you've never heard of the Green Men?'

'Sorry; never.'

'Right. Look, I was sent to Stockholm because our Intelligence had become interested in the Green Men; it was believed to be a propaganda network — well, espionage, since you prefer that word — planning to start a revolution in Russia by spreading the rumour that the Czar would betray the nation by making a separate peace with Germany.'

'Because of Tannenberg?'

'Partly, and partly because the Czarina was German born, and has a brother fighting on the German side.'

'Do you really think it matters to the Russian peasants, the bulk of the population, that Ernest of Hesse is a German princeling in the Kaiser's army? They've probably never even heard the fellow's name,' said Joe.

'It's up to the Green Men to make it matter. And it could be done by way of Rasputin.'

'He's been lying low since he came back to Petrograd.'

'He wasn't lying low in Moscow a few nights ago,' said Dick. 'Didn't you know he'd gone to Moscow?'

'You bet; it was well advertised in the newspapers. Seems he took a vow last summer after he recovered from the wound that woman gave him, to make a pilgrimage to one of the shrines in the Kremlin.'

'His pilgrimage took him to a nightclub called "Yar", a few evenings ago. And I was there.'

'You went to Moscow to keep an eye on Rasputin?' said Joe.

'Yes, I was sent to Moscow to get a line on his contacts, if I could. The brute is so well guarded in his apartment here, with an army of plainclothesmen protecting the Little Fathers' beloved Grigori, that it isn't easy to get close to him. Especially after the stabbing in Siberia. So my assignment was to start fresh as a Moscow businessman — I know the milieu pretty well — and find out, if I could, how the money was flowing from Germany, through Stockholm, into the hands of Rasputin.'

'I don't believe he's all that interested in money. But go on!'

'It wasn't too difficult to get to meet him in Moscow, and I saw some interesting faces in his entourage. But within forty-eight hours the whole thing blew up at the "Yar" nightclub.'

'You went there with him?'

'I was there, but not with him. He came in late, and very drunk, with his hangers-on — men and women too — and after he'd drunk another bottle he began to sing and dance and howl like a Siberian wolf, breaking glasses and upsetting tables and crockery, until at last the manager and his staff intervened. Rasputin barricaded himself behind the furniture and made a wild speech at the pitch of his voice, saying they dare not touch him, he was protected by the Little Father and the Little Mother, "Matushka" as he calls her, who ate out of his hand — but he didn't say "hand". "I can make the old girl do anything I want", he yelled, "I've got what she likes best!" And then, just in case any of us had missed the point — he exposed himself.'

Dick Allen grinned savagely at Joe's face of disgust.

'The manager had sent for the police by this time,' he went on, 'and they arrested him. They had to.'

'You mean Rasputin's in *prison* in Moscow?'

'No such luck. He was arrested in the name of General Djunovski, the chief of the gendarmerie, supported by General Adrianov, the Prefect of Police. But in spite of that he was released at once, pending an investigation into the affair at the — very — highest — level.'

'Guess who,' said Joe.

'Exactly, guess who. And if, after these public insults to herself, the Czarina goes on protecting Rasputin — if at least a hundred witnesses are overruled, or never get a hearing — if the press censorship is clamped down on the story — then it may mean the fall of the monarchy.'

'And Russia will leave the war.'

'Exactly.'

Joe Calvert got up and poured himself more bourbon from the bottle imported by the American Embassy. He knew they had come to the crux of the matter — the desperate anxiety of the western Allies that Russia should continue the fight. The month of March had brought them two major reverses: the massacre of Neuve Chapelle and the failure of the Royal Navy to force the Straits of the Dardanelles, the gateway to Constantinople and the Black Sea: if Russia made a separate peace now the victory of the Central Powers was assured.

'You're kidding yourselves,' he said.

'We're what?'

'Kidding yourselves, if you think the Russian monarchy depends on Rasputin. Sure, the empress protects him — and I wouldn't bet on those two Moscow cops keeping their jobs — because she believes he's a holy man, and a holy man who has the power to cure her boy whenever he gets sick. But that's only part of it, Dick! You can't say the future of the Russian Empire depends upon a mad monk and a kid! For my money — and I've been following the whole thing pretty closely — the real danger to the monarchy, and the prosecution of the war, lies in the rotten, I mean rotten to the core, relationship between the Czar and the Duma.'

He was still standing by the drinks tray, and Dick looked up at him consideringly. The greenhorn of last summer had acquired authority; he spoke as if he was sure of himself, and knew what he was talking about. Young America comes of age, thought Richard Allen, and answered seriously:

'I think you attach too much importance to the Duma.'

'And why not? God damn it, why shouldn't the Duma be important? I know it's not the House of Commons. I know it isn't Congress. But it's all they've got as an elected assembly, a debating forum, and every time they pass a resolution he dislikes, the Czar simply winds up the session. He sulks out there at Czarskoe Selo and won't even receive the Ministers. That's where the inefficiency of this country begins, Dick — in the Alexander Palace at Czarskoe! That's why all the war supplies they bought from their Allies, and from us; coal, guns, munitions, are rusting and rotting on the docks at Archangel, because they can't even run a railroad efficiently! The Duma votes for a Munitions Council, the Czar says no dice. They try to sort out the arms shortage by indicting the War Minister —'

'And he's protected by the Czarina and Rasputin,' Dick interrupted. 'It's no good, Joe; everything comes back to those two —'

'— And the Green Men. I wouldn't care if your Green Men were as thick on the ground as the Green Mountain Boys in Vermont in 1775, I still say you can't pin every muddle in this country on Rasputin. You can't blame him for all the quarrelling between the Army Medical Service and the Zemstvo Red Cross; the like of which I've never witnessed in my life. Nor for the way the civil servants oppose everything that the county councils try to work out along with the town councils to get quarters and food for all those wretched refugees. Don't worry, Dick; I'll keep my ear to the ground for anything I can hear about your Green Men, but I think they're a damned sight less important than the Bolsheviki.'

'Most of whom are now living in Switzerland.'

'Don't you believe it! Those five members of the Duma who were tried and found guilty of conspiracy against the Empire — tried in a regular court of justice, and not by Rasputin — and packed off to Siberia only last month were Bolsheviki, meeting in "illegal assembly", as the prosecution called it, to debate Lenin's "Defeatist Thesis" that the victory of Germany will mean the downfall of the Czar. That's it, short and sweet! Lenin may be living in Zürich, but his instructions to Russian socialists to work for the defeat of Russia have been in circulation as an underground pamphlet for at least the last six weeks.'

'Have you seen one?'

'No, but I — what in hell is that?'

A tremendous explosion, which made the wooden shutters rattle and the porcelain stove shake in its brick foundation, sent its sound waves echoing across the city.

Both Joe and Dick were on their feet, but neither spoke. Some flakes of whitewash fell from the ceiling, and they could hear a trickle of dust behind the walls. Then the babble of an excited house broke out, and the doors were slammed, and feet ran up and down the stairs.

'Terrorists!' said Joe. 'The Winter Palace!'

'A hospital depot now —'

'But the girls go there,' said Joe. 'The young Grand Duchesses. I met them both there, the night they opened a barracks for the refugees — you stay still,' he went on urgently. 'I'm going up to the attics to find out.'

'You won't see much from a building this high.' But Joe was out of the flat by the back door and running up the service stairs to the attics, which he knew were divided into boxrooms and a few bedrooms for menservants, whom few tenants in the Italianskaia had employed since the outbreak of war. There he found a dozen people who had had the same idea as himself, and some had already opened two or three skylights and climbed up on chairs or storage chests to scan the sky. It was brilliantly illuminated by tongues of flame, which flickered against the rainfilled clouds and the dust of the great explosion to cover Petrograd with a lurid purple pall.

Joe took his turn at peering out, listening to the opinions of his neighbours (one of whom was convinced that the Kaiser's Zeppelins had got through to Petrograd) and hurried back to Dick.

'Well?'

'It's not the Winter Palace, that's for sure. It's a whole lot further to the east.'

'Oh my God!' said Richard Allen. 'Can it be the Arsenal?'

Joe stood aghast. The Arsenal of Petrograd occupied two huge building complexes, one on each side of the Liteini Prospekt near the Alexander Bridge across the Neva.

'If it's the Arsenal half the Liteini Prospekt must have gone up too,' he said. 'And it's awful goddamned close to our embassy. I think I ought to go and see.'

'I'm coming with you.'

Richard Allen began to put on his padded garments and gold pince-nez, the accoutrements of the Moscow merchant. As the legal tenant of the flat, he checked the heat of the porcelain stove and made sure the kitchen light was out while Joe fetched his own overcoat and fur hat. Before Dick opened the front door he stopped in the dark little hall and said to the American:

'You've caught Russian fever now, like the rest of us. You hear a bang and you think of a bomb. You feel a blast and the first word you say is "Terrorists!"'

'Oh, for God's sake, cut it out!' said Joe.

'Because if it is the Arsenal, then the only word is "sabotage".'

They met nobody on the staircase, everybody was in the attics or the street. Wherever the fire was, it was blazing wildly enough to send umbered shadows dancing on the yellow and white façades of the Italianskaia as the two young men hurried towards Sadovaia Street. There was no question of getting through to the American Embassy, for heavy police patrols were already clearing the main arteries for the passage of the fire engines and ambulances, likely to be quite inadequate to a disaster assuming an epic scale. At least three policemen assured Joe that the embassy was not in danger, neither was the Tauride Palace nor the Smolny Convent, all of which were in the same locality: the explosion had taken place at the Okhta munition works on the east side of the Neva.

'I'm afraid there's no doubt about it,' said Dick, who had been making his own enquiries among some of the more responsible elements in the crowd that was fast degenerating into a rabble. He spoke in French; English would hardly have been in keeping with the personage he was trying to create, and Joe answered in that language, 'It really is the Okhta?'

'Yes. The most important explosives factory in Petrograd, perhaps in the whole of Russia. And this in the middle of the advance! The factory that made everything from rifle bullets to machine-gun parts, and where the workers hardly ever went on strike! The munitions crisis will be twenty times worse than it was before.'

'They'll have to make an effort to bring on the Archangel stores.'

'Which will be a mere drop in the bucket compared to the weekly production of the Okhta.'

'You going to blame this on Rasputin too?'

Dick bared his teeth in a grin. They were slowly forging their way southwards through the crowd, in the direction of the Nevski Prospekt. Here and there old men and women were kneeling at the edge of the pavement, crossing themselves and praying aloud.

'They're praying to Saint Andrew and Saint Catherine to intercede for them,' said Dick. 'They say the explosion is a sign of God's wrath with Russia. This means another spiritual crisis, of course. Another excursion into the dark night of the Russian soul. All this, right on top of the Dardanelles — !'

'Where are we heading for?' said Joe.

'We might as well go back to the Astoria and have a drink — I've got a room there, by the way, in the name of Shulkov, and I'm expecting a call from Moscow within the next hour. If the Okhta disaster doesn't foul up the whole telephone system, that is.'

'I might try calling our embassy, just to make sure — ' Joe began, and then, pointing across the street, he interrupted himself to say, 'Look, Dick! Isn't that Mara Trenova?'

'You've got better sight than I have, old chap. That girl in the red fox hat, holding on to a fellow's arm, beside the tram stop?'

'She's not holding on to him, stupid, she's *struggling* with him! My God, he's going to hit her! It *is* Mara Trenova, I tell you!'

'He hasn't hit her, and she's got away from him,' said Dick, peering short-sightedly at the lighted corner of the Nevski, where the surging crowd made it difficult to judge the movements of any two figures as the tram cars set down and took up their passengers. 'Look, Joe,' he said, himself grasping the American's arm, 'even if it is the Trenova girl, don't interfere. You haven't been seeing her, so keep it that way. There's enough trouble afoot tonight without getting involved with —'

He had meant to say 'with one of Russia's eternal victims', but the far-fetched phrase died on Dick Allen's lips as Joe gave him a light slap on the shoulder, said, 'Call me at the consulate tomorrow!' and threaded his way through the crowd on their side of the pavement with a footballer's grace. He had never lost sight of the red fox hat, and soon caught up with Mara, walking stiffly and as if blindly, back up the Nevski in the direction of the Winter Palace.

'Good evening, Mara Ivanovna,' he said as he came abreast of her. 'Can I be of any help?'

She looked up at him, startled, and he saw tears and dirt on her pale face.

'Mr. Calvert!' He had spoken to her in Russian, and she hardly knew how to address him, having heard him object, in what seemed like another life, to 'Yusuv Yurievich'. She said uncertainly, 'Thank you, I'm very glad to see you, but I don't need help.'

'I was afraid you were in some kind of trouble — or distress.'

'I'd just — just heard of a friend's death. Well, not a friend exactly, just someone I knew . . . It shocked me.'

'*Not* Simon Hendrikov?'

Her sudden peal of laughter, cutting through the noise of the avenue, was as shocking to Joe as her stained face and bare hands, which he now saw were bruised and bleeding at the base of the palms.

'Oh no, not Simon Karlovich, Mr. Calvert. He's making splendid progress, with the whole imperial family to fawn over him and feed him with black grapes and champagne. No, just an acquaintance. Somebody you would never have dreamed of knowing —'

'Come on now,' said Joe, 'you don't know what you're saying. You got caught in that crowd, didn't you, and everybody was pushing and shoving like mad, and you stumbled and hurt yourself, wasn't that it?'

'My coat,' said Mara, looking down at the wet stains above her knees, 'yes, somewhere back there, I must have fallen — it was silly of me.'

'Not silly at all, on a night like this.' Joe looked about him. They were nearly at the Hotel Europa. He couldn't take her in there, bedraggled as she was, and the few teashops still open were crammed with soldiers and their girls. 'We're just five minutes from my place,' he said. 'Come back and wash your hands and let me make you a cup of tea.'

'Oh, but —'

'And don't tell me you were hurrying home to mother, because you were walking in the opposite direction.'

'All right.' Mara made no further protest, but let him take her arm, and walked round the corner to Joe's flat as if it were quite natural for her to go alone to a man's rooms. In the flat he helped her off with her coat, and gently drew the torn woollen gloves from her hands.

'Let me take your hat too,' he said. 'Red fox. The colour suits you.'

'One of Dolly Hendrikova's cast-offs. Just right for me.'

'You're not a cast-off person. Don't rate yourself so low, and now come and wash those hands.'

He showed her to the bathroom, found her a clean towel and a bottle of iodine, and went to the primitive kitchen. The samovar from which Varvara drank tea all day long was not quite cold, and he had a hot glass of tea, well sugared, ready and waiting when Mara Trenova came out of the bathroom, looking much refreshed.

'Sit in the basket chair and drink your tea,' he said. 'And don't let any false modesty stop you from telling me this: were your knees cut too? Because if so, you're going to need more first aid.'

'No, it's all right. My coat and skirt and things protected them.'

'Somebody really barged into you, to make you fall like that.'

'I suppose so.' He was watching her, drinking the sweet tea

179

greedily. She had accepted the version of someone knocking into her just as she accepted his first suggestion that she must have stumbled and fallen in the crowd. Joe wondered if either version was the truth. He remembered the short thick-set man struggling with her in the half-darkness at the corner of Sadovaia Street.

'This is Captain Allen's flat, isn't it? You told us about renting it, that night of the dinner at the Hotel Europa.'

'That's right. I've been here ever since.'

'It's very nice. And Captain Allen, is he still in Stockholm?'

'Still in Stockholm.' Mara put down the empty glass and said, in her prickly, defensive way:

'I was very sorry not to be able to return your hospitality. But really I can't invite anybody to my humble home.'

'I told you already, don't underestimate yourself.'

Joe pulled his own chair up to Mara's and took one of the abraded hands, now brown-streaked with iodine. She let him stroke it gently, and seemed to relax, but he felt that she was still trembling.

'You had a bad fright,' he said. 'Were you anywhere near the munitions factory at the time of the explosion?'

Mara shuddered. 'Near enough.'

'Then no wonder you were scared, I didn't like it much myself.'

'Do you think they've got the fire under control by now?'

'If they haven't, a whole lot of tenements must have been gutted. God! I hope they got the people out in time.' He slipped his arm round her thin shoulders.

'This friend of yours, whose death upset you so, was he killed in action?'

'I suppose — you could say — he died for what he believed in.'

'That's as much as any man can do. Mara! Please don't cry!'

But she wasn't really crying, she was looking at Joe Calvert with the unfocussed look which had alarmed him on the Nevski Prospekt. And while she murmured, 'You're very sweet to me,' it changed unmistakably into a look of invitation. He leaned forward and lifted her out of the basket chair and into his embrace.

He kissed her cheek and then her lips, cradling her in his lap and feeling her warm against his chest and thighs. She was very light, but there was a strength in her arms as she locked them round his neck which told Joe that Mara Trenova was his for the taking, God knew for what reason, but certainly not for love. And he loved her no more than his occasional café pick-up, but there was something about her, something corrupt and bitter, which had fascinated him since the night they met. Now she was in his arms, and to the bitterness was added the aphrodisiac of a strangely mixed perfume, compounded of his own soap and some cheap scent like appleblossom, and a chemical smell which reminded him of the lab. at school.

He raised his head and saw that she was watching him between her half-closed lids. As he met that calculating look, so far removed from tenderness or even lust, he identified the smell. It was picric acid.

Picric acid, extensively used in the manufacture of explosives, whether explosives were made in the Okhta Works or in some cellar in the back alleys of Petrograd.

He didn't know, didn't want to know, what she had been doing. It was none of his business, whatever Dick might think. But he also knew he couldn't take Mara Trenova to bed, as she obviously meant him to do, to consume him, to blur his perceptions of — what? Feeling like his Bible namesake escaping from Potiphar's wife, feeling like a chilled, emasculate, useless fool, he kissed Mara lightly and said:

'You're feeling better now, aren't you? Come on, cheer up, and I'll take you out to supper at "The Bear".'

CHAPTER TEN

THE pious Russians who knelt to pray in the streets of Petrograd on the night of the munitions factory disaster, and crowded the churches of the capital next day, were soon justified in their belief that the tragedy was a bad omen for the war. Within a matter of days the western Allies and the troops of the British Empire were defeated in their first attempt to attack Turkey by land in Asia Minor and Gallipoli. Although Enver Pasha and the Young Turks might have dragged Sultan Mohammed V into a dangerous adventure, a far greater man than Enver was prepared to confront Turkey's enemies, and on the heights called Ariburnu, above the landing beach which came to be known as Anzac Cove, Colonel Mustafa Kemal repelled the western invaders and took the first giant step into his own dramatic future.

On the heels of Kemal's victory, the German advance began. It came a few days too late for Italy, for the Italian government, convinced that the Russians had defeated Austria, slipped down off its congenial position on the fence of neutrality and stabbed Austria-Hungary in the back with a formal declaration of war. Then the German war machine went into action in the northern sector of the long front. The immense German superiority in weapons and fire-power was felt once more, and while in Flanders the battle of Second Ypres was raging, the Russians had to surrender the great fortress of Przemysl, the prize they had held for two months only.

At the time the Germans began their drive through Poland, the Russian casualties amounted to four million men, and it became necessary to consider calling up the Second Category, the *opolchenie*, of untrained men between the ages of eighteen and forty-three. It was an extreme measure, for the Second Category had only been called up twice in Russian history — in 1812 against Napoleon I, and in 1854, during the Crimean War. There was now not a town, not a village, not an *isba* in Russia which had not given its toll of young men to the war.

June came round again, the war was nearly a year old, and in spite of the lengthening shadows over the Empire there were girls in Russia who still nursed a secret happiness. One was the Grand Duchess Olga, who by good fortune had her sweetheart close to her. Simon Hendrikov, discharged from hospital and pronounced fit for light military duty, was in the Marine Guards barracks at Czarskoe Selo, one of the élite body — now largely composed of war veterans — whose special duty was to protect the imperial family. As the summer dawn broke earlier and earlier, the Czarina was edified by her eldest daughter's early morning visits to the little Znamenia church near the palace. Olga had always been less willing than her sisters to give herself up to the long services, the frequent hours of prayer which fed the Czarina's mystical fervour, and the mother encouraged the humble walks on foot to the Znamenia and the brief devotions which, Olga declared, sustained her all day long in hospital and city.

The real refreshment, of course, was the half-hour she spent with Lieutenant Hendrikov before they went to their respective duties. Their meetings were not furtive, for they walked openly in the park, and fed the deer now turned out for the summer, and gathered branches of lilac, purple and white, for the wards of the palace hospital. The 'botanists' knew all about their idyll, for the secret police were botanising as usual among the shrubberies and the rose parterres, and the Cossacks cantering along their perpetual round of the avenues of Czarskoe Selo knew something about it, for they often saluted the young officer of the Garde Equipage who had just saluted his princess before she entered the gates of the Catherine Palace. The three girls who made up the rest of the group which had once signed itself OTMA may have suspected it, but they said nothing. The Czarina was in a state of exalted ignorance, for she had but two aims in life at that time, to get the Grand Duke Nicholas removed from the supreme command, and to contradict the foul lies, as she called them, which were circulating in Petrograd about the sainted Father Grigori's behaviour in a vile Moscow nightclub, where of course he had never set his holy foot.

The Czar was at GHQ at Baranovichi.

There came a fine June day when Olga was relaxing contentedly after a night on duty at the hospital. She had slept undisturbed for most of the morning, her mother being at a Red Cross meeting in the city. Then she had a wing of chicken, a peach and a glass of wine, played the nursery piano to Alexis's balalaika, and saw the boy off for a drive in his donkey cart, Alexis holding Vanka's reins and Marie sitting watchfully beside him. Anastasia had received an imposition from Monseur Gillard and was dolefully studying French verbs.

'Come on, you silly kid, and I'll hear your pluperfect subjunctives,' Olga called at last. Tatiana was at the hospital, and Olga had taken a leisurely bath in the solid silver tub used by all the sisters, and washed her hair with a lotion scented with her favourite essence of tea rose. The four girls had no personal maids, but they had several attendants, young women of good family who, but for the war, might have become maids of honour to the Grand Duchesses. One of them was brushing Olga's bright hair as she sat near the window in her white cambric wrapper and listened to Anastasia stumbling through the subjunctive mood.

It was a drowsy, peaceful scene, broken suddenly by a knock at the door.

'Come in!' said Olga.

The door opened to admit a fair-haired young footman, who had only recently entered service in the private apartments of the palace. He bowed apologetically.

'Your Imperial Highness, Father Grigori requests the honour of an audience —'

'Stand back, little brother!'

Rasputin motioned the footman from his path. He strode into the pretty feminine room, almost stumbled over a footstool, and clutched at the back of a chair to steady himself. Wearing the coarse, knee-length tunic of a peasant with a worn leather belt and high boots, his hair matted and greasy, he automatically raised one dirty hand in blessing.

'Where's Matushka?' was all he said.

Olga had risen to her feet, tying the ribbons of her wrapper across her young breast, while the French grammar in her lap fell to the floor, and Anastasia, who had risen too, moved a step backwards in dismay. The girl with the brush stood petrified behind Olga's low chair.

'*What* did you say?' asked the Grand Duchess disbelievingly.

'I said, "Where's Ma?" Where *is* the old girl?' said the monk.

Olga looked at the footman, standing at attention by the open door. 'Go to the Commandant of the Palace,' she said. 'Tell him to call four Cossacks of the Escort and bring them to me at once. And hurry!' She turned furiously on Rasputin. 'Her Imperial Majesty is at the Winter Palace,' she said. 'Your spies should keep you in better touch with her movements. And His Majesty, my father, forbade you years ago to enter these apartments.'

Rasputin's eyes narrowed. He took two steps towards Olga, and she felt the smell of stale brandy and foul breath.

'So!' he said. 'Little kittens are growing long claws, are they? Little Olga plays at being the great Catherine, eh? What would a sceptre feel like in that pretty hand? No, no!' He changed to a wheedling tone. 'Your faithful Grigori was only joking. But Olga Nicolaievna, lovey, little sister, Grigori needs Matushka's help. Batiushka Czar is far away, out of reach, and I need help today —'

'What sort of help?'

'My boy,' the monk said cunningly, 'my only son. They say he must be called up with the Second Category. A soldier, Grigori's boy Mitia, the mainstay of the family, the poor little family at Povrovskoe! This must not be. Tell Matushka she must write a line, an order to set the poor boy free —'

'Other men's sons have gone to the war, and given their lives for their country,' said the Grand Duchess Olga. 'Why should yours be exempt?'

'Ah, now you argue, now you're willing to bargain, like a country girl!' said Rasputin. His magnetic eyes, half closed, travelled all over her body with the sensuous look which had overcome the resistance of a thousand silly women in the so-called society of Petrograd. 'And what a lovely country girl you'd be. Gold hair, white breast, strong legs to clasp your lover with, when the handsome lieutenant takes you into the bushes after the village fair —'

'You're wasting your time, glaring and grimacing,' Olga said. 'I'm not a subject for hypnosis.' The first shock of the monk's appearance was over, and she was completely in command of the situation. Rasputin seemed to feel it by instinct. He said, more calmly, 'I'll ask Matushka to give me my son back as I have often given her back her own. And you, little sister, I'll give you something extra, to make up for having offended you: I'll tell you the secret of the Green Men.'

'Who are they?'

'What, you've never heard of the Green Men? They're friends of mine, good friends. Most of them live in Sweden, with the trolls who dig the precious metal from the secret mines. But *their* friends, my friends too, they live in Russia. Some here, some there, some in Siberia. *I* call them the Greenishes. Wouldn't you like to know what Batiushka Czar should call them?'

'I neither want to know nor care,' said Olga. She had heard the tramp of the Cossacks coming down the gallery, and sighed with relief. The fair-haired footman flung the door open, the Commandant and his escort came in.

'In what way may I serve Your Imperial Highness?' the soldier said.

'Order your men to take Grisha Rasputin and escort him from the palace and the grounds,' said Olga. 'He is to be put out at the gate leading to Srednaia Avenue, where he has friends. He is never again to be admitted to this part of the palace. Warn the sentries accordingly, and you —' she turned like a fury on the footman, 'you there — what's your name — Ivan! You are dismissed for a grave breach of trust, and if I ever hear of you in the imperial service at any time or place, I'll have you flogged.'

It was the Romanov temper, which had skipped a generation: the rage which the Commandant, at least, was old enough to remember in Alexander III. He saluted hastily. He said, 'Happy to serve Your Imperial Highness!' and ordered his men to take Rasputin and the footman from the room. The young man walked out in silence. Rasputin could be heard swearing horribly all the way to the top of the stairs.

'I'll get dressed now, please,' said Olga to the young attendant. The girl was thankful to hurry away to the big dressing-room next door, to lay out the first summer cotton that came to hand, and Anastasia moved closer to her sister.

'Olga — won't mamma be terribly angry?'

'Probably.'

'Because you know she's going to say just what *he* said, that he's saved Baby, over and over again —'

186

'Alexis is very tired of being called Baby, or haven't you noticed? Why don't you run away, and see what he and Marie are up to? I think you know your verbs quite well enough by now.'

'Oh, thank you, Olga!' The child was glad to escape. When Olga was dressed she went downstairs to the library, where nobody would think of looking for her, and persuaded the librarian to lend her one of the forbidden books, so as to compound her act of defiance. Protesting, he gave her Tolstoy's *Resurrection*, which she had dipped into furtively before, and then he sat down to work at the Czar's neglected stamp collection, while Olga took her place by the open window and began to turn the pages of the book.

She was quite incapable of reading the text, because her brain was occupied by the scene with Rasputin and its inevitable consequences. He went straight to Ania, and she telephoned to mother at the Winter Palace, she thought. Then mother went directly to the Srednaia, to get a full account of my misdeeds. Well! I'm glad I did it; it was high time.

Olga mechanically turned the pages of *Resurrection*, looking at the illustrations by Leonid Pasternak, showing the thief and prostitute Maslova in the courtroom and on her way to Siberia. Maslova stood alone in the emptying courtroom 'After the Sentence', behind her stood a guard with a drawn sabre, his heavy left hand on her arm. She wondered if the Cossacks had hustled Rasputin out like Maslova, delighted — she was sure of it — to have her authority to lay rough hands on the charlatan. I wish I could send him to prison, she thought, and looked vengefully at the pictures in *Resurrection* of the prisoner gangs stumbling through the Siberian snow to Tiumen, to Ekaterinburg. Poor Maslova, more sinned against than sinning! Her fate seemed remote from the life of an Imperial Highness, safe in her father's palace of Czarskoe Selo, who had nothing to fear but the sound of her mother's limousine purring round the long driveway by the lake.

It came, and there was a silence as if the palace held its breath, which lasted for perhaps a quarter of an hour. Then Tatiana, rather out of breath herself, appeared at the library door.

'Oh, there you are!' she said to Olga. 'I've been looking for you everywhere.'

'You're back early.'

'Mamma telephoned to the hospital. She wants to see you in the drawing-room.'

The private drawing-room of the Czarina had been decorated at the time of her marriage in pale green, with spindling Chippendale furniture. Through the years innumerable portraits of her family had been added to the walls, which were dominated by a huge painting of Marie Antoinette, for whom the Czarina had a special cult. There were flowers in profusion, and among the nick-nacks on the glass-topped tables a number of devotional books and slim volumes of poetry, all bound in limp mauve leather and embossed with the Czarina's favourite emblem, the swastika. The Czarina herself was standing by an étagère of mauve sweetpeas, forced in the palace hothouses. She was still wearing the dust cape she used for motoring, and twisting a long pair of beige suede gloves between her hands.

'Olga!' she said, and by the very tones of her voice her daughters knew that she was in a state of barely suppressed hysteria. 'Olga, I sent for you — I want to hear the truth from your own lips — could you, dared you, insult Our Friend today, here in this very house?'

'I'm sure you've already heard the truth, with a few additions, from himself and Ania,' said Olga.

'Never mind about Ania; leave Ania out of this. Father Grigori, the best friend we've ever had or ever will have, came here in great distress to ask a favour of myself. You repaid him for years of prayer on our behalf, for interceding at the throne of the Most High for Baby's very life, by sending for soldiers to remove him from our home like a common thief —'

'Or a common drunk,' said Olga. 'He may have sobered up before you ran to comfort him at Ania's, but he was tipsy when he lurched into my bedroom, where I was sitting only half-dressed —'

'Drunk!' cried the Czarina. 'That's a lie! So you have joined the pack too, Olga: the enemies who are hunting Father Grigori down! "Grisha Rasputin", he says you called him — the insolence, the disrespect —'

'That's what he calls himself,' said Olga, 'when he's drinking and singing in the bath houses, naked with the women of the town.'

'Olga!'

'And if there's a pack,' said Olga mercilessly, 'it's a pretty big one. It's composed of all the Duma, half the High Command, most of the daily press, my grandmother — and my father.'

The Czarina collapsed into an armchair, and waved back Tatiana, who had started to her side.

'Tania, go to your room and rest, darling —'

'Stay where you are, Tatiana,' Olga said. 'Let's have this out once and for all; it affects you as much as it does me. You can remember, and maybe the Little Pair can too, the night five years ago when Rasputin came into our rooms when we were all in our nightdresses, and he tried to tickle us and play kissing games with us, until the nursemaids ran to bring our governess to make him stop. Oh yes, we had a governess then! Madame Tutcheva, the only educated woman who ever took charge of us, and she complained to papa about Rasputin, and papa forbade him ever to come near our rooms again. Of course you had your revenge; you sent our governess away, and today Rasputin was too drunk to remember the rule, or thought he could take a chance while papa was at the Stavka. And then he must have bribed that new footman to admit him by the private stair —'

'So you took it upon yourself, you had the impertinence, to dismiss one of my servants —'

'I would dismiss the Commandant of the Palace himself if he betrayed us to Rasputin. Mother, when will you understand that by the favours you show to this *strannik* — for that's all he was, a wandering hedge-priest, living by charity and his wits until *you* raised him up — you're destroying the people's faith in you, and in all of us? Stolypin made my father send him home to Siberia once. After what he did today, mightn't it be possible to have him sent back again?'

'The people's faith!' cried the Czarina, catching at the words. 'What people? The good Russian men, the peasants, worship Father Grigori as they worship their Little Father the Czar. The people who hate him are only certain people in Saint — Petrograd: that rotten town, not an atom Russian, and I know who they are! Aunt Miechen and her horrible sons, and Nikolai Mihailovich, who has detested me since I was a girl of seventeen, when your father fell in love with me; and Paul's wife, and even Dmitri now! All the people hate *me*, because they know I have a strong will, I don't change my mind, and that they can't bear! But I am strong because I'm blessed by Grigori! I can even bear the wounds you've dealt me, Olga! Oh, my heart . . . my heart!'

Clutching the right side of her body, the Czarina fell heavily across the arm of her chair. Tatiana ran to kneel beside her mother.

'Palpitations,' said Olga, tugging at the long embroidered bell pull. 'I'll tell them to send the doctors. She'll be all right.'

She said a word to the anxious ladies-in-waiting in the ante-room and went upstairs. It was a long time until anyone came near her. Then she rang for her girl attendants, enquired for the Czarina and was told Her Majesty was resting comfortably in bed. Olga said she would like to have a supper tray in her own room at eight o'clock. She had been on night duty for a week, and so was not due back at hospital until eight next morning.

A tray of eggs and fruit, with the pot of coffee she had especially asked for, made its appearance in due course, and Olga fetched her cigarettes from the pocket of her hospital cape. For the first time in her life she smoked in her own bedroom in the palace. And as she smoked she thought over the scenes of the day, not without a sense of triumph, and not without reflection on Rasputin's curious references to the Green Men and the Greenishes. Was he merely babbling because he had drunk too much brandy? Or were the Green Men real, who if they were Rasputin's friends could only be ranged on the side of evil? She was trying to think of German regiments which wore green jackets — huntsmen, Jägers — when, the tray having been removed and fresh coffee brought, Tatiana at last came in.

'Olga, this has been a dreadful day!'

'You missed the worst of it.'

'Oh yes, sweetie, I know Father Grigori was very naughty, and deep down inside her mamma knows it too, but still — to have him thrown out!'

'I was only sorry I couldn't do it with my own hands.'

'Olga, why do you say such things, when you know how it upsets mamma? She's sent the most dreadful telegram to Bar-anovichi.'

'Where I should think father has other things on his mind than Rasputin and me.'

'Maybe, but why don't you come downstairs now, and say you're sorry, and then you can both kiss and make up?'

'Because I'm not sorry, and I'm not a baby now, Tania. I did my best to tell her the truth tonight, but if she won't listen —'

Tatiana, with a gesture of despair, went into the dressing-room. When she came out she had her nightdress and wrapper over her arm.

'Going to bed already? It's only nine o'clock.'

'I know, but mamma's in such a nervous state, and they don't want to give her veronal. I think she might sleep if I went to bed . . . I'm sorry, Olga. I know it's your turn, but she wants me to sleep with her tonight.'

'You're very welcome. And you might take your snoring bulldog with you, if you want to do me a real favour.'

'You don't have to quarrel with me too,' said Tatiana sorrowfully. 'Come along, Ortipo.'

The Grand Duchess Olga had one more visitor before the palace clock struck half past nine. This was the Heir to the Throne, who in white pyjamas and carrying his big grey cat in his arms, slipped into her room with a quick glance behind him.

'Alexis!' exclaimed his sister, 'you ought to be in bed and sound asleep.'

'I can't go to sleep in the daylight,' said the boy, 'so when Zilchik went down to dinner I thought I'd come along and see you.'

'Cat and all?'

'Yes, I brought Pussy too, in case you were feeling a bit lonely. I'd like him to stay with you all night.'

'That's very sweet of you, Alexis.' The big spoiled cat, now sniffing suspiciously at the place where Ortipo had been lying on the rug, was as welcome to Olga as the snoring bulldog, but she knew the gift of his company was the most important Alexis had to offer, and she pulled the boy close to her and gave him a hug.

'Olga, is it true you've been very naughty?'

'I don't think so. I think I've been very sensible, but then grown-up people have different ways of looking at the same thing.'

'I expect so.' The beautiful blue-grey eyes, so like their

mother's, were turned thoughtfully on Olga's face. 'I wish papa were here.'

'Oh, so do I.'

'But anyway I brought you my sugar ration.' From the pocket of his pyjama jacket Alexis produced a small white linen package and handed it to Olga. 'That's my handkerchief for tomorrow morning,' he said anxiously. 'It's perfectly clean.'

It was, but the effect was somewhat spoiled by the collection of assorted nails which the Czarevich, an inveterate hoarder, had wrapped up with two cubes of beet sugar, and Olga stifled a giggle.

'Are the nails for me too?'

'No, just the sugar. Don't you want to eat it now?'

'You eat one bit and I'll save the other for my last cup of coffee. You're sweet, Alexis, but honestly Monsieur Gilliard will have a fit if he comes up and finds you're not in bed.'

'All right.' Alexis crunched contentedly. Then he flung one arm round Olga's neck and gave her a sugary good night kiss. His lips were close to her ear when she heard him whisper, 'I don't like Father Grigori very much myself!'

When he had gone she settled down to *Resurrection*, which the librarian had thoughtfully sent up to her room.

'The cell in which Maslova was imprisoned,' she read, 'was a long room twenty-one feet long and sixteen feet wide, occupied by fifteen persons. Two-thirds of the room was taken up by shelves used as beds. By the door there was a dark spot on the floor on which stood a stinking tub —' She laid the book down in disgust. So those were the conditions of women prisoners, politicals or criminals, on the long road to Siberia! The dimensions of the room she shared with her sister were almost exactly the same as the den occupied by Maslova and her fourteen companions in misfortune. But this beautiful room, into which Rasputin with his foul breath had stumbled, affected Olga now as something like a prison cell. She threw her hospital cape round her shoulders and went into the broad gallery, warm with the sunset light.

Alexis was not the only wakeful one among the imperial children. The door of the Little Pair's bedroom was ajar, and through it Olga could hear Anastasia, in a very good imitation of her own voice, declaiming:

' "You are dismissed for a grave breach of trust, and if I ever hear of you in the imperial service at any time or place, I'll have you flogged." ' The dramatic pause was filled by Marie's uncontrollable giggle.

It was a great temptation to go in and say 'I don't think it's very kind of you to imitate your own sister!' but Olga conquered it. The complaint would be so exactly in their mother's tone of martyrdom, and after all, what did it matter? She went on, past the two men on duty at the entrance to the bedroom corridor, to the top of the main staircase of the Alexander Palace.

In Quarenghi's beautiful Palladian design the two wings of the palace, the one occupied by the Czar and his family, the other by the suite and by occasional guests, were joined on the outside by a colonnade and an enormous paved court and on the inside by the State apartments which were so seldom used. Only a few chandeliers were lighted above the well of the stairs, and the vast rooms of state were dark, but when the Grand Duchess appeared on the staircase lights sprang up above her head, and hands in white cotton gloves carried candelabra from room to room until at last each one was brilliantly lit, to honour the passage or anticipate the whim of a girl in a cotton dress, with a nurse's cape lying loose on her young shoulders.

Olga entered the great Crimson Hall. The Cossacks and the footmen were already there, immobile, brought at her approach from their supper or their wine, sixteen of them ordered by fours against the marble walls. She walked slowly beneath the portraits of the reigning empresses, Catherine I, Anna, Elizabeth, Catherine II, who had all done better for Russia than most of the men who followed them. And among the Russians there was a stranger face, not strange to Olga, although it was younger far in the picture than in the photograph which always stood on her mother's writing table. It was a state portrait of her English great-grandmother, Queen Victoria.

Queen at eighteen. A constitutional monarch, bred to that idea of democracy Olga often heard her own father deride. Who told her prime minister on the day of her accession — their English tutor had taught Olga the words — 'It has long been my intention to retain the present ministry at the head of affairs.' What calm, what self-possession! Supposing

Victoria had had to say 'It has long been my intention to retain Rasputin at the head of affairs'?

Never.

The great entrance doors, meant for ambassadors, were swung open as Olga approached. And now a major-domo, or a chamberlain, or some minor functionary with a gold chain of office round his neck was bowing, and asking if he should send for a limousine —

'No thank you. No.'

She crossed the courtyard in the shadow of the great nude statues of the games players, which they called Babochnik and Svayachnik, and walked slowly towards the palace gate. It was a beautiful white night, still rosy in the west, and the sky above as purple as the lilac blossom she had gathered the day before with Simon Hendrikov. The guards at the gate could see her coming; she heard the words of command rapped out by a sergeant, and saw a young officer emerging hurriedly from the guard house on the other side of the public avenue. For a moment she hoped that by one chance in a thousand Simon Hendrikov was the commander of the guard. Then, as the great gates with her father's monogram on the grilles swung slowly open, she recognised another man and stood still as he saluted her.

'Happy to serve Your Imperial Highness!' he said breathlessly. 'May my men have the honour of providing an escort to the hospital?'

The word roused Olga from her reverie. 'No thank you, Captain Vlashkov,' she said with a smile. 'I'm not going to the hospital, not just yet. In fact I'm not going anywhere. Good night!'

She turned away, hearing the clink of swords in scabbards and the clang as the gates were shut at her back. And Olga Nicolaievna walked towards the palace where lights sprang up at the passing of a girl who wasn't going anywhere, with the sick conviction that they were all bound hell-for-leather on the road to nowhere.

'At four o'clock, you say, my granddaughter comes off duty?' The agreeable, coaxing voice of the Empress Dowager came along the telephone wires from Petrograd to the palace hospital at Czarskoe Selo. 'No . . . no, princess, certainly not. I wouldn't dream of asking any privileges for her. Don't say anything until she's free. Then you might ask one of your assistants to tell her she is to come straight to me instead of returning to the Alexander Palace... What's that? Yes, I myself will inform Her Majesty. Just tell the Grand Duchess one of my own cars will be waiting to bring her here ... Thank you very much, princess ... What a noble work you are doing for our brave men.'

The Empress Dowager listened with a smile to the farewells, dictated by protocol, of the chief surgeon of the palace hospital, and laid down the telephone. She had got her own way again, as she had been getting it for nearly fifty years — ever since a pert little princess, born Dagmar of Denmark, had arrived in St. Petersburg as the bride of the future Czar Alexander III. A beautiful dancer, a superb skater, she had been dancing and skating over all the trials and difficulties of her great position from that day forward, and although she had always kept aloof from politics she had more political sense in her little finger than her daughter-in-law the Czarina had in her whole mystical and muddled brain.

It was only half past two, at least two hours before Olga could be with her, but the Empress Dowager, ramrod straight at sixty-eight, had never yielded to the temptation of an afternoon nap. Before she left the desk where her telephone stood she wrote several letters, and carefully re-read the evening paper which had prompted her telephone call to the palace hospital. Then with a lady-in-waiting she walked for some time in the gardens of the Anitchkov Palace, her city home for many years — the Anitchkov, that world within a world, with the vibrant life of Petrograd flowing past it on one side, along the Nevski Prospekt, and the Fontanka Canal flowing past Quarenghi's splendid portico on the other.

Marie Feodorovna had never been as beautiful as her sister Alexandra, now the Dowager Queen of England, but she had what the French called *du chien*: a lively little face with large dark eyes, a twenty-inch waist still, and a great deal of attraction. She had never relaxed into old ladyhood, nor into boudoirs and negligées, and she was trim and erect in a plain black dress with a pearl 'dog collar' when she sailed across the carpet of the Red Drawing-room to greet her granddaughter with a kiss.

'Now tell me what you've been doing, you naughty girl, to get your name in the papers!'

'*My* name in the newspapers?' Olga looked genuinely astounded. 'Granny — is it something to do with my Soldiers' Committee?'

'Committee indeed! It's something to do with that awful man Rasputin! You didn't know? Read this.'

Olga read, on the front page of *Vechernaia Vremia*, an editorial complimenting her on having 'the clarity of vision and the energy' to take the advice consistently given by the Suvorin group of newspapers and 'banish the charlatan Rasputin from the imperial palaces'.

'Banish!' said Olga. 'Palaces! He'll be back.'

'I'm afraid he will, he or another like him. Rasputin is not the first, you know. Are you old enough to remember Philippe Vachod?'

'Monsieur Philippe, the Frenchman? Who gave mamma a bell that rang when evil influences came anywhere near her? She has it still.'

'No doubt,' sniffed Marie Feodorovna. 'But my concern is with you, Olga. It's most unpleasant to see my grandchild's name all over the front page of a rag like this — and heaven knows what *Grashdanin* and *Rech* will make of your exploit. You had better tell me yourself what happened.'

As she described Rasputin's invasion of her bedroom, Olga had the pleasure of seeing anger take possession of her grandmother's little crumpled face, and ended triumphantly:

'Anyway I don't care, I've got father on my side!'

'You've heard from him? Your mother told me she had telegraphed.'

Olga took a crumpled telegram from the pocket of her apron and held it out. The Empress Dowager read aloud:

' "My girlie must remember all Our Friend has done for Sunbeam and forgive his mistake, which will not be repeated. Kiss mamma, sisters, Baby from loving old papa, and be agooweeone." H'm! That's clear enough, at all events.' She peered again at the telegram through her gold lorgnette. 'Is that an English word, *agooweeone*?'

'Four English words, it means "a good wee one". Don't you remember, that's what mother used to say to Alexis when he really was a baby, "Sleep well, and be agooweeone"?'

'Yes, but your father needn't telegraph to you as if *you* were a baby. It doesn't matter! He obviously means to send Rasputin away this time.'

'Does he? I only hope you're right, grandmamma.'

'Your mother knows about this telegram?'

'It arrived before breakfast, and she read it first.'

'I talked to Tatiana too, this afternoon. She said your mother refused even to see you before you went to hospital.'

'It was all my fault!' cried generous Olga. 'I said far too much yesterday, I was so angry about Rasputin, and I made her ill. She has one of her terrible headaches today.'

'Or a backache, or a stomach ache, or pains in all her limbs. There never was a greater sufferer than your poor mother. Oh, I knew how it would be, when she and Nicky were engaged! She had to go off at once to take a cure for rheumatism at Harrogate. And a few months later, when she came to us at Livadia, when your dear grandpapa was dying, she complained all the time of pains in her legs. Pains in her legs indeed! A young princess, twenty-two years old, does not permit herself to have pains *anywhere*, when the ruler of her future country is passing away!'

'But you're such a Spartan, grandmamma! Mother tells us her health was ruined by having five babies, so close together, and nursing us all.'

'I had a large family too, and I was never a penny the worse for it ... Of course I ate raw ham,' said the Empress Dowager reflectively.

'Raw *ham?*'

'Every day, before I got out of bed. It's the best thing in the world for morning sickness. Remember that, my dear, when your time comes.'

'I don't believe my time will ever come.'

'No? Well, we'll see about that, and as quickly as we can, too. But now ring for tea, Olga, I know you always enjoy an Anitchkov tea; at least you did when you were in the schoolroom. And take off your veil so that I can see your hair. H'm! When did you last have it properly dressed?'

A retinue of servants brought in tea tables and trays, and while they were in the room the old empress contented herself with saying, in French:

'How do you suppose the story of what happened yesterday appeared in the papers today?'

'I've been wondering about that.'

'Which young lady was in the room with you at the time?'

Olga told her. 'But she would never have given the story to the press,' she said. 'She wouldn't know how to, any more than I do.'

'No, I don't believe she would. The general — impossible. One of the Cossacks?'

'I think it probably was the fair-haired footman. I sent him away too, you see.'

The Empress Dowager smiled. 'I didn't know that. Dismissing the staff — no wonder your mamma was angry.'

'He betrayed his trust,' said Olga obstinately.

'Yes, well, that can't be helped now. What I'm concerned with is *your* future. First of all, I'm not going to have you exposed, day after day, to your mother's sighs and sulks.'

'Mother can't help sighing and sulking, it's in her nature.'

'I know it is.' Marie Feodorovna closed her lips firmly on what she wanted to say, which was, 'And I've had to put up with her sulks for twenty-five years, ever since poor Nicky fell in love with her. Especially after she came among us as his wife, determined to set the Family at loggerheads, and snub the whole of Petersburg society!' Reminding herself that Olga was the woman's daughter, and that the woman, according to her lights, was a most devoted mother, she contented herself with saying, 'She inherited her difficult nature from your other grandmamma, Princess Alice. All that religious fervour, all that wild enthusiasm for some "man of God" or another, all that domineering tactlessness — ' She pulled herself up short.

'Did you know my other grandmamma?'

'Yes, quite well, when my sister Alix was first married and living in England. Queen Victoria used to be very cross with Alice of Hesse, until of course her tragic death sanctified *her*. But all that doesn't concern *you*, my dear. I only want to see you happily married, and established in a home of your own.'

'Easier said than done, granny dear.'

'That sounds rather melancholy. You don't regret sending away the Rumanian prince?'

'Oh *no*!'

'I'm glad, I could never picture you in Bucharest. Olga Nicolaievna to be the future queen of that semi-Oriental, self-indulgent little country — !'

'Married to that semi-Oriental, self-indulgent boy.'

'Your mother pressed it because of the Orthodox religion, didn't she?'

'I suppose so.'

'Does the faith you were baptised in mean a great deal to you?'

'If you mean the Christian faith, it does. If you mean the Orthodox form of worship, I don't think it means any more than the Lutheran service did to you, when you gave up your church to marry my grandfather.'

'I wish to heaven,' said the Empress Dowager piously, 'that your mother's conscience, all those years ago, had been as accommodating as yours. After all, as I used to say to her, what do the rites matter? It's only another way of worshipping our Saviour. You agree? Then, my darling, let me tell you about a little plan I've made for us. You've been nursing for nearly a year without a break. It's June, the best time for a trip to Denmark. Suppose you and I take a little holiday, and visit Copenhagen? It's a long time since you've seen your Danish relatives.'

'Granny, you're sweet, but I can't give up the hospital just because you think I need a holiday.'

'And then we might spend a week or two in London. You could do even more good in London than you're doing here,' said the old lady cunningly. 'The English know so little about Russia. Or rather, what they do know is all bad propaganda, spread by that wretched Socialist, Ramsay MacDonald. You see I realise what is going on! If you were there, the eldest daughter of the Czar, going about with Queen Mary to all those wonderful public works of hers, meeting the people who count — the Ministers — the generals — you would show them another side of Russia, wouldn't you?'

'Possibly. And among the people who count, would you include the Prince of Wales?'

'He's at the front with his regiment, my sister writes.'

'But if you and Queen Alexandra asked especially, he could be brought home at a day's notice, couldn't he?' Olga laughed. She got up and kissed her grandmother's delicately powdered cheek. 'Oh darling, you never give up! I believe you're still trying to make a match between me and poor David of Wales.'

Marie Feodorovna caught at Olga's hand, noted automatically that the nails were untended, and whispered,

'To see you Queen of England, Olga! My dream ever since you were born!'

Olga pulled her chair closer to her grandmother's. 'Listen, dear,' she said, 'I told my father I would never marry away from Russia. And now I know I can never marry without love. David was fifteen and I was fourteen when we were last in England, that time at Cowes; what possible feelings, grown-up feelings, could there have been between us two? Now he's twenty-one, and I'm nearly twenty; and if our families make us marry, then we're forced into a loveless marriage — just as Aunt Ducky was forced in her first marriage, or poor Aunt Olga with the Prince of Oldenburg. Haven't you seen enough of that, granny, close to home? Oh, I know you were one of the lucky ones. You accepted the man your parents chose, and you've often told me you and grandpapa were happy together. But it doesn't always work out that way, and this is 1915, after all, not 1866. The Prince of Wales only wants to get himself into the firing line, I'm sure he doesn't want to marry now, and I'm also sure the King and Queen won't force him into marriage.'

'If they don't, they may live to regret it,' said Marie Feodorovna. 'Princes and princesses should marry young, it's their first duty, and if Georgie and May don't arrange the right match for that boy soon, he may lead them a pretty dance when he grows older.'

'I'm sure I'm not the right match, granny dear.'

The Empress Dowager sighed. 'I only want you to take a little time and think it over. But in the meantime, here's what I want you to do —'

She asked Olga to spend a month with her at the Anitchkov Palace. It was too tiring for a girl, going from hospital to those endless committee meetings, those visits to refugee shelters, those charity performances; and then there were the battleship launchings, two within the next two weeks. Why stay at home to be scolded and treated like a child? It would be so convenient to be in Petrograd. 'And it would be company for me,' the old lady said wistfully. The girl realised that she was lonely with her elderly court in the enormous palace.

'Granny, you're very sweet to ask me, but I can't give up my job, even to please you. It would be deserting, just like a soldier at the front.'

'You make too much of that most unsuitable "job", as you call it.'

'Perhaps I do. Tania's a better nurse than I am, and I think Marie'll be better than both of us, when she starts next September. But I've got to go on trying—'

'Don't be ridiculous, child. There are ten hospitals in Petrograd where you can give your services for a few weeks, if it means so much to you, and I know a dozen young ladies who'd be delighted to take your place at the Catherine Palace. You might very well spend every morning at the British Red Cross hospital; that would please our Allies, and Dmitri would like it too, I'm sure.'

A lovely smile brightened Olga's face. 'Dmitri's hospital!' she said slowly. 'I'd forgotten that. Yes, that might work out very well.'

The Empress Dowager fiddled with the gold watchguard looped into her black silk belt. 'Olga,' she said, 'is there a definite reason for your wishing not to leave Russia? You've been looking very happy lately. You ought to look exhausted, and I must say your grooming has been shamefully neglected, and yet you're prettier than ever. Almost as if you were in love. Do tell me, Olga—is it Dmitri?'

'Dmitri and I are the best of friends. But there's no more between us than that, nor ever will be.'

'I know when you were children your parents thought it would be a happy match for you.'

'It didn't work out that way,' said Olga lightly. 'Remember Dmitri's four years older than I am. As we grew up, his fancy fell on my cousin Irina, not on me.'

'But she preferred Felix Yusupov, I don't know why.'

'Felix and Irina seem to be very happy, and now they've got a dear little girl. Mashka's perfectly foolish about that baby! What does it feel like to be a great-grandmother?'

'It makes me feel like an ancestor, my dear. And don't try to change the subject, we were talking about you.'

'We *are* having a heart to heart, aren't we? Please, granny, don't plan any more marriages for me. I don't want Dmitri, I don't want the Prince of Wales, I don't want awful Carol—'

'Then what *do* you want?'

'Only to be loved.'

CHAPTER ELEVEN

THE sunlight of the white nights still lingered over Petrograd, but inside 'The Red Sarafan' it might well have been mid-winter. The little restaurant was always dark, lit only by oil lamps and occasionally by candles, and always crowded for half the day and half the night.

Above the door on a little alley, not much cleaner or more inviting than the alley which housed The Children's Castle, a street sign swung. It was the kind of sign which elsewhere in that district of illiterates showed the wares the wretched shops were selling, but instead of a leg of pork or a loaf of bread the restaurant sported a painting of a buxom peasant girl wearing a scarlet sarafan, a bright pinafore dress with shoulder straps over an embroidered blouse. The girl was laughing; a handkerchief was tied over her fair hair, and her strong arms were akimbo. It was an image which had no relation to the regular customers of 'The Red Sarafan', who were almost all under-nourished, unhealthy and discontented.

They were also noisy. There was always somebody holding forth at 'The Red Sarafan', somebody reciting his own poetry (usually beginning with exclamations like 'Howl!' 'Kill!' 'Dogs!') or somebody singing to the balalaika; and the noise of the performers and the critics round the wine-stained tables made it possible for many private conversations to go on in the alcoves at the back of the room. There on a summer night sat a square-shouldered man who looked better fed than any other there, who indeed had put on weight since the winter: the editor of *Castle Comments*, Jacob Levin.

He had just refilled the glass of his secretary, Mara Trenova, who had joined him, hot and thirsty, a few minutes before.

'Feeling better?' he said indulgently.

'Much.'

'You looked as if you needed that. Everything cleared away at the office?'

'Sergiev was just locking up when I left.'

'Good.' It was the evening of press day, they had earned their glass of wine.

'Jacob, I've got something to tell you.'

He had something to tell her too, but you couldn't beat Trenova. She *had* to talk first, blurt out whatever was in her mind; it was one reason why Levin had given her so many black marks on her last report.

'What is it, Mara?'

'My mother's going to spend the rest of the summer in the country.'

'Where in the country?'

'Oh, not too far from here. At Koivisto in Finland, the Hendrikovs have a dacha there. It seems they've taken pity on my mother, so lonely, daughter out at work all day —'

'And half the night, eh?'

'— And so they've asked her to keep the place open, keep it tidy, be a sort of housekeeper in fact, just for the professor and his wife. Dolly won't be going there this summer, she's too busy nursing.'

'Meantime Dolly's brother is rising in the world.'

'Rising, how?'

Levin flicked his thumb and finger at the evening paper, folded at the programme of tomorrow's ceremony, the launching of the battle cruiser *Poltava* at the Vassili Island yards. 'In the suite of HIM the Czar,' he read aloud, 'HH the Grand Duke Dmitri Pavlovich, ADC; Admiral Nilov, Commander Sablin; in the suite of HIH the Grand Duchess Olga, Madame This, Countess That, Lieutenant Simon Hendrikov.'

'That old snob of a professor will be overjoyed,' said Mara.

'You're not very civil to your mother's benefactor. But what about you? Shall you stay on all by yourself in the Yamskaia?'

'Yes, of course, I've nowhere else to go.'

'That might have certain definite advantages.' Levin yawned, stretched his legs, and shouted to the panting waitress to bring more wine.

'Mara, let's get down to business. Here's *my* news. I'm off to Moscow at the end of next week — no, not on a business trip — for good.'

'Jacob, why?' He saw her eyes dilate in the candlelight, and that was all.

'Two reasons. One, now that it's official about the Second Category, I mean the call-up in September, I stand a fair chance of being combed out and sent off to the marshes round Lake Naroch, mutilated hand and all. Two, that our publisher and boss has had a strong hint from a friend across the river, you know, in police headquarters near Peter and Paul, that *Castle Comments* ought to suspend publication for a while.'

'But why to Moscow?'

'Ah yes, that's reason three. The Party thinks I'll be more useful there than here.'

'Will you take me with you, Jacob?'

'I think the Party may have other plans for you.'

'I'm not a member of the Party. I'm perfectly free to look for a position with some other publication, or anywhere I can find a job.'

'Oh no, you're not.'

His maimed hand fastened on hers with the touch she found perversely exciting, and beyond the spear of candlelight Mara saw the crowded room swinging in a maze of heat.

'Listen,' said Levin, 'there's no need to drag this out. When Rostov recruited you at the Xenia he sent you to me because he thought Ivan Trenov's daughter, full of fire and guts, might have considerable revolutionary potential. My first job was to kick all that SR nonsense out of you — the heroines of *Narodna Volnia*, the Czaricides, and all the beloved comrades whose names have been consigned to oblivion by most of us. You learned fast enough, and it's only a matter of time till you can be accepted as a Party member. But in another way you've been a disappointment. You turned out to be useless as a comrade for direct action.'

'Give me time,' said Mara resentfully.

'You've had six months. And I knew you would be hopeless with a gun the first time I took you out to the marshes for target practice — remember?'

Mara looked away. She remembered the winter Sunday, and the long tramcar ride along the main road, lined with wooden houses which grew shabbier with every verst, on the way to the Finnish frontier. And then the waste land, half marsh and half scrub pine and birch, where they were out of earshot, out of sight of anything but the shore ice of the Gulf of Finland, and all her limbs seemed to freeze as she stood there firing at the target, with only the Nagan in her hand for warmth. She remembered the dingy *traktir*, halfway to the city, where coarse food and contraband vodka had warmed her as if she were recovering from frostbite. There Levin had taken her to bed, and the surrender of her virginity, which she had anticipated as a moment of romance and beauty, had become a brutal, painful struggle in a room with dirty blankets and a red-hot stove. Yes, she remembered the marshes.

'You're no use at all with firearms,' Levin repeated. 'You couldn't hit a barn door at ten paces, and as for throwing a hand grenade, you can't even throw a tennis ball! Admit it now, if you were to stand outside the Vassili-Ostrov works tomorrow, when the Czar and his retinue go by, what chance would you have of eliminating any one of them? Even the little Grand Duchess — or her ADC?'

'I thought the Party line was against assassination, for the present.'

'It is, because we want Nicholas the Bloody to work out his own damnation. But you couldn't pull the trigger, could you now?'

She shook her head.

'And then that night at the Okhta Works — you lost your head and made a scene in the street, just because you'd seen young Stepan blown to pieces when he placed the charges wrong! A kid you hardly knew, and yet you were sobbing and carrying on because Stepan had the guts to give his life so that children not born yet would have a better life than ours —'

Mara crushed down the thought of the children who had been killed in the Okhta disaster, when the fire licked through the workers' tenements across the Neva. She said painfully:

'You've said all that before, Jacob. You only want to go on punishing me because I went home that night with Joseph Calvert —'

'And how many nights since then?'

'Not so very many. Joe Calvert is really what you try to be — a dedicated professional. His job comes first, and I come nowhere, so there's no cause at all to be jealous.'

'Jealous!' said Levin, and his coarse face crinkled in a smile. 'Trenova, you could go to bed with half the Baltic Fleet for all

I care! If you like going to bed with me, fine, but it doesn't give us any claim on one another. We're comrades in the struggle, and that's all.'

'In that case,' said Mara, trying to keep her voice steady, 'I think it's time I went home. I'll come in to the office tomorrow morning, and pick up my wages.'

'Sit down,' said Levin, dragging her roughly backwards as she rose, 'I haven't finished talking to you. Drink your wine and listen to me.'

Mara picked at the fastening of her shabby satchel, her head lowered.

'You can't be allowed to walk out with your nose in the air, like some little bourgeoise stenographer whose sister's husband has found her a job in one of the Ministries. You know too much. You're in it with us now.'

'You can trust to my discretion, Jacob, absolutely.'

'I trust nobody. I watched you making your dis-coveries — oh, you were sharp enough for that! You looked like a cat with a saucer of cream when you found out about the messages from Lenin going out to the cells in the provinces along with the candy classics, tucked in between the pages of *Pikovaya Dama* and *Voina i Mir*. And then the code in the *Comments*, in the Letters to the Editor — how did you find that out, by the way?'

'I worked out all those page and paragraph references for myself.'

'You see? You're sharp enough, as long as we keep you away from firearms. Now here is what you do. You come in tomorrow and get your money, just as you said. In the evening we have a final celebration in my room at the Hotel du Nord, before the train leaves for Moscow. You have a couple of days to see your mother off to Finland, and on Monday you start your new job at *Pravda*.'

'But I don't want to work for *Pravda*! *Pravda*'s liable to be raided any day!'

'No, they'll be in the clear for a bit, now that the editor's been sent to Siberia, along with the Bolshevik Five. There's practically a new staff at *Pravda*, and they need all the help they can get. I've recommended you as an editorial assistant, chiefly on the strength of those fillers you've been writing for *Comments*. You've got a flair for that sort of thing — that and caption writing. You'll get on all right.' Levin slapped his pockets, feeling for his cigarettes.

'What if I absolutely refuse to work for *Pravda*? It's a Bolshevik paper. And I'm not a Party member.'

'You will be,' he said. 'And you won't be going among strangers. I've fixed a job for Sergiev, quite a good one. He doesn't mean to be a copyboy for ever.'

'I hoped I was going to see the last of Sergiev tomorrow. Frankly, Jacob, he makes my flesh creep — '

'That's too bad, because he'll be there to keep an eye on you. Sergiev reports on you, you report on Sergiev, and the Party member on the staff reports on both of you. That's how it's done, my dear, and very effective too: now let's have something to eat and another bottle.'

Which was possibly why Mara Trenova was loitering, next morning, with two weeks' salary from The Children's Castle in her purse, at the Vassili Island end of the Nicholas Bridge. For during the leisurely drinking of the second bottle of Crimean wine, which along with the heat and noise of 'The Red Sarafan' had made her head spin more than ever, Jacob Levin had talked so much about firearms, her own inefficiency with firearms, and the uselessness of firearms in getting rid of all the evils which preyed on the workers of Russia, that Mara had come, almost in a state of trance, to the place where she could see the Czar's procession pass from the launching of the battle cruiser *Poltava* from the Vassili-Ostrov yards. As usual, neither the time of the launching nor the route to be taken had been announced in the press, but the island site narrowed the possibilities of arrival and departure, and Mara had guessed correctly that the carriages and the cavalry would not cross the new Palace Bridge. So she left the tram herself at the Admiralty stop, and walked down river and across to the island by the Nicholas Bridge, which Dolly Hendrikova and she had once known so well as the way back to the Xenia School after a holiday. She knew she had guessed right when she saw the crowd of spectators behind the police cordon. 'They' had gone by, an old apple-seller told her, but 'They' would be coming back this way again; and Mara stood on the kerb and reckoned how many paces it was from there to the carriageway, and at what moment some better marksman than herself would raise his gun and fire.

Her head was splitting, between the effects of last night's wine and her anticipation of the night ahead (for it would be the last night) in Levin's shabby room in the old Hotel du Nord, opposite the Nicholas Station, where so many revolutionaries had lived under so many aliases, and her dread of the future. She had been expecting carriages and Cossacks, and the motors came up so quietly that she almost missed the Czar as he went past, saluting mechanically, with smudges so dark beneath his eyes that they looked like bruises.

'Retreat, retreat — how can the Little Father smile?' growled a man in the crowd, but the cheerful applewoman called out, 'Look at the sweetings! Look at the lovely couple!' and Mara realised that the noise coming up with the hoofbeats was one name, shouted by five thousand shipbuilders, suddenly unanimous:

'Ol-ga! Ol-ga! Ol-ga!'

The Grand Duchess Olga, flushed with success, was driving in an open motor car with her cousin the Grand Duke Dmitri Pavlovich. She had a bouquet of flowers in her lap, and one white-gloved hand waved steadily at the crowd. At her grandmother's desire she wore a very small hat, so that her face could be seen, and she remembered to look up, from time to time, at the windows of the high buildings on the embankment, where students and office-workers, not all of them friendly, had waited to see the Czar go past. Olga's was a new face to them, a young and pretty face, a change from the sour, set faces they knew too well, and some of them applauded, even against their will.

'*She* launched the battleship,' said a well-informed man in the surging crowd round Mara Trenova. 'The workers asked for her, at the last minute. Said they thought she'd bring good luck —'

'Can't bring any worse luck than *he* does!' said a cynic.

'Look at her with her best boy, will you?' cried the applewoman. 'When's the wedding, lovey dear?'

The Grand Duke Dmitri, overhearing, took Olga's free hand in his own and sketched a kiss. He was easily the handsomest young man in the Family, tall, with regular features and thick blond hair, and the one who most resembled the Czar Alexander II, the liberator of the serfs. He grinned companionably at his cousin as the car turned right on the Nicholas Bridge, and told her she looked wonderful, had risen to the unexpected occasion at the launching 'like a real trouper', and God! how he could use a drink.

The watching faces disappeared from the windows facing the Neva, the crowd scattered, the show was over. But Mara Trenova, when the carriageway was clear, walked out from the kerb into the middle of the street and calculated that for any marksman who, unlike herself, could hit a barn door at ten paces, the distance would have been ten paces — exactly.

The Czar, who knew the jealous scene his wife would make if he stayed in the city to lunch with his mother, drove straight back to eat consommé and mutton cutlets at Czarskoe Selo. In Olga's honour, her grandmother had arranged a luncheon for thirty guests in the Anitchkov Palace, with a *zakuski* table filled to overflowing for the gentlemen, and sprays of Crimean roses at each lady's place. The launching of the *Poltava* was not needed as the excuse for a party, because the pleasure-loving old lady had given several such luncheons since her grand-daughter had come for a holiday to Petrograd. She obstinately called it a holiday, for although Olga spent four hours every day on duty in the wards of the hospital on the Palace Quay and three in the committee rooms of the Winter Palace, there was time for hairdressers and manicurists and above all dress-makers to be brought in bevies to the Anitchkov. Olga accepted all they did for her with pleasure: she knew, as one female to another, that it was her grandmother's way of spiting the Cza-rina, who — as the older empress said with a sniff — 'always dressed those poor dear girls as if they were an English parson's daughters'.

Olga enjoyed the party, as she enjoyed everything these days. Her grandmother invited girls of her own age, and their brothers or young husbands at home on leave, to all of whom she was her friendly, lively self. The younger generation went home and told their parents that Olga Nicolaievna was very different from what her mother had been, years ago; and it was high time that casual charmer, Dmitri Pavlovich, took himself in hand, just as his bosom friend Prince Felix Yusupov had done, and settled down to matrimony with that delightful girl. Before the launching lunch was over there were knowing smiles on many faces when Dmitri took Olga into one of the window bays to admire the view over the Fontanka Canal, which both knew by heart. But there was nothing loverlike in what the Grand Duke said:

'What time d'you come off duty tomorrow, Olga?'

'Twelve o'clock as usual, why?'

'Could you come down and see me when you're free? I won't keep you long. Olga, I've *got* to talk to you alone. Not in a mob like this.'

'But my father's going back to the Stavka at Baranovichi tomorrow morning early. Aren't you going too?'

'Well, that's just it. There may not *be* any Baranovichi by tomorrow.'

'Oh, my God,' she said. 'The German advance! Is it so bad?'

'So bad the C-in-C is thinking of moving the Stavka to the Dnieper river.'

'I'll join you as soon after twelve noon as I can.'

'Thank you, dear.'

Olga took her leave of the company and went to change her dress. It was one of her grandmother's orders that she was not to drive through the city in her nurse's uniform, which was to be kept at the hospital, just as her grandmother had ordained that on public occasions the Grand Duchess was to be accompanied by two ladies-in-waiting ('And *young* ladies,' she insisted, 'not some of those old frumps of your mother's, stumbling about and peering through their spectacles') and also by an ADC. It had been the simplest thing in the world to persuade the Czar that a devoted former member of his own bodyguard, Lieutenant Simon Hendrikov, was just the right person to be his daughter's ADC.

Once inside the Winter Palace, it was also a simple matter to shake off the ladies-in-waiting. They too were involved in committee work for the different war charities, and in that great warren of the Romanovs most of the committee members spent their time hunting about for meetings which might be held in any of the thousand rooms. The Malachite Hall was their final rendezvous, and provided Olga was there at the end of the afternoon, pensively inspecting the famous door knobs made of great red balls of garnet held by golden claws, or looking at her reflection in the Empress Anna's bridal mirror, no lady would have dared to question where she had been in the meantime.

Within an hour of her arrival from the Empress Dowager's luncheon, she was leaving the Winter Palace by an unpatrolled staircase which led to the doorway of the New Hermitage.

Simon Hendrikov watched her coming down the steps, in the shadow of the ten grey granite monolithic figures which guarded that doorway, and thought how slim and light she looked by contrast, and how clever she had been to wear an inconspicuous summer dress, grey-green like carnation leaves, and a hat with a veil of the same shade. He hoped he was equally inconspicuous in the undress uniform of the Garde Equipage, with a flat cap, and without the aiguillettes of an acting ADC. Olga was his only concern, that day and always, as he stepped forward to salute her, and to refrain, with difficulty, from kissing the laughing face so nearly on a level with his own.

'I did it! I did it! I don't have to be back until five o'clock! Now we can go for a real walk!'

'You're sure you'll be all right?'

'Of course. Who's going to recognise me, dressed like this?'

'Half Petrograd saw you this morning, it seems to me.'

'Yes, but people were expecting to see me then, they aren't now,' she answered sensibly. 'Hurry, Simon! We ought to get away from here!'

'This way, then.' He led her down from the river front of the palace, where the sentries were on duty, along the side of the Winter Canal, between the great buildings and out to the Millionnaia. He felt better when they were away from that princely street and crossing the vast Square where her ancestor, Alexander I, was remembered by his column. There were a great many men about, coming and going to the General Staff Headquarters with portfolios under their arms, none of whom gave a second glance at the young officer and the girl by his side.

Olga looked over her shoulder at the Winter Palace. 'It looks so different from here,' she said. 'I wish they hadn't painted it that hideous shade of ox-blood red.'

'My father says Rastrelli meant it to be porcelain blue.'

'Rastrelli was crazy about porcelain blue, look at the Catherine hospital. Aren't you glad to be away from there?'

'As long as I can be in Petrograd with you.'

'Petrograd!' she said. 'Imagine being free to *walk* along the Nevski Prospekt, and when the shops are open, too!'

They had emerged on the great avenue at the level of the Police Bridge over the Moika Canal, and Olga looked longingly at a cinema on the far side of the street.

'Is that the only cinema in Petrograd?' she asked.

'No, there's another one. The Parisiana and the Piccadilly, they're called. I don't know why they both have foreign names.'

'Allied names, at least. And where's the Astoria Hotel?'

'It's at the far end of the Morskaia.'

'I suppose we couldn't go there and have tea?'

'Good heavens, *no*!'

Olga laughed. 'It's all right,' she said, 'I realise you think people would know me there. And I don't really want tea, I only wanted to look inside. I remember three years ago, when the Astoria was opened, I nearly broke my heart because they wouldn't let me go to the gala dinner with the British Ambassador and Lady Georgina Buchanan. Oh well! This is much more fun, isn't it?'

And Simon, touched and adoring, wondered if there was another girl in Petrograd who was getting as much fun out of walking down the Nevski Prospekt on a fine summer day, amused at everything, and finding such ordinary things so new and strange. He felt increasingly confident that no one would recognise her, even when she stopped beside one of the street kiosks and mischievously pointed out a selection of postcard photographs of herself in nurse's uniform, all veil and white apron, with nothing but a tip-tilted nose and a firm chin turned to the camera to indicate the girl inside the dress.

'It doesn't do the Grand Duchess justice,' he said hastily, and almost pulled her away from the stand. Olga said with a giggle, 'Justice! It's a libel! Jaguelski really is a rotten photographer — he makes all of us look awful except my sister Tatiana, and nobody can spoil *her*.'

'Nobody can spoil you, Princess.' He didn't mean photography, and she knew it; she gave Simon the smile he loved before she turned away to identify, with delight, the famous English Shop which purveyed so many things to the imperial children, from picture puzzles and tennis balls to golden syrup for school-room tea and the round brown cakes of Pear's soap which had once been a feature of their bath time. He got her past the Hotel Europa without incident, and then, of course, she wanted to cross the street and buy something, anything, in the bazaar called the Gostinnoi Dvor.

Simon was afraid, for her sake, of the old, rambling, two-storey building, with its warren of tiny shops dating from the eighteenth century. Unable to rid himself of the idea that they had been followed, he suggested that there were better shops in the Passage, only a few minutes' walk from where they stood. And there he led her, past a basement tearoom with cheap saffron buns in the window, and a men's outfitter showing shoddy summer suits, for the shops on the Nevski grew dustier and less inviting the nearer they came to the Fontanka Canal. But inside the Passage there was a perfumer's, and a jeweller's, and a shop with suede handbags in pastel colours, and there was a theatre, presenting *The Three Sisters*, and far down the Passage there was one of Petrograd's two cinemas, announcing a matinée performance of William Farnum in *Young Lochinvar*.

'A movie! An American movie! Oh, Simon, do let's go!'

He hadn't the faintest idea what the title meant, but Olga was quick: she looked at the stills in their glass case outside the door, and of course the lurid coloured bills were showing cowboys, one with a girl perched behind him on the saddle and the dust rising beneath the horses' hoofs.

'You can't want to see a show like this,' he said.

'Oh, but I do. We never get to see a decent movie! Don't you remember those awful evenings at Livadia, in the riding school?'

'With "short selected subjects for instruction and amusement"?'

'Selected by my dear mamma,' she said, and Simon choked on a laugh. The Czarina's selections, and more particularly the cuts Her Majesty made in any item remotely romantic or exciting, had caused some ribald comment in the Guards' mess at Livadia. He realised that Olga for the first time had said 'mamma' instead of 'the Czarina'.

'We did once get to see Max Linder,' he reminded her.

'Simon, I want to see *this* show! And hurry, it's going to start in five minutes!'

'Well, come inside the lobby, then, don't stand about outside.' The lobby was empty. The woman in the little kiosk said the house was nearly full. But Simon was able to get two seats in the back row, with a chance of being seated on the aisle himself, and at least the house lights had been dimmed before they went inside.

It was amazing how many young people had preferred watching William Farnum to walking in the Summer Garden on such a fine afternoon. They applauded the pianist, coming in and settling her beads and bangles before attacking a tinny piano; they applauded frantically the extinguishing of all the lights as the credits began to roll up on the screen: William Farnum in *Young Lochinvar*, based on the famous poem by Sir Walter Scott. The distributors had balked at the expense of translating the sub-titles into Cyrillic characters, and the audience sat in docile ignorance until the picture began. And then it turned out to be a very simple story, as easy to understand in Calcutta as in Petrograd or in New York.

They saw the little dusty cow town in the Wild West, where a rancher forbade his only daughter to have any dealings with one of his cow hands,

'He's a low-livin', no-account coyote'

said the sub-title, and Simon whispered to Olga:

'You speak English, don't you?'

'I thought I did.'

'Is that Farnum, the peasant?'

'S-sh.'

Simon smiled. While the screen father ranted at his daughter, and told her she must marry another rancher,

'A great guy, with ten thousand head of cattle'

his eyes were for his princess and not for the star. She had folded back her veil, and her charming profile, nose tilted, lips parted, was lifted in complete absorption to the screen. Olga paid no attention to her surroundings, although the cinema was small, with hard wooden seats, and the atmosphere, thick enough to cut with a knife, was made up of sweat, scent, hair-oil, cachous and stale fish. There was enough light from the flickering images on the screen to show that most of the audience were boys in uniform, young enough to be the first draft of the Second Category, with their arms around their girls. Greatly daring, Simon slid his own arm behind Olga, cushioning the hard back of the unpadded seat, and to his joy she moved slightly towards him, so that he felt her slimness and her warmth against his side, while she never took her eyes from the screen.

A grand wedding was planned at the ranch house, beginning with a barn dance. The unwilling bride and her groom stood up together. William Farnum appeared in the doorway and told the scowling rancher that he claimed a dance.

'Let's you and me really show'em how, honey'
was what the sub-title made the dashing cow hand say. He danced the girl through the open door, threw her on his saddle, jumped up in front of her, and rode away triumphant with his friends cavorting all around them.

'Young Lochinvar wins his bride!'

The show was over. The audience clapped and cheered, and Simon Hendrikov got the Grand Duchess Olga Nicolaievna through the lobby and into the Passage ahead of the stampede of her father's troops.

'Oh Simon! Oh! wasn't it heavenly! How I wish I could tell my sisters all about it!'

'You enjoyed it better than the short selected subjects?'

'Don't be silly, there's no comparison. William Farnum, wasn't he marvellous? I only wish I'd understood the words.'

'They must have been in American.'

'Probably. And now, before we go back — can't we just *walk* through the Gostinnoi Dvor?'

She was terribly persistent, with the Romanov persistence, but Simon still refused to take her up those ramshackle wooden stairs and through those crowded corridors where the exits were so few. Luckily, Olga was attracted by the outdoor booths, set between the wall of the bazaar and the trees on the verge of the Nevski Prospekt, and he followed her from one to another, from the ice-cream stalls to the soft drink stands, and from there to the little cart where a fat woman in a white apron was selling the meat patties called *pirozhki*.

'Simon, do look at the chocolate books!'

They were neatly arranged on a candy stall, the familiar slabs of chocolate tied by orange ribbons to the little books bound in greyish paper, and Simon said, 'That's funny! I never saw them on sale in the bazaars before. My sisters and I used to buy them out of our pocket money, at a rather fancy confectioner's on the Island.'

'I know, Konradi's. Aunt Olga used to have parcels of them

215

sent from there, and we were given them when we went to lunch with her on Saturdays.'

'Would you like to choose one now?'

'Oh please! But you choose, that used to be half the fun of it, having someone else choose, and not knowing what you would find inside.'

'That's why they're bound in a plain paper.'

Simon bought the packet on the top of the pile, and gave it to the smiling girl.

'Want to open it now, or wait until you get back — ?' He couldn't say aloud 'get back to the Winter Palace', but that was what he meant. The holiday afternoon was very nearly over.

'Now, of course, I can't wait.' She untied the orange ribbon carefully and lifted the little book from the wrapped chocolate.

'Lermontov's *Poems*, how gorgeous, they're my favourites . . . Oh Simon, look!'

She was holding something out to him in the shadow of the trees, and he saw dismay invade the face which had been, for so short a time, so happy. He took the thing in his hand, the cartoon which had been folded between the leaves of Lermontov. It was a viciously clever drawing of a gigantic Rasputin, holding two tiny figures on his knees. One, in military uniform, with his face vacant above his heard, was the Czar Nicholas II. The other, wearing a crown, and a dress cut so low that her almost naked breasts were rubbing against Rasputin's tunic, the Czarina.

They were both clutched in Rasputin's giant hands, shaped like claws. Underneath, four words were written:

'*The Ruler of Russia.*'

'How dashing it feels,' said the Grand Duchess Olga, 'to be drinking champagne in a bachelor's apartments, and before luncheon too!'

'It would be more dashing still,' suggested the Grand Duke Dmitri, 'if you didn't mean to rush away to have lunch with your grandmamma.'

'You think I ought to go on drinking champagne, and then spend the afternoon with you?'

'Something like that.' The young man looked at his guest with amusement. She had arrived rather late; the bells of Peter and Paul, just across the Neva, had chimed the '*Kol slaven*' at midday, and two quarters, before Nurse Olga had come off the ward, changed out of uniform, and run down the private staircase of the palace he had turned into a hospital to Dmitri's own apartments on the ground floor. Now she was affecting sophistication, and quite delightfully. She had even complimented him on the big living-room — he refused to call it by any more formal name — which he had designed in collaboration with the men who had made the stage sets of the Imperial Russian Ballet famous in every civilised capital in Europe.

Dmitri had come back to the palace which his widowed father had left empty, following on a second and typically Romanov morganatic marriage, after the Czarina had made it clear that he was no longer a welcome inhabitant of the Alexander Palace at Czarskoe Selo. The cause of the trouble had been his intimacy with Prince Felix Yusupov, then a bachelor himself; 'decadent, and degenerate' being two of the mildest adjectives 'that German *hausfrau*', as he thought of her, had applied in their wild-oat days to Yusupov. So Dmitri Pavlovich had left his 'Uncle Nicky' and 'Aunt Alix', as he called the rulers who were in fact his cousins, and behold! Yusupov was now a model husband and father, and he, Dmitri, was about to appeal for help to the eldest of the long-legged girls who only yesterday were making sand-castles on the beach at Livadia. He respectfully offered his cigarette case to Olga Nicolaievna.

She was sitting in an armchair entirely covered with zebra skin, which unlike her mother's furniture had not come from the Tottenham Court Road, and which made a striking background to Olga's golden head. Dmitri touched the pale silk of her summer dress.

'Pretty frock,' he said, 'you do look so pretty since you came to Petrograd. Olga, don't you think it's time you gave up the hospital?'

'Stop nursing? Why on earth should I?'

'The men don't like it, and it's not fit work for you.'

'But it *is* fit work for your own sister, Marisha, and my Aunt Olga at Kiev?'

'They both took up nursing to get away from Petrograd, Marisha because of her divorce and Olga Alexandrovna because she wanted to escape from a miserable marriage. But you

217

and Tatiana are young girls, the daughters of the Czar, and please forgive me, Olga, "cheapen" is a horrible word to use, but some of the men think it cheapens you to go among them as a servant, washing their feet and bandaging their wounds —'

'They haven't read their Bibles, then.'

'They don't read the Bible, they kneel to their ikons. And they think the Czarina should be like an image in an ikon, all pearls and gold. They simply don't understand it when they see her in an apron and a veil.'

'That's true enough,' said Olga thoughtfully. 'I remember at one of the first hospitals we ever visited, at Vilna I think it was, one of the wounded men called me over just as we were leaving the ward. And he said, "Little sister, who's the old lady the boys carried in on their clasped hands?" I told him it was the Czarina, Alexandra Feodorovna, who was too lame to walk upstairs. He got quite angry. He said, "You lie, little sister, everybody knows Alexandra wears cloth of gold, and lives in a palace eating off gold plate and praying for our souls: she wouldn't come here in an apron, like my old woman back home, to see the likes of us." '

'You see?' said Dmitri.

'Yes, I do see, and I think it's very hard. If we did stay in our palaces and brought out the gold plate instead of our nice English china, you know what the left-wing press would make of that. If Tatiana and I empty slops, and go down on our knees to scrub floors, then we're told we're making ourselves too cheap. It's so unfair, so miserable, that everything we say or do is wrong!'

'I've never found it easy to be a Romanov.'

'Oh, *you*!' she said resentfully. 'Is that what you asked me to come here for, to give me a sermon about nursing?'

'No. Your father meant to telephone to you this morning. What did he say?'

'He only said he wasn't going back to Baranovichi.'

'Right, and now tell me, how long are you going to stay at the Anitchkov?'

'Indefinitely, I imagine — why?'

He answered her obliquely. 'You had a row with your mother about Rasputin, didn't you?'

'The biggest row of my life. But father patched it up when he came home.'

'Of course. And what you did was splendid, Olga; the night the newspapers reached GHQ with the story, we asked His Majesty's permission to drink your health.'

'And he granted it?'

'Yes, he did.'

'Sometimes I think I'll never understand him,' said his daughter.

'But as I remember,' said Dmitri, cautiously refilling Olga's glass, 'you were rather fond of Grigori Efimovich, when you were a little kid.'

'Yes, then, maybe, but not after I was old enough to understand his very convenient message: that the more you sin and the worse you sin, the more certain you are of redemption.'

Dmitri laughed. 'Olga, would you say I was crazy if I asked you to go back — oh, not tomorrow, but next week — to Czarskoe Selo?'

'But why?'

'Because the children need you, and because some of us are very worried about your father's health.'

'Father isn't ill, is he, Dmitri?'

'It's not so much that he's ill as that he's taking medicines that make him ill.'

'*Badmaiev!*' She spoke the name so loudly that Dmitri came quickly to her side and took the half-empty champagne glass from her suddenly limp hand. 'Olga!' he said, 'are you all right? I didn't mean to frighten you. I didn't know you knew.'

'Rasputin's friend,' she said with trembling lips. 'Anna Virubova's friend! Oh yes, I knew. Anastasia came home from the Srednaia with a story about meeting him along with father, and how father was going to take a bottle of Tibetan Elixir to the front with him — Dmitri, are they drugging him?'

'I'm afraid so. I haven't heard about the elixir, but Badmaiev has been sending him some stuff to take for — for a stomach complaint we've all been suffering from, and it makes Uncle Nicky wildly excited and then terribly depressed, and — well, the doctors are worried, that's all; and I thought you could help.'

'How, please? Even if I go with them to Ania's every time they visit her, and make sure father doesn't leave with a bottle of dope in his pocket, how can I stop *any* of that gang, say

Sister Akulina, smuggling out the stuff to mother at the hospital? How can I check all the couriers that travel between home and GHQ? My mother would send on any medicine, any wine, as long as it was blessed by Father Grigori! Dmitri, I'm sorry, but it isn't my responsibility! If only we could get rid of Rasputin —'

The slim young man in the grey civilian suit, so quietly distinguished in the bizarre décor of savage colours which Bakst had created for him, sat very still on the arm of Olga's chair.

'How would you propose to get rid of him?' he said.

'By persuading father to send him back to Povrovskoe.'

Dmitri relaxed. 'That has been tried,' he said.

'This might help in the persuasion.' Olga opened her big silk bag and handed her cousin the package Simon had bought outside the Gostinnoi Dvor. The slab of chocolate was unopened, the orange ribbon tied again round the *Poems* of Lermontov, the cartoon called 'The Ruler of Russia' was ready to slip out and hand to him. The young man examined it in silence.

'Where did you get this, Olga?'

'A friend bought it for me.'

'Nice friends you have, I must say.'

'It wasn't done on purpose! My friend bought it from a stall on the Nevski Prospekt, out of a hundred other chocolate packs. Sold on the public street, Dmitri, and the police don't even interfere!'

'They will now, don't worry, I'll see to that.' He dropped the little book and the cartoon in his pocket. 'I'm sorry you had to see that rubbish, or even know it existed. Selling on the streets, that's new.'

'New?' Olga caught at the word. 'You mean you've actually seen that — that trash before? Are there other pictures like that going the rounds?'

Dmitri could have told her that he had seen far worse, that the police, civil and military, had their work cut out to suppress the pornographic drawings of the Czarina, Anna Virubova, and Rasputin, sandwiched together in a writhing climax of arms and legs. He had too much respect for Olga's integrity to put her off with a lie or a caress. He only answered her with one word, 'Yes.'

Two anxious days followed for Olga. Marie, whom she consulted by telephone, told her papa was taking a new kind of tea, imported from Outer Mongolia by Badmaiev, which would cause Divine Grace to descend upon him. Some of this was given to Sunbeam, as Alexis was still called by his parents, but the boy spat it out of the schoolroom window and refused to take any more.

'And don't *you* take any, Bow-Wow — nor Tania, nor Imp —'

'It's far too precious for the likes of us. Olga, when are you coming home?'

'Soon, but I've several things to do in Petrograd, and you know how granny is. She keeps saying she'll miss me terribly —'

'We miss you here,' said Marie, and Olga laid down the telephone feeling that Dmitri was right: her first duty lay at home with the other members of OTMA, and with Alexis. But there were engagements to fulfil, including a charity ballet performance at the Maryinsky Theatre, and she carried them out attended by her two ladies and by her acting ADC, Lieutenant Hendrikov.

During those two days the tremendous German advance started which was to result in the recapture of the whole of Galicia and Bukovina, and in the north a part of Courland as well. To train the Second Category and transport them to the front was obviously going to demand a major effort from a War Ministry which so far had made nothing but mistakes, and a big comb-out of all the garrison troops began. Even Simon Hendrikov, so recently discharged from hospital, was ordered to report to a medical board.

Whatever he felt about his interview, he was smiling when on the third afternoon, Olga having found another opportunity to escape from the Winter Palace, his princess joined him in the shadow of the New Hermitage.

'I've got a droshki waiting on the Millionnaia.'

'Oh, wonderful, I've never ridden in a droshki. But I thought we were going to your home this afternoon?'

'If you still want to. But as it's quite a long walk to the Fourth Line, I thought you'd rather drive.'

'Of course I want to! I've been looking forward to it!'

But on the pavement of the Millionnaia, while the *isvostchik* was whipping his weary old horse towards them through the dusty sunlight, Simon said urgently:

'You do understand, don't you, that my mother and father won't be there? They went to Finland yesterday. I — I didn't tell them there was a possibility you might honour our home with a visit—'

'Oh, don't, Simon, you sound like someone presenting a purse of gold to a war charity! Darya Karlovna will be there, she told me so this morning. Let's get in.'

The droshki set them down under the linden trees of the Fourth Line, and the porter, bowing low, looked inquisitively at the veiled lady accompanying Professor Hendrikov's only son. Simon opened the door of the flat with his latchkey, and scowled at the sight of strapped trunks and tin boxes blocking the rather narrow hall.

'What a mess,' he said, 'I didn't want you to see the place like this. And Dolly ought to be here to welcome you.'

'With the ikon and the bread and salt?' she laughed. 'I think this is fun. Am I to come in here?'

Simon was holding open the door of the living-room. The bay windows were wide open, and the Island's summer smell of lime blossom, tar and salt water filled the room. For that reason it was at once more pleasing to Olga than the Grand Duke Dmitri's splendid living-room where scented pastilles burned, and heavy net curtains shut out the light and air.

'I told you it wasn't as nice as the dacha,' said Simon, watching anxiously as she walked round the big table to inspect the bookcases and the 'problem picture' of the young mother and her child.

'The dacha's special. But this is such a friendly room, Simon. It feels as if a lot of people had enjoyed eating and talking and living here ... Do you suppose vodka was *her* downfall?' she said mischievously, tilting her head at the picture of the girl with the baby and the ringless hand.

'You're very quick, Olga Nicolaievna. Most people don't see the vodka bottle until they've looked two or three times. If they bother to look at all, that is.'

'The artist was clever, he hid the bottle on the floor by her skirt. Poor thing! I suppose that's what they call narrative painting.'

'Talking of narratives, I telephoned my father about that

222

movie we saw. He promised to look out Scott's poem for me, but I don't see anything like English poetry here. It may be in the study.'

Olga followed him into the professor's study, where all was unnaturally tidy, with nothing on the desk but a big calf-bound volume of Scott with a paper stuck between the pages.

' "Lady Heron's Song" from *Marmion*,' Simon read aloud.

'How clever of your father to know where to look!'

'You read it, Olga. Read it and tell me what it says.'

Olga read:

'O, young Lochinvar is come out of the west,
Through all the wide border his steed was the best,
And save his good broadsword he weapons had none,
He rode all unarm'd, and he rode all alone.
So faithful in love and so dauntless in war,
There never was knight like the young Lochinvar.'

'It's very long,' she said, reading on silently, 'But — yes, I understand it now. They took a tale of chivalry and made a Wild West movie out of it, and why not?'

'That verse you read, what does it say in Russian?'

She translated to the best of her ability. And Simon asked if Lochinvar had been a prince or a nobleman.

'No, just a soldier, I think. It says he had a sword.'

'And he was faithful to the girl he loved.'

' "So faithful in love and so dauntless in war",' said Olga. 'Like you, Simon.'

'Oh, my darling!' The word had been spoken at last between them, spoken and avowed; and Olga was in Simon's arms, close held, with her lips parting beneath his eager lips, which he lifted from hers only to say again and again, 'I love you!'

She took her hat off and laid her cheek against Simon's with a sigh of happiness. And now he was free to touch her hair, her bare throat, at last her breast, until desire was made manifest in both their bodies, and Olga broke away from him with a gasp —

'Dolly —'

'Dolly won't be home until four o'clock,' Simon said roughly. 'Don't be afraid, the maids are here. But I wanted to be alone with you, we're never alone, I had to tell you that I love you —'

'Tell me again.'

At that whisper of acquiescence Simon almost lost his head. But he drew Olga gently to the battered old leather sofa, for once not covered with piles of students' essays, and there in his arms the princess whose one desire was to be loved heard that she was adored, idolised, worshipped, but above all had the heart's whole love of Simon Hendrikov. She held his head between her hands, feeling the blood beating in his temples and touching his crisp chestnut hair, watching his hazel eyes grow dark, tracing with one finger tip the square lines of the face that pleased her more than any other, until Simon interrupted his long-suppressed words of passion to say:

'I was such a fool a year ago, Olga! That day in the country, by the river, saying I was jealous of any marriage planned for you! Wanting you to stay for ever a young girl, so that I needn't picture you the wife of any other man! I wonder how I dared to say it — I, who have nothing to offer you, not even a Baltic title, let alone a name descended from Rurik —'

'The Romanovs aren't descended from Rurik. We're just a bunch of parvenus compared with him.'

'Try telling any courtier that. I'm a man without a title, or estates, or money —'

'You have your good broadsword, like young Lochinvar.'

Olga smiled, and Simon even laughed, until the meaning behind her words struck him, and he said almost in awe, 'You mean you don't care that I'm not a baron or a prince? That if it were humanly possible — but I know it's not — that you would marry *me*?'

'Yes I would, my darling.'

He kissed her until the breath almost left her body, and then he said, 'But why me? Why me, *dushenka*? There must be a thousand men like me, ready to fall in love with you: why should I be the one?'

'Because we're right for each other.'

Simon knew that, beyond all hoping, it was true. The Czar's daughter and the professor's son, in the simplicity of their view of life and the harmony of their physical natures, were the right match for each other. But even in his triumph Simon felt that he had said too much, had forced her to her own avowal,

224

and between kisses he begged Olga to believe that he would have waited — would have been silent in the present as in the past — except that they would be parted very soon.

'*What* did you say?' Olga raised her head from Simon's breast. 'Why should we be parted soon? You're coming back with me to Czarskoe Selo next week.'

'Darling, no. I had a medical board this morning, while you were at the hospital. I've been passed fit to rejoin my battalion, or what's left of it plus the new intake. They're stationed at Odessa now.'

'But that's ridiculous! You're not nearly fit for active service yet!'

'No, but Odessa's only a replacement depot.'

'It's also a staging point for the Turkish front. Next month you may be sent to Armenia or the Caucasus, or — anywhere!'

He thought it was entirely possible.

'I shall speak to the Czar at once,' said Olga.

'Darling, don't. You have to understand, I must go where I'm sent, it's all in the line of duty. And I owe my life to His Majesty. Without him I would have died in that filthy station yard at Warsaw. And look what I've got, along with my life! Four wonderful months of seeing you nearly every day. Those early mornings in the park, and being in your escort here in Petrograd, and now this — this joy.'

'Such a short joy!' said Olga, and there were tears on her dark lashes. 'But Simon, it won't be for ever that we'll be apart. You'll get leave, you'll come home; *we* may go to Livadia in the spring, and travel by Odessa ... and the war must end some day. Then I think there'll be big changes for us all. I don't know what they'll be exactly, but a lot of the old rules and traditions are being thrown overboard already, and who knows what the future may have in store for you and me?'

With his lips on hers Simon heard the door-bell ring. 'There's Dolly, ten minutes early, confound her!' he said. 'Darling, stay where you are.' There were voices in the hall, a man's, a girl's, not Dolly's, and some guttural words from the Lettish maid. Simon hurried out.

'What's the matter?' he said. 'Whose is the — good God, Mara, what are you doing here?'

The porter and the maid were pushing a heavy leather

portmanteau into place alongside the pile of luggage already in the hall, and Mara Trenova, slightly out of breath, was flexing the fingers of her right hand.

'A bit too heavy for the young lady, *barin*,' said the porter. 'I carried it upstairs for her.' His cap was in his hand, his eyes darting in all directions. Simon gave him a coin.

'All right, Stepan,' he said. 'Now, watch out for Darya Karlovna, I'm expecting her any minute. She'll come in a droshki, tell the driver to wait . . . Well, Mara Ivanovna,' he said as the man withdrew, 'that wasn't much of a welcome, was it? I didn't know you were coming to stay with us.'

'Don't be ridiculous, Simon, of course I'm not. I brought mother's portmanteau, it's to go to Finland by carrier with Madame Hendrikova's luggage. You did know mother had gone to Koivisto, didn't you?'

If he had heard it, Simon thought, it was in another life, the life before the one begun less than half an hour ago. He stammered that of course he knew, it was a fine idea, the weather in Finland was fine too, he thought, and at last, 'Won't you come in?' The Lettish maid asked if she should bring the samovar.

'Yes — no — yes, it doesn't matter,' Simon said. He ushered Mara into the living-room. The Grand Duchess Olga had not stayed in the study, and he was glad of that. She was looking at the books in the glass-fronted bookcase, wearing her hat again, like any friend of Madame Hendrikova's who was paying a social call. Mara looked at her with amazement. Then the Xenia training told; she swept her curtsey, while Simon said, 'Your Imperial Highness, may I present my sister's friend, Miss Mara Trenova?'

'How do you do,' said Olga cordially. 'I know who you are, Dolly's clever schoolfellow, she's often told me about you.'

'I'm flattered, Madame.'

'You're not doing nursing work, are you?'

'I'm obliged to earn my living, Madame.'

Simon opened his mouth to explain about The Children's Castle and shut it again. He knew quite well who published the candy classics, and by consequence the cartoon of Rasputin as the ruler of Russia. Suddenly aware that the high collar of his tunic was undone, he explained that Mara Ivanovna had an interesting job on a literary review.

'But I left it last week,' said Mara. 'I'm starting another job next Monday.'

'I think that's wonderful,' said Olga. 'Imagine being so independent!'

'I wouldn't care to change jobs with Your Imperial Highness.' It was Mara at her worst, defensive and gauche, and Simon was not surprised at the slight frost in Olga's 'Really?' and the deliberate misunderstanding in her reference to war nursing. He thanked heaven that Dolly came in then, happy in her greeting to both guests, and was followed by the beaming maid, who brought the samovar nobody wanted and made an immense clatter with the tea-things.

'Stepan said you wanted the droshki to wait?' said Dolly.

'Yes, so that Her Imperial Highness may go straight back with me to the Winter Palace,' Simon said. It was nearly an hour before they need meet the ladies-in-waiting, but this situation, with Mara Trenova's dark eyes travelling from one to the other, was too complicated for him. Olga was quite at her ease. She had sat down, at Dolly's shy request, to sip at a glass of tea, and looked up smiling at the mention of the palace.

'Lieutenant Hendrikov has been showing me parts of Petrograd I've never seen before,' she said, 'and the Fourth Line is one of the pleasantest of all.'

'I can show you other streets not nearly so pleasant,' said Mara Trenova. 'Where I live myself, for instance. You wouldn't like that much.'

The Grand Duchess raised her eyebrows at the tone, and Dolly said, 'But, Mara Ivanovna, your apartment's very nice. So — compact.'

'I imagine Her Imperial Highness has very little idea of how the poor live,' said Mara.

'On the contrary,' said Olga, 'I see the poor every day. Those who come to the hospitals to visit the wounded, and many of the soldiers' families my care committee tries to relieve. My sister and I visit the refugees at the Narva Gate shelter, every week of our lives.'

'We all know the Narva Gate — shelter, do you call it? The refugees *you* see have been bathed and clothed and fed and taught the words of thanks to say to the kind visitors. They're not representative.'

'Perhaps not,' said Olga. 'But when we go as near the front

as we're allowed, we take our turn to work in barns and stables without water, with only straw for beds, where the refugees come in — sometimes wounded, always covered with sores and lice, always half starving. Have you ever worked in any place like that?'

'No.'

'You should try it some time.'

'Madame, I don't have to go to the front to see people covered with sores and lice, and starving. I could show you sights like that not two miles from the Anitchkov Palace.'

'Where?'

'If we take that droshki, waiting outside, and cross the Neva, past the Xenia School and the Maryinski Theatre — which of course you know very well indeed — we'd come to the Jews' Market, where the people your grandfather deprived of their rights live in a stinking ghetto. We'd go on down the Zabalkanski, and I'd show you what they call civilian barracks, with the tiny rooms, the *kamorki*, where three or four families live together, with one chair and one table for ten people, and only their rags of washing hung on lines from wall to wall to separate them for the sake of decency. That's where the workers live, Your Imperial Highness, that's the kind of den they go back to from the war factories —'

'And you were never in a place like that in your life,' Simon interrupted. 'You got all that out of some subversive book.'

'But there *are* such places?' the Grand Duchess asked.

'Yes, there are, unfortunately,' Simon said, 'but the people in the *kamorki* are the real down-and-outs, the "dark people", the kind of riff-raff you find in any great city, not only Petrograd.'

'But I'm concerned with Petrograd,' said Olga. 'Mara Ivanovna, would you like to take me to the Zabalkanski now?'

'She's not going to take you anywhere!' said Simon angrily. He was suddenly furious with Mara for her ill-timed arrival and her strident introduction of a theme he knew only too well. And Olga had been provoked into accepting her challenge! He recognised her reckless tone, though he had seldom heard it before: it was the voice her sisters would have called 'Olga never saying No to a dare.'

'There's nothing to be afraid of in the Jews' Market, or the Zabalkanski either,' said Mara, as if she read his thoughts.

'All right, Mara Ivanovna, we all know you're a rebel,' he said. 'But it's my duty to protect the Grand Duchess, and I won't allow her to be jostled in the Market, or exposed to the insults any lady would risk in the *kamorki,* where even the Petrograd police won't go. It's no use, Your Imperial Highness,' he said, as Olga impatiently took up her bag. 'If you insist, I shall telephone to the guardroom of the Winter Palace, and a detachment of the Convoy Cossacks will be here in just as short a time as it takes them to saddle up. You must decide if you want their escort, or if you'll come back in the droshki with me.'

He turned to the window, to make sure the droshki was still there. The driver was sitting patiently on his box, chewing sunflower seeds.

When Simon looked round, all the girls were on their feet, and Olga was pulling on her gloves. She was still intent on Mara Ivanovna, and seemed to ignore her sarcastic smile.

'Simon Karlovich called you a rebel,' she said to the other girl. 'Are you more than that? Are you a revolutionary?'

'You would be a revolutionary, Madame, if you lived in the Zabalkanski.'

'Perhaps I should,' said Olga Nicolaievna. Then her irrepressible gaiety flashed out as she added, 'But don't you think my name's against me?'

CHAPTER TWELVE

LIEUTENANT HENDRIKOV received his movement orders for Odessa three days later, one day after he had been in attendance on the Grand Duchess Olga at another battleship launching, this time performed by the Czar himself. They had no opportunity for anything but a formal and public leave-taking, and the speed of Simon's removal from the scene sent Olga home to the Alexander Palace with anger in her heart.

She remembered Rasputin's gibe at her as 'a country girl . . . when the handsome lieutenant takes you into the bushes — ' and wondered if the spies of the *staretz*, or perhaps Anna Virubova herself, had told him about the morning meetings in the park with Simon, which they had never attempted to keep secret. Then, if Rasputin told her mother, how easy it would have been for Alexandra Feodorovna to drop a hint at the War Ministry, where the Minister owed her so much, and have the inconvenient lieutenant sent from Czarskoe Selo to Odessa. It was just the sort of feminine tit-for-tat her mother would enjoy, and Olga's head was high, her greeting cool, when she reappeared in the mauve boudoir. But her sisters squealed with joy at the sight of her, wearing one of the beautiful dresses their grandmother's couturier had made, and she, in turn, exclaimed at the sight of Marie in a probationer's overall.

'You've started in hospital already, Mashka?'

'Last week. I didn't tell you on the telephone, I wanted it to be a surprise.'

'And how's it going? Aren't you exhausted? We were, at the start.'

'Oh, I am too! Last night I went with papa and mamma to spend the evening with Ania, and I was so tired I fell asleep on the sofa and had no idea what was going on!' Marie gave Olga a significant look.

'You poor old thing,' said Olga lightly. 'I thought you weren't going to start nursing till September.'

'I couldn't wait after I heard about Nurse Cavell.'

'Who's she? Oh, that poor woman in Brussels, yes, I read about her.'

'I've started a scrap-book about Nurse Cavell.' And Marie showed her sister a blurred newspaper photograph of Edith Cavell, the matron of the Red Cross hospital in Brussels, who had just been tried and found guilty by the Germans of assisting English, French and Belgian soldiers to escape over the Dutch border.

'I thought heroines had to be beautiful — and young,' she said. '*She's* fifty!'

Olga looked at the thin, self-contained face beneath the nurse's bonnet. 'She looks very calm and brave, doesn't she? I think she's wonderful, Marie.'

'Imagine saving the lives of two hundred men! Why can't *we* do things like that!'

'Two hundred would be something,' said Olga grimly. For this was at the time when the Russians had surrendered Warsaw, and after Warsaw, Vilna, and the loss of millions of men had been in vain.

'Do you think the Germans will really dare to shoot her?' said Marie, still thinking of the heroine.

'Granny says the Germans are equal to any devilry.'

'We must all pray for her,' Tatiana said.

If her young deputy couldn't keep from falling asleep on Anna Virubova's sofa, Olga felt it was high time she was there to act as watchdog. She proposed herself as a companion to her father and mother every time they went to visit the lame woman, and sat up bored but alert while Sister Akulina handed round the insipid refreshments, to which the Czar sometimes added a bottle of cherry brandy, carried in the pocket of his tunic. There was never any sign of Rasputin, or Badmaiev; a young officer called Soloviev was present once or twice who spoke familiarly of them both, but no mysterious Tibetan cordials were offered, and Madame Virubova's conversation was as boring and banal as it had ever been. It was hardly possible to think of the crippled woman, now obese from lack of exercise, as dangerous, and yet Olga's intuition told her where the danger lay. It lay in the telephone which linked Anna Virubova with Rasputin's flat and with the palace. It lay, at the very end of the long coil of intrigue, in the double bed where a passion unquenched by years and suffering was

231

consummated, and where on the dark verge of sleep the Czar heard his wife's whispers, prompting him to act like Peter the Great, like Ivan the Terrible — to be Russia's saviour.

From half-hints dropped by Ania, from conversations halted when she went in to her mother's boudoir, Olga realised that the new intrigue centred on one thing: her mother's jealous hatred of the Commander-in-Chief. All her persuasions were directed at getting the Czar to relieve him of his command and send him to the Caucasus with some meaningless title like Viceroy, while the Czar took over the supreme command himself. But the Czar appeared to be in no hurry to act, or to visit the little provincial capital of Mohilev, to which the Stavka had removed from Baranovichi. The governor's house, standing in the woods above the Dnieper river, was ostensibly being made ready for the Grand Duke Nicholas Nicolaievich and his staff. Meanwhile the Czar transacted business with his Ministers, played with his boy, went for long walks with his ADCs, and at night read aloud to his wife, whose failing health had caused her to give up nursing at the palace hospital.

On the day when Nicholas II told his family, in his quiet way, that he intended to assume the supreme command, Olga escaped from her mother's open jubilation in the course of the afternoon. It was very hot, and she went into the park with a novel and a parasol, hoping for an hour alone, in a rose arbour near the entrance to the palace and with the book closed on the rustic table, to collect her thoughts. She was surprised to hear male voices from the arbour, one of them the eager voice of her brother Alexis.

'Olga!' he called as soon as she came into view, 'do come here! See who I'm entertaining! Monsieur Rodzianko!'

They were all on their feet as Olga came up; Alexis, and his Russian tutor, and the President of the Duma, Michael Rodzianko, who had once jovially described himself to Alexis as 'the biggest, fattest man in the whole of Russia'. He was not looking jovial now; the polite smile which accompanied his bow was forced, and as she gave him her hand to kiss Olga said, in an attempt at gaiety, 'Are you playing truant from the Duma, *monsieur le président?*'

'He came to see papa, and papa's too busy to talk to him,' Alexis interrupted. 'So he came out with me instead.'

'It's not quite as bad as Alexis Nicolaievich makes out,' said

Rodzianko, with a laugh as forced as his smile. 'My audience with His Majesty had to be postponed for a little while. And I've been in the hands of an accomplished host — '

Olga looked at the silver tray on the rustic table, which held chilled wine, fruit and cakes, and smiled. 'The Czar had a number of audiences to give this afternoon, I know,' she said. 'May I join your party?'

'We shall be honoured, Madame.'

'Alexis,' said the Russian tutor pleadingly, 'our lesson should have begun half an hour ago — '

'All right, I don't mind coming now, if Olga's going to sit with Michael Vladimirovich. Goodbye, sir,' said Alexis, holding out his hand to Rodzianko, 'I'm most awfully glad to have seen you again.'

'What a charming child,' said the President of the Duma, as the boy and his tutor hurried off towards the house. 'I'm glad I arrived in time to spare him half an hour of Russian grammar. He tells me the subject doesn't appeal to him at all.'

'We'll never make a scholar of him,' said Olga, and the tall, stout man surveyed her with appreciation. He was uncomfortably warm in the black frock coat required for an audience with the Czar: she looked as cool as springtime in a thin dress of greenish grey. It was the dress she had worn to walk with Simon on the Nevski Prospekt.

'I last had the pleasure of meeting Your Imperial Highness at the launching of the *Poltava*,' he said, and began to compliment her on her great personal success that day. But Olga cut him short in her characteristic way. 'Monsieur Rodzianko,' she said, 'you know so much: can you tell me anything about the Green Men? Do you know who they are, and what they do?'

Rodzianko sat astounded, silent under her blue direct gaze until he dared be silent no longer, and then he chose his words with care.

'As it happens I do know a great deal about that — organisation. You will permit me to say that I am surprised Your Imperial Highness has ever heard of them.'

'Rasputin mentioned them.'

He remembered then — the story so well publicised in the Petrograd press, of this girl's confrontation with Rasputin. He made up his mind that she deserved the truth, whatever use she made of it, or however far, in that palace of intrigue, she was to be trusted. He spoke as precisely as he would have spoken in the Duma:

'The Green Men are a body controlled by German agents in Stockholm, but operating in this country. Their object is to obtain places of power for their associates through the manipulation of Rasputin, and also to enrich themselves by the financial transactions of which his staff obtain inside information. Am I making myself clear, Madame?'

Olga nodded.

'The leader of the group is the banker Manus, one of the few Jews who has a residence permit and the right to do business in the capital. He has a confederate called Manuilov, a journalist and suspected forger, already enriched by the sale of stolen state papers. There are other names, equally unsavoury, which I need not mention to Your Imperial Highness. They are a decided menace to the good government of Russia. They meet weekly for dinner at Rasputin's apartment on the Gorokhovaia, where he is lavishly entertained by Manus, at whose expense the dinners are supplied.'

'Did the police find out all this?'

'The details were given me by an Englishman, who has been working on the Stockholm connection. We have checked with our sources here, and the facts are true.'

'Do you intend to make any arrests?'

'Arrest the friends of Rasputin?'

Olga's eyes fell. She might as well have said, arrest Rasputin.

The statesman leant across the table, and spoke urgently. 'Madame — Olga Nicolaievna — you've already proved your strength and courage. Do, I beg you, give me your support in the matter which brought me here today. I asked for an audience by telephone — I knew His Majesty was unwilling to grant it, just as now he is unwilling to see me — because he thinks of me as an upstart, a challenger to his authority, and too often as the voice of doom. I've warned him for years about Rasputin, and His Majesty has never paid the least attention to my warnings. If I told him what I've just told you about the Green Men he would only laugh at me. But I haven't come to complain of Rasputin today. I've come to warn him that if he persists in his intention of taking command of the armies he will put himself in a desperate situation. He will be blamed for every defeat and every failure. If he dissolves the Duma — as he is almost certain to do, as soon as we oppose his wishes — the workers of Petrograd will come out on strike. Not at our call, but because they have men behind them who know how to profit from every difficulty. Strikes in the war factories mean more defeats, more blame for the Commander-in-Chief. In the end, it will cost him his command — if not his throne.'

He saw that he had touched her to the heart, for Olga's face was very pale, and her voice shook as she said, 'Do you really think the dynasty may be endangered?'

'On my solemn oath, I do, Madame.'

'Then *you* must tell him so, and not you alone! Get the generals — get all the leaders of the Duma to put their views before him. He's not unreasonable, but — ' She stopped, but they both knew what her next words would have been, 'But he only listens to my mother.'

'Will *you* speak to him, urge him to see reason, as only a daughter can?'

'But he treats me like a child!' she said. 'Whenever I talk politics he laughs at me. But I will tell him, you have my word for it, that he mustn't quarrel with the Duma, because the Duma represents the people, whom he loves.'

Rodzianko looked at the pretty, flushed face admiringly. 'Madame,' he said, 'I wish to God *you* were the Heir to the Throne!'

'The fat fool had a great deal to say for himself today,' the Czar observed tranquilly to his wife, when the whole family met at the dinner table. 'He threatened me with dire consequences if I dissolve the Duma.'

'As you will, of course, darling.'

'Certainly, if they continue to make seditious speeches about me.'

Three of his listening daughters took his words as gospel, and even Olga knew better than to interpose at such a moment. As far as the supreme command of the army went, she was not sure of her ground. It was surely significant that even the head-quarters had been moved in the general retreat from the advancing Germans, but it had been a basic principle of the scanty instruction in history she had received that Russia *always* tempted her enemies to advance deep into the country and then destroy them. Think of Poltava! Think of Napoleon, driven back to the Beresina! These were the classic examples which the Czarina, in her exaltation, was never tired of quoting. But Olga was unable to persuade herself that her father was the reincarnation of Peter the Great or General Kutusov.

Everything fell out as Rodzianko had predicted. The Duma President was snubbed, the Duma suspended, the strikes began. The members of the Family telegraphed, asked for audiences, wrote letters of protest at the whole business of the State's being left to — Who? — while the Czar took up the exacting duties of supreme commander. The Czar smoked and smiled: was silent, and prepared to leave for Mohilev.

Olga tried once, though she knew it was useless, to make him change his mind. All she got for answer was an allusion to the birthday of the long-suffering Job, and the solemn words: 'Perhaps a scapegoat is needed to save Russia, and if so, I mean to be the victim. Come to the Znamenia church and pray with me, my dear.'

The last person to try was the Grand Duke Dmitri, and he, reckless as ever, stook a special train from Mohilev to beg 'Uncle Nicky' to leave 'Nikolasha' in command. It was two hours after his arrival before he was able to reach Olga by telephone.

'Dmitri! Where are you?'

'At Pavlovsk. Listen, Olga, I've *got* to have a talk with Uncle Nicky. I've called half a dozen times, and he won't even come to the telephone — '

'What do you expect me to do?'

'Fix it up for me. Beg Aunt Alix to let me come over in the car — '

'She won't listen to me, and neither will he, if it's about Mohilev.'

'Of course it's about Mohilev! It's going to be an absolute disaster if he throws out Nikolasha. The troops adore Nikolasha, they'll follow him through thick and thin — '

'Several millions of them have followed him to their deaths in the past twelve months.'

'Yes, we've had defeats, terrible defeats, but Nikolasha's not the *emperor*! If we have another summer like this one, the troops will throw your *father* out, and then where'll we all be? He's got to stay in the rear where he can't do any damage —'

Olga lost her temper. 'Now that's quite enough of that! You make my father sound like a perfect fool! Who are you to judge, at your age, and only an ADC? My father had a thorough military training —'

'Yes, just enough to make him look good at the summer manoeuvres at Krasnoe Selo. He had a few years in the army when he was a youngster, just like me, he doesn't know a damn thing more about how to handle troops in action than I do.'

'But he'll have General Alexeiev as his Chief of Staff, won't he?'

'Oh, to hell with Alexeiev! Olga, if you love me, you'll get me an audience today, before nightfall — they're waiting at Mohilev to hear —'

'*I* can't do it, but maybe Tatiana can.'

As usual, Tatiana could. Dmitri was invited to a family dinner that evening, and then to play billiards with the Czar. There were no equerries present. The click of balls became the murmur of voices, and eventually Dmitri emerged from the billiard room with a radiant face. The elder girls were hovering in the green drawing-room; he seized them round their waists and danced them troika-fashion to the private door.

'It's all right!' he exulted. 'Thanks to you two. What a pair of bricks you are! Uncle Nicky's given me his absolute promise to call off the whole thing and let Nikolasha stay. Hurrah!'

Two days later the Czar blandly and characteristically broke his promise to Dmitri, and placed himself at the head of his armies.

For once it seemed as if the evils of the long-suffering Job were to be spared the Czar. He took the supreme command at the Stavka, with General Alexeiev as the effective commander in the field, exactly at the moment when the German advance lost its impetus after five devastating months. The winter was not far away, and behind the frozen lines the Russian generals had time to plan the campaign of 1916, with only one new anxiety in the south, where Bulgaria had entered the war on the side of the Central Powers.

All was so calm at Mohilev that the Czar took the great decision, only six weeks after his first arrival, to fetch Alexis from the schoolroom to share his life at the Stavka and his visits to the troops. The boy, of course, was wild to go. He had been in excellent health for months, and was feeling neglected by his busy sisters; soldiers, real fighting soldiers, seemed likely to be better playmates than the few little boys he was ever allowed to meet. His mother, equally of course, was in terror for Sunbeam's safety, but he set off with such a retinue of doctors, tutors, sailor attendants and orderlies that 'the womenfolk', as he loftily called them, could hardly feel anxiety when he left them in his father's care.

He had adopted a device for himself that autumn, something in the style of the Prince of Wales's *Ich Dien*, but not so terse. 'Prayer to God and service to the Czar will never be in vain' was to be the boy's motto, and he scrawled it on the flyleaf of all his schoolbooks, often with the signature *Alexis* beneath it in a variety of fancy capital As and underlining, as if the writer were practising for the time when he would sign himself Alexis II. He was very much the Czarevich when he kissed his mother's hand on the station platform, and gravely saluted his admiring sisters. He was extremely proud of wearing the uniform of a private soldier, complete with military cap and top boots, 'instead of those kiddy sailor suits I used to wear', he said.

The letters from both father and son made delightful reading to the ladies left behind at Czarskoe Selo. Alexis had a camp bed in his father's room at Mohilev, with a *lampadka* burning constantly in front of his favourite ikon. He had a typewriter, and a silver bowl for his bedtime fruit instead of a silly china saucer. The girls read with resignation that he also had a new kitten, called Zubrovka, for which he wanted a collar and a bell.

To these practical details the Czar added that the troops cheered Alexis wherever he appeared, and the publicity pictures ('this sort of thing seems to be needed now') were excellent. The Allied liaison officers enjoyed his chatter and fun, and he had had the time of his life at Reval with the British submariners who had penetrated the German sea defences in the Baltic. At Odessa he had been almost mobbed by the townspeople. It was all a huge success, though Monsieur Gilliard might shake his head over neglected lessons, until the day when the letter said 'Alexis has a little cold . . . we are giving up our visit to Galicia . . . we are going back to Mohilev' . . . and then the telegrams.

Then the telegrams. Very severe bleeding from the nose, summon the specialists, we are on our way home. Bleeding can not be stopped, he is growing very weak, pray for him. And then the last, pathetic message, from Vitebsk: please let there be nobody at the station when we arrive tomorrow.

There was 'nobody' in the official sense, no courtier, no station master, when the blue imperial train drew gently into the private station at Czarskoe Selo. Only the tragic mother, the anxious girls, were there to see the faithful sailor, Nagorny, step warily to the ground with the half-conscious boy, wrapped in blankets, in his arms. Nagorny had held the Czarevich against his shoulder all through the terrible night, when to let the boy lie back upon his pillows might have been fatal.

They took him, with the blood still oozing from the plugs inserted in his nose, back to the palace where his hospital bed was waiting for him. Professor Feodorov, who had cared for him in other attacks, was in attendance, and he told the parents not to give up hope. The head cold, with the sneezing and catarrh, had unfortunately caused a tiny blood vessel to break inside the Czarevich's nose, but the doctors would proceed to a cauterisation of the nostrils, which would give relief.

The haemorrhage was halted, the boy had spoken and even taken a little beef tea, when Rasputin in his peasant dress arrived at the Alexander Palace. He was escorted to the forbidden bedroom floor as an honoured guest. He smiled at Alexis from the doorway of his room and made the sign of the Cross in the air. 'God bless you, little Aliesha,' he said in his resonant voice, 'you will soon be well and strong again.' He added to the unshaven Czar, the weeping Czarina, 'Don't be afraid, my dears. Nothing will happen to the Little One.' And then stood, with an exaggerated air of humility while the imperial couple knelt to kiss his hands.

'So Rasputin wins again,' said Olga, alone with Tatiana in the room from which she had had Rasputin ejected in the summer. 'Along he comes when that poor kid is cured, and gets away with all the credit.'

'How do we know when the cure took place? Father Grigori prays for Baby all the time, he told us so. Today he blessed him and promised he would be well. And he *is*!'

'Rot!' said the Grand Duchess Olga. 'They've been feeding us up with tales like that for years. Today you and I *saw* it happen. The doctors cauterised the nose, the bleeding stopped. Not by faith healing. By medical science!'

'What does it matter, if Baby's going to be all right? Honestly, I can't think straight any more — '

'I can,' said Olga. 'I think this is the worst thing that's happened to Alexis yet.'

'Oh, Olga, it's nothing like the Spala time! He seems quite comfortable already — sitting up in bed, and asking to see Joy, and his cat.'

'Yes, but don't you see? All the other times the internal bleeding began because he fell, or knocked himself against something, like last summer on the *Standart*. He hurt himself outside and then he started to bleed inside, that's what we were always told. But this time it was only a cold, Tania! He didn't trip, or bruise himself. He only sneezed, or blew his nose, as anyone might do! And that made him bleed so much he nearly died last night! Just because of a cold in the head!'

'Oh, it was far worse than a cold. He burst a blood vessel in his nose, the doctors said.'

'Yes, but *why* did it burst? I'm going to find out the truth this time, Tania; we've got to know.'

'You know they don't like us to ask questions. Mamma used to tell us it was because Alexis is a boy, and we're girls, so he's made differently from us — '

'Yes, she made a big sex thing out of it, trust her. Do you remember all her blushing and stammering about what she called the curse of womanhood? And telling us, even this year, that the stork had brought Irina a dear little baby? I'm going to tackle Feodorov tomorrow morning.'

But Professor Feodorov was far too skilled in turning aside questions on the Czarevich's health to reveal anything to Olga. It was Dr. Botkin, officially her mother's physician, but who often cared for the children too, who told her the truth at last. Perhaps he was exhausted by the strain of the child's dangerous haemorrhage, perhaps he was weary of the long dissembling, or perhaps he felt compassion for the girl of twenty who knew nothing of her own fatal inheritance, but he told her, in the privacy of his little study, that there was a scientific name for her brother's malady, which as far as medical science knew, was incurable.

Haemophilia. The female always the carrier, the male always

the sufferer. A disease where a blow, a fall, a bruise could cause the internal bleeding which knotted the muscles, cramped the limbs, stopped — as she had seen so often with Alexis — the very power to walk.

'You say the *female* is the carrier, *she* transmits the disease? Then it was mother who gave this — awful thing to Alexis?'

'That's been her tragedy, Olga Nicolaievna.'

'But how did *she* get it?'

'From her own mother, one of those little boys died of it. And *she* carried it from Queen Victoria, who also lost a son through haemophilia.'

'And Aunt Irene, is she a carrier too? Is that why *her* little boy died, and Waldemar is — delicate?'

'Alas, yes, that's the reason why.'

'But Aunt Victoria, she must be all right? The Battenberg boys are both strong and well, I know!'

'Yes, because Princess Victoria is not a carrier. Not every woman, in every family, transmits the malady. Sometimes it skips a generation and then reappears in the next —'

'I see,' said Olga, and Dr. Botkin wondered at her calm. 'It's like that game called Russian roulette, they say our young officers used to play. Hold the pistol to your head, fire, and with any luck the chamber will be empty! Am I a carrier or am I not? Get married and find out!'

'Dear Olga Nicolaievna, I know this has distressed you very much ... I do beg you won't tell Her Majesty what I've disclosed to you in confidence —'

'No, no, of course not,' Olga said almost abstractedly. She was putting the thought of her mother aside for a time: the guilt, the self-tormenting she had undergone explained so much. 'Alexis is the one who matters. Can he be cured?'

'I told you, my dear young lady, that no cure has yet been found for haemophilia.'

'But doctor, those other boys you spoke of, they died when they were younger than Alexis — little children, and he's at an age when he can be sensible, and learn to take great care of himself, can't he?'

'That's what we'd all begun to hope. But this new attack, the haemorrhage starting from a winter cold, the most ordinary of ailments ... this has shown us all, all the Czar's medical advisers, that the life of the Czarevich hangs by the merest thread.'

241

He allowed her to weep then, with her head on her folded arms, crouched over his work table; while the only words he could hear under the tangle of Olga's golden hair were 'My father! Oh, my poor father!' It was all new to her, the thought that her brother might die young, and never reign. Dr. Botkin, like the Czar and the Czarina, had lived with that thought for nearly twelve years.

When Olga raised her head at last, and felt for her handkerchief, and pushed her hair back from her wet eyes, he knew that she was fully aware of that other thought, which he had not dared to put into words. She voiced it at once, and with a smile which gave him pain to see.

'Thank you, Dr. Botkin,' said the Grand Duchess Olga. 'I'm grateful to you for telling me the truth. My sisters and I *have* wondered, and worried, and made wild guesses, for a long time now. Do many of the people who are closest to us, know?'

'Monsieur Gilliard does, but he's the soul of discretion, as you're aware. None of the Family, I think.'

'And I'll say nothing to my sisters, at least, not just now. But they'll have to be told some day, and probably quite soon. Because I understand quite well what you've been trying to tell me — that not one of us is a fit wife for any man.'

CHAPTER THIRTEEN

A FEW weeks after the bitter truth of her inheritance was told to Olga, she received a new and surprising proposal of marriage.

With great self-command, she told Tatiana nothing of Dr. Botkin's revelations. When asked, she answered 'I couldn't get a thing out of him we didn't know already!' and Tatiana had not persisted; she was deep in the old farce of pretending that the sudden return of the Czarevich was due to 'a really bad cold; poor darling, he wanted to be at home in his own bed!' Watching the faces of the courtiers as they listened to the story, Olga began to wonder how many of them believed it. She had a feeling that there were smiles and raised eyebrows behind their backs, just as in hospital there was often an ugly ripple of laughter in the wards when some man roughly declined the offering of a holy picture, and said 'How about a good tumbler of vodka, little sister, that's more in my line than your saints!'

The sad and funny thing in the latest fiction about the boy's illness was that the last place where Alexis wanted to be was in his own bed. He wanted to be back at Mohilev, in a man's world, and much more than his sisters' he wanted the companionship of 'Zilchik', his tutor, who had been with him at Mohilev and could endlessly discuss with him the garrisons they had visited and the soldiers they had met. Failing Zilchik Alexis made do with Olga. In spite of his bouts of illness and the constant petting and pampering, there was a tough, unsentimental streak in the boy which found its counterpart in his eldest sister, and to her, when they were alone, he was able to communicate what it felt like to go aboard the British submarines, lying sheathed in ice in Reval harbour, or to see the Russian wounded in the field dressing station at Rovno humbly touching the Czar's greatcoat as he knelt on one knee beside their stretchers and wished them well.

At Odessa in November he had seen Lieutenant Hendrikov,

one of a detachment of the Garde Equipage which had re-sumed its old duties as a bodyguard. 'And I'm jolly glad Simon Karlovich was there,' he said importantly, 'because the people really went wild at Odessa, and he helped to keep them back from the car. Honestly, Olga, it was *me* they wanted to touch that time! They kept shouting out "The Heir! the angel! the pretty boy!" all the way to the parade ground. Papa was so pleased.'

'I'll bet he was.'

'I asked Simon Karlovich if he wanted to send his love to you, and he said you knew all about that already. What did he mean?'

'Now, Alexis, don't be sly, and let's have a game of domi-noes!'

'I'm sick of dominoes. Papa plays every evening with the ADCs, and when I've finished my lessons he makes me play too.'

'It's high time you had lessons to do again.'

'That's what Zilchik says.'

The boy was not supposed to laugh, or sneeze, or do any-thing which might start another nasal haemorrhage, but it was difficult to keep him quiet when his new cat, Zubrovka, arrived in a basket from Mohilev (the satin lining torn to shreds) and promptly began to fight with Pussy, the grey Persian. Anna Virubova had just given Anastasia a little Pekinese called Jimmy, and when Jimmy and Joy added their barking to the fray, the sickroom, so-called, became, said the Czar, more like a bear garden. Entirely reassured about his heir's recovery, he went back alone to the Stavka at Mohilev.

Once more established as the man of the family, Alexis de-cided to keep a diary. Kind-hearted Marie helped him to rule the lines in a new book stamped '1916', and he started out in the footsteps of all his royal and imperial ancestors, who had been trained to keep diaries in their own schoolroom days. But with so little to chronicle the entries soon tailed away into the classic Forget What Did, and Alexis, teased by his sisters, an-nounced that he would make a proper start as a diarist when he went back to Mohilev. His father wrote that he was greatly missed at GHQ.

With the man of the house in bed by seven o'clock, the evening in the private apartments seemed long and intensely feminine. Madame Virubova, who called in her wheel-chair twice during the day, spent four hours with the Czarina every evening, talking about her imaginary love affairs and listening to the stories of Alexandra Feodorovna's happy childhood in Darmstadt, which had long ago reduced her daughters to strangled yawns. There was reading aloud, that favourite occupation, although the girls missed their father's attractive voice in the readings, and their mother's choice set Olga's teeth on edge. Alexandra Feodorovna had discovered an English book called *Through the Postern Gate*, over which she shed sentimental tears. The action took place mainly in a garden which, the Czarina said, reminded her so much of her sister's garden at Walton-on-Thames, where she and her future husband had once spent some happy and carefree days. Olga took the book upstairs after the first emotional reading aloud. It was not very long, and she finished it before she went to sleep.

'What did you think of it, childie?' he mother asked next day.

'I thought it was awful. It nearly made me sick.'

'Sick? That beautiful, tender story?'

'Very tender, just like underdone beef. That awful heroine, with her "stately presence", and poor "Guy, slight and boyish", that she played with on the beach when he was six and she was sixteen, and called him "Little Boy Blue"! How *could* he fall in love with a woman who kept on saying "Why was I not your mother?" Enough to put any man off for life, I should have thought.'

'Ten years is no great difference between a woman and a man.'

'Oh yes, it is, mamma, but that's not the point; what's so false is the way Christobel keeps *on* about feeling like his mother, even after he's grown up. "I knew my Little Boy Blue had no mother" — she can't stop talking about it, ever.'

'You don't know what *you're* talking about,' said the Czarina, whose presence at that moment was very stately indeed. 'When you meet the right man, Olga, you'll find out that every woman has the feelings of a mother for the man she loves. He's her first child, it's such a beautiful relationship . . .'

Olga heard the fantasy out in a polite silence. When she turned away to return Mrs. Barclay's masterpiece, in its mauve binding, to its place next to *The Rosary*, she formed with her lips the one word 'Bosh!' which caused Anastasia to burst into a fit of laughter and be sent from the room in disgrace.

After this lesson in love it was refreshing to find the Czarina in an unsentimental mood when the offer for Olga's hand was received.

It came out of the blue, on a day of heavy snow, with a twenty-four hours' warning which caused some surprise at the Alexander Palace.

'Olga,' said her mother, coming unannounced into the girls' sitting-room, 'I've had an extraordinary letter from Aunt Miechen.'

'Goodness, what does *she* want?'

'Wants to come to tea tomorrow, to have a confidential talk with me, and especially wants to have a word with you.'

'Me? What have I been doing wrong?'

'You know that best yourself,' said the Czarina darkly, and Olga began to think aloud about her recent committees and receptions — had she forgotten a name, a face, or an attentive word to one of Aunt Miechen's friends? 'I can't think of anything,' she said, 'We'll have to wait and see.'

'You'll be sure to be at home?'

'What's tomorrow? Thursday; yes, I'll be at home.'

'And try to make yourself look nice, you're getting far too fond of slopping around the house in uniform.'

Olga grimaced, but next afternoon she took care to brush her hair to its liveliest gold, and put on a dark red dress made for her most important public functions. It was only four months old, and seemed too loose already; Olga drew the waist-belt a notch tighter, and asked her attendant to bring a single strand of pearls.

Aunt Miechen, otherwise the Grand Duchess Marie Pavlovna, widow of the Czar's Uncle Vladimir, believed in keeping her relatives up to the mark: a dress had to be more elaborate, a tea more festive, when she graced the Alexander Palace with her presence. This seldom happened, except on state occasions, for Miechen and the Czarina had been at daggers drawn since the seventeen-year-old Alix of Hesse, painfully shy and stiff, had been unmercifully snubbed by the handsome young married woman on her first appearance in St. Petersburg society. The awkward princess had become the adored wife of the Czar, but Marie Pavlovna, self-confident, brilliant and worldly-wise, still treated her as a girl from the country, and her daughters as Cinderellas who were never even invited to the ball.

Aunt Miechen had a daughter of her own, married and living in Greece, and three sons for whom she had once been very ambitious. They were not young men now, and Kirill, the eldest, was the man who had cut his own career short by marrying the divorced wife of Alexandra Feodorovna's brother. The second, Boris, who was nearly forty, had for long lived the totally uninhibited life of a Romanov bachelor, and the third, Andrei — not rash enough to risk a morganatic marriage — had spent many happy and domesticated years with the ballerina, Mala Kchessinskaia, and the son she had borne to him.

That any one of these grand-ducal cousins could be the subject of a confidential talk with the Czarina was beyond Olga's imagination. Probably another attempt to get mamma to give a ball, she thought; for Aunt Miechen was the most brilliant hostess in Petrograd, and while the sovereigns sat drinking their own cherry brandy with Anna Virubova her salons were always filled with outstanding people in diplomacy and in all the arts of which she was the patron. Olga knew the great lady was arriving by train from town, and that a half-company of cavalry had been sent to escort her to the palace. She waited until she heard the horses clattering across the great forecourt, and a few minutes more, and then went quietly down to the green drawing-room, waiting for her mother's summons.

It came in less than a quarter of an hour: a bell ringing, a maid of honour curtseying, and then the Grand Duchess Olga was admitted to her mother's mauve boudoir and kissing the air exactly one inch from Aunt Miechen's cheek.

'How are you, my dear? Not too busy, not too tired, I hope?'

'Thank you, aunt, I'm very well. And you?'

'Aunt Miechen is in splendid form,' interrupted the Czarina. 'She has come to us with the most remarkable proposal I have ever heard.'

'Perhaps you would like to explain matters to the dear girl?' beamed Aunt Miechen, and the Czarina snapped, 'Tell her yourself, Marie. I'll have nothing to do with it.'

Olga looked interrogatively at her father's aunt. Marie Pavlovna wore a dark blue dress of fine cloth, with a sapphire brooch and earrings, just visible beneath her tiny sable bonnet.

She was a robust, handsome woman in middle life, whose vigour made the Czarina's once dazzling beauty seem sickly and faded. She smiled.

'Come and sit beside me, Olga dear, and don't stand looming over me like a young giantess.' The Grand Duchess reached forward and took Olga's hand. 'The fact is, I'm here to speak for my son, your cousin Boris. He begged me to come here myself and open the — the matter nearest to his heart, on his behalf. He has just told me, and of course his brothers, what none of us suspected: that ever since you left the schoolroom, his heart has been given to you.'

'I never suspected it either,' said Olga. 'I can't even remember when I saw my cousin Boris last.'

'He respected your youth, my dear, and your great devotion to our wounded heroes. He wanted to wait until you were at least twenty, before he spoke.'

'But he hasn't spoken yet,' said Olga. 'What am I supposed to do? Say "Oh, Aunt Miechen, this is so sudden"? Isn't Boris brave enough to do his own courting?'

'So you will give him permission to address you, when his military duties permit?' said Aunt Miechen swiftly.

'Oh certainly, he may *address* me,' Olga said, over her mother's furious gesture. 'Then I can ask him one or two questions myself.'

'Such as?'

'Well, Boris is twice my age; doesn't he really think that's rather too big a difference?'

'Not where there's a genuine attachment —'

'If Boris can convince me that there *is*! And then, Aunt Miechen, I should want to ask him if that Zina person, that lady who has shared his home here for so long, will pack her bags and leave before Boris is married, or if she'll stay on and make it a *ménage à trois*.'

'Olga, let me tell you, no well-brought-up girl ever referred to such subjects in *my* young day —'

'Probably not in your young day: at the court of Mecklenburg-Schwerin, wasn't it?' said Olga, who knew that Aunt Miechen hated to be reminded of her German provincial origins. 'But there's a war on, aunt, or hadn't you realised it? I know all Boris's Zinas and Zizis are just meant to be fun, a young man sowing his wild oats — and poor old Boris has had time to sow a whole provinceful of wild oats — but that doesn't mean a modern girl can close her eyes to it.'

'Boris will be grateful for your interest,' said his mother, her nostrils quivering. 'May I tell him that the Grand Duchess Olga does not entirely reject his addresses?'

'Tell him to ask my father, if he's such a stickler for etiquette. I think I know what father's going to say.'

'*I* shall write to Nicky tonight,' said the Czarina, getting a word in at last. 'I shall tell him that a used-up, half worn out, blasé man has dared to propose — at second hand — to a pure girl half his age — '

'My dear Alix, how you love to dramatise yourself,' said Marie Pavlovna, rising with amazing swiftness from her sofa. 'I'm sure poor Nicky will understand, far better than you do, how important it is to get dear Olga settled in a home of her own, and with a member of the Family, who understands all her little fads and fancies — '

'You make me feel like an old maid, Aunt Miechen.'

Miechen laughed, a hard little laugh. 'Scarcely an old maid at twenty,' she said, 'but the years pass, faster than you realise. You're too thin now, and you ethereal blondes don't keep your looks for ever. Haven't you found it so, Alix? ... I shall tell poor Boris not to give up hope. If Nicky will kindly grant him leave from his duties, perhaps he will be able to storm Olga's hard heart himself — and to assure her that any little difficulty she may feel sensitive about will of course be cleared away before the wedding.'

'Aunt Miechen managed a great deal better than we did,' said Olga, when her mother returned from making the adieux which protocol required. 'We were rude and excited, but she kept so cool. She made it sound as though she'd won.'

'She's had a long training in duplicity.'

'I wonder how Madame Zina Rashevskaia would like hearing herself called a little difficulty, something to be swept under the carpet to the tune of wedding bells?'

Olga laughed as she said it, but it was a bitter laugh, and the Czarina said remorsefully, 'I shouldn't have let Miechen upset you. I oughtn't to have sent for you, only I wanted to let her hear you speak your mind yourself. Otherwise she would have said I wanted to keep the whole thing a secret, and have something else to blame me for.'

'She didn't upset me, mother.'

'You stood up to her so well, lovey, far better than I did at your age. Now I must get a letter off to your papa — there's a courier leaving for Mohilev at six, I know.'

The Czarina sat down at her writing desk and opened her well-worn letter case. Olga said, 'You're not going to write him all of that, are you?'

'Why not?'

'Oh, I don't know.'

Alexandra paused with the pen in her hand. 'Don't worry, dear,' she said. 'I won't tell papa what other thoughts have filled your little head and heart. Even the best of men can't understand that a young girl has holy secrets which others cannot share —'

It was the exact, the sickly note of 'Little Boy Blue', and Olga said rebelliously. '*What* holy secrets? What are you talking about, mother?'

'Don't you still think rather too often about Dmitri? I had so hoped you were beginning to get over that! He's not reliable, my dear. Felix got him into a wretched set, and they say he's undermined his health with drinking and late hours —'

'Dmitri's a darling, and I won't listen to a word against him. But Boris! Mother, you don't know how humiliated I feel, to have been proposed to by Miechen, on behalf of Boris Vladimirovich!'

'Of course the whole thing is Aunt Miechen's idea. She thinks that by marrying you Boris would be nearer to the throne.'

'How could that be? I'm not in the succession to the throne! In Russia, no woman ever is.'

There was silence in the mauve boudoir, where the Czarina sat in her flowing mauve teagown, so exactly matched by the scented Parma violets massed in the shallow bowls by Baccarat. Then she said carefully, 'Boris wants to call himself the Czar's son-in-law, that's all.'

Olga had hardly time to consider all the implications of the Grand Duke Boris's second-hand and second-rate proposal when the Grand Duke Dmitri, on the following day, came on the telephone.

'Dmitri! Where have you gone to ground this time?'

'I'm back at Pavlovsk. Special leave to see Marisha, she's got a week off from her hospital at Pskov.'

'Oh good.' In any other house than the Czarina's, it should have been possible to invite two favourite cousins to come to dinner, but Olga knew better; she asked discreetly, 'When shall we see her — and you too, of course?'

'My last visit wasn't a great success, was it? . . . Olga, are you there? What we were wondering was, could you come to tea with all of us at Pavlovsk this afternoon? . . . Splendid! Try to come about four, and you and I can have a long talk first.'

There was for once no need to give notice of her movements, for the Czarina had announced that she would be engaged all afternoon with Monsieur Goremykin, the venerable prime minister. More and more, since the Czar became Commander-in-Chief, she had tended to think of herself as the regent, summoning Ministers from Petrograd to secret conclaves, after which the couriers were sent flying with long unpunctuated letters to Mohilev. Olga ordered a troika and a sleigh for half past three. It was a beautiful winter afternoon of hard, glittering frost, the very day to drive behind horses along the short two miles to the palace of Pavlovsk.

Two pairs of white-gloved hands made the bearskin lap robe secure round Olga's waist and attached it by loops to the side knobs as soon as she was settled in the sleigh. She was wearing the sables which Simon had admired, with the addition of a sable muff which she held up to her face, in the classic gesture of a Russian lady, as a protection from the frost and from any lumps of frozen earth and snow which might be thrown across the screen of bright blue netting on each side of the sleigh. The driver, himself shapeless in furs, cracked his whip as they dashed out into the avenue. The sleigh bells began to ring.

The way to Pavlovsk lay between an avenue of Christmas trees, pines thickly embossed with the long winter's snow, on each side of which lay the handsome houses of those members of the Family whose ancestors had followed the Romanov empresses to Czarskoe Selo in the bygone days. The girl wondered if there was one of those houses left which her parents could enter as friends, one in which the Czarina's folly had not made half a dozen enemies. She was glad to be going to Pavlovsk, where a few congenial people lived remote from politics: Dmitri's grandmother, the widowed Queen of Greece, and the young Serbian princess who had married Prince John Romanov, and now Marisha, who like Olga asked only to be loved. There was no pomp at the beautiful yellow palace built by the son of Catherine the Great, no Cossacks, no secret police. Two sentries presented arms as Olga's sleigh swept through the iron gates, and two more came to attention at the entrance to the palace. But almost before the footmen had helped his cousin free of the bearskin lap robe, the Grand Duke Dmitri came running out to greet her, shrugging himself into his grey overcoat, and saluting, with his hand to his fur hat, before he kissed the hand in the little suède glove.

'What an entrance!' he said admiringly. 'My frost princess, you should live surrounded by furs and snow!'

'And tall guardsmen!' she mocked him. 'Where's Marisha?'

'Sound asleep, but Helen meant to wake her as soon as we saw the sleigh. Come on, let's go for a walk. It's not too cold for you, is it?'

'*Walk?* Look at my shoes!'

'The paths are hard, you won't get your feet wet. And there's something I want to show you in the park.'

She said 'All right!' and tucked her hand companionably through the arm he offered. It was still daylight, although the ghost of a full moon had already appeared in the February blue, and a freshet of water could be seen among the ice of the little Slavianka river. A few wax candles, which the dowagers of Pavlovsk preferred to electricity, were lit in the windows of the palace.

'It hasn't changed much since his day, has it?' said Dmitri, looking up at the statue of their ancestor, the Czar Paul I, which stood alone in the forecourt.

'D'you know that if I'd been a boy they were going to call me Paul?'

'After *him* or after my father? I suppose my papa was still in favour, back in '95.'

'Granny says it was after the emperor. She was against it, just to annoy mother, I imagine; but when you consider that Paul I was murdered by his own son, it didn't seem a very good omen for Paul II.'

'Sometimes I'm sorry you weren't born a boy,' said Dmitri.

252

Olga laughed. 'What an ugly little wretch he was,' she said, still looking at the statue. 'Isn't that a grotesque nose! That's supposed to be what I inherited from him.'

'You've a very pretty nose,' said Dmitri, studying the charmingly tip-tilted profile under the becoming sables. 'Do you remember when you used to call it "my humble snub"?'

'Of course I was only fishing for a compliment. But oh, Dmitri, people *are* beginning to grow old when they start saying "Do you remember"!'

'Wait till you see what I've got to show you, down here in the park.'

'How *is* Marisha, Dmitri? Exhausted, I suppose?'

'She's been working awfully hard at her hospital, but she looks well in spite of it. She's bobbed her hair!'

'*Bobbed?*'

'Cut it short, round by the ears. It's the latest fashion abroad, and I must say it suits Marisha.'

'We'd never be allowed to cut our hair.'

'Dear Olga, not *your* lovely hair!'

Olga stopped short at the top of the path leading down to the Slavianka. 'Is this what you wanted to show me?' she said incredulously, and Dmitri laughed. In the wide, safe space between the frozen river and the little Temple of Friendship which Cameron had built, the prettiest of all the follies of the Pavlovsk park, there stood a magnificent snow mountain, far higher than any ever seen at Czarskoe Selo, with its ascent ladder frozen into the rear, and toboggans protected by a tarpaulin at one side.

'Alone I did it!' said Dmitri. 'Well — almost alone, with the assistance of Marisha and four creaking stablemen, veterans of the battle of Plevna, I'm inclined to believe —'

Olga giggled. 'Oh, come on, they couldn't be as old as that. It really is a beauty, though!'

'The poor little kids were playing on such a miniature one, I couldn't bear to see it. So we started in with river water and buckets, and that's how we ended up. You should have heard the nurses shrieking when I took the kids down on the toboggan!'

'I'll bet! Alexis would be wild with envy.'

'Want to have a run yourself?'

'All bundled up in furs? I haven't tobogganed since I was in the schoolroom.'

'That's not so long ago. Come on, I'll help you up.'

There was something in the frosty air, the solitude, the unusual sense of freedom, which made Olga willing, as ever, to accept the unspoken dare. She hardly needed Dmitri's hand to guide her up the ladder, he pulling up the toboggans with his other hand, until they stood together on the little platform at the top.

'It *is* high, Dmitri! You go first, like you used to do!'

'Right.'

He crammed the fur hat down on his blond head and was off, the runners of the toboggan striking sparks from the snow chute that was as hard as iron, flying down and down to brake and stop by the barrier formed by a hedge of young fir trees.

'Come on!' he shouted up to the excited girl, and Olga answered with a mock-dramatic cry as she launched her toboggan:

'Farewell, my youth!'

Then she felt the joy of that almost flight, that headlong, downward dash through particles of ice that stung her cheeks to crimson, down through depths of green and blue where the snow took on the colours of the sea, until she too braked to safety, and held out her hands to Dmitri.

He lifted her off the toboggan and into his arms. He kissed her as he had never kissed her in his life before, and Olga, hungry for love and aching with the strain of the months since Simon went away, responded to Dmitri's kisses. She put her arms round his neck like the child she still was, thrilling as he stooped from his great height to hold her closer still, as if their two bodies, so embraced, could hold back the oncoming darkness of the Russian night.

It was possible that if Dmitri Pavlovich had spoken the right words then, had turned to lead her up the path back to the palace in the shelter of his arm, the course of two lives might have been altered, and one life saved. But all he said when he released her was, 'Darling Olga, that was fun! No, don't let's go back just yet. There's something I want to say to you while we're alone. Something about your father.'

'We can talk indoors, surely. It's too cold to hang about in the snow.'

'Come inside the Temple, then, it's warm in there.'

He pushed open the door of the hall used for concerts before the war; now dismally empty with its seats piled round a statue of Catherine the Great as Ceres, goddess of plenty, but certainly not cold.

'You're right, the stoves are hot. I wonder why?'

'Helen had them lit this morning, in case the kids got their clothes wet tobogganing,' said Dmitri.

'I hope she had candles brought in too, if you're going to keep me here long.' Olga felt chilled and irritable, somehow and against her will defrauded.

'Cigarette?'

'Thanks.' It was dark enough inside the hall for the match to light up Dmitri's smoothly handsome face. 'Olga, this isn't going to be easy to say, and all I can do is blurt it out: I hear you've refused to marry Boris Vladimirovich.'

Over a heart-beat of anger she retorted, 'How quickly gossip travels in the Family!'

'Gossip! Isn't it true?'

'Of course it's true. Oh, I didn't say no to Aunt Miechen, not in so many words, because I thought it was impertinent of her even to make the offer, but she knew what I meant all right. I wouldn't touch her precious Boris with a ten-foot pole.'

'Olga, d'you know *why* that proposal was made, just at this time?'

'Not for love of me, I'm sure.'

He brushed that aside. 'Because Boris, with all his faults, is not a fool. He gets around, he meets more people than I do. He's quite aware that things are going very badly for your father — both at the Stavka and in Petrograd.'

Olga was silent. She had picked up a child's toy, a windmill abandoned on one of the piled chairs, and was whirling it with her forefinger.

'We who're close to him at GHQ — Olga, please believe me, I hate to tell you this — we know he's not equal to the responsibilities of a Commander-in-Chief. He doesn't even try to do a fair day's work! He sees Alexeiev in the morning, and some others of the Staff as well, and he always has luncheon with members of the different Allied missions. But in the afternoon he does gymnastics, or goes for a long walk if it isn't snowing. In the evening he pastes snapshots into his albums, or sits for a couple of hours over some kind of puzzle, or a game of patience. His last big activity, when Alexis was at GHQ, was listening to Alexis say his prayers.'

'You don't have to be cruel and sarcastic about religion.'

'I'm being cruel to be kind. Religion's at the root of all the trouble — not our own true Orthodox faith, but the vile perverted superstitions Uncle Nicky's picked up from Rasputin. Do you know he never goes for a walk without Rasputin's walking stick, or gives an audience without holding an image Rasputin sent him in his hand? Your mother told him to comb his hair with Rasputin's comb before he took any important decision, and he *does* it, Olga, he *uses* the filthy thing, I've seen him do it! Last month your mother sent him a little bottle of wine from Rasputin's saint's day feast — Saint Grigori, can't you picture it? and Uncle Nicky was so excited he drank the stuff straight out of the bottle —'

'Drank that wine!'

'Ah!' said Dmitri, 'that hit you hard — I thought it would.'

'Do you wonder?' said Olga. 'I told you when we were at your apartment in Petrograd that I couldn't possibly keep mother, or Ania for that matter, from sending anything Rasputin wanted sent, to Mohilev. Oh, my poor father? How did it affect him, the feast day wine?'

'It didn't affect him right away. But when it was time for *zakuski*, about an hour later, he drank a glass of vodka, which as you know he very seldom does, and ate nothing. He maundered all through luncheon about a character in a book called Little Boy Blue, and a little red gate and a brick wall covered with fruit outside your aunt's house at Walton — it was embarrassing. The Allied generals couldn't help exchanging glances — they probably thought poor Uncle Nicky was drunk.'

'I wish he had been,' said Olga sadly. 'But Dmitri, I don't think it's so terrible to go for long walks in the afternoon, even at the Stavka. It's no worse than spending a whole morning making a snow mountain, is it? And things will change as soon as the thaw begins. Father will get away from Mohilev and be with troops again, and everything will be quite different.'

'But whether he's at Mohilev or at the front, he won't be at home or in Petrograd, and that's where the real danger lies.'

'You're thinking of my mother, aren't you?'

'Of course I am. She's not even regent, but she's behaving as if she were the sovereign. Believe me, Olga, I've learned to quail — and so has Uncle Nicky — at the sight of the couriers arriving with her letters from Czarskoe Selo. Dismiss this Minister, promote that one, stop the trial of the War Minister and his conniving wife — there's nothing too great or too small for her to interfere in. And only two days ago she asked him to accept Goremykin's resignation and make Boris Stürmer prime minister —'

'Goremykin was coming to see her this afternoon.'

'Probably signing his resignation this very minute. To make room for Stürmer — with the German name and the German sympathies. Can't Aunt Alix realise that it's fatal for her to make that man her protégé?'

Olga threw the little windmill on the floor. The sunset light had almost died away, but the full moon was shining brighter, and the Russian colours of the windmill's sails, white, red and blue, were turned in its pallor to a uniform silver grey.

'What d'you expect me to do about it?' she cried in the high petulant voice of a schoolgirl.

The young man moistened his lips. 'To see straight, Olga. Because if things go on the way they are, with Aunt Alix and Stürmer and Rasputin running the country, we're heading straight for revolution. A far worse revolution than the disturbances of 1905.'

'Have you tried saying this to my father?'

'Have *I* tried! Everybody has tried — my own father, and the older cousins like Nikolai Mikhailovich, and poor old Nikolasha before he got shopped to the Caucasus, and Rodzianko speaking for the Duma, time and time again. None of us did any good. Nothing will do any good at all ... unless the Czar can be persuaded to abdicate.'

'*Abdicate!*'

'Yes, Olga. Give up the throne, and take Aunt Alix to live quietly at Livadia, away from war and politics ... before anything worse can happen to them.'

'Do you remember the grand-ducal oath you took when you were sixteen? The Romanov tradition, that the girls get a diamond necklace on their sixteenth birthday, and the boys pledge allegiance to the Czar as head of the Family, as well as sovereign? Does your allegiance include asking your sovereign to give up his crown?'

'I don't care a damn for any outworn tradition. What concerns me is the future of our House — and Russia.'

'But the House of Romanov comes first with you? I see.' Olga laughed scornfully, but her face was grave, and her cousin's silence forced her to say, 'If father really were to abdicate, is Alexis old enough to be crowned Czar?'

'Alexis is the Heir, and some people think he could reign with a council of regency until he comes of age.'

'But you don't?'

'I know what's the matter with Alexis. Do you?'

'Dr. Botkin told me, after they had to bring him home before Christmas. How did *you* find out?'

'Indirectly, from something one of the British officers said about the Spanish royal family. He'd been an attaché at Madrid before the war, and he learned that two of King Alfonso's sons suffer from haemophilia. Apparently they don't make any secret of it there.'

'Unlike us. And did this man say the boys got it from Queen Ena?'

'Alas yes, she's what they call a carrier, through her grandmother Queen Victoria.'

'Like my poor mother.' Before the pity in Dmitri's face she said with a kind of bravado, 'At least it's got nothing to do with *your* side of the Family!'

'No. But you understand why we daren't try to rally army support to poor little Alexis, because —'

Dmitri left the sentence unfinished. But Olga could fill it in with the words of Dr. Botkin: 'because the life of the Czarevich hangs by the merest thread.'

'After Alexis,' the Grand Duke went on, 'the next in the line of succession is your Uncle Michael. I remember the prayers for him in church as heir-apparent, years before Alexis was born.'

'Poor old Uncle Misha, with his famous morganatic wife!' said Olga. 'Do you think he'd be much of a success as Floppy the First?'

'No, I don't. And that's when we come to the ambitious Boris and his two brothers, the grandsons of the Czar-Liberator.'

'You're a grandson of the Czar-Liberator too, Dmitri.'

'But I'm not ambitious, dear.'

'You can't mean that *Boris* wants to be the Czar?'

'No, but he rather fancies himself as the consort of the reigning Czarina.'

It took a moment for his meaning to sink in. Then Olga, seizing the lapels of her cousin's greatcoat, and striving to see his face in the brightening moonlight, exclaimed 'Me! You think I could succeed to the throne, and reign as the Czarina? You're out of your mind.'

He took her in his arms again, in an attempt to regain the physical harmony they had both felt at the bottom of the snow mountain.

'No, I'm not crazy, dear. You are the logical choice. You're Uncle Nicky's eldest daughter, and you've made yourself immensely popular since the war started. Everybody admires the way you stood up to Rasputin. And remember how those sailors and those shipyard workers cheered you at the *Poltava* launching? Remember the Allied ambassadors applauding, that night at the concert in the circus? You made more friends in the one month you spent at the Anitchkov than your mother did in more than twenty years in Russia. Don't shake your head! I know all about the Law of Succession. Paul I declared by imperial ukase that no woman could reign in Russia after him, because he hated his mother, the great Catherine. Your father need only sign a rescript revoking that ukase, and a new law stands.'

'Do you think he would ever sign a ukase making over the throne to me? My mother wouldn't let him, to begin with.'

'She can be stopped from interfering, by force if need be,' said Dmitri. 'What we are planning could be the dawn of a new day for Russia.'

'Planning!' she echoed. 'Do you realise that what you're saying is high treason?'

'It won't be treason if the plan succeeds. If you stand fast on the letter of the law, we'll make your father sign the ukase when he signs the act of abdication. If he refuses, the army will carry you to Petrograd and the Winter Palace, as her soldiers did for Catherine the Great.'

'She usurped her husband's throne, and later had her husband killed,' said Olga. 'Aren't we a charming family? Now you

259

and your friends want me to usurp my brother's throne, in the expectation that he'll die an early death. Who *are* your friends, by the way? You didn't dream this up all by yourself.'

'I'm not at liberty to reveal their names.'

'Except for Boris Vladimirovich, who seems to have shown his hand too soon.'

The Grand Duke plucked up courage. She had objected, of course, and made a girl's fuss; but the deed was done, and at least she had not refused point blank. He said urgently, 'I know all this has been a shock. But think it over, Olga; try to see it from everybody's point of view. Uncle Nicky will be perfectly happy with Aunt Alix at Livadia, and poor little Alexis may well be thankful to be spared the burden of the crown. Whereas you, Olga — strong and generous-hearted — '

'I don't want to think about it any more just now. Let's go back and talk to the Queen and Helen and Marisha . . . B-rr! I'm cold, and I can hardly see the way to the door.'

'It's over this way; take my hand.'

'If you were an experienced conspirator you'd have a dark lantern to light us back.'

'The moon is bright enough.' Dmitri pulled open the door. Between the Temple of Friendship, garlanded in carved grapes, and the river, the snow mountain reared up its great height in the moonlight, and Olga shivered again.

'That thing looks like a scaffold now . . . Dmitri!'

'Yes?'

'I don't know much about how the army put Catherine on the throne, a hundred and fifty years ago. Mother always made cuts in Professor Petrov's lessons, because she said Catherine was a disreputable woman . . . Don't laugh! I do know it was Prince Orlov, Catherine's lover, who engineered the *coup d'état*.'

'Well?'

'If I agree to your plan, depending absolutely on my father's abdication, do you intend to play Orlov to my Ekaterina?'

'If you want me to.'

'And if I tell you I'll have nothing whatever to do with it?'

Dmitri sighed. 'Then I suppose I'll have to think of something else.'

CHAPTER FOURTEEN

'WE ought to say, "Thank God for our good dinner!" as we used to do when we were little, eh, Dolly?' said Simon Hendrikov.

'It was a wonderful dinner, Joe!' said Dolly, and Joe Calvert beamed. They were all sitting round the table in Joe's rented flat in the Italianskaia, with the windows open to the summer night.

'Glad you enjoyed it,' he said. 'I can't flatter myself you were treated to home cooking, but I wouldn't wish Varvara's efforts on to any of my guests. Specially when it's a celebration for Simon Karlovich's return to Petrograd.'

'I'm flattered,' Simon said, 'but isn't it something new for the Europa to send out meals to private houses?'

'I wouldn't know. I fixed it up with them about six months ago, and they've been sending food round ever since.'

'I wrote to you about the lovely dinner Joe gave father and mother and me at our New Year,' said Dolly, with a faint touch of complacency, and Simon agreed with a smile. During a pleasant evening he had been quietly amused by his sister's little proprietary airs towards Joe Calvert, and Joe's devoted attention to everything Dolly said. He had never imagined having an American brother-in-law, but from hints dropped by his parents, and Dolly's sparkling eyes, he thought this might come to be. After all, Dolly was nineteen now, and prettier than ever.

'You were saying you hadn't seen Mara Trenova since her mother's funeral,' Joe began, when Varvara had lumbered out with a tray of dishes, and Dolly pouted.

'*Not* a very cheerful subject for a celebration, poor Madame Trenova's death,' she said. 'It was very sudden, just three weeks ago. The Finnish doctor said she must have had a heart condition for a long time.'

'And never had a check-up, I suppose.'

'Probably not. Mara travelled to the dacha with papa and

me. We buried her at Koivisto, you know: it seemed the best thing to do. And at least she wasn't alone, mamma was with her when she had the last attack.'

Joe changed the subject. 'Any chance of your getting to the dacha before your next posting, Simon Karlovich?'

'If I'm very lucky. You've been there, haven't you?'

'Your mother kindly asked me for the Easter weekend. My first break for over six months, and I surely did enjoy it.'

'More than I enjoyed *my* Easter,' Simon grumbled. 'I expected to be back at Czarskoe Selo by the end of March.'

'Simon was looking forward to the Easter reception, and exchanging the resurrection kiss with all the little Grand Duchesses,' said Dolly slyly. '. . . Never mind, Simon, you'll be there tomorrow, and they'll soon be back from their visit to Mohilev.'

It was too much to expect shiftless Varvara to draw the cloth, and Joe set a tray with bottles and glasses on the white damask. It was new, like the damask table napkins, for he had recently replenished Dick Allen's modest stock, and bought some delicate glasses to replace the tumblers Varvara regularly smashed. There was even a bowl of ragged flowers in the middle of the table and another on the writing desk, in Dolly's honour, for Joe was trying to make the bleak little flat seem more like a home.

The telephone rang sharply.

'Who can that be, at eleven o'clock at night? Will you excuse me, please?' said Joe.

He picked up the telephone. 'Who? . . . Good Lord, we were just talking about you. How are you?' he put his hand over the mouthpiece and said 'It's Mara Trenova!' Simon, with interest, watched the back of Joe's neck slowly turning red.

'He's *what*? . . . I didn't even know he was in Petrograd. Where did you . . . well, have you called a doctor? . . . But surely if he's as bad off as you say . . . All right, I'll come as fast as I can. What's your number on the Yamskaia? . . . Right, I'm just leaving.'

He hung up without a word of goodbye, and turned to the Hendrikovs.

'That was Mara,' he repeated unnecessarily. 'She's got that friend of mine, you met him once, Dolly, Richard Allen, at her apartment. He's been in some sort of accident, cut his arm or something, and she wants me to come and take him away. Extraordinary girl!'

'He's the Englishman father knows, isn't he?' said Simon. 'Where do you suppose she met up with him?'

'Or why she didn't call a doctor. Look, I'm really sorry about this, but I guess some funny business has been going on. She made it seem like Dick had been drinking hard, and I just don't believe it.'

'I'll come with you,' said Dolly, jumping up. 'If there's been an accident, I can help.'

'I'll come too,' said Simon. 'I'll get a droshki from the rank outside the Europa.'

'Before we go anywhere,' said Dolly, very much in charge, 'I think we should put out some sheets to air. Perhaps Captain Allen ought to go to bed as soon as we bring him back.'

'I hate to have our evening end like this.' But Joe got fresh bed linen from the cupboard in the hall, and helped Dolly to spread it out in the warm living-room before they all went downstairs. Not much was said until they found a droshki. There was a traffic jam at the corner of the Nevski Prospekt, where three soldiers in well-worn uniforms were objecting to being refused entrance to a tramcar.

'That's one of the stupidest things they've done yet,' said Joe. 'Depriving the military of the right to ride the street-cars.'

Simon made no reply. There was much else to get accus-tomed to in this city from which he had been absent for nearly a year, above all the endless queues for food and fuel. There was now very little meat on sale, although the Europa Hotel had sent a leg of roast lamb to Joe Calvert's dinner table as a matter of course. Lena, his mother's one remaining maid, had told him that the great subject of rumour in the food queues was the scandal of the municipal cold storage depot beyond the Baltiski railway station, where the refrigerators were overflowing with rotting animal carcases, once intended as beef for the army, and now, because of the lack of transport to the front, fit only to be taken to the glue factories by horse-drawn carts.

The square in front of the Vladimir church smelled as if some of the carcases had been piled there too, for the street cleaners had come out on strike, and beneath the empty market stalls and on the cobbles there was a thick layer of straw and vegetable refuse. Some beggars were pawing it over in the hope of finding food.

'It's a lousy section for a girl like Mara to be living in,' said Joe. 'I thought she'd got a worthwhile job with some newspaper.'

'She's not with a newspaper at all now,' Dolly said. 'She's employed as a stenographer in a commercial office — hides and tallow, I think she said.'

'Can't be much money in hides and tallow these days.'

There was a knot of loungers in front of the tenement where Mara Trenova lived. They muttered and move unwillingly aside at the arrival of a droshki with an officer in the uniform of the Garde Equipage, but a girl in nurse's dress was rightly a privileged person, and Dolly, followed by Joe, went unmolested up the steep stone stair. Simon remained standing by the droshki, to make sure, he said, that the *isvoschik* didn't pick up another fare. In fact he wanted to avoid the irritation of a meeting with Mara Trenova.

The bell pull outside the door of her flat was broken, and the tongue waggled uselessly in Joe Calvert's hand. He knocked on the thick panel. After a few minutes the door was slowly opened, in the semi-darkness it appeared by nobody. Then Joe looked down and saw, somewhere between his waist and his shoulders, the huge head of a hunchback with suspicious eyes peering through a tangle of dark hair.

'Mara Trenova sent for me,' said Joe, and then she was there, saying 'Thank you, Joe! What, Dolly, you too?' and drawing them into a room with an empty grate, a kitchen table covered by a checked cotton runner over oilcloth, and a long sofa or daybed on which Richard Allen lay breathing heavily. One arm, bandaged with strips of towelling, lay across his chest, and a tin pan full of blood-stained water stood on the kitchen table.

Dolly Hendrikova began to examine the bandages, and Joe asked Mara what in the world had happened.

'*I* don't know,' she said with an affectation of bravado. 'I was at "The Red Sarafan" with my friend Mr. Sergiev' (she indicated the hunchback, standing like a sentry by the kitchen door) 'when we saw Mr. Allen arguing with some men at the entrance. We thought he'd been drinking, which was none of our business, but when we left ourselves a few minutes later we saw him leaning against the wall with blood dripping from his sleeve. I brought him here for first-aid treatment, but then he became unconscious, and the best thing I could think of was to send for you.'

'Quite right,' said Joe, and Dolly, looking up, said, 'You were smart to put on a tourniquet, Mara. The bleeding seems to have stopped. Is there another piece of towelling, please?'

'Plenty. How lucky you could come along, Dolly! Were you spending the evening at Mr. Calvert's flat?' Dolly was tearing up a strip of towel, and Mara went on without waiting for an answer, 'It was only a shallow cut inside his arm.'

Joe looked at the hunchback and then at Mara. Another year of independence, of God knew what else, had changed her greatly. Her sharp features were sharper than ever beneath a thick black fringe, for Mara, though not for reasons of fashion, had cut her hair short, and the heavy leather belt she wore gave an almost masculine look to her dark jacket and skirt.

'I was sorry to hear of your bereavement,' he said.

'Thank you. And thanks to Dolly's parents, my mother had one good year — perhaps the happiest she ever had, since my father died.'

'Are you going to stay on alone in this apartment?'

'For the present, yes . . . See, now he's coming round.'

Dolly had laid a cloth soaked in cold water on Dick's forehead, and as the drops ran down his cheeks he moaned and stirred on the couch.

'He looks younger than when I saw him last,' said Dolly in a whisper.

'He's shaved off his moustache, that's why.' Joe thought that a thin blue suit, which might have been worn by anybody, instead of the padded garments of the Moscow merchant, also made Captain Allen look slighter and younger; and at that moment the Englishman opened his eyes and said, 'Good Lord! All of you! Awfully sorry to be such a nuisance! Where have you brought me to?'

'You mustn't talk, Mr. Allen,' said Dolly Hendrikova.

Dick levered himself up on his sound elbow, gave a groan, and set his teeth.

'Dolly, don't you think he needs a doctor?' said Joe, and Mara hastily intervened.

'It would take too long. No doctor is ever in a hurry to come to the Yamskaia — '

'I've got nine American doctors cooling their heels not very far away,' said Joe, 'and a droshki waiting outside. Dick!' he said urgently, as Captain Allen succeeded in sitting up, 'do you think you can make it as far as the street?'

'I can try.'

'That's the best plan!' cried Mara. 'What do you want now, Dolly? Material for a sling? Will this do?' She took a whole, clean roller towel from a cupboard, cut it open with the kitchen shears, and held safety-pins while Dolly arranged the make-shift sling.

'I hope to God his wound doesn't open again, jolting over the cobbles,' muttered Joe. He braced himself beneath Dick's weight and remembered thankfully that Simon was waiting in the street below. Dolly put her arm around Dick's waist.

'Thank her — please,' Dick gasped, and Mara Trenova said, 'It's all right!' She spoke in English, and the silent hunchback scowled. 'You were kind to me when I was in distress, Joe. I'm glad I could do something for your friend.'

It was not till the following evening that Joe heard the complete story of the incident at 'The Red Sarafan'. By that time Dick was in good heart, having been doctored and nursed all round the clock by members of a newly arrived American Red Cross team who had volunteered to care for prisoners of war in Russia. Varvara, amazed and dismayed at finding her former master in the spare room bed, had slippered in and out all day with glasses of tea and bowls of buckwheat gruel, and although he had been ordered to remain in bed Dick had felt able to get up in the afternoon and make a laconic telephone call to the British Embassy.

'They're sending a car for me in the morning,' he told Joe, swirling round in one of the new glasses the very small ration of bourbon and branch water which Joe allowed him. 'They want me to rest up there for the next few days.'

'I should hope so. You must get leave for a couple of weeks, and go fishing. Well no, not fishing with that arm, but you could go to one of the embassy dachas, couldn't you?'

'I could not. In a couple of weeks' time I expect to be in Archangel, not exactly a holiday spot.'

'What're you going to do in Archangel?'

'An interpreting job.'

'Something to do with your pleasant evening at "The Red Sarafan"?'

'No, that was a hangover from my last assignment. Just a hunch I had, which didn't quite pay off.'

'I'll say it didn't. Now come clean, Dick, you always tell your story backward; begin at the beginning.'

'All right, I'll come clean, but just let me ask you one question. In your Service, is everything so compartmentalised, as well as departmentalised, that you don't know what problem your colleague in another branch is working on?'

'I'm not quite sure I follow your thinking,' said Joe cautiously.

'Well, here's an example. There was a very decent chap here before you, Murchison I think his name was?'

'Ned Murchison. He was posted to Berlin when I came to Petersburg in June '14.'

'Right! I remember wishing him luck at the Fourth of July party, where I met you for the first time. Now, you're both in the consular service, you're both neutrals, you could communicate by diplomatic bag, but tell me, have you ever heard of Ned Murchison from that day to this?'

'He could be posted to Jericho for all I know.'

'Precisely. Well, that's the way we operate too. Not on a personal but on a departmental scale. In other words, I may have wasted the two years I spent loosely attached to our Legation in Stockholm, trying to track down the flow of German gold from Germany to Petrograd.'

'I'd hardly call them wasted years.'

'They were, because I was concentrating on the flow of German money from Stockholm to the ring running Rasputin. Now I know the really big German bribes go through Stockholm and out again to Bern and Zürich.'

'To the Social Democrats in exile? The hard-core Marxists?'

'Exactly, to the Bolsheviki. As a matter of fact, to two chaps living in Switzerland for years. Of course, Whitehall knew all about it. Even I was told that Baron von Romberg, in Bern, was one of the German ambassadors whose embassy covered an intricate spy ring. But Bern was in one Whitehall dossier, and Stockholm was in another, and it wasn't until I picked up a cross-reference in Reval that I started to follow up the trail myself.'

'The cross-reference being Alexander Keskuela,' said Joe tranquilly.

'*Eh?*'

'We've got considerable material on him in our embassy files. We're not as dumb as some of you think we are, you know.'

'Then you know that Alexander Keskuela, born in Esthonia, arrived in Switzerland September 1914, is one of the key contacts with the man who calls himself Lenin — Vladimir Ilyich Ulianov, author of the "Defeatist Thesis" that Russia should be defeated by Germany to prepare the way for the class war. Keskuela was on to that as soon as the stuff was printed. He got £20,000 out of the German government, cash down, to finance Lenin's and all the other Bolshevik publications, as long as they hewed to the same party line.'

'That's about the figure we've got.'

'What have you got on Parvus?'

'Nothing.'

'Oh well now, Parvus. He's a bird of a very different feather. Keskuela has this excuse, he's an Esthonian patriot, and thinks the downfall of Czarism will mean an Esthonian Socialist Republic. Parvus is an old pal of Trotsky's. They were in the first Petersburg Soviet together, back in '05, but after a turn as financial adviser to the Young Turks, he got to like his little comforts, and by the spring of last year he was nicely established in a suite at the Baur au Lac, one of the most expensive hotels in Zürich. His official reason for living in Switzerland is that he's running a translation bureau called the Scientific Institute. The profits wouldn't pay for even a chauffeur's room at the Baur au Lac if it weren't a front for the German-Bolshevik finance machine. Parvus is the man who distributes the money to finance strikes in the Russian war factories. The railway workers, the chaps at the Baltiski, the Putilov, the Obukhov works — Parvus, sitting pretty in the Baur au Lac, is the man who brought them all out. He'll foot the bill for Lenin to come back to Russia, when the right time comes.'

'Which will be when?'

'Perhaps never, if this summer's offensive succeeds. But

there's no reason to suppose it'll succeed any more than the great attacks of 1914 and 1915. Less.'

'In other words, German money is behind the Social Dems. and their Bolshevik leadership, inside and outside of Russia. And the right time for Lenin to stage a *coup d'état* will be when the Czar's regime collapses from its own inertia.'

'That's one way to put it,' said Dick Allen, and lay back on his pillows.

'You getting tired?'

'No, carry on.'

'If Parvus and Keskuela are both outside Russia, what took you to "The Red Sarafan" last night?'

'Some news I had about one of Parvus's young men at the Institute. He and his mother left Russia for Switzerland a few years ago, ostensibly for the kid to study at Zürich University, and they bought a villa on the Dolderberg outside the town. I know Boris Heiden came back to Russia for a few months last year, but since then he took out Swiss citizenship, which means he can come and go to Germany as he likes. We believe he's one of the couriers between Lenin and his paymasters in Berlin, so when we picked up his trail on the way back to Petrograd I thought I'd like to check on who he was seeing here.'

'A youngster, is he?'

'Twenty-eight and looks younger, according to his description. Medium height, fair-haired, slim: everything we have on him stresses his marked resemblance to Alexander Kerensky, the Labour leader.'

'That's an odd coincidence.'

'My information was that this fellow Heiden might try to make contact with one of Lenin's agents at the "Sarafan" last night — it's a notorious meeting-place for the comrades, and I wonder it's never been raided by the Okhrana. So I went there for a look-see. I had some food and a half bottle of wine — which was sealed, and opened at the table — and listened to the music for a while. Then I had some brandy, brought in a glass, and after that I knew I had to get outside fast. There was a scuffle at the door, but I don't remember much until you were there in Mara's kitchen, and you know the rest.'

'Somebody slipped you a Micky Finn, I guess.'

'Somebody tried to knife me, and I don't mean just a slash up my inside arm. Joe, was I delirious, or was there really some sort of a dwarf hauling and shoving at me, when Mara got me up those stairs?'

'There was a poor misshapen creature along with her, called Sergiev, she said.'

'Could it have been Sergiev who was carrying the knife?'

'In that case I don't see Mara acting as the good Samaritan.'

'I'm not so sure. They say there are a lot of women like Mara in Switzerland — Russian exiles, fagging for the Bolsheviki, making the tea and copying the manifestoes. Women who would stick a knife in your back one minute and dry your feet with their hair the next. I don't think Mara Trenova's made up her mind if she wants to be a revolutionary or a saint.'

The Russian summer offensive of 1916 *had* to succeed. Nobody connected with the plan of campaign, from the Czar and his effective commander in the field, General Alexiev, and all the epauletted and bemedalled officers of the Stavka, to General Brusilov, chosen to spearhead the attack, dared to envisage anything less than total victory.

For some of them, and perhaps most of all for the Czar, it was a matter of personal prestige. It was galling to think that the only conspicuous Russian success since winter ended the German advance in 1915 had been achieved by the Grand Duke Nicholas, recently relieved by the Czar of the supreme command. Sent to a remote theatre of operations, 'Nikolasha' had distinguished himself by the capture of the key Turkish city of Erzurum, and followed it up by taking Trebizond on the Black Sea. It was proof of what nobody had really doubted, that the Grand Duke was a first-rate professional soldier, but scarcely a matter for great rejoicings. Meantime the French were engaged in the catastrophic defence of Verdun, and the British were about to open the equally catastrophic battle of the Somme. A Russian offensive on the grand scale would relieve the pressure on both the western Allies, and it was Simon Hendrikov's bad luck that he reported at Czarskoe Selo at this precise moment of history, when the advance was all that mattered, and nobody was interested in the return of an officer from the replacement depot at Odessa. The Guards were stationed, as a combat unit, in the Lithuanian sector of the front, where the enemy invariably attacked in great strength, and subject to the calculated losses, Lieutenant Hendrikov might expect to become a replacement there himself. Meanwhile, the papers confirming his captaincy were lost somewhere in the files of General Staff Headquarters.

The members of the imperial family seemed preoccupied too, in their different ways, when Simon saw them for the first time after they all came back from Mohilev at about ten o'clock one summer night. It was true that it was late, and only a few of the privileged courtiers had been invited to be at the station, but Simon could remember arrivals and departures when all the Grand Duchesses had made a point of greeting the members of the bodyguard by name. Now Tatiana seemed more intent than ever on her mother's comfort, while the younger girls and Alexis were equally concerned with sorting out the leashes and baskets of the various pets. The maids and valets were swarming round the luggage, and the Grand Duchess Olga, the last to leave the train, made her way round them without a look to right or left. Only a sidelong glance, and the corner of a smile, helped Simon to persuade himself that she had seen him in the uncertain light of the station lamps.

Next morning, long before the bugles sounded for parade, he went to their old rendezvous at the Znamenia church. He hardly dared hope that Olga would come to meet him. Their second parting had been much longer than the first, and this time he had not returned as a wounded hero, but simply as a run-of-the-mill subaltern who had spent a year shuffling papers in a transit camp outside Odessa. He had no right to hope that the Czar's daughter would be faithful to the memory of a few passionate words spoken in his father's study on another summer afternoon.

He knew that Olga's correspondence, as she neared her twenty-first birthday, was still as strictly supervised as when she was ten years old, and his only way to send her messages had been through Dolly. He wondered if she thought of their relationship as something in a story or a play, as illusory as *Young Lochinvar*, and in one sense Simon Hendrikov had not been as faithful in love as Farnum's cowboy, or the hero of Scott's poem. He had been physically unfaithful to his hopeless ideal not once but many times during the drudging months at

Odessa, and he wondered if Olga, too, would some day break under the strain of a romantic love with no hope of sexual fulfilment. He had heard it said more and more often that she would end by marrying her cousin Dmitri.

There the wondering ended, for she was coming towards him between the birch trees, with the early morning sun sending her long shadow ahead of her on the wet grass. She was thinner, and looked taller, dressed as he had never seen her dressed before, in a short skirt with a plain white silk blouse, and one of the new belted jersey coats slung round her shoulders. She was smiling as she came, but he saw that Olga's face was graver; the old eager friendliness was gone.

'Simon!' she said, and gave him her hand to kiss. 'I knew you would be here this morning! But what a long, long time you've been away!'

He was too diplomatic to say, 'Every time I put in for leave it was refused!' He said, 'It's been ten times as long for me,' and saw Olga frown at the courtier-like speech.

'I was hoping you would come for Easter,' she said.

'I had a railway pass for Easter, but then there were the troops from Erzurum to shift, and all Easter leave was cancelled.'

'I had the most beautiful Easter egg for you, painted with the Marine Guards' emblem.'

'May I have it now?'

'I gave it to Alexis, he's collecting regimental eggs.'

'I had a beautiful egg for you too.'

'Keep it until next year.'

'But what about the Easter kiss?' and Simon took Olga in his arms.

She had kissed him in the shelter of the Znamenia church last summer, with kisses as fresh as the lilac which grew round the walls, but now Olga put her hand against Simon's chest and said mischievously:

'Too late, it'll soon be midsummer! Don't you remember your Pushkin —

> "Gone is the resurrection kiss,
>   But yet to come: you swore it me!" '

'*Do* you swear it me, Olga darling? Do you?'
'Yes.'

272

Twenty minutes later the Grand Duchess Olga strolled home through the Alexander Palace park, swinging her jersey coat by its collar and humming a little tune. She felt exhilarated, lightened in the heart which had been heavy during the week at Mohilev. It was not her first visit to the Stavka, and while her sisters exulted in the freedom of the woods and river (always accompanied by the mob of ragamuffins whom Marie attracted from the peasants' and railway workers' huts) Olga had watched and worried over the future. She saw that what Dmitri said was true: the Czar was not soldier enough, not man enough, to cope with the duties of a Commander-in-Chief. He was as much interested in acquiring a sun-tan, or in rowing on the Dnieper, as he was in the strategy of the summer offensive, and when they all attended the showing of a French film made on the battlefield of Verdun, Nicholas II had no professional comments to make. He showed only the tepid interest which he might have shown in *Young Lochinvar*.

Olga herself was hardly aware of the damage done to her spirit by the veiled suggestions of her cousin on the day of their last ride down a snow mountain. She had brooded over a possible future which contained both her father's abdication and her brother's death until she was hardened to both these ideas, and to the thought that it might even be her duty to allow herself to be proclaimed empress to save the nation from a revolution. But if her ambition was kindled — and Olga Nicolaievna was a true Romanov in her ambition — it was quenched almost immediately by the knowledge of the taint in her own blood, the game of Russian roulette that she must play if she ever dared to marry. There was no one to whom she could open her heart, not even her understanding grandmother, for the Empress Dowager, sick of her children's involvement with Rasputin, had gone off to Kiev. She had a child there too, her own daughter Olga, to whom the war had brought freedom: over the Czarina's anger and Rasputin's open disapproval, Olga Alexandrovna had won the Czar's consent to ending her miserable marriage by divorce.

But now Simon Karlovich had come back, and perhaps some day she would tell him her troubles. Even in that brief encounter by the church, Olga had felt they were still as right for each other as she had felt in Petrograd: that he was the man she could rely on through whatever troubles lay ahead.

Meantime, it was a beautiful summer morning, and as she came near the garden entrance of the palace she saw the family breakfast table being set on the wide balcony where the Czarina liked to sit in the early morning sun. Closer at hand, she saw Alexis standing near the lake. He had his spaniel Joy at heel and was holding a basket of bread, for Alexis loved to feed the deer which wandered freely in the park. The little fawns were nuzzling up to him to be stroked. The boy had grown very much since the New Year, and while waiting for new uniforms to be made he was dressed for the first time in well-cut dark blue suits, like an English schoolboy. He was wearing a dark suit now, with a white shirt and a blue tie, and looked more like a youth of sixteen than a boy barely twelve. He was tanned from the river excursions with his father, and his hair glinted like copper in the sun. It struck Olga that if the doctors were wrong, and his health continued to improve, Alexis Nicolaievich would soon be a man. He might even be the Czar of All the Russias in ten years' time. How had she dared to think of usurping his inheritance? But then Olga thought of what she might be in ten years, an unmarried woman of thirty, a mere appendage at a young imperial court! Who would Alexis bring home as his bride, and what consideration would he have for his old maid sister? I'm not my brother's keeper, she thought impatiently. If my father abdicates, I shall do whatever I think is best for Russia.

CHAPTER FIFTEEN

THE Grand Duchess Anastasia's fifteenth birthday was due to fall in June, a year short of the time when she would receive the traditional diamond necklace and be presented to society at a court ball. Marie, a year earlier, had good-naturedly allowed her ball to be postponed indefinitely, but the *enfant terrible* of the family was clamouring for 'a real grown-up dance' that summer.

'And I want it before, not after, my birthday,' she said, 'because all the handsome young officers will be going off to the front. After all, Olga and Tania had plenty of fun before the war, now it's my turn!'

A ball was ruled out, but the Czarina consented to a small dance in the great unused state rooms of the Alexander Palace, and Olga invited Simon Hendrikov at their very first meeting by the Znamenia church. She was looking forward to the dance as eagerly as the birthday girl. A real dance, with a string orchestra, and new dresses for them all— the Grand Duchesses had been deprived of such gaieties for years. And then, even while the chefs were preparing the cake and the ball supper, and the hothouses were being ransacked for roses and heliotrope, news was received at GHQ which caused the Czar to cancel his youngest daughter's party.

It was not the news of the Battle of Jutland. That had already been greeted with angry tears by the Grand Duchesses, who still remembered a happy day aboard HMS *Lion*, and the attractive young British sailors of whom so many had met their death in the cold waters of the North Sea. But Russia, with her own warships penned up at Kronstadt, where the German submarines kept their doomwatch outside the harbour, was remote from the inconclusive battle between the Royal Navy and the German High Seas Fleet. It was the news of Lord Kitchener's death which shocked the world.

Kitchener, Britain's Secretary of State for War, and a man of immense prestige, had been personally invited by the Czar to visit the Russian battlefronts and report to his own government on the essential needs in military co-operation and supply. He died on his secret voyage to Archangel, going down with HMS *Hampshire* when the cruiser struck a mine off the coast of Orkney; and with him perished, in the long Atlantic rollers under Marwick Head, the only initiative Nicholas II had ever taken as Commander-in-Chief. He made his usual, fatalistic references to the birthday of the long-suffering Job, and desired his wife to cancel the dance for Anastasia.

Who wept, and said it was a great shame, and they never had any fun; but who became more reasonable when Tatiana quietly reminded her of court festivities which had taken place at the time of other tragedies, and the very bad impression this had made on all classes of society.

'But it's not like court mourning, is it?' said the child.

'No, but the British Ambassador and his party couldn't possibly come, unless it were made a matter of absolute protocol, and you wouldn't want that, would you?'

'It's not as if Lord Kitchener were a *relation*.'

'Cheer up, Imp,' said Olga. 'We'll plan something nice for your birthday itself, and then you can have a lovely dance in the winter, along with Marie.'

The Czarina herself had other ideas. 'It does seem too bad to put it off, after all the preparations. Such a disappointment for poor Anastasia, and Sunbeam, too, was looking forward to it! His first dance, and really it was time he had some ballroom practice!' Their mother thought she would telegraph to Mohilev.

'I'd leave it, mother,' counselled Olga. 'I think papa has really made up his mind this time. Lord Kitchener was someone very special.'

'Perhaps,' said the Czarina with a shrug. 'But Father Grigori told Ania his death may be a blessing in disguise. You know Our beloved Friend dreads what England may do in the peace negotiations. Later on Lord Kitchener might have done Russia harm.'

'The Germans would love to hear you say that, wouldn't they?'

Olga's barb, planted where the Czarina was most sensitive, provoked another clash between the mother and the daughter, already parted by Alexandra's jealousy of her husband's love for Olga, and the youth and beauty of her eldest child. For several days the Czarina sulked, and spoke to Olga only in the presence of others. This was noted by the whole court — that strange, disaffected court, cut off from the intimate life of the imperial family by the empty rooms of state, and yet aware of every least shift of allegiance, every facet of disagreement in the little group of people they were pledged to serve.

Olga told Simon Hendrikov the whole thing, at the meetings they contrived early and late in the two palace parks. In the woods by the Chinese Pavilion, among the sedges on the verge of the lake near the Turkish bath-house, she blurted out the story of the drowned Lord Kitchener, and the drowned British sailors, and her horror at the increasing death toll of the war. Simon soothed her and kissed her, falling in love with her all over again, but now in a different way — as if their love was not hopeless, but might some day be openly acknowledged in a world of change. He was not to know how much Olga Nicolaievna left unsaid, nor that the story of the quarrel with her mother was one justification for her vision of herself as the reigning empress.

But Simon was gone within a month, not to the northern sector of the front but to the Stohod river. There what was left of the Imperial Guard was to advance to Kovel, one of the objectives of Brusilov's offensive which now began.

It relieved the German pressure on Verdun, but in all other respects it followed the pattern laid down in 1914 and 1915: a brilliant start, the routing of the Austrians, the capture of half a million prisoners who clogged the trains and the highways. And then the whole thing slowing down: no guns, no shells, no transportation, and the Germans moving east with disciplined precision. In all, the Germans had to take fifteen divisions from Verdun and the Somme to crush Brusilov. It was popular to blame the Czarina for the defeat: she, the German traitor, and her creature Rasputin, had ordered the Czar to 'stop the massacre' just when 'victory was within the Russian grasp'. It was true that Rasputin intervened. It was not true that victory was possible. The Guards stood on the Stohod and died almost to the last man.

In the two previous winters of the war, the coming of the snow had seemed to blanket Russia from the outside world. The snow slowed up all the reactions to the war, giving the generals time to plan, the war profiteers time to send their money out of the country, and giving even the young survivors time to marry and engender children in a false dream of peace. But not in 1916. That winter everything moved faster, except where the dead lay on the battlefields and on the vast steppes remote from the fronts where the Little Father Czar was still only at one remove from God. In Petrograd, from the warm, well-provisioned clubs and restaurants to the slums of the Lavra and the Zabalkanski, everybody knew that something was moving under the surface and would presently burst in fire through the snow.

Joe Calvert knew it, just as he knew, as soon as he heard of Kitchener's death, what sort of 'interpreting job' it was that took Richard Allen to Archangel almost before he was fit to travel. Joe was in his seat in the public gallery of the Duma, where he was now as familiar a figure as the ushers, on the day at the beginning of November when Miliukov, the Kadet leader, openly denounced the Czarina for engineering Stürmer's appointment to the Ministry of Foreign Affairs as well as the premiership which he already held, and Joe heard the Duma's deep-throated roar of approval. Joe met all the speakers, Rodzianko, Purishkevich, Alexander Kerensky, and reported on them weekly in the painstaking, pedestrian letters to his uncle which without his knowledge were now being read by the Secretary of State.

A naval commander who, by courtesy, bore the name of Yakovlev knew it, even while his ship, the *Askelod*, was on her way from Devonport to the new Russian harbour of Murmansk, and Mara Trenova knew it, hurrying between the hides and tallow merchant's office where she earned a modest salary, to the cellar where *Pravda* was printed, where she earned nothing but the satisfaction of believing that as a copy editor and caption writer she was helping to bring about the Revolution. And a man in Switzerland, who went by the name of Lenin, and who had once despaired of ever seeing the Revolution, began to think his hour was not far off.

The Czarina was doing everything possible to hurry on that hour. Launched on a Valkyrie ride of power, supported by her dark angel Rasputin, she went from excess to excess. After making Stürmer Foreign Minister, she forced the Czar to accept a man named Protopopov as Minister of the Interior,

278

with the control of the Okhrana and the civil police. Protopopov was suspected of being a syphilitic, as such treated by Badmaiev, the 'Tibetan wizard', who had brought him to the attention of Rasputin. He was known to have been in touch, immediately before his appointment, with leading German agents at Stockholm. The Duma clamoured for his dismissal as well as Stürmer's.

'The Czar rules and not the Duma.' So the Czarina wrote again and again to her husband at Mohilev, her self-will strengthening with every warning from Rodzianko, every letter from her relatives, every appeal to send Rasputin away and interfere no more in politics. Olga, alone in the Family, believed that Rasputin was not the key to the situation. He had fed Alexandra Feodorovna's mystical religious fervour, it was true. But far more than mysticism, the dominant in her nature was the will to power. Much stronger than her weak-willed husband, she now demonstrated, as she made and unmade Ministers, that she shared the same personality, the same manic drive to power as the man she hated — her first cousin, Kaiser Wilhelm II.

One woman came from as far away as Moscow to make a personal appeal to the Czarina. This was her sister Ella, the widow of the Grand Duke Sergei and now the Mother Superior of the Martha and Mary convent, a nursing sisterhood which had done much good in the city where the Grand Duke was assassinated. She arrived by train, rather late in the evening, tired but still beautiful in the pearl-grey robe of fine wool with the white wimple and veil of the habit designed for her by a famous painter. Rooms had been prepared for her in the visitors' wing of the Alexander Palace as if to keep Ella at a distance from her sister, and there her nieces kept their Aunt Ella company while she ate some supper and asked her usual impersonal questions about their hospital work. Then she went to the Czarina, who received her in cold state, with two ladies-in-waiting and a gentleman usher in the drawing-room, before Ella was taken to the mauve boudoir for their private talk.

It did not last long. All those making polite conversation in the drawing-room heard the Czarina's terrible cry as her sister, ashen-faced, made haste to leave the hot mauve room. 'I hope I never see you again! Never! Never!' It was left to Olga to take her aunt by the hand and lead her, blind with tears, to the apartments she had left so short a time before.

'Like a dog! She drove me away like a dog!' Ella kept saying, as they went down the marble corridors to the white and gold doors guarded, in honour of the Grand Duchess, by two of the Ethiopian attendants. But it was not Her Imperial Highness Elizabeth Feodorovna, not the Mother Superior of a nursing sisterhood who fell sobbing on the velvet couch inside the doors. It was simply a woman, cruelly rejected by her sister, her nearest relative in Russia, for daring to protest against Rasputin and his sinister influence; for begging that sister to go to Livadia and stay there 'for her health's sake' at least until the spring.

'Aunt Ella, dear, please don't cry! It'll be all right in the morning, just you wait and see!' The Grand Duchess's maid brought sal volatile, and Olga signed to her to leave the room.

'I shan't be here in the morning. I shall go back to Petrograd by train tonight. There are twenty houses where I'll be made welcome —'

'Yes, yes, of course, but there *isn't* another train tonight... Yes, maybe, we could get a special, but it *is* late, and you're so tired, coming all the way from Moscow. Stay till the morning. Try to get some sleep.'

Olga coaxed her aunt into taking off her habit, and helped her into a dressing-gown. It hardly seemed to belong to a convent life, being made of the finest embroidered lawn, and in it Ella looked still young and lovely when Olga loosened the gold hair so like her own. Even when her tears were dried with a handkerchief soaked in eau de cologne, Ella was too agitated to relax. She talked about the trains — a time-table — the connection to Moscow — her regret that Dmitri, who had lived in her house as a child, was far away at Mohilev — her anxiety about Marisha, who had a new love younger than herself — and so on, aimlessly, disjointedly, until after a long sigh she said:

'I suppose all this is my fault.'

'But you were never fooled by Rasputin, Aunt Ella.'

'I wasn't thinking about Rasputin. I was thinking that if I hadn't married your Uncle Sergei, Alix would never have come to Russia, or met Nicky.'

'Oh come now, that's just silly,' said Olga affectionately. 'You might as well say mamma could have gone to visit Aunt Irene in Prussia, and married there. And she did stay, often, with Aunt Victoria in England, but she didn't marry an Englishman. She and papa met at your wedding, we all know that; only they would have fallen in love with each other wherever they met.'

'Yes, but what I meant was, it was from me she learned to love our Orthodox faith. I found it beautiful and comforting when I came to Russia as a bride, but she went further, deeper into the mysticism which only Rasputin could satisfy. And then the *hating*, Olga! How she hated everyone who didn't bow down to her as the young empress — *that* she never learned from me — and yet I never had such a happy home as hers.'

Olga sat uncomfortably silent, and her aunt went on:

'Couldn't you persuade her to go to Livadia, Olga? It's the only possible alternative to what may be in store for her, if your father abdicates.'

Olga's fingers tightened on her aunt's hand. 'Do you really think my father is going to abdicate?'

'If he's no longer competent to rule . . . if *she* continues to rule in his name . . . And some of our cousins hate her even more than she hates them. They want to have her shut up in a convent, if not in prison — unless Rasputin goes.'

'Then Rasputin will have to go.'

'That's what Dmitri says.'

'Have you been discussing all this with Dmitri?'

'I haven't seen Dmitri for months — well, weeks,' said his aunt in some confusion. '. . . You must forgive me, Olga dear, I've spoken to you much too frankly, but it's better you should know the truth. God knows, my only concern is for you and your dear sisters, and what is to become of you and little Alexis!'

'We'll be all right, aunt. And now you must really get some rest, it's nearly midnight. I'll come to you soon as you send for me tomorrow morning.'

She stooped to kiss her aunt good night. But Ella kept hold of Olga's hand, and her grey eyes were inscrutable as she looked up at her niece and said:

'Dmitri thinks Alexis is too young to rule.'

So that was one more tiny piece of the jigsaw puzzle presented by two people whose meeting and whose marriage had created such unusual problems for their children. Once, a younger Olga had thought of them only as papa and mamma, two people beyond all human questioning. Growing up, she had learned for herself their weakness and their strength, and now was learning more from other people. There was a grand-mamma, who had been afraid of the stiff German princess as a bride for her son, and Aunt Ella, who held herself responsible for Alix's religious fervour, and above all there was Dr. Botkin, who had revealed her dreadful legacy of haemophilia. Olga knew much, now, of what was driving this man and this woman towards their destiny. Before December was half over, the last piece of the puzzle came almost by chance into her hands.

It came when she was in a mood to seize at anything, any prospect of freedom from the dreariness which seemed to settle on the palace after Aunt Ella, icily calm, had given her blessing to the assembled Household and departed with a mounted escort to the station at Czarskoe Selo in the black darkness of the winter morning.

But before she discovered more of her father's past, out-wardly simple but more enigmatic than her mother's, Olga had a brief message from Simon Hendrikov. She had learned before the end of October that he had come safely through the fighting near Kovel and was with a reserve battalion at Minsk, but that was a verbal message passed on by Dolly by telephone to the palace hospital. Now Dolly, greatly daring, brought his letter to the Winter Palace on one of Olga's committee days. There were hospital wards in the Winter Palace now, as well as the repositories for medical supplies, and a young nurse from the British Red Cross hospital had no great difficulty in pass-ing the sentries.

There was no opportunity for a private word, for two of the Czarina's younger ladies-in-waiting were in the small room used as an office for the Soldiers' Families Relief Committee, but Dolly ventured to say:

'We were all hoping you would visit our little hospital yes-terday, Madame. The Grand Duke Dmitri spent two hours in the wards, and everybody was so pleased!'

'I thought His Highness was at Mohilev.'

'He told us he had forty-eight hours' leave.'

'Ah well, when you had the Grand Duke Dmitri you didn't need me,' said Olga. 'But thank you very much for coming, Darya Karlovna.' Dolly dimpled, and went away delighted. Olga, before she could read Simon's letter, reflected that Dmitri had undertaken a round trip of at least fifty-six hours to spend forty-eight in Petrograd, in his apartment with the hospital wards above, and wondered what pressing business or pleasure had brought him to the city.

Alone in the bedroom where she had laid her furs, the Grand Duchess opened Simon's letter. It was short and to the point.

My Princess,
We have now received orders to entrain for Petrograd, and will be at the Guards barracks until the middle of February. This means I can expect, by the duty roster, to be at Czarskoe Selo from then until the end of March.
I hope you will let me see you and be with you again. But there must be no more secret meetings. They are not fair to you. Give me the right to tell His Majesty that I love you. Once you said we were living in a changing world. Princesses have married commoners before now, even in the world we know. And my heart is yours always,

Simon

She memorised the words before she destroyed the single sheet of paper. They were very clear in her mind as she left the Winter Palace by the throne room of Peter the Great, and stopped to look at the red velvet throne under the draped canopy. It always seemed such a little throne for such an enormous man.

Now she had two alternatives, both seemingly impossible — to marry Simon Hendrikov, knowing her tainted blood, or to take the power in an army *coup d'etat* and ascend that little, waiting throne.

She hoped all evening for a telephone call from Dmitri, which never came.

Her father's past rose before her unexpectedly, next day, when owing to an emergency change in Tatiana's hospital schedule Olga took her sister's place at a reception organised by the Refugee Committee.

'I admire your devotion, Olga Nicolaievna,' said the lady-in-waiting, as they settled themselves in the limousine for the drive to Petrograd. 'It's a presentation of purses, isn't it? Very tiring for you, especially after yesterday.'

'It's very disappointing for the people, not to have Tania,' said Olga gaily. 'Still, they do expect to see one of us, so I must go. I wonder when we'll be able to trust Anastasia with a Committee!'

She was fond of Countess Gendrikova, the youngest of her mother's ladies, and forced herself to laugh and talk on the way into the city. They were late, even by Russian standards, for the occasion, and apologising for Tatiana Olga had no time to glance at the list of those to be presented. The routine began, the names were called, the generous donors (they were nearly all women) came up to curtsey and kiss Olga's hand. She distributed a testimonial, a medal, sometimes both. It was very like a school prizegiving. The Malachite Room, where the ceremony took place, became unbearably hot.

'Madame Mathilde Kchessinskaia.'

The dancer curtseyed to the ground, and lifted her vivacious face to Olga's with a smile.

'My thanks, madame, and my congratulations.'

The prescribed words came mechanically, and Olga put the certificate and the medal into the little gloved hands. She listened to the citation, read aloud. Russia's *prima ballerina assoluta,* who had opened a hospital ward in her Petrograd residence and turned her dacha at Strelna into a convalescent home for the wounded, had recently undertaken a dancing tour across the empire from Reval to the Caspian Sea. All the fees for her share in the performances were in the purse now to be handed to Her Imperial Highness . . . At this point the eulogy was interrupted by applause.

'I'm one of your admirers, madame,' said Olga. 'I'd like to have a word with you after the ceremony. I want to hear more about your remarkable tour.'

The ballerina curtseyed again and returned to her little gilt chair at the back of the hall. When she was brought to Olga in a small salon where tea was immediately served, the girl had recovered from her surprise, although she was still not sure of what she was going to say. It was quite impossible to say to Mala Kchessinskaia, at the very top of her profession, the adored for so many years of the Grand Duke Andrei, fulfilled both as an artist and as a woman, 'Were you once, and are you still, my father's mistress?' She began to talk about the tour.

'How could you possibly go on stage, night after night, in places like Tiflis and Baku, after travelling for hours in a crowded train? Didn't you get very tired?'

'Sometimes,' Kchessinskaia smiled. 'But I was lucky enough to have a wonderful new partner, who was a great support to me. Has Your Imperial Highness seen Vladimirov dance in Petrograd?'

'Did he appear in the tercentenary performance at the Maryinski?'

'Only in the ballet. He was understudying Fyodor Surov then. Vladimirov is very young, you know: he only graduated from the School in 1911 — the summer I celebrated my twenty years on the imperial stage.'

As she spoke, she touched an ornament pinned to her grey velvet dress — a diamond eagle pendant with a rose sapphire drop, the imperial gift which marked that twentieth anniversary. Looking at her, Olga could hardly believe that she was forty-four, the same age as the haggard, worn-out empress, for the ballerina, delicately built, had the complexion and the vitality of a much younger woman. Seen without the advantage of stage make up and lighting, she was no beauty; it was the piquancy and sparkle of her expression which gave her charm. It was not a face which concealed secrets, like so many faces at the court, and Olga was suddenly convinced that there was no truth in the rumours, so acceptable to the jealous Czarina, that this woman had taken bribes for placing orders with the army contractors.

She said, 'You had no partner when I saw you dance at Krasnoe Selo, just before the declaration of war.'

'In the mazurka? That's my favourite solo number. And — *A Life for the Czar* has always had a very special meaning for me.'

There it was — the opening which Olga was too inexperienced to handle. And the dancer, as if sensing this, went on:

'I saw *you* that night, Madame, closer than I ever saw you before. Of course I remember you as a child, when the Empress Dowager used to bring you and your sisters to the matinées, but the imperial box at the Maryinski is a very long way from the stage! In that little theatre at Krasnoe I felt quite close to you when I was standing in the wings ... You looked so lovely in your pink dress. I could see His Majesty was very proud of you.'

'But it was you he looked for that night, madame. He saluted you at your dressing-room window, as we left the theatre.'

With a little laugh, quite without the bitterness Olga knew in her mother's laughter, Kchessinskaia said, 'That window! It has rather special memories for both of us. Outside that window, in my first summer season at Krasnoe, your father used to stand and gossip with me before the performances. He was only the Czarevich then, of course: a young lieutenant in the cavalry.'

'And after the performances?'

'Afterwards we became very good friends. I think he knew he could trust me, for he told me all about the beautiful princess he hoped to marry, in spite of the difficulties in their way ... Those were happy summers at Krasnoe.' She lifted one expressive hand in a dancer's gesture. 'I have never seen him alone since his wedding day.'

It was a finished, stage performance, and yet Olga knew instinctively that it was sincere. She also knew that beneath the smoothness, the sweet sympathy, there was a will of steel, that a passionate tigress breathed beneath the tame domestic cat. I bet *she* never felt like a mother to him, nor called him Little Boy Blue, was Olga's thought.

'There's a stretch of road on the Moscow highway,' said Kchessinskaia, 'that I can never pass without remembering our farewell. You know where the short cut to Volkhonski joins the high road, before the approach to Czarskoe Selo? That was where we said goodbye, twenty-three years ago ... It's almost my only unhappy memory of our companionship.'

'You were fortunate in your youth, madame.'

'Yes, my friends and I were young together in happier times than these.' The ballerina smiled at Olga, and she was not acting now. 'Tell His Majesty that I shall always remember what he used to call me. *Radouchka*, bringer of joy.'

CHAPTER SIXTEEN

WHAT burst in fire through the snow was the murder of Rasputin. The first intimation that the charlatan had reached the end of his course on earth came very quietly to the Alexander Palace at Czarskoe Selo. It was a beautiful December morning, with deep snow on the ground but clear blue skies. Alexis, brought home from Mohilev on Monsieur Gilliard's plea that lessons were being totally neglected at GHQ, recruited Anastasia as soon as their midday break from school work came round, and the pair of them had a lively snowball fight beside the frozen lake. Then with the help of some of the gardeners, they planned the foundations of a snow mountain, 'the biggest ever!' said Alexis. 'Bigger than the one Cousin Dmitri built last winter for the little kids at Pavlovsk!'

'You never saw that one.'

'No, but Olga told me all about it.'

Mr. Gibbs, the Czarevich's other tutor, called Alexis indoors for an English lesson, and Anastasia sat down near her mother's table in the morning-room to sign 'OTMA' on some of the vast pile of Christmas cards which the sisters would send out.

'I thought you had a French essay to finish before luncheon,' said her mother mildly. 'Can't the cards wait until the afternoon?'

'I've got to see about the Christmas trees for the hospital in the afternoon, mamma. And the big one we always have in the *manège.*'

It was all normal and cheerful enough. There was nothing in the tapping of Anna Virubova's walking sticks, as she limped across the parquet of the next room, to indicate that this was anything but her usual morning visit. But the sight of Ania's pale face, puffy with tears, and her bulging eyes, was a certain prelude to disaster.

'Ania, lovey, what has happened?' cried the Czarina. She tried to rise, and the loose pages of her writing pad were scattered on the floor.

'It's Father Grigori. Dearest, beloved Majesty, they telephoned to me from Petrograd. His bed hasn't been slept in. He didn't come home at all last night.'

'Not come home? But you told me yourself he had agreed to go to supper with Felix Yusupov —'

'At the palace on the Moika — to meet Princess Irina —'

'Irina's in the country. Ania!' cried the Czarina, as the first hint of the terrible truth dawned upon her, 'why didn't you tell me that before? If he was asked to meet Irina, then his enemies may have been preparing a trap for him —'

'I didn't think it mattered,' whimpered her cringing friend. 'I thought it would be all right, because Dmitri Pavlovich was going to be there too. I only warned our dear Father Grigori not to drink too much wine —'

'Too much wine!' The Czarina had struggled to her feet, and was clutching the back of her armchair. 'They may have given him *poisoned* wine! Oh my God, what shall I do, what shall I do?'

'Dearest Majesty —'

'Be quiet, Ania,' said Anastasia, 'can't you see you've terrified my mother?' She put her young arm round the Czarina's trembling body. 'Mamma, come and lie down. It'll be all right soon, they'll find Father Grigori any minute, he can't be very far away.' The child hardly knew what she was saying. And the Czarina, deaf to comfort, whispered 'Oh, my heart!' and collapsed between her armchair and the floor.

It was the first time the youngest Grand Duchess had ever been faced with such an emergency. She handled it quietly, pulling at the bellrope, sending two footmen running for Dr. Botkin and the Czarina's principal dresser, Madeleine, and got rid of Anna Virubova, while the Czarina was being carried unconscious to her bedroom, by ordering a sleigh to take her home. 'You can do far more good in the Srednaia, Anna Alexandrovna,' she said with a touch of Olga's decision. 'Go back and start telephoning to everybody you can think of who might know where Father Grigori is now. Start by ringing up his housekeeper. And don't come back here until my mother sends for you.'

'Would you like me to call the hospital, my dear?' said the lady-in-waiting on duty gently. 'Don't you think one of your sisters should come home?'

'I'd like to wait for half an hour, Isa. You know, all this may be a false alarm. He may have stayed for breakfast at the Moika, and then gone for a sleigh ride into the country with Felix, it's such a glorious day.'

'As you wish, Anastasia.'

But before the half hour was over one of the chamberlains was bowing before Anastasia Nicolaievna, with a message that the Minister of the Interior desired to speak on the telephone with Her Imperial Majesty.

'I'll take the call myself.' The main telephone of the palace was in the Czarina's mauve boudoir. The girl went to pick it up, and Baroness Isa, who followed her, was struck by the coolness of her greeting.

'This is the Grand Duchess Anastasia speaking, Monsieur Protopopov. Her Imperial Majesty is indisposed, and can't talk to you at present ... No, I can't say when, her doctor is with her. You may give me the message. What? They discovered this *when*? ... After Monsieur Purishkevich talked to the police?'

The baroness, watching, saw the girl's fingers curl into the palm of her free hand, and shook her head warningly at Dr. Botkin, who had come to say the Czarina had recovered from her fainting fit. They both waited until Anastasia laid down the telephone. But before either of them dared to speak she picked it up again and said to the palace operator:

'Please get me the Grand Duchess Tatiana at the hospital.'

'I think we'd better all go back together,' said Tatiana to her sisters fifteen minutes later.

'What, three of us come off the wards and all go panting home,' said Olga, 'just because Rasputin is lying blind drunk in some bath house, or bawling dirty songs in a cheap cabaret?'

'Felix wouldn't go to a public bath house any more than he'd go to a cheap cabaret.'

'Don't you believe it! Felix hasn't reformed all that much. He's quite equal to a bit of fun when Irina's not at home.'

'But he invited Father Grigori to *meet* Irina.'

'Tania's right, Olga,' said Marie. 'We know he went away with Felix, because his people saw them leaving, and Grigori Efimovich was all dressed up for the occasion. And you've heard what the Minister told Anastasia.'

'All you've got to go on,' said Olga argumentatively, 'is that a policeman heard shots in the courtyard of Felix's house on the Moika and went to investigate. He saw this man Purishkevich, who shouted out, 'We've shot Rasputin!' or 'We've killed Rasputin!' or some such nonsense. So why didn't the police go inside and look for the body, if they believed what Purishkevich said was true?'

'Because Dmitri was indoors with Felix,' said Tatiana patiently. 'You know the police have no right to enter any house while a Grand Duke is there. Not without a special warrant, and perhaps not even then — papa would know.'

'We've only the Minister's word for it that Dmitri *was* there,' said Olga. 'You two go home if you want to. I'm staying here till I come off duty at two o'clock.'

She went home on foot across the parks, trudging through the snow in her fur-lined boots, with her head bent before the wind which had sprung up as the winter day turned to an early twilight. She usually went to the side door, or the garden entrance, but when she saw the line of motors in the great forecourt the Grand Duchess Olga passed through the great colonnades and halted on the threshold of a hall usually silent and empty. It was filled with men, nearly all in uniform, with a few women among them, courtiers who in the secluded life led by the imperial family were seen by them only at irregular intervals, but who had all emerged from their obscure if well-paid posts for this exceptional occasion. In the inner circle of their group was the Minister of the Interior, himself surrounded by men in frock coats, with leather portfolios under their arms, who appeared to be arguing with him and with each other.

Silence fell as Olga entered, and she was greeted by low bows and curtseys. The lady-in-waiting who had been with Anastasia earlier in the day came quickly to her side.

'How is my mother, Isa?' said Olga in a low voice.

'She is — very tired, Your Imperial Highness. Shall I announce —'

'No,' said Olga. Then, raising her voice, she said to the Minister, 'Are you holding a public meeting, Monsieur Protopopov?'

'N-no, Madame.'

'Then be good enough to come with me.'

The officers, saluting, made way to let them pass. Olga led the sweating Minister to an anteroom where the Czar's guests waited to be received in audience: a high-ceilinged room, with hunting trophies on the walls, and tables spead with uncut magazines.

'What was the meaning of that extraordinary scene?'

The bejewelled empresses in their satin décolletages, gazing from the portraits in the Crimson Hall, were no more commanding than the girl whose fur *shuba* was thrown back to reveal a nurse's dress, and Protopopov licked his lips.

'Madame, the murder of Grigori Efimovich has roused great excitement, here as in the city—'

'Murder? The police have found the body, then?'

'Not yet, but it can only be a matter of hours —'

'Then how do you know it's murder?'

'One of the miscreants has confessed, Madame.'

'The Deputy, Purishkevich?'

Yes, Purishkevich. Who had talked too much, and who undeniably was drunk when the police reached the Yusupov palace. But whose story — repeated when he was sober — was that he and a doctor (doctor an unstable witness, had fainted early in the numerous attempts at murder) —

'The *numerous* attempts?'

'Alas, yes. These two men had joined Prince Felix Yusupov and the Grand Duke Dmitri in a plot to kill Grigori Efimovich Rasputin by administering poison. They invited him to one of the — er — intimate little suppers he was known to enjoy, in a — h'm — luxuriously furnished room, a cellar room, in the Yusupov palace. There was music, balalaika and gramophone music —'

'Never mind the entertainment, Minister.'

'He drank poison in the wine, he ate poison in the cakes, and he *enjoyed* it!' burst out Protopopov. 'Prince Felix shot him with the Grand Duke's Browning, and he rose to his feet with the bullets in his body as if he were rising from the dead! He staggered as far as the courtyard. They beat him with a club there, and even then he nearly reached the gate! It was Purishkevich, according to his own confession, who fired the shots which killed the holy man.'

'So you have a full confession, but no body?'

'Exactly, Madame.'

'And nothing to support a drunken exhibitionist's confession? No traces that murder was actually done?'

'There was a pool of blood in the courtyard of the palace. Prince Felix said he had shot a dog.'

Olga's lips twitched. 'Who knows?' she said. 'Perhaps he had.'

'Surely, Madame, there is no question of condoning —'

'One moment,' she interrupted him coldy, 'I understand why *you* are here: Her Majesty naturally required a full account from you in person. But who are these officials you appear to have brought with you? Are you holding a trial of the princes in their absence — and in the absence of the Czar?'

'Madame, I'm trying to save the princes from their folly!' cried the Minister. 'These gentlemen are the legal advisers to my Ministry, part of the permanent secretariat, and three more from the cabinet of the Public Prosecutor. I asked them all to accompany me to Czarskoe Selo, to explain to Her Imperial Majesty that what she wanted done was legally impossible, totally against the laws of the Russian Empire —'

'What she wanted done?'

'She wanted Prince Felix and the Grand Duke Dmitri to be taken before a firing squad and shot.'

Then he saw the girl's composure break, and heard her cry: 'A summary execution! My God, have we *all* gone mad?'

There was indeed a double element of madness and of farce in what remained of the darkening day at the Alexander Palace. The farce was supplied by Anna Virubova, whom the Czarina insisted in bringing away from her own little house and installing in the rooms recently occupied by the Grand-Duchess Elizabeth Feodorovna. 'They will murder Ania too!' insisted the Czarina, and so the crippled woman arrived in a wheel-chair, escorted by her bewildered, elderly parents, and of course by the indispensable Sister Akulina. The private lift stuck between two floors with Sister Akulina and some of the baggage in it, and the holy woman's screams indicated very little trust in Providence, or in the palace electricians who got the lift in motion after an hour's delay. Madame Virubova herself, once she was certain of the imperial protection, had to be firmly told not to use the telephone, as she was jamming the little switchboard with her frantic calls to every place in Petrograd where Rasputin, alive or dead, might be. Tatiana told her again and again that the lines must be kept open for a call from Mohilev. Everybody hoped that the Czar would telephone, but he contented himself with sending a telegram saying he would return from GHQ as soon as possible.

Olga read the brief message over and over, and tried to find some meaning in it. Was her father, like his wife, grief-stricken at the disappearance of the Friend who had swayed his judgment and corrupted his intentions for so long? Or was he simply relieved? Would he return in time to save his young cousin and his niece's husband from the fate the Czarina had demanded for them both?

The only way to allay her madness was to issue a warrant committing them both to house arrest. Even when she was assured that this had been done the Czarina went from one excess of anger to another. 'I could kill them! I could kill them with my own hands!' she kept repeating through the night, until Alexandra Feodorovna slept the sleep which only veronal could bring.

It was nearly midnight when Olga crept downstairs to her mother's mauve boudoir. She had been haunted all evening by the thought that while Felix Yusupov was held inside a palace protected by an outer wall, gates and a courtyard, where able-bodied servants were armed and ready to defend their master, Dmitri was alone in his apartment on the Neva embankment, with only his elderly valet and perhaps a soldier-servant to act as bodyguard. He could be taken out and killed at any time — if anyone could be found, or paid, to avenge Rasputin.

'I suppose I'll have to think of something else.' Dmitri's words, as they stood beside the snow mountain, came back to Olga with new force. Worse still, she remembered what she had once said to him in the very room where he was now a prisoner: 'If only we could get rid of Rasputin!' So many people must have spoken as she did, unthinkingly, but Dmitri and his friend *had* thought of something else, they *had* got rid of the tainted creature. And they might have to pay for it with their own lives.

At last she picked up the telephone and asked to be connected with the Grand Duke Paul. Dmitri's father, as the Czar's only surviving uncle, was not without influence in the Family, although since his return from banishment following a morganatic marriage he had taken little share in public affairs. He lived with his second wife and family in Czarskoe Selo. The telephone rang again and again in his beautiful home, but not so much as a footman answered. At last the palace operator said:

'Exchange says the telephone is out of order, Madame.'

'Try to put me through to the Grand Duke Dmitri in the city, then.'

Olga listened for the ringing tone in vain. There was a vibrant silence on the line, and then the sleepy voice reported:

'His Highness's telephone has been disconnected, please Madame.'

'Thank you.' That was it, then — Dmitri was held incommunicado, and beyond help.

Next morning, Olga waited only to hear that Rasputin's body had not been found, and went by motor to the hospital, in time to relieve a delighted young nurse of the last two hours of her night duty.

At the winter solstice it was still night at nine o'clock in the morning, and all the artificial lights were burning in the Catherine Palace when an orderly brought a message: Captain Hendrikov was on the telephone.

'Captain Hendrikov'! It was the name Olga had wished but hardly dared hope to hear. She ran through the long corridors where the great Catherine had walked in state, and ran, as Catherine never ran, upstairs three steps at a time.

'Simon!'

'Is it you, Princess?'

'Oh Simon darling, I'm so glad to hear your voice! Are you calling from Petrograd?'

'Yes, from the barracks. We came in yesterday afternoon. I know what's happened, Olga Nicolaievna; is there anything I can do to help?'

'I can't remember *when* anyone said that to me! Oh Simon, it's so wonderful to have you back! Tell me, is my cousin Kirill Vladimirovich in Petrograd?'

'The Grand Duke? No, he's still at Mohilev.'

'Oh. I thought — but it doesn't matter now you're here. I'm so terribly worried about my other cousin — Dmitri.'

She felt rather than marked a slight hesitation in Simon's reply. 'His Highness is under house arrest, isn't he?'

'Yes, and I want him to be under guard as well.' Olga explained the situation, and the disconnected telephones. She said she was afraid 'some of Rasputin's followers' might break in through the hospital wards on the upper floors of Dmitri's palace: of her real fear she dared not speak. 'Could you get in touch with Dolly?' she pleaded. 'She's living-in at the British Red Cross hospital now. She would know if *anything* has been done to make sure of Dmitri's safety. And if she says there aren't any soldiers there, couldn't you order a bodyguard yourself?'

'I'll go straight to the Palace Quay and find out what's happening, Princess.'

After the babel of yesterday's conflicting voices, Simon's voice was steady and reassuring. Olga smiled.

'Is there much disturbance in the city?' she asked him.

'More like general rejoicing. They say the Kazanski church was crowded yesterday, everybody was lighting candles before the ikon of St. Dmitri, and it was the same thing at the church of Vladimir. I haven't been out of barracks yet, but my mother telephoned this morning, and she said most of the houses on the Fourth Line were illuminated last night. D'you remember the Fourth Line?'

'I remember everything. Oh Simon, please come soon!'

Simon Hendrikov laid down the telephone, despising himself for what he left unsaid. Would she have liked to hear that along with the candles round the ikons of St. Dmitri, simple folk were placing picture postcards of herself, the pictures in nurse's uniform which she had laughingly declared to be a libel? Dmitri and Olga, the ideal couple, the two most attractive members of the whole Family, were already paired off in the minds of those still loyal to the monarchy as a hope for the future. In the mess the night before, Simon's colonel had gone so far as to discuss the proposal, now an open secret, to declare the Czar unfit to rule and raise Alexis to the throne under the regency of the Grand Duke Nicholas Nicholaievich. 'The best of both worlds, gentlemen!' the colonel had chuckled. 'The Heir succeeds, and we get Nikolasha back again, to give us another victory like Erzurum!' There was no limit to the euphoria in the army on the night when the story of Rasputin's murder had spread all over Petrograd.

Alexis and Nikolasha made a strong combination, but

would it be as strong as Dmitri and Olga? Especially if she was fond of him, as her anxiety for the Grand Duke's safety clearly showed. Much as he loved her, Simon smiled at Olga's calm assurance that a newly promoted captain could fall out a bodyguard and march it off to protect a man under house arrest, all too likely soon to be on a charge of murder. It was not arrogance, it was the Romanov certainty that a bodyguard would always be forthcoming, and the irony was that this bodyguard was intended to protect the man Simon regarded as a serious rival.

Being free to leave the barracks, he went out through the ornate iron gates and looked for a droshki. There was not one to be seen, something unusual in that district, the heart of the garrison quarter, where the Tauride Palace stood. The imperial double eagle flag was drooping in the frozen air above the palace, and Simon wondered if the Deputies were in session, listening to Monsieur Purishkevich plead his right to parliamentary immunity for the murder of Rasputin. He crossed the bustling avenues to the embankment of the Neva.

There all was hushed under the snow. The wide river was frozen from bank to bank, and as happened every winter a number of people, shapeless and sexless in their heavy wraps, were taking short cuts from one shore to another along the footpaths on the icy surface. Above their heads the cathedral chimes were ringing *Gospodoi pomiloui.*

Simon walked on the river side of the embankment, saw two city policemen standing guard outside the Grand Duke Dmitri's residence, crossed the quay and passed outside the heavy door. There was a side gate, unguarded, opening on a courtyard where a British Red Cross ambulance was standing, and Simon walked straight in at the hospital entrance with no challenge from the white-haired porter, who rose from his stool and bowed as the young officer asked authoritatively for Darya Karlovna Hendrikova. He was invited to walk upstairs to the hospital floors.

'I don't think much of the Grand Duke's house arrest,' he said to Dolly when their greetings were over, and told her why.

'Only two city policemen at the door?' she said, puzzled. 'There were six when I came on duty at eight o'clock, and four on the side gate as well.'

'They've been withdrawn, then. Exactly what the Grand Duchess was afraid of!'

He described Olga's anxiety, and Dolly shook her head. 'If there *is* a break-in,' she said, 'there's nobody here to stop it. Simon, what are we going to do?'

'She asked me if the Grand Duke Kirill was in town. He's not, but if he were, I don't believe he'd lift a finger to help. I'm going to Czarskoe Selo to see the Grand Duke Paul!'

'Simon, you can't, not in that uniform!'

'In civilian clothes, then.'

'Doesn't matter if you're out of uniform. You're a serving officer, couldn't you be court-martialled for interfering with the course of justice?'

'Justice!' said Simon. 'But you're right, Dolly. Somebody else must take the message, only — who?'

'Somebody quite impartial. Outside the whole thing. And clever, able to speak Russian —'

'You wouldn't be thinking of your admirer, Plain Joe Calvert?'

'Joe would like to do it, but he'd quote at least three rules of the American Foreign Service saying why he shouldn't. No, but I know the man who'd go to the Grand Duke Paul, and make him act! Captain Allen, at the British Embassy.'

'Would he be willing?'

'I think he would, for me.'

The body of Rasputin was found on the morning of the third day. The amateur conspirators had flung it into a hole in the Neva, so badly weighted that it soon floated into the current, which washed it under the ice into one of the canals. The doctors who performed the autopsy found that Rasputin had survived poison, bullets and blows, and pronounced him dead by drowning.

By that time the Czar had returned from GHQ. By that time, too, the Grand Duke Paul had joined Dmitri in Petrograd, along with the distinguished officer who had been Dmitri's tutor, and other friends. Outside, patrols from His Majesty's Regiment, one of the special security regiments of the Household, guarded all the entrances to the palace where the Grand Duke was under house arrest.

The Czar did not interfere with these arrangements. Neither did he oppose his wife's desire to be solely responsible for the burial of the *staretz*, once 'Our Friend', and now canonised as 'Our Dear Martyr'. The body was taken to a resting-place on the way to Czarskoe Selo, prepared for the grave by Sister Akulina, and then, early in the morning of the fifth day after the murder, buried in a corner of the palace park. The service was short, the mourners few, but all the young Grand Duchesses were present with their parents.

Then the Czar made known the punishment of the two principal plotters. Nobody could touch Purishkevich, a member of the Duma, nor was Dr. Lazavert an important conspirator. But Prince Felix Yusupov was banished to his estates in Kursk province, and the Grand Duke Dmitri Pavlovich was also to be removed under guard from Petrograd, and posted to military duty at Kasvin on the Persian front.

'I won't have them shot, Alix, make up your mind to it,' he told his wife, and to the older courtiers, who murmured discreetly that the sentences might be too severe, the Czar would only say, 'I spared their lives, which is more than my father would have done. Let them be content with that!'

It was not until several days after her father's return that Olga was able to speak to him alone. She was admitted to his study just after Alexis emerged, rushing stormily past her and down the corridor, and the Czar was smiling when she entered the room.

'I hope you're in a gentler mood than Tiny,' he said whimsically. 'He's gone off furious with me because I didn't bring his new cat back from Mohilev.'

'Is that Verushka? We've heard a good deal about Verushka since he came back himself.'

'I can't keep track of all the names he gives them, and I didn't make matters any better by telling him that the little brute got out of her basket down at the station and was last seen wriggling away beneath a pile of railway sleepers.'

'He really is cat crazy. I thought Zubrovka's kittens might have kept him happy: she had five, all in one litter.'

'Still, it's wonderful to see him so bright and well,' said the Czar. 'Now, what can I do for you, my dear?'

'Father, I don't quite know how to begin.'

The Czar's face changed. 'I see,' he said, 'you've come to add

298

your voice to all the petitions I've had from the Family to pardon Felix and Dmitri Pavlovich.'

'Not exactly.'

'What then?'

Olga stood with her hands linked behind her back, as when she had recited Pushkin and Lermontov to her father not so many years before.

'I've come to beg you to commute the sentence on Dmitri,' she said. 'Leave him at Kasvin for two months or three, but not more, his health won't stand it. That's what makes his punishment so much harder than Felix Yusupov's. He'll have a very pleasant spring in Kursk, in his own house, with Irina and the little girl. But poor Dmitri isn't strong enough for the Caucasian front.'

Nicholas II turned over a pile of letters on his desk. 'That's the point his grandmamma makes,' he said negligently. 'Dmitri's weak chest. Considering that her own husband was assassinated in the evening of his days, I should have thought the Queen of Greece might have known better than plead for a murderer.'

'I thought all the Family had written to plead for Dmitri.'

'They did, here's their letter, with no fewer than sixteen signatures. Including even your dear Aunt Miechen's. Would you like to see what I've written across it?' He turned the document for Olga to read the words: *Nobody is allowed to commit murder.*

'But Dmitri swore to his father that he didn't fire a single shot!'

'And Dmitri's father would swear anything to me.' The Czar drummed his fingers on his desk. 'Incidentally, my personal police sent me an odd report upon my uncle Paul. It seems that before Father Grigori's body was discovered, a man from the British Embassy visited him in haste and secrecy. Immediately after, Paul persuaded General Voieikov to double or triple the military guard on Dmitri.'

'There *was* no military guard, the morning after he was arrested. Only two city policemen. Easy to overpower in an attempt to kidnap Dmitri.'

'To kidnap him? Olga, how do you know all this?'

'I suspected it. And I sent a man I trust to find out what was going on at the Palace Quay.'

'I believe I can almost guess his name. Was it Captain Hendrikov?'

'Yes.'

'An officer of my Garde Equipage, asked by my daughter to interfere in an affair under the jurisdiction of the civil power. Did you put your request in writing to this man?'

'No, we were talking on the telephone.'

'Good. Then I think I'll order an investigation by the young man's commanding officer, who *may* decide to proceed to a court-martial.'

'I advise you to do nothing of the sort.'

'You advise *me?*'

'Because if anybody tries to break Captain Hendrikov, I'll make it publicly known that the police guard on my cousin was withdrawn, was totally inadequate after the first few hours. And I have witnesses at the British Red Cross hospital who saw them marched away.'

'On the orders of the Chief of Police, no doubt.'

'Who takes his orders from the Minister of the Interior. And *he* takes his orders from my mother.'

'Do you realise what you're saying, Olga?'

'Perfectly. If you'd been here that first night, you'd have known she'd stick at nothing to get revenge for Rasputin. It's entirely due to Simon and his British friend that Dmitri was alive next day. And perhaps — a little due to me.'

The Czar lay back in his chair, his face was very pale. 'Pour me a glass of water, please.' She brought him the glass and he drank thirstily. The skin of his face was drawn and wrinkled, as if the man had been scorched by some fierce inner fire.

'Are you in love with Simon Hendrikov, Olga?'

'I've been in love with Simon for a long time.'

'You know that nothing can possibly come of it?'

'But he loves me.' She smiled. 'I'm not asking for permission to marry him.'

'It would never be granted. You, the Czar's daughter —'

'You gave my Aunt Olga permission to marry Colonel Koulikovski two months ago, after her divorce from Uncle Peter. And she was a Czar's daughter too.'

'That was the outcome of a very long attachment, following on an unfortunate first marriage. You can't say you've been forced into marriage against your will.'

'As Aunt Olga was. You can call it what you like, father: "a very long attachment" is as good a phrase as any; but the truth is that Aunt Olga, in the end, has done exactly what she wanted, she's made a new life with the man she loves. As Marisha hopes to do! As they all did, your uncles and cousins, when they married divorcées, or women not their equal in rank, or didn't marry their mistresses at all! Nikolasha, Kirill, Andrei, your Uncle Paul, my Uncle Misha — every one did just exactly as he pleased; and yet they can be sanctimonious about it like Boris, when he had the nerve to ask me to marry him, with Zina Rashevskaia actually living in his house! Why shouldn't I have a little happiness, with the man who loves me too?'

'But this is what your mamma has always said, "Let the others behave badly if they must! It's *our* family the good Russian people take for their example!" And dear mamma and I *have* set an example of virtuous living, for which we can only give thanks as the time draws closer to our silver wedding. That'll be in 1919, Olga, not so far away now.'

'But when you were a young man you did exactly what you pleased too, didn't you — when you were in love with Madame Kchessinskaia?'

The Czar started. 'I've only loved one woman in my whole life,' he said. 'And that was the girl I married.'

'I don't know that *that* makes it any better,' said Olga. ' — Oh, don't think I'm blaming you! I don't see how any man could resist Kchessinskaia, even now. I think she's adorable! She brought her dancing fees for the Refugees, when I was there, and we talked afterwards.'

'About — old times?'

'Only about some happy times. The dressing-room window at the Krasnoe theatre, and a pet name you used to have for her —'

'*Radouchka?*'

'Bringer of joy,' said Olga, and went to put her arms round her father's neck. 'Oh, my poor father, I'm so glad you had some joy once!'

She could tell that the Czar was moved when he said, 'What is it you want, my darling?'

'Some joy for me too.'

'This young man?'

'If you would only allow him to be near us for a little while. He's true and loyal, father, you don't know how true! Whatever he did to protect Dmitri, he only did it to please me.'

'I thought you came here to plead for Dmitri, and now you're pleading for Simon Hendrikov.'

'But I do still ask you to forgive Dmitri! Oh, not at once, because my mother would be furious, and I know he can't come back to Petrograd. But take him away from that terrible Kasvin soon. Banish him to the Crimea if you must —'

'To enjoy the fine weather,' said the Czar. 'I wonder you don't ask me to turn Livadia over to him outright. No, Olga, I will not pardon Dmitri. You don't know what doom he and Felix may have brought upon us.' He gently put Olga's clinging arms aside and took a letter from his desk. 'A courier came in today from Mohilev, with all the mail which arrived after I left. This was among them — my last letter from Father Grigori. He must have written it just before he was trapped into going to that fatal supper party. Read it, and see what Dmitri and Felix have done to me and mine.'

'A letter from Rasputin!'

Olga recognised the peasant's handwriting — sprawling, illiterate, unmistakable.

'I write and leave this letter behind me at St. Petersburg. [Olga read aloud] I feel that I shall leave this life before the first of January.

Czar of the land of Russia! If you hear the sound of the bell which tells you Grigori has been killed, you must know this:

If your relatives have wrought my death, then no one of your family will remain alive for more than two years.

They will be killed by the Russian people.'

CHAPTER SEVENTEEN

'WHAT fools they are,' said Mara Trenova, 'to think the Russian people give a damn for the Grand Duke Dmitri.'

She was standing at a window of the old Hotel du Nord in the great square opposite the Nicholas Station, which had been closed to the public since before midnight. It was now nearly two in the morning, and while she and her friends were perfectly capable of talking and drinking tea or anything else available until dawn, it was irritating to be confined to a hotel room by order of Nicholas the Bloody. The departure, under guard, of Dmitri to the Persian front had taken everybody by surprise. The Znamenia Square had been fenced off, the hotels and lodging houses in which the square abounded told to close their doors, and at one a.m. two companies of Cossacks had cantered in to police the approaches to the station.

'All this for one common or garden little royal murderer,' said Smirnov at her elbow. 'Our people didn't get the red carpet treatment when *they* took the road to exile.'

There was a growl of assent, but at the same time there was a fascination in the spectacle of the vast square, completely empty but for the Cossacks riding round and round as if they were in the ring at the circus. The horses had to be kept moving, even with their blankets on, for the night was bitterly cold: 1917 had come in with blizzards and freezing temperatures which broke the records of most people's memory. The snow of the Znamenia Square had been flattened by many feet all day long, but there was always a new powdery carpeting which the wind blew up in eddies round the horses and their red-clad riders.

'What are they expecting us to do?' asked one of the six or seven men and women huddled together for warmth at the uncurtained window. 'Rush out and stage a last-minute rescue?' There was a laugh, through which Mara heard the voice of Sergiev telling Sasha to put another log into the stove. Sergiev was no longer a copyboy at the *Pravda*. As Jacob Levin had predicted, he was ambitious, and now he had Mitia for a slave at the office, and Sasha, in whose room they were meeting, to put his own logs on the fire. Sasha was a deserter, whose first-hand stories about the brutality of his officers and the starvation of the men had run for three underground issues of *Pravda*, which made the boy feel important; besides, he had money from his father to pay for the protection his new comrades in Petrograd were giving him.

'Tired, Mara?' Smirnov put his arm round the girl and pressed her strongly to his side.

'Yes, I am tired, Smirnov. It's been a long day.'

'But worth it, now we can see the better days ahead.'

'Oh, yes!'

'The cars are coming now,' said someone. 'We should have had binoculars.'

'*Only* binoculars?' The ugly laugh came again. Smirnov, unobserved, sketched a playful little bite on Mara's neck, somewhere between her high collar and her hair. She gave him a side-glance of surprise. Her comrades disapproved of public endearments; their sexual drives were sublimated into politics for a good deal of the time, but Smirnov, a recruit from Georgia, had a reputation for adventures more lighthearted than the singleminded revolutionaries liked. It was something new for him to make advances to Mara Trenova, but she remembered that Smirnov, too, had a room in the hotel, and was probably hunting for a temporary bedfellow. She decided to go with him if he asked her: it was far too late, even when the police barriers were removed, to go back on foot to the Yamskaia through the snow.

Smirnov, with his healthy colour, tumbled black hair and black southern eyes, was at least more physically attractive than his fellow-Georgian, the bespectacled and bearded Agabagov, who was huddled next to Sasha on the dingy couch. It would be pleasant enough to share Smirnov's bed for one night, even in the Hotel du Nord, in a squalid room which would inevitably bring back memories of Jacob Levin. Mara resented her own bourgeois dislike of those memories, but she never admitted that her whole attitude to men and sex had been conditioned by Simon Hendrikov's rejection, Jacob Levin's brutality, and Joe Calvert's cool indifference into an aridity of flesh and spirit which made her almost incapable of physical satisfaction. She was Trenova, a good comrade, a good worker for the revolution, and that was all.

'There he is!'

There had been enough blowing on the frost which encrusted the double windows of Sasha's room to give everybody a good view of Dmitri's tall figure, in the grey Guards greatcoat, on the pavement between the two limousines. His father, nearly as tall as himself, got out of a car and stood beside him, accompanied by someone unrecognisable in furs.

'Who's the girl?'

'Probably that sister of his.'

'Not your friend Olga, eh, Trenova?'

They saw the young Grand Duke's hand rise and fall, acknowledging the salute of the captain of the guard. He turned and walked between them under the overhanging roof of the station, and the rest of his party followed him into the darkness.

'And now for the private coupé, the champagne and chicken sandwiches, and then the bed made up with silken sheets,' said one of the young women, named Sofie. 'The show's over, dears. I wonder when they'll fall out the Cossacks, and let us all go home?'

'Don't go yet, comrades,' said the deserter eagerly. 'There's enough tea for all of us left in the samovar.'

'We might as well go through the plans for our operation across the river,' said Agabagov, and the others agreed. The dingy plush curtains were drawn again across the windows, and the group settled down around the stove. Operation 'Across the River' was the name for an intended raid on the beautiful house which the ballerina, Kchessinskaia, had built about ten years earlier, and which to the revolutionaries was one of the great symbols of Czarist corruption. Agabagov had suborned the dancer's housekeeper. She had already shown him over the house while her mistress was absent, and would open the doors to his commando when the day came. Mara listened to his greedy description of the Empire drawing-room hung with yellow silk, the conservatory, the larders, the cellar. The loot would be tremendous.

She herself was sitting on the floor with a cushion between her back and the wall, and a sketching block and pencil in her hands.

'Get some inspiration?' Sergiev growled.

'I think so. Show you later on.'

She took out a pencil and began to sketch. Mara was not a trained commercial artist, but she had a talent for turning out line drawings in which the action was suggested by little stick-like figures, and these were adapted for propaganda by Efron, one of the men sitting on Sasha's bed and noisily drinking his tea through a precious cube of beet sugar held between his teeth. Efron was a professional. They were all professionals, dedicated Party members, regarding Trenova with the faint if indulgent suspicion she owed to her Social Revolutionary past. She knew now that she would never be in the front rank of the struggle, like Maria Spiridonova and Katarina Brech-kovska, two of her SR heroines who were still alive after many years in the Czar's prisons. She was not considered suitable for direct action, although she had been issued with a Mauser pistol for self-defence when the revolution should begin. She knew she would never have the patience Brechskovska had shown until her arrest in spreading Marxist beliefs among the peasants and the pilgrims on their way to the holy city of Kiev. But she had a gift for the stinging phrase, the jingle, the slogan, although she acknowledged that she had not invented anything so good as the two simple slogans which the shock troops of the red daybreak would shout: 'All Power to the People!' and 'Bread! Peace! Freedom!'

'Show me,' said Efron, sliding to the floor beside her. 'H'm! Not bad!'

Mara had drawn four little sketches, in which the two limou-sines were shown as horse-drawn prison vans, with Dmitri standing between them. The hand which had been raised in salute was now seen clawing at a crown slipping from his head; in the last sketch he was trying to retrieve it from the gutter with a dripping sword.

'Can you do anything with that, Efron?'

'I'll get to work on it right away, and bring it round to the Yamskaia first thing in the morning for you to do the cap-tions.'

Mara was about to say 'All right!' when her thigh was pinched between Smirnov's thumb and forefinger, and she changed the words to 'Ten o'clock would be better, I'll be ready at ten.'

Efron was still studying her sketches. 'A strip of four, I think, like the others,' he said. 'I'm just wondering if we couldn't get a woman in here too. The sister — we haven't done anything on her.'

'Or Olga again,' suggested Smirnov. 'Wasn't she supposed to be sweet on him at one time?'

'I thought so, when I saw them together after the *Poltava* launching,' Mara said. There was no need to tell the comrades that on a day very soon after the *Poltava* launching she had seen with her own jealous eyes that the Grand Duchess Olga had fallen in love with Simon Hendrikov, and that he was deeply in love with her. There was no need to say anything at all, because the girl Sofie was squealing:

'Yes, do Olga, do her all over again! That Rasputin and Olga cartoon was the best you've ever done!'

'I must have another look at it,' said Efron, and Sofie at once gave him a copy from her handbag. 'I carry it around,' she said, 'People were *yelling* at it in the "Bi-Ba-Bo" last night.'

'Just an idea I had in a food queue,' said Mara modestly. It was true that on the day Rasputin's body was found she had been in one of the endless bakery queues, trying to buy half a loaf of bread, and had heard one of the shawled women shuffling forward behind her telling her neighbour that the Czar's daughter Tatiana had been present at Rasputin's murder, dressed as a boy.

'What would she want to see a horrible thing like that for?' marvelled the neighbour, and the first woman explained:

'Because he raped her, see, in her own bed at the palace, when she was only twelve years old, and she wanted to be there to see 'em cut his balls off, that was why!'

From this promising beginning Mara and Efron had devised a strip of four images: one of Olga naked on a four-poster bed with crowns on the bedposts, with Rasputin crouching over her; and three showing the murder and the fictitious castration. In these, Olga was not merely dressed as a boy, she was wearing the uniform of the Chevalier Guards, with huge breasts bursting out of the tunic, and Dmitri in the same uniform was nuzzling her back. The strip, circulated underground, had had a huge success, and Mara had never confessed, even to herself, that she had substituted Olga for the Tatiana of the street woman's fantasy, because she remembered only too well the proud and lovely face, the eagerness of the girl who had wanted to be shown the Zabalkanski, and because she wanted to degrade that girl by every means in her power.

The four young sisters in their palace at Czarskoe Selo knew nothing of the slanders of the food queues, any more than they knew about Mara Trenova's cartoon strips or the series Sergiev was writing for an underground paper under the title of 'The Lovers of the Grand Duchesses'. The hunchback himself was impotent, but the wealth of scatological detail implied a vast experience, and the details were better understood by his readers than they could ever have been by the Czar's younger daughters, who thought 'taking a lover' meant becoming engaged to be married.

Marie, at least, used the word 'lover' for the man who made the first proposal for her hand. This was one consequence of the disastrous extension of the war to Rumania, where two German armies, invading the country by the Carpathian passes and the valley of the Danube, had ended a lightning war with the capture of Bucharest. The Rumanian court and government fled to Jassy, and Prince Carol, now the Crown Prince, travelled to Petrograd with the prime minister, Bratianu, to ask help from Russia as the long-term protector of the Slavs.

'But I never dreamed he would ask leave to marry *me*!' Marie marvelled, after an official dinner party at which she had listened with her usual sweetness and docility to Carol's account of the mountain fighting in his country. 'Imagine having a lover, at my age!'

'Well, that's it, Mashka, you really are too young,' said Tatiana reasonably. 'That's just what papa said to Prince Carol.'

'Lots of girls are married at seventeen,' said Marie.

'But you don't mean you would even *think* of marrying Carol?' said Olga, and added tactfully, 'even if he is a lot nicer than he used to be.'

'Well, who *are* we going to marry, if we don't start marrying soon? I think Carol's very nice. I'd love to be in the mountains with them all, riding with the guns like his mother does, and bringing in the wounded under fire, and cooking their meals over charcoal braziers —'

'Being a heroine, in fact,' said Anastasia slyly, and was amazed when Marie, the target of so much of the family teasing, suddenly burst into tears and ran out of the room.

'Go after her, Imp, and apologise,' said Olga. 'You really hurt her feelings.'

'Her nerves must be like fiddle strings,' said the girl, repeating what she had heard someone say about the Czarina. But she obeyed, she was very fond of her sister Marie, and Olga, left alone, thought that what Marie really wanted was not the showy Balkan prince, nor even adventure with the troops alongside his courageous but theatrical mother Queen Marie: it was what drove so many girls into an early marriage — the desire to get away from home. If the ambitious Carol did eventually win a Romanov princess for his bride, it would be because Marie Nicolaievna was not determined, like the Olga of nearly three years ago, 'to live and die in Russia', but to lead the rough-and-tumble Balkan life which would suit her so much better than the tense silences of Czarskoe Selo.

They had all lived through the first weeks after the Rasputin murder in a state of shock. The Czarina, when she appeared among them, sat for long periods in her chair staring fixedly before her and saying nothing, but she spent most of her time in her mauve boudoir alone or with Alexis, with whom she invariably shared her meals, such as they were. She only roused herself to express passionate anger against her sister Ella, who had telegraphed to the Grand Duke Dmitri congratulating him on what she called his patriotic deed, but in truth she was no more separated in spirit from her sister than she was from her own four girls. The only one who could rouse her from her frozen grief was her own creation as Minister of the Interior, Monsieur Protopopov, who had taken up spiritualism, and presently announced to the Czarina that he was in touch, through the spirit world, with the martyred Rasputin.

The Czar's apathy was of a different sort. The Allied ambassadors who saw him during January 1917 found that his memory had almost completely gone, and that when talking his dark eyes moved aimlessly in a face so drawn and wrinkled as to be nearly unrecognisable. He sent for his brother Michael, who had done better in the Caucasus than anyone expected, and seemed to find some pleasure in going to tea with Michael at the palace of Gachina. He listened unmoved to the Duma President's reports of the shortage of food supplies in the armies and the cities, and the strikes in the great war factories — all of which, Rodzianko warned, was bound to end in revolution. He still declined to grant a workable constitution or a ministry responsible to the Duma.

Almost the only positive thing he did after punishing his cousin Dmitri and Felix Yusupov for the murder of Rasputin was to arrange for the posting of Captain Simon Hendrikov to Czarskoe Selo, and inform the Minister of the Palace that the Marine Guards officer was to have the entrée to his home. So now Olga had a 'lover' too, a young man who was actually allowed to take tea with her in one of the smaller salons of the guest wing — both of them comfortable but ungrateful beside the blazing pine logs while the blizzard howled across the park outside.

'I wish it was summer! I wish we could go for walks!' Olga sighed in the dusk of a February afternoon.

'I wish I could take you hundreds of miles away from here,' said Simon.

'Where would you take me to? Your dacha?'

'We'd start at the dacha. But it wouldn't be winter —'

'Of course not, it would be summertime. With all the furniture exactly in the same place, and everything happening just as it did three years ago — except that we wouldn't have Mashka and Anastasia along.'

'And we wouldn't have to go back to the *Standart*,' said Simon, falling in with her mood. 'My God, I remember that night so well. Everybody felt honoured because His Majesty came to dinner in the mess, and I could hardly talk, let alone eat, because I thought you might have come on deck, and I was missing another chance to be with you.'

Olga smiled. 'I remember lying in a deck chair that evening, watching the stars come out, and wishing —'

'What did you wish, Princess?'

'For the world to be different, I suppose. We didn't know *how* different it was going to be. Let's go on pretending. Where'll we go to when we leave the dacha?'

Neither of them had seen much of the world outside Russia. They had to settle on Copenhagen, which they both knew, although Simon had explored the summer beaches and the winding oldworld streets while Olga had only lived at the palace of Amalienborg. 'My grandmother wanted to take me back two years ago,' said Olga. 'I didn't see how we could possibly go.'

'I haven't been in Copenhagen since my sister Betsy married, back in 1910.'

'Granny's always ready to plan a trip. Her latest idea is to take us all off to the Crimea.'

'Are we still pretending, Princess?'

'No, this is absolutely true. She was terribly upset about what happened to Dmitri, and now she's worried about my sisters and me. She says if mamma won't take us to Livadia, she'll open up her own palace at Ai Todor, so that all of us can have a winter holiday.'

'Olga!' Simon seized her hand. 'It's the best thing that could possibly happen. You must go!'

'But you said you were so happy, now that we're meeting every day —'

'I'd be happier still if I knew you were out of danger,' said Simon grimly. '*Dushenka*, please believe me, it's the wisest thing to do. Surely when His Majesty goes back to Mohilev, you can persuade the Czarina to go south — perhaps only for a few weeks, until things are more settled in Petrograd — and take all of you with her?'

'You think it's important that my mother should go too?'

'Very.'

'But she thinks her popularity has never been greater!' Olga answered him obliquely. 'She gets hundreds of letters and telegrams every day, sympathising about Rasputin, and thanking her for all the good she does, and everything!'

'Ninety-five per cent of those messages are written at the Ministry of the Interior.'

'You mean Protopopov . . . ?' She didn't flare up, she took it calmly; Simon saw with compassion that Olga Nicolaievna knew the truth as well as he did.

'I'd love to go to the Crimea,' she said uncertainly, 'it's so wonderful there in February. Think of the bougainvillaea, all rose and purple on our white walls, and the freesias and cyclamen growing wild over the terraces, down to the shore! And the hot sun at noon, instead of snowstorms and icy cold . . . But we couldn't go now, Simon. Not until the Allied Delegates have held their conference, and they haven't even left for Murmansk yet.'

'There's always one thing more to stay for,' said Simon Hendrikov. 'Olga, for God's sake, don't let it be the one thing too many!'

'And don't you be so gloomy,' she said with forced cheerfulness. 'Even if Petrograd *is* badly disturbed, we're perfectly safe out here. We've got the Cossack Escort, the Marine Guards, the Railway Regiment, and His Majesty's Own Regiment all here for our protection: don't you think that's enough to look after five women and a boy?'

'If the regiments are loyal, yes.'

'How can you possibly think they're disloyal?'

'How can you risk believing that they're not?'

Always one thing more. That was the sombre thought in Simon's mind when he rose that evening in the Marine Guards' mess to drink the health of His Imperial Majesty, and listened to the fervent exclamations of 'God bless him!' repeated up and down the long, silver-laden table. Always one thing more to stay for, and of all fatuous things to take any risks for, the Inter-Allied Conference was certainly the worst. Even a junior officer, who knew nothing except how to fight on the Vistula or the Stohod, knew that the latest discussion between the Allied Powers was doomed to failure from the start.

Very probably the British delegation headed by Lord Milner, and the French, headed by the Minister for the Colonies, Gaston Doumergue, were quite aware that they had set out on a useless errand as they began on their Arctic voyage, round the North Cape and through the Kola Inlet to the town ambitiously called Port Romanov at the head of the new Murmansk railway. They found in it a sample of Russia at its worst, with heaps of stinking refuse and untidy piles of fir logs between the little wooden houses which looked like workmen's huts, and what was far worse, huge stockpiles of munitions rusting on the makeshift quays. The train into which they were ushered was the first to travel the new Murmansk railway from end to end. It took three days to reach Petrograd after a nine-hundred-mile journey along the single track, which was wretchedly ballasted and inclined, through the tundra and the frozen forests, and when the delegates arrived in Petrograd they found sporadic strikes in progress, and agitators openly haranguing the food queues even in main arteries such as the Liteini Prospekt. The official talks with their Russian colleagues degenerated into farce: who, they felt, could promise more aid to a country so obviously unable to help itself? The six million Russian losses were written off as an heroic but useless sacrifice by Allies who, in February 1917, had reason to fear their own countries would lose the World War — unless the one country missing, the one great Ally, should at last decide to take the field.

Meanwhile, of course, there were the usual empty celebrations. The delegates stayed at the Hotel Europa, and were lavishly entertained by society. The Grand Duchess Marie Pavlovna, 'Aunt Miechen' to her relatives, gave them a dinner so magnificent that the Empress Dowager telegraphed from Kiev, demanding at least equal splendour at the Alexander Palace, where the British, French, Italians and Rumanians were to be entertained on the last Saturday evening of their stay. She even gave some instructions about how Olga was to be dressed which aroused the Czarina's never long dormant jealousy.

'Such a fuss,' she said, while three of her own six dressers were with the young Grand Duchess, 'sending to the Treasury for the Empress Catherine's coronet! I'm surprised Granny didn't insist on the imperial crown.'

'We all wish you felt able to meet the delegates yourself, mamma,' said loyal Tatiana. 'And papa must wish it most of all.'

'But Olga's going to look simply lovely,' said Marie. 'Do you know she spent the whole afternoon reading notes about the guests, and memorising not only their names but what they look like in their photographs?'

'Taking a leaf out of Aunt Miechen's book, I suppose,' sniffed the Czarina. 'It really isn't necessary to remember these people's names; a smile and a bow are all they can expect.'

'But you keep telling us we ought to talk,' objected Anastasia.

'Not on state occasions . . . Olga, come in and let us all see you. Yes, you look very nice.'

The younger girls were speechless as Olga came slowly towards them. She wore a court dress of white silk, revealing whiter shoulders, with the diamond necklace of her sixteenth birthday, and the red riband of the Order of St. Catherine. The little coronet the Empress Catherine had worn as the wife of the Czarevich, before the path to power opened out before her, was made of two separate bands of priceless rubies, set between diamonds, and crowned, as if it had been made for her, Olga Nicolaievna's golden hair.

'You're not wearing rouge, are you?'

'Oh mother, certainly not!'

'She's excited, that's all,' said Anastasia. 'Oh, how I wish I could be in the drawing-room when you walk in!'

'Yes, but it's all wrong,' said the Czarina pettishly. 'You're half in court dress and half out. You should be wearing a *kokoshnik* and a veil with the coronet, and you should have a train falling from your shoulders too.'

'Trains aren't worn in wartime,' said Olga. The sick woman's jealous pinpricks made no impression on a girl exultant at playing, for the first time, one of the leading roles on a state occasion, and confident in the beauty which she saw reflected, only half an hour later, in the admiring eyes of many men. She 'made the circle' with the Czar at eight o'clock, pacing in her white and diamonds through the great flower-filled reception rooms where fragrant wood burned in the porcelain stoves, and contriving to say something friendly and personal to each of the Allied statesmen. In that she succeeded better than the Czar, who confined himself to such banalities as 'Is this your first visit to Russia?' and 'Did you have a comfortable journey from Port Romanov?' His sombre eyes only brightened when as they sat down to a simple wartime dinner, served from the gold plate and priceless glass which had been in storage for years, he saw his daughter talking animatedly with the laughing guests who sat near her at the foot of the table. In his heart he acknowledged that her mother, as a hostess, had never even made anybody smile.

It was all over in a couple of hours. The State dinner was only a show-piece, not intended as an occasion for private talk, and carriages were ready to take the guests back to the station shortly after ten. The Czar and his daughter said the good-nights required by protocol, and by protocol were thanked: a

French delegate, who had appreciated the champagne, was the only one to step out of line in the diplomatic circle and press an undiplomatic kiss on the Grand Duchess Olga's hand.

'*Mes hommages, Altesse!*' he said. 'How well a crown becomes your lovely head!'

'*Je vous remercie, monsieur.*'

She walked pensively, alone, up the great staircase. Tatiana was still with their mother, and only the three dressers were waiting in the warm bedroom. Olga asked for a glass of water, and to be left alone for a quarter of an hour.

'Your Imperial Highness has a headache!' said the chief dresser, all solicitude.

'No, but I want a cigarette.' She went as far as to light one while the women were in the room, and almost immediately threw it into the open stove. Cigarettes had no place in her brief magnificence; they belonged to the nurse's uniforms and the jersey coats of summer mornings, not to the coronet of the Empress Catherine. Olga, sat down at her dressing-table, and saw a thousand sparks gleam, in the light of the chandeliers, from her necklace and the diadem. She put her hands up to the coronet and found it too securely fastened to be removed without help. It was still hers to wear for a few more minutes — the crown which, if she had listened to Dmitri, might, on a thousand to one chance, have been hers for life.

The Czarevich Alexis was bored and irritable. He wanted, more than anything in the world, to go back to GHQ at Mohilev, but his father lingered at Czarskoe Selo, procrastinating, still temporising with Rodzianko and all the others, even including his brother the Grand Duke Michael, who brought him warnings of famine and the outbreak of a general strike. He told Alexis that it might be some time before any train could take them back to Mohilev — 'The snow is clogging the permanent way, Sunbeam,' he said, 'don't you know over a thousand railway engines are out of action?'

'I wish you wouldn't call me Sunbeam, you know I hate it. Nobody calls me Sunbeam at Mohilev! And the permanent way isn't clogged round Petrograd, Zilchik and I saw a lot of trains running yesterday.'

'Well then, you had an interesting outing: didn't you enjoy it?'

'Not as much as I used to,' said the boy. 'I don't know what's the matter with everybody these days. The people at the stations don't seem to want to talk to me any more! I bow, but they don't always bow back; they just stare, or look away.'

'You've grown so tall, they probably don't recognise you.' The Czar spoke abstractedly, but Monsieur Gilliard, who had observed his pupil's distress at the unfriendliness of the railway people, pointed out in private that the boy was really pining for companionship. The Swiss tutor went even further: he said that Alexis was too much with his mother, in her present state of health, for his own good.

'You're right, monsieur, we've been neglecting him,' said the Czar, and the tutor permitted himself to laugh. There was no danger of Alexis being neglected in that palace, where his health had been the chief concern for years, but now, as he said, the boy was splendidly well, and he needed to play with boys of his own age, or older. The Czar agreed, and plans were made to invite a group of cadets from the military school in Petrograd for an afternoon of games in the snow at Czarskoe Selo.

It was the happiest and noisiest occasion at the palace for many a day. Alexis was enchanted to be with soldiers again, and although the soldiers were only boys of seventeen and eighteen they might well, on the next call-up, find themselves in the front line of the Russian Army. With the cadets he skated on the frozen lake (his hands crossed with Nagorny's) and played a fast and furious war-game with snowballs for ammunition. But the success of the afternoon was the snow mountain, now very high, and the lads went down in quick succession, braking their toboggans to a grinding halt and running round the base of the mountain to start again.

'Just look at Nagorny, waiting for Alexis at the foot like a mother hen with a duckling,' said Olga who with Simon by her side was among the score of spectators who had come out to look on. The sailor-servant never took his eyes off his charge, who was not allowed to come down the slide alone; as fast as Alexis reached the foot Nagorny picked him off the toboggan he shared with one of the cadets.

'Just look at the driver, he's as white as a snowman,' said Simon, indicating the tall cadet who had steered Alexis down the snow mountain.

'He must have got well plastered with snowballs in the war-game,' said Olga. The tall cadet was laughing, and very flushed. They saw him wipe his brow with a handkerchief as he took the toboggan from Nagorny and ran off to the starting place.

'Alexis Nicolaievich is having the time of his life.'

'Yes, and it isn't over yet, they're going to have a wonderful tea as soon as it gets dark.'

'Olga,' said Simon in a changed voice, 'here comes Her Majesty.'

It was the first time he had set eyes on Alexandra Feodo-rovna for many months. He saw that she was haggard and pale, and there were traces of grey in the hair visible beneath her fur hat, but she was not permanently crippled, as rumour said she was. She carried a walking stick, but so did many of the ladies on that frosty day, and she was smiling at the boys as she talked easily with Monsieur Gilliard.

'I'm glad she's come out to see the fun,' said Olga.

'Her Majesty is looking well,' said Simon. 'Have you spoken to her yet about going to the Crimea?'

'Oh, Simon, how you harp on that! One would think you were anxious to get rid of me.'

'Of *you — dushenka*, girl of my heart —' He took her fur-clad arm so violently that Olga moved away and whispered, 'Don't! People will see! And I must go in now, Simon. Tatiana and I are going to preside at the boys' tea. They're going to have blinis and plum cake, isn't that a nice mixture?'

'Blinis for *tea*?'

'Alexis always asks for blinis on a special occasion. I bet those boys are hungry enough now to eat a dozen each!'

So it seemed, when the cadets came ravenously into the dining-room prepared for them. The blinis were served smok-ing hot, delicious little pancakes of buckwheat flour with every possible accompaniment already on the table: saucers of sour cream, chopped onions, burbot roe from the Gulf of Finland, chopped hardboiled eggs, smetana, and for those with a sweet tooth, fresh butter and raspberry jam. There were pitchers of milk and light beer on the long table, set between platters of cut plum cake and other good things, and Olga and Tatiana offered tea with sugar and lemon.

There was only one boy who seemed to have no appetite,

317

and that was the tall cadet who had driven Alexis on the toboggan. He was still flushed, although the sports were over, and now his eyes seemed to be paining him, for he was blinking even in the soft candlelight. Alexis was sitting beside him, anxiously pressing him to eat.

'Olga,' he said to his sister, as she came up to pour their tea 'this is my friend Peter Arkadeivich, and he says he isn't a bit hungry!'

'Perhaps he doesn't like blinis,' suggested Olga, as the tall cadet leaped to his feet. 'Would you rather have a meat patty, Peter Arkadeivich? I can't believe you're not hungry, after tobogganing all afternoon!'

'I beg Your Imperial Highness not to trouble,' said the boy in a hoarse voice. 'I do like blinis very much, and these are excellent. It's just that I'm so thirsty, if you please — '

'Then you must have some tea. Here's a cup, and when I've poured out for the others, I'll bring you more.'

She moved on down the table, but she kept her eye on them, for Alexis was clearly delighted with his new friend, and chattering like a magpie. He ought to see more nice boys like these, she thought, and presently went back to sit between Peter Arkadeivich and the cadet on his other side, asking the friendly questions that were second nature to her, about their homes and families. Peter Arkadeivich had beautiful manners. He spoke to his sovereign's daughter clearly and concisely, as he was taught at military school, but he had to apologise more than once for coughing, and Olga said sympathetically:

'You've caught a little cold, haven't you, Peter Arkadeivich?'

'It's nothing, Your Imperial Highness.'

'I'll tell them to mix a honey drink for you, and that'll make your throat more comfortable.'

Alexis told Olga later on that Peter Arkadeivich (champion of the school sports last summer and a candidate for the artillery) thought his sister was terrific. He went to bed a happy boy, saying he wished every day could be like this one.

But the days which followed were like those his sister knew so well, with the Czar still fighting the Duma, and threatening to dissolve the session which had resumed after a short winter recess, and the President, Rodzianko, warning him more than once that each report he made at Czarskoe Selo might be the last. The terrible winter conditions were still slowing up railway transport, and now nearly sixty thousand supply trucks were laid up at different stations on the routes to the front, but plans for the next offensive were going forward, and the tracks were open between Petrograd and Mohilev. The Czar prepared to return to GHQ. Characteristically, he took the same evasive action as in the summer of 1915, when he told Dmitri he would give up the idea of assuming the supreme command. This time he told Rodzianko that he would appear personally before the Duma on a given day, raising hopes that even at the eleventh hour he would agree to a constitutional ministry, and then, on the night before, he left his home and went back to Mohilev.

His farewells to his family were short and hurried. The Czarina, who dreaded the effects of their separation, was in tears, and Alexis was almost as distressed at being left behind.

'But you'll bring Verushka back with you next time, won't you, papa?'

'Who's Verushka — oh yes, the cat. All right, I will, if I remember.'

'You've got to remember.' Alexis kissed his father; he was not too big for kisses, although he was nearly as tall as the little Czar.

'Don't kiss me, father, I've got a streaming cold,' said Olga from the background.

'Yes you have, poor ducky, and Tania too,' said their father fondly. 'Better have hot lemon drinks and spend tomorrow in bed.'

'That's what we mean to do.'

They were still in bed, and in a raging fever, when Simon Hendrikov came to the palace two evenings later, and asked, according to custom, for the honour of an audience with the Grand Duchess Olga.

He waited in the little salon, just long enough to begin feeling anxious, until Marie came to greet him in her forthright way.

'I'm awfully sorry, Simon Karlovich,' she said, barely acknowledging his bow, 'both my sisters are ill in bed. I can't even tell Olga you're here, because Dr. Botkin and mamma are with her now.'

'Ill in bed? Good heavens, Marie Nicolaievna, what's the matter?'

'I'm afraid you'll laugh, Simon — they've both got measles.'

'Laugh? I'm not laughing! Measles can be horribly uncomfortable for a grown-up person. Is Olga — are they both feeling miserable?'

'I'm afraid they are, just at present, and the worst is, Alexis seems to be coming down with it too.'

'What absolutely rotten luck.' He saw that Marie was pale and strained. 'Haven't you all *had* measles?' he said angrily.

'Not us, we were far too well taken care of. But the doctors say the girls'll be much better by tomorrow; if you like to bring a little note next time you come, I'll see that Olga gets it.'

'You're very kind, Marie Nicolaievna, but that's what I came to say: I won't be here tomorrow. I've been ordered to the Marine Guards barracks at Petrograd.'

'Who ordered that?' the girl asked sharply.

'The commander of the Garde Equipage, the Grand Duke Kirill. He wants two companies detached from Czarskoe Selo.'

'Because of the rioting that's started in the city?'

'I'm afraid so, yes. But don't tell your sister — yet.'

'I won't, the doctors say they're to be kept very quiet. Good luck to you, Simon Karlovich, and come back soon!'

He kissed the girl's hand, and kept it for a moment in his own. 'Give her my love,' he said. 'Poor Olga! How in the world did *they* contrive to catch the measles?'

'We know exactly how,' said Marie Nicolaievna. 'One of the cadets, a boy called Peter Arkadeivich, was coming down with it that day they were all playing with Alexis on the snow mountain.'

CHAPTER EIGHTEEN

It was March in the western world; it was still February by the Russian calendar when the long-awaited revolution erupted in Petrograd.

Joe Calvert had a ringside seat for it, since during the early days he was often at the American Embassy in the Furshtatskaia, not far from the Tauride Palace where the Duma was in session. It was nearly a year since Ambassador Marye had asked for his recall for reasons of health — reasons not accepted by the Czar's government, which at once suspected an intended American affront. His successor, Ambassador David Francis, was a jovial gentleman of sixty-seven summers, who since his elderly wife had chosen to remain at home liked to surround himself with members of the Foreign Service, irrespective of rank, who could play a good game of poker. Mr. Francis had achieved fame in the United States as the organiser of the St. Louis Fair.

It was not a poker session which took Joe to the embassy on the day the shooting started in the streets. The career officers of his Service were meeting almost daily for an informal briefing session after the Washington cables and the local press digests were read, because for over a month it had been apparent that the United States was preparing to enter the war, and not by the road of conciliation. President Wilson had played his chosen role of mediator up to the hilt, and as lately as the New Year it seemed as if the Allies, with victory still far from their grasp, would have to accept his mediation and with it a compromise peace. Then the Germans, in one of their classic crises of dementia, had announced a policy of unrestricted submarine warfare as the only means of bringing Britain to her knees. Early in February the United States severed relations with the German government, and so, on President Wilson's appeal, did most of the Latin-American states. The Emperor Franz Josef had just died, and Gavrilo Princip, still in prison, was dying; as the Great War became a global war few remembered that it had begun with just two shots fired in a Sarajevo street.

The rioting which started the day before Simon Hendrikov, much against his will, was forced to leave Czarskoe Selo had pursued what was for Petrograd a normal course. The strikes in the war factories became a general strike, the tramcars stopped, the bridges were raised, and crowds of demonstrators were cleared by the military from the main thoroughfares. When Joe went to the Furshtatskaia for the briefing it seemed as if Ambassador Francis was preparing to go out, for his Russian driver was waiting with his team at the front door. The ambassador owned a Ford touring car, an object of great interest to the public, which was driven by his Negro valet and majordomo, Philip Jordan, but in the bitter winter weather he was using his sleigh. The horses were snorting and pawing a little under their warm blankets. In the grey day the American flags, worn in each bridle over the horse's outer ear, struck a note of lively colour. After the firing began the ambassador was persuaded to send the sleigh back to the stable and cancel the engagement he had made for lunch.

At the same time there was no real danger. Joe gave the Liteini Prospekt a wide berth, and took short cuts across the Gardens to his flat without seeing any incident, although a confused yelling and stampeding from the direction of the Nevski Prospekt suggested that the Cossacks had got the strikers on the run. Eveything was normal in the Italianskaia, and he was mildly surprised when Varvara, not usually so attentive, pulled open the apartment door before he could take out his key.

'The master is here, *barin*,' she said with a toothless smile, and Joe laughed. Captain Allen was still the master of the house to Varvara, and his tenant slapped him on the back as he rose rather stiffly from the basket chair beside the stove.

'Where've you come from this time, you old horse-thief?'

'From Murmansk, for my sins. Helping to shepherd our delegates aboard the minesweeper that's going to take them back to Aberdeen took a lot longer than I anticipated.'

'Must have done,' said Joe. 'They left here quite a while ago.'

'Their train broke down at Kem, with three hundred miles to go,' said Dick. 'That's when an interpreter really came in handy. I got stuck at Kem myself on the way back. What a dump! It was the last straw for the Allied delegates. They'd been told it was possible to haul over three thousand tons of war supplies daily, across the tundra; now they've seen for themselves it's barely possible to handle one.'

'Well, have a drink,' suggested Joe. 'I don't need to ask Varvara if there's enough lunch for two, she always breaks out the emergency supplies when the master comes home. You staying long in Petrograd this time?'

'If I can get a room at the Moskva, but I hear it's choc-a-bloc with Siberian escapees and Social Dems. from Finland these days.'

'You'd better bunk in here, if you don't mind the little room.'

'Thanks, Joe, I'd like that. I'll pick up my stuff at the embassy — it'll only be for a day or two.'

He studied the contents of his glass in silence. Joe had never seen him look wearier or more depressed, even after the knifing incident at 'The Red Sarafan'.

'What's the news from Washington?' Dick roused himself to say.

'Nothing special.'

'H'm.' Dick's mind seemed to go back to his last journey. 'They used too much German POW labour for it,' he said, and Joe knew he was talking about the Murmansk railway. 'No wonder there's not a trestle bridge that can be trusted, from one end of the line to the other. If Nicholas knew what was good for him, he'd order Trepov to get his repair gangs on the job — and at the double.'

'First they've got to make the trucks available, to bring in the war material.'

'I wasn't thinking of the war material. I was thinking of the personal safety of the Romanovs. Murmansk's the only port open in the whole of Northern Russia, and they may need that perishing railway if they have to make a quick getaway.'

'You think things are that bad?'

'Of course I do, and you do too. The strikes which German money paid for, and the rioting, and the scandals, were all planned months ago. Nicholas has thrown away all his chances, and the Duma won't be able to control the situation. Make no mistake about it, Joe — the revolution is about to begin.'

'And then?'

'Then, even if President Wilson declares war tomorrow, it'll be too late for some nice kids out at Czarskoe Selo. And if they packed their bags tonight and arrived incognito at the British Embassy, we couldn't get them out through Finland now. It would have to be the Murmansk route, and I tell you — just one more freeze-up on the tundra, just one more hold-up at Kem, and you can write off the Romanov family as another casualty of the war.'

'Let's hope things won't look quite so grim tomorrow.'

But tomorrow, and the day after that, came and went, and half of Captain Allen's predictions were proved true. The Duma, now in constant session, rejected an imperial ukase from Mohilev ordering them to suspend their sittings. Instead, they sent Nicholas II their final advice to grant a constituion, adding, from the pen of Rodzianko, 'Tomorrow it may be too late!' By the time the lethargic emperor at last gave his consent, it was too late. The troops refused to continue firing on the crowds. They threw away their rifles and embraced the workers who swarmed across the barricades made out of captured vehicles and uprooted trees. A soldier in one of the crack regiments shot an officer and roused his comrades to mutiny. One by one the finest regiments of Petrograd — the Transfiguration, in which the Czar himself was a colonel — the Volinski and all the others, now manned only by boys and the disaffected comb-outs from the replacement depots, broke ranks and went off singing to the Duma.

For many of them the rallying point was Preobrazhenskaia Ploshad, the great square of the Transfiguration Regiment, but almost as many made straight for the Tauride Gardens round the palace Catherine II had built for her lover, Prince Potemkin. The Americans, from their embassy windows, saw them stumbling and shouting down the Furshtatskaia. The military attaché identified the regiments by their insignia, for all were now marching under a new banner — the red flag.

'Here comes the Garde Equipage,' he threw back over his shoulder. 'And — my God, yes it is! the Grand Duke Kirill's right out there in front!'

'You're kidding!' But it was true, they all recognised the tall figure of the Czar's first cousin, Aunt Miechen's eldest son, marching under the red flag, with a red ribbon on his coat. He had been punished, years ago, for marrying without the Czar's permission: banished, deprived of his rank, estates and decorations, and even after the sentence of banishment was lifted, snubbed and humiliated at the imperial court. There was just the suspicion of a smile on his handsome face as he led his men towards the Duma. Now, aligned with the Czar's enemies, it was his turn to punish the Czar.

'I'm going to try and get inside the Duma,' said Joe Calvert, grabbing his fur hat.

'Going to see the last act?' someone said.

'Or the curtain-raiser.'

While the overture to the last act of the Imperial Duma was being played, all was peaceful at Czarskoe Sélo.

The illness of the older girls and their brother had roused the Czarina from her torpor of grief for Rasputin. The maternal instinct, so very strong in her, revived with her children's need, and although trained nurses were at once brought from the palace hospital, it was their mother who bathed the girls tenderly and prepared the few sips of cooling drink Alexis was allowed. She put on the uniform with the red cross worn at the beginning of the war, and in fresh white limped from the girls' big bedroom to her son's little one, listening to Alexis cough, holding him up in his bouts of sickness and all the time terrified that some minor, internal blood vessel would break and precipitate catastrophe.

The Czar wrote sympathetically but abstractedly, saying it would be better if 'the chicks' all came down with measles together, and got it over.

'He wouldn't say that if he knew how ill poor Olga and Tania are,' said Anastasia to Marie. 'Dr. Botkin says it's far worse having measles after you're grown up.'

'You and I are nearly grown up, Imp, so we must pray that we don't get it too,' said Marie in a voice as frightened as she felt. 'Because there's nobody else left now.' Anastasia nodded, she knew exactly what her sister meant. No one really close to them was there to take charge in those days when courtier after courtier seemed to be called for urgent reasons to Petrograd, and then telephoned regrets that the train strike prevented his return. The two loyal ladies-in-waiting whom the girls knew as 'Nastinka' and 'Isa' could be counted on to come into service in their turn, and so could Mademoiselle Schneider, the Czarina's Reader, but the men left behind were old men, bound entirely by the traditions of a former age. The Czarina seemed not to notice the defections. One of her closest friends, Madame Dehn, a simple good-natured creature who had once gone on a pilgrimage with Rasputin, had come to visit her from Petrograd, and with Lili Dehn for confidante she seemed to feel the need of no one else, not even Anna Virubova. 'And wouldn't you know Awful Ania would get measles too?' said Anastasia disgustedly.

'She probably thinks it's the sincerest form of flattery. You must never go into her bedroom, 'Stasia, remember that!'

'Mamma told me not to.' The youngest Grand Duchess carried innumerable messages from the private apartments to Anna Virubova's sickroom in the guest wing, where the crippled woman was being nursed through the measles by Sister Akulina. 'Thank you, darling,' the Czarina said a dozen times a day. 'What would I do without you? You're my legs!'

'I wish I were a brain, and not a pair of legs!' said Anastasia. 'I wish Olga or Tania would get better, and tell us what to do! When I ask mamma about the troubles in the city, she tells me to go away and do a nice jig-saw puzzle; and yet she sits there crying and whispering to Lili, and burning papa's letters with her diaries in the boudoir stove!'

'I'm going to send for General Voeiekov.' And Marie did so, much to the surprise of the Commandant of the Palace, who found the strong, gauche Grand Duchess suddenly invested with the dignity he remembered in her grandfather, Alexander III. Yes, he was bound to admit to Her Imperial Highness, there had been serious rioting in Petrograd, and in fact the Winter Palace and the Admiralty were being attacked, at that very moment, by disloyal troops, but two leading members of the Duma had gone to consult His Majesty at Mohilev, and reinforcements would soon be on their way from General Alexeiev's command to the capital.

'Is it true there have been mutinies in the Navy too?' said Marie.

Well, yes, there had been disturbances at Kronstadt, but there too the situation was well in hand.

'And at Helsingfors?' Marie persisted.

'There are no recent reports from Finland.'

'Why not?'

'Madame, the telephone lines are down in the Grand Duchy.'

'Surely the telephone lines can be repaired.'

'It will certainly be done tomorrow, Your Imperial Highness.'

The girls went upstairs to their room. Monsieur Gilliard was pacing up and down the gallery, he said the doctors thought Alexis was a little better. They all three looked out from one of the great windows across the snowy park, and saw the Cossacks of the Escort riding slowly, at the prescribed interval, along the boundary made by the nearest avenue.

'Ten o'clock, and all's well!' said Monsieur Gilliard. 'Please God we'll have good news from Mohilev in the morning!'

'And please God all the sick ones will be feeling better,' said Anastasia, so soberly that Marie caught at her hand when they were alone in their room.

'Are *you* all right, Anastasia? Do you want me to take your temperature?'

'Don't be silly, you're not on the ward now! I'm perfectly all right.'

'Good, but I think we ought to gargle with permanganate, and drink some quinine and water before we go to bed.'

'Will that keep us from having measles?'

'It's the only thing I can think of. And we simply mustn't be ill now!'

'Can't we have some tea as well?'

A scared maid from the old nursery wing brought them tea, and said she didn't know what had happened to the footmen. They sat up in bed in their white nightgowns to drink it, pleased by the unusual treat, and so concerned with the need to keep well that when they woke in the grey morning the Grand Duchesses said almost simultaneously 'How do you feel?' and laughed with relief when the answer was 'I feel fine!' But when they went in their dressing-gowns to whisper at their sisters' door, the nurse on duty shook her head. The usual adult complications had set in: Olga's eyes and Tatiana's ears were badly affected by the disease. There was no question of even peeping in at them that day.

It was Monday, the beginning of a new week, when with a little effective generalship there might still have been room for hope. But the Czar's message from Mohilev, when it came, was only an order that the riots in the capital should cease forthwith, and that order was impossible to carry out. General Khabalov was still holding the Winter Palace, but as no food had been provided for the loyal troops it was doubtful how long their loyalty would last. The experienced regiments ordered to reinforce the garrison of Czarskoe Selo were not within two hundred miles of their objective, for the revolutionaries had cut or blocked the railway line, and the roads were barricaded. As for the garrison itself, it was melting away. The mounted men were seen no more on the avenues: the Escort, the Railway Regiment, the Personal Regiment, the personal police were all on their way to Petrograd and the victorious Duma. Rodzianko himself, as a last gesture, telephoned to the Czarina, and with rough compassion told her: 'When a house is on fire it's best to leave it. Pack your trunks, Madame, and go!' There were so many people in the President's room, so many hundreds more pushing and shouting in the corridors outside, that Rodzianko could hardly hear the answer of the woman he had mistrusted and opposed so long. And yet the low intense words registered, and came back to him later:

'My children are dangerously ill and can't be moved. I will never leave my children!'

The Marine Guards at this time were still on duty at the Alexander Palace, for the Grand Duke Kirill had not yet made up his mind to go over to the revolution. In the early dusk every man was mustered to guard the various entrances, and some light artillery mounted in the great forecourt after news was received that a rabble of soldiers and workers was on the way from Petrograd to take 'the German woman' prisoner. They came by train and trucks and stolen automobiles, many drunk, all singing and shouting, and were welcomed and given food by the Czarskoe Selo militia. By the late evening the beautiful mansions of the Czar's Village were lit by flaming torches as the mob caroused up and down the avenues. The power station was seized, and electricity cut off in the palace. The lifts stopped running, and only the strong arms of Madame Dehn and the grit of little Anastasia enabled the Czarina, lame and half fainting with anxiety for her husband, to climb the stair to the rooms where her ailing children lay.

But the Garde Equipage stood firm behind the closed gates,

and the terrible cold, the eighteen degrees of frost which came with the darkness caused the mob to withdraw at last, and go off to fraternise with their new comrades in the militia barracks. Their yells died away and dissolved into singing in the distance.

'I must go out myself and thank our brave defenders,' said Alexandra Feodorovna.

'I'll come with you, mamma,' said Marie. 'No, not you, 'Stasia, you've been sniffling a bit since tea time. Are you all right?'

'I'm fine,' said Anastasia, hastily pocketing her handkerchief.

'Good, but stay indoors with Lili, we won't be long. Mamma, don't you think we might ask the Guards to come into the hall in relays, and give them all some tea?'

'I don't know, Mashka, we've never given them tea before.'

'There's never been a night like this before,' Marie said grimly. She slung a fur cape round her shoulders and went out, carefully supporting her mother down the icy steps. They went slowly along the lines, talking to the men, who were half frozen, and accepted the offer of tea with incredulous pleasure. Twice on the first trip, and twice on the half dozen walks she took between the courtyard, and the gate, Marie's cape fell off into the snow, and every time it was picked up and carefully wrapped round her by some rough fellow with the ice of his own breath whitening his moustache.

Inside the hall Anastasia was in her element, presiding over the samovars, and directing the servants, such as were available, in passing tea and great slices of buttered bread to the men as they came in. Marie helped too; she had taken her exhausted mother back to Lili and her ladies, and then went outdoors and in, although her back was beginning to ache and her face and hands to burn in spite of the cold. She felt her fur hat very tight across her brow, but every time she raised her hand to ease it Marie realised her head was bare.

'Isn't this fun!' exulted Anastasia. 'I've found some men who were on the *Standart* on our last cruise, look, those three over there. Do go and talk to them, Mashka, it's just like being on the yacht again!'

'I only wish Simon Karlovich was here.'

'Poor Olga wouldn't like him to see her now, all over spots.'

Marie laughed wearily. But she went to talk to the men from the happy *Standart* days, and to all the others who came so awkwardly into the palace of the Czar, until at midnight it was decided to stand down half the guard, and relieve the others in two hour rotas until midnight. The servants, without asking permission, had gone to bed; the two girls were left alone in the candelit hall.

'Should we blow the candles out, Marie?'

'They'll burn down to their sockets by and by. Let's go and ask the night nurse how the others are. And then let's go to bed.'

They looked at each other, both very flushed, shivering even in the warm hall. Then Marie said reluctantly:

'How do *you* feel now?'

'I feel absolutely awful.'

'So do I.'

The mounting of the guard at the Alexander Palace on that winter night was one of the last attempts to defend the Russian monarchy. By the time Marie and Anastasia woke early next morning, miserable in the onset of measles, their cousin the Grand Duke Kirill had ordered the remnants of the Garde Equipage back to another barracks near the Moika canal, from where he would presently lead them to the Duma. Others had preceded them there, for almost the whole cabinet, and many other leaders of the Czarist regime, had gone to the Tauride Palace on that wild Monday night to seek protection from the revolutionaries. Last of all came Protopopov, whining, cringing, disguised. He and his fellows were assured that the Imperial Duma did not shed blood, but this did not save them from imprisonment. They were all confined in due course in the fortress of St. Peter and St. Paul.

Next morning Joe Calvert found not an inch of space available in the public galleries of the Duma, where he had taken his unobtrusive seat so many times in the past. It seemed as if twenty separate meetings were taking place in the galleries alone, and as many more in every corridor as speeches and arguments, restrained for so long, broke out among the elected Deputies, the officers of the regiments which had gone over, and above all among the men who burst into the building waving the red flag and singing the *Marseillaise*. Pushed from one side of the Catherine Hall to the other, Joe was at least present for the eclipse of the old reliables of the Duma, men like Rodzianko and Prince Lvov who had struggled with the Czar's stubborn apathy for years. He saw them superseded, whatever their nominal functions were to be, by the brilliant young leader of the Social Revolutionaries, Alexander Kerensky.

Kerensky occupied the rostrum for hours that day. Slim and blond and only thirty-six, he poured his eloquence in torrents over the crowd. The beautiful voice which he had used to such effect as defence counsel in the great labour trials grew raucous as the day wore on, but the words never failed him. Alone, Kerensky stemmed the tide of hatred which flowed into the hall as it filled with armed soldiers, workmen, students, all dedicated to anarchy rather than a new form of government. The only concession he made to them — and he made it quickly and willingly — was the opening of the Budget Committee room to their leaders who, following Trotsky's example after Bloody Sunday in 1905, had made themselves into a Soviet of Soldiers' and Workers' Deputies.

It was in one of the eddies of the crowd which followed this announcement that Joe found himself side by side with Mara Trenova, who in her fur hat, her suit with the worn leather belt and her high boots looked not unlike a soldiers' Deputy herself.

'Hallo, Mara Ivanovna!' Joe managed to gasp. 'Come to see the red dawn breaking?'

'It has broken at last, thank — thanks to a few brave men,' she said. 'Now the real work begins. Guchkov and Shulgin have left for GHQ, to persuade Nicholas Romanov to abdicate; we can go on from there tomorrow. All power to the people!'

'Sounds great,' said Joe. He pulled her into a corner of the hall, where stacked arms and greatcoats made a slight protection against the swaying mass. 'Only what they seem to be shouting is "All power to the Soviet!" '

'It's the same thing,' she assured him. 'Kerensky himself helped to establish the Petrograd Soviet.'

'And what d'you think of *him*?' Joe was tall enough to see Kerensky's fair head bobbing above the rostrum; the rest of a physically insignificant man was hidden from sight. But Mara followed the jerk of his chin.

'Kerensky? I used to meet him often at the Hendrikovs, when I was at school with Dolly.'

'Yes, I know you did, I've met him there myself, but what d'you think of him now?'

'Too much war talk. He mustn't forget the desire of the workers for bread, peace and freedom!'

'I remember where you were very thrilled at the beginning of the war when he and his friends told the workers to defend their country first, and the revolution would come afterwards.'

'Oh, at the beginning of the war!' she said impatiently. 'Aren't six million Russian dead proof enough that we were willing to defend our country? Now it's surely time to put an end to the useless massacres! The workers want a government that'll make peace with Germany, and that's what Kerensky must be made to understand!'

'From what I've heard him say today, the new government would want to go on fighting, right alongside the Allies.'

'Our Allies have made sacrifices too,' said Mara. 'They'll understand our position better than a neutral.'

Joe bit his lip. It was the old sneer with which any Russian could win an argument about the war: America was neutral, an American couldn't understand. But before he could speak a young man with a black beard and spectacles pushed aside the pile of coats and weapons and seized Mara by the arm.

'We're going "Across the River" now, Trenova!' he shouted above the din. 'Don't you want to see the fun?'

'Oh I do, I do!' Joe Calvert heard her say, and without another look or word for him she was off, arm-in-arm with the bearded man and another of the same Georgian type, all three pushing their way somehow out of the Tauride Palace. Joe followed them within an hour. He had been there since eight o'clock that morning, and it was nearly eight at night, but only hunger and fatigue drew him from a scene where fresh orators harangued the crowds on every subject from taxation to illiteracy. He thought, as he had often thought on Madame Hendrikova's evenings, what amazing stamina the Russians had for talk.

In the Tauride Gardens behind the palace, once famous for

332

their snow mountains, hundreds of men who had no hope of entering the building had made a kind of bivouac, with charcoal braziers burning on the snow, and even one or two field kitchens dispensing food of a sort. The stacked arms and the glint of bayonets made it seem as if an army on the march was camped round the Duma, and in fact a fair proportion of the army had come exulting from the surrender of the Winter Palace. Joe picked his way unchallenged through the mob. Once in the Furshtatskaia, only two blocks from the American Embassy, he drew in several gulps of the fresh icy air. The snow was falling in soft flakes on the almost empty street.

The last rumour he heard in the gardens — spluttered out by a soldier who insisted on kissing him and doing a little bear-dance in the snow — was that Nicholas II had abdicated.

It was not true then; the monarchy lasted one more day, during which the Soviet and the Duma hammered out a compromise for the creation of a provisional government. Then the Czar signed the instrument of abdication, exactly eleven days after his return to GHQ, and was taken back under close arrest to the palace where his wife was already a prisoner of the State.

Unless the end of March brought a severe snowstorm, as sometimes happened, the worst of the Russian winter appeared to be over within ten days of the Czar's abdication. The Fourth Line, as Joe Calvert walked along to call on the Hendrikovs, was lighted by fitful sunshine which gave a foretaste of the coming spring. The lime trees were still sheathed in ice, but snow had begun to slide off the roofs, and patches of black earth were appearing in the little city gardens.

Madame Hendrikova herself opened the door to him.

'Welcome, dear friend!' she said. 'What a long time since you've been here! What incredible changes we have seen!'

'It seems like a long time to me,' said Joe, hanging up his coat and hat. His Russian lessons had ended nearly six months earlier, and he had not seen Madame Hendrikova since. Even in the dim hall he could see that her hair was now quite grey, but she was as erect as ever, wearing a neat plaid silk blouse with a fountain-pen clipped to the breast pocket, and a wrist watch on a leather strap instead of the old silver fob she used to brandish at her tardy students. 'I called the hospital,' he said, 'they told me Dolly was having the day off, so I thought — '

'You're very welcome, and Dolly will be glad to see you. She has another visitor today, someone you know — '

It was Captain Richard Allen. He was sitting at a table already set for tea, between Dolly and her father, and seeming quite at home in the familiar living-room. His presence and Dolly's blush so disconcerted Joe that after he had greeted the professor and his daughter he could find nothing better to say to Dick than, 'I didn't know you were back in Petrograd.'

'I've been around. All well at the Italianskaia?'

'No damage done so far.' And then the maid came in with the samovar, over which Dolly undertook to preside, giving Joe a chance to say quietly to her mother:

'I've been wondering about your son, madame. Dolly said you had a telephone call a week ago?'

'We haven't heard since then, but you know what the telephone's been like.'

'He's still at the barracks on the Moika?'

'As far as we know.' It was said with a glance at Professor Hendrikov, and Joe took the hint at once. He turned to Simon's father.

'Dolly's been telling me,' he said, 'that you played quite a part in the abdication of the Grand Duke Michael.'

'Oh, I wouldn't say that, my dear boy,' said the professor, brightening up, 'I only provided what Dolly says I'm so fond of, namely pens, ink and paper.'

'I'm not really clear, as to how it all came about, sir.'

'I don't believe the Grand — I mean Michael Alexandrovich, is quite clear on the matter himself. Of course it came as a great surprise to him.'

'Because he must have thought if his brother did abdicate, the Czarevich Alexis would succeed.'

'So everybody thought. But then there was the question of the child's health, and the father couldn't face a possible separation from the boy, so he named his brother as his successor on the throne.' The professor coughed.

'But nobody really imagined Michael would wear the crown?'

'He least of all! By good luck he was in Petrograd — with the Putiatins in the Millionnaia — and when he joined us he proved most willing to sign an act of abdication on his own

334

behalf. I had to smile when Kerensky said to him, 'Promise us not to consult your wife,' and he said, 'Don't you worry, she's out at Gachina!' He knew, poor devil, that the Countess Brassova had been very ambitious to wear a crown.'

'So you composed the abdication document?'

'Not I, no indeed! I literally did supply the paper from my writing case, but the statement was drawn up by my old friend Vladimir Nabokov, of the *Rech*. He was as quick and clever as always, it didn't take *him* long! And when Michael Alexandrovich signed his name, somehow we were all aware that the Romanov dynasty had come to an end, that there would never, in our new world, be any room for a pretender to a toppled throne. It was all over in five minutes, and Kerensky was extremely moved. He shook poor Michael warmly by the hand, and said "Monseigneur, you're one of the noblest of men!" and all of us applauded. It was yet another triumph for Alexander Kerensky.'

'And for you too, my worthy father,' a new voice said.

'Simon!' cried Madame Hendrikova.

Perhaps he had come in very quietly, or perhaps they had all been riveted by Professor Hendrikov's story; however it was, Simon Hendrikov had arrived unnoticed, and was standing in the open door, with one shoulder against the jamb. He was in uniform, but the uniform looked as if he had slept in it for days, and the fur hat in his hand as if it had been rolling along the gutters. To four of the people present it seemed that he had been drinking; to Richard Allen, the one most competent to judge, Simon Hendrikov was one of the walking wounded, suffering from the internal bleeding of his own lost cause.

'Sorry if I startled you,' said Simon between drawn-back lips. 'I didn't want to interrupt father's gloat over the downfall of the Romanovs — or was it over the triumph of his own little genius, Alex Kerensky? Sorry if I turned up to remind you that there *are* still men living who haven't forgotten the oath of allegiance they took to His Majesty the Czar.'

'My dear boy, don't exaggerate,' said his mother, gathering her wits about her. 'We're delighted to see you. We've all been wondering where you were — '

'You didn't have to worry,' said her son. 'I told you when I was allowed to telephone — one man, one call — that I wasn't far away. I've been confined to barracks all this while, with the rest of the Politically Suspect — that's what they're calling us now, Politically Suspect — me and about twenty more who had the wits to see what our great commander, Kirill Vladimirovich, was up to. Mind you, I had my suspicions, when they pulled some of us out of Czarskoe Selo! Kirill wanted to have us under lock and key in the Moika if we refused to join him on his great march to the Tauride. Under the red flag! Well, I've been spared that disgrace, never mind what it cost me —'

'Simon, do stop' said Dolly. 'You're tired out, you're not yourself. Let me pour you a cup of tea —'

Simon looked at her owlishly. 'That's where you're wrong, my dear sister,' he said, 'I never was more myself than I am at this moment. And I don't want tea. Buckets of tea! That's the great Russian prescription for every malady. Thank you, I had enough vodka to float the *Standart* on my way here.'

'On your way from the Moika?'

'Who said anything about the Moika? I've been to Glinka Street. Wanted to see for myself if it was true what they were saying, that the red flag was flying from Kirill Vladimirovich's house. It was too. Bastard of hell! He broke his oath to his soveriegn, and disgraced the whole Garde Equipage when he marched them off to the Duma to suck —'

'Take it easy, Simon,' said Joe.

'Oh, you're there, are you?' said Simon as if he realised Joe's presence for the first time. 'And Captain Allen, too; that's fine. I did you a good turn when Dolly and Joe picked you up in the Yamskaia, now it's up to you to do something for me.'

'If I can,' said Dick. Joe Calvert thought he was the only one able to listen to Simon without dismay or embarrassment: his pale eyes showed only an appraising interest.

But Simon had gone off on another tack.

'You know, I blame you for a lot of this,' he said to his father. 'You and your pet Kerensky. You had him here night after night, listening to him and buttering him up, and now, by God, he's Minister of Justice in the Provisional Government *and* a leading figure in the great Petrograd Soviet! How's that for a double turn? You and your lectures on the French Revolution! You thought I was too dumb to understand what you were getting at, didn't you? But Jesus, I could listen, I used to listen in this room night after night, to your seminars getting your views on Mirabeau and Danton, and all they did to overthrow the Bourbon tyrants, until a little man like Alex Kerensky thought *he* was Mirabeau — at the very least; now he thinks he's Bonaparte! That's what they call him when he goes raving and tearing through the Tauride, spouting speeches like the one I heard him make this afternoon. Napoleonchik, that's what they call him! Not Bonaparte, Napoleonchik! The pocket Napoleon!'

'As a matter of fact they call him Speedy,' said Richard Allen.

Simon's jaw dropped. 'They call him what?'

'Speedy. The police call him that. He moves around the town so fast, they can't keep up with him.' Seeing that he had stopped Simon's tirade, he went on placidly, 'My dear old chap, you said you needed help, and if I can I'll help you. Just tell me this: are you absent without leave from your quarters?'

'I've got a twenty-four hour pass.'

'Of which you've already wasted some at Glinka Street and the Tauride. And also in several bars, of course. Now what do you want me to do?'

'It's something only father can do, not you,' said Simon sulkily. 'Father, I want you to go to Kerensky and arrange for my transfer into a Line regiment — any regiment that's serving at the front. On the Vistula, on the Stohod, anywhere. Kerensky wants to carry on the war against the Germans. So do I. I'm not going to break the oath I took to the Czar, not me.'

Dick looked warningly at the shaken old professor, and said, 'I think that can be arranged, perhaps tomorrow morning. After you've had a bath and food, and a good sleep.'

'Ah!' said Simon, with the cunning of the partly sober, 'I know what you want to do. You want to hustle me off to bed before I put my foot in it. Before I disgrace my dear papa, the great liberal historian, godfather of the Russian Revolution. Well, I'm not going to play your game, so don't you think it. I've got to have twenty-four hours for myself, no, not twenty-four left now, say twelve. Because first I'm going out to Czarskoe Selo to see my girl.'

'What girl?' his mother asked, and Dolly began to cry.

Captain Allen's voice for the first time had a parade-ground rasp in it. 'Don't be a damned fool,' he said. 'If you go out there in your present mood you'll get a bullet through your head.'

'How'd you know?'

'Because I was there myself this morning,' said Dick, and Joe wondered fleetingly in what disguise the Englishman had visited a palace now guarded in strength by the soldiers of the Soviet. As if he had read Joe's thoughts, Dick explained:

'I went in under a safe conduct, as a special messenger from the British Embassy.'

'Did you — see any of them?' Simon got out.

'Certainly not. I had an interview with the new Commandant, Korovichenko, that was all. Their Majesties are both being held incommunicado at present, as prisoners of State, and the young people are still in their bedrooms, convalescing.'

'But they're not prisoners?'

'Not officially, no. The two older girls are making a pretty good recovery from the measles, I was told. Alexis is better, Anastasia never was very ill, but unfortunately the Grand Duchess Marie is still lying between life and death. Apparently she was coming down with measles the night she went in and out to the Marine Guards in the courtyard, giving them tea and all that, and the chill she caught turned into pneumonia.' Dick paused. 'If it hadn't been for that, I really think they would have made a bolt for it at the last minute, but of course it would've been fatal even to take the poor girl out of bed.'

'The Garde Equipage was in the courtyard!' said Simon. 'And I wasn't there.'

Professor Hendrikov cleared his throat. 'Simon, my dear lad,' he said, 'we all respect your feelings. You've been closer to the imperial family than most of us, and naturally you're concerned about their fate. I'm sure they're in no danger, because Kerensky is in charge of them, and everything is settling down so fast. There can hardly have been a major revolution since recorded history began which was carried out with so little bloodshed or looting, apart from Madame Kchessinskaia's house, which was occupied and pillaged by some hotheads on the first night. And even that was only a symbolic act — '

'Sorry to disagree, professor,' Dick Allen interrupted, 'it hadn't anything to do with symbolism. I believe the taking of the Kchessinskaia house was ordered by somebody who hasn't arrived yet, to provide a command post for his future operations. It's very convenient for the Soviet's GHQ at the Finland Station — '

'You're thinking of Lenin,' Joe Calvert stated rather than said.

'Oh, to hell with your symbolism and your Soviet!' Simon Hendrikov burst out again. 'What I want to know is, what's going to happen to the imperial family? Will they be allowed to travel south under a trustworthy escort, and live quietly at Livadia?'

'Too easy,' said Dick with the ghost of a smile. 'Even Kerensky couldn't bring that about. What my ambassador is trying to arrange is their safe conduct to England, as soon as the children are well enough to travel. King George is waiting to receive them all, and the Germans are willing to give them some sort of a *laissez-passer*.'

'*England!*' said Simon, with something horribly like a sob. Dolly put her hand on his bowed head. 'Oh, don't, my dear,' she whispered. 'You must try not to mind so much – if it's what would be best for *her*.'

CHAPTER NINETEEN

OLGA's convalescence was a fume of dreams. She had suffered from nightmares during the worst days of her illness, nightmares in which they told her that her father was no longer Czar, that her mother was under arrest, and that their children were under lock and key in their palace home, and sometimes her dormant intelligence told her that those evil dreams were true. Very often, too, she had bad dreams about Simon Hendrikov. She saw him lying again in the charnel house of neglected wounded at Warsaw, or imagined him dead in the last stand of the Guards on the Stohod, and often, equally painfully, she was in his arms, on the verge of the act of love, and felt him torn from her body in the very moment of satisfaction. Sometimes, raging and frustrated, she heard him speak to her from behind the iron fences of the palace park, now made out of bayonets: he spoke the lines from *Young Lochinvar* which she had read to him on a summer day in the Fourth Line, or else he said, as he had said then, 'I wanted to be alone with you, we're never alone!' That sent her back to Lermontov, and the poem which haunted her on the night long ago when Simon was on his way back to her in the hospital train, and she raised herself on her pillows, reciting:

> I want to be alone with you,
>   A moment quite alone,
> The minutes left to me are few,
> They say I'll soon be gone

and going on through the poem to the poignant lines:

> And say I died, and for the Czar,
> And say what fools the doctors are,
> And that I shook you by the hand,
> And spoke about my native land

until her mother, sitting by her bed, held her hands and said,

340

'Hush, Olga, you're disturbing Tatiana!' To which Olga replied coherently, 'But she can't hear a thing we say.'

When her mother told her by daylight what had been only whispered in the darkness of her nightmare, that her father had abdicated and was coming home to them, the girl waited until she could ask one of the doctors for a piece of paper and wrote the news for Tatiana to read. *Father has abdicated* — in Olga's widely spaced writing, the fact seemed more brutal when the paper was held out to Tatiana's urgent hands and consternation spread across her lovely face. But once the truth was told there were no lapses into nightmare. A strong constitution reasserted itself, and it was only Olga's obstinate refusal to face a changed world which kept her dreaming through that strange convalescence, when one by one the doctors and nurses who had cared for them were allowed by the jailers to leave their palace prison, and were seen no more.

Olga's last defence against reality was to shelter behind the condition of her eyes. She was forbidden to read until she had completely recovered from all the side effects of measles, and bandages soaked in soothing lotion were tied over her inflamed eyelids. When the bandages were finally removed, she asked for a disfiguring green shade. She always wore it when her father came to sit with them: it was too painful to look at his stunned and beaten face.

A spring day came when Olga's sense of fun returned, and she wrote on Tatiana's pad that they looked like two of the three wise monkeys — Hear no Evil and See no Evil, and was rewarded by hearing her sister laugh for the first time since their illness began. Ten minutes later the green shade had been thrown away, and Olga was looking critically at her own reflection in the mirror. Her hair had lost its sheen and her face its colour, but she felt strength coming back with every breath, and when Tatiana fell into a light doze Olga for the first time ventured outside their rooms to see the world.

At first sight it had only changed in one respect: there were no footmen on duty in the gallery. There was only Alexis, curled up in a window seat with Joy, and the boy and the dog hurled themselves into her arms like one being in their delight at seeing Olga again.

'You don't know how glad I am to see you, Olga,' said Alexis, when the kissing and exclaiming were over. 'You're the only person around here who ever gives me a straight answer to a straight question.'

'That's a very serious thing to say.'

'Well, but it's true! Zilchik used to tell me things, but now when I ask him anything important he tells me not to be inquisitive or go bothering mamma and papa. Look, I don't mean to bother them. But when I try to talk to mamma she only cries, and papa says he was born on the birthday of the long-suffering Job, and that's why everything went wrong.'

'I don't think that was really why, Alexis.'

'Nor do I. After all, how do we know papa was born on the same day as the long-suffering Job? There's nothing about it in the Bible.'

'I think it tells about Job in the *Lives of the Saints*, or so papa once said.'

'It's an awfully long time ago, but never mind. What I want to know is, who's going to be the next Czar of Russia?'

'The *next* Czar?'

The boy's face grew red. 'Well, there's got to be a Czar, hasn't there? Papa told me he was too tired to carry on, and Uncle Misha was tired too, and nobody seems even to have thought of me!'

'They probably thought you were too young, Alexis.'

'They might have asked me, anyway.' He kicked the wood of the window seat. 'But now Monsieur Kerensky says there's going to be an election soon, so perhaps I'll have another chance, what do you think?'

'I don't suppose they're planning to elect a Czar, whatever else they do. I think we have to face it, dear, people are tired of the Romanovs —'

'But *why*? What did *we* do that was so wrong? You and the other girls and me?'

If Olga had given her brother the straight answer he hoped to have from her, she would have said, 'We were born of the wrong parents, at the wrong time.' But she equivocated, like all the others, and said, 'The Russian people are more tired of the war than they are of the Romanovs. Maybe when peace comes, they'll change their minds again.'

'But we'll be living in England then.'

'I'm sure we won't be in England all our lives, we're only going there on a long visit.'

342

'That's good. But we won't be going in the *Standart*, I'm afraid.'

'The *Standart* doesn't belong to us any more.'

'That's what mamma said. It seems incredulous — incredible,' said the boy. 'I can't believe I'll never see my friends on board again, nor my regiments, nor the officers at the Stavka — ' His lips quivered ominously.

'Come on, Alexis,' said his sister bracingly, 'let's not sit here moping and feeling sorry for ourselves. Do you know I haven't been out of doors for weeks? We'll go for a stroll in the garden, just as far as the lake and back — '

'If they let us,' said Alexis doubtfully.

'Why shouldn't they?'

The brother and sister walked to the head of the great staircase. All was silent in the hall below. The King Charles, sensing a walk to come, rushed barking down the red-carpeted stairs.

'Get back, you Romanov scum! Get back to your own quarters!'

A soldier in a filthy uniform, with felt boots split at the uppers, had appeared from one of the side rooms where the Cossacks of the Escort had waited for their turn on duty. He was trailing his rifle by its sling. The spaniel frisked down the remaining steps and ran towards him, wagging its tail.

'Joy! Joy!' The little creature halted at its master's anxious call. The soldier raised his rifle and took aim at Joy.

'No!' screamed Olga, and 'No, comrade, no!' cried Monsieur Gilliard, who had appeared in time to run downstairs, heedless of the rifle, expostulating in Russian so bad that even the soldier smiled. He pretended rage and stamped his foot, and used the weapon to wave them back upstairs. No one spoke until they were safely in the schoolroom with the door shut. Then the Swiss tutor turned on his pupil in the anger of a great relief.

'I've told you again and again, Alexis, you must never let Joy or Jimmy out without their leads.'

'I forgot.'

'That brute might have killed the dog,' said Olga, shivering. 'And we weren't doing anything, we were only going for a little walk.'

'I've seen that fellow before. He's one of the Soviet soldiers, who don't allow us the slightest indulgence,' said Monsieur Gilliard. 'And my dear Olga Nicolaievna, we only go for walks when *they* permit it, and then under their escort. Just for the time being, just until Their Majesties and you get leave to go to England, we shall all have to remember that we're their prisoners.'

It would have been less strange, the girls in their innocence occasionally said — after Marie had quite recovered, and Tatiana had got back most of her hearing — if they had been taken in to the city and locked up in one of the bastions of Peter and Paul, political prisoners, fed on bread and water, instead of sharing the world divided between home life and imprisonment. They were not State prisoners; this Monsieur Kerensky assured them on more than one of the flying visits which, living up to his nickname of Speedy, he paid to the former emperor and his family. As Minister of Justice in the Provisional Government, Kerensky had the sole responsibility for the Romanovs: as a famous defence lawyer he felt obliged to assert the liberties of some of his charges. The young ladies were held in protective custody only, and not subject to interrogation, he chivalrously said, even while he ordered the Czar to live apart from the Czarina, until an investigation was opened to determine if she had been in treasonable communication with the enemy. The husband and wife were permitted to have their meals together in the presence of guards, provided they only spoke Russian, which in spite of much tuition had never been Alexandra Feodorovna's forte. The Czarina was unexpectedly docile. She had been alarmed by the arrest of her two friends, Madame Dehn and Madame Virubova, although the former was released after a very brief imprisonment. Ania was in the fortress prison of Peter and Paul, a warning to others that the Provisional Government had its eye on the friends of Rasputin.

Gradually they all shook down together into a new way of living. They still had servants to wait on them, and food no worse than Alexandra's own menus, but they had no friends, for the brilliant court which the Czarina had affected to ignore had vanished at the first breath of revolution. Two very old men, two foreign tutors, four devoted ladies, made up the little circle which walked in the park, sawed wood, planted seeds as the days grew longer, in full view of the Soviet soldiers and those of their friends able to take the train trip from Petrograd to look at the Romanovs through the park fences as they might have looked at wild beasts in a zoo.

'I don't know how papa can do it,' Olga confessed. 'First clearing the snow away and then laying out a kitchen garden, with everybody staring and sneering, and those brutes in uniform trying to trip him up with the gardening tools, or yelling at him to go back if he moves ten paces beyond the bridge! Why can't he stay in the library, and work on his stamp collection? Dmitri said he was keen enough on that at GHQ.'

'You know he's accustomed to a lot of exercise,' said Tatiana. 'He really hates to feel confined.'

'Don't we all.' Olga herself longed for the freedom of the park and the lilacs coming into bud by the wall of the Znamenia church, but she stayed indoors for much of the exercise time rather than face the mocking eyes outdoors. To the old church she did go one Sunday with her parents, to give thanks for Marie's recovery and pray for the success of the Russian army which Kerensky had launched in a new offensive against the Germans, but when she saw her father piously crossing himself at the name of the Provisional Government Olga turned her head away.

The darkness of Good Friday came, followed by the joy of Easter Sunday. Alexis was passionately eager that Easter should be as beautifully observed as ever, with all the drama of the Orthodox rites, the midnight mass and the clergy walking round the church with tapers in their hands in search of the vanished Christ. He wanted — they all wanted — to renew the joyful greeting, when the priest says to the people, 'Christ is risen!' and the people answer. 'He is risen indeed!' Alexis wanted the exciting presentation of the Easter eggs, and the friends and retainers streaming through the palace to exchange the resurrection kisses with the Little Father and his family.

'No Easter eggs this year, Treasure,' his pale mother told him sadly.

'Why ever not?'

'Colonel Korovichenko won't allow us to order any.'

'Then can't we get out some of the old ones and polish them up?'

'If you like. You can take some of the Fabergé eggs from my boudoir.'

'Alexis is really thinking of the supper,' said Anastasia. She was as gaily impudent as ever, having been less ill than her sisters, and only despairing that the attack of measles, from which Marie had risen as slim as a willow wand, had not melted one ounce from her own obstinate puppy fat.

'Who wouldn't think of the supper?' said the boy. '*Pashka* stuffed with preserved fruit, and lovely melted sugar dripping off the *kulich* — we'll have those, won't we mamma?'

'If Colonel Korovichenko says we may.'

But the Commandant had no patience with such bourgeois notions. The Romanovs were allowed to give one glass of wine to their servants as an Easter present, and even that meant a row with the soldiers' soviet, which having held a meeting to debate the point, demanded a glass of wine for every soldier too. Olga stayed upstairs in her room. She knew she was behaving badly, and she didn't care. If her family chose to act like saints and martyrs, turning the other cheek to their enemies on Easter Day, she admired them for it; she couldn't live up to their example. Olga Nicolaievna had been stripped of the title of Grand Duchess: she could not at once forget her imperial past; nor the fact that in this very palace only a year ago, and for all the years she could remember, a thousand courtiers, soldiers, guards had thronged the halls where now a few men in tattered uniforms argued over their right to a free glass of wine. She remembered the Crimson Hall on other Easters, when the uniforms of the whole Empire shone in a kaleidoscope of ostrich plumes, crimson caftans, Arab turbans and vermilion tunics, and white-gloved servants carried salvers laden with good things from one guest to another. She remembered the Easter eggs, the hundreds of eggs carved from amethyst, from gold, from opal, with the tiny toys inside which Fabergé made for the delight of little princesses. They had received just one egg on their first Easter as prisoners — an offering which the brave old Queen of Greece carried from Pavlovsk and handed through the grilles of the locked gates to a good-tempered guard.

It was not until after dark that another egg was brought, this time in a small square package with no address, but which one of her mother's dressers took straight to Olga.

'Madame, a man and a girl brought this gift to the gate half an hour ago. They insisted it was for you, and only you: the sentries accepted it and sent it in.'

'The sentries did!' marvelled Olga. 'They can't be Soviet sentries, then!'

'No, Madame, the *sovietski* troops were relieved at eight o'clock by men of the Sharpshooters Reserve. And they are — loyal.'

'At least they're kind,' amended Olga. 'A man and a girl, you say. Have you any idea what they looked like?'

'A pretty girl, the soldier said. The man was older, rough, one of the "dark people", as the saying goes.'

'Thank you.' For a wild moment she had hoped it was Dolly Hendrikova and Simon, but an older man, a peasant, hardly sounded like the Marine Guards officer she knew. But Olga's intuition was so far right that when the woman left her alone, and she opened the small package, the first wrapping inside the cardboard container was a note from Dolly.

'Your Imperial Highness,' the schoolgirl scrawl began, 'My brother has exchanged into a Line regiment and left for the western front. He bows to you and begs you to accept his Easter blessing. I bow respectfully to you and kiss your hand. — DKH.'

Inside more wrapping paper was an Easter egg. It was the cheapest-looking egg Olga had ever seen, being made of satin in a crude shade of cherry red, with a huge 'XB' for 'Christ is risen' in diamanté ribbon writing on one side. It looked like the kind of egg sold in the Petrograd bazaar where she had never been allowed to go, the Gostinnoi Dvor. And inside, a paper folded between the two halves was more precious to Olga than all the jewelled Fabergé toys of the past, for it contained two lines in Simon's own handwriting:

Gone is the resurrection kiss,
But yet to come: you swore it me!

'He remembered that; how wonderful!' she said softly; and she remembered too, in the darkness of this sad Easter Sunday, the glowing morning of their reunion less than a year ago when Simon had come back from Odessa many weeks too late for Easter. She had teased him with the lines from Pushkin, with her hands on the breast of his tunic, and then she 'swore it

347

him', that kiss, next year, on the Easter morning that would find her a prisoner and Simon on his way back to the front. And brave little Dolly had risked coming to the palace prison to bring his Easter message to the girl he loved! Olga went to bed in a mood between happiness and tears, with the paper folded underneath her pillow. It was not until the middle of the night, when there was no sound in the room but Tatiana's even breathing, that she awoke suddenly as if a voice had called her, and with a pang of purest terror recalled the whole of the verse which Russia's greatest poet had written:

> *Your beauty in the grave's abyss*
> *Has vanished, and your misery;*
> Gone is the resurrection kiss,
> But yet to come: you swore it me!

At Easter the former Czar seemed to have regained all his old fatalistic composure. He had convinced himself that the abdication signed at the request of nearly every general in his army had succeeded in its purpose, which was to avoid the horrors of civil war in Russia. The Provisional Government was carrying on the struggle against Germany, in accordance with the oath he had sworn in the Winter Palace, and he waited trustingly for them to arrange his transportation to a new life in England. 'And at least,' he said cheerfully to his family, 'I've no beastly papers to sign now.'

Even his wife was reconciled to a future in the land where so much of her childhood had been spent. In England, as a granddaughter of Queen Victoria, she had a position of her own, whereas she had been outraged at a well-meant suggestion by the Grand Duke Paul that the imperial family should take refuge in his villa on the outskirts of Paris. 'Life in a suburb like Boulogne-sur-Seine!' she fumed. 'Does Uncle Paul expect us to do our own housework and marketing?'

'I think that would be rather fun,' said Marie.

'Can I go to boarding-school after we get to England, and play netball and hockey like the girls in our school stories?' said Anastasia.

'It's not so long since you wanted to have a grown-up dance,' said Tatiana, whose hearing was improving every day.

'There's nobody to dance with now.'

'They're not in much of a hurry to send us anywhere,' said Olga. She felt that the guards were more aggressive, the people who watched them at exercise more insulting, and the Minister of Justice more vague about his plans for their future. Still —

'I've every confidence in Alexander Feodorovich Kerensky,' said the former Czar. 'He really is a most valuable man, with a sincere love of Russia. I only wish I'd met him sooner.'

'Well, why didn't you?' The words trembled unspoken on Olga's tongue. 'Why didn't you go to the Duma, as they begged and begged you to do, and meet him there? Why didn't you grant a responsible ministry and a real constitution? Why did you have to get all of us into this horrible mess?

'It's the complacency that makes me sick,' she said later on to Tatiana. 'That, and the condescension. I believe papa still thinks of himself as the God-anointed monarch, who just *might* consent to speak to an elected Minister of Justice —'

'I take it, then, you won't be joining papa's history class this term?' said Tatiana, dryly for her.

'I don't much care for his own interpretation of history.' And when the parents told the children what an interesting syllabus they had prepared, so that lessons need not fall behind this summer, Olga said curtly that at twenty-one she thought her education was completed, and would beg to be excused from her mother's lectures on religious systems and Monsieur Gilliard's extension course in French.

'But you ought to come to history,' said Anastasia, after a few mornings when all the older persons in the diminished entourage had been pressed into service to give lessons to the younger. 'Honestly, Alexis is a riot!'

'What does Alexis do?'

'Asks a lot of questions father doesn't want to answer. About Peter the Great and *his* son Alexis, and how Peter had him tortured to death rather than let him reign. And Alexander plotting to kill Paul I, so that he could be the Czar instead of his father, and, you know, all the Romanovs who got rid of anybody who came between them and the throne —'

'Professor Petrov used to give us very milk-and-water stuff compared with that.'

'Or else Alexis is smarter than the rest of us,' suggested Anastasia. Olga said it was very likely. Under Anastasia's sharp

349

eyes she refused to say what she really felt: that Alexis had found a way to show his fierce resentment at being dropped from the succession. Later she was sure of it, when she opened one or two of his history books to see if passages so critical of the Romanovs were really included in the text, and discovered that the fly-leaves had been torn out with large jagged tears which suggested temper.

'Prayer to God and service to the Czar will never be in vain' was what the child had taken as his motto and written in all his books. Did his disavowal, at least of 'service to the Czar' mean that Alexis had been completely disillusioned by his father's abdication? The only word of reproach Olga had ever heard him utter was a complaint that Nicholas had forgotten to bring the new cat, Verushka, home with him when he left Mohilev under arrest, as if the cat had become in his mind a substitute for the crown. That was a relapse into childhood, but the elaborate teasing about Romanovs who never reigned or were betrayed by their nearest and dearest, was vengeance on an adult plane. She almost felt relief, though of a painful sort, when the emerging adult came to her in tears next morning and threw himself into her arms like a baby, sobbing that the *sovietski* soldiers had killed all the collies — and the little fawns — and *Vanka*!

'Brutes! Beasts! Devils!' Vanka, that cleverest of all their pets, the circus donkey who would go to anyone for a sweet or a caress, who had trotted confidently up to the the two-legged animal armed with a rifle in the very moment before the shot rang out! 'Don't cry, Alexis, please don't cry!'

'But *why*, Olga? The baby deer hadn't done them any harm!'

'They were ours, that was enough. Here's my handkerchief —'

'What if they try to hurt Pussy and Zubrovka?' — with a sob.

'Cats are awfully good at looking after themselves, Alexis. But maybe it would be a good idea to let them live in the kitchens now, and they'd get more to eat. After all, you still have both the dogs —'

'And I'm never, never going to let Joy off his lead again.'

Olga was very gentle with her brother for the rest of that day, and the gentle mood continued after he had gone to bed.

She endured another reading aloud of *Through the Postern Gate*, and after the saga of Little Boy Blue and his motherly sweetheart had turned her parents' mind to the happy days at Walton-on-Thames, she even looked out some of the song albums bought at that time, and played accompaniments for her mother's singing. Alexandra Feodorovna had never had more than a pretty voice, and now it cracked and broke piteously in the upper register, but Nicholas leaned on the piano and looked at her as if she were lovely Alix of Hesse again, and he the Heir to the throne of All the Russias.

> If we must part, oh! why should it be now?
> Is this a dream? Then waking would be pain,
> Oh, do not wake me —
> Let me dream again!

'Beautiful, Sunny, beautiful! You wrote those words into my diary at Walton, do you remember?' said Nicholas, and to Tatiana there was something very touching in the way the grey-haired, grey-bearded man bent lovingly over his wife's hand. Then Marie asked for 'Abide with me', which she had always called 'Nurse Cavell's hymn' since it became known that the brave Englishwoman, shot by the Germans in 1915, had repeated the words along with the clergyman who visited her cell on the night before her execution. The poignant hymn sent most of the party upstairs in a subdued mood. But Olga, going to bed, sang 'Do not wake me, let me dream again!' with a very sarcastic inflection, and said as she put the light out:

'Do you suppose those two are ever going to wake up to reality?'

CHAPTER TWENTY

REALITY was in the outside world, far from Czarskoe Selo, where President Woodrow Wilson took the plunge at last and declared war on Germany. Immediately, Ambassador Francis found himself one of most sought-after men in Petrograd. Until then he had been somewhat isolated in his embassy, playing poker with his staff or taking walks along the Neva with Madame de Cram, a charming lady met on shipboard; a few days after America entered the war Mr. Francis was so busy that he called at the consulate and asked for Vice-Consul Calvert to be seconded to the embassy on a temporary basis.

'They tell me he's the finest linguist at our disposal,' said the old gentleman, lighting one of the cigars he smoked all day long. 'Sure, we've got Russian interpreters on the payroll, but how do I know when they're tellin' me the truth? I need Calvert right beside me, at least until this here mission they've wished on us has come and gone. And don't tell me his consular duties are any more important than that; why, most of our commercial interests in Russia have been at a standstill since the war began.'

'They won't be at a standstill for long,' said the consul. 'Not now we've entered on a war of resources, as Mr. Wilson told the Congress. "Oil, steel, money, bread!" he said; but it's going to take a lot of American know-how to get them all to Russia.'

'It's a mighty slender life-line, I'll allow.' The elderly ambassador stood looking with young Joe and the older consul at the huge map of the Russian Empire stretched over nearly the whole of one wall in the consul's office. Over the vast landmass, stretching from the Gulf of Finland to the Bering Sea, only the thin track of the Trans-Siberian railway extended all the way from east to west, with its Pacific terminal reached, through Manchurian territory, at Vladivostok.

'I think our declaration of war is going to teach the Russians to take a new look at their own maps,' Joe ventured. 'Everything's been geared to the capital for generations. Now Vladivostok will come into the limelight, when our war material starts arriving there.'

'Wonder what the Japs'll say to that,' said the ambassador, chewing his cigar. For there, due west of Vladivostok, lay the little offshore island, the country of the silent ally which had declared war on Germany in August 1914, and never fired or heard a shot in anger since.

'Well, that's the President's headache,' continued Mr. Francis, neither of the other men having broken the silence. 'Japan, eh? Wonder if the Root Mission'll plan a little stopover in Tokio en route for Petrograd? We'll have to arrange the red carpet treatment for 'em in Vladivostok, that's for sure. Well, Consul Caldwell is a great little fixer, they tell me.'

'And a first-rate officer,' said the consul. 'Trouble is, Mr. Ambassador, the Service is mighty thin on the ground in Russia. Caldwell in Vladivostok, Consul-General Maddin Summers in Moscow, some representation in places like Irkutsk, and that's about it.'

'Which is another way of saying you don't want me to borrow Calvert. What do you say to it yourself, Joe? Like the idea of working at the embassy for the next few months?'

'I'm here to work, sir. There's just one thing —'

'Speak your mind, son,' said Mr. Francis encouragingly.

'Now that we're in the war at last, I'd like to resign from the Service and join the army.'

At which both the older men became eloquent. The waste of time, the waste of training, the waste of a valuable Russian language qualification were all set against a step which might land Joe Calvert in some job on an army post in a middle-western city instead of with the death or glory boys in France. 'Give it till the Root Mission's been and gone, and then we'll talk again,' said the ambassador. 'I'm going to need all the young guys like you that I can get to handle old Elihu and the other members of his mission. The good old USA has voted a credit of $100 million to the Provisional Government, and Elihu Root is going to make damned sure we get our money's worth.'

'But the Root Mission won't be here until June, Mr. Ambassador,' objected Joe.

'I'll keep you busy in the meantime, son. You know Kerensky personally, don't you?'

'Not very well. But I've met him several times at a friend's house over the past few years.'

'You've got the entrée to his office at the Tauride?'

'Well yes, sir.'

'Bully for you,' said Mr. Francis. 'I hear they call him Speedy now. Okay, Joe, whenever you catch Speedy on the wing, you just pass on this piece of thinking: No fight, no dough. That's what Uncle Sam wants, action; and Kerensky'd better be prepared to deliver the goods.'

Joe felt more reconciled with his conscience after that brief talk, and after a far from brief cable (prompted, he suspected, by the ambassador himself) from his uncle at the State Department, reminding him that his job in Petrograd was, as the senior Calvert biblically said, in the forefront of the battle. He felt free to move around more in the city, to see the effects of the first month of revolution, and indeed to enjoy some of the places where poetry and rhetoric now flourished as they had never done before.

Mara Trenova saw him come in to a café called the 'Vienna', with Dolly Hendrikova on his arm, and two other couples, the men obviously young Americans, sitting down with them at a candle-lit table not far from the piano. She felt a quick annoyance at being there with Efron, the cartoonist, in his rough clothes, and Smirnov, whose boredom was obvious to everyone who looked their way. Smirnov was about to throw her over; their affair had not lasted long. And Dolly seemed so pleased and happy! I was a fool to come to the 'Vienna' at all, Mara thought angrily. It's a rotten, black-market, bourgeois place.

I have lost my way
This is the wrong city and the wrong midnight

She had heard a very handsome young man called Boris Pasternak reciting his own verses in 'The Red Sarafan' only two nights before, and those lines had stuck, oddly, in the head of a young woman who had been sure of her way ever since her first talk with Professor Rostov in one of the little classrooms at the Xenia School. This was not the time to give way to depression, with the first battle won for democracy, and the second, the greater, nearly ready to begin! *Pravda* had come out of its cellar and was no longer an underground publication. With a new office on the Moika, and a man called Molotov as editor, *Pravda* had given its first post-revolution issue away free and then sold an unbelievable one hundred thousand copies of the second. It was a useful, solid achievement, far more important in the long run than direct action, whether carried out with picric acid or a Mauser pistol.

It was humiliating to be concerned with the presence in the 'Vienna' of Dolly Hendrikova and Joe Calvert and their friends: concerned to the point of getting up and following them when they finished their drinks and left, looking at their watches, just as someone was about to recite Mayakovsky's fighting poem, 'LISTEN, YOU SWINE!' Efron and Smirnov merely looked up and nodded as Mara left the table. She went out quietly, so as not to disturb the reciter, and loitered until Joe's party had collected their coats and fur hats. Then she followed them to the Nevski Prospekt and northwards. It was nearly ten o'clock, and as they had checked their watches she supposed they had an appointment for ten, no doubt in some Czarist stronghold, a mansion where an elaborate supper was set behind shuttered windows, and the guests, drinking champagne, would proceed to plan a rescue of the Romanovs. Mara realised that she was light-headed, though not from the glass of adulterated wine she had drunk in the 'Vienna'. Hunger was her trouble: it was some time now since the supplies at the Kchessinskaia house had come to an end, satisfying though it had been to raid the kitchens on the night the ballerina's venial housekeeper had turned over the place to Agabagov and his gang. It was even more satisfying to think of the owner of the house, Russia's one and only *prima ballerina assoluta,* flying for her life across the Alexander Bridge with an old shawl tied round her head like any of the cleaners at the Maryinsky Theatre. Imagine Kchessinskaia slinking along in the shadows, like the jealous woman whose fantasy of exposing a Czarist plot and handing over Joe and Dolly to the Soviet militia exploded as soon as Mara came into the glow of light outside the big cinema at the corner of the Morskaia. Light which revealed the American dream in all its global supremacy, shining on the letters above the entrance:

Douglas Fairbanks
in
THE AMERICANO

After that exposure of Dolly's frivolity (and not Dolly Hendrikova's alone, there was a long queue of people shambling in to see the American movie) Mara was determined to prove her own seriousness by attending a concert at the Maryinsky Theatre in aid of the victims of the revolution. It was difficult to get anyone to go with her, for Kerensky was to be the principal speaker, and her friends refused to take Kerensky seriously, but finally the girl Sofie, tired of dressing up in the contents of Kchessinskaia's wardrobes, good-naturedly agreed to make the effort. And when they got to the theatre even Sofie, nibbling sunflower seeds, was impressed by the sight of the imperial box, once draped with blue and gold in honour of the Family, now occupied by thirty old revolutionaries who only three weeks before had been confined in Schlüsselburg prison, or even further away in their long Siberian exile. For Mara Trenova it was a dream come true to see and hear Vera Figner, one of the founders of the People's Will assassination group, who had carried the explosives in at least one train attempt on the life of Alexander II, and Katarina Brechskovska, now a fat old lady clinging with exaggerated affection to Kerensky's arm.

'Comrade Brechskovska seems more excited about the American gold than our fallen comrades,' Sofie scowled, and Mara found herself making lame excuses for the old women. Figner was sixty-five; age and imprisonment had destroyed her eloquence, and she stood on the Maryinsky stage like a mummy or a memorial to the past. But Mara's heart was full when Spiridonova came down to the footlights and held out her arms to the cheering audience. Spiridonova was still only thirty-one: it was ten years since she had shot and killed the brutal Luzhenovski, a leader of the repressions which followed Bloody Sunday, and with her burning eyes and big sulky mouth she represented a kind of perverse femininity which drew an unexpected response from Mara Trenova.

'You fancy her, don't you?' said Sofie shrewdly, and she laughed when Mara in her pedantic way began to recite all that the thin woman on the great stage, with her broad ugly face and dark hair parted in the middle, had done for the sacred cause of the revolution. 'I still say you fancy her, and welcome!' she said scornfully. 'All these SR fogies are dead on their feet, and they don't know it.'

In her heart Mara admitted the girl was right. The show was dragging terribly. It had begun with the *Marseillaise*, played in the slow time preferred by the revolutionaries of 1917, and was to end with a funeral march no gayer than the lugubrious speeches of the returned exiles. Kerensky was billed as the star turn, but 'Speedy' was not on his best form that afternoon. He was visibly worn out by weeks of oratory, for he harangued mass audences nightly as Robespierre harangued the Jacobins, and even his flow of ideas, his lyrical metaphors, had begun to sound flat. His voice was not helped by the acoustics of the great theatre, and he had fallen back on exaggerated gestures and grimaces to make his points. With his right hand stuck in the breast of his coat, his left sawing the air, he seemed with his contorted face to be trying to dominate his audience with something like Rasputin's hypnotic power.

He was not the great leader the revolutionaries had hoped for, but they had not much longer to wait for leadership: the great man was on his way.

Early in April the long and careful preparations made by Parvus, Keskuela and other agents operating between the German government and the Bolsheviks in Switzerland were completed, and Lenin and his followers set out to return to Russia. At the expense of Germany, they were to be transported across German territory in a sealed train and from the port of Sässnitz to Malmö in Sweden by ferry. The Swedes, having permitted German agents to operate in their country for years, made no objection to a continuation of the journey north to Haparanda, from which frontier post the group stepped on to Russian territory in the Grand Duchy of Finland. Lenin, who had opposed the war consistently since 1914, was the best investment the Germans ever made, and worth more to them in his own person than several armoured divisions.

If the neutral Swedes received the transit passengers calmly, the neutral Swiss gave them a noisy send-off from the main station at Zürich. The large supplies of sugar and chocolate laid in by the Bolsheviks were confiscated by customs men before the sealed train started, and as it drew out of the station a crowd of indignant Switzers bellowed 'Goodbye spies! German spies! Don't come back!' The answer, from behind the shuttered windows came in the singing of the *Internationale*, which the Bolsheviks liked better than the *Marseillaise*.

There were only thirty-two persons in the party, which included Lenin's wife Krupskaia, and his mistress Inessa Armand, and the sound of their singing was soon drowned by the turning of the wheels and the engine's whistle as the train made for Germany. But the sound swelled to a roar, an animal yell of triumph, when seven days later another train drew into the Finland Station at Petrograd, and a crowd of thousands surged forward to cheer their returned hero, Vladimir Ilyich Lenin.

Most of them like Mara Trenova, were seeing him for the first time. Years had gone by since he left Russia, where he had suffered imprisonment and Siberian exile, but as he climbed up to the roof of an armoured car outside the Finland Station, and was seen in the light of the torches, it seemed as if every man there knew Lenin's face by heart and for ever.

He was forty-seven years old, eleven years older than Kerensky, but physical exercise had kept his stocky figure agile, and as he stood on the armoured car with his hands in his overcoat pockets, smiling, he was the embodiment of a controlled sexual power very different from Kerensky's romantic force. His fur hat was pushed back on his head, revealing a big domed forehead, a craggy nose, and a chin adorned with a reddish-brown beard: there was something Mongolian about the whole cast of his face. His supporters yelled and swarmed around him. There had been a fresh fall of spring snow that morning, so that the Finland Station and the buildings round about were covered in white. Between the white roofs and the black mass of people stretched a sea of red flags, a leaping, living thicket of torchlight, and in the middle stood the dark figure on the armoured car which dominated the scene. Mara Trenova, pushed mercilessly forward by the movement of the crowd, saw that all round the car stood a double rank of Soviet soldiers with their fingers on the triggers of their rifles. With a pang of foreboding she saw that the people's leader was guarded as closely as any Czar.

When Lenin had kept them waiting long enough for anticipation to become so keen that even breathing was stilled, he raised his right hand in a smooth simple gesture to shoulder level, with the palm opened towards the throng. Broad, short-fingered and virile, that hand never moved as he spoke his opening words in a voice resonant but without passion, un-dramatic but totally assured —

'Dear comrades, soldiers, sailors, workers,' said Lenin (and every man in the crowd knew that the words were spoken to himself alone) 'the Russian revolution made by you has begun. It has opened a new epoch.' The orchestrating hand moved once, and without rehearsal, in a spontaneous gesture, the red flags were lifted higher.

'All power to the Soviets! From here our prophetic words will spread across the land: Hail to the world Socialist revolution!'

CHAPTER TWENTY-ONE

WITH the arrival of Lenin, the fate of the Romanovs became a matter of grave concern to the Provisional Government. Some members of the Family had already slipped away from the revolutionaries, including the Empress Dowager and her daughters, who had reached their palaces in the Crimea, while others moved quietly on to their dachas in Finland. The most fortunate of them all now turned out to be the Grand Duke Dmitri, whose punishment had taken him safely out of the path of the revolution to the frontier of Persia. But the prisoners at Czarskoe Selo were the real problem, especially when the first plans for their departure were shattered by the British Cabinet.

'We shan't be going to England after all, my dears,' said Nicholas to his daughters, trying to speak lightly, when Kerensky broke the news.

'But why, papa?'

'It seems we'd be most unwelcome guests. Mr. Lloyd George thinks the very sight of me would cause a general strike, and stop the war effort in all the factories and ports. And Ramsay MacDonald, that man Lenin's friend, has told the British I'm no better than a common murderer.'

'What have they got to do with it?' said Tatiana indignantly. 'The King is your cousin, you were to go to London as *his* guest —'

'That's a constitutional monarchy for you,' said her father. 'Poor Georgie has to bow to the will of his idiotic cabinet ... Don't let's talk any more about it now, and don't say anything to poor mamma.'

The girls saw that their parents' sense of rejection was acute; they had both been very fond of their English cousins. The first sense of hopelessness began to chill the spirits of them all.

One afternoon in early June the four sisters were sitting beside the lake, trying to ignore the stares and sometimes the jeers of the soldiers patrolling the bridge behind them. They were still pale and drained of energy, and although they had been under the public gaze all their lives, they were now morbidly sensitive about their appearance. The long bright hair of all four, so carefully brushed and tended, fell out in handfuls after the measles. On medical advice it had been cropped almost to the bone, and although the girls wore silk headscarves indoors and out, they all felt they were disfigured. When old Count Benckendorff, who still styled himself Grand Marshal of the Court, came looking for Olga, she nervously twiched the headscarf further across her brow.

'Your Imperial Highness,' he said with a bow, 'my profound apologies for disturbing you. A messenger is here from Monsieur Kerensky, with an urgent request that you will talk to him in private.'

'A messenger from Alexander Feodorovich? Are you sure it's me he wants to see?'

'He asked for you, Madame, and there's no doubt he has the authority —' On a tiny salver, as if conjured from his pocket, the Count presented a note with the letterhead of the Ministry of Justice, and signed under a few lines of writing with the unmistakeable single name, Kerensky.

'Where have you put this man, Count Benckendorff?'

He was in the old waiting-room where Olga had questioned Protopopov after the murder of Rasputin. The room had not changed since that night; the heads of big game still stared beadily from the walls, and the magazines for the month of February had been laid out but not cut.

The envoy from Petrograd was studying a tapestry hanging above the empty fireplace. He swung round as Count Benckendorff ceremoniously announced. 'Her Imperial Highness the Grand Duchess Olga Nicolaievna,' and acknowledged her titles with a slight smile and a slighter bow.

At the first glance, Olga thought it was Kerensky himself. The man before her had the same blond, crew-cut hair, the same aggressive nose, and the slender, supple build. But the features were more Slavic, and the voice, when the young man spoke, was more staccato than Kerensky's.

'Good-day to you, Citizeness Romanova,' he said.

'You want to speak to me?' said Olga bluntly.

'In private, if you please, citizeness.'

'You may leave us, Count Benckendorff.'

'Happy to serve Your Imperial Highness,' said the Marshal of the Court, with a vindictive glance at Kerensky's envoy. He laid the salver and the paper on a table near the door as he bowed himself out of Olga's presence.

'Be good enough to state your business,' Olga said. 'You have a message from the Minister of Justice?'

'Indirectly, yes. That is, Alexander Feodorovich knows the nature of my mission, and signed a gate pass admitting me to what I suppose we must still call a palace. I'm a member of the Petrograd Soviet of Soldiers and Workers, citizeness.'

The words were rapidly spoken, but Olga had time to snatch at a fleeting resemblance, and an almost forgotten memory.

'Haven't I seen you before?' she said.

The Slavic features creased in a wider smile. 'Ah, you're beginning to remember,' said the man. 'Try a little harder. Here in this very palace . . . in another kind of livery . . .' He pulled down his ill-fitting khaki tunic and drew himself up.

'I recognise you now,' said Olga. 'You're the footman who brought Rasputin to my rooms.'

'And my name?'

'How should I remember your name?'

'You called me Ivan, very glibly, then. Of course we were all Ivan to you and the rest of the Romanovs, weren't we? Just another pair of hands, wearing white gloves in case a drop of honest sweat should ever touch you or your belongings . . . sixteen thousand of us there were in all your palaces — your obsequious slaves.' He hissed the words at her, and Olga answered indifferently:

'I really never counted them. I wonder if there were many like you among what *we* called, and what fools we were, our faithful servants? You, who took a bribe from Rasputin, and money, I imagine, from the editors of the gutter press of Petrograd when you sold them the whole story —'

'I, whom you had thrown out of the palace, saying next time you would have me flogged —'

'If I'd had my wits about me I'd have had you shot.'

The man in khaki and high boots burst out laughing. 'Bravo, citizeness,' he said. 'You're true to your principles, anyway. I always told my comrades you had twenty times the guts of

362

your father: with you on the throne our victory might have been postponed for years.'

'Which is as good as admitting that when you were Ivan the footman you were already a member of the Bolsheviki, here in our home as an agent of your party?'

'Exactly' — with a bow. 'Only you must call us the Communist party now, not Bolsheviki. That's the latest directive from our GHQ at the Kchessinskaia house, by order of Comrade Lenin himself.'

'And afterwards? Did you go underground, as I believe the saying is, when you were rather forcibly removed from my service?'

'I returned to my mother's home in Switzerland, and continued to serve the Party there.'

'And now you're back in Petrograd, a member of the Soviet. Why have you come here today? To gloat over us in our imprisonment? Or have you anything constructive to say?'

'What a girl you are!' said the young man admiringly. 'Always forthright and to the point . . . I've never been accused of being a ladies' man, but I must say, if I were, you'd be the girl for me.'

'You flatter me, Ivan. Or should I say Colonel? Are you a Soviet officer now?'

'Just a humble *apparatchik*, so far. But wouldn't you be more comfortable sitting down?'

'Thank you, I prefer to stand.'

'Very well, now let us be serious. It must have been a severe blow to your pride, wasn't it, when your loving cousins in England declined the pleasure of your company? H'm? You don't want to answer that one, I see. Did you know that Comrade Trotsky, as soon as he arrived from Canada to join Lenin, began pressing for a State trial, a grand showpiece put on before the whole world, bringing your father and mother to justice on a charge of high treason?'

'I don't believe there will be such a trial, as long as Kerensky is Minister of Justice.'

'He may not be at the Justice ministry for ever — or for long. But one thing is clear, and he has told you so himself: you and your sisters are not State prisoners. Three of you were war nurses. We'll stand on that record, and overlook the Romanov name.'

'Am I supposed to express my gratitude?'

'It isn't necessary. Now!' His voice was sharp. 'I've come to tell you something, important to you all. A message has been received from your aunt in England, through the British Ambassador, offering a permanent home to your sisters and yourself. Provided you can leave within a week, you're free to go.'

'Leave in a week? B-but I don't understand,' stammered Olga. 'I mean, how can we? How would we travel? How could we even leave the country, the way things are?'

'It would be possible,' the man said stolidly. 'You could be escorted through Finland and then across the Gulf of Bothnia. One at a time, of course, because the four of you, travelling together, would probably be recognised, but you would meet in Stockholm and go on from there. You could be free and in London within a month from now.'

Olga was silent. The idea was so unexpected, the plan so suspiciously easy, that she had no idea what to say. Except —

'Would my brother be allowed to leave with us?'

'No.'

'Why not? He's only a child, and a delicate child too; what harm can he possibly do you in a foreign land?'

'He was born the Heir, and in a few years he could rally the monarchists around him anywhere. He's the representative of the legitimist principle —'

'While you and your friends represent the illegitimate principle?'

The pale boyish face flushed with anger. 'Citizeness, you're throwing my birth in my teeth —'

'I know nothing whatever about your birth, and care less. I don't even know your name.'

'My name is on the pass, you should have read it. But then you're very careless about names, Citizeness Romanova!'

'What do you mean by that?'

The voice which had been staccato suddenly became shrill. 'What possessed you all to sign your names on the loving message we found in Rasputin's coffin?'

'*I* sign my name to a loving message — you must be crazy!'

'You went to his funeral.'

'My mother was beside herself with grief. We didn't dare refuse.'

'You knew his body was dug up and burned?'

'I heard about it later. It happened when I was ill.'

'They found a holy picture, with your names on it, laid beneath his cheek.'

Olga gave a long shuddering sigh. 'A holy picture,' she said. 'Now I understand. There must be thousands of such pictures in existence, we used to sign them by the boxful for the troops. And somebody took one of them to put inside Rasputin's coffin. Sister Akulina!' she exclaimed, as recollection came. 'She had charge of everything. She did it to compromise us . . . Was *she* one of your Party, too?'

'A very useful and experienced agent, citizeness.'

Olga made a helpless gesture with her knotted hands. 'So many traitors,' she whispered, 'everywhere we turned! And you were one of them! Why have you come here to help me, if you mean to help me? Or is this another trap, like Sister Akulina's?'

'No, it's not a trap, Olga Nicolaievna. It's a fair offer to give you a chance to save yourself. Because Kerensky seems to have sized up your parents pretty well. He thinks you'll never hear about the message from England, unless you hear it from our side.'

'I suppose that's possible,' she said, and sighed. 'I know they think we must all stay together. Do they know already?'

'They'll hear about it when Kerensky comes tomorrow.'

'Then I'll wait until the next day before I say anything to my sisters.'

The man shrugged. 'That's your affair,' he said, 'but don't delay too long.' He turned to retrieve his cap from the stone mantel, and looked up at the tapestry.

'I remember that thing,' he said, 'from the days when I used to usher your father's visitors into this very room. Marie Antoinette and her children, isn't it?'

'Yes. It was copied from the Vigée-Lebrun picture, and presented to the Czarina by the French government.'

'I understand the former Czarina had a great admiration for Marie Antoinette?'

'Only as a very unfortunate queen and woman.'

'I needn't ask if you've read the works of Marx or Hegel, citizeness?'

'Not a word.'

365

'Marx revised one of Hegel's statements in a very illuminating way. He pointed out that great events and personalities may well recur on the stage of history, but the second time they appear in farce, not tragedy. In other words, if Alexandra Feodorovna has ambitions to play the Queen of France, and die nobly on the guillotine — take care she doesn't drag the rest of you into the farce as well.'

He moved towards the door, and Olga said reluctantly: 'Thank you for coming.'

'You can get in touch with me through Colonel Korochivenko,' he said. 'He'll know where to find me, as long as I'm in Petrograd.'

'Are you going back to Switzerland?'

'No, but I'm expecting to be sent to Finland fairly soon.' His hazel eyes gleamed. 'I may be your escort from Helsingfors to Abo one of these days. Make up your mind, Citizeness Romanova! And don't forget the old saying, "It is later than you think".'

He sketched a salute with two fingers to the peak of his cap and went out quietly. Olga waited until the door closed behind him. Then she took Kerensky's *laissez-passer* from the salver and read his envoy's name:

Boris Heiden.

The thoughts of Karl Marx on farce and tragedy in history came back to Olga many times in the weeks that followed; never more vividly than on the night the Romanovs were taken away from the palace at Czarskoe Selo.

They were to go as a family. That had never been in question: the former Czar and Czarina had taken it for granted that their children would accompany them everywhere, and the latter had said vaguely, in answer to Olga's casual enquiry about an invitation from Aunt Victoria, that perhaps there *had* been some kindly idea of that sort, but of course papa and mamma could never let their chicks go to England alone. But before that it had been settled among the girls themselves, for the younger three hardly took time to consider Heiden's offer.

'I can never leave mamma,' said Tatiana quietly, and Marie and Anastasia had protested a good deal less quietly that they couldn't possibly be parted from their parents and Alexis.

366

'Unless any of us wants to go alone?' said Anastasia slyly. 'Do you, Olga?'

'No, I'll stay.'

'That's settled then. Hurrah! OTMA for ever!'

'And even if papa can't go to London now,' offered Tatiana, 'things are much better here than they were at first, since Colonel Kobilinski became the palace commandant.'

But when they were alone Tatiana said, 'I don't want you to think I'm living with my head in the sand, Olga. There may be bad times ahead, worse than we've known yet, but I still think we ought to stick together. Whether we can make a go of it depends very much on you.'

'Why on me?'

'Because you're the strongest and the cleverest of us all. But I don't know if you quite realise that from here on you and I have got to think of mamma and papa as if they were the children, and we the parents now. We have to make allowances for all the foolish things they say and do. And sometimes you're terribly impatient and sarcastic with them both.'

'I don't see why they shouldn't hear the truth, once in a while.'

'Could you keep it to "once in a *great* while", my dear?'

'I'll try, Tatiana.'

And she had tried, not always with success, during those blazing summer weeks when everything had gone wrong again. When the advance ordered by Kerensky, now prime minister and Minister for War, had failed miserably, as it was bound to fail when thirty-one Russian divisions, freed by government decree from any sort of discipline, had faced one hundred and sixty-four German divisions bound to knock Russia out of the war once and for all. When Lenin chose this moment to attempt a *coup d'état*, and blood ran again in the streets of Petrograd before the government won and the Communist leader fled to Finland. When the American missions arrived with their teams of experts, whose expertise was swiftly confounded by the total breakdown of what passed for technology in Russia. The former Czar's complacent comments on the 'liberal republic's' difficulties had been hard for a spirited girl to listen to in silence.

Nicholas seemed not quite to understand that it was because of the 'July Days', as the attempted Communist *coup* was called, that he and his family were sitting in the small hours of a stifling August morning in the Crimson Hall of their palace prison with their friends, servants, dogs and baggage disposed around them, waiting for orders to get aboard a train taking them to an unknown destination. Kerensky had had a bad scare in the July Days. He knew that Lenin had very nearly triumphed: that he had only been driven away because of the revelation that he had been in the pay of the Germans, something the average Russian was not yet prepared to stomach; but if Lenin came back, and next time, won? Then what would become of the ex-imperial family? Kerensky, and the select few he let into the secret, made plans to remove them to a place of safety.

'Only until the elections are over,' Nicholas told his family. 'Once the new Constituent Assembly is in session, Kerensky says we may return to Czarskoe Selo, probably in November.'

'Where can they possibly take us, for a short stay of three months?' wondered his wife.

'I think it might be to some fine old Russian city like Kiev or Novgorod. Alexis, you and I'll be able to study history where it all happened.'

'I'd rather go to Livadia,' said the honest child.

'We're probably going further east than Novgorod, and we may be away for longer than three months,' said Tatiana. 'We've been told to take plenty of warm clothing with us.'

'Kerensky knows what he's doing,' said Nicholas confidently. 'Travelling by rail, going east, the nearer we'll come to Vladivostok. Eh, chicks? How would you like to see Japan?'

But that had been before the farce began, the dismal farce now being enacted in the Crimson Hall. They had come downstairs at eleven p.m., the train was to leave at one, and now it was four o'clock in the morning, with everybody arguing and running to and fro, and the soldiers' soviet solemnly making speeches, and taking votes on what to do next. Their problem was the transport of the family's luggage, provisions and other belongings to the trucks waiting to take everything to the Alexandrovski Station: at the station the problem was getting the railwaymen to put the train on the line at all. Kerensky ran from the hall to the telephone and back again: he sent messengers to the station in staff cars, he conferred with the palace commandant until poor Colonel Kobilinski, who had been severely wounded earlier in the war, collapsed in an armchair and fell asleep with his mouth open. Alexis was asleep too, with his head on his mother's shoulder. He had been very lively early in the night, and very impressed when the priests from the Znamenia church came in chanting and bearing aloft the ikon of the Virgin of Znamenia to bless the travellers. But after a couple of hours, during which it seemed to his sisters that he never stopped fidgeting and stumbling over their feet, always with Joy's lead wound tightly round his wrist, the boy said, 'I know it's a beautiful Russian custom to sit down with your friends and think kind wishes before going on a journey, but this is ridiculous!'

'Alexis is quite right,' said Olga softly, as she watched sleep overtake him. 'What fools we all look, sitting here hour after hour, and getting nowhere!'

'I like watching the soldiers,' said Anastasia. 'Some of them are funnier than the clowns at Cinizelli's circus.'

'I hadn't thought of the circus. I was thinking *we* all look like the refugees at the Narva Gate, when Tatiana's committee ran a shelter there. With our bags and bundles, and our heads tied up in silk scarves like very grand *babushkas*—'

'You hate to go away, don't you, Olga?' said sympathetic Marie. She had Jimmy, the Pekinese, on her lap, along with one of the jewel boxes which they all carried.

'Yes, I'm sorry to be going.' Olga said no more than that: there were no words to express her desolation at leaving the home they knew and loved the best, the hospital — now un-visited since their imprisonment began — where she had tried to serve, the wooded alleys and river banks where she had walked with Simon Hendrikov. Even the Crimson Hall was a reproach to her, with the Czarinas whom she had not dared to follow watching from the walls, and the young Queen Victoria looking down haughtily at the descendants who had lost their throne. The curtains had been left open, and daylight began to touch the sleeping faces, some stubbled, all grey with fatigue, and the empty tea glasses, the spat-out sunflower seeds on the floor of the great hall. Somebody said 'Here comes Speedy!' as Kerensky rushed back from yet another argument on the tele-phone. There was a sudden rustle of movement, and the great entrance doors were pulled open. A voice said, 'Now, Colonel Romanov!' and then they were on their way.

Tatiana had to run back at the last moment for the cushion from her mother's chair. It was a gift Alexandra cherished, having been filled with rose leaves by Tartar women for their empress, and the scent, still delicious, filled the motor car which took her to the station with her husband, Alexis, and Olga. The other girls crowded into a second car, and Kerensky headed the procession. It was nearly six o'clock and the sun had risen. They looked out eagerly at the familiar park, where the dew lay on the grass, but already they were at the open gates, and a cavalry company swung in behind the cars as they went through. All the way to the station the girls heard the familiar and now totally unreal clatter of a Sovereign's Escort.

One friend alone was there to greet them on the platform. This was General Tatischev, a former cavalry officer whom Nicholas had invited to accompany him as an ADC. Tatischev, now an elderly man with many civilian responsibilities, had not hesitated for a moment. 'Give me enough time to pack my bag,' he had said, and with his old army valise by his side he had waited stoically at the station through the long hours of the night. He gave immediate help in supervising the unloading of the baggage, while the Czar gleefully pointed out to his daughters that the train was flying the Japanese flag and carried the emblems of the Japanese Red Cross Mission. 'I told you so!' he said cryptically. 'I told you Kerensky knew what he was doing! Come, girlies, time to get into the train!'

The steps, of course, had been forgotten, and the coaches were extremely high. Alexandra Feodorovna's stiff limbs failed her, and she landed on her hands in the entrance to the coach. In darkness, she was carried inside a coupé and laid flat on the long seat. The girls scrambled in somehow, Nagorny lifted Alexis up out of his father's arms, and one by one the whole entourage was dragged aboard.

'Oh, poor mamma! Have you really hurt yourself?'

'My hands — '

'Feel her hands, Tatiana.'

'They feel scratched, but I can't see. Open the window, Imp!'

'I can't, it's boarded up.'

'Why are we in total darkness? Where's the light?' That was

their father's voice, and then came Tatischev's, 'I have matches, Sir.'

The train started with a lurch, the match flared up. 'There, mamma, it's not too bad,' said Tatiana. 'Your cushion saved you from a nasty graze. Marie, there's a little first-aid kit in my handbag.'

'Let me take the matches, general,' said Olga Nicolaievna. She knelt on the floor, as close to Tatiana as she dared, holding up the little flame in the darkness to which they had been translated from the bright day outside. The train gathered speed. They were on their way, protected by the flag of Japan. Whether their journey into the unknown would end in Japan or not, she had no means of telling. But Olga knew that the further east they went the closer they must come to the grim territory which lay between them and the Pacific Ocean. Like all the political exiles who had preceded them in chains and handcuffs, the Romanovs themselves were on their way to Siberia.

CHAPTER TWENTY-TWO

THE July Days which were to alter radically the fate of the Romanovs began quietly for Joe Calvert. Joe's troubles had started earlier, and were to last longer, with the arrival of the USS *Buffalo* at Vladivostok in the month of June. She brought to Russia an Ambassador Extraordinary in the person of Senator Elihu Root, General Scott, the US Chief of Staff, and other distinguished Americans who all lived up to the prediction of Ambassador Francis in expecting the red carpet treatment, and got it.

Materially, the treatment was easy to provide. The former emperor's train was placed at the disposal of the Root Mission for their long journey to Petrograd on the Trans-Siberian Railway, and with their advisers, experts and escort the delegation filled the eight blue-painted coaches and overflowed into Alexandra Feodorovna's grey and lilac boudoir. In the capital Kerensky played host to them at the Winter Palace, where sumptuous suites were renovated to receive the Americans. There were not many great houses to which they could be invited, because those which had not been looted in the spring revolution were locked and shuttered, their owners far away, but the red carpets went down at the Astoria, the Europa and the Hotel de France, and Ambassador Francis kept open house at the Furshtatskaia.

That part of it, Joe conceded, was all right. There had been a flurry just before the Mission arrived, when all the press releases and set speeches had to be rewritten when it became known that President Wilson refused to allow the United States to be called an Ally; he insisted on the expression 'Associated Power', but there were plenty of people who could cope with that one, and also with the thirst of the special correspondents assigned by American newspapers to cover the mission to revolutionary Russia. What worried Joe, after what now seemed like the golden years of neutrality, was the infighting which started the moment the imperial train pulled into the Nicholas Station. He knew, of course, that they had domestic troubles: Ambassador Francis was no favourite with the career officers of the Foreign Service, some of whom went so far as to declare that his close friend Madame de Cram was a German agent; but none of them had expected to be taken over so vigorously by the 'old Russia hands' accompanying Senator Root. General Judson, who had been an official observer in the Russo-Japanese War of 1905, and Arthur Bullard, the Secretary of the American Friends of Russian Freedom, who as a freelance had witnessed the political troubles of the same year, struck Joe as seasoned players to beware of when the chips were down, and he waited in trepidation for the fur to fly between the Russian railroad men of the Trans-Siberian and the Advisory Commission of Rail Experts headed by John F. Stevens.

On leaving the Mission gave a farewell dinner to the Allies, with an invitation list so all-embracing that even Vice-Consul Calvert and Captain Richard Allen joined the company in the Malachite Hall.

'Very stout fellows, your delegates; not troubled at all by memories of the past,' said Dick, as the two men walked away together.

'They *haven't* any memories of the past,' said Joe. 'The war began last sixth of April, don't you realise that?'

'Well, I do, old chap, but it didn't seem my place to say it. Jolly good dinner, jolly good speeches, any old how; one good thing about sitting down to dinner at six o'clock, you get the whole agony over before nine.'

'With any luck they'll be gone the day after tomorrow.'

'Expressing complete faith in the future of Russia.'

'And leaving one hundred million US dollars behind them in the present,' said Joe, stopping to light a cigarette. 'Also a fragrant memory of Senator Root's opinion that the Russians are just an infant class in the art of being free, needing kindergarten material to teach them how to join the democratic community.'

'Did he say all that?' said Dick admiringly. 'No wonder you're looking a bit off-colour these days. Cheer up, Joe, at least they haven't started sending you propaganda material like the newsreel on the Battle of Arras I saw run off at our consulate today. Our new Department of Information must have odd ideas on what will make the new Russian army want to fight.'

'Are you going to show it to the girls?' said Joe with a grin. He indicated a company of the new Women's Battalion of Death, swinging back across the bridge from a parade ground on the other side of the Neva. They were great strapping girls, sweating in heavy uniforms and high boots, and wearing black and red flashes on their sleeves. ' "Red for the revolution that shall not die, black for death rather than dishonour",' quoted Joe. 'Poetical fancy, isn't it?'

'You wouldn't call it poetical if you'd seen Mrs. Pankhurst taking the salute from 'em outside the Astoria,' said Dick. 'That's all we needed to complete the picture, a visit from the good old British suffragettes. Joe, I'd rather fight Spion Kop all over again than face the Battalion of Death; what do you say we walk over to the Island and see the Hendrikovs, and get the taste of a lot of things out of our mouths?'

'At this time of night?'

'It's barely half past nine; they'll be talking away for hours yet. Besides, Dolly has twenty-four hours off from hospital.'

'You seem to follow Dolly's schedule pretty closely these days.'

'Any objections?' The tone was so different from Dick Allen's usual sleepy acquiescence that Joe glanced at him in surprise. He shrugged instead of taking up the challenge. Dick and he were friends of three years' standing, but their friendship, so much interrupted by the Englishman's absences, had never progressed beyond a certain point. And three years of Joe's neutrality, of his guarded tongue, had made a barrier between them and complete confidence. They walked across the bridge in silence.

'Lights everywhere!' said Joe cheerfully, glancing up at the Hendrikovs' windows when they turned in to the Fourth Line. 'Cousin Timofey must be in full cry tonight.'

But the one who was crying was Dolly. They heard her sobs as they entered the front door, for once wide open, above the sound of agitated voices on the second floor. They looked at each other and dashed upstairs. On the landing they found Dolly, clutching an unknown young woman, also in tears. Two men they had never seen before, one in naval uniform, were trying to soothe them both.

374

'What the hell is the matter?' gasped Dick. 'Dolly — your father — is anybody ill?'

'No, I don't think so — I don't know!' wailed Dolly. 'We've had such a terrible fright. Three Red sailors came, and forced their way in ... if it hadn't been for Commander Yakovlev I don't know what would have happened ...'

'You hear, Mikhail?' cried the unknown young woman. 'It'll be our turn next! If those roughs from Kronstadt can force their way into *this* house, you and I may be murdered in our beds tonight, and Mitia too! I'm leaving first thing in the morning, whatever you may do!'

'Why didn't the *dvornik* warn us, that's what he's paid for!' said Mikhail, presumably the lady's husband, and Joe, from long experience, realised that a typical Russian argument had only just begun. With a touch on Dolly's arm he slipped round the group and into the apartment.

The first thing he saw was the hatstand and the hall table, both lying on their sides. In the living-room the glassfronted bookcase had been smashed and emptied of the books, which had been soaked with oil from the hanging lamp, and there were knife slashes across the pictures and the upholstery of the various chairs. The windows were starred but not broken. Professor Hendrikov, very pale and breathing heavily, was lying on the sofa in his study, where, as in the hall, all the books had been toppled on the floor, and Madame Hendrikova, for once dishevelled, was holding smelling salts beneath his nose.

'What happened, for God's sake?' said Joe, and Madame Hendrikova tried to smile. 'Some unwelcome visitors,' she said. 'Red sailors, very drunk ... I'm so glad to have you here, dear Joe!'

'Dick's here, too. Shouldn't I get some brandy for the professor?'

'I don't suppose there's any left.' It was true; Joe's quick investigation revealed nothing but the fine cut crystal decanters, smashed to pieces, in front of the sideboard's open doors.

'Where are the maids?' he called, and Madame Hendrikova answered, 'There's only Lena, and she locked herself in the kitchen.'

'Sensible girl.' Joe hurried down the corridor and released the terrified Lett. 'Go and help your mistress,' he said, 'the professor isn't well.' But Joe's strong arm was neeeded to help the shaken old man to his room, and by that time Dolly, Dick, and the naval officer were back in the living-room with the front door closed.

'This is Commander Yakovlev, Joe Calvert,' said Dick briefly. 'I met him last time I was up at Murmansk, he's in the *Askelod.*'

The commander bowed. 'I'm very glad I was able to help,' he said. 'I'm back on leave, and came to visit my cousins Dr. and Mrs. Martov (you saw them a few moments ago) just as Miss Hendrikova managed to escape from those ruffians and called out to me —'

'And he was *armed*!' said Dolly. 'They were going to — they said they were going to burn down the house —'

They saw, they smelt the oil spilled across the books, and Commander Yakovlev nodded. He was, Joe noted, a pleasant-looking man, with a weather-beaten face and dark hair growing to a peak on his forehead. His uniform was well-worn but very spruce.

'Kronstadt!' he said deeply. 'We think things are bad enough at Murmansk, but here —'

'Yes, but why this house and not another?' Richard Allen said. 'Simple people, living very quietly, with nothing much worth looting — why pick on them?'

'I'm very much afraid it's because our son's an officer,' said Madame Hendrikova, coming quietly back to the living-room. 'At Kronstadt the hostility to the officer class is terrible.'

'What, burn the flat down and probably the building along with it, just because your son was an officer in the Garde Equipage?' said Joe.

'Dolly, I'm very worried about your father,' said Madame Hendrikova, evading the question. 'I think we ought to get the doctor.'

'I'll telephone, madame,' said Joe, rising.

'They pulled the telephone out of the wall when they broke in. Lena will go, our doctor lives in the next Line. And now I must go back to sit with my husband, Commander Yakovlev: I don't know how to thank you for your rescue and protection.'

The naval officer bowed over her hand. 'If there is anything anyone can do, I know Madame Martov will be glad to help,' he said. 'I shall hope to have good news of Professor Hendrikov from her.'

'Thank you.' Dolly went to see him to the door, and Joe and Dick were left staring at each other.

'What a bloody awful mess,' said Dick, stirring the broken glass and sodden paper with one foot.

'Don't worry about it, Dick,' said Dolly, returning. 'Lena and I will clean it up as soon as she comes back from the doctor's.' She was very calm now, with red spots like rouge on her pale face, and she said, 'Oh, do let's sit down!' with a sigh that showed her weakness in the relief from strain.

'Are *you* all right, Dolly?' said Joe. 'Nobody seems to be concerned about you.'

'Father was the only one they actually struck. Oh, but if it hadn't been for Commander Yakovlev —'

'He seems like an all right guy,' said Joe.

'Were those men armed?' said Dick abruptly.

'Only with those knife things sailors carry. That's what they slashed the pictures with.'

'Dirks. And Yakovlev's navy pistol was enough to scare them off?'

'Thank heaven, yes!'

Joe had found a bottle, overlooked in the back of the sideboard shelves. 'I don't know what this is,' he said, sniffing, 'some sort of plum brandy, probably. You'd better drink some, Dolly, you look all in.'

'And now perhaps Dolly will tell us the truth about this — incident,' said Richard Allen gravely, when she had sipped from the bottle's metal cap. Dolly opened her eyes wide.

'You mean about why those wretches came?'

'It wasn't just because your brother's a serving officer at the front.'

'It was mamma who said that, poor darling,' Dolly said reluctantly. 'You know how her generation are always trying to *pretend*! She heard what the soldiers said, we all did, even Commander Yakovlev — goodness knows, they were shouting at the pitch of their voices — but it was just too much for my mother to accept . . .

'Was it something about Simon and the Grand Duchess Olga?' said Joe gently.

'Did you know too?'

'It wasn't hard to guess, when I saw him here just after the revolution.'

'What those ruffians said was that we were enemies of the people and friends of the Romanov murderers,' Dolly faltered. 'They said this was the place where the Grand Duchess Olga met — met her secret —'

'Her secret lover,' Dick finished it for her.

'Richard, how can you? I told you at Easter, when we went out to Czarskoe Selo with his gift to her, that it was just worship from afar! Poor Simon, how could it be anything else, with that wonderful girl?'

'But she did come here?' said Joe.

'Just once. And I was here too, for part of the time.'

'How could those fellows know a thing like that?'

'Because somebody else was here as well,' said Dolly, and her pretty face grew hard. 'Mara Trenova. She betrayed them. And I could *kill* her for it!'

Mara Trenova, like Joe Calvert, had spent a harassing summer. There had been a great upheaval in the *Pravda* office, just at the moment of its renewed success, when a former bank robber called Joseph Stalin, more recently an exile in Siberia, had returned to Petrograd immediately after the revolution and proceeded to take over the paper. With Molotov out and Stalin in, there were the usual firings of lesser members of the staff, and among those who lost their jobs was the hunchback, Sergiev, who disappeared completely from his former haunts. Mara kept hers 'by the skin of her teeth', as Stalin told her — and she was more afraid of Stalin than of any terrorist met in the days of Jacob Levin — because the cartoons she and Efron worked on together had achieved a certain fame. Stalin even mentioned the cartoons to Lenin, when the great man visited the *Pravda* office, now reopened not far from the huge silent palace where Felix Yusupov and the Grand Duke Dmitri had lured Rasputin to his death.

'Good! Very good!' said Lenin, rubbing his hands and laughing his hard laugh. 'We might be able to use something in this line in our cinema propaganda, by and by. That'll be the great medium of the future, don't you agree, Comrade What's-Your-Name — Trenova?'

'Yes, comrade.' Mara had no views on the cinema, except to feel annoyance at the American films which so many people who should have known better seemed to enjoy seeing, but she was prepared to be hypnotised by Vladimir Ilyich Lenin. Seen close, he was quite as impressive as the orator of the Finland Station, and much more so than Stalin, with his vulpine features and his thick moustache covering a brutal mouth. Lenin had a trick of closing one eye while he was preparing to summarise his opinion of a cartoon or an editorial, which gave his face a kindly, comical look: he used his face as he used his short, strong body, to express power and reliability. On this visit to *Pravda* the expressive face was smiling and conciliatory; he slapped Stalin on the back and praised him as a man of action. The demoniac power of the leader on the armoured car had been exchanged for a homespun comradeship which very nearly made Mara Trenova accept him as the hero she had waited to worship all her life.

Nearly, but not quite. For Mara's chronic jealousy was aroused by Lenin's companion, a woman who was said to be one of his few intimate friends, and high in the councils of what they were all trying to remember to call the Communist party. Her name was Alexandra Kollontai. Born, like so many of the revolutionaries, into an aristocratic family, she had become famous in her twenties as an agitator in the textile strikes of 1898, was exiled, had worked with Lenin for at least ten years. Mara Trenova hated her on sight, the mild little woman with soft blue eyes and hair just tinged with grey, whose eloquent and personal exposition of free love had earned her the name of the Red Rose of the Revolution.

'Is he sleeping with her?' she asked when the distinguished visitors had left, and the men in the newsroom laughed.

'Catch him! She says sex is like drinking a glass of water, have it or go without; he says keep all your strength for the world revolution. How'd *you* like that, Trenova?'

'She's got a handsome sailor about half her age, down-river in Kronstadt. Dybenko's got strength to serve the revolution, and the Red Rose too,' said one of the reporters.

'Wouldn't mind a piece of her myself.'

'I bet it's not all world revolution in the Kchessinskaia house. Not when they get going on the Grand Duke Andrei's champagne.'

'There can't be much left for them. *We* had all we wanted at the beginning, when *they* were still in Switzerland,' said Mara.

'That's right, you were with Smirnov then, in the good old Agabagov days. Been there for supper lately, Trenova?'

No, and that was where the jealousy began, of course. But Lenin had praised her drawing, and Mara was stimulated to produce the best series since she had drawn Olga Nicolaievna in the arms of Rasputin. It showed Maria Bachkarova, the peasant woman who founded the Battalion of Death, leading her girls — enormous of buttock and breast — to the service at St. Isaac's cathedral when their standard was consecrated, and then the girls behind the lines, performing other services for Kerensky's soldiers. But immediately after that success came the failed *coup d'état*, when the machine-guns rattled again along the Nevski Prospekt, and Lenin, after haranguing his followers from the balcony of the Kchessinskaia house was forced, as his enemies said, to 'do his disappearing act again'. For Mara the worst aspect of the clash between government and Communists was a raid on the *Pravda* offices, and the total destruction of the printing presses by government troops. She was thrown out of work, and after a few weeks of desperation was thankful when Stalin offered her a job on the paper hastily vamped up to take *Pravda*'s place, and called *Rabochi Put, The Workers' Path*.

During the July Days Joe Calvert tried in vain to keep in touch with his friends in the Fourth Line. He soon realised that the three sailors who had planned to destroy Dolly's home were only the advance guard of a greater force from Kronstadt when he heard of the two destroyers which sailed up the Neva in support of Lenin, carrying Communist crews which terrorised the town. The sailors were finally overcome, and taken to the prison of Peter and Paul, but Kerensky, true to his belief that the Revolution must shed no blood, carried out no executions for mutiny, and the men were soon released. Like all the American staff Joe was kept close to his embassy during those anxious days, and when they ended the next crisis was the arrival of forty men representing the American Red Cross. They had been issued with army uniforms before sailing from San Francisco, and as they all had the assimilated rank of colonels they at once became known to the Americans in Petrograd as The Haitian Army.

Once these worthies had been found hotel rooms and office space, embarking on a career of wrangling and dissension which beat all the quarrels of the Russians, Joe was able to telephone to Dolly Hendrikova at her little hospital to suggest a meeting.

'How's your father, Dolly? How are they both?'

'Much better, but mother was terribly anxious about papa last week. He could hear the firing, and the yelling from the Neva, and it upset him badly. But the doctor says he's able to travel now, and they're going to the dacha in a few days' time.'

'Swell idea, and you're going too, I hope.'

'Not right away.'

'Oh, Dolly, you can't stay on your own in Petrograd!'

'I can't even *talk* any longer,' she said in a whisper, 'meet me in the Summer Garden, by the kiosk, at noon?'

'I'll be there.'

It was a convenient meeting-place between her hospital and his embassy, and Joe reached it through almost empty streets. The tempo of Petrograd life had been grinding to a halt since the revolution, and now the cracks in the imperial façade were very obvious. The St. Petersburg of 1914 had turned into a neglected place, a vista of lifeless palaces beside a river foul with the refuse of three days of street fighting and oily with the miasma of a stifling summer.

The Fortress bells were ringing the *'Kol slaven'* as Joe reached the kiosk, which had nothing to sell but apples and a few children's toys, and saw Dolly coming towards him down one of the long unweeded avenues. He hurried to meet her, so fresh and neat in her Red Cross uniform, and they found a stone seat as far as possible from the children's playground, where a bush of fading lilac gave them the illusion of privacy. And there Dolly told him firmly that of course she couldn't give up the hospital, they were short-staffed as it was, and what about last summer, when papa and mamma had gone on holiday without her?

'This summer isn't last summer,' said Joe grimly. 'And you certainly can't be in that apartment, at any time, all by yourself.'

'Oh no, the apartment's going to be closed up. And you know I've got about a dozen cousins and their wives and husbands, to go and stay with if I ever have another twenty-four hours off.'

'I do know it, but what I hate is having you walking around the town alone. Good God, look at what happened last week!'

'Last week we were too busy with the civilian casualties to listen to the firing. Please don't fret, Joe! Mamma and papa are very willing for me to stay here, they want *somebody* to be waiting to welcome Simon when he comes back from the front.'

If he comes back from the front. Joe and Dick Allen both believed that Captain Hendrikov's third campaign would be his last, but it did no good to say so: he only asked gently, 'Have you any news at all?' and Dolly shook her head.

'Won't you get *any* leave to go to Finland? You had two weeks last year.'

'I'm going to try to work right through to the end of November. After that, we'll see.'

'What's so special about November?'

'If father can get a substitute to take his classes, we might spend the winter with my sister in Copenhagen.'

Joe felt blank. He wanted her to be out of danger, but Copenhagen, after his three years in Russia, seemed to Joe Calvert to be in another world. He hardly heard what Dolly was saying, something about 'Richard' having advised Professor Hendrikov to transfer his account from the Imperial Bank of Russia to the Private Bank in Helsingfors, and deposit his securities there as well.

He hadn't meant to tell her what had been in his mind for months, for Vice-Consul Calvert, with nothing but his modest salary, had little to offer a girl; but there she was beside him, so pretty and engaging, and soon, perhaps, to be right out of his reach! He blurted out:

'I worry about you, Dolly, I can't help it, you're so little and cute, and you'll be all alone if — if Simon doesn't come back. Please give me the right to take care of you, then and for ever. I love you so much, and I'll try so hard to make you happy. Please say you'll marry me. Please!'

Her hazel eyes were fixed so trustingly on his, and her lips were parted as if to whisper Yes. Joe's arm was round her already, and when Dolly put her hand in his free hand he was sure it was all right. Her words, when they came, were like a douche of cold water in his face.

'Joe!' she said, 'dear Joe! I've had a feeling you would ask me that some day, and I did so hope you wouldn't. Because I hate to hurt you — and I've got to tell you, I don't think I could ever be your wife.'

'Why not?'

'Because, deep down, I don't think you love me enough.'

'Dolly!'

'Was that an awful thing to say? I didn't mean to be unkind. I know you're very, very fond of me, just as I'm fond of you. And *you're* so kind, Joe! If I were ever in any trouble I'd come running straight to you, and if I said Yes and we got married I think we *would* be happy together, "right now", as you say. It's not "right now" that scares me, it's the future.'

'We would share the future, Dolly sweet —'

'Oh no we wouldn't, because I'm not rèally the right girl for you. You only think so because I'm *here*, and we've known each other for three years, and you've been a little bit in love with Russia all that time. I saw it happen to you, right at the beginning, and my mother saw it too. You were fascinated by St. Petersburg from the very first moment, and I suppose I'm a tiny part of Petersburg, so it wasn't too difficult to think yourself into being in love with me. But I'm not nearly clever enough for you, Joe. You've a brilliant career ahead of you, everybody says so —'

'*Everybody?*'

'All the people who've met you at our house, including Nabokov and Kerensky, and they're pretty good judges, don't you agree? And Richard thinks that some day you'll be the American ambassador to Russia — maybe twenty years from now —'

'What'll Russia be like by that time, I wonder?'

'I don't know, but when you come back to live in that great palace on the Furshtatskaia, you ought to have an American lady as Madam Ambassadress, not silly little Dolly Hendrikova from the Fourth Line, who wouldn't know what to say to the diplomatic corps —'

'Who would charm every man in the diplomatic corps.'

Dolly shook her head. 'It's no use,' she said. 'I'm not even clever enough to make you understand.'

'I certainly don't understand why you're talking about an outside chance, that may or may not come up twenty years from now.' Joe hesitated. There was one thing he didn't want to say, but it came out. 'Are you turning me down because there's somebody else?'

Dolly grew pink and compressed her lips.

'Sometimes lately I wondered if it was Dick Allen.'

'Please, Joe! I do like him very much —'

'You're twenty, and he's nearly forty —'

'I don't think age makes any difference.'

'When did it start between you and him, Dolly?'

'I suppose — after we found him hurt that night in Mara's flat. He seemed so young then — changed somehow —'

'He can change into anything he wants to be,' said Joe. 'And he's a loner, has been all his life. I shouldn't think he'd ever want to settle down.'

'How boring you make marriage sound!' said Dolly with a flash of temper, and Joe asked quickly, 'Are you engaged to him?'

'Not officially.'

'Then can I go on seeing you?'

'Of course you can! We'll meet at Cousin Timofey's, just like we used to do at home. And maybe I'll *be* at home quite soon again, when father and mother come back to settle the university thing. After all, they'll be less than fifty miles from Petrograd. It isn't as if they were going to Siberia!'

CHAPTER TWENTY-THREE

A FAMILY which had gone to Siberia was scattered forlornly along the docks of a river port on a sultry August midnight, guarded by three hundred men of the Sharpshooters' Reserve.

Not only history but chance was now shaping the destiny of the Romanovs. The chance that Alexander Kerensky, as a child, had been impressed by a photograph of the governor's house in remote Tobolsk, an ancient town in the Ural region of Siberia, and as head of the Provisional Government decided that the Romanovs could spend the winter there before an attempt was made to get them away to Japan. He had no reports on the actual state of the governor's mansion, very dilapidated by 1917, nor apparently did it occur to him that a town two hundred miles from the railway line and accessible only by river steamer in summer, by a frozen dirt road in winter, was hardly a suitable base for an escape attempt.

It did occur to several members of the former Czar's party when they were ordered to leave the train at Tiumen. Until then, their spirits had been rising steadily. When they were clear of the environs of Petrograd, and the shutters were taken off the train windows, it was exhilarating to see the countryside again, and like old times to sit in the dining car, enjoying well-prepared meals, and see the villages go by. The windows were boarded up when the train stopped at a station, but that did not happen often in their four days of travel. One early morning they stopped so long at a place called Ekaterinburg that they began to think their journey would end there. But the train went on across the mountains, and soon Nicholas was able to show his boy the great pillar with 'Europe' on one side and 'Asia' on the other, and tell him, 'Now you're really in Siberia!'

'You were one of the first people ever to travel on the Trans-Siberian railway, weren't you, papa?'

'I suppose I was, from west to east. I laid the first stone of the east-west line at Vladivostok in 1891. Long before I could persuade your dear mamma to marry me!'

'And then you went on to Japan, and a wicked Japanese tried to kill you.'

'He did indeed. Dear Greek Georgie saved my life that day, and carried a scar on his own skull to prove it.'

'If you had been killed, papa, would Uncle Misha have been the Czar?'

How he harps on that, thought Olga. But Nicholas replied tranquilly, 'No, my next brother would have succeeded me. Poor fellow! You children never knew your Uncle George. He was an invalid, and had to live in the Caucasus. He died there when he was only twenty-seven.'

'What was the matter with poor Uncle George? Did he have pains in all his joints, like I used to do, and was he carried about sometimes, instead of walking?'

'No, nothing like that. He had a lung complaint, that was why he had to live in a dry climate. The air of St. Petersburg didn't agree with him at all.'

'I don't think it's agreed with us very well.'

Tatiana changed the subject by asking Alexis if he remembered the Great Trans-Siberian Easter Egg which Fabergé had made for the Czar in 1900, and which ever since had been kept with other precious objects in a locked glass case. Alexis had sometimes been allowed to take it out and look at the tiny model of the imperial train which it contained, with gold carriages, a platinum engine and rubies for headlights. This, of course, led to a general discussion of whether the Trans-Siberian Easter Egg had been packed, and if so in which box or valise: in those early hours of their east-bound journey they were often agitated about treasures left behind. Meanwhile the Siberian landscape rolled on in all its vastness beyond the windows of the train, and now and then they caught a glimpse of the old Siberian highway, running slightly to the north of the modern railroad. It was the Chain Track, down which so many political prisoners had stumbled with their hands in fetters on their way to the mines or to Sakhalin.

In the old days there had always been two trains in the imperial convoy, one going ahead to make sure the line was neither mined nor bombed before the sovereigns went by. Now the Romanovs themselves were in the leading train, and the soldiers travelled with the baggage in the second, so that the family party could almost forget they were not on an excursion, perhaps to some town where they would be greeted as of old with the banners, the ikons and the chanted Te Deum. But awareness of captivity came back with a rush when they reached Tiumen, and were told their journey would continue by steamer to Tobolsk. There Colonel Kobilinski, in terror for the security of his prisoners if the local dockers staged a demonstration, ordered his soldiers to line the wharves and the decks of the steamer *Rus* on which they were all to embark. It was three o'clock in the morning before the last of the baggage was carried aboard.

Alexis and his mother went to their berths at once, the others stayed on deck to watch the scene on the dock. Eugene Kobilinski, short, dark and nervous, was here, there and everywhere, urging speed; the soldiers, who since the revolution had been permitted by an order introduced by the Petrograd Soviet to disobey any unacceptable form of military discipline, slouched and smoked and took as long over the job as they pleased. But at least there was no demonstration, perhaps because at that hour of the morning the Tiumen dockers were too tired to stage one; the *Rus* cast off her mooring ropes, blew her steam whistle, and departed.

After their broken night it was mid-morning before the party gathered on the first-class deck. In peace-time it had been the preserve of government officials en route for the far north, and the wealthy Siberian merchants who traded in fish, skins and furs, while the steerage was reserved for peasants, Kirghiz and Buriat tribesmen, and 'politicals' going to imprisonment in the Beresov district beyond Tobolsk. The latter had been guarded by armed Cossacks, carrying the deadly whip called the *nagaika*, while the Sharpshooters, lounging on the steerage deck with their tunics unbuttoned, seemed to be taking their duties lightly enough. But Alexis, exploring the steamer with Nagorny, reported that their rifles lay ready to their hands.

'Does anybody know when we dock at Tobolsk?' Olga asked, and her father himself said, 'Not till tomorrow afternoon. About half past four, according to Colonel Kobilinski.'

'It's a long way from Tiumen,' said Marie.

'It's a long way from anywhere.' There was nothing to be

seen for hours of their voyage: nothing but the steppe on either bank, and the vast Siberian skies above, the horizon marked only by the receding line of the Ural mountains beyond which Europe lay. There was something hypnotic about the beat of the engines and the ripple of the Tobol river, something ominous about the silence of the few figures which could be seen from time to time as they approached a village. The last time they had made a river voyage together was on the Volga, during the tercentenary celebrations, when the peasants waded waist deep into the water to catch a glimpse of their Batiushka, the Little Father Czar. Nobody alluded to that triumphal voyage. Nobody so much as mentioned Rasputin when the *Rus* passed his native village, Povrovskoe. The former Czarina sat with her head bent over her embroidery, and the girls respected her silence. But everyone was remembering the dead man's prophecies, 'You will visit my home, whether you want to or not,' and that other, still more ominous, 'If I die or you desert me, you will lose your crown and your son within six months.' The boy was safe beside them, with Nagorny chasing him all over the boat, but the crown had gone in three months, not in six, and out of the brilliant court and Guard of the Czar of All the Russias the man who had worn the imperial crown had now only two gentlemen in attendance, his childhood playmate Prince Dolgoruki and the faithful Tatischev. Alexandra Feodorovna had with her the lady styled her Reader, Ekaterina Schneider, who began to teach her Russian at Harrogate, where as Princess Alix of Hesse she took a cure for rheumatism at the time of her engagement; and the young Countess Gendrikova. This was the court of Nicholas and Alexandra, on board the *Rus*, on their way to prison.

'I wonder if we're going to like this place,' said Alexis doubtfully, when the steamer arrived at Tobolsk. The scene was strange, and perhaps frightening to a child, for the ancient town was situated on high bluffs above the waters'-meet where the Tobol river flowed into the mighty Irtysh. There was a roar from the falls and a sudden absence of sunlight, as the high cliffs threw their shadows over the *Rus* and her passengers. Or else Alexis was perceptive enough to feel what his elder sisters felt: that even when they were allowed to take a brisk walk away from the dock and along the towing path — a walk very welcome after nearly seven days in the train and boat — they were still in a place saturated by centuries of imprisonment. Among the historic buildings which dominated the cliffs above the Irtyish was the Swedish Tower, built by the Swedes whom Peter the Great took prisoner at the battle of Poltava, and for two hundred years since Poltava the Romanovs had consigned their enemies to Tobolsk. The Dekabrists had been brought here in the reign of Nicholas I. The Poles who staged the Warsaw rising of 1863 had ended their days here. Now to Tobolsk came the man crowned as Nicholas II; the tables were turned; he and his were prisoners.

'I don't know if we're going to like Tobolsk,' said Anastasia, as she and Alexis scampered ahead of the others down the towing path, 'but I'm awfully glad we're going to live on the boat for a few days, aren't you?'

'Oh yes, I like the boat, and I've got to know some of the soldiers, too.'

'Some of them are very nice.'

'Eugene Stepanovich is nice, he really worries about us.' For Colonel Kobilinski, before his charges were permitted to disembark, had made a horrified inspection of the governor's mansion which had looked so pleasant in a photograph, thirty years before. It was filthy. He ordered cleaning and renovating which would take at least a week.

For that one week, during which the *Rus* was still their home, the rather desperately gay, holiday feeling which they had all cultivated since leaving Czarskoe Selo prevailed among the Romanovs. Every excursion among the paths and fields beyond the bluffs was a treat; the sun shone, and the pallor of their confinement became a healthy tan; father and son found the river life as fascinating on the Irtysh as on the Dnieper in the days when the Czar was also the Commander-in-Chief. Marie talked tirelessly to the soldier escort, and was soon a mine of information on their homes and families. Alexandra Feodorovna remained aboard the *Rus*, always with somebody to keep her company: she never complained of her heart now, but the sciatica was growing worse, and she was often in great pain. It made her smile of thanks all the more touching when her children brought back tiny posies of Siberian flowers, growing so sparsely on the edge of the steppe, as long ago they had carried her the wild roses of the Crimea.

They could forget for hours at a time, in such surroundings, that they were in captivity. Every now and again they had a sharp reminder in a barked order or a scowling face, or as when Olga, throwing a tennis ball to Alexis, strayed unintentionally off the permitted path. They were playing near the river, and the boy threw the ball so straight and hard that his sister missed the catch, and had to go scrambling down the bank to bring the ball back. They were beginning to learn that even an old tennis ball was a treasure, that nothing must be lost, and she was laughing when she found it in the wet gravel; but then a heavy body jumped down the bank behind her, and one of the guards took Olga roughly by the arm. It was the first time any of them had touched her, and it was only by an effort that she caught back the words, 'Take your hands off me!' She had learned already to smile ingratiatingly as she said:

'I was only picking up my brother's ball.'

'You'll stay where we can see you if you know what's good for you.' He gave her arm a shake. 'Understand?'

'Yes, I understand. Will you let me go now, please?'

But the man kept her in his grasp until they had both clambered back to the footpath, and then he took the tennis ball away from her and put it in his pocket. 'Too good an excuse, chasing after a thing like that,' he growled. 'Don't try to run away again, little sister.'

'I wonder where he thinks we're going to run to,' Olga said lightly to Alexis, a rather frightened spectator of the scene. She called to the girls, and they all sat in a ring to play guessing games, while the soldiers walked suspiciously up and down. But for the rest of that day she felt the heavy hand on her arm, and remembered the picture of Maslova in *Resurrection* — 'After the Sentence', with the soldier starting the condemned woman on her way to prison and Siberia.

Their own prison, the governor's mansion, was ready for them at last. It was not a large house, so that all their companions except the faithful Gilliard were to sleep in another house across the street. Alexis had a small bedroom to himself, with Nagorny in a smaller one next door, but the sisters found they were expected to share a large corner room, in which four plain bedsteads had been placed.

'It's rather like a dormitory in one of your old school stories, Imp,' said Olga as she looked around.

'Good idea, let's call it the OTMA dormitory,' said Marie, who was always cheerful.

'The beds are softer than the ones at home,' said Anastasia, bouncing on a spring mattress, and Tatiana, untying her silk headscarf, said, 'Thank goodness! We won't have to wear these things indoors.'

'We're almost presentable now.' The four heads, the golden, the red-gold, the shades of brown, were clustered together in the dressing-table mirror, and Olga said, 'I do believe you're going to have little curls, Mashka.'

'So I am' — much gratified.

'Do you remember how shocked mamma was when you told her Marisha had bobbed her hair? We'll all have bobbed hair, by and by.'

'I don't think it quite makes up for measles.'

'Let's go and see what it's like downstairs.'

It was quite roomy, quite well furnished, and the commissar representing the Soviet, by name Makarov, seemed to have no objection to what Colonel Kobilinski had done to make his charges' lot more comfortable. There were no guards posted indoors. But almost immediately after their arrival a fence was erected all round the house and its neglected dusty grounds: not too high to prevent the Romanovs from seeing across it from their bedroom windows, but quite high enough to prevent any of the townspeople from seeing in. The hopes Nicholas had cherished of being allowed out on the steppe for an occasional day's shooting, were dashed at once. He took to sawing wood as a means of exercise.

By the time September came in, with cooler and thinner airs, they had settled down to some kind of routine. Lessons began again, and Alexis once more displayed remarkable dexterity in asking questions which had some bearing on their own fate, this time in English history. King John and Magna Carta, King Charles at war with his parliament, King James chased off his throne by the revolution of 1688 — 'I'd no idea he knew so much,' marvelled Anastasia.

'Some of those stories were in the picture books they used to send from England. I do remember something about King Charles up an oak tree —'

'Don't mention it to Alexis, he hasn't discovered that one yet.'

'I'll be glad when Mr. Gibbs gets here, and takes over the English history class from poor papa.' For the English tutor, as devoted as his Swiss colleague, was following the Romanovs to Siberia, and hoped to reach them before the rivers froze. The last loyal member of their entourage, Baroness Buxhoeveden, whom they called Isa, had been operated on for appendicitis about the time they were removed from Czarskoe Selo, and could easily have made that an excuse for staying in Petrograd. She, too, was determined to reach Tobolsk as soon as she could get a travel permit.

Mr. Gibbs brought no reassuring news. General Dukhonin's offensive had been a failure, and under German attacks the Russian troops were deserting by whole companies. A general named Kornilov had attempted to establish a military dictatorship in Petrograd, and to defeat him Kerensky had to call in the help of the Soviet. Trotsky, who had remained in the capital when his leader fled to Finland, had organised a body of Red Guards who helped to defeat Kornilov, but remained under arms. It was the first overt threat of civil war in Russia.

The former Czar heard all this with his accustomed calm. But when he was alone with the men he regarded as his ADCs, he said for the first time that he was beginning to regret his abdication. He had been persuaded by unscrupulous men that it was necessary for the good of Russia, to spare Russia the horrors of civil war, and now since the July Days Russian had been fighting Russian, and what might not the future bring? He longed for news, and the shortage of reliable news was one of the severest trials in the governor's mansion as September slipped into October, and the only break in the monotony was the weekly outing to church on Sunday, with Alexandra Feodorovna pushed in a wheel-chair between a file of armed soldiers, while the citizens of Tobolsk stood on tip toe behind them to see those who had been their rulers trudging through the autumn mud.

There was an erratic telegraph service between Tobolsk and Petrograd, and a still more erratic delivery of newspapers to the prisoners. Nicholas received a few belated copies of the The Times which they all read until the paper was reduced to shreds, but the soldiers' soviet, after a long discussion, voted to suppress The Times unless every word was translated into

Russian for their approval. After that the prisoners relied on the local paper, such as it was, and the local lending library, which supplied them with tattered copies of standard Russian novels. There was no censorship of the girls' reading now, and Olga read *Resurrection* again, from pages spattered with food stains and tobacco crumbs. She felt the same strange affinity with Katerina Maslova, tramping with the chain gang across Siberia, through towns whose names had a new significance: Tiumen, Omsk, Ekaterinburg.

'The cell in which Maslova was imprisoned was a long room twenty-one feet long and sixteen feet broad, occupied by fifteen persons.' She had read that first in her pretty bedroom at the Alexander Palace. Now she and her sisters shared a room of almost exactly those dimensions. Should they be thankful that instead of fifteen they were only four?

The Czar, in his delightful way, read aloud to his family. They had to hear about Little Boy Blue again, while the girls bent their heads decorously over the drawn-thread work they were doing, on coarse local linen with silks brought from their home, to fashion into Christmas gifts. They had *The Rosary*, for Alexandra Feodorovna's sake, and *Greenmantle* for Alexis, who never tired of the adventures of Richard Hannay. They had read it earlier in the year, and Nicholas, in his simple way, was still amazed at the skill of 'the writer fellow' who had described the battle of Erzurum only a few months after the Grand Duke Nicholas had won it.

'I wish I knew if Nikolasha's had a chance to read it himself,' he said, and his wife smiled indulgently at the once hated name.

'I wonder if anybody'll ever write a book about us,' said Anastasia.

'*I* wish I had another book by John Buchan,' said Alexis.

'I'll get you *The Thirty-nine Steps* some day,' said Mr. Gibbs. 'It's about Richard Hannay too.'

'Oh, wonderful! And no girls messing about in it?'

'Not a girl,' said the tutor, with a smile of apology at the four sisters.

'There's a girl in *Greenmantle*,' said Anastasia. 'Hilda von Einem. And she's in love with Sandy —'

'Yes, but they don't start *kissing*, and all that rot.'

'No, because she's a villainess,' said Marie seriously. 'I like a book to have a real heroine, very beautiful, who does brave deeds.'

'Oh, Mashka!' Olga said, 'when will you ever realise that you're a heroine yourself?'

'*Me*?'

'That night at Czarskoe Selo,' said Olga, 'the last time with the Garde Équipage. When you went out and in, trying to help mamma even though you were feeling ill, and got pneumonia . . . You were ready to give your life for all of us that night. I call that being a real heroine.'

'Like Nurse Cavell?'

'Exactly like Nurse Cavell.'

Reading, and talking about the people in the stories, helped to pass the time, but they were all hungry for news of the real people who had once been their friends. Alexandra wrote faithfully to Anna Virubova, though without much hope that the letters would reach her. Madame Virubova had been removed from Petrograd by order of the Provisional Government, and was now in the great fortress prison of Sveaborg, outside Helsingfors, to which Kerensky had also consigned Badmaiev, the Tibetan wizard of the Rasputin days. But others were free, who might have written, and did not, to the sovereigns on whom they had once fawned, and it was not until the end of October that a letter came from the far distant Crimea with news of all the Family.

It was written by the Empress Dowager from her palace at Ai Todor, and after many loving messages and condolences the old lady continued in her usual debonair strain:

' "How I wish the dear girls were here with us in the Crimea" ' [Nicholas read aloud] ' "The young people contrive to amuse themselves in spite of everything, and the autumn has been so fine that the beach parties go on until all hours by the light of bonfires and the moon." That sounds very pleasant, doesn't it?'

'It doesn't exactly sound as if they were missing us,' said Tatiana. 'Please go on, papa.'

' "Michael and that impossible wife of his are still at Gachina, and I hope she's proud now of what her liberal friends

394

have done to destroy the monarchy. Sometimes poor Misha seems as far away from me as you, beloved Nicky, but at least they have left him some freedom of movement. I am glad to have both my daughters close to me. Xenia is thankful to be able to see Felix and Irina — they, and little Irina, are well — and all her boys are as healthy and noisy as ever. Olga, needless to say, is very happy with her baby son." '

Nicholas paused. 'How old is my sister Olga?' he enquired. 'Thirty-five,' said Marie. 'Imagine Aunt Olga with a baby!'

' "I don't know if you've heard the great news about Ducky and Kirill. They wisely left Petrograd and went to Finland, and after they reached their manor dear Ducky gave birth to a son and heir." '

The Czar stopped again. 'Now Ducky *must* be over forty,' he observed.

'Forty-one,' said his wife. 'She and Kirill must be very happy to have a son at last.'

'Everybody's having babies,' said Anastasia.

'Except us,' said Marie.

'Does granny say anything about Marisha?' said Tatiana.

'Marisha married Prince Putiatin soon after we left home,' said Nicholas. 'And Dmitri — what's this about Dmitri? Sometimes I can't read her writing.

' "Dear Dmitri has behaved so loyally and nobly. The Provisional Government, so-called, sent him word that his exile was over and asked him to return to Petrograd. He replied that he was on the Persian front by the Czar's orders, and would respect them by staying there until the war is over." '

'Very correct of Dmitri,' commented Nicholas.

'Does Motherdear say anything about his health?' asked Alexandra.

'No, she goes on to another matter,' said Nicholas with a twinkle in his eyes. 'Listen to this, girls.'

' "The latest piece of gossip from Odessa, unconfirmed as yet, is that Carol of Rumania has entered into a morganatic marriage with a young person rejoicing in the name of Zizi Lambrino. One feels so much for that wild boy's parents, poor Missy of Rumania will be beside herself." '

'There goes my only hope of matrimony,' said Marie solemnly.

'We hadn't a chance, Mashka; the Zizis and the Zinas always win,' said Olga with equal gravity. Suddenly they were all laughing wildly, even their mother, in an almost hysterical reaction to this glimpse of a world which was going on without them. But even though she laughed till she cried, and had to search for her handkerchief, Olga was impressed by her mother's quiet acceptance of so much good news about her old enemies. Kirill, who had betrayed her when he marched his men to the Duma under the red flag. Felix and Dmitri, the murderers of Rasputin, even Ducky, her much disliked former sister-in-law — all these were names which would once have roused her to passionate denunciations and contempt. 'How good she's trying to be!' the girl thought, and she touched Alexandra's white hair with a spontaneous kiss before she kissed her hand and said good night.

Before many nights had passed the family's painfully achieved calm and hopefulness were shattered by news of the outside world brought them by a shaken and reluctant Kobilinski. He walked in as the whole household was having evening tea, for the younger children had been acting a little play, as they were fond of doing, and everyone available had been in the audience. The drawing-room was warm and cosy, the samovar was steaming, it was a pleasant Russian domestic scene.

'Sir,' said Eugene Kobilinski, 'I feel you ought to know that despatches have been received by telegraph from Petrograd. The news they convey is very — very disquieting.'

'Well, out with it, man!'

'If these despatches are correct, there must have been a rising in the capital. Lenin is said to have returned, and the Red Guards hold the key points of the city. Kerensky is in flight. And the Winter Palace — the palace, Sir, when the message ended — was being shelled by a battle cruiser from Kronstadt, the *Aurora*.'

'Good God!'

It was an hour before the news, in all its implications, was thoroughly discussed. Kobilinski, desperately worried about the news Lenin's triumph would have upon his men, went to the guardroom but promised to remain within call. Nicholas was so sure that new telegrams would arrive before midnight, contradicting what they had already heard, that he and his wife were only willing to retire when their gentlemen volunteered to sit up for a couple of hours and pass on any news which might come in. The men settled down to play cards in the dining-room.

It was nearly one o'clock when Olga came downstairs in her stocking feet. As keyed up as anybody in the house, she had only partly undressed and was unable to go to sleep. When there was silence in the 'OTMA dormitory' she slipped out: the drawing-room stove would still be warm, and an hour with a book, beside a good oil lamp, might enable her to relax, might ease the appalling sense of their helplessness in this dead heart of the Siberian steppe. The moonlight was flooding cold into the hall.

She had almost reached the shelter of the warm room when the dining-room door was opened, and through the crack she heard General Tatischev's voice, decisive and resigned:

'Well, gentlemen, if Kerensky has really thrown in his hand the game is up. Personally I knew when I left Petrograd that I shouldn't come out of this alive. I only ask two things: not to be separated from the Czar ... and to be allowed to die with him.'

CHAPTER TWENTY-FOUR

On the bleak, late autumn day after the cruiser *Aurora* came upriver from Kronstadt to anchor in the Neva off the Winter Palace, Joe Calvert woke up to discomfort in the shabby apartment on the Italianskaia. The heating in the building had not functioned for several days, and Varvara had apparently neglected to start the wood fire in the living-room stove. He went into the kitchen to complain, shivering in his dressing-gown, and found it empty. Joe damned the transport delays, and the food queues where the old woman spent so much of her time, and prepared to make his own coffee. There was no water in the kitchen tap. There was no water in the bathroom taps either, and he was only able to shave by using some of the drinking water he kept in a glass pitcher. Fuming and dabbing at his chin with a square of lint, Joe breakfasted off the remains of the water and two dry biscuits, and let himself out into the empty street. He hoped Varvara would have some decent food ready, and his bed made, by the time he went back to the apartment.

A day and a night passed before Joe Calvert returned to the Italianskaia, and he never saw or heard of Varvara again. She had been killed as she shuffled across the street on her way to work, knocked down, with her skull cracking against the kerb, by a Red Guard truck careering round a corner on its way to seize one of the telephone exchanges as part of the plan which Lenin and his henchmen had worked out to gain control of Petrograd. Joe, as he hurried through the public gardens, could hear the sound of shouting from the top of the Liteini Prospekt, and when he saw a dense crowd of men struggling round the Prospekt end of the Alexander Bridge he guessed that the troops or police, or both, had received orders to raise the bridges to prevent the workers crossing from the northern quarters into the centre of the city. He went no nearer than the corner of the Furshtatskaia to investigate, but made for the embassy door, in front of which several American cars were parked. He guessed that on a day when trouble was so obviously brewing many of the newcomers to Petrograd had left their own offices to gather at the one place where reliable news was likely to be had.

Vice-Consul Calvert found that, as he had expected, the handsome entrance hall was full of men with serious faces, and, as a pleasant surprise, that a cup of hot coffee was immediately available. It was not served in the usual embassy style, for the kitchen coffee-pots had been dumped on a marble-topped console table with a few cans of condensed milk, dripping stickily from raggedly punched holes, and the big cups had no saucers, but it was blessedly hot and stimulating after his cold-water breakfast. While he drank it one of the attachés told him that the Red Guards had control of the water supply and other public utilities, with all the railway stations. 'Looks like Lenin learned his lesson last July,' the man said. 'He's making sure of the key points before he tries another *putsch*.'

'I thought Trotsky and Kamenev were masterminding the next operation.'

'Sure, but Lenin will hog all the credit.'

'Either way it's a pretty poor look-out for Mr. K.'

The ambassador was not present. Only a few days earlier he had advised Washington that public sentiment was turning against the Bolsheviks, and more demonstrations were not to be expected — an error of judgment which probably accounted, Joe thought, for the sardonic smiles of some of the senior officers of the Foreign Service clustered round the coffee table. They were preserving a diplomatic silence. The man doing most of the talking was Raymond Robins of the American Red Cross, whom the embassy officials regarded as arrogant, tactless and high-handed to the last degree.

He was a striking-looking man in his early forties, with an actor's mobile face, strong features and jet black hair. In uniform as one of the 'colonels' of the Red Cross Mission, otherwise known as The Haitian Army, he had arrived in Petrograd just before the July Days, and so far had had no direct contact with Lenin, for whom he had developed an almost fanatical hero-worship. It was not a popular view-point at the American Embassy, and Joe felt relieved when the press attaché drew him, with his second cup of coffee in his hand, into one of the side rooms.

'Joe, I hate to ask you, but none of the Russian translators has shown up today, and the Governor's asking for the press digest. Could you bat out a few lines for him?'

'Sure. Glad to do it.' Glad to have something to do, was what he meant, but the file of newspapers to work on was much smaller than usual.

'Looks as though the press is going out of business too,' he said. 'Where's Stalin's paper, *Rabochi Put?*'

'Mr. K. sent three companies of Cossacks yesterday, to close it down.'

'And the Cossacks obeyed orders, did they?'

'They did yesterday. What they'll do today is anybody's guess.'

There was really not much in the papers except a few communiqués from Mohilev, still the site of GHQ, and a list of additional foodstuffs to be rationed by the end of the week, but Joe Calvert was a two-finger typist, and the digest took longer than it need have done. He had just finished, straining his eyes after the electric light flickered and went out, when the press attaché came back and said briefly, 'Governor wants you.'

Ambassador Francis, who still liked to be called by the title he had held as Governor of Missouri, was making a gallant effort to look dignified and statesmanlike when Joe entered his room. For once he was not smoking a cigar. He wore a frock coat, which he called a Prince Albert, with immaculate white slips to his waistcoat, and a handsome gold watch chain spanned his considerable girth. But beneath the façade Joe saw a tired old man in a job too big for him, and thought compassionately that David R. Francis was finding Petrograd, 1917, a good deal more complicated than the St. Louis Fair. The Counsellor and the First Secretary, looking harassed, were also in the room.

'Mr. Calvert,' the ambassador began, 'you once told me you had the entrée to Kerensky's office at the Tauride. D'you happen to know your way around the Winter Palace?'

'Not exactly, sir. I was there at the Root Mission's farewell dinner last summer, when you and Mr. Kerensky were the guests of honour.'

'In the Malachite Hall, yes, of course you were. And that's plenty good enough to be going on with. I'm going to send a little rescue party along to the Winter Palace right now, and I want you should go along with them in case they need an interpreter.'

'To rescue the Ministers, sir?'

'Kerensky,' said the Counsellor irritably. 'Kerensky alone, of course. The Ministers will have to take their chance.'

'Fact is,' said Mr. Francis in a more kindly tone, 'I've been in touch with Mr. Kerensky, off and on, this morning. He doesn't want to admit it, but it looks as if this city will fall to the Bolsheviks before midnight, and if they take the power the first thing they'll do is ask the Germans for an armistice.'

Joe nodded. It was the old bogey, constantly in the minds of the Allies.

'Whereas if Kerensky takes off, and rallies what's left of the army at Pskov, he has a fair chance of saving the situation. The Soviet has no power outside Petrograd — none at all.'

'Quite so, sir; but do you think he has any chance of getting through the city, past all the Bolshevik checkpoints, without being arrested, or even shot at sight?'

'He says he's willing to risk it. Thinks the shock element of seeing him appear may turn the trick. Now, before you leave, is there any angle you can think of which may be useful if he gets awkward at the last minute and refuses to go? You used to meet him socially, you said.'

'I never knew him really well. But enough to know that he's a very proud man — well, conceited if you like — and I'm pretty sure he'll never accept protection under the American flag.'

'He's not too proud to ride in an American car, I hope?'

'Very few Russians know one make of car from another. But he won't want to go down in history as having passed the Bolshevik checkpoints flying the Stars and Stripes.'

'Something in that,' conceded the ambassador. 'But I don't see why he should kick at the flag, considering what he's costing the United States.' He turned to the Counsellor. 'Did you see Caldwell's last report from Vladivostok? Over half a million tons of American military stores lying on the wharves there, and not a single unit of the Asiatic Squadron to protect as much as a packing-case! I'm going to cable Washington to have the *Brooklyn* sent to Vladivostok, licketty-split, if Lenin comes to power ... All right, Calvert, off you go, Captain Riggs can take you in his car. Use your own judgment about the flag.'

Joe went back to the hall to collect his coat. The excitement seemed to be rising; not only had Raymond Robins reached his peroration and was quoting poetry, as he loved to do, but a much younger man with a Stetson hat on the back of his head had stolen half his audience, and was shouting:

'He's there! He's back! Lenin's at the Smolny, and he's holding them in the hollow of his hand! Damnedest thing you ever saw, Lenin with his beard off, and a wig over his big bald head. But that voice, you couldn't possibly mistake it, ever —'

'Excuse me, Mr. Reed,' said Joe, pushing past the vehement young man.

'What's all the hurry, Calvert? Don't you want to come back to the Smolny with me and see democracy in action?' John Reed had an open, laughing face and a breezy, back-slapping manner. Joe Calvert thought of him as the poor man's Jack London.

'I've been watching democracy in action for the past three years, while you were cutting capers down in Mexico,' he said. It was unlike Joe to be gratuitously disagreeable, but among the clashes of personality which distinguished the American community he had to admit that his clash with John Reed, a man of his own age and background, Harvard 1910, who had blossomed out as a Communist and a draft dodger, was as violent a clash as any. He ran down the steps furiously and jumped into the military attaché's car.

The struggle for the Alexander Bridge seemed to have ended with a strong force of Red Guards in command of the approach, and Joe looked up anxiously at the Grand Duke Dmitri's palace as they went by. He saw a Red Cross flag fluttering from the roof, but the British flag had gone, and his heart was gripped with a new fear for Dolly Hendrikova's safety. But there was no possibility of halting on the way to the Winter Palace; they went, as directed, to the Hermitage entrance, and after the minimum of explanation with the sentries, were told that the prime minister would join them as soon as possible. The Americans waited in an anteroom. In the hall beyond they could see women in uniform, and some of the boy cadets. It was not a very convincing force to repel a possible attack.

Kerensky ran downstairs with the speed which had earned him his nickname, and came gaunt-faced and hollow-eyed to shake their hands. He was ready to go, and had a car of his own waiting. He told Joe he meant to go first to Pskov and then if necessary to Mohilev, while at the same time directing an operation to capture the wireless station at Czarskoe Selo, the most powerful in the whole of Russia. In the semi-military uniform he had affected since becoming Minister for War, Kerensky looked capable of doing all three things at once, and it was evident that he was living on his last reserves of nervous force. The departure did not take long. He said a brief goodbye to his staff, and got into his own car with Colonel Kuzmin, the commander of the Petrograd district, and an aide. The rest of the party piled into the car belonging to Captain Riggs, from which the owner ruefully removed the American flag.

'I guess that's the last I'll see of my automobile,' said the soldier, looking rather bleakly after the procession as it drove away. 'Think he's going to make it?'

'He might. Want to walk back through the square and see what's going on?'

'Okay.'

The enormous square was only half full of people, and the huge Winter Palace showed no sign of life. Nobody came out on the balcony today, and Joe remembered how he had stood on the fringe of a vast throng of half a million people, cheering their Little Father, on the day when the Court was in and the People were out, on a summer Sunday of 1914. He listened absently to what his companion had to say of Kerensky's gall in sleeping in the Czar's bed in that palace, and driving in the Czar's own car.

Kerensky's reckless departure was successful. He passed all the Bolshevik checkpoints without hindrance, the Red Guards being apparently stunned by his audacity, and was on the highroad to Pskov before it was fairly realised that he had left the Winter Palace. And by the early evening the Palace Square was crowded again, with a crowd which had come not to cheer but to triumph: a crowd waiting for the signal of revolution, the single blank shell fired at the Winter Palace by the cruiser *Aurora* at nine o'clock that night. Then came the cannonading from across the Neva, as the batteries of the fortress of Peter and Paul attacked the palace with shell after shell. The firing was not very accurate but the effect on morale was enormous. The women, the rear-guard of the Battalion of Death, surrendered first and came out under promise of an amnesty; the boy soldiers held out a little longer. Finally, in the small hours of the morning, the Ministers of the Provisional Government accepted their defeat. When they came out under arrest, white-faced in the glare of the torches, the cheering crowd could be kept back no longer. They surged forward into the palace of the Romanovs, singing:

> Arise, ye prisoners of starvation!
> Arise, ye slaves of want and fear!

They knew that at last the Court was out and the People were in, and this time the People were there to stay.

There was little sleep that night for those who chose to remain in the American Embassy. The visitors of the morning drifted back to their hotels in the late afternoon, when the demonstrations seemed to be ending in a stalemate, but as the cloudy, rain-streaked daylight faded to an early darkness, Joe Calvert was among those who volunteered to stay in the building with the duty officers and the ambassador's household. Poker was a distraction in the early part of the evening. Then the firing began, just as they were all sitting down to a meal neither dinner nor supper, and the plates were pushed away as the Americans listened, and tried again and again to get news on the telephone which sometimes ceased to function for an hour at a time. The cadets of the military school were still holding out in their own building on Vassili Island, in the central post office, in the Astoria Hotel, and in the Engineers' Palace. By four in the morning the city seemed to be quiet. The exhausted men slept in armchairs and on couches, and only the US Marines posted outside the code and file room remained awake. It was still dark when someone shook Joe Calvert's shoulder and whispered, 'Telephone for you — the British Embassy.'

Half asleep, he stumbled to the telephone in the press attaché's room.

'Joe? Dick here. Thank God I've found you. I've been calling the flat for half an hour.'

'Half an — say, what time is it?'

'Just on eight. Joe, I've got Dolly here, she spent the night in the embassy.'

'Dolly? But what about the hospital?' He was dazed with fatigue and had a crick in his neck; none of this was making any sense.

'The Bolshies cleared them out when they were fighting for the bridge. Wanted to occupy Dmitri's palace, something symbolic I suppose. Lady Betty brought Dolly here because she'd nowhere else to go—'

'What about the wounded?' Joe was still trying to sort out the facts. Dolly at the British Embassy, he couldn't visualise it; Dolly under Dick's protection he could imagine only too well.

'The Red Guards put in their own medical orderlies. Now wake up, Joe, what I want you to do is get hold of a car and take Dolly over to the Italianskaia.'

'What, back to the flat? She'll be a damn sight safer in your embassy.'

'I doubt it,' said Dick grimly. 'I'm looking out of a window right now, and I see the Reds hauling field guns into Suvarov Square, as hard as they can go. They mean to blast the cadets out of the Engineers' Palace, and I wouldn't be surprised if they had a bang at the embassy as well.'

'Good God,' said Joe, now fully awake, 'I'll grab a car and be with you in ten minutes. How about you? Are you coming to the Italianskaia too?'

'Not likely,' said Dick. 'I'm off to the Smolny with General Knox. Those damn fool girls in the Women's Battalion are being held in some barracks instead of turned loose and sent home as they were promised. I don't know if we can stop a mass rape, but we'll do our damnedest to stop the order for a mass execution.'

While exhausted men in the Allied embassies snatched a few hours of sleep after the surrender of the Winter Palace, the triumphant revolutionaries continued their marathon session at the Smolny Institute, the aristocratic girls' school taken over as their headquarters. In the beautiful white and gold hall where the Smolny girls had danced through the generations from the minuet to the mazurka, bearded and sweating men, some of them heavily armed, jostled for a place to see and hear the leaders of the Military Revolution Committee, and to bellow the magic formula, 'All power to the Soviets!' The greatest ovation was reserved for Lenin, now named as chairman of the Council of People's Commissars.

The law-making started immediately, and went on through the daylight hours. Decrees to end the war by negotiation with the enemy, to end the private ownership of land, to abolish ranks and titles, to adopt the western calendar, followed each other in quick succession, the only approval necessary being the roars of satisfaction from the body of the hall. And with the law-making came the punishments; from the order to arrest Kerensky to the creation of People's Courts to try counter-revolutionaries and all the enemies of the Communist regime. The young cadets who surrendered during that day did so under an amnesty, like the women defenders of the palace, but many a body in cadet uniform was found in the canals for days to come. The women soldiers were more fortunate, for after the urgent appeal of General Knox they were set free.

There had been heavy street fighting in Moscow, but by the time Joe Calvert drove back to the Italianskaia in the early evening Petrograd seemed orderly enough. A reduced tram service had been started, and some shops had opened for business, while the theatres announced performances as usual. Thankful for the lull, Joe ran the embassy Ford, which he had kept since morning, into the courtyard behind number 365. He took out the ignition key, went round to the front of the house and ran upstairs.

Dolly was badly scared when he brought her home in the morning, and he could do no more than strip his own bed, give her cold clean sheets and pillowcases, and beg her to get a few hours' rest, before he had to go back to his post of duty. But when he opened the front door that evening he smelt a savoury smell of cooking, and there was Dolly, coming flushed and smiling out of the kitchen with one of Varvara's coarse blue aprons tied over her own blue dress.

'Dolly! Are you all right?'

'Oh yes! I had such a lovely sleep, and now I'm getting supper ready!'

She looked so pretty, and it was a welcome such as he had never had to the bleak little flat. Joe took Dolly in his arms and kissed her heartily. She kissed him too, but they both knew they kissed as friends, not lovers, and he made no attempt to hold her back when she rushed into the kitchen and began stirring something in a saucepan with a long iron spoon. 'What *are* you fixing?' he said, 'it sure smells good.'

'I found some canned meat and vegetables in your cupboard, enough for a good stew.'

'Isn't the gas ring working?'

'The gas is still off, but I found a little spirit stove on the top shelf in the hall.'

'Must be some of Dick's stuff, I never saw it before. And how about Varvara?'

'She didn't appear, but the maid in the next-door flat was so nice, Joe, she helped me to carry up the water.'

'*Carry* the water?'

Dolly gaily explained that the water had been turned on at a standpipe in the courtyard for an hour that afternoon, and the tenants had filled buckets and jugs as long as they were able. There were two full pails in the bathroom and one in the kitchen, and it was drinkable; she would make tea by and by. Also, she had started up the stove in the living-room.

'You're a great little sport,' said Joe, 'I just hope you didn't get tired out. Put out your little heater for now and come and have a drink. Dick telephone?' he ended casually.

'The telephone's still out of order, Joe.'

'It's been out all day.' He had a quick wash in the bathroom basin, using about a pint of the precious water, and went back to the living-room, where he saw the table had been set for three.

'Do you remember how you used to order sherry cobblers?' Dolly asked, when he began to rummage in the depleted drinks cupboard.

'Do I not! I haven't even sherry, straight, to offer you, but how about a glass of cherry brandy? It's hardly an aperitif, but it certainly is warming.'

'That would be very nice.' He poured it, glad to see the bottle was nearly full, poured three fingers of rye for himself, and collapsed into the creaking basket chair.

'Poor Joe, are you exhausted?'

'It's been quite a day.'

'And it — really — is all over?'

'Or it's just beginning.' He wondered if she fully realised what the new revolution meant. She sat there looking into the open stove where the birch logs were crackling, so young and so composed, and she had made her shabby place of refuge into something so like a home that Joe Calvert was half prepared to fall in love with her again. He had not seen much of Dolly Hendrikova since their talk in the Summer Garden. She had turned him down so definitely, had made her preference so clear that day, that his pride forbade him to hunt after her when her parents went away to Finland. When they did meet, she was always sweet and friendly, but somehow not as open and appealing as she had been — as she was now, sitting by his fireside, and telling him eagerly about the excitement at the hospital and the great kindness of the ladies at the British Embassy.

'Dick and I really shanghaied you this morning, didn't we?' he said.

'Shanghaied?'

'Well, kidnapped. Carried you away to our own den. But we didn't mean you to turn into a maid of all work —'

'Getting supper ready isn't being a maid of all work —'

'It was a very sweet thing to do . . . Dolly, listen, I've still got the car, it's right here in the yard. Where would you like me to take you, after we've had something to eat? To your Cousin Timofey's?'

To his surprise Dolly blushed. 'Richard didn't say anything about going to Timofey's,' she said.

'*Richard* didn't — ?'

'No. He wants to take me to Finland, tomorrow if he can. He doesn't think I ought to stay in Petrograd.'

'I told you months ago you should have gone to Finland with your parents. And how does Dick propose to take you to Koivisto — by train?'

'He said by train.'

'*If* he gets a travel permit, and that won't be tomorrow. The Bolsheviks have closed the main stations for the next few days.'

Dolly was not listening to him, but to the sound of a key in the door. 'That must be Richard now!' she said delightedly. 'Shall I —'

'You must.'

Joe listened for less than a minute to the sound of their greeting. The shy laugh, the deep voice saying her name, the movement of two bodies into a close embrace were not meant for his ears. He kicked the living-room door shut with one foot. Then he turned to the flawed mirror which hung beside the writing table and had a hard look at Vice-Consul Calvert, thin-faced and sallow, with his eyes reddened from the sleepless hours and even his brown hair dusty from the neglected streets of Petrograd. It wasn't a face to attract a girl, he thought, but then he remembered Dick's chameleon face with the round pale eyes, and wondered why it had to be Joe Calvert who was the odd man out.

He felt even more the odd man out an hour later, when leaving Dick and Dolly in the light and warmth of their little oasis in the desert of the city, he set out in the embassy Ford for the Fourth Line. There was one more small service he could render Dolly, and by doing it he would also give them time to discuss the plan of escape which Dick had very briefly out-lined at the supper table. It sounded like a heavy risk to Joe, but with Dick in charge it was probably not more risky than the far shorter journey across Petrograd in an American car on a night when the Red Guards were in a mood to commandeer any and every form of transport. He took the back streets and the longest way round, approaching Vassili Island by the Nic-holas Bridge, and there on the embankment of the Neva he was stopped by a Red patrol.

He presented his diplomatic passport, which only one of the six men gaping at the car was able to read, but the word *am-erikanski* several times repeated seemed to impress them all. They let him pass without even pulling aside the mica flaps which served as windows for the car, and as Joe drove over the bridge in low gear he saw, looking back, that they were all moving off towards the big square where the Xenia School had stood. There was no patrol on the Island side, and no living creature visible. Only the body of a policeman, swinging from a lamp-post in the bitter wind, showed that the revolution had passed that way.

No lamps were lit on the Fourth Line, and Joe guessed that this was one of the areas where electricity had been cut off. He left his acetylene headlamps burning to show him the way to the familiar door. To his surprise it was open, and the hall and staircase yawned black before him. He had brought a flashlight, and by its pencil-thick beam Joe was able to insert Dolly's latch-key and try to open her father's door.

It was bolted top and bottom on the inside.

He dropped the latchkey in his pocket and felt for the gun which, by recent permission, all the American consuls were allowed to carry. With one hand closed round it, he raised the other to the electric bell, remembered that the power was cut, and knocked heavily on the panels. There was a faint shuffling movement inside the flat.

'Simon!' he said, with his lips close to the keyhole, 'Simon! Is that you?' It might be a thief, or a whole gang of looters; with the gun in his hand he was ready to take a chance.

Then a voice, very hoarse but still recognisable, said 'Who's there?'

'Joe Calvert.'

'Are you alone?'

'Yes.'

The bolts were dragged back, the chain rattled, and the beam from the flashlight revealed Simon's haggard face.

'Come in, quick!' was all he said, but he seized Joe's hand in a strong clasp, and when the door was made fast again he added, 'There's a lamp in the kitchen. Come on!'

Joe followed Dolly's brother to the kitchen, where he had never been before, and by the light of a little oil lamp he saw a packet of Finnish flatbread lying open in a ring of crumbs on the deal table, and the rags of an army uniform upon the floor. He then saw that Simon was wearing a thick tweed suit, obviously made before the war and hanging loose, and a dark fisherman's jersey with a turtle neck.

'Is Dolly all right?' was the first thing he said.

'She's perfectly safe, we've got her at the Italianskaia right now.'

Simon nodded. 'What are you doing here, Joe?'

'I came to get some things she wants to take to Finland. But good God, Simon, where have you been? Dolly's been worried sick about you. The last time anybody heard of you was at the end of July —'

'I was wounded at Malodechno,' the Russian said, in a tone of complete indifference, 'and my arm went back on me as well. I couldn't write at all, Joe, and then they kept moving us about after the retreat.'

'But three months, man! Where have you come from now?'

'I was discharged from hospital at Pskov at the weekend. Came on by train until the strike began, and then I got a lift in a truck as far as the Narva Gate. I walked from there.'

'No wonder you're out on your feet. Come into the living-room and sit down.'

There was oil in the big ceiling lamp which Professor Hendrikov had liked so much, and by its soft light Joe saw that Simon's eyes were unfocussed and glassy, his broad shoulders slumped as he sat down in the nearest chair. He had brought the packet of bread from the kitchen.

'This came from Koivisto,' he said inconsequently. 'Real Finnish flatbread. How did that get here?'

'Your mother probably left it behind when they were here at the end of September. Simon! You knew your parents were in Finland, didn't you?'

'Oh yes,' he said in the same tone of indifference as he had used about his wound. 'I had a long rigmarole, about that from Dolly, I couldn't make head or tail of it. All about some drunks breaking in, and Commander Yakovlev coming to the rescue, and father — how is my father now?'

'Much better since they went to Finland. And Dolly's going there tomorrow, Simon, did you understand what I was telling you?'

'There won't be any trains running tomorrow.'

'Dick Allen knows another way; he's going to take her. If you know what's good for you, you'll go along with them, and you won't stop going till you're all in Copenhagen.'

'Just because Lenin and his gang have staged another revolution?'

'Exactly.'

'Sorry, Joe, but I've got other plans.'

'Such as?'

Simon had been turning the packet of flatbread in his hands. Now he placed it on the table with exaggerated care, as if food were an object for reverence, and said in the same dull way:

'I *was* going to the hospital to look for Dolly, but that's all right. So now I can go straight to the Yamskaia and have a word with Miss Trenova.'

'With Mara? What the hell for?'

'According to Dolly, she was the one who sent the sailors here to wreck the place.'

'That's never been proved to my satisfaction.'

'You always did stick up for her.'

'I don't, but you've got too much at risk to go charging off to that end of town. You're quite liable to be arrested as a counter-revolutionary. Besides,' he was suddenly inspired to say, 'she's probably still at the Smolny. She was there all last night, I heard; a fellow I know called John Reed was talking to her at four o'clock this morning. Leave her alone, there's a good old boy! Come straight back with me to Dolly, and have a square meal and a good night's sleep, and Dick will do his best to get you both away.'

The unfocussed eyes wandered round the room, and Simon said irrelevantly, 'It looks queer without the pictures and the books.'

It was not only the books and pictures that were missing. The spaces on the wall where the still lifes had hung, with the vast canvas of the unmarried mother, the baby and the vodka bottle, showed how faded the wallpaper was, and the boarding over the splintered windows made the bare room look like a shelter for refugees. The warmth and grace of one Russian way of life, which Joe Calvert had enjoyed so much, had gone for ever.

He stood up. 'I'm not going to hang around here, it's too damned dangerous.' He was thinking of the open street door, and the possible checkpoints on the way back to the Italianskaia. 'I wish you'd show me which is Dolly's room and help me find her things. She wants two wool dresses and her fur coat.'

Simon got up obediently. But what he said had no bearing on his sister's clothes.

'Is it true the Czar and his family are at Tobolsk?'

'They've been at Tobolsk for nearly three months.'

'And nobody's made any attempt to rescue them?'

'How could they, Simon? We all hoped against hope they'd be allowed to leave for England, and when Ramsay MacDonald and Lloyd George queered that pitch they weren't so much removed to Tobolsk as just spirited away. I *have* heard of monarchist groups plotting a rescue, but I don't believe it's ever been tried.'

'I see.'

'That sort of thing wouldn't be in your future plans, would it?'

'I'll show you where Dolly's room is.'

They packed a suitcase quickly by the light of the hand lamp, and Simon fetched a heavy civilian overcoat and some belongings of his own. Back in the living-room, pulling down the oil lamp to extinguish it, he said to Joe, 'One good thing, there's hardly anything left for the looters. Or the squatters, whoever moves in first.'

'One better thing, and it's thanks to Dick Allen, your father and mother transferred all their assets to Finland when they left. They won't arrive penniless in Copenhagen.'

'I'd better check the drawers of my father's desk, in case he left any other papers, hadn't I?'

'Take the flashlight. There's no light in the study at all.'

Simon closed the door between the two rooms. For Joe Calvert's benefit he went through the motions of pulling the drawers open noisily: they were empty, of course, and he had expected nothing less from his mother's efficiency. He only wanted to be in the study alone.

When he came back to the apartment, ravenous, filthy and exhausted, his only desires had been animal, to eat, to splash his face and hands with the last drops of water in the taps and to get out of this tattered uniform. But the contact with Joe had roused him from that brutish state. His mind was alert to the luxury of thinking about Olga. In this room, where he now stood alone in total darkness, he had held her in his arms, had kissed her, had listened entranced to the confession of her love. She rose before him so vividly in the dark that he could almost see her golden hair and the lovely hollow of her cheek beneath the high Slavic bones and the dark blue eyes. He heard her voice again, reading *Young Lochinvar*, saying the lines he had learned by heart, and telling him:

' "So faithful in love and so dauntless in war" — like you, Simon!'

He struck his strong left hand into the right which was almost useless now, as if he were taking a vow, and said to himself:

'*Dushenka moya!* I'll save you — if I can.'

413

CHAPTER TWENTY-FIVE

AFTER she overheard General Tatischev's dry acceptance of the fact that their Siberian imprisonment might end in death, Olga passed through a period of deep depression. She was on the eve of her twenty-second birthday, and life was so strong in her that she refused to accept the fact of dying: what she feared as the first result of the Communist revolution was the staging of a State trial, probably in Moscow, of her father and mother. She knew that this had been one of Trotsky's aims from the moment he returned to Russia. But she betrayed her anxiety to no one, and her sisters' chief concern seemed to be the problem of keeping warm in a draughty house as the terrible cold of a Siberian winter closed down upon Tobolsk.

There was no immediate shortage of money, although the Provisional Government which paid their expenses had been swept away, and the political changes were not felt at once. Soviets were being formed all over Russia, and in the Ural region there were two very powerful Soviets at Ekaterinburg and Omsk, but Tobolsk, with its twenty-seven churches to twenty thousand inhabitants, remained the same God-fearing backwater it had been for so long. The onset of winter, coinciding with the revolution, cut the town off from all propaganda which could not be conveyed by telegraph.

The two representatives of the Petrograd Soviet who had replaced Makarov at the end of September were not Bolsheviks, but old-line Social Revolutionaries, and one of them, at least, was quite well disposed towards the Romanovs. They regarded it as part of their duty, however, to encourage political discussion among the soldiers assigned to guard the imperial prisoners, and Colonel Kobilinski found it increasingly difficult to assert his authority over the Sharpshooters. The units drawn from the 1st and 2nd Regiments became impassioned revolutionaries; the men from the 4th were good-natured, and sometimes played games with the younger girls and Alexis.

Nicholas and his gentlemen spent hours every day in discussing each scrap of news that came their way. There were fruitless debates on the defeat of Kerensky, who had failed to lead the remnants of the army to the recapture of Petrograd, and was now in hiding. There were even longer debates on Lenin, whom the former Czar roundly denounced as a German agent, and the armistice he had concluded with Germany and Austria as the preliminary to a treaty of peace. Nicholas had never appeared more broken, even in the first days after his abdication, as when news of the armistice was received: the oath he swore in the Winter Palace, never to make peace while an enemy remained on Russian soil, was one he had taken as solemnly as his marriage vows. From the British, who had denied him a refuge, and the Americans he expected nothing, although their warships were keeping station outside the Artic ports and Vladivostok. General Foch had already advised French intervention at Odessa, but more was probably to be hoped – said the former Commander-in-Chief gravely — from the new Volunteer Army which General Alexiev had at once begun to raise.

This was talk among men, confined to the dining-room; in the drawing-room Alexandra Feodorovna seldom alluded to politics now. She sat knitting thick wollen stockings for Alexis, who at every opportunity practised skiing up and down the yard, and her only complaint was the restriction of church services to one mass on Sunday mornings. But the evening prayers in which the whole family joined were a comfort, and Olga especially enjoyed the simplicity of these gatherings and the blending of the girl voices in hymns once intoned by the splendid Russian basses and baritones of the Orthodox church. She and the young lady-in-waiting, Countess Nastia Gendrikova, wrote some simple verses to supplement the old favourites. Sometimes a young deacon from the church where they were allowed to go on Sundays joined them to intone the evening liturgy, and after a time Olga noticed that Deacon Vasiliev often joined her father and the other gentlemen in the dining-room when the ladies wrapped their shawls round their shoulders and hurried upstairs to their glacial rooms. Alexis was usually in bed by that time, and under the ill-fitting door they could see the glimmer of the cherished lamp which always burned beneath his favourite ikon.

415

Olga watched the deacon; she watched her father's increasing cheerfulness and the return of something exalted and excited in her mother's face which reminded her of other days, and she decided to take counsel with Monsieur Gilliard. She knew him much better than the two Russians acting as ADCs to the man they still called the Czar; she also knew, for it had been thoroughly tested, the Swiss tutor's utter reliability. It was not easy in their cramped quarters for any two people to talk privately, but one morning at exercise time, when her father released Gilliard from work with the two-handed saw, Olga fell into step beside him and drew attention to her brother's increasing skill on skis.

'He hasn't got much room to practise in, poor fellow,' said the Swiss.

'No, and yet he hardly ever complains. I've only once heard him say, "Oh, if I could only take my skis outside the gates, just once, even for ten minutes!" Usually he's as patient as they are.' She indicated Marie and Anastasia, who were taking turns at pushing each other on a swing rigged up not far from the wood pile.

'I wish Tatiana and you could find more outdoor pastimes.'

'Well, we're a little old for swinging, don't you think ? And so are *they*, of course. Eighteen and sixteen — they ought to have something better than a rotten old swing! Saddle horses. A motor car all their own. Lots of friends —' She sighed. 'I hate the waste, for them.'

'I hate the waste for all of you.' He remembered the summer when Olga Nicolaievna was eighteen, that wonderful last summer before the war and the lovely girl who had enjoyed every moment of it. She looked much older now than twenty-two. Olga's hair had grown to the length of a short bob, not unbecoming, but it was an ashy blonde in colour, no longer living gold, and she looked pale and pinched as she huddled inside her thick cape.

'Dear Monsieur Gilliard,' she said. 'I've known you for such a long time, haven't I? Longer than any of the other friends who were brave enough to throw in their lot with ours —'

'You were barely ten when we started our French lessons. I remember Her Majesty bringing you and Tatiana into my classroom for the first time. I was very nervous and Tatiana was very shy, but you smiled and were ready to be friends, right from the start.'

'I think you were more afraid of us than we were of you! So, after twelve years, may I ask you a very important question?'

'Of course.'

'You and Mr. Gibbs are free to come and go in the town — '

'With a military escort,' the man put in.

'With an escort, yes. But you go to the shops, and the public library, you meet people. Tell me, do you ever hear, do you ever see the faintest sign, of any plan to rescue us, to set us free?'

'I wish to God I could say yes.'

'So there's nothing to be expected from the townspeople. If any help comes, it must come from outside. But from where?'

'I've asked myself that a thousand times,' the Swiss said between his teeth. 'This is the right time for it, before the rivers freeze, and before the Bolsheviks take over Tobolsk as they took Ekaterinburg. Kobilinski's on our side, I know, and if the soldiers from the Fourth were on guard, it could be done. If only there were a few brave men outside to help us — '

'Have you ever heard my father speak of any?'

Monsieur Gilliard seemed to regret his outburst. He said, with his usual reserve, 'His Majesty may discuss such matters with his ADCs, Olga Nicolaievna. Certainly not with me.'

'But you've heard something? You sit with the ADCs in the evening, you have your meals together. You *must* know if there's something in the wind. Or have you given up hope, like General Tatischev? Do *you* think you'll never get out of here alive?'

'Has the general said that to you?'

'I've heard him say it, I don't know if he believes it. But you must tell me the truth, whatever it is, because I'm beginning to think our lives may depend on what's planned now.'

'I've only heard one thing,' her old friend said reluctantly, 'and this His Majesty told me, just the other day: there are three hundred Russian officers at Tiumen, preparing to lead a force to Tobolsk to set us at liberty.'

'Thank you,' said Olga from her heart. 'Only the other day,

you say? Then perhaps there's still time for me to talk to father and mother. To find out what they're planning for us now.'

'You won't betray my confidence, I hope?'

'Of course I won't.'

So even in this tiny community of prisoners they were breathing the old infected court atmosphere of secrecy and intrigue. Olga said as much to Tatiana, when they snatched a moment to be alone together, and the older sister told the younger of her fears.

'If they're planning some crack-brained scheme that'll turn the guards against us, we'll be separated and put into a *real* prison,' said Olga grimly, and Tatiana for once agreed with her. 'Three hundred of our officers in a little town like Tiumen, a likely story!' she said. 'We must speak to papa tonight.'

'Yes, but not a word about the three hundred. We can't give Zilchik away.'

As it turned out, the young deacon stayed late at the mansion that night, and it was easy for Olga, when she and her sister followed their parents to their bedroom, to begin by saying:

'Father Vasiliev comes to say evening prayers for us nearly every night now, doesn't he?'

'I think I'll just look in and make sure that Baby is nicely tucked up,' said Alexandra. She was wrapped in a long shawl, like both the girls, but a fleecy dressing-gown lay ready on the opened bed, and the room, hung with ikons and family portraits, was not without its comfort.

'Please, mamma, wait a minute, there's something we really want to ask you,' said Tatiana, and the Czar, looking amused, asked if it wasn't rather late to hold a family conference.'

'We can't help wondering if Father Vasiliev is carrying messages — if he's in touch with any of our friends outside,' said Olga. 'If so, we think we ought to know about it.'

'They've stumbled on our secret, Alix; I think we'll have to let them share it,' said Nicholas. 'We didn't want to raise your hopes until the time was ripe,' he said to the girls. 'But it soon will be. Three hundred brave men, officers of my army, are at Tiumen, preparing to come to our rescue. Your mamma has conferred a beautiful name on them: the Brotherhood of St. John of Tobolsk, and at her wish they've taken the swastika for their emblem.'

He spoke in a low voice, and the high-flown name had to be repeated for Tatiana, whose hearing was still impaired.

'There are three hundred Reds on guard duty here alone, and other regiments in the town,' said Olga. 'I hardly think they'll stand by and let the Brotherhood whisk us away.'

'A great many of the townsfolk have shown their loyalty, and all the clergy are on our side.'

'Including Father Vasiliev, of course?'

'He's the chief local agent of the Brotherhood.'

'Who's the agent in Tiumen?'

'Nicky dear, I think you've told them quite enough,' said Alexandra Feodorovna. 'We've been warned not to expect help until after Christmas —'

'Then the helpers will have to come by road,' said Tatiana, 'with the telegraph giving warning at every post station they go through.'

'Who's financing the Brotherhood?' said Olga. It was another of the blunt practical questions her mother had always disliked.

'They can't very well reveal their sources,' she said, 'but Yaroshinski, who managed my hospital train, has undertaken to forward a large sum to Tiumen.'

'I thought he was in prison,' said Olga. 'He was a confederate of Manuilov, whom Rodzianko had arrested. Oh mamma, what have you got yourself into this time?'

'I think Lieutenant Soloviev is a most trustworthy man,' said Nicholas mildly, and Olga caught at the name.

'Is he the head of the organisation in Tiumen? Lieutenant Soloviev? What Soloviev is that? Not *Boris* Soloviev?'

'A trusted friend we used to meet at home,' said her mother.

'In Anna Virubova's home, you mean,' said Olga contemptuously. 'I met him there once myself. Do you remember him, Tania?' she said, raising her voice. 'He'd been in India, studying theosophy with Madame Blavatsky. Badmaiev brought him out to Czarskoe Selo, along with the Tea of Divine Grace and all the rest of the rubbish, and then to crown his career he married Grisha Rasputin's daughter. Rasputin's son-in-law, planning to rescue us! Oh, father!' she cried passionately, 'how can you be fooled by such a story! How can you trust anyone connected with the man who did us so much harm before? I wouldn't go as far as the yard gate with Boris Soloviev, and I won't let the others, either! What he means to do is betray us to the Bolsheviks —'

Alexandra was weeping by this time, and protesting against the insult to the memory of Our Dear Martyr, while her husband made his accustomed reference to the long-suffering Job. But Olga stood her ground and got his promise — for what it was worth — to have no more transactions in secret with Tiumen. 'Not unless we all know about it,' she said firmly, and Nicholas retorted, 'Are *you* planning to set up a soviet, my girl?'

Whether the swastika brought bad luck to the Brotherhood, or whether the Brotherhood existed only in Soloviev's imagination, there was certainly no sign of an armed force on the frozen highway as the bitter winter days grew shorter, and the *Rus* came to her moorings for the last time until the spring. What did happen, with far-reaching consequences, was that on the Russian Christmas Day the young deacon, Vasiliev, publicly intoned the prayers for the long life and health of the imperial family, which had been forbidden to be sung in churches since the abdication.

It was the signal for the soldiers of the guard to begin a real harassment of their prisoners. This was not constant, because when the men of the 4th Sharpshooters were on duty there was always friendliness, but surly or friendly, there were now guards inside the house as well as out. The Czar was forbidden to wear epaulettes on the shoulders of his increasingly shabby uniforms. Letters were neither collected nor delivered, and the sense of isolation became acute. The brave lady-in-waiting who had risen from a hospital bed to join her imperial mistress at Tobolsk was not allowed to enter the governor's mansion at any time, and local people who had liked to leave little gifts for the prisoners were chased away with threats. Finally, the two Socialist Revolutionary commissars were recalled to Petrograd, and replaced by two Bolsheviks of a very different stamp.

The one ray of light in the gloom was the good health and good spirits of Alexis. He had had no recurrence of the bleeding since the nasal haemorrhage of two years back, and seemed to thrive in the winter weather. He was full of jokes and mystifications about the changing of the Russian calendar to western time, which took place in January, and announced that in 1918 they must all have two birthday parties, on the old date and the new. His own fourteenth birthday was due in August. 'It's a long time to wait,' he said.

As soon as the snow was really deep he clamoured for the building of a snow mountain bigger than any before, and one Monday morning, after a particularly heavy overnight snow-fall, they all started work. It took days to get it as high as he wanted, for it was so cold that the water froze in the buckets before it could be poured on the rising slopes, but everybody helped — the tutors and Nagorny, and all the girls. The friendly soldiers of the 4th Regiment were smitten with the fever and carried water willingly. They too were eager for toboggan rides.

'Is it as high as the snow mountain Dmitri built for the little kids at Pavlovsk?' Alexis asked, when the mountain towered above the fence and the chute was smooth and ready for the toboggans.

'Oh, higher, I should think,' said Olga. 'He hadn't nearly as many people to help him as we have.'

'But they were all free,' said Alexis pensively. It was odd, his sister thought, how often he mentioned the snow mountain he had never seen, the slide built beside the Slavianka river on the winter day when Dmitri wanted to raise her to the throne. Imprisonment, and the ugly shadow of Rasputin which still lay across their lives, had so chilled the warm responses of Olga's body that the sexual memories of that afternoon, of Dmitri's kisses and his close embrace, had no longer any power to move her. All she retained of the snow mountain at Pavlovsk was her own prophetic cry, 'Farewell, my youth!' She felt so strongly that her youth was over that when the new mountain was at last complete she was prepared to be a spectator with her father and the older men. It was only to please Alexis that she pulled herself up the ladder to the top of the toboggan run. But once on the platform, with the lively young faces looking up at her from the yard, and the novelty of a view into an unknown Tobolsk street, some of the excitement of life came back to Olga Nicolaievna. With a shout of 'Here I come!' she launched herself down the icy track in a sparkling illusion of liberty.

CHAPTER TWENTY-SIX

WHEN Richard Allen used the back stairs in the old house on the Italianskaia he was accustomed to knock a little warning on the door before he opened it with his own key. On the evening in late February when he went there for the last time he omitted the warning, slid the key in noiselessly, and signalled to the two trembling girls behind him to wait on the landing. Once inside, with the door closed behind him, he said experimentally, 'Joe?'

Joe came out of the living-room at once. 'Hallo!' he said. 'Where have you been hiding yourself? Something up?'

'Are you alone, old man?'

'Absolutely.'

Dick relaxed. 'Thank God for that. One never knows from day to day, and I was afraid you'd have some Russians quartered on you.'

'I'm still pleading diplomatic immunity. Well, don't stand there, come on in!'

'I'm on a job,' said Dick gravely. 'We've got visitors.' He opened the door behind him. 'Will you come in now, please?' Joe heard him say.

The two girls who came in were very young. When they were in the lighted room, and slowly taking off their heavy overcoats, Joe saw that the eldest was not more than sixteen, the younger her junior by perhaps two years — the youngest 'visitors' Dick Allen had ever brought to his place of refuge.

'This is the American friend I was telling you about,' Dick said cheerfully. 'Mr. Calvert. I'm sure he'll be glad to make you a cup of tea.'

The elder girl whispered her thanks. Joe saw that they were both badly shaken, and drew forward two chairs to the stove.

'Come and sit down,' he said. 'You must be tired. Have you come a long way?'

'No,' Dick answered for them, 'but they've a long way to go, and I must change my clothes before we start. Princess,' he said to the girl, 'will you and your sister try to rest for ten minutes, while I talk to Mr. Calvert? Then I'll explain to you exactly where we're going, and what I want you to do.'

'We're in your hands, Captain Allen,' she said. She had taken off her rough woollen cap, and fair hair as fine as floss silk fell round her shoulders. She put it back with one beautifully manicured hand.

'I don't have to ask you who they are,' said Joe, as he followed Dick into the kitchen and filled the kettle from the water bucket. 'I know. I saw them with their father and mother once, at an embassy reception.'

'Yes, well, the Cheka arrested their father early this afternoon. He's in the Shpalernaia Street prison, and their ass of a mother wasted hours at Cheka headquarters trying to intercede for him before she came to the embassy and was put on to me. Now she wants the kids taken across the border. Fool of a woman — they should have left a year ago, but she hung on hoping to save their houses and their art collection, and now, of course, she can only think of life or death.'

'She isn't going too?'

'Won't desert her husband in his hour of need. Won't realise that a Romanov prince hasn't a hope of going free until the day he walks out of his cell to face the firing squad — I've got to change.'

He poured two glasses of vodka from the bottle in the kitchen cupboard and led the way to the little bedroom, which was glacially cold. Joe drank his at a gulp, he had taken to vodka at last, and the warmth spread gratefully through his body while he listened to Dick talk.

'I don't mind admitting this one's a bastard,' said the Englishman, pulling some rough garments out of the wardrobe and taking off his jacket. 'Those poor little devils are in a state of shock. They saw their father arrested, and the Cheka men rampaging through the house, and then their mother went into screaming hysterics which lasted for about an hour. It was her maid who kept her head. That's the maid's clothes the girls are wearing. Joe, have you got a car?'

'Every last car we had went off with the ambassador and his staff to Vologda.'

'Oh, hell, I never thought of that. It would have been a help

423

if you could have driven us to the Okhta station, like you did the night I took Dolly over. Well, there's nothing for it, we'll have to take the tram.'

'You're going through the forest?'

'What else? I daren't risk crossing the ice with those two babies. They haven't got white clothing, and there's no time to get any; what's more, the moon is at the full. And too many escapees have lost their nerve when the arc lights from the Kronstadt forts are switched on. Besides, I'm getting a bit too old for the ice caper.'

Dick had been changing his clothes as he talked. When he took up his untasted glass of vodka he was dressed as a Petrograd working man, in a heavy frieze coat reaching to his knees, and his trousers tucked into shabby knee-high boots. Like Joe, he drank his vodka at a gulp. 'God, I'm tired!' he said.

'How long are you going to keep this racket up?'

'Oh, a little while longer, I expect. Now that the ambassador's gone back to London, some of us had better hang around.'

'Isn't Dolly getting impatient to see you again?' Joe was rather proud of himself: he could say her name without the slightest pang.

Dick smiled, and when he smiled, in the dim light of a ten-watt lamp, he did look young again, as young as on the night when Dolly found him wounded, and looked at him with new eyes. 'The wedding's fixed for June,' he said.

'Congratulations! I suppose I have to say the best man won.'

'You're a good sport, Joe. Now I must get back to my ewe lambs.'

'Just a minute,' said Joe Calvert. 'When do you expect you'll be back from Finland?'

'Day after tomorrow, with any luck.'

'I'll probably still be here.'

'How d'you mean, probably?'

'I've been recalled,' said Joe. 'The cable came in yesterday. Recalled to Washington for re-posting. Proceed immediately, you know the sort of thing.'

'Can't proceed immediately when you're leaving Russia. Exit permit, travel warrant, it all takes the devil of a time. You'll be here all right! We'll have a long yarn when I get back, Joe, and meantime congratulations to you too. I'll bet you're glad to be let off Vologda.'

'Vologda sounds like a living death.'

When Joe carried the tea into the living-room the two young girls seemed more at ease. There was even a little colour in their pale faces, and both listened attentively to what Dick Allen had to say.

'The princess asked me to take you to Imatra, to your aunt at the Valtio Hotel. That means a rather difficult route across the border, because as you know General Mannerheim is fighting the Reds in Finland, and the front in Karelia is what soldiers call "fluid", and we don't want to run into any action. So there may be a delay here and there before we can cross the border.'

'But the Germans aren't in Karelia, are .they?' said the younger girl. She was pretty, Joe saw, and trying hard to be composed. 'Papa was so worried when the fighting began again.'

'No, the Germans aren't in Karelia. But they're not a hundred miles from Petrograd, which was one reason the princess entrusted you to me. Mr. Calvert's ambassador left Petrograd for that same reason, and went away to a little town called Vologda, on the Trans-Siberian railway. Now we're taking the train too, only we go north from the Okhta station, and it'll take us four hours to reach our destination. You may be able to sleep a little in the train.'

'I feel as if I'd never sleep again,' said the girl with a shudder.

'Now, when I knew we were going to take a trip together I sent a Russian friend of mine on ahead of us, and when we leave the train he'll have a sleigh and horses waiting. When you're alone with Ivan and me you can talk as much as you like, but try not to talk in the tram or in the train. Your voices might give you away, you see, and you'll have to keep your gloves on all the time. Try not to cry, try not to think. This is one big thing you can do for your mother, to put up with being tired as well as unhappy, and maybe hungry too, for a few hours between now and tomorrow morning, and then she'll know you're out of danger.'

The girls had beautiful manners; they stood up at once when Dick said they must go, and thanked Joe for his 'very kind hospitality'. He wished them Godspeed, but he felt uneasy once they were gone. He had felt uneasy, in fact, ever since Dick Allen said, 'I don't mind admitting this one's a bastard.'

The same feeling of unease had been with Dick Allen for the whole of his journey. It had all seemed to go smoothly enough in the north-bound train, where he was sure nobody suspected them to be other than a boorish, half-drunken workman and his two frightened daughters, and when they got to Grusino Ivan had been waiting there with the sleigh and the horse, himself bundled up in furs and with extra wraps for his passengers. Then they drove west towards the Finnish border, along the snowy back-roads Dick had come to know so well on his old fishing trips, while the two girls huddled together for warmth in the piercing cold. They were alone and unchallenged in the moonlit forests. But when they reached the first staging point on their route Dick's uneasiness became acute. The peasant, Igor, whose hut they always used, was surly; it was getting too risky, he grumbled even while he took their money, the Finns were fighting each other on Lake Ladoga. He objected to turning out in the middle of the night to find the men who would take them along the next stage on the way to Imatra.

But he left on snowshoes, and the girls fell into an exhausted slumber. Dick watched them in the firelight of the peasant's hut. The little one, whose name was Ludmila, had cried herself to sleep in her sister's arms, and they were lying, curled up like two puppies, on the battered couch where Dolly Hendrikova had rested on the night he brought her along this road to safety. But Dolly had not been sleepy, she had chattered happily about their future plans, and she had kissed him — his Dolly, who had seen something in a battered old soldier she could love. He thought about the wedding in June and rose noiselessly to his feet. Ivan, who had been sitting on a stool by the fire, got up too.

'He's been away an hour longer than usual,' said Dick in a low voice. 'I hope he hasn't run into any trouble on the border.'

'I've been worrying,' the young man confessed. 'I was beginning to think we should have carried straight on without him.'

'The poor old nag was ready to founder, and I don't know the footpaths on the other side half as well as the guides do. Besides, the girls had to get some rest.'

'I thought I heard his footsteps then.'

'Look out, Ivan, and make sure it's him.'

'It's him all right, and he's alone.'

Dick slipped his revolver back into its holster, and gently aroused the girls. The peasant came in, as surly as before, but he had passed on the word to their friends across the border, who would be waiting with a sleigh on the far side of the river.

'You hear that, Princess Rita?' Dick said cheerfully to the older girl.' We've got to walk for an hour, I'm afraid, but it's easy going, and then you'll see a big black and white post, and when we're past it we'll be safe in the Grand Duchy.'

It was not easy going, and they walked for nearly two hours before they came in sight of whatever safety there might be in a Finland torn by civil war. The girls stepped out bravely at first, but they began to stumble and lag behind, and the two men dared not raise their voices to urge them on. They took Rita and Ludmila by the arms, and pulled them along the forest paths, at some places deep in snow. They half carried them along the last mile to the frontier post, where a frozen river which marked the border glimmered in the light of the setting moon. To his huge relief Dick saw two men in white cloaks waiting on the far side.

Ludmila was terrified of the river. The ice would break, and they would all be drowned, she sobbed, and her sister, too, had reached the breaking point.

'It's no use, we'll have to carry them,' said Dick. The two Finns had come down to the river bank, and were making urgent signs. They pushed back their white hoods, and Dick recognised two trusted guides. Suppressing a groan he lifted Ludmila up in his arms. The trudge through the snow had exhausted him as well as his charges, and the leg wounded in the Boer War, so long ago, felt as if it would give way beneath him. He was up to the knees in water as the ice cracked and broke beneath his weight.

'Come on, Ivan,' he said between his teeth. He was afraid of letting Ludmila fall, and was thankful that the Finns in their high boots came more than halfway to meet them. He gladly passed the weeping child into their arms.

'Where's the sleigh?' he demanded, as soon as they stood gasping on the Finnish bank.

'Just beyond the trees. Be quick, captain, we can't waste time. There's a Cheka patrol out on the border tonight —'

'A *Cheka* patrol?'

'So the foresters say. Can you walk, young lady, or must we carry you to the sleigh?'

'We can walk,' said Rita bravely, and the other Finn seized a hand of each and began to hurry them up the bank and into the protecting trees.

'Halt, you over there! Halt or we fire!' The dreaded challenge rang down the frozen river; the moonlight shone on the black leather jackets of the special police emerging from the trees to the north.

'The patrol!' cried the remaining Finn. 'Run for your lives!'

Dick Allen took a few steps, and fell. He scrambled up, his knee refused to bear him, and he jerked out his revolver and fired a few shots. He knew that it was useless, he was outnumbered ten to one, and the Cheka men were upon him. He raised his hands high above his head.

Joe Calvert made arrangements to leave Russia without a great deal of trouble. His exit permit was issued with only a day's delay, and at the cost of standing in line for nearly three hours at the Finland Station he had obtained a travel warrant and the possibility, though not the actual reservation, of a seat in a 'soft' coach in the train to Helsingfors. He packed his belongings into two valises, said his official goodbyes to the few Americans remaining in Petrograd, and was ready to leave Russia in a matter of hours.

He was very glad to go. The months since the revolution had been a terrible strain, as the 'Extraordinary Commission', the Cheka, established a police network far more efficient and brutal than the Czar's Okhrana, and hunger and disease took their toll of the civilian population. The seizure of all private assets, including safe deposit boxes, raised endless problems at the consulate, and at the embassy, while the ambassador remained in Petrograd, there had been constant friction.

Ambassador Francis made his position perfectly clear from the first. He thought Boshevism 'a foul monster', and ad-

428

vocated America's early and violent opposition to it. 'Colonel' Raymond Robins, on the other hand, continued to admire Lenin and called Trotsky 'the greatest Jew since Christ'. Sometimes Joe Calvert thought himself the only man in the Furshtatskaia who had not made an inflammatory speech for or against the new Russian government, or threatened to 'take a poke' at one of his fellow-Americans.

It was beginning to grow dark, for the February afternoon was overcast, when he heard the familiar knock on the service door, and waited for the sound of Dick's latchkey. Instead of that the knock came again, and Joe felt a sudden alarm grip his body. He had no fear of a looting raid, for when the Kronstadt sailors put into action the new rule that all property belonged to the community, and came looking for furniture and bedding, they came right up the front stairs and threatened to break in the front door. Diplomatic status had not saved Joe from one such invasion. But this might be another kind of trap, and he began to sweat. The last thing he wanted was a run-in with the Bolshies, within a few hours of his going free.

He went to the back door and said, 'Who's there?'

'A messenger from Dick. His friend Ivan.'

Joe undid the bolts reluctantly. There was a dim shape on the service landing, a shape of furs and mufflers, and Joe caught the gleam of white teeth in a bearded face. The man slipped quickly past him into the flat.

In the feeble light of the living-room Joe saw an unmistakably Russian face, the face of a young man disfigured by an old scar and heavy recent abrasions, but smiling anxiously.

'Mr. Calvert? Please forgive me for coming without warning. Captain Allen told me some time ago how to get here. He wanted me to tell you if anything went wrong for him. And — I'm sorry to bring bad news — he is now in the hands of the Cheka.'

Joe felt his very bones go soft, and he motioned to the newcomer to sit down. All he could say was, 'When was this?'

'Just before first light, yesterday morning, on the Finnish border.'

'*Yesterday* morning?'

'It took me all of thirty-six hours to get back to Petrograd. I wouldn't have got away at all, if it hadn't been for Dick.'

'Just a minute.' He fetched what was left of the vodka from the kitchen. It was the only stimulant he had to offer an obviously exhausted man.

'Where is he now?' he asked as he handed Ivan a glass.

'Thank you, this is good . . . He's at the Shpalernaia Street prison. You knew he was taking people across the border?'

'I knew something about it. I even heard him mention your name the last time he was here, if you're the Ivan who was to meet him some place up the line.'

'That's right. I was one of the Russian group who worked with him. I — used to be an officer in the Garde Equipage.'

'You'd better tell me the whole story,' said Joe. He listened in silence, and at the end his only query was, 'What do you think went wrong?'

Ivan shrugged. 'It looks as if Igor's gone over to the other side. He probably alerted the Cheka patrol at the same time as he went to bring the Finnish guides. What puzzles me is what the Cheka men were doing so far away from Gorokhovaia Street. We used to think of Rasputin when we said "Gorokhovaia Street", now it means something worse.'

'How do you know they took him to the Shpalernaia?'

'Two of our people here saw him being taken in.'

'How did he look?'

'Badly beaten up.'

'Okay,' said Joe, getting to his feet. 'So the thing to do is spring him, as fast as we can.'

'If he's alive.'

'They'll keep him alive, all right.' To make him talk, of course, to give away the names of his group and their pathetic customers. 'Four o'clock,' he said, looking at his watch. 'I'm going to the Smolny. You'd better go to the British Embassy and tell them what you've just told me.'

'Dick always said nobody at the embassy could protect him if he ever got into trouble. And haven't they all gone back to England?'

'Ask for the naval attaché,' said Joe. 'He stayed on, and if anyone can help, he will. Now let's go through the details once again.'

When he was sure the story was fixed in his brain, Joe poured the man called Ivan another small measure of vodka and put the rest into his travelling flask. Dick would need it if he were still alive to drink it, and Joe had heard of enough summary executions to know that this was open to doubt. As he shrugged himself into his fur-lined greatcoat he said to his exhausted visitor:

'Did you know a man called Simon Hendrikov in the Garde Equipage? You did? Any idea where he is now?'

'Still in Petrograd. I believe he hangs out round the Lavra quarter.'

'I wish to God he'd gone with his family to Copenhagen.'

'Is that where they are?'

'Thanks to Richard Allen.'

Grey Petrograd was like a ghost town now, but at the end of its short avenue the Smolny Institute was ablaze with light. The sentries carried their rifles at port arms; the row of machine-guns which Joe remembered from his visits to the commercial section was protected by tarpaulins from the falling snow. He knew the drill: the challenge which came as soon as he walked up the steps beneath Quarenghi's eight white columns, under the pediment on which the red flag flew, and then the armed escort to a crowded guardroom. Joe told the duty officer that he wanted to see Comrade Mara Trenova, 'employed' — as he knew from something John Reed had once let drop — 'in TEO, the theatrical section of the People's Commissariat for Education'. It sounded knowledgeable, and after the slow examination of his own papers Joe was allowed to fill up the endless forms in triplicate, while the soldiers breathing down his neck grunted their amazement that the *amerikanski* could write such a beautiful, running Cyrillic script. He completed each form with a flourish: 'Nature of business — cultural.'

Then he waited for half an hour, oppressed as always by the constant racket and tramping going on inside the Smolny, where comrades were addressing meetings, carpenters hammering away at new partitions, deputations arriving from Soviets outside the capital, and delegates from the different workers' unions coming in to present their fraternal greetings to the Commissars. Gradually his lungs adapted themselves to the odours of the Smolny, of soup made from horseflesh, clothes stiff with sweat and grime, and that other stench which proved that sanitation at the seat of power was no better than elsewhere. He was glad when a girl messenger wearing felt

431

boots and some sort of military uniform came to conduct him to the theatrical section of *Narkompros*, housed in a former classroom with some of the girls' desks left in, and a few matchboard partitions dividing it into cubicles. Mara Trenova's was slightly larger than the others. She leaned across a desk heaped with papers to offer him her cold hand.

'You're quite a stranger, Mr. Calvert; I hardly expected to receive *you* here,' she said in a tone as dry as her skin and hair. She had a pencil stuck behind one ear.

'I only discovered the other day you'd gone to *Narkompros*,' said Joe easily. 'Last time I heard, you were working on a newspaper.'

'*Rabochi Put*; yes, we survived Kerensky's last-ditch attempt to destroy us,' she said with her bitter smile. 'After the revolution the editor found me a cinema job in TEO.'

'And how d'you like making movies?'

'I've got nothing to do with the actual production! I write scripts and continuity, and also I'm head of research for the whole theatrical section.'

'I bet that keeps you busy,' said Joe. 'I saw your name on the credits for last week's show at the cinema in the Passage.'

'Oh, you do go to see our films?' She actually blushed with pleasure. 'I did the linking shots for that — between each scene, a Czarist emblem. A hand holding a pair of handcuffs or shaking a knout, just a simple symbol, but quite effective.'

'Very effective, I thought.'

'We have great plans for more truly cultural productions. Just at present, you understand, the need is for quite elementary propaganda films.'

'Suited to your great mass audience,' said Joe. He wondered how much longer he would have to spend on buttering her up, when Dick's life might hang on a matter of minutes, but he didn't dare rush her; he had always known Mara Trenova for an unbalanced creature, who responded well to praise. He was prepared to continue his praises of the rubbish which had replaced Douglas Fairbanks and William Farnum in the cinemas of the Nevski Prospekt, but Mara herself, as if recalled by the word 'cultural' to her own duties, looked at her watch and said,

'Well, what can I do for you, Joe? I take it this is an official visit?'

'It is and it isn't,' said Joe. 'It's an emergency.' As briefly as possible he asked her to arrange for him to meet Vladimir Ilyich Lenin, to ask for clemency for Richard Allen, in the Shpalernaia prison. Before he could finish, he felt her hand over his mouth, and the trembling of her body as she stood beside him.

'Are you mad to talk about the Cheka here? Are you crazy, to think I'll do your dirty work for you?'

Joe Calvert shook himself free. 'I thought you liked Dick Allen,' he said. 'You helped him once, when he was knifed in "The Red Sarafan".'

'That was quite different! I only knew him then as *your* friend —'

'He's still my friend, and he's the man Dolly Hendrikova is going to marry, one of these days —'

'Is that any reason I should help him to avoid punishment?'

'Considering what you did to the Hendrikovs — yes.'

'What *I* did to the Hendrikovs?'

'The day you betrayed them to the Kronstadt sailors, for a cheap revenge on Simon and — Olga Romanova.'

This time Mara put her finger to her own lips at the word Romanova. 'That's the name one must never say,' she whispered. 'What do you mean about the Kronstadt sailors?'

He quickly described the wrecking of the flat, and Dolly's conviction that Mara had revealed the Grand Duchess Olga's visit to the terrorists.

'What a fool Dolly is,' she said contemptuously. 'I never told anybody about meeeting — that girl — in the Fourth Line. But somebody else saw her then, and told his friends. The doorman!'

'Stepan? I sometimes wondered about that. But he disappeared after the July Days, and couldn't be questioned, by me or Dick either. And Dolly was so sure —'

'Stepan was one of us,' said Mara. 'He used to report on everybody in that building, and their visitors. I know it was a man called Yakovlev who had him dismissed from the job.'

'A common spy, and one of "you",' said Joe. 'Oh, Mara, do you never feel ashamed?'

'Not when I think of the better world I'm helping to construct.'

'The world of the Cheka and the Shpalernaia prison?'

'Or your world, in which I'm suspected of betraying people who were once my friends? My mother's friends?' Mara's voice softened. 'Joe, you don't understand. I have no power, absolutely none, to go to Comrade Lenin to beg for an English spy — yes, a common spy, and one of *you* — because I would put myself under suspicion of sympathising with the counter-revolutionaries.'

'I'm not asking you to beg for Dick. I'm asking you to get me an interview, that's all: I'll do the rest myself.'

'I would have to put the request through at least two other people before it would reach his office, and even if he agreed to see you it might take a week —'

'So let's get started,' he said, and Mara Trenova gave in.

'I'll send your name upstairs,' she said, 'but you won't get away with "nature of business — cultural" when it's to do with *him*.'

'Write this down,' said Joe, for she had dipped a steel pen in the ink, 'write "the case of Captain Richard Allen, a British subject, unlawfully detained at the Shpalernaia prison". That way, the cards are on the table!'

'Don't blame me if you find yourself in the Shpalernaia too.' She sealed the sheet of paper and rang a table bell for a messenger. 'You do realise it may be hours before you get an answer? I'm sorry I can't ask you to wait here, but I'll take you to the canteen and see you get a glass of tea, and I'll tell the upstairs messengers where you can be found. Will that do?'

Joe picked up her hand and kissed it. He felt grateful and angry and sorry for her, with her thin burned-out face, all at the same time.

'We don't go in for bourgeois manners here,' she said.

'Mara, it may be bourgeois, but let me just say this: thank you for me, and thank you for Dick Allen too. He once said you hadn't made up your mind whether to be a saint or a revolutionary. I'm going to tell him you turned out to be a saint.'

'Perhaps I was really meant to be a martyr.'

Joe spent two hours in the canteen. It was crowded, but he was allowed to occupy a small table by himself. Aware that he was under surveillance by the four burly men at the next table, he

434

did his best to look unconcerned, and not as if several trains of thought were simultaneously starting and clashing in his brain. Dick in prison and undergoing interrogation by the Cheka — that was the overriding theme; but he had time to think of Dolly, who had depended on Joe Calvert as a help in trouble, and her brother Simon, who had talked so ardently about rescuing the Grand Duchess Olga from Tobolsk, and was hanging about in Petrograd, a down-and-out among the human refuse in the Lavra. The final worry was his own departure, for the train to Helsingfors left officially at ten, and as the hands of the canteen clock passed eight Joe began to wonder if he would be kept waiting until after ten o'clock, and then shown abruptly to the door.

It was eight-fifteen when they came for him, and as he was taken back to the guardroom where his fur hat and greatcoat had been locked away on his arrival, Joe was certain these items would now be returned to him as a preliminary to expulsion. This time, however, he was carefully searched, and he was glad that the gun he had carried during the revolution was in one of his suitcases at the flat. The envelope with his train ticket and other documents got the closest scrutiny before it was returned to him with his passport, and when the examining officer was satisfied that Joe was not carrying firearms, vitriol or a hand grenade he was told curtly that Comrade Lenin would see him now.

The upper floor of the Smolny, evidently reserved for top-ranking members of the Soviet, was even more crowded and bustling than the halls below. Men and women in and out of uniform were hurrying from room to room, always with piles of paper or leather pouches in their hands, and Joe, side-stepping to avoid a girl who came charging at him with a steel filing tray, was hit squarely in the face by a door, opening outwards, which some energetic official must have opened with a kick. One of his soldier escorts asked him, with a guffaw, if he were hurt. Joe, feeling blood oozing from a cut above his eye, made no reply.

They came to a door guarded by two sentries with fixed bayonets, who after a word with the escort permitted Joe to pass. He was admitted to Lenin's presence with one eye rapidly closing, and blood trickling down his cheek.

With the other eye, he could see that he was in a little room, sparsely furnished with a high wall desk, a small desk, now vacant, for a secretary, and a large table illuminated by a single cone of light coming from a green-shaded lamp swung low from the ceiling. It lit up the bald head, the great domed forehead, and the cold eyes of the new ruler of Russia, Vladimir Ilyich Lenin.

'Mr. Calvert — ' Lenin began in English — 'Good heavens, have you been fighting?'

'I had an argument with a door, coming along the corridor,' said Joe. 'One of your staff came out with the devil of a rush!'

Lenin smiled. 'We're making a new nation,' he said, 'so naturally we're all in a hurry. But let me see if I can find something for that nasty cut. Do take a chair!'

He disappeared behind a partition which seemed to divide what had once been a much larger room, and Joe heard the murmur of a woman's voice. He knew that Lenin lived on the premises, in the simplest manner possible, with his wife Krupskaia. He remembered diplomatic complaints, in the old days, that the Czarina listened from a hidden balcony to the Czar's discussions with ambassadors and with his Ministers. Joe wondered if Krupskaia performed the same listening service for Lenin.

The chair which Lenin had indicated was too far from his work table for Joe to see clearly the papers in the open dossier lying on the bare top, but he could recognise, upside down, his own identity photograph and Dick's, each attached to a closely typed foolscap sheet. He held his handkerchief to the bleeding cut with a feeling of despair.

Lenin came back with a small piece of sticking plaster which looked as if it had been used before, and a glass of water. 'This seems to be all we have by way of first aid,' he said cheerfully. 'You prefer your handkerchief? Very well. I'm sure they have some iodine downstairs.' He sat down at the table and drew the dossier towards him. 'Our records show you have a remarkable grasp of Russian, Mr. Calvert. My English is rusty, but I would prefer to use it during this interview.'

'First let me say, sir,' Joe began formally, 'that I'm grateful to you for *giving* me the interview, especially at such short notice.'

'It is rather unusual, isn't it?' said Lenin. 'If this were Washington, do you think the President of the United States would make himself so readily available to, say, a young vice-consul of the French Republic?'

'New methods for new nations,' Joe retorted. 'I needn't apologise for my rank in the Foreign Service, Mr. Lenin. The proper person to wait upon you in this matter is His Excellency the British Ambassador.'

'Who fled the country over a month ago. I believe a person from the embassy is here, bombarding Trotsky with requests for an interview. You showed better judgment in coming straight to me. I haven't met many Americans as yet. The last, or perhaps the first, to come with a similar petition to this room was your own ambassador, before he left for Vologda. A charming old gentleman, a hopeless amateur of course.' Lenin tilted his chair back, and in a characteristic gesture, stuck his middle fingers in the armholes of his waistcoat. 'I believe he was connected with what you call show business before he became ambassador?'

'He was at one time the Governor of Missouri, Mr. Lenin. And the petition, as you call it, he addressed to you on behalf of his Rumanian colleague was entirely successful.'

'The Rumanian was being held on a technical charge, Mr. Calvert; deportation was a sufficient punishment in his case. Now you have come to plead for someone who under our new laws is a criminal — the counter-revolutionary, Richard Allen. Caught redhanded by the special police in the act of smuggling two members of the Romanov family across the frontier into Finland.'

'Two girls in their teens, who never did any harm to anybody —'

'I'm sure you'd say the same of the former Czar's daughters, and no doubt Allen would try to get *them* across the border, if he could.'

'That's a mere hypothesis, and in the present case, let me remind you, Captain Allen can plead diplomatic immunity to Russian jurisdiction. He ought not to be held in the Shpalernaia prison without a trial.'

'He can no longer plead diplomatic immunity, Mr. Calvert. Allen is, and has been for years, a member of the British SIS — the Secret Intelligence Service. Since the revolution, he has ranked as the number three man in their apparatus in Russia. You know the organisation, I suppose?'

'I've heard of the SIS, and I know it exists solely in opposition to German Intelligence. We're still at war with Germany, Mr. Lenin! And so are you.'

Lenin smiled. 'The peace treaty will be signed within the next few days,' he said.

'Which means that counting the troops withdrawn from Russia since last September, Germany will be able to throw forty more divisions into her next attack on the Allies in the west.'

'Which means, as I see it, the imperialist countries will be weakened, and the world revolution brought nearer, by a still greater slaughter.'

Joe's whole head and face seemed to be throbbing. He pressed the handkerchief to the cut above his eye again. To his limited vision the figure of Lenin seemed to swell to a giant size. His reddish beard had grown again, and between the pointed beard and the heavy forehead his features were inscrutable. If the slaughter of tens of thousands meant so little to him, how could Joe Calvert persuade him to spare the life of one Englishman? He said desperately, 'If you consider Richard Allen is a criminal —'

'A political criminal, Mr. Calvert; that's why he was arrested by the Cheka and not by the border guards.'

'Very well. If you refuse to grant him clemency, or even to give him a fair trial, will you allow me to visit him tonight, in the Shpalernaia?'

Lenin glanced down at the page headed by Joe's identity photograph. 'Tonight?' he said. 'I thought you were leaving for Helsingfors at ten.You must be a very devoted friend of this man Allen! You shared a flat with him for several years?'

'He's been there, off and on, since his posting to Stockholm. You could say I shared his flat, but not his activities. I'm his friend.'

'I've thought of a way to test your friendship,' Lenin said. 'I can't grant clemency to a counter-revolutionary and let him go free, but neither do I intend to stage a trial for a spy like Richard Allen. The one who'll be brought to justice, for the whole world to see, is Nicholas Romanov. What I can do for the man Allen, and I will do it on one condition, is what I did in the case of the Rumanian diplomat: I'll order him to be deported.'

438

Joe moistened his lips. 'What's the condition?'

'I'm not a novel reader, Mr. Calvert. Fiction has always appeared to me to have nothing to do with the proletarian struggle. But when I was living in England I did read some novels by a so-called proletarian writer, Charles Dickens. One was called *A Tale of Two Cities*. Have you read it?'

'I have.'

'Dickens was not a Marxist writer, naturally. He was a sloppy sentimentalist, like our would-be comrade in arms, Ramsay MacDonald. But one character has always stuck in my memory, though I really don't know why: the English lawyer who went to the Conciergerie prison, and took the place of his friend condemned to die by the guillotine.'

'The whole point of the substitution being that Sydney Carton closely resembled the condemned man.'

'Whereas you and your friend are quite unlike, and we mustn't strain the credulity of the warders at the Shpalernaia. Oh, and there was one other interesting point: the lawyer — Carton you call him? I'd forgotten that — was in love with his friend's wife. Is there any complication like that in your case?'

It was one of the flashes of insight which gave Lenin his demoniac power over the minds of men. Joe Calvert acknowledged it at the same time as he replied steadily, 'Captain Allen is a bachelor like myself.'

'I see. So what I propose is this: *we* rid ourselves of a reportedly unresponsive and intractable prisoner, and you do a service to your valued friend, on this condition: that he takes your place on the train tonight, travelling in your name, and keeps your identity until he crosses the Swedish border.'

Joe's hand travelled instinctively to the wallet in his inside pocket, which contained the precious travel warrant. 'And me?' he said hoarsely. 'When can I apply for another permit to leave Russia?'

The big forehead was raised a fraction, the cone of light, so bright in the darkness, caught a gleam of amusement in the small merciless eyes.

'You, Mr. Calvert? I think we may want to keep you with us for a long time yet.'

Less than six weeks from that talk in Lenin's cold, shadowy

room, Joe Calvert was finishing dinner with his uncle in a brilliantly lit and overheated suite in the Biltmore Hotel in New York City.

The menu had been of his own choosing: shad roe, grilled steak and french fries, green salad with thousand-island dressing, and chocolate ice-cream. He had thought about it all the way across the Atlantic in a British ship with strict rationing and a captain extremely nervous about submarines.

'Gee whittakers, what a good dinner!' he said when the waiters had wheeled out the service table. His uncle answered, 'You can do with a bit of feeding up!'

The senior Joseph Calvert belonged to the same lean and rangy type as his nephew, but even in his youth he had never been such a 'string bean', as he thought of the gaunt young man before him. The kid was twenty-nine, and looked forty, which might do him some good with the old fogeys at State, and certainly his London tailoring did his slimness credit. 'You wait until tomorrow night and the spread your mother's getting ready for you. Poor Vinnie — I reckon she started planning it the moment she got the cable with your sailing date.'

'I just wish I could speak to them this evening.'

'All your dad's fault, he won't have the telephone in the house. Only thing I'm sorry about is, you weren't in Baltimore *last* night to hear the President's great fighting speech in the Armory.'

The Sunday papers were scattered on the floor, stacks of them: the words of the President's peroration stared up at Joe from the front page of the *New York Times*:

Germany has once more said that force, and force alone, shall decide whether justice and peace shall reign in the affairs of men. There is therefore but one response possible from us: Force to the utmost, Force without stint or limit, which shall make Right the law of the world.

'I've listened to an awful lot of great fighting speeches in the past four years,' he said wearily.

'You'll feel better after a good night's sleep,' his uncle said. 'Let's have a highball and relax. Scotch? How much ice? Soda?'

'Just for the hell of it, I'm going to get me some fresh cold water from the spigot.' Joe went into the bathroom, came back with his tie loosened, and sprawled in an oversprung, velvet armchair. 'Good God,' he said, 'what luxury! The water runs, the can flushes, the towels are clean — in another minute I'll wake up and find I'm dreaming.'

'You had it rough the past few months.'

'Not as rough as some.'

'Well, in any event, it's a great foundation for the future. (You haven't taken to cigars yet, I see.) And it's your future I came up to New York to discuss with you, because I don't want you *or* me to put a foot wrong when we get back to Foggy Bottom tomorrow morning. First off, I want to check through all the details as to how you got out of Russia. I'm seeing Secretary Lansing in the morning, and we ought to make sure that both our stories jibe.'

'There's only one story, uncle. Tell it the way it happened.'

'Right! You gave up your seat in the train to this Englishman, and the Reds brought him along in an ambulance. Two guys from the Red Cross had come to the station to tell you goodbye, and when you didn't show they checked around and found you were being held in protective custody at your apartment. Then they just about tore the town apart, and got through to old Dave Francis at Vologda, and at the end of a week the Reds let you get on the freedom train too. Is that about right?'

'Just about. It was Wellwood and Tasker who started it all, and the ambassador was first-rate too. But the one who really helped me to get away was Raymond Robins. All right, shake your head, I used to feel that way about him too — I thought he was some kind of a ham actor, and that was all. But he has the inside track with Trotsky, and he never let up on the kind of international scandal it would make, an American vice-consul in protective custody and all that, until finally they got sick of it at the Smolny and let me go. My guess is they were too busy celebrating their precious treaty with the Germans to bother about the likes of me.'

'Brest-Litovsk, and a pack of trouble for the rest of us.' Mr. Calvert shook his head. 'But let's get back to you. My advice is, soft-pedal Robins when you tell your story. He's coming back next month, and my guess is he won't even be received by the

President. Nobody takes him seriously now. As for Sissons, all that stuff he wrote about Lenin and the money he took from Germany is going into the inactive files, where nobody may read it for the next fifty years. Now you're as hot as a pistol, Joe. You did a great job in Russia, and everybody knows it, I've seen to that. I've arranged for you to meet Mr. Lansing, and Newton D. Baker, the Secretary of War. Talk about inside tracks — Secretary Baker sure has the inside track with the President! A good interview with Mr. Baker, Joe, and you're all set for a really plum job at State — if you talk about the right people and the right things.'

'As we say at the Smolny, keep your nose clean.'

'How's that again?'

'I'm not sure I want a plum job at State. What did you have in mind?'

'The new Russian desk they're planning to set up in May.'

'If I'm not posted back to Europe, I'm going to join the army. How do you think I felt last month in England, when the big attack was on? Our troops in action for the first time? All those German divisions released from Russia, so damned nearly breaking through? I was surprised the British girls didn't snow me under with white feathers —'

'Now take it easy, boy! Take it easy! Maybe I can fix up some sort of a deal with Newton D. Maybe — oh, hell, you kids are all the same! Can't I get it through your fool head that if you stay alive, and yes, okay, keep your nose clean, you just might end up an ambassador yourself?'

Mr. Calvert's exuberant view of his nephew's future did not seem to be shared by anyone in Washington. Joe reported to his immediate superior in the Foreign Service, was congratulated on five years of good work and told to take a three weeks vacation before his Russian language qualification exam. It was all very flat, and his interviews with the Secretary of State and the Secretary of War did not take long. Mr. Lansing was reserved and impatient, Mr. Baker relaxed and cheerful, but both men showed interest in only ten minutes of Joe's four years in Russia — the interview with Lenin. He was made to go over that word for word in the presence of stenographers.

Mr. Baker alone took the subject of the interview a little further, and asked what became of the Englishman, Captain Allen.

'He was badly beaten up in the Shpalernaia, sir; he's been recuperating in Copenhagen.'

'Does he know he owes his liberty to you?'

'The British naval attaché was working closely with the Red Cross men, that night at the Finland Station. He got in touch with Captain Allen later, and gave him a pretty good idea of what happened. I got a very nice letter from Captain Allen while I was in London, and one from his fiancée too.'

'No more than you deserved! One more thing, Mr. Calvert: when you left Russia, it wasn't on a deportation order, was it?'

'Just as an ordinary traveller.'

'So you weren't declared *persona non grata* by the Bolsheviks?'

'No, sir.'

It was an odd little coda to his interview with the Secretary of War, but Joe forgot about it before the train pulled into Baltimore and he saw his father and mother on the platform. It was a very happy reunion, and though his mother of course shed tears and his father pump-handled his arm to a painful degree, they all settled down to each other very quickly, and five years seemed to be bridged even before they were ready for Mrs. Calvert's welcome-home supper. It turned into a kind of running buffet, for the neighbours drifted in and out all through the warm April evening, bringing young people whom Joe remembered as knickerbockered kids on bikes, or young married women with babies in their cribs at home whom he remembered as debutantes at the Bachelors' Cotillions. They were all delighted to have him back. Nobody was at all interested in Russia.

His father was interested in gardening, and in moving little flags on a map of the western battlefront, where General Foch and the Allies had succeeded, but only just, in containing Ludendorff. Mrs. Calvert was interested in the rationing which had been imposed in January — America's 'heatless, meatless, wheatless, sweetless days' — in movie stars like the Biograph Girl, now identified as Mary Pickford, and above all in President Wilson's second marriage to a charming widow. It was all very relaxing, and Joe felt no desire for wilder amusements. He had had an exhausting week of sex and drink in London.

Baltimore had changed very little in five years, and if Joe's

443

old flames were married there was a new crop of 'belles' with delicious slurred voices, pretty faces, and shining bobbed hair. There were more automobiles parked in the pleasant suburban streets, and more telephone subscribers (although not Joe's father), but very little else that was modern: it was hard to believe in Baltimore that the nation was at war. When Joe went to Washington — and his uncle was in almost daily touch by telegram, setting up appointments for him with this or that official who had 'pull' — he was amazed at the swarming streets and office buildings, the pace and tempo of the capital. After Petrograd it took a bit of getting used to.

He was very glad to be out of Petrograd. He appreciated the comforts and the efficiency of his own country as never before. The Russians had got themselves into the devil of a mess, and it was not Joe Calvert's business to care how they got out of it. He considered all the loose ends of his Petrograd life to have been neatly tied up when he got Dick Allen's neck out of the noose and sent him off to Dolly, and no one was left there whom he regretted, or to regret him. Only it was curious how often, as the beautiful spring days went by, and the dogwood and fruit blossom flowered in the public gardens and by the ornamental waters of Washington, he found himself thinking of the city on the Neva — of the Fourth Line, and the smell of tar, salt and linden — even of the maddening, dirty, exciting corridors of the Smolny.

The men he met in Washington were vitally interested in Russia, but not in the Russia Joe Calvert had known so short a time before. The emphasis had shifted from Petrograd to Siberia. This was not because of the imprisonment of the Romanovs, for any Congressman knew that to evince the slightest sympathy for Nicholas the Bloody was a quick way to lose the Jewish vote, but because of a new development during the weekend when President Wilson made his 'Force to the utmost' speech against Germany: the beginning of a Japanese armed intervention in Siberia.

It started very quietly. With an immensely valuable stockpile of Allied war material on the wharves at Vladivostok. With a few Allied warships in the harbour, keeping an eye on it. With a few 'incidents' between Communists and Asiatic shopkeepers, and a few brawls between seamen, nothing out of the ordinary in an ocean port. Then, on an April day, a few hundred Japanese Marines were set ashore 'to protect Japanese property'. It was a very small, token force, and there was no fighting, nothing to suggest any great international repercussions — .

The same situation as at Sarajevo.

One day after he had been on home leave for two weeks Joe received a telegram from his uncle, summoning him to Washington: 'come quickest', the message ran, 'important news'. Mr. Calvert's messages were always urgent, but Joe went off to the train in good spirits; he thought there might be word of his next posting. He found as soon as he met his uncle that Secretary Newton D. Baker had arranged for him to meet President Wilson at the White House.

Joe's first feeling was one of consternation, his second, that if he'd known he would have worn a different tie.

'I told you Newton D. was a great fixer,' Mr. Calvert chuckled as they walked up Pennsylvania Avenue, 'but I sure kept my fingers crossed yesterday. The Cabinet meeting was cancelled, and I thought maybe today's appointments would be cancelled too, after the President hurt his hand in that damned tank.'

'Hurt his hand in a *tank*?'

'Yeah, that show tank they set up, something to do with the Liberty Bond drive, I guess. The injury wasn't mentioned in the press, but Mr. Wilson's hand was badly burned on some bearing, or something he was pulling himself up by, when he was inspecting the tank yesterday morning.'

Joe stopped in his stride. 'D'you think it was the work of terrorists?' he said.

'Terrorists? In *Washington*?'

'Well, uncle, why would any part of a stationary tank be hot enough to burn a person, unless there was a deliberate hook-up in the electrical system?'

'Nonsense, boy, it was an accident, Mr. Baker told me so himself. He was the only one who got to see the President after it happened.' They walked on rapidly. 'Terrorists, huh? Seems to me you spent too long in Petrograd.'

Joe laughed. He remembered Dick Allen telling him long ago that he was getting Russian fever, like everybody else. When you hear a bang, you think it's a bomb. A show tank, wired up for the Presidential visit — it didn't sound like an accident.

'Now don't get started on terrorists,' said Mr. Calvert crossly, as they parted at the gates of the White House. 'Don't mention the Romanovs. Just answer the questions he puts to you — he's a great question and answer boy — and say, there's one sure-fire way to know if you've got his interest, it's when he puts the flowers on the floor. What flowers? The roses, or whatever, that the new Mrs. Wilson fixes in a bowl on his desk with her own hands. Fresh every morning, and of course he doesn't want to hurt her feelings, but what he likes is a bare desk, all the time. And when he's really interested in what you're saying, he sets the rose-bowl on the carpet and gets into his stride.'

Except for the roses the desk was bare, with one folder on its polished surface. That was the only thing the large airy room of the President of the United States, Commander-in-Chief of the armed forces, had in common with the little room at Smolny, where Lenin believed himself to be making a new nation, and the man with the lean Scottish face who gave Joe a courteous greeting was Lenin's exact opposite in habit of mind and heritage. There were no soldiers with fixed bayonets outside President Wilson's door; nothing but the flag behind his chair and the Presidential seal to indicate his office, and yet Joe Calvert knew that in two months of his own thirtieth year, from the Smolny to the White House, he had travelled between the two poles of the world's power.

'I hope your hand is better, Sir,' he said diffidently. When the President was seated the injured hand lay rather inertly on the desk top, expertly bandaged and taped with snowy lint.

'Much better today, but it's still throbbing a bit,' said the President. 'It was a silly thing to happen, all my own fault.' He smiled. 'The last time I saw you, Mr. Calvert, you were a sophomore at Princeton, trying out for the team.'

Joe Calvert was sophisticated enough to know that the 'recollection' stunt was the one politicians pulled most often, implying not so much a good memory as a well-trained team of secretaries, and yet it always worked. He had only seen Woodrow Wilson on the public platform since he ceased to be the president of Princeton University: he had almost forgotten the younger, comparatively carefree man who had been such an impassioned, shouting, cheering, supporter of Princeton football. 'I didn't make the team, Sir,' he said.

446

'Not that team, no; but you played well for our side in Russia. I've been reading your final report with great interest.' He opened the folder, and Joe braced himself for the usual questions about his meeting with Lenin. But the President wasted no time in going over that ground: he had the written account before him, and that was enough. He started the question and answer conversation which Joe's uncle had warned him to expect.

What did Mr. Calvert know of General Alexeiev, the former Czar's Chief of Staff, who had led the first armed opposition to Bolshevism? Of Admiral Kolchak, a potential leader, who was on his way back to Russia via Peking? Of the Cossack Ataman, Kaledin, whom the Allies were backing in South Russia? Of the general called Skoropadski, who seemed to be siding with the Germans in their occupation of the Ukraine? Was there any hope that Kerensky might lead the fight again?

'I don't think so,' said Joe. 'He escaped to Finland in January, about the time the Communists murdered the Kadet leaders in their hospital beds. It was rumoured that he was back in Petrograd in disguise, but no reliable informant can swear to having seen him.'

'Pity. We sunk a lot of dollars in Mr. Kerensky . . . You were in Finland yourself, of course, on the way home. What's your opinion of General Mannerheim?'

The President's line of questioning was perfectly clear to Joe. The Commander-in-Chief, who must hesitate to divert any part of the American war effort from the western front, was now being forced to consider military intervention in Russia. Mannerheim was the only White General who had really tackled the Red menace, on the smaller scale of his own land, and Joe Calvert said as much.

'He gave me lunch, Sir, in his railroad coach, *and* a safe conduct through his lines to Torneå-Haparanda. I could see he felt the civil war was as good as won then, even before von der Goltz brought in the Germans on his side.'

'The British put Marines ashore at Murmansk last month, in case the Germans advanced that far north.'

'I should say we've nothing to fear from a German advance through Finland as long as Mannerheim is in command. But what happens when he wins the war is anybody's guess. He's not the head of government, Mr. Svinhufvud is, and it was

Svinhufvud who went to Berlin and came to an agreement with the Germans.'

'Ye-es,' the President drawled. 'I haven't been given an appreciation of that aspect of the matter.' He moved his bandaged hand and winced.

'Can I help you, Sir?'

'If you'd put this bowl of roses on the floor. Thank you.' Mr. Wilson stretched his arms across the desk top and flexed the shoulders which bore so much responsibility. He asked Joe Calvert the key question:

'In your view, is an Allied intervention in Russia likely to succeed?'

Joe looked rather desperately round the stately room. It was very quiet, except for the hum of a mower in the gardens of the White House. Mrs. Wilson's roses were so perfect that not a petal had fallen when Joe set them on the floor.

'Mr. President, I'm not a military expert, and I haven't been in Russia half as long as some other members of the Service—'

'Mr. Calvert, in the White House time is not measured by weeks or months or years, but by deep human experience. And I think your experience in Russia went very deep with you. Don't be afraid to speak your mind.'

'Well then, frankly, I don't think a military intervention against the Communists is likely to work out. The Allies—the Associated Power would get no support from the Russian generals, because they're already quarrelling among themselves, and landing small forces at so many different points means no co-ordination. And then the Communists are certain to make a great appeal to patriotism. Yes, Sir, I know Lenin came to power on the peace plank, but he'll kick it over if the issue's big enough, and Trotsky just might turn out to be some kind of a military genius. He licked the Red Guards into shape fast enough; with new enemies to face I think he'd do the same with the Red Army.'

'Ye-es,' the President drawled again. 'That's very clear. Thank you.' He looked beyond Joe for a moment, out of the window, as if he were seeing as far as Vladivostok. Then, with a brief glance at the folder on his desk, he said, 'I admired your persevering attendance at the Duma, Mr. Calvert. I read a digest of your letters to your uncle, occasionally; they became more vivid as you became more proficient in Russian. What took you to the gallery of the Tauride Palace, week after week?'

'I got interested in it, Sir.'

'Yes. Well, as Mr. Lenin dissolved the Constituent Assembly by force of arms when his own party failed to win the elections, I doubt if anyone will be going to the Tauride Palace for some time to come.' He paused. 'Mr. Calvert, I want you to go back to Russia in a few weeks' time.'

'To Vologda, Sir?' It was a horrible thought. Back at Vologda on the Trans-Siberian railway, cooped up with that grumbling poker school of refugee ambassadors! He was reassured by President Wilson's smile.

'Mr. Baker thought you would do well at Vologda, say as assistant military attaché. Your English friend, Captain Allen, found that quite an elastic term! But we don't want to send you back by Petrograd. You could be very useful at Vladivostok, working with Mr. Caldwell, and as of the first of April you would have full consular rank.'

'Thank you, Sir.' The President stood up, and Joe did too. The interview was over. Against all his expectations, but perhaps not altogether against his hopes, he was being posted back to Russia.

'Mr. Baker told me of your wish to join the army, which does you credit, Mr. Calvert. We can't second a valuable man like you from the Foreign Service at the present time. But if things develop as we anticipate in Siberia, I think I can arrange for you to be commissioned,' said the Commander-in-Chief.

449

CHAPTER TWENTY-SEVEN

AT the same time as the American Cabinet was considering armed intervention in Siberia, Simon Hendrikov achieved his goal, and entered the vast province beyond the Ural mountains.

It had taken him nearly six months to get as far as Tiumen, within two hundred miles of his princess, after his strength had been carefully built up from a neglected wound, semi-starvation and exposure to the cold, until he was able to sustain the character assigned him by the leader in the most competent plot yet devised to rescue the imperial family.

Simon was travelling on the Trans-Siberian railway in the comparative luxury of what had once been a 'soft' coach for six, and was now occupied by only sixteen people, all provided with food packets and in some cases with flasks of cold tea as well. He was posing as a sackman, one of the black marketeers who left Petrograd with empty sacks and came back with bulging ones, sacks filled with food from the provinces where food was still obtainable, but Simon's sack was far from empty on the outward trip. It contained the uniform of a Red Guards officer, which he intended to wear after he was through Tiumen, and the body of the former owner was probably now polluting the Neva after having been tipped into the appropriately named Drainage Canal.

In the first frenzy of Lenin's revolution, when officers like Simon Hendrikov were liable to arrest on sight as counter-revolutionaries, he had gone to earth on the banks of the Drainage Canal at the point where it flowed into the Neva near the Lavra, the great complex of Alexander Nevski which contained eleven churches and four cemeteries, all of which had for many years offered a refuge to fugitives from justice. There, until the snows began late in November, he had slept in the Tikhvin cemetery, moving with other shadows like himself from the tombs of Tchaikovski and Glinka to the tomb of

Dostoievski, and creeping out by day for a bowl of kasha or a patty and tea at the kind of eating shop where the down-and-outs of the Larva went. When sleeping rough became impossible he found a bed of sorts in the attic of what had been a beautiful home on the Millionnaia, abandoned by its former owners, and now the resort of ex-officers like himself, anarchists who were misfits even in a Communist society, and professional thieves. The latter helped him to obtain forged papers and a forged labour book, without which he could neither obtain work nor leave the city.

Simon had realised, within a few days of his return to Petrograd, that he could never hope to go off alone to Tobolsk and, single-handed, carry off his princess from her Siberian prison. For that he needed funds and helpers. Some time after Christmas he learned from one of the vagrants of the Millionnaia that the former Grand Marshal of the Court, Count Benckendorff, had organised a supply line to the imperial family, whose own funds had run out since the fall of the Provisional Government. They had dismissed many of their servants, and were now actually in debt to the tradespeople of Tobolsk. He went to see the old gentleman, whom age and infirmity had prevented from accompanying the prisoners to Siberia, and learned that his stepson, Prince Dolgoruki, was the ADC in attendance on the Czar (as Benckendorff put it) and thus one of the chief links between him and the outside world. Simon also heard for the first time of the Brotherhood of St. John of Tobolsk, and eagerly asked to be told how to join them.

The Grand Marshal shook his head. 'Be patient for a few more weeks, my dear Hendrikov,' he said. 'I've sent half a dozen young men like yourself to Tiumen, and so far not one of them has come back to give us an accurate report of any real attempt at a rescue or an escape. Wait until we know more of the facts.' He sighed. 'I'm not quite satisfied with our agent in Tiumen — Rasputin's son-in-law.'

'I thought we'd heard the last of Rasputin,' said Simon. 'What's the son-in-law's name?'

'Soloviev. He seems genuine enough, but — I'm sending one more officer to Tiumen next week to size up the situation. Would you like to have a talk with him before he goes? Vassili Yakovlev is his name — he was in the ill-fated *Askelod* at Murmansk.'

'Commander Yakovlev?' said Simon, brightening. 'I've met him once or twice, and he did my family a very good turn last summer. Can I meet him here?'

'I would rather not,' said Benckendorff. 'I think the friends sheltering my wife and me will begin to object if too many young men are seen coming and going; we don't want to invite the attentions of the Cheka.'

Eventually Simon and Yakovlev met in a *traktir* near the Warsaw Station, which was always full of people hoping to obtain travel warrants, so full that two men, one very shabby, talking in a corner, passed unnoticed. Yakovlev, in civilian clothes, looked reasonably prosperous. He was extremely guarded with the younger man, giving away no details about himself or his mission to Tiumen, but practically ordering Simon to 'Get out of that thieves' kitchen on the Millionnaia and get yourself back into condition. I can find you a job, if you've got a labour book. It won't be worth much, but you'll draw decent rations, and if you can hold it down for a month, I'll be here for another talk exactly four weeks from today.'

'I'll hold it down.' Simon was not so sure that he could, when he found out what the job was: medical orderly in a huge general hospital near the Baltiski Station. The building was nearly a hundred years old, and almost falling down, the wooden floors and walls were impossible to keep clean. Simon carried pails of water, emptied sluices, scrubbed the operating theatre and acted in emergencies as a stretcher bearer. He loathed the work, but he soon realised how well Yakovlev had placed him. The Baltiski General was a far better hideout than any abandoned house, especially since the dangerous state of the dark streets, where men were assaulted and even murdered for whatever they had in their pockets, had caused Trotsky to order the Red Guards to clean up the robbers' dens. Nobody questioned a diligent medical orderly, at a time when a typhus epidemic had begun to hit the city, largely as a result of the water shortage and the condition of the sewers. Also the rations, while coarse, were regular, and Simon's health improved in spite of the long hours, When he was given a big bowl of cabbage soup and a hunk of fresh bread for supper, he sat over the food in torpid animal pleasure. It was only in dreams that he remembered another hospital, where he had been a Palace Pet, with an empress and her lovely daughters at his own bedside.

When he kept his appointment with Yakovlev, he saw satisfaction in the other man's eyes, but Yakovlev said nothing but, 'Wait for ten minutes and then follow me up to the Fontanka,' before he drained his glass of tea and pushed his way out through the crowded *traktir*. Simon, as he obeyed, could see the man walking slowly trim and well-knit in his decent overcoat and fur hat, up the long, dreary avenue which led to the Fontanka on its way to meet the Neva at Galerni Island. It was a dismal part of Petrograd, and in the steadily-falling snow there was no one to spy on the two when Simon caught up with Yakovlev on the embankment of the Fontanka Canal. There Yakovlev held out his hand.

'You've got back in shape, well done,' he said briefly. 'I thought you would, but I had to make dead sure. We don't want any weaklings in our operation.'

'There *is* an operation, then?' said Simon eagerly. 'Have you been to Tobolsk?'

'I didn't go as far as Tobolsk, because I didn't want anyone we may meet there to remember my face when we go in as a group.' It was still a Romanov face, Simon thought, although Yakovlev was dark where most of the Romanovs were fair; but the look was there and made him think of Olga. 'I've been to Tiumen,' Yakovlev went on. 'I met some of the incurable romantics who call themselves the Brotherhood of St. John and couldn't rescue a dog from a burning kennel, let alone the Czar of Russia.'

'Did you hear how *he* is — how they are?'

'Well enough, but kept in very close confinement now. Living on army rations. Bullied by a real swine of a Commissar, Hokrianov, a former stoker. I only wish I'd had him in the *Askelod*.'

'And Soloviev, Rasputin's son-in-law?'

'A fake and a charlatan, like Rasputin before him. Nearly all the money poor old Benckendorff collected for the imperial family has stuck to Lieutenant Soloviev's greasy paws. So now I'm sure of that, I mean to bypass Soloviev, and mount the rescue operation on my own. With hand-picked men. Do you still want to be one of them?'

'I do. I'll follow you, Yakovlev — I haven't forgotten what

453

you did for my parents and my sister, that day in the Fourth Line.'

Yakovlev smiled. 'Can you ride, with that arm?'

'I don't see why not.'

'Because we'll have to take them out by road, before the river traffic opens. And the Czarina's a liability; she can hardly move now, except in a wheel-chair.'

'And the boy?'

'In splendid health.'

'Well, then, the sooner the better, I should say.'

'We'll have to wait to operate out of Moscow, after the government goes there next month.'

'What's the government got to do with it?'

'I'm a government employee. Rather a valued one, I think.' He smiled grimly at Simon's look of surprise. 'You see, I handled the problem rather differently from you and all the death or glory boys. When I came on leave from Murmansk last summer I let it be known I was a convert to the gospel preached by our own ratings — who killed my Captain in the first revolution and shot the Admiral later on — and when the *Sovnarkom* took over, nobody sang the *Internationale* louder than Vassili Yakovlev. I've a nice berth at the Admiralty — Commissariat section, providing double rations and extra vodka for those swine down at Kronstadt, whom Trotsky called in my presence the fine flower of the Russian revolution.'

'I couldn't do that,' said Simon flatly.

'Do what?'

'Act a part like that, every day of my life.'

'I don't suppose you could, Hendrikov; every man to his trade. By the way, my immediate superior at the Admiralty is Captain Gordienko. You may remember him as a petty officer in the *Standart*, back in '14.'

'Remember him!' Simon remembered Gordienko, posted at the rail to help Alexis board, on the day the *Standart* started her last summer cruise, and how nearly he and the sailor, Derevenko, had let the child fall between them. Had that been a put-up job, like so many other things? 'What makes me want to vomit,' he said, 'is to think how many traitors *they* had round about them, even among those they called their friends.'

Yakovlev nodded, and the Romanov look was clear upon his

face. 'That's why I'm working for *Sovnarkom,* and cheering Comrade Lenin,' he said. 'They taught us some useful lessons in infiltration.'

And that was why, on a night in April, a sackman with a Red Guard uniform in his sack struggled out of an overcrowded train at Tiumen.

Yakovlev was not to know that what had caused the closer confinement of the Romanovs, with increasing spites and deprivations, was their last great pleasure — the snow mountain.

The young people had enjoyed it for exactly a month before the day when their parents for the first time climbed up the ascent ladder and stood upon the platform at the top. It was no wonder the guards stared and muttered, for Alexandra Feodorovna had never been seen out of doors since the church privileges ended after Christmas, but it was a sunny March morning, and she was encouraged to hobble out of the house on her husband's arm.

There had been recent orders from Petrograd about the disposition of the guard which had brought the prisoners all the way from Czarskoe Selo. The unit of the 4th Regiment of Sharpshooters was to be withdrawn, and replaced by more politically reliable men, young troops from the neigbourhood of the capital, and on that pleasant March day they were to start the long trek back to the railroad at Tiumen. They had always been friendly to their prisoners, even kind, and the goodbyes in the yard — especially to Marie, their favourite — were cordial. Then Alexandra, who had snubbed so many aristocrats in her time, had the unlucky idea of climbing to the top of the snow mountain to wave to these humble men as they marched off.

She stood there, leaning on her husband's arm and Tatiana's, for long enough to see them go, and then to watch Alexis make one descent of the chute in Nagorny's clasp. The boy was so delighted to have his mother watching them that the fun on the snow mountain grew fast and furious as the afternoon wore on. Tea was a cheerful meal. Meantime, the soldiers' soviet was holding a meeting to discuss the unprecedented action of Citizeness Romanova.

Such discussions took a long time, for each one opened with

a debate on the right to debate the matter in hand, and in this case there were two schools of thought, and everybody had to have his say. Some of the comrades thought Alexandra had climbed the mountain to signal to counter-revolutionaries mysteriously hidden in the street. Others believed she had exposed herself to the risk of assassination, for which her guards would of course be blamed. After a long, enjoyable evening of argument and speechification, the two schools united in a unanimous decision: the snow mountain must be destroyed.

Demolition work began next morning and went on all day. Picks were required, and a great deal of brute strength. The work had been well done, and it seemed as if a few of the toiling soldiers came to regret their decision, for some shamefaced looks were directed at Alexis and his younger sisters, standing disconsolate in the snow. Hokriakov, the Bolshevik Commissar, came out with his colleague Rodionov to gloat over the children's dismay. He was an ignorant and brutal man, with the vindictive mediocrity of many of those like him who had climbed to minor authority in the Party, and he enjoyed swaggering through the rooms of the Romanovs in the black leather jacket which had come to be recognised as the uniform of the Cheka.

He took up a heavy hammer to lend a hand in the work of destruction. No one was quite sure what happened, and certainly none of the children was anywhere near him, but the snow mountain had been sufficiently undermined for a large block of ice to slide forward unexpectedly and knock the hammer out of Hokriakov's hand. It fell on his foot, and the pain was sharp. Hokriakov hopped on the other foot, swearing.

Olga came forward from her place in the shelter of the stone entrance to the house.

'Let me have a look at that, Commissar,' she said. 'Your foot may be bleeding.'

'So what would you like to do — rub salt in it?'

'Don't be ridiculous; come in and take your boot off,' she said, with such authority that Hokriakov followed her into a little cloakroom beside the door, and with an oath took his high boot off. Olga gently removed a matted sock and studied a singularly unpleasant foot.

'It's a very bad bruise, and you may be lame for a day or

two,' she said. 'Anastasia, be nice, and run to the kitchen for a basin of hot water.'

'Isn't my foot clean enough for Your High-and-Mightiness?' growled the ex-stoker.

'I've seen dirtier feet in hospital,' she told him. 'We clean them up before we put the bandage on.'

She washed the injured foot carefully, applied some ointment on a lint pad, and made the bandage fast. The Commissar, like Anastasia holding the first-aid box, looked on in silence.

'I never thought the day would come when I'd have a Romanov at *my* feet,' he said with an attempt at swagger. But when Olga drew the sock on, and looked round for the boot, he took her chin into his powerful fingers and tilted her face up. The blonde hair fell in strands across her forehead, under the knitted cap she had not stopped to pull off, and the blue eyes were steadfast on his own. 'You're not such a bad wench, Romanova, after all,' he said, and added a word to which he was not accustomed — 'Thanks.'

'I hope you've all heard about the latest flirtation — Olga and the Commissar,' said Anastasia when the family assembled for tea. There was a shout of laughter. The joke lasted the whole evening, for the evenings were sometimes terribly long. They tried to break the monotony with charades and little plays, Nicholas and Anastasia surprisingly good in a Chekov play, *The Bear*, and Alexis willing to play any part — even a girl's. But the fun had gone out of his days with the destruction of the snow mountain, and Joy was getting old now, and less willing to play in the icy yard. Olga invented a game called Happy Times, which sometimes amused him in the evening. Each person had to recall some time, or place, or meal which had been pleasant in the past, and the boy liked asking questions about the years before he was born, the games his sisters played then, the lessons they had learned.

'Was my christening a Happy Time, Olga?' he asked when they had gone through every court ceremonial she could remember.

'It was for me, because I was your godmother, and delighted to have a little court dress made specially for the occasion.'

'And my godfathers were the whole Russian Army.'

'Not exactly,' said Nicholas quietly. 'All the combatant soldiers in the war against Japan.'

'Oh yes, that war. I don't expect anybody had as many god-fathers as me, ever.'

'No. But I'll tell you who didn't have a Happy Time,' said Olga, 'and that was the old lady who carried you to the font. She was so blind and lame they were afraid she'd drop you in and drown you. So she wore a pair of tennis shoes, with rubber soles, under a satin dress —'

'I bet everybody else thought she was crazy.'

It was not easy to play Happy Times, when each day was so dark and so monotonous, and such news as reached them was increasingly bad. Not a word was heard of the old empress and her family in the Crimea, but it was said that the Grand Duchess Ella had been arrested in her own convent in Moscow, and the Grand Duke Michael taken from his palace at Gachina to house arrest at Perm. The only good news was of Dmitri, who when the Bolsheviks took power went from the Persian front to Teheran and a refuge in the British Legation. He had applied for a commission in the British Army. 'Oh, good for Dmitri! Good for him!' cried Olga with some of her old exuberance when she knew that Dmitri, at least, was free.

Amazingly, their parents continued to bask in their fantasy of freedom. The Brotherhood of St. John must act soon, before the thaw set in and while the frozen rivers could still be crossed by vehicles; Our Dear Martyr's son-in-law had promised, and was sure to keep his word. The Soviet government was in Moscow now, and the Germans had sent an ambassador to Moscow, Count von Mirbach: there was a whisper that Mirbach, too, was trying to organise a rescue. 'Well, really!' said Alexandra Feodorovna, 'I must decline to take advantage of the Kaiser's kind arrangements! After what they've done to your father I'd rather die in Russia than be rescued by the Germans!'

'You're tempting Providence, mamma,' said Olga.

'It's not as if we'd be going to *live* in Germany,' coaxed Tatiana. 'And honestly we do need somebody to help us out of here.'

'Where shall we live, we've never discussed that,' said Marie. 'Mamma, you don't want to go to Paris, and we obviously can't go to London now. Why don't we plan to go to Copenhagen? The Danish cousins are good fun.'

'They haven't lifted a finger to help us, any more than our

English cousins have,' said Alexandra bitterly. 'One place I will *not* go to is Switzerland. Imagine living in Swiss hotels as ex-royalties, like the Serbs and the Greeks; imagine being snap-shotted by tourists and interviewed for the American press!'

'I'd love to give interviews and allow my picture to be taken by anyone who wanted! I think Switzerland sounds like fun,' said Anastasia to Olga, later.

'Switzerland sounds like heaven.' Olga was growing fright-ened, though she never showed it. Instead of replacements from the Czarskoe Selo garrison, the new and augmented force at the mansion was composed of Red Guards from Omsk, a strongly Bolshevik town, who shouted obscenities and scratched filthy drawings on the fence, whenever the girls went into the yard. The Commissar had forgotten his brief grati-tude, and egged them on. Olga felt that a ring of hate was slowly tightening round them, from which the Romanovs never would escape.

Poor Marie regretted, to the end of her life, that in a final dredging up of memories for Happy Times, she was the one who told Alexis about a summer journey when the four small girls were allowed to get out of the imperial train to picnic and play, and their play had taken the form of sliding down the grass of the railroad embankment on silver trays taken from the dining car. She told him how the courtiers had joined in, and how one old general had looked particularly silly, coasting along in gala uniform with all his medals, but Alexis cared nothing for the general: he wanted to try sliding on a tray himself. And perhaps because they had all, even Nagorny, begun to take his good health for granted, nobody was aware that Alexis had borrowed a tin tray from the kitchen and was about to use it as if the staircase was an indoor version of the snow mountain.

Until they heard the crash at the bottom of the stairs.

He was carried to his room and Nagorny undressed him, while Dr. Botkin stood ready to examine him for any bumps or lacerations. He had a bruise on his forehead, which was bleed-ing slightly, and a lump the size of a hen's egg on one knee — just the kind of damage an ordinary schoolboy might do to himself at any rough sport, and so his sisters bracingly told him, at the same time as they were telling him it was nearly bedtime anyway, and why didn't he have a supper tray in bed?

But before long the forced cheerfulness was at an end, the dark blue swellings made their appearance, and the dreadful haemophilia, always latent, declared itself again. The bruised blood seeped from the knee along the thigh, the leg cramped fast against the thin boyish body, and his mother, beside herself with grief and anxiety, was praying to the soul of Rasputin to intercede in heaven for her child.

It was the worst attack Alexis had suffered for six years. The time aboard the *Standart*, the time of the nasal haemorrhage, had been nothing like as bad as this. Dr. Botkin tried everything that had helped in the past, and even the Commissars, once they were sure the boy was not shamming, told him to draw on the local hospital for anything he might need. But there was nothing to be done, nothing but wait and hope that, as some physicians believed had happened without the prayers of Rasputin, the haemophilic bleeding would stop of its own accord. Later, the torture of leg irons might have to be imposed to release the locked limb from its rigid cramp against the body; in the meantime, with Dr. Botkin always reluctant to administer morphine, the poor boy's only release from pain was fainting.

He was very brave for the first two days, and then pain mastered him. They heard him crying and then screaming, high spasms of screaming, until finally, as his anguished sisters huddled in their cold room, they heard him sob:

'I want to die, mother! I can't bear such awful pain much longer! Mother, please, I want to die!'

It was the voice of an adult human being, in the grip of torment. But his mother's voice, hoarse with tears, soothed him with the words of his infancy:

'Hush, Baby, be agooweeone. Hush, my Sunbeam, mother's holding you fast. Sleep well and be agooweeone.'

By the twenty-second of April the worst of the attack was over. Alexis was unable to stand, much less walk, and his old bed-ridden life began again, but he was out of pain. That was the day when a small troop of horse cantered up to the governor's mansion at Tobolsk, and Alexandra Feodorovna, smiling for the first time for many days, limped into the girls' room to tell them the rescuers were there at last.

'They're in the Red Guards uniform, but I *know* they're

members of the Brotherhood!' she exulted. 'Good Russian men — some of them mere boys. I haven't seen such kindly faces for a long time. Now they'll be in touch with us at once —'

'They'll stable their horses and have some food first, whoever they are,' said Olga.

'And if they really are our rescuers,' said Tatiana, to humour her mother, 'don't you think we ought to start doing what we've often talked about — sew some of our jewels into the clothes we're going to wear?'

The selection of the garments and the jewels kept them occupied for an hour, while Alexis dozed in the next room, until a maid came to beg 'Her Imperial Majesty' to go downstairs. There, Kobilinski was waiting to present to both the Majesties an emissary from the Moscow Soviet, Special Commissar Vassili Yakovlev.

It hardly sounded like a rescuer, but the prisoners felt some degree of confidence in the well-built, well-spoken man in the dress of an ordinary seaman, who so obviously belonged to the world they had left behind. Over tea, he made social conversation, showing some knowledge of the theatre and the arts; he was extremely courteous to the girls. He only seemed disconcerted once, when on enquiring for the missing member of the family he was told that Alexis Nicolaievich had been seriously ill, and might be confined to bed for weeks. 'I shall bring my own doctor to see him in the morning,' he declared. Yes, he had a doctor, and a hundred and fifty men, fully armed with machine-guns, and a telegraph operator to keep him in direct touch with the Kremlin.

'He's a very pleasant fellow, but he's not a rescuer,' said Nicholas, when the unexpected guest had gone.

'At least he's a Special Commissar,' said Olga, determinedly cheerful. 'I only hope he outranks Hokriakov, and sends away that horrible crowd from Omsk.'

'I wonder what he came for,' mused the Czar. 'He reminds me of somebody, I don't know who.'

The Special Commissar came back next day with an army doctor who visited Alexis, conferred with Dr. Botkin, and went away. The Romanovs were still completely in the dark about Yakovlev's mission, and what the powers of a Special Commissar might be. These were revealed next day, and only to

Colonel Kobilinski, after prolonged telegraphic exchanges with the Kremlin, but not until Commissar Yakovlev had had a few words with Comrade Hendrikov in the neglected saddle-room which was one of the outbuildings of the governor's mansion.

'It's no good, Simon, that poor kid can't be moved. Our man is certain of that, and his sisters must stay with him.'

'Oh God, the kid again! The measles, and now this! Can't he be packed into a *tarantass*, with his mother?'

'The doctors told me jolting in a *tarantass* would be the death of him. Sounds a bit extreme, but that's what they said —'

'And I suppose there's no question of leaving him behind?'

'You know them better than that.'

In the glow from a stable lantern, their only light, Simon's face was very pale. His head was aching, his heart torn with the strain of being so near to his princess and still unable to set her free. 'So what are you going to do?' he said.

'I'm going to take the Czar and possibly the Czarina. I *must* leave with him, I've my orders from Sverdlov, and the Red Guards they sent along with us at the last minute know what those orders are. It's leave with him or be shot ourselves — there's no alternative.'

Simon jumped at the Czarina's name. 'Then if Her Majesty goes,' he said, 'one of the Grand Duchesses must go with her. They'd never send a sick woman off on a trip like this without one of her daughters. For God's sake, Vassili Vaslevich, make sure the Grand Duchess Olga accompanies her mother!'

'It's because of her you're here, isn't it?'

'Did I make it obvious, when we were talking back in Petrograd?'

'Not at all. It was — something those ruffians from Kronstadt shouted, when I was hustling them downstairs after they broke into your father's flat.'

'Dolly told me about that.'

'Simon, I promise you, I'll do everything I can. But you know you gave me your word to follow me, and my first job's to get the Czar clear, to spare him the public trial Sverdlov and Lenin are setting up in Moscow. I've got to persuade those Reds they sent along with us that I've my orders to go east to Omsk, not west along the track to Moscow, and even if we get to Omsk we've still got half the Empire to cross before we're within sight of the Pacific. We have the guns and I'm prepared to stand and fight along the way if I must, but let's get out of Tobolsk without bloodshed. Agreed?'

'Agreed, if Olga Nicolaievna can go too.'

Next day, it seemed as if she might. By that time Yakovlev had produced all his impressive authorisations from Moscow: the letters signed by Jacob Sverdlov, President of the All-Russian Congress of Soviets, whose rank in the Party was almost equal to Lenin's, threatening Colonel Kobilinski and all the men under his command with instant death if the Special Commissar's orders were not carried out. These orders were to take the entire Romanov family under escort to Moscow, and they represented months of acting a part, of intrigue in high places, of sheer bluff, by the one man who had the strength to plan, and so far to carry out his plan, the escape for the prisoners which Kerensky had vaguely visualised — along the clear track of the Trans-Siberian to Vladivostok and Japan.

Yakovlev's master plan had foundered on the building of the snow mountain, and its aftermath.

The order for the Czar to go to Moscow dissipated at a blow all the Christian resignation his wife had shown during more than a year in captivity. She raged as she had raged in the days of Rasputin — as if Kobilinski, Yakovlev, Nicholas himself, were the Ministers she made and unmade with a stroke of the pen in the months before Rasputin's murder. He should not go, she raved; and when Tatiana persuaded her that he must go, they were powerless to prevent it, she insisted in outspoken language that she must go as well. He had thrown away the crown, she cried, when he was all alone at Mohilev, and God knew what he might say or do or sign in Moscow if she were not by his side to prompt him and advise! Then she was told that she might go, with the Grand Duchess Olga to keep her company: the Czar might take Prince Dolgoruki or General Tatischev. She ordered Olga to prepare for the journey, and went to throw herself upon her son's bed, and clutch the weeping, bewildered Alexis to her breast.

For a few hours, while the preparations were going on, Simon Hendrikov thought the miracle had happened, and that he would hold Olga in his arms again. He felt light-headed at the very thought. He must have been light-headed in fact, for his face and hands were burning, and at the evening meal his tongue seemed thick in his mouth when he exchanged a few guarded words with the other members of Yakovlev's silent company. He even stumbled when he went up a rickety wooden stair to their temporary sleeping place to put his few possessions in an old valise. Everything was strapped up, they were all ready to go.

'But are *they* ready?' he said in an undertone to Yakovlev in the deserted mess hall. 'I thought we were to leave before midnight.'

They both listened to the soughing of the wind. It had the sound of spring, and they heard the drip of water from the eaves.

'The roads are going to be liquid mud,' Yakovlev said. '... They had tea at half past ten, they said goodbye to everybody before half past eleven, and now it's nearly two. God *knows* what's causing the hold-up —'

'You can't hurry them, I learned that at Livadia —'

'Yes, but this isn't a holiday, it's a matter of life or death.'

What was holding them up was Alexandra's last-minute decision that Olga should not be the daughter to accompany her to Moscow. 'Olga's the eldest, and has the most authority with Colonel Kobilinski,' she argued feverishly. 'With Baby ill, she's the right one to take the responsibility. Olga and Tania, together, can manage the whole household and look after Baby too. Olga, what do you think yourself? Shouldn't Marie be the one to come with papa and me?'

'As you wish, mother; only the Commissar did say it should be me.'

'As if it mattered!' her mother said impatiently. 'He only meant one of you girls; any one. Papa and I alone will be expected to talk to this man Sverdlov and his confederates, neither you nor Prince Dolgoruki will be asked for your opinion. Marie, hurry and get ready to come with us. All the rest of you do what you can to help her.'

It was after three when Prince Dolgoruki came out and said that 'Their Imperial Majesties' were ready to start the journey. The *tarantasses*, rough Siberian springless carts in which two passengers and a driver could travel in discomfort, had been waiting in the yard for hours. The horses were brought out and backed in between the shafts, the mounts of the escort were led out of the stable. There were nearly two hundred of them now, for a detachment of Colonel Kobilinski's men had insisted on riding rearguard: they were openly suspicious of the strangers from Moscow.

Simon sat his horse with the reins gathered up in his left hand; his right arm, like his head, felt numb. He saw the servants putting a mattress into one of the carts. That would be for the Czarina to lie down on, with Olga sitting by her side. He was glad to see the servants had brought rugs and blankets too.

The Czar came out, looking up at the troopers with a vague smile. He was to travel alone in one *tarantass* with Commissar Yakovlev. Then the Czarina came, and her husband and Prince Dolgoruki helped her to her place. The doorway was suddenly filled with people watching them depart.

There was no sound in the courtyard where the snow mountain had stood, and which was now churned into mud by the horses' hoofs, except the faint jingling of their harness. Simon saw a tall shape in a long fur coat, heavily veiled against the sleet, climb into the *tarantass* beside the Czarina. He thought of the moment when dawn broke over the steppe and he would see Olga's face again. He wondered at what point along their eastward journey it would be safe to reveal himself to her.

Yakovlev got into the *tarantass* beside the man he had taken out of his prison-house, and a sergeant gave the words of command. Simon wheeled his horse, and gave one look backward at the lighted door.

It was then he saw Olga — not, as he had believed, on her way to safety, but standing with another girl's arm round her, and her own hand lifted in farewell. The shawl fell back from her fair short hair, and Simon saw his princess, at the breadth of a filthy yard; and as her hand went to her mouth he knew that she had seen him too. His impulse, the strongest impulse of his life, was to dismount and run to her side, to seize her and hold her against them all. But the column was moving through the open gates, and someone snatched at his reins and pulled his horse back into line. He had time for one look at the face of his idol, still beautiful to him, and then the breadth of the world was between them once again..

It was Tatiana's practical good sense which saved Olga from

complete collapse. Stunned by the glimpse of Simon, over-joyed that he had come to the very gates of her prison, she was yet more shaken by the knowledge that only her mother's in-curable meddling had prevented her from being on the dark road south with Simon now. But Tatiana had not recognised Simon Hendrikov, and she immediately drew her sisters back into the warm house.

'We can't do anything more to help them now,' she said. 'We must go to bed and try to get some sleep, there's a lot to do tomorrow morning.'

What there was to do occupied all the sisters fully. It con-sisted in looking through all the trunks in the attic, to which they had at last been allowed access on behalf of the travellers, and discovering how many of their garments and personal pos-session had been looted. They had few summer dresses or light shoes left, very little indeed but their heavy winter clothing, and spring was on its way. Hokriakov, challenged by Olga, told them their fancy clothes had been distributed among the workers whose need was greater than theirs.

'Do you think I believe that for a moment?' she said con-temptuously. 'Your soldiers stole our things and sold them to buy vodka.' It was only the intervention of Colonel Kobilinski, whom she had asked to be present, which prevented the Com-missar from striking her.

'Don't provoke them too far,' said Tatiana uneasily. She was making lists of what remained to them, always a congenial employment for Tatiana, but she was nearly as much on edge as Olga. The news coming in of flooding rivers and highways washed away made it seem as if a confrontation in Moscow was not the worst danger to be feared for their parents and Marie. It was a great relief when a telegram from Marie announced their arrival at the railhead at Tiumen, but then silence fell again, and there was no word that they had reached Moscow. There was no news at all until Colonel Kobilinski's men came back.

The commandant asked to see Olga alone, and told her their strange story. First, they said, Commissar Yakovlev had said they were to travel to Moscow by way of Omsk. It was not the direct way but it was a possible way, and nobody had ques-tioned the Special Commissar's decision.

'But he was taking them east instead of west,' interrupted Olga.

'Exactly, and if he could have got Their Majesties through Omsk he might have got them safely through to the Pacific. But sixty miles west of the town the train was stopped by members of the Omsk Soviet, and Yakovlev ordered to go no further. He said he only took his orders from Moscow and insisted on going into Omsk to telephone.'

'He was in constant touch with Moscow while he was here, I know.'

'In touch with President Sverdlov, every day. Oh, he had the right credentials, no doubt of that! So he went off to Omsk, with a Red Guards officer who had fallen sick along the way, to put the man in hospital. But he couldn't get round Sverdlov this time. He came back to the train, where the local Soviet was mounting guard, and said Comrade Sverdlov had ordered him to deliver his prisoners to the Soviet at Ekaterinburg, east of Tiumen.'

'And is that where they are now?'

'Presumably, but my men left them at Tiumen, and came back by road.'

'What an extraordinary story,' said Olga. 'First east, then west, and nowhere near Moscow. Eugene Stepanovich, I *know*, I feel certain that Yakovlev planned a rescue attempt. What do you think went wrong?'

Kobilinski hesitated. 'You know I'm no politician, Your Imperial Highness. But I'm inclined to think this man Yakovlev was double-crossed by Sverdlov — which means Lenin, of course. He obviously had their confidence up to a point, and as we know the German Ambassador has been bringing pressure to bear on the People's Commissars to get Their Majesties out of Tobolsk. So what was simpler than to let Yakovlev bring them away, and make sure he was intercepted, before he could move far in either direction, by one or other of the Ural Soviets?'

'That's just what frightens me,' said Olga, for the ferocity of the Ural Soviets was notorious. 'Oh, if they had been taken anywhere else than Ekaterinburg!'

Colonel Kobilinski tried to reassure her.

'Perhaps it's only a halt on the way to Moscow. We shall hear more in a day or two,' he said.

What the terrified girls heard was that their parents and Marie were imprisoned in a house called the Ipatiev Dom, and that Prince Dolgoruki had been arrested and taken away, for no reason given, as soon as the train reached Ekaterinburg. Yakovlev sent a telegram to Colonel Kobilinski which might have been entitled 'Failure of a Mission', for it read:

> Take the detachment with you
> and depart
> I have resigned
> and I am not responsible
> for any consequences

Across the steppes of Siberia summer followed winter in the course of one week, or so it seemed to the nomad tribes which resumed their wanderings, or to the townsfolk of Tobolsk watching the *Rus* cast off her moorings and set her course again down the mighty river.

In the governor's mansion all seasons were alike to the imprisoned. Alexis a little better, the rooms a little less icy, the snow in the yard all gone — these were the only perceptible differences. There was no longer any attempt at study, or acting plays, or the game of Happy Times. There was only an increasing fear of their jailers, whose severity increased with every day.

Colonel Kobilinski, heart-broken, was relieved of his command and ordered back to Petrograd. When he was gone the last check on the two Commissars was removed, and Hokriakov was ingenious in new harassments. One day he ordered the keys to be removed from all the doors, and the bedroom doors to be left ajar at all times. Often the girls awoke to hear the breathing of a soldier, standing still — more terrifying than a prowler — just inside their sleeping-room. The other Commissar, Rodionov, made a rule that none of the girls was to be seen at a window at any time; the sentries were given orders to fire if anyone was seen looking out.

Alexis was partly exempt from this ruling, because the Commissars allowed him to be wheeled to the window of his room and back again in his mother's old wheel-chair. They seemed to think that looking across the yard at the occasional passer-by would encourage him to start walking, but the fact was that although he wore the torturing leg brace for hours together, the child could hardly take a step alone. The news of his illness got out in the town, and although few of the citizens of Tobolsk came near the governor's mansion since the advent of the Red Guards from Omsk, one intrepid schoolboy was arrested in the act of climbing up to look over the stockade into the yard. His defence was that he wanted to see the poor little Czarevitch, who was so ill. He was taken out and shot.

Hokriakov had a congenial time cross-examining Alexis about a 'plot' between the two boys, and pointing out what happened to a brat who didn't obey the benevolent orders of the new revolutionary state. The former Heir to the Throne put an end to the scene with a good deal of dignity, by squaring his shoulders on the pillow and saying, 'Go away, please, you're making my head ache.' But he paid for it with a sleepless night, and his head was still aching next day. As he told Olga, he couldn't get that other boy out of his mind.

On a Sunday in May, two weeks after a sad, late Easter, when the doctors thought Alexis might be fit to be carried aboard the *Rus* in a few days, the two Commissars gave a final demonstration of their power. The priests and nuns who had been allowed to come on Sundays, to hold a service with the little household at an improvised altar in the drawing-room, were seized and stripped, on the grounds that they were carrying secret messages or firearms. The cries of the nuns and the coarse laughter of the soldiers conducting the search rang in the children's ears for hours, and when the time came for evening prayers the Commissars went on a new rampage. Through the house they went, tearing down the ikons from the bedroom walls and throwing them out of the windows with the valuable miniatures of her children which Alexandra had been forced to leave behind. Finally the ikon which had accompanied Alexis to the Stavka was wrenched off its hook and sent smashing into the hall with the lamp which had shone upon it all night long since the boy could remember anything at all. His sisters, herded into their bedroom by a grinning lout with a bayonet, heard Monsieur Gilliard remonstrating in his bad Russian, and Nagorny growling, and then the sound of one heavy blow. Who was the victim, they could only guess.

Tatiana and Anastasia undressed and fell asleep at last, while Olga lay down fully clothed upon her bed. She had kept some stubs of candle for emergencies, and by the light of one of them she studied Tatiana's lovely face and Anastasia's merry one, which looked older and more purposeful in sleep.

469

She thought of Marie at Ekaterinburg, and not for the first time she blamed herself that she had not overridden their parents' selfishness and accepted Boris Heiden's offer to get them all away to England while there was time. Or if, before the measles began, she had listened to Simon Hendrikov's advice to leave for the Crimea.

A faint scratching at the door, standing ajar, brought her off her bed in a moment. Nagorny or Gilliard — it had to be one or the other, and in the darkness she heard the sailor's voice.

'Your Imperial Highness!'

'Is it Alexis?'

'He's asking for you.'

'I'll get a candle.'

Shading it with her hand she crept out to the landing. In the faint light a bruise stood out upon Nagorny's cheek. Olga touched it very gently. The healthy blood had dried already, and the sailor dropped to his knees and kissed her hand. There was no sound in the house except the murmur of voices from the improvised guardroom at the door.

'What if they come upstairs?'

'They won't get past me if they do.'

'No, no, you must warn me, we can't have any trouble. Stay by the door, Nagorny — please!'

Olga slipped inside her brother's room. By the candlelight she could see him sitting up in bed, with the dog Joy looking warily from his basket at the far side of the room. She set the stump of candle in its saucer on the bedside table, dropped on her knees, and slid her arm round the boy's thin shoulders. 'You've brought a light, Olga,' he murmured. 'Oh, I'm so glad!'

'Sh-h, we mustn't talk too loud. What's the matter, darling — are you missing mámma?'

'You know I always miss her,' he said reproachfully. 'But — I got to feeling scared in the dark, without my ikon and my dear *lampadka!*'

'We heard them — taking it away, and we were all so sorry. But there's nothing to be scared about, Alexis; God doesn't need a lamp to see us by.'

'You believe that, don't you, Olga?'

'Absolutely.' She made her confession of faith with no sense that she was talking to a child. Alexis had taken another step

470

forward into manhood; even his voice seemed deeper, and the planes of the man's face were coming through the childish curves. His hair had not been cut since his illness began, and it fell over his brow and ears, the colour of a bright copper penny.

'Well, that's what I wanted to ask you about,' he said. 'Do you think God's angry with me now?'

'Angry with *you*? But why?'

'Because when I was hurting so, after I fell downstairs, I kept telling mamma I wanted to die, I wanted to die, and it isn't true! I want to live, Olga! I *don't* want to die!'

'You mustn't talk like that, not now, when you're getting better all the time. Think, in just a few days we'll be out on the river again, on our way to father and mother and Marie, and Nagorny and you will sit on deck and watch everything that happens on the steamer—'

'I want to live, even if I'll never be the Czar.'

Olga's head dropped on the pillow beside her brother's. Through tears, she heard him whisper, 'And I meant to be such a good Czar, and go down in history —'

'Did you, Alexis?'

'I meant to grant a constitution, and have Monsieur Rodzianko for my prime minister, like they do in England, and tell him to build hospitals and schools, and never, never go to war —'

The child's dream, she saw, had been very strong. He must have been dreaming it in the days of Dmitri's fantasy of putting her upon the throne, the days when in her headstrong way she had indulged the fantasy, telling herself that she was not her brother's keeper, and that if her father abdicated she would do whatever was best for Russia ... She saw now that the Empress Olga had never had a chance of reigning, any more than the Emperor Alexis: they were two leaves blown on the great gale of revolution which might some day sweep across the world.

'I wish you'd say something good to me now, like mamma does —'

'Oh, Alexis, I'm not nearly good enough myself.'

'You're my godmother, you should be able to say *something*.'

'Would you like us to say the Lord's Prayer together?'

471

'I've said it twice tonight already. Once with Nagorny, and once with Zilchik, after they took away my *lampadka*. Say some of that hymn you and Nastia made up, the one you wrote into that book mamma gave you at the New Year. The one about patience.'

'I can't remember all of it, but I'll try.' She heard Nagorny shift his position by the open door and knew that he was listening too.

> 'Give patience, Lord, to us Thy children,
> In these dark, stormy days to bear
> The persecution of our people,
> The tortures falling to our share.'

'Say about "the hour of utmost dread".'
Olga went on:

> 'Lord of the world, God of Creation,
> Give us Thy blessing through our prayer,
> Give peace of heart to us, O Master,
> This hour of utmost dread to bear.'

Her arm was growing cramped beneath the boy's weight now, light though it was; she moved slightly, and settled him more deeply on his pillows.

'They're going to kill us, aren't they?' he said.

'Oh, Alexis!'

'Will it hurt very much? Olga, what'll it be like to die?'

She was going to whisper something about saying a prayer, something better than her poor verses, but then Olga found the inspiration, or the grace, to say:

'Do you remember when you were so ill in the train, that time coming back from Mohilev, and they couldn't let you lie down flat in bed? Nagorny held you in his arms the whole night long, didn't he?'

'Yes, they told me afterwards: all night long.'

'I think when our time comes to die — when we're old, old men and women — it'll be just like that. Like being taken into very strong arms, and then held fast through the darkness.'

She felt his breathing relax, and Alexis said drowsily, 'Very strong arms, I like that. For all of us?'

472

'All of us.'

'Then I won't mind — so —'

By the candle flame she saw the dark lashes sweep his cheek as sleep descended. Very cautiously she took her arm away and blew out the light. Very gently she laid her forehead against one of the boy's long hands.

Am I my brother's keeper?

Yes.

CHAPTER TWENTY-EIGHT

WHEN the German Ambassador, whose help Alexandra Feodorovna had disdained, was shot dead in Moscow, it was the most discussed assassination — in Russia at least — since the now almost forgotten murders at Sarajevo. It started a series of reactions in the All-Russian Congress of Soviets, then in session in the new capital, and brought Lenin back to Petrograd for the first time since the seat of power shifted from the Smolny Institute to the Kremlin.

He was to speak in the Maly Theatre, and Mara Trenova saw the red flags going up round the railings of the Michael Square and in clusters at the windows of the Hotel Europa as she walked to work on a hot summer morning.

When the Smolny was dismantled the TEO had moved to temporary offices above a concert hall on a corner of the Nevski Prospekt not far from the Catherine Canal. The section was due to move to Moscow in September, but there were propaganda films in production and other projects to be completed before then, and the TEO was working at full-strength. There was little time for comradely greetings as the members arrived and settled down to work, and Mara was not aware of any special chill in the atmosphere as she hung up her jacket and knitted cap and went to her desk beside the window.

The premises were too small to be partitioned off, and several times during the morning, when Mara lifted her head from her work, she met the speculative gaze of the section chief, Ilya Korv, whose face was familiar wherever the new propaganda posters could be pasted up in Russia. He was a big fair man nearer fifty than forty whose humorous, kindly expression and powerful shoulders made him a natural model for the Productive Peasant, the Punctual Traindriver, and other mythic heroes of the new Russia.

When the morning's work was nearly over he crossed the room and perched on a corner of Mara's desk. 'You're down to see the rushes of the anti-Romanov picture at six o'clock, aren't you?' he began.

'Yes, *Coronets and Loving Hearts*. It's ready for subtitles, Maltsev said.'

'Any outside assignment before that? No? Then I'd like you to investigate the children's theatre show we've had complaints about over on Vassili Island. There's a performance at three o'clock.'

'That's the animal show.' Mara opened a letter file. ' "Subversive indoctrination . . . insults to Marxism and the heroes of the Winter Palace . . ." — that's pretty strong for poor old Rudov and his beasties!' She looked up with a smile, but Korv's grey eyes were cold. 'We've had three different complaints from citizens living in the Maly Prospekt,' he said. 'There must be something in it. Come and have your soup with me and let's talk.'

'All right.' Mara went to get her cap and jacket. Her summer suit of dark green linen was three years old and needed pressing, but it had been of fairly good quality to start with, and she looked better dressed than most of the women workers in *Narkompros*. The customers in the National Kitchen across the Prospekt were noticeably shabby, and in the hot, close room their infrequently washed clothes and bodies gave off a disagreeable smell. Mara's appetite was gone before she and Ilya Korv, after standing in line for ten minutes, secured bowls of beet soup and hunks of black bread, and looked around for seats.

'Over here,' said Korv, indicating two vacant stools at a table occupied by young soldiers of the new Red Army, sweating in their coarse grey uniforms. 'Aren't we going to sit with the others?' she said, for there was no canteen at the temporary office, and most of the workers ate their midday meal at the National Kitchen.

'We're all right here,' Korv smiled and nodded at the soldiers, who had stopped eating to stare at them. 'Before I forget, I've got kind remembrances to give you, from an old friend of yours I saw in Moscow.'

'Jacob Levin?'

'What put Levin into your head?'

'I saw his photograph in one of the Congress pictures. He was with the Presidium, only four seats away from Comrade Sverdlov — '

475

'Yes, he ranks high in the Moscow Soviet these days. But it wasn't Levin who sent his regards. It was Comrade Sergiev, who used to work with you on *Castle Comments*.'

'He was the copyboy on *Castle Comments,* when I was Levin's secretary.'

'He's a war correspondent for *Pravda* now.'

'I know, I've seen his by-line. Isn't it strange to be talking about war correspondents when only six months ago we were dedicated to eternal peace?'

Korv looked quickly at the soldiers. They had lost interest in the man and the girl and were deep in their own conversation. He said in a low voice, 'We're at war because of the Czarist counter-revolutionaries and their foreign allies. The Japanese are landing troops by the thousand, the Czechs are fighting all along the Trans-Siberian. Comrade Lenin himself has said our first task must be the creation of a mighty Socialist army —'

'And words like "motherland" and "patriotism" are respectable again.'

Ilya Korv sighed. 'Out of your own mouth,' he said. 'Comrade Mara, this is what I wanted to talk to you about. We held a meeting last night, after you left the office, to discuss your sarcastic criticisms of our just resistance to the foreign aggressors. Your fellow-workers feel that you are introducing a subversive element into our group which must not be allowed to develop into open dissidence. By a majority vote, I was elected to warn you accordingly.'

Mara's pale face had flushed an ugly red. 'What about the minority vote?' she asked. 'Was that in my favour?'

'On the contrary. The meeting was unanimous in its disapproval of your recent unco-operative attitude: the minority vote was for public reprimand. What I am giving you, as privately as possible, is an official warning.'

'A warning against what?'

'Comrade, listen to me. From the moment the Fifth Congress opened, according to every other member of the section, you championed the Social Revolutionary, Maria Spiridonova. Who consistently attacked Comrade Lenin in the vilest terms. I was there on the opening day, I heard her. She accused Lenin to his face of betraying the peasants and treachery to the nation in concluding peace with Germany. We know she sent

Blumkin to kill the German Ambassador in the hopes that Germany would be goaded into resuming the war with us — '

'We also know that Trotsky sent a Lettish regiment and a detachment of armoured cars to surround the SR party headquarters — '

'Because the SRs were planning a *coup d'état* to take the power from the people's leaders, and frustrate all the hopes of our glorious revolution.'

'You can't deny that Spiridonova has been absolutely consistent in her own beliefs,' said Mara.

'Spiridonova's beliefs have landed her in jail.'

'*What?*'

'She was arrested just before dawn this morning, and taken to prison in the Kremlin. Lenin will announce it in the Maly Theatre tonight ... Don't you want your bread? You musn't waste it.'

She dumbly pushed the hunk of bread across the table. The soldiers were getting up to leave, and shouldering their rifles and their packs.

'Why are you telling me this about Spiridonova now?'

'For your own good. I know, we all know, how much you used to admire her, and it's true she was a good revolutionary in her day. But now Maria Spiridonova has been declared an enemy of the state, and if you say one more word in her defence, you'll be dismissed from the People's Commissariat for Education.'

'I can get another job at *Pravda,* or *Rabochi Put.*'

'Nobody can move from job to job at his own free will. You might be put to work with the "mofectives" — the morally defective children. But more likely you'd be directed into a munition factory. Either way you'll have less time to spend at "The Red Sarafan", where it's reported that you're seen far too often — '

'Surely I can do what I like in my off-duty hours?'

'There are no off-duty hours for a good servant of the state. Now, Comrade Mara!' (for Korv saw tears of anger in her eyes) 'you *must* believe that I'm your friend. Last night I carried the majority with me when I proposed this warning should be given in private. I marked you for the children's assignment today so that you won't be in the office while you're so overwrought. Stay in the park all afternoon and think calmly over what I've said. Clear your mind of all subversive thoughts, and come to the meeting in the Maly prepared to give a hero's welcome to Lenin.'

Ilya Korv smiled, his poster smile, so natural, which brought out the laughter wrinkles at the corners of his eyes. One of his large hands, still calloused from his beginnings as a sheet metal operative at the great Putilov Works, closed over the girl's clasped hands. 'Good comrades both?' he said.

'Good comrades ... You're very kind, Korv. I wish I had met someone like you when I was young.'

The man laughed. 'How old are you, Comrade Mara?'

'Twenty-three.'

'I'm more than twice your age.' He patted her hands, and released them. 'Poor child, you've missed your father.'

Mara Trenova walked slowly away towards the Neva. Too stunned by the news from Moscow to be aware of the passersby, she noted automatically that pictures of Lenin, clenched fist raised above cloth cap, were being pasted on the billboards which stood outside such overspill government offices as the TEO. Far down the Morskaia she saw the red flags at the windows of the old General Staff Headquarters. Just over the Police Bridge, outside the cinema, there were coloured posters called 'The Workers Fight Against Foreign Aggression!' — the model was Ilya Korv in a workman's shirt and trousers, his sleeves rolled up over his powerful forearms, with a hammer raised to strike.

The children's theatre accused of subversion was at some distance, in a shabby park on the Maly Prospekt in the centre of Vassili Island. It could be reached directly by the Sixteenth Line off the University Quay, but Mara had time to kill, and she instinctively headed towards the Fourth Line, which she knew so well. She passed the corner where she had stood to watch the Grand Duchess Olga pass, on her way from launching the *Poltava* three years earlier, and walked into the empty roadway to calculate the distance, as she had done then. Ten paces exactly from the pavement to the carriage. You couldn't hit a barn door at ten paces, said that ornament of the Presidium, Jacob Levin. You couldn't pull the trigger, could you now?

Each flat in the Fourth Line had been divided up for

workers' families, and lines of shabby washing adorned most of the balconies. Across the middle of the street, strung between two tall lime trees, was a grimy banner, red lettering on white, announcing that 'The Rule of the Proletariat is the Death of the Bourgeois Horde!' It was a slogan now to be seen in every propaganda hall in Russia, and must have been displayed in the Fourth Line as part of the May Day celebrations. One end of the banner was attached to the tree outside what had been the Hendrikovs' living-room window.

Now who would have thought that Plain Joe Calvert, always so correct and cautious, would be the man to put his hand in the fire for the friend who had cut him out with Dolly Hendrikova? Mara had not forgotten Joe's brief appearance at the Smolny. It had brought her the fresh breath of a different way of life and a recollection of old times. From then, she dated the overt criticism of the regime which now threatened her with relegation to a *Rabfak* or the instruction of 'mofective' children, and her increasing disillusionment with Lenin. Lenin who, gossip said, had done a deal with Plain Joe Calvert and had been outwitted by the Americans. Lenin, who had sent Maria Spiridonova back to the prison where the Czar had kept her.

She came to the park at last. There was a sign above the gate picked out in electric light bulbs, meant to be switched on when electricity supplies permitted, which made one of the favourite Bolshevik statements: 'Children are the Flowers of Life'. So many bulbs were missing that the sign read Chi r n are t Flowe s of L e, and the flowers themselves looked pale and woefully undernourished as they went along the dusty path leading to the children's theatre.

It had been opened by an old star of the circus, long famous for his animal acts, in a tumbledown wooden hut which might once have held the gardeners' implements. Rudov himself, whom Mara remembered seeing as a child, was taking the money at the door, and for the price of admission — thirty kopecks only — she received, instead of a ticket, a small bag of carrots chopped in rings and a sprig of parsley. This, no doubt, was the 'counter-revolutionary waste of food' mentioned in one of the letters of complaint.

Inside the hut, Mara found herself one of the few adults present. The benches were crammed with children, keyed up to an anticipation which broke into applause when a bear cub

479

dressed in a blue smock climbed up to the stage and made them a courtly bow. Then he pulled a cord to display a curtain bearing the title of the show, which was 'Hares of All Lands, Unite!' and a hare appeared, holding up a book with wooden pages, entitled in huge letters *Das Kapital*.'

This was the signal for the cub to pull a second curtain, revealing a stage set of the Winter Palace and the Palace Square. The palace was manned by an army of rabbits, wearing hats and holding rifles, whose sensitive noses twitched anxiously as they peered out of the windows at the empty square. The hare holding *Das Kapital* turned the wooden pages with a sound like a clapper, which was the signal for an army of twenty hares, hatless, to appear from the wings and storm the palace. They dragged in miniature cannon, which let off cannon balls; the rabbits replied with rifle fire from the windows. After much firing, and frantic cheering from the audience, the rabbits laid down their rifles and surrendered, and the victorious hares, having occupied the Winter Palace, raised the red flag from the roof. The bear cub repeated his performance with the curtains, and all the actors streamed into the auditorium to receive the carrots and parsley, and many caresses, from the hands of the delighted children.

The whole thing was over in about half an hour. Rudov told Mara it would be repeated twice more that day. The old clown spoke ingratiatingly, as he would never have done when he was one of the kings of the Russian circus, billed as The Inimitable Rudov; she suspected that he guessed from her workmanlike suit, and the heavy satchel slung from her shoulder, that she represented some sort of officialdom. 'I hope the lady enjoyed herself?' he said anxiously, and spoke about his animals, and the patience required to train them. She congratulated him and walked away. There was a stone seat near the entrance where it was possible to write her notes.

It would have been so easy to send in the kind of report the letter-writing busybodies wanted, about the reduction of a great national event to the level of a circus trick, and so on — a report which would probably have added Rudov to the bursting population of the Shpalernaia prison. Instead, Mara began, 'For thirty kopecks, the price of a cup of tea at a National Kitchen, the lucky children of Petrograd are able to see, at the Rudov Theatre in the Vassili Park, a remarkable dual illus-

tration of Pavlov's theory of conditioned reflexes and Meyerhold's principle of audience participation.' That was the
carrots and parsley, of course, but it would do the trick, it was
just the sort of pompous rubbish to be acceptable at *Narkompros*. She wrote a full page of description and praise, omit-
ting any reference to *Das Kapital*, and ending with the words,
'This is a delightful entertainment for young people, and if
there were more shows like it there would be fewer mofective
children in Petrograd.' She had to substitute 'Petrograd' for
'St. Petersburg' at the end of her report.

Later, after long wanderings through the park and the grass-
grown streets of the Island, she returned to the empty TEO
office and laid it on Ilya Korv's desk for him to read next
morning. She had heard his voice when she passed the open
door of the concert hall, and knew that he was there already,
with Maltsev, the producer of a movie of which she knew
nothing but the title. *Coronets and Loving Hearts* — it was an
exposé of imperial vice, she had been told. If so, the title was
far too complimentary.

About twenty people were scattered about the concert hall,
which had been used for some time to show the rushes of
TEO's propaganda films. *Coronets* began on time, with the
symbols of Czarist oppression she herself had chosen coming
up on the crawl sheet, over the credits: the knout, the
handcuffs, the chained prisoners toiling across the snows of
Siberia. Then came the opening shots of the four Grand Duchesses, dissolves from their photographs in court dress, taken
together and separately. The photographs were completely out
of date, having been taken before the war, so that Anastasia
appeared as quite a small girl, but they made the point of
elegance and luxury, complemented by a background of sofas
with satin cushions, fur rugs, and vases full of exotic flowers.
The two younger girls wore white ribbons in their flowing hair,
and only Olga and Tatiana were wearing coronets. But when
the film proper began it was clear that, if not the coronets, the
'loving hearts' were applicable to all four: it was simply a pornographic movie of the sexual promiscuity of the former
Grand Duchesses.

Mara was sitting at one side of the room, at a table with a
lamp just strong enough to light the page of her reporter's
notebook. It made her conspicuous in the dark hall, and she

saw one or two men turning to look at her, as if wondering what a young woman's reactions would be to the perversions on the screen. The producer had employed four actresses, each with a faint resemblance to one of the Grand Duchesses, and by a skilful use of make-up, had made that resemblance more positive. It was quite clear who they were meant to be, and clarity was assured by repeated cuts to the original photographs. The effect of the total sexual commitment of the girls — shown copulating with grooms, footmen, sailors, guardsmen, inevitably with Rasputin and ultimately with animals — was greatly heightened by the contrast between the four innocent, girlish faces of the real photographs and the indiscriminate whoring on the screen.

When the lights went up at the end of twenty minutes there was a good deal of applause, but the clapping was slow and lazy, as if it came from lax hands; and the spectators rose and moved away with curious, satiated lassitude. Ilya Korv's face, when he came up to Mara's table, was no longer the humorous kindly face of the Ideal Worker, but slack-lipped and moist with sweat.

'Strong stuff, eh, Trenova?' he said, and squeezed her arm. She shut her notebook hastily: she had written only a few words.

'It should have an excellent effect,' she said primly, and some man guffawed in the background.

'I'll want your subtitles in the morning, Trenova,' said the producer. 'I want to rush a print straight to Ekaterinburg.'

'We must arrange a showing in the House of Special Purpose,' said Korv with a laugh. 'Don't be late for the rally, Comrade Mara.'

'What's the House of Special Purpose?' Mara asked.

'It's where Nicholas the Bloody and his brats are locked up at Ekaterinburg.'

'Why do they call it that?'

'Use your imagination, Trenova!'

Korv turned away with his arm round Maltsev's shoulders, and Mara was free to go to the dreadful lavatory and retch. She had eaten nothing since the soup, and her empty stomach was contorted by the spasms induced by utter disgust, shot through with the recognition of personal guilt. What she had seen on the screen was very little worse than the cartoon strip she herself had devised of Rasputin's violation of Olga; only the animation, and the inclusion of the younger girls, and above all the bestiality made it worse. And Lenin himself had called the cinema 'the great medium of the future' — Lenin, who had consigned those girls to a house whose sinister purpose was clear enough. He means to have them all killed in cold blood, she thought. As tomorrow he may order the execution of Spiridinova.

It was impossible to think of returning to her wretched home. She went instead, and as an act of defiance, to 'The Red Sarafan', where there was always company. But when she got there a young man was reciting a poem by Blok, and she sat down to listen:

> Rancour, rancour to make one weep,
> To make one's blood seethe in dismay,
> Rancour sanctified, rancour black and deep,
> Comrade, on this day – vigil keep!

A waitress lounged up to Mara's table and asked what she wanted to drink. It was this girl who was later to depose that 'Trenova had been drinking heavily', though in fact she only drank two vodkas at 'The Red Sarafan'. But Mara was not used to vodka, and the drinks went quickly to her head.

> To bring all bourgeois to ruination
> We'll fan a world-wide conflagration.
> World conflagration, fed by blood,
> Bless us, O Lord!

The performance was over; it had been a day of performances. Blok, and Hares of the World, and something she had to write sub-titles for. She opened her satchel and felt for her thick notebook. She had rammed it far down in the bag, upon the detritus of labour card, ration book, accreditations and identity papers, and all the TEO pamphlets she was obliged to carry. Mara rummaged in the darkness and came upon something cold and hard. It was the loaded Mauser she had carried through the two revolutions.

She laid the pistol on top of all the layers of papers and took out her notebook. The waitress, bringing the second vodka, saw that Mara Trenova was writing busily, like so many of the failed writers who used the ambience of 'The Red Sarafan' to bolster their misfit personalities. Nobody paid any attention when the scribbled page was crumpled up and dropped beneath the table. But it was retrieved and produced later as proof of her mental derangement: instead of sub-titles for 'a valuable cultural film' it was scribbled over with the words: 'Bread, peace, freedom = Famine, war, oppression' followed by 'Blood and rancour = Leninleninlenin.'

Mara had promised to be in time for the rally, and she was. She went no further than the foyer of the Maly Theatre, where her press card, and her reporter's notebook, gave credibility to her statement that she was covering Comrade Lenin's arrival for the TEO. Ilya Korv and his whole section were already seated, and nobody challenged Mara Trenova's right to be there. A thin girl in a green suit, with an open satchel swinging from her shoulder, attracted nobody's attention.

Lenin, who had enough German blood to hate the feckless Russian unpunctuality, arrived on time. He stopped in the doorway of the Maly to greet the chairman of the Petrograd Soviet, who had organised the rally, between the evening sunlight in the Michael Square, filled with cheering people, and the bright foyer. He was about ten paces away from the half-educated, bitter and frustrated girl whose hero worship had turned to rancorous disappointment in him and in the world. He was the perfect target whom her first owner, Jacob Levin, had trained and taunted her to kill, except that Levin had been thinking of the old Czar and not the new.

'You couldn't pull the trigger, could you now?'

She took the pistol from her open bag and snapped off the safety catch. It was heavy in her hand, too heavy, but there was no time to worry about that. She pulled the trigger at ten paces and saw blood streak out on Lenin's big bald head. Then the rain of blows upon her own head and body felled her to the ground.

When Mara Trenova fully recovered consciousness she knew that she was in the Fortress of St. Peter and St. Paul. She had become aware of that hours earlier, when the quarter chime of 'Lord, have mercy upon us' began to penetrate her coma, and she even knew, from what the warders said as they dragged her back from her summary trial, that she was in the Trubetzkoi bastion. It was the strongest place in the entire prison, reserved for the chief enemies of the state. The Dekabrists had preceded her here, and the assassins of Alexander II; Anna Virubova had spent months in the bastion, listening as Mara was listening to the sound of lapping water from the Neva running just under the level of the ventilators. To have achieved imprisonment in the Trubetzkoi must be accounted Mara Trenova's last success. She already knew from the charge read at her trial, indicting her for 'the *attempted* murder of Vladimir Ilyich Lenin', that she had been in that, as in so much else, a failure. Bruised from head to foot by her beating, held up between two warders, she remembered little else of the summary court, except that her only words of defence had been 'I am Ivan Trenov's daughter!' and that she had felt a cloudy, professional indignation that her name was being mispronounced Ternova.

The cell was in total darkness, broken only by a ray of light from the corridor, coming through the warders' spyhole. They had taken everything away from her except her stained and torn clothing, her satchel and the gun as a matter of course, and even her watch and her mother's wedding ring. But when she was able to lift her head from the pillow stuffed with seaweed, and sit up on the iron bed built, like the table, into the wall of her cell, Mara knew what time it was: the cathedral bells so far above her dungeon were chiming the midnight *Kol slaven*, 'How glorious is our Lord in Sion', which none of Russia's new masters had yet thought to stop.

She felt her way to the iron washstand and splashed her face with cold water she found there. She had a premonition, as the midnight chime brought the sound of movement all through the Trubetzkoi bastion, that she would never hear the cathedral chimes again. When the four armed men came in, carrying chains and lanterns, Mara felt only thankfulness that they were disposing of her quickly. There would not be another day of the terrible interrogation to make her name her accomplices in the 'plot'.

> I have lost my way
> This is the wrong city and the wrong midnight –

These were the only words Mara could recollect when she

was led out with a line of the condemned of that day, although one older woman seemed to be praying, and two men in the tattered remnants of the Horse Guards uniforms were muttering the words of the old national anthem. They were taken into a little yard in the heart of the fortress, with the blank wall of the Mint on the right and the Trubetzkoi bastion on the left, like a great squat blockhouse behind its palisade. Then she realised that facing them was a line of Red Guards armed with rifles, and like the other woman she began to scream and struggle, writhing in her chains. She was aware that someone was tying a cloth over her eyes, and in that darkness the words of the *kontakion*, which she had heard and mocked so often came back to her and destroyed her illusion that she was dying a martyr's death:

> All we go down to the dust
> And weeping o'er the grave we make our song:

The rifles blazed out across the prison yard —

> *Alleluia! Alleluia! Alleluia!*

CHAPTER TWENTY-NINE

WHILE Lenin was recovering from the shallow scalp wound received in the foyer of the Maly Theatre, it was announced that his would-be assassin, now executed, was a counter-revolutionary and White agent. Her name was variously given in the newspapers as Martha or Maria Ternova, an accomplice of the woman Spiridonova who had instigated the murder of the German Ambassador. On the principle of guilt by association, all 'Ternova's' former colleagues were assigned to other employment, in the war factories or the institution for defective children.

By that time the Romanov family had been united for about six weeks, and the group left behind at Tobolsk had almost forgotten the nightmare of their journey to Ekaterinburg.

The trip downriver to Tiumen had been quite different from their first journey on the *Rus*. Alexis had to be carried aboard, and so far from moving about the ship or even sitting on deck to watch the passing scenery, he was locked in a cabin with Nagorny and made to stay there for the whole two days. Olga and her sisters were a little better off, because they had a new companion: Baroness 'Isa' Buxhoeveden, who courageously followed them to Tobolsk and then was forbidden to visit them, was at last allowed to join the sisters on their journey to Ekaterinburg. She had much to hear from them, and also much to tell of what she had gathered in Tobolsk. Commissar Yakovlev, forced to abandon his charges to the Ural Soviet, had courageously gone on to Moscow and confronted Sverdlov with a complaint of what he called contradictory orders. He had not been punished for his boldness, for he was seen drinking with Sverdlov that same night, but it was later given out that he had defected, and was fighting with the White Army raised by Admiral Kolchak.

Olga listened to this with interest and hope. It was clear from all Isa said that the townspeople of Tobolsk had taken Yakovlev at his face value as a Special Commissar, and the men who accompanied him had attracted no attention in the town. If he had succeeded in joining the Whites, it was possible that Simon had done so too, and would at least be among his own kind; she was burning with impatience to see and question Marie. Meantime, Isa's courageous presence was a great help. She had not been crushed by imprisonment like Countess Gendrikova and Mademoiselle Schneider, and was able to cheer up these old friends. The gentlemen admired her, and as the *Rus* made her way downstream there was a spurt of renewed hope in the tiny court surrounding the former Grand Duchesses.

It was extinguished at Tiumen. There for the first time the three girls and Alexis were exposed to the fury of an angry crowd as they made their way, carrying as much of the luggage as they could, from the steamer to the train. Members of the local Soviet wanted to arrest them and try them for treason on the spot, and the squad of soldiers conducting them to Ekaterinburg had to push their way through the crowd with fixed bayonets. The Tiumen Reds had made sure that no luxuries nor even comforts would be provided in the grimy fourth-class carriages into which the Romanov party was pushed. The cushions they brought with them had to be laid along one wooden seat for Alexis, while the girls and Nagorny sat, uncomfortably close, on the opposite side.

The older ladies, with General Tatischev and the two tutors, were herded into another fourth-class carriage, and forbidden to talk to 'Nicholas the Bloody's youngsters'. Before the wood-burning train started its two hundred mile journey across the steppe their hearts were wrung to hear Alexis crying and asking for a drink of boiled water. There was none to be had, and no water in the lavatory: hot, hungry and miserably uncomfortable the boy and his sisters were slowly carried west.

'Ekaterinburg at last! Wake up, Alexis!' said Olga cheerfully, when the outskirts of the town were seen in the late afternoon of the second day. The boy had been dozing, with his head in Anastasia's lap; he sat up drowsily and rubbed his eyes.

'Will papa and mamma be at the station to meet us?' he asked. He was evidently thinking of Czarskoe Selo and the imperial comings and goings, with the station staff bowing, hats in hand, and the limousines waiting beside the neat flower-beds outside.

'Oh, I shouldn't think so. They'll be waiting at the Ipatiev House, all ready to give us a nice tea, I hope ... What is it, Tania?' Her sister was worriedly consulting one of her neatly written lists.

'What *I* hope is that we'll be able to have baths and change into fresh clothing,' said Tatiana. 'All the underwear was packed in the Vuitton trunk. And I'm nearly sure I saw it left behind on the platform at Tiumen.'

'I bet those horrible people robbed us right and left,' said Anastasia.

'Never mind, we know where the most important things of all are,' said Olga, and the sisters exchanged glances. Every jewel they possessed had been carefully sewn into the hems and seams of the skirts and jackets they were wearing.

'We're stopping! But there isn't any platform! Oh, bother, they're taking us into the freight yard!' They were all talking at once, as the train shunted backwards and forwards, over-shooting the points, so that baggage fell off the racks in all directions, until it came to a halt at last in the grimy locomotive yards outside the town of Ekaterinburg. A detachment of Red Guards, walking along the track, told the passengers roughly to get away from the windows and pull down the shades 'if you know what's good for you'.

'When may we get out?' Olga asked.

'When we say so, citizeness, and it won't be until the coast's clear. There's people in this town would like to tear you murderers limb from limb.'

'I don't believe I ever killed anything bigger than a fly,' said Anastasia in a small voice, after the patrol had gone by. 'Oh, Olga, I do so want to be with papa and mamma and Marie!'

'We'll have to be patient a little while longer, sweetie.' And all Olga could do was to set them an example, for their patience wore very thin as the long light evening turned at last to darkness, and still they remained in the locked coach, waiting for release. Nobody bothered to tell them that the inhabitants of Red Ekaterinburg had been roused against them, not only by the local Soviet, which was violently Bolshevik, but by the arrival of five hundred Kronstadt sailors, who had been drinking and terrorising the town for days. Nobody told them that fighting had broken out in Siberia between the Red Army and a large, well-disciplined body of Czech prisoners of war, big enough to form an army corps, who wanted to go back to Europe and fight the Germans but were perfectly willing to remain in Russia and fight the Reds. This new phase of the civil war had further enraged the people against their former Little Father the Czar, the man they held responsible for all their miseries.

His son and daughters were not allowed to leave the train until next morning. They plucked up hope when they saw a line of one-horse cabs, drawn by wretched animals, creeping into the freight yard, and Olga, risking a shout or even a shot, put her head out of the window to see what was happening.

'There's a soldier getting into the carriage where Isa and Nastia are,' she reported. 'Oh, I hope they're allowed to come and join us now!'

But the Red officer, accompanied by a suspicious Commissar of the local Soviet, was making other arrangements for the former ladies-in-waiting, and comparing a file of photographs in his hand with the anxious faces in front of him.

'Sophia Buxhoeveden, Pierre Gilliard, Sidney Gibbs. You, and you, and you. Take your stuff and get out of the train, you're free to go. Don't you understand me, citeeness? Go to any damned place you want to; you're no further concern of ours. Now the woman with the German name — you, Schneider — and Anastasia Gendrikova, and Tatishev, former general — you with the beard — you're under arrest. Leave your luggage, you won't be needing it again.'

'Lieutenant,' said the old general sturdily, as the horrified women began to cry, 'I am entirely at your disposal. But these two ladies have done nothing to deserve arrest, any more than I have. Take me if you must, but let them go free.'

The Commissar took Nastia's trembling chin in a hard grip. 'This here's not a bad-looking lass,' he said. 'What would you do with yourself if I let you go, my dear?'

The gentle young countess drew herself up and said very clearly, 'Serve my empress till the day I die!'

'Take them away.'

The Romanovs were hustled from the train after the three prisoners were removed, and the three so inexplicably set free watched in horror as they saw Tatiana stumble and fall, trying to keep Jimmy the Pekinese in her arms and carry a heavy suitcase at the same time, and Anastasia, equally burdened, keeping tight hold of Joy the spaniel's lead. They heard the cry of execration which went up from the crowd mobbing the freight yards as the cabs drove away. They saw the suitcases and trunks taken from the baggage car and dragged along the ground, bursting open even before the crowd rushed in to loot them, snatching at clothes and boots and books indiscriminately, and literally tearing the fur coats apart. One packing case contained letters, no doubt treasonable, and therefore to be handed over to the Soviet for despatch to Moscow, but when all the letters were found to be in English interest waned, and they were scattered like confetti about the yard. A fine rain finally dampened the popular enthusiasm. The letters in Alexandra Feodorovna's clear, elegant penmanship were trodden deep into the mud. They were all letters she had written to her husband at the Stavka, and taken by him to Tobolsk, and on one, which fluttered in the Siberian wind longer than the others, could have been read the words:

... the Czar rules and not the Duma! Please, my Nicky, Russia's saviour, be agooweeone and keep Stürmer and Protopopov, Our Friend advises it ... and remember me loves oo, Little Boy Blue.

'Oh, my Olga, my first-born darling, my good, brave girl! I knew you'd take care of the others, and bring them safe to me!'

For once Alexandra's emotionalism did not jar on Olga, as she clasped the weeping, white-haired woman in her arms. For once she did not feel that Alexandra was the child, and she the mother, when after the long strain of the journey from Tobolsk she gave the burden back to the hands which first had ruled her life. In that greeting, that embrace, the mother and daughter were closer than ever before, and the frictions of the four war years were all but forgotten.

They were all tearful and emotional when the girls ran into the Ipatiev house, Nagorny following with Alexis in his arms, and it was not until he had been thoroughly kissed and cried over that the boy exclaimed,

'But where's Zilchik?'

'Yes, what have you done with them all?' said Nicholas cheerfully.

'Aren't they here already?' said Olga blankly. 'We saw three of them going away with the soldiers.'

'They'll be here any minute,' said Marie.

'Or else they've been taken to another house,' said Tatiana. 'Remember, they weren't allowed to live in our house at Tobolsk.'

'Perhaps Nagorny can tell us something — '

But the sailor had been too occupied with 'His Imperial Highness' to pay any attention to the older ladies and gentlemen.

'We'll hear in the morning,' said Tatiana firmly. She was determined not to let their reunion be spoiled by worry. But they never saw their friends again, for General Tatischev, the countess, and Miss Schneider, were taken to join Prince Dolgoruki in prison, and from there they were all taken to be shot. As for Monsieur Gilliard, he and the English tutor and Baroness 'Isa' lived at the freight yard for ten days, until they were thrown out of the town, sleeping in one stationary train after another, and by day visiting the British consul in an attempt to get help to the Romanov family. It was hopeless; there were ten thousand Soviet soldiers in Ekaterinburg.

But on the first night the family could keep up a pretence that everything was going to be all right, even though the newcomers quailed at the sight of the guards, indoor and outdoor, who occupied all the ground floor of the Ipatiev house. There was a cellar below that, so far unoccupied, and above were the five rooms allocated to the family, Dr. Botkin, and their few remaining servants. The windows were covered with whitewash, and a high stockade had been built right round the house.

'It's a real prison, isn't it?' said Olga to Marie. It was difficult to find privacy anywhere in five crowded rooms, and the four girls were once again to share a bedroom, but Tatiana and Anastasia were with their parents in their room, and Nagorny was putting Alexis to bed.

Marie shook her curly head. 'It's pretty bad,' she admitted. 'You'll hate the Commissar, Avdiev — he's drunk half the time, and even when he's not he's so insulting! He comes in when we're eating, and takes food off our plates with his dirty hands, and says we must learn to share it with our betters — '

'Oh, horrors!'

'The guards are beastly too. They shout dirty words at us when we go out —'

'Oh, we *do* go out?'

'For an hour in the afternoon. But it's really pleasanter to stay indoors.'

'I can imagine.'

'Olga dear, you look so tired. Why don't you lie down for a little while?'

'Not when I've got you all to myself. Marie, tell me, darling, did you know Simon Karlovich was with Yakovlev's men?'

Marie looked quickly at the half-closed door. There was the usual soldier lurking in the hall.

'I've been wondering if *you* knew,' she said. 'I didn't dare to write.'

'I saw him right at the end, just as you went away. Marie, when did *you* see him — or did he speak to you?'

'Yes, he did. It was at the last *isba* we stopped at before we got to Tiumen. It was morning, still very dark, and papa and mamma were indoors having coffee. I went out to the *tarantass* for something mamma wanted, and suddenly he was right there beside me, with the muffler, like they all wore, pulled away from his face. I knew him at once, but I didn't dare speak, there were so many of them around, so I just smiled. And Simon said, very quick and low, 'Tell her I adore her, and I'll try again,' and that was all.

'Oh, Marie, you darling! Oh, how marvellous to get his message! How I wonder where he is, and what he's doing now!'

Marie looked troubled. 'Olga, I hate to tell you this, but Simon was left behind at Omsk. He got ill, he must have been ill that day outside Tiumen, because he was the one who was taken into Omsk when Yakovlev went in to telephone. And I'd got quite friendly with some of the soldiers by that time — they told me the man who went off in the car was coming down with typhus.'

'With typhus — and all alone at Omsk! Marie, he may be *dead* by this time! Oh, Simon, I'll never see you again —' Olga burst into tears, and Marie stood aghast. In more than a year of imprisonment she had never seen her eldest sister cry.

'Olga, please don't, you mustn't, or you'll set us all off, you know you will! Olga, you've been so brave, and stood up to

493

everything — can't you just be happy with his message, and knowing he came all that way to see you, and that he wanted so much to try again?'

Olga held out her hand for a handkerchief. 'I'm sorry, Marie,' she said. '. . . I thought all the loving was knocked out of me. But I was wrong.'

'At least you've known that a man loves you. We never did.'

'Oh, Marie!' Olga's eyes were still full of tears. But she made a great effort; Marie was right, they mustn't all start crying on this happy evening of their reunion. She dried her eyes, and combed her short fair hair. There had been no hope of a bath, of course, and the Vuitton trunk was certainly missing: she would have to put on a clean cotton dress over the garments she had travelled in.

'What wardrobes!' she said, trying to be natural, nodding at the built-in cupboards in the corners of the room. 'Right up to the ceiling. We'll have to stand on your shoulders, Mashka, if we want to get at the top shelves.'

'It's a queer house altogether, the Ipatiev Dom.'

'I *thought* that was what they called it, you've all said so in your letters. But the man at the station called it something else — '

'Did he, Olga? It's called the Ipatiev House because a man called Ipatiev built it, they moved him out to put us in.'

'Yes, but after we got out of the train I heard the commissar tell the cab driver to take us to the House of Special Purpose — have you ever heard it called that, Marie?'

'Sometimes.'

'What do you suppose it means?'

'I'm afraid to ask.'

Gradually and painfully, they settled down to life in the House of Special Purpose. They were all up and dressed by eight o'clock for an inspection by the Commissar, Avdiev, who drunk or sober insisted on a head count every morning. After that, with any luck, they were given black coffee and stale bread for breakfast, and occupied themselves as best they could until two in the afternoon, the appointed time for the main meal of the day. Sometimes it did not arrive till four or five, for although they had a cook and a kitchen boy in their own service, there was nothing to be cooked: the food was brought in from a Soviet communal kitchen, and sometimes sampled — or even spat in — by the guards. Nicholas and the girls walked up and down the yard in the afternoon, when their vision was extended to include the red flag flying on the roof of the house where they were imprisoned, and a cross surrounded by machine guns on the dome of the Church of the Ascension in a neighbouring square. They listened, sometimes gratefully, to the sounds of life and freedom going on all around them. Ekaterinburg was a busy place, a mining town built for the most part of wooden one storey houses, but having in the centre the spacious homes, surrounded by gardens, of the men who had made fortunes in the gold and platinum mines of the Urals. The town was entirely in the hands of the Communists. The leading hotel, called the American House, was the head-quarters of the Cheka, and it was a Cheka man, Jakob Yurovski, who presently replaced Avdiev in charge of the prisoners.

Whether Avdiev or Yurovski was the Commissar in charge, the guards themselves were equally intolerable. They were drawn from the local factory workers, bloodthirsty and rancorous to the last degree, and they persecuted their charges, the girls especially, by every means in their power. Olga and her sisters had become accustomed at Tobolsk to the men prowling round their rooms at night: at Ekaterinburg the orderly officer made the rounds of the house twice every hour during the night, and the other twelve men of the inner guard were free to come and go as they pleased through the family rooms. Here, too, there was a new humiliation: each prisoner had to be accompanied to the lavatory by a grinning and interested member of the guard. It was too much for Anastasia, who returned from the first such expedition in floods of tears.

'Imp, darling,' Olga comforted her, 'try not to think it matters. They're only animals, just poor resentful dogs, and you wouldn't mind Jimmy or Joy coming into the lavatory with you — would you?'

'A — dog wouldn't stare at you, and say such awful things —'

'I know, it's horrible, but just pretend they aren't there. Look through them, that's what I do! They're punishing us because we were born Romanov, all right, let's *be* Romanovs!

495

Chin up, Anastasia! Each one from now on pretends she's Catherine the Great!'

It helped a little. They were OTMA again, a closed corporation, walking up and down the yard arm in arm, four abreast, ignoring the catcalls and obscenities of the men on duty. They took turns in amusing Alexis, whose spirits were very low. The faithful Nagorny was the first of their sad little company to go, for Nagorny struck a guard intending to steal a gold chain with images belonging to Alexis, and for that the penalty was death. They tried to keep it from Alexis, but he guessed, and Olga could only be thankful that their mother was there to pet and coax her 'Sunbeam', and assure him that his dear Nagorny was safe, safe for ever, having only gone ahead of them for a little while.

Olga saw with awe that Alexandra Feodorovna had come to terms with death. She was grateful whenever a priest of the Orthodox faith was allowed to come to them, and scrupulous in the forms of the morning and evening prayers, but the old religious fanaticism, the mystic longings Rasputin had known how to exploit, seemed to have dropped away. With a beautiful and inspiring serenity and faith she waited for whatever the future might bring. Her husband's ties to earth were stronger. He still believed in the possibility of a rescue, and at the end of June kept his family up and fully dressed for several nights, on the strength of a letter signed 'Officer' which the cook had smuggled in to him. It gave some explicit plans for an escape, but whether it was in earnest or a cruel hoax they never knew.

Olga felt this episode most cruelly, because it raised her hopes that Simon Hendrikov had come to Ekaterinburg and meant to try again. With half her mind she knew it was a fantasy, for if Simon was still alive he might well be in a Bolshevik prison, but she clung obstinately to her dream of Young Lochinvar and to the message he had whispered to Marie. When their father, after several wakeful nights, had to admit that no help was coming, she said sadly to her sister:

'It's no use, Mashka, it was just another wild idea, like the Brotherhood of St. John of Tobolsk. Nobody can get us out of here unless the Czech Legion can arrive in time. And they're still east of Tiumen, over three hundred miles away, even if they capture every station on the railway it may take them weeks to fight their way into Ekaterinburg. And where will we be when they come? Still here, doing our little bits of laundry in a bucket of dirty water? Or cleaning out our room?'

'I think housework's fun,' said Marie stoutly. If Olga was still the leader, Marie, just past her nineteenth birthday, had emerged as a girl of great character, as strong in personality as in her body. She was also very pretty, with her brown curls and huge blue eyes, and as she said, running her hands down her slim flanks, 'there's one good thing about a prison diet — nobody'll ever call me Fat Little Bow-Wow again!' The soldiers never shouted at Marie, but they watched her as she swung up and down the yard with her hands in the pockets of her cotton dress, and sometimes they whispered together and licked their lips.

The time came when what Olga had begun to dread, took place. They were all asleep in the darkest hour of the night when their door was quietly opened and two soldiers came in, one with a dark lantern in his hand. They were drunk, but far from incapable, and they were even willing to parley with the frightened girls. The guards had drawn lots, they said, for who got the chance, and they had won; now they were going to take 'the two cute little young ones' down to the cellar.

'Just a moment.' Olga had slung on her dressing-gown, while Tatiana, who had only heard half of what was muttered, put her arms round her younger sisters. Olga pushed the men out to the landing. From the mere fact that they were whispering and not shouting, she guessed that they were afraid of the commandant, just as she was afraid of her father hearing them and coming out to see what was wrong. That they were absolutely set on their vile purpose was quite apparent; one of them actually had his Nagan pistol in his hand as he told her in explicit terms that he meant to have a woman, and couldn't face his mates again unless he did.

'Yes, but not one of my sisters, they're very young, you'd frighten them,' said Olga, and the one without the gun said the younger the better. He wanted the one with the curls, she swung her hips at the boys when she went by.

Olga braced herself against the door. 'I won't let you interfere with any of my sisters, and that's flat,' she said.

'Maybe you'd like to come with us yourself, you stuck-up old bitch?'

'If you force me to, I will.'

The sudden raucous shout of laughter was like a blow. 'Hark at her, Stepan, she's asking for it! Little sister, we'd have to be hard up to take on the likes of you! Better take a look at yourself in the mirror, you old crow!'

He tore the front of Olga's nightdress open, and spat between her breasts. At the same time the voice of the orderly officer, preparing to make his rounds, was heard calling from the hall.

'Coming, comrade!' 'Just doing a night patrol, comrade!' The two men clattered downstairs without a backward look. And Olga stumbled down the corridor into the lavatory, ripped off the hem of her nightdress, poured water from the enamel jug on it and rubbed her defiled breast until the white skin was an angry red. Then she looked at herself in the cracked mirror. *Old* bitch, *old* crow — the stinging adjective had hit its mark. In this moment of utter humiliation, Olga saw that the thin, haggard face staring wildly back from the mirror was close to being the face of an old woman. A line from *Resurrection* came into her mind, the words of the woman taken prisoner to Siberia: 'I had ceased to be a human being and had become a thing.'

She went back to her sisters and calmed them. The men had been quite reasonable, she said, and she didn't think they would come back again. Nor did they, for within a few days all the men under Avdiev's command had gone along with himself, and Jacob Yurovski, the new commandant, kept a tighter discipline in the House of Special Purpose.

The inner guard Yurovski brought with him to the house were all men from the Cheka headquarters at the Amerikanski Dom. Some of them were Russians, but others were prisoners of war who had shown a special aptitude for police work, among them being at least one German. Others spoke a language which Alexandra Feodorovna thought she could identify as Magyar. All wore the black leather jackets of the Cheka, and went about their duties with a cold professionalism very different from the ranting of Avdiev's louts.

The outer guard, which numbered fifty, had been replaced, but the replacements were still local factory workers, and Yurovski himself had lived in Ekaterinburg, running a photographer's business, before he joined the Cheka. Bearded and bespectacled, he was possessed of a cold hate for the monarchy, hating with the special intensity of a Jew who believed that the Romanovs alone were responsible for the pogroms which had regularly swept through the villages and ghettos of Imperial Russia. He came to the House of Special Purpose at the moment of Mara Trenova's attempt on Lenin's life — an attempt which started off a real Red terror of cruelty and oppressions, and this wave of terrorism exactly suited the mood of Yurovski and of the Ural Soviet, which had never intended, once he was in their clutches, to let the former Czar leave Ekaterinburg alive.

The Romanovs, who were no longer allowed to read the newspapers, knew nothing about the campaign of ruthless repression which was filling the prisons and the scaffolds of Russia. But they knew from the sounds beyond the stockade that there was much movement in the town, and one afternoon they actually heard a man shouting 'The Czechs are west of Tiumen!' before a guard ran up and herded them into the house. It was something to think about with fear and hope. They dreaded Yurovski's reaction if the Whites fought their way into Ekaterinburg. They watched his face when he came near them as if they could read the news of battle in his eyes.

The sixteenth of July began badly. They had no piano now, but they often sang Russian hymns after morning prayers, and one of the guards confessed afterwards that he had been touched to hear the fresh young voices lifted in 'The Cherubim's Song'. But this morning Marie suggested Nurse Cavell's hymn, still her favourite, and they all began to sing the English words:

Abide with me, fast falls the eventide,
The darkness deepens, Lord, with me abide.
When other helpers fail, and comforts flee –
Help of the helpless, O abide with me.

Almost before the first verse ended, Yurovski was in the living-room, icily telling them that to sing, as well as to speak, in any foreign language was absolutely forbidden, did they understand him? The girls nodded dispiritedly and went back to sew in the stifling bedroom. They had very few clothes left now, and those required constant mending.

At some time before the main meal of the day the little kitchen boy disappeared. The cook, whose only employment was brewing the coffee and warming up the tepid food sent in from the Soviet kitchen, came in wringing his hands to say the *sovietski* guards had taken the little boy away and he hadn't come back, what was to be done? Nothing, obviously. The fate of Nagorny was in all their minds, though it was hard to know what the kitchen boy, a meek little soul, could have done to offend the guards. They were now so small a company that the loss of even the least member left a gap. They still had the cook, a valet and a lady's maid for Alexandra Feodorovna, but Dr. Botkin was the only man left for Nicholas to talk to, and they had given up hoping to see the six good friends parted from them at the railway station. The girls and their father went out to the yard for exercise, and here unusual noises warned Nicholas that some pieces of light artillery, probably machine-guns, were being dragged into place against the stockade. The machine-guns on the roof of the church still pointed menacingly in their direction.

'Do you think it means the Czechs are coming near, papa?' asked Tatiana.

'I don't know, my dear, I wish I did.'

'But you hope so, don't you?'

'I hardly know what to hope for, any more.'

They were ordered to keep away from the stockade, and presently were herded indoors. It was still very hot inside the house. Supper was served, and the man who brought it from the communal kitchen said he knew nothing about the missing boy. Alexis began to worry about him and wonder if he had been shot like the poor boy in Tobolsk. To calm him, Dr. Botkin went upstairs and began to tell him stories, while his father and mother settled down silently to a game of bezique. Seeing them absorbed, Tatiana proposed to her sisters that they should go up to their room and talk.

'What's there to talk about?' yawned Olga.

'We could play Happy Times,' said Anastasia. 'We haven't played that for ages.'

'I ought to mend the lace on my petticoat, it's beginning to rip.'

'You're not supposed to strain your eyes, you know,' said careful Tatiana.

'It's only nine o'clock, it'll be light enough to sew for an hour yet.'

'Oh, come on, Olga, you can do that tomorrow,' said Marie, and Olga gave in. They went upstairs and sat on their iron beds. Since the weather became so hot they were allowed to open their window at night, but as iron bars had been fixed across it since Yurovski came, their view was even more depressing than before. They played Favourite Meals as part of Happy Times, with Olga choosing the caviar which the Ural Cossacks brought every spring as a present to the Little Father, and Marie saying she'd always wanted to eat *zakuski* and drink vodka with the men. They played Favourite People, which was not a success, because their favourites were scattered far and wide, or dead, and then, after their parents came upstairs and whispered good night at their door, they began in whispers themselves, so as not to rouse Alexis, to play the Happiest Time of All.

'I wonder why we never thought of that before,' said Olga. 'Anastasia, you begin.'

The girl, who had just passed her seventeenth birthday, pretended to be deep in reflection. 'My long life!' she said lightly. 'I think I've been happiest when we were acting. Even at Tobolsk, it was such fun acting with father in *The Bear*.'

'You're far and away the best actress of us all,' said Marie.

'I like pretending to be somebody I'm not. If we ever get away from here I'd like to be an actress, acting a scene in prison, and knowing as soon as the curtain fell I would be free ... Now you, Tania.'

'My happiest time? I think it was when the English sailors came to Kronstadt, just before the war. We had such wonderful fun!'

'Olga?'

'Oh, I don't know. My first dance, I suppose. Do you remember that dance at Livadia?' She had said the first thing that came into her head, and a girl's first dance was a perfectly conventional choice. She was touched to see Tatiana's thin face light up as her sister said, 'We all thought you looked beautiful that night, and so grown up! We leaned over the balcony and watched you opening the ball with Dmitri.'

'We thought Dmitri was going to fall in love with you,' said

Anastasia shrewdly, and Olga said, 'So did I!' She remembered a pale pink dress and a diamond necklace, and Dmitri's arm holding her lightly as they waltzed in the marble ballroom at Livadia.

'I never went to any ball, but I disgraced myself the first time I wore an evening dress and high heels at a dinner party,' said Marie. 'Do you remember that blue dress, and how I tripped and fell? And father looked round and said, "Of course – it's fat Marie!" Yes, you can all laugh – it was terrible! What I think were our happiest times were the cruises on the *Standart*, we always felt so — free. And then I loved going ashore for picnics, like that heavenly day in Finland, Olga, when we went to tea at Simon Karlovich's dacha.'

Olga flashed her sister a quick look of gratitude. She said that just to please me, bless her, and let me know she hasn't forgotten about Simon, she thought. Oh, if I could have just one day, only one, with Simon, in Finland, in the woods!

It was still daylight when they went to bed, and the House of Special Purpose was ominously quiet. Olga, who had been sleeping badly, lay awake for a long time. Through the partly opened window, between the bars, she could see a few stars in the darkening summer blue. They made her think of the night aboard the *Standart*, after her visit to the dacha, when she had swung lazily in a cushioned hammock on the deck, and wondered if she was falling in love with Simon Hendrikov.

It was a gentle thought, and Olga was smiling when she fell asleep. It was only an hour later when her father came to wake them, saying they must rise and dress quickly, they had all been ordered to go downstairs. 'All of us,' he said, 'the servants and Dr. Botkin too. Marie, go and help to dress Alexis. Just put a few things in one of the suitcases, they say we won't need much.'

'What's happened, papa? Where are we going?'

'Yurovski wants to move us away from here for a few days. The Czechs have outflanked the city and are coming close; I suppose he's afraid of an attempt to rescue us.'

He was obviously very excited and eager. The girls hastily put on the suits into which they had sewn their jewels, though it was too warm for jackets, and they decided to wear no hats. Anastasia took the Pekinese in her arms, and Alexis was carried out of his bedroom by his father, who declared that the boy's legs were growing too long for his poor old papa, and Dr. Botkin helped Alexandra Feodorovna, who clung painfully to the banister.

'Come this way,' said Yurovski, waiting in the hall. 'You'll have to wait a few minutes, the motors haven't arrived yet. My men are in the rooms on this floor, but you'll find some chairs in the cellar.'

It was an empty room, not twenty feet square, lighted only by stable lanterns. The time was only a little past midnight, and there was still some light in the sky, which the lanterns seemed to turn to a deeper blue.

'What a queer place!'

'It doesn't seem to be used for anything.'

'I was rather expecting to find some of our missing luggage, tucked away down here. Are you quite comfortable on that hard chair, mamma?'

'Joy! Joy!'

The boy's cry, which they had heard so often, reached Olga's ears too late for her, or any of them, to stop the spaniel. He had twitched his leash out of his master's lax grip, and ran in terror, a streak of brown and white, out of the cellar in the House of Special Purpose.

'You've been told again and again to keep him on his lead!'

'Oh, Anastasia, do go and find him and bring him back!' pleaded Alexis, nearly in tears.

'Thanks, I'd rather not. There are two men in the corridor with bayonets. It's all right, Alexis! He can't get out of the yard.'

'He'll be waiting for us when we get into the motors,' said Marie.

'I don't hear any motors. Oh, Olga, do you think they'll *hurt* him?'

'They're not hurting him at all, I can hear him barking. Move over this way a bit, Alexis, you're really too heavy for papa.'

Olga sat down on the edge of a chair and took part of her brother's weight against her shoulder. It was only then that she saw the writing on the wall — two lines from Heine, written over the previous day's date, as if the German member of the Cheka had been down clearing out the cellar —

> Balthasar was on that same night
> Murdered by his slaves

There was hardly time for the words to sink in before the cellar door was flung wide open, and the Cheka men, headed by Yurovski, burst in with drawn revolvers in their hands.

She knew, with a great spasm of terror, that the hour of utmost dread had struck. She was aware that her mother had clutched her crucifix, that her father, with one arm round Alexis, was trying to rise and stammering 'What are you — ?' or 'What do you —' at the same time as Yurovski choked out 'Your friends are — you are guilty —' and the shrieks and the revolver shots rang out together.

Olga flung herself across her brother. The first bullet caught her in the shoulder and spun her round. The second, in her chest, knocked her to the floor. They were falling, writhing, moaning all around her, and the men from the corridor, armed with rifles, were clubbing the dying girls with rifle butts. The cellar reeked of fear and death. Then the last bullet struck her in the throat, a tide of blood poured from her mouth, and Olga was at peace.

CHAPTER THIRTY

SIMON HENDRIKOV reached Ekaterinburg on an autumn day, when the wind was whipping along the dusty streets, and sullen skies gave promise of an early winter.

Joe Calvert was waiting for him at the redbrick railway station. The freight yards behind, where the Romanovs had been locked up for the whole of one night in May, were now filled with Allied armoured cars, and the passenger station was full of men dressed like Simon himself, in Russian uniform with a red and white badge representing the Lion of Bohemia.

'Simon, it's good to see you. You're looking well.'

'So are you. I suppose I ought to call you Lieutenant Calvert now!'

'Don't kid me, captain. I'm embarrassed that my uniform's so new. I only got my release from the consular corps when the President decided to send an American Military Mission to the Czechs.'

'So you said in your letter.'

They were awkward with one another, making trite conversation, in this first meeting after so much had happened to them both. Joe Calvert said, to cover the awkwardness:

'I wish I'd known you were in Tiumen when I came west three weeks ago. It was a big surprise, when I got here, to read your name on the roster of Russian officers serving in the Czech Legion.'

'I haven't been at Tiumen very long. I was at Omsk for more than two months, after the Czechs got me out of prison, and took me on the strength.'

'You had a bad go of typhus before that, didn't you?'

'Yes. But as I couldn't have acted the part of a Red officer much longer, you could say the typhus saved my life. If I had any reason for living left.'

'I've fixed a car,' said Joe gently. 'We have to pick it up at Czech HQ. You'll want to report in anyway, and then they'll arrange about your billet.'

'No billet needed. I only got a short pass, and I'll have to go back to Tiumen on the night train.'

'Tough going, but the trains are running better now. Up this way.'

The Cheka had been flung out of the Amerikanski Dom when the Czech troops entered Ekaterinburg on the twenty-fifth of July, and it was now the headquarters of the Czech Legion in that area. There was only one way to get there, and that was up the long hilly Liberty Street, past the House of Special Purpose, still conspicuous because of its stockade, and the white and green flag of the Independent Siberian Government flying where the red flag had flown. There were sentries posted at the gates, and Joe was not surprised when Simon identified the house at once. He stopped and said, 'Is that the place?'

'Yes.'

'Why the sentries?'

'Everything inside's been locked and sealed, until the full investigation can begin.'

'Have *you* been inside?'

'Oh no. It was sealed off long before I got here. Mr. Gibbs and Monsieur Gilliard went in, right at the start — they had a whole lot of guts, those two — and Gibbs told me everything about it.' He added gently, 'You wouldn't want to see the cellar, Simon.'

It was an odd thing to say, for the man was a soldier, who had seen death all around him for four long years. But the horror of the spattered cellar, where a hasty washing had not removed all the blood from the walls and floor, was surely something the man who had loved Olga could not bear to see.

'I don't want to see inside the house. I only want to see the place where they were buried.' Simon moved on a few paces. 'Was that the yard where they were let out for exercise?'

'I believe it was — it must have been. The Czarevich's pet dog was found there, half-starved, when the Czech troops came in.'

'Little Joy? The spaniel?'

'Yes, it was a King Charles. One of General Knox's ADCs is going to take it to England with him.'

'I've seen Alexis playing with his dog a hundred times.'

He thought of Joy gambolling at the foot of the snow mountain, climbing wet-pawed into the car where he sat with Olga by his side.

'Here we are at HQ,' said Joe. While Simon was talking to the Czech commanding officer he lit a cigarette and strolled up and down the hall of the Amerikanski Dom, thinking about the ordeal immediately ahead. To say that Simon Hendrikov was looking well was a mere figure of speech: the man had had typhus fever, a spell in a Bolshevik prison before the Czechs took Omsk, and finally a crushing blow, and he showed it in his face and manner. But Joe was glad he had arranged for the young man to come to Ekaterinburg. He was more disturbed by what Simon had just said about the place where the Romanovs were buried.

The part of the forest to which they were bound was only one of the places in Siberia where the Bolsheviks had attempted to wipe the Romanovs from the face of the earth. After the murders at the House of Special Purpose, the Grand Duke Michael had been shot dead at Perm; at Alapaevsk the Czarina's sister, the Grand Duchess Elizabeth, had been killed with five Romanov princes, all of them flung living down a mine shaft; and others were in the Fortress of Peter and Paul awaiting execution. Ten thousand Russians had died in the Red terror: the British Embassy in Petrograd had been stormed and the naval attaché killed; in Moscow the Allied diplomats had to take shelter from the mob in the American consulate. All American citizens other than the military had been ordered to leave a country which had deliberately cut itself off from the world. All this was certainly known to Simon Hendrikov: there was one hideous special circumstance in the deaths of Olga and her family which he had just revealed he did not know.

Joe decided to take the bull by the horns. When Simon reappeared he drew him into a tiny anteroom, hardly bigger than a cupboard, where there was a brief chance of privacy.

'Simon,' he said, 'are you sure you want to go through with this? To take that drive, I mean?'

'That's what I came for, isn't it?'

'Sure it is. But there's one thing I'd better explain first. Out there at the Four Brothers — the Czar and his family aren't actually buried there —'

'But I thought that's where they were taken, afterwards —'

'Yes, they were *taken*, but then the bodies were destroyed, they weren't buried.'

'How, destroyed?'

Joe told him the brutal truth. 'They were dismembered at the site, and the remains were dissolved with sulphuric acid, and burned in a petrol bonfire.'

Simon's square-cut face turned white. He swallowed a rush of bitter water to his mouth. It was clear that he had no words to express his horror. Joe went on, 'It was the peasants from Koptiaki who broke the story first. They were coming into town with a mess of lake fish to sell, and they saw the cars, and the flames. They went back to the place later and found a lot of — objects, which helped in the identification.'

'But there must have been *some* remains!'

'The bones are at the bottom of the mine shaft now, and the frost is setting in. There's nothing more to be done about it until the spring.'

'But if no bodies were found maybe they aren't dead at all!' The hazel eyes lit up with hope, the fanatic hope which Joe had encountered in others who refused to believe the Romanovs were dead. 'There was a story going the rounds in Omsk,' Simon said, 'that they'd been helped to escape and taken to a yacht in the White Sea, and that they're all on the yacht still, sailing round and round until the war is over —'

'Like the Flying Dutchman,' said Joe sadly. 'Don't wish that on them, whatever you do. Just try to accept that their troubles on earth are all over now.'

'But Olga Nicolaievna, and her sisters, and the boy — their lives were only beginning.'

Joe gripped his arm and piloted him out to the street. An army car was waiting, and beside it a Czech driver and his sergeant armed with a rifle snapped to attention and saluted as the two officers came out.

'Up the Koptiaki road, Jan,' said Joe. 'You know the place.'

'Do we need an armed escort?' Simon asked. He spoke in French, and Joe answered in that language that there had been cases of Red snipers lurking in the woods and it was best to take no chances. The war between Russia and the west was only beginning; he had a notion that it might last in one form or another for the next fifty years. But —

'Simon,' he said, 'The war in Europe is as good as won. Germany and Austria will sue for peace any day. Don't you think it's time you made some plans for the future?'

'I haven't got a future now.'

'My God, man, you're only — what is it — twenty-seven? You've a long life ahead of you. You'll recover from all this. When the Czech Legion goes home, to their new independent country, and I go back to my job in Vladivostok, I want you to come along with me. I'll get you a visa for the United States, and we'll work out some sort of job idea once you're there.'

Simon actually laughed. 'I don't know any job but soldiering,' he said, 'and I can't speak two words of English —'

'Learn it, then. Go *on* to England, if you like that idea better; Dolly and her husband will see you get a start. And you've got all the rest of your family in Copenhagen. You're not exactly alone in the world.'

'Thanks, but talking about ideas, I don't like the idea of sponging on my relatives. Too many people have been doing that since the revolution . . . Joe, I appreciate you want to help me. But I'm quite satisfied with the job I'm doing now, fighting the Reds. If you people would send us more men and arms, we'd get it over all the sooner.'

Joe shrugged his shoulders. It was the old cry, echoing through all the countries of the world since the murders at Sarajevo: More men! More guns! In Siberia Lieutenant Calvert was as much convinced as Plain Joe Calvert had been in Washington that Allied intervention in Russia could only make a desperate situation worse. But the President's military advisers had thought otherwise, and by the time the Japanese landed over seventy thousand men in Siberia, Mr. Wilson had been persuaded to order landings at Murmansk, Archangel and Vladivostok, of forces quite insufficient to their task in numbers and morale. Trotsky had responded to the challenge, as Joe had foreseen. He was making the Red Army into a great and disciplined fighting force.

The army car was slowing down as the road became a mere cart track, going deeper into the forest round Ekaterinburg. Yurovski and his gang had not brought the bodies of their victims, flung into the bottom of a truck, much more than ten miles out of town.

'Better stop here, Jan,' said Joe in Russian. 'We're liable to break a spring if we go much further. You two wait here till we come back.'

He led Simon down a path to a clearing blackened by fire, where four pine trees stood sentinel above a disused iron mine working, with their bare trunks slashed and scarred like the saplings growing up around them.

'Is this the place?' said Simon. Instinctively he lowered his voice.

'This is the Four Brothers mine, Simon.'

'They ought to call it the Four Sisters now.' His face was suddenly convulsed. 'But they'll be forgotten, all of them! They might as well never have lived, if it was only to end like this!'

'They won't be forgotten, not as long as decent Russians live.'

'Ah!' said Simon Hendrikov, 'and you've been telling me I should get out of Russia! Well, Olga didn't run away, and neither will I. I'll stay in Russia till the day I die, and fight her murderers.'

Joe walked a few paces across the clearing. There were the marks of tyre tracks and spades, used for digging up the ground where many pathetic relics of the Romanovs had already been found. Simon seemed unwilling to put his foot on the burned patch, as if it truly was a grave. Joe heard the anguished voice behind him saying, 'I never could do anything to help her ... We had so little time together ... but I loved her better than my life.'

He waited a few minutes before he looked round. When he did so he saw Simon's lips moving, and supposed he was saying a prayer. But Simon was not praying. He was only repeating the words of the pledge he and Olga had once made to one another:

Gone is the resurrection kiss,
But yet to come: you swore it me!

I swear it, Olga, he promised in his heart. He said aloud:

'Come, Joe, we must go back.'

They walked back to the waiting car in silence. The skies were leaden over the Four Brothers, and soon the snow would come, to cover all.

ALSO BY CATHERINE GAVIN

THE FORTRESS

The American privateer who sailed under British Letters of Marque soon became a legend in the Baltic. Alix, Brand and Joe were stared at when they went ashore together – the beautiful fair girl in the fisherman's jersey, the tall American who always held her by the hand, and the wiry fellow with black curly hair were the most discussed trio in the whole of Gotland.

'Something for everyone, a beautiful woman, swashbuckling men, heroic battles – and all historically accurate. If Catherine Gavin had been teaching me history, I would have remembered a lot more. Enjoyed it more, too.'

Daily Mirror

THE DEVIL IN HARBOUR

How can a rough young trawlerman from Aberdeen adapt to life as a naval officer at the time of the Battle of Jutland?

How does a minister's eighteen year-old daughter at Scapa Flow react to the knowledge that there is a traitor in her family?

Why should a famous Russian dancer, devoted to the Allied cause, become the mistress and tool of a German secret agent?

'THE DEVIL IN HARBOUR shows again Catherine Gavin's superb sense of history, her capacity for dramatising the character and thrust of an age with the clear and moving images of the personal conflict. She takes us from the restaurants and theatres of Petrograd to the high seas off Jutland, always with unshakeable confidence and skill.'

Los Angeles Times

AVAILABLE IN CORONET BOOKS

CATHERINE GAVIN

☐	14984 1	The Fortress	60p
☐	12946 8	The Devil In Harbour	50p
☐	04354 7	The Moon Into Blood	40p
☐	15116 1	The House Of War	40p
☐	16335 6	Give Me The Daggers	45p

JAN DE HARTOG

The Peaceable Kingdom

☐	16657 6	Book I The Children Of The Light	50p
☐	16873 0	Book II The Holy Experiment	50p

ELIZABETH GOUDGE

☐	15149 8	The Middle Window	45p
☐	02875 0	The Rosemary Tree	45p
☐	15105 6	Green Dolphin Country	75p
☐	15104 8	Scent Of Water	40p

All these books are available at your bookshop or newsagent, or can be ordered direct from the publisher. Just tick the titles you want and fill in the form below.

....

CORONET BOOKS, P.O. Box 11, Falmouth, Cornwall.

Please send cheque or postal order. No currency, and allow the following for postage and packing:

1 book – 10p, 2 books – 15p, 3 books – 20p, 4–5 books – 25p, 6–9 books – 4p per copy, 10–15 books – 2½p per copy, 16–30 books – 2p per copy, over 30 books free within the U.K.

Overseas – please allow 10p for the first book and 5p per copy for each additional book.

Name ....

Address ....

....